DAWN POWELL

◆

ANGELS ON TOAST
THE WICKED PAVILION
THE GOLDEN SPUR

◆

DAWN POWELL

◆

ANGELS ON TOAST
THE WICKED PAVILION
THE GOLDEN SPUR

◆

With an introduction by
Gore Vidal

Quality Paperback Book Club
New York

This edition created specially in 1989 for Quality Paperback Book Club by arrangement with Jacqueline Rice and the Estate of Dawn Powell.

Grateful acknowledgment is made to the following people, who helped in the preparation of this volume: Howard Frisch, Al Silverman, Jacqueline Rice, Gore Vidal, and the staff at the Elmer Holmes Bobst Library at New York University.

Dawn Powell, the American Writer

Gore Vidal

◆

Once upon a time, New York City was as delightful a place to live as to visit. There were many amenities, as they say in brochures. One was something called Broadway, where dozens of plays opened each season and thousands of people came to see them in an area which today resembles downtown Calcutta without, alas, that subcontinental city's deltine charm and intellectual rigor.

One evening back there in once upon a time (February 7, 1957, to be exact), my first play opened at the Booth Theatre. Traditionally, the playwright was invisible to the audience. One hid out in a nearby bar, listening to the sweet nasalities of Pat Boone's rendering of "Love Letters in the Sand" from a glowing jukebox. But when the curtain fell on this particular night, I went into the crowded lobby to collect someone. Overcoat collar high about my face, I moved invisibly through the crowd, or so I thought. Suddenly a voice boomed... tolled across the lobby. *"Gore!"* I stopped;

everyone stopped. From the cloakroom a small, round figure, rather like a Civil War cannonball, hurtled toward me and collided. As I looked down into that familiar round face with its snub nose and shining bloodshot eyes I heard—the entire crowded lobby heard: *"How could you do this?* How could you *sell out* like this? To *Broadway!* To *commercialism!* How could you give up *The Novel?* Give up the *security?* The security of knowing that every two years there will be—like clockwork—that *five-hundred-dollar advance!"* Thirty years later, the voice still echoes in my mind, and I think fondly of its owner, our best comic novelist. "The field," I can hear Dawn Powell snarl, "is not exactly overcrowded."

On the night that *Visit to a Small Planet* opened, Dawn Powell was fifty-nine years old. She had published fourteen novels, evenly divided between accounts of her native Midwest (and how the hell to get out of there and make it to New York) and the highly comic New York novels, centered on Greenwich Village, where she lived most of her adult life. Some twenty-three years earlier the Theater Guild had produced Powell's comedy *Jig Saw* (one of *her* many unsuccessful attempts to sell out to commercialism), but there was third-act trouble, and despite Spring Byington and Ernest Truex, the play closed after forty-nine performances.

For decades Dawn Powell was always just on the verge of ceasing to be a cult and becoming a major religion. But despite the work of such dedicated cultists as Edmund Wilson and Matthew Josephson, John Dos Passos and Ernest Hemingway, Dawn Powell never became the popular writer that she ought to have been. In those days, with a bit of luck, a good writer eventually attracted voluntary readers and became popular. Today, of course, "popular" means bad writing that is widely read while good writing is that which is taught to involuntary readers. Powell failed on both counts. She needs no interpretation, and in her lifetime she should have been as widely read as, say, Hemingway or the early Fitzgerald or the mid O'Hara or even the late, far too late, Katherine Anne Porter. But Powell was that unthinkable monster, a witty woman who felt no obligation to make a single, much less a final, down payment on Love or the Family; she saw life with a bright Petronian neutrality, and every host at life's feast was a potential Trimalchio to be sent up.

In the few interviews that Powell gave she often mentioned as her favorite novel—surprisingly for an American, much less a woman of her time and place—the *Satyricon.* This sort of thing was not acceptable then any more than it is now. Descriptions of warm, mature, heterosexual love were—and are—woman's writerly task, and the truly serious writers really, heartbreakingly, flunk the course while the pop ones pass with bright honors.

Although Powell received very little serious critical attention (to the extent that there has ever been much in our heavily moralizing culture), when she did get reviewed by a really serious person like Diana Trilling (*The Nation,* May 29, 1948), *la* Trilling warns us that the book at hand is no good because of "the discrepancy between the power of mind revealed on virtually every page of her novel [*The Locusts Have No King*] and the insignificance of the human beings upon which she directs her excellent intelligence." Trilling does acknowledge the formidable intelligence, but because Powell does not deal with morally complex people (full professors at Columbia in midjourney?), "the novel as a whole ...fails to sustain the excitement promised by its best moments."

Apparently to be serious a novel must be about very serious—even solemn—people rendered in a very solemn—even serious—manner. Wit? What is that? But then we all know that power of mind and intelligence count for as little in the American novel as they do in American life. Fortunately neither appears with sufficient regularity to distress our solemn middle-class middlebrows as they trudge ever onward to some Scarsdale of the mind, where the red light blinks and blinks at pier's end and the fields of the republic rush forward ever faster like a rug rolling up.

Powell herself occasionally betrays bewilderment at the misreading of her work. "There is so great a premium on dullness," she wrote sadly (Robert Van Gelder, *Writers and Writing,* Scribner's, 1946), "that it seems stupid to pass it up." She also remarks that it

> is considered jolly and good-humored to point out the oddities of the poor or of the rich. The frailties of millionaires or garbage collectors....Their ways of speech, their personal habits, the peculiarities of their thinking are considered fair game. I go outside the rules with my stuff because I can't help believing that the middle class is funny, too.

Finally, as the shadows lengthened across the greensward, Edmund Wilson got around to his old friend in *The New Yorker* (November 17, 1962). One reason, he tells us, that Powell has so little appeal to those Americans who read novels is that "she does nothing to stimulate feminine day-dreams [sexist times!]. The woman reader can find no comfort in identifying herself with Miss Powell's heroines. The women who appear in her stories are likely to be as sordid and absurd as the men." This sexual parity was unusual. But now, closer to century's end than 1962, Powell's "sordid, absurd ladies" seem more like the comic Carol Burnett than the dread Alexis of *Dynasty* fame.

Wilson also noted Powell's originality: "Love is not Miss Powell's theme. Her real theme is the provincial in New York who has come on from the Middle West and acclimatized himself (or herself) to the city and made himself a permanent place there, without ever, however, losing his fascinated sense of an alien and anarchic society." This is very much to the (very badly written) point. Wilson finds her novels "among the most amusing being written, and in this respect quite on a level with those of Anthony Powell, Evelyn Waugh, and Muriel Spark." Wilson's review was of her last book, *The Golden Spur*; three years later she was dead of breast cancer. "Thanks a lot, Bunny," one can hear her mutter as this belated floral wreath came flying through her transom.

Summer. Sunday afternoon. Circa 1950. Dawn Powell's duplex living room at 35 East Ninth Street. The hostess presides over an elliptical aquarium filled with gin, a popular drink of the period known as the martini. In attendance Coby—just Coby to me for years, her eternal escort; he is neatly turned out in a blue blazer, rosy-faced, sleek silver hair combed straight back. Coby can talk with charm on any subject. The fact that he might be Dawn's lover has never crossed my mind. They are so old. A handsome young poet lies on the floor, literally at the feet of E.E. Cummings and his wife, Marion, who ignore him. Dawn casts an occasional maternal eye in the boy's direction, but the eye is more that of the mother of a cat or a dog apt to make a nuisance. Conversation flows. Gin flows. Marion Cummings is beautiful; so indeed is her husband, his eyes a faded denim blue. Coby is in great form. Though often his own subject, he records not boring triumphs but improbable disasters. He is always broke, and a once distinguished wardrobe is now in the hands of those gay deceivers, his landladies. On this afternoon, at home, Dawn is demure, thoughtful. "Why," she suddenly asks, eyes on the long body beside the coffee table, "do they never have floors of their own to sleep on?"

Cummings explains that since the poet lives in Philadelphia he is too far from his own floor to sleep on it. Not long after, the young poet and I paid a call on the Cummingses. We were greeted at the door by an edgy Marion. "I'm afraid you can't come in." Behind her an unearthly high scream sounded. "Dylan Thomas just died," she explained. "Is that Mr. Cummings screaming?" asked the poet politely as the keening began on an even higher note. "No," said Marion. "That is not Mr. Cummings. That is Mrs. Thomas."

But for the moment, in my memory, the poet is forever asleep on the floor while on a balcony high up in the second story of Dawn's living room a gray, blurred figure appears and stares down at us. "Who," I ask, "is that?"

Dawn gently, lovingly, stirs the martinis, squints her eyes, says, "My husband, I think. It *is* Joe, isn't it, Coby?" She turns to Coby, who beams and waves at the gray man, who withdraws. "Of course it is," says Coby. "Looking very fit." I realize, at last, that this is a *ménage à trois* in Greenwich Village. My martini runs over.

To date the only study of Dawn Powell is a doctoral dissertation by one Judith Faye Pett (University of Iowa, 1981). Ms. Pett has gathered together a great deal of biographical material, for which one is grateful. I am happy to know, at last, that the amiable Coby's proper name was Coburn Gilman, and I am sad to learn that he survived Dawn by only two years. The husband on the balcony was Joseph Gousha, or Goushé, whom she married on November 20, 1920. He was musical; she literary, with a talent for the theater. A son was born retarded. Over the years a fortune was spent on schools and nurses. To earn the fortune, Powell did every sort of writing, from interviews in the press to stories for ladies' magazines to plays that tended not to be produced to a cycle of novels about the Midwest, followed by a cycle of New York novels, where she came into her own, dragging our drab literature screaming behind her. As doyenne of the Village, she held court in the grill of the Lafayette Hotel—for elegiasts, the Lafayette was off Washington Square at University Place and Ninth Street.

Powell also runs like a thread of purest brass through Edmund Wilson's *The Thirties*: "It was closing time in the Lafayette Grill, and Coby Gilman was being swept out from under the table. Niles Spencer had been stuttering for five minutes, and Dawn Powell gave him a crack on the jaw and said, '*Nuts* is the word you're groping for.'" Also, "[Peggy Bacon] told me about Joe Gousha's attacking her one night at a party and trying to tear her clothes off.... I suggested that Joe had perhaps simply thought that this was the thing to do in Dawn's set. She said, 'Yes: He thought it was a social obligation.'" Powell also said that "Dotsy's husband was very much excited because the Prince of Wales was wearing a zipper fly, a big thing in the advertising business." A footnote to this text says that Dawn Powell and Wilson carried on a correspondence in which she was Mrs. Humphrey Ward and he "a seedy literary man named Wigmore." Later, there is a very muddled passage in which, for reasons not quite clear, James Thurber tells Dawn Powell that she does not *deserve* to be in the men's room. That may well be what it was all about.

Like most writers, Powell wrote of what she knew. Therefore, certain themes recur, while the geography does not vary from that of her actual life. As a child, she and two sisters were shunted about from one midwestern farm or small town to another by a father who was a salesman on the road (her mother died when she was six). The maternal grandmother made a great impression on her and predisposed her toward boardinghouse life (as a subject, not a residence). Indomitable old women, full of rage and good jokes, occur in both novel cycles. Powell's father remarried when she was twelve, and Dawn and her sisters went to live on the stepmother's farm. "My stepmother, one day, burned up all the stories I was writing, a form of discipline I could not endure. With thirty cents earned by picking berries I ran away, ending up in the home of a kindly aunt in Shelby, Ohio." After graduation from the local high school, she worked her way through Lake Erie College for Women in Painesville, Ohio. I once gave a commencement address there and was struck by how red-brick New England Victorian the buildings were. I also found out all that I could about their famous alumna. I collected some good stories to tell her. But by the time I got back to New York she was dead.

Powell set out to be a playwright. One play ended up as a movie while another, *Big Night*, was done by the Group Theater in 1933. But it was World War I, not the theater, that got Powell out of Ohio and to New York in 1918, as a member of the naval reserve. The war ended before her uniform arrived. Powell wrote publicity. Married. Wrote advertising copy (at the time, Goushé or Gousha was an account executive with an advertising agency). Failure in the theater and need for money at home led her to novel writing and the total security of that five-hundred-dollar advance each of us relied on for so many years.

Angels on Toast was the first of Powell's novels to become, if not world famous, *the* book for those who wanted to inhabit the higher, wittier realms of Manhattan where Truman Capote was, later and less wittily, to camp out. It is 1940. War had begun to darken the skyline. But the city's magic is undiminished for the provincial Ebie, a commercial artist whose mother is in the great line of Powell eccentrics. Ebie lives with another working woman, Honey, who "was a virgin (at least you couldn't prove she wasn't), and was as proud as punch of it. You would have thought it was something that had been in the family for generations." But Ebie and Honey need each other to talk at, and in a tavern

> where O. Henry used to go... they'd sit in the dark smoked-wood booth drinking old-fashioneds and telling each other things they certainly wished later they had never told and bragging about their families, sometimes making them hot-stuff socially back home, the next time making them romantically on the wrong side of the tracks. The family must have been on wheels back in the Middle West, whizzing back and forth across tracks at a mere word from the New York daughters.

Brooding over the novel is the downtown Hotel Ellery, where for seventeen dollars a week Ebie's mother, Mrs. Vane, lives in contented squalor.

> BAR and GRILL. It was the tavern entrance to a somewhat mediaeval looking hotel, whose time-and-soot-blackened façade was frittered with fire-escapes,... its dark oak wainscoting rising high to meet grimy black walls, its ship-windows covered with heavy pumpkin-colored chintz.... Once in you were in for no mere moment.

In its remoteness, this world before television could just as easily be that of Walter Scott.

It is also satisfying that in these New York novels the city that was plays so pervasive a role. This sort of hotel, meticulously described, evokes lost time in a way that the novel's bumptious twentieth-century contemporary, early talking-movies don't.

> Another curious thing about these small, venerable, respectable hotels—there seemed no appeal here to the average customer. BAR and GRILL, for instance, appealed to seemingly genteel widows and spinsters of small incomes....Then there were those tired flashes in the pan, the one-shot celebrities, and on the other hand there was a gayer younger group whose loyalty to the BAR and GRILL was based on the cheapness of its martinis. Over their simple dollar lunches (four martinis and a sandwich) this livelier set snickered at the older residents.

Ebie wants to take her mother away from all this so that they can live together in Connecticut. Mrs. Vane would rather die. She prefers to lecture the bar on poetry. There is also a plot: two men in business, with wives. One has an affair with Ebie. By now, Powell has mastered her own method. Essay beginnings to chapters work smartly:

> In the dead of night wives talked to their husbands, in the dark they talked and talked while the clock on the bureau ticked sleep away, and the last street cars clanged off on distant streets to remoter suburbs, where in new houses bursting with mortgages and the latest conveniences wives talked in the dark, and talked and talked.

The prose is now less easygoing than it was in the early novels, and there is a conscious tightening of the language although, to the end, Powell thought one thing was different *than* another while always proving not her mettle but *metal. Angels on Toast* ends with a cheerfulness worthy of Shakespeare in his *Midsummer Night's Dream* mood: everyone where he or she should be. I can think of no one else who has got so well the essence of that first war-year before we all went away to the best years of no one's life.

The Wicked Pavilion (1954) is the Café Julien is the Lafayette Hotel of real life. The title is from *The Creevey Papers* and refers to the Prince Regent's Brighton Pavilion, where the glamorous and *louche* wait upon a mad royal. From Powell's earlier books, the writer Dennis Orphen opens and closes the story in his mysterious way. He takes no real part in the plot. He is simply there, watching the not-so-magic wheel turn as the happy island grows sad. For him, as for Powell, the café is central to his life. Here he writes, sees friends, observes the vanity fair. Powell has now become masterful in her setting of scenes. The essays—preludes, overtures—are both witty and sadly wise. She also got the number to Eisenhower's America as she brings together in this penultimate rout all sorts of figures from earlier novels, now grown old: Okie is still a knowing man-about-town and author of the definitive works on the painter Marius, Andy Callingham is still a world-famous novelist (based on Ernest Hemingway), serene in his uncontagious self-love, and the recurrent Peggy Guggenheim figure is back again as Cynthia, an art gallery dealer. One plot is young love: Rick and Ellenora who met at the Café Julien in wartime and never got enough of it or of each other or of "the happy island," Powell's unironic phrase for the Manhattan that she first knew.

A new variation on the Powell young woman is Jerry, clean-cut, straightforward, and on the make. But her peculiar wholesomeness does not inspire men to give her presents; yet "the simple truth was that with her increasingly expensive tastes she really could not afford to work.... As for settling for the safety of marriage, that seemed the final defeat, synonymous in Jerry's mind with asking for the last rites." An aristocratic lady, Elsie, tries unsuccessfully to launch her. Elsie's brother, Wharton, and sister-in-law, Nita, are fine comic emblems of respectable marriage. In fact, Wharton is one of Powell's truly great and original monsters:

> Wharton had such a terrific reputation for efficiency that many friends swore that the reason his nose changed colors before your very eyes was because of an elaborate Rimbaud color code, indicating varied reactions to his surroundings.... Ah, what a stroke of genius it had been for him to have found Nita! How happy he had been on his honeymoon and for years afterward basking in the safety of Nita's childish innocence where his intellectual shortcomings, sexual coldness and caprices—indeed his basic ignorance—would not be discovered.... He was well aware that many men of his quixotic moods preferred young boys, but he dreaded to expose his inexperience to one of his own sex, and after certain cautious experiments realized that his anemic lusts were canceled by his overpower-

> ing fear of gossip....Against the flattering background of Nita's delectable purity he blossomed forth as the all-round-He-man, the Husband who knows everything. ...He soon taught her that snuggling, hand-holding and similar affectionate demonstrations were kittenish and vulgar. He had read somewhere, however, that breathing into a woman's ear or scratching her at the nape of the neck drove her into complete ecstasy. ...In due course Nita bore him four daughters, a sort of door prize for each time he attended.

The party is given by Cynthia now, and it rather resembles Proust's last roundup: "There are people here who have been dead twenty years," someone observes, including "the bore that walks like a man." There is a sense of closing time; people settle for what they can get. "We get sick of clinging vines, he thought, but the day comes when we suspect that the vines are all that hold our rotting branches together."

In 1962 Powell published her last and perhaps most appealing novel, *The Golden Spur*. As so often was the case with Powell, the protagonist is male. In this case a young man from Silver City, Ohio, called Jonathan Jaimison. He has come to the city to find his father. Apparently twenty-six years earlier his mother, Connie, had had a brief fling with a famous man in the Village; pregnant, she came home and married a Mr. Jaimison. The book opens with a vigorous description of Wanamaker's department store being torn down. Powell is now rather exuberant about the physical destruction of her city (she wrote this last book in her mid-sixties, when time was doing the same to her). But there are still a few watering holes from the twenties, and one of them is The Golden Spur, where Connie mingled with the bohemians.

Jonathan stays at the Hotel De Long, which sounds like the Vanderbilt, a star of many of Powell's narratives. Jonathan, armed with Connie's cryptic diary, has a number of names that might be helpful. One is that of Claire Van Orphen, a moderately successful writer for whom Connie did some typing. Claire gives Jonathan possible leads; meanwhile, his presence has rejuvenated her. Her career is revived with the help of a professionally failed writer who studies all of Claire's ladies' magazine short stories of yesteryear; he then reverses the moral angle:

> "In the old days the career girl who supported the fam-

> ily was the heroine, and the idle wife was the baddie," Claire said gleefully. "And now it's the other way round. In the soap operas, the career girl is the baddie, the wife is the goodie because she's better for *business*. ...Well, you were right. CBS has bought the two [stories] you fixed, and Hollywood is interested."

Powell herself was writing television plays in the age of Eisenhower and no doubt had made this astonishing discovery on her own.

Finally Cassie, Peggy Guggenheim yet again, makes her appearance, and the famous Dawn Powell party assembles for the last time. There are nice period touches. Girls from Bennington are everywhere, while Cassie herself "was forty-three—well, all right, forty-eight, if you're going to count every lost week end." She takes a fancy to Jonathan and hires him to work at her gallery. By the end of the novel, Jonathan figures out not only his paternity but his maternity and, best of all, himself.

The quest is over. Identity fixed. The party over, Jonathan heads downtown, "perhaps to 'the Spur,' where they could begin all over." On that blithe note Powell's life and lifework end, and the magic of that period is gone—except for the novels of Dawn Powell.

ANGELS ON TOAST

◆

To

Max Perkins

ALL CHARACTERS IN THIS BOOK ARE FICTITIOUS

I

THERE was a bottle of Robinson's B.E.B. right in Lou's bag but Jay Oliver wasn't interested.

"The hell with cooping up here in the compartment," he said. "Let's go down to the club car. I like to see people."

"I don't," said Lou. "I got things on my mind."

The porter brought the ice, glasses and soda.

"Okay," sighed Jay. "I might as well stick around a minute."

He sat down and kicked his shoes off. They lay on the floor jauntily toeing out, reddish brown, sleek, very much Jay Oliver. He crossed his stockinged feet on the seat opposite and viewed them complacently, marked the neat way the crimson clocks in the gray hose matched the herring-bone stripe in his blue suit.

"Paid four fifty for these socks," he stated briefly.

Lou took his suit coat off and hung it in the closet. He had put on about ten pounds in the last year, but there was something about a little extra weight that gave a man a certain authority, he thought. All right so long as it didn't get him in the middle and he'd have to watch it so that he didn't blow up like his old man had. One ninety was all right for five-eleven—he could carry it because of his big shoulders—but two hundred was the beginning of the end. Even this ten pounds made him a touch short of wind and made sitting around in his clothes uncomfortable. He undid his collar—he wore a separate white with his new imported colored shirts,—hung up the tie, a Sulka clover-leaf pattern, over the hanger, then sat down beside Jay's feet.

"Some shirt there, Lou," said Jay. "What'd it set you back?"

"Eighteen bucks," said Lou. "I swore I'd never wear a pink shirt but it was the goods that got me. Feel that material."

"Say!"

Jay leafed over the *American* and folded it at the sporting page so that the crouching figure of a Northwestern star, football under arm, seemed ready to whiz past Lou in a perpetual touchdown. Jay was still a little sore because Lou wouldn't wait over for the fight that night and plane out the next day, but he'd get over it. Lou hadn't told him that he had his reasons for booking the General. You don't have to tell all you know.

"If we got to take a train, why couldn't we have taken the bedroom train on the Century?" complained Jay. "Give me the New York Central any day. I took the Commodore Vanderbilt out of New York last month and slept like a baby. Not a jolt."

"Ah, you can't beat the General," said Lou. "You got to admit the Pennsylvania's got a smoother roadbed."

So far as he was concerned Jay could get out if he wanted to and let him do some thinking. Jay was all right, Jay was his best friend but a little bit of Jay went a long way. Lately, although their businesses were not the same, they seemed to be in everything together, and you can't have even a best friend knowing every damn move you make. Or was Jay his best friend? Jay was Whittleby Cotton and Whittleby Cotton was really his best friend. If Jay was ever eased out there his successor would be Lou's best friend.

"What's your wife think of your opening a New York branch?" Jay asked.

"What would I be telling her for?" Lou wanted to know. "I don't go round looking for trouble."

He was still disturbed by Mary refusing to say good-bye to him. He had been jumping in and out of town at a minute's notice for years, hell, that was his business, and she had never uttered a peep until this morning. What did she know? What did she suspect?

"You just got back from New York three days ago," she had said. "We've scarcely had one evening together since I got back from my cruise. I can't understand why you can't handle these things by telephone the way other men do."

"Honey, you wouldn't understand even if I told you," he answered breezily. "I'd be wasting my time."

"I really believe," she said in a low voice and then he realized she was serious about it, "you *prefer* being away from home."

So he explained how tricky his New York contracts were and how he had to keep feeding them in person,—telegrams and telephone calls were never effective, but while he was talking she quietly rose and left the table, her coffee and the toast she had just buttered, untouched on her plate. He had always been glad Mary had been so well brought up that she wouldn't dream of making a scene; but this silent indignation could get your goat just as much as a couple of plates flying through the air. He started to go after her, then shrugged, you can't let these things get you. When he called out good-bye to her a few minutes later there was no answer from behind the closed bedroom door. The baby had been sick so he did not dare stop to say good-bye to her either, for fear she might be sleeping. Outside he looked up at the bedroom window, half-expecting Mary to be there waving good-bye, but the shade was drawn to shut out the sun,—that meant she had one of her headaches,—those headaches, he suspected, that came from controlling her feelings too well. It annoyed him now that such a little thing as his wife's unusual parting mood should cross his mind when he had so many important things to think of,—a lot more than old Jay could ever guess. There was the matter of his ex-wife showing up in Chicago, old Fran whom he'd never expected to see again. As long as she hung around town there was the danger of Mary finding out he'd been married before. He was a close-mouthed man and after he and Fran broke up, so long as she seemed unlikely ever to bob up again, he saw no necessity for going into all that business with the new friends he made in Chicago. By the time he and Mary were married it would have been senseless to bring up the matter. No reason why not, but it would be hard to explain that the sole reason for his keeping it secret was that he liked to forget the ups and downs of his life before he settled in the West. With old Fran running around Chicago, goodness knows what Mary was likely to hear. Smart man that he was he had certainly outsmarted himself in not making some deal with Fran last time he saw her to keep out of his territory. It was not like him to make such mistakes.

What really was on Mary's mind, he wondered. A little fleabite, that's all it was, but that closed silent door of hers leaped out of the page of Jay's newspaper where the touchdown hero should be. It stuck out of flying Indiana villages, diminished, it winked at him from the highball glass in his hand. Lou clenched his fist and socked the green plush cushions. He could handle anything if he only knew what it was, but he hated being tormented with these trifles he did not understand. His wife not saying good-bye to him and then Judge Harrod, his wife's uncle, cutting him, sitting back there in the club car this very minute smoking a Perfecto and reading *The Atlantic Monthly* as intently as if it was the stock closing news,—so intently that he did not see Lou's outstretched hand.

"Nuts," said Lou clearly and finished his drink.

Jay freshened up their glasses.

"Flo will tell Mary you're getting N. Y. offices," he said cheerfully. "Flo can't keep her trap shut five minutes."

Sure, Flo would tell her. That is, if Mary gave her the chance. Flo had met them at the Drake for lunch and heard them talking over the plans. Jay's main office had been in New York for years so he had plenty of suggestions, and Flo put in her oar now and then, as if she was an old New Yorker. Mary wouldn't mind not having been told the business details, she never showed much interest in the office anyway, but what would hurt her would be the fact that Lou hadn't asked her downtown for lunch when Jay had his wife down, especially when she loved eating in the Cape Cod Room as Lou well knew. Those were the things that hurt Mary, and the things that were least important to Lou. The point was that Jay took care of those little matters because he had a guilty conscience, but you couldn't explain that to Mary or she'd remember it someday when he, Lou, might have a guilty conscience himself and be fixing it up with a nice luncheon. Jay figured that if he buttered up his wife before every trip and brought her a present afterward it gave him his freedom.

"Personally, Lou, I'd take the Rockefeller Plaza office," said Jay. "It's central, and you got your address. Unless you think you'd get more prestige out of the Empire State building. Personally, I don't think you will."

Was anybody asking for advice?

"You don't need a whole floor, you know," pursued Jay. "You don't need a lot of antique furniture. All you need is a desk, a telephone and a good-looking receptionist."

"I suppose you'll pick her out," said Lou.

"I could," said Jay. "I know how to pick."

"I was thinking of a nice older type," said Lou with a straight face. "Lavender gray marcel, lorgnette, class, yes, but the mother type."

Jay gave a snort of laughter.

"Get a blonde and let me age her," he suggested. "Listen, Lou, no kidding, though, you don't need to set up a palace suite like you've got in Chicago. In New York when they see a swell suite of offices they think Chase National's just about to take over. Keep it simple."

How about letting Lou Donovan take care of his own business in his own way?

"I got my eye on a log cabin," said Lou, "unless you think I could do with one of those Hudson River coal barges."

"Indiana is a lousy state," said Jay looking out the window. "Take South Bend. Or Terre Haute. Flo wants to buy a melon farm down by Vincennes but I say if we buy any farm it'll be in Pennsylvania. That's a state."

"You going straight to the Waldorf?" asked Lou. "I got a suite reserved if you want to bunk with me."

Jay took out a pearl-handled knife and began paring his nails.

"Can't stay at the Waldorf," he said. "That's where I stay when I'm with Flo. I'll be at the Roosevelt."

"Looking for a little party?" Lou asked.

Jay shook his head.

"Ebie?" Lou asked, getting the idea finally.

Jay nodded.

"Getting on at Pittsburgh," he said.

Lou shrugged.

"Give me a hand with her if any of Flo's relations pop up, will you?" Jay asked.

Lou didn't say anything. Jay made more trouble for himself taking chances that way, saying good-bye to his wife at one station and picking up Ebie at the next. And like as not he would go into the club car any minute now and try to promote the first skirt he saw till Ebie got on. If he, Lou, was as scared of his wife as Jay was of Flo he'd give up running around, or else get out and stop making excuses. Lou used to run around but since he'd been married to Mary he kept out of trouble, still doing what he liked when he liked but in out-of-the-way sectors and on a strictly casual basis. Jay was forty, all tied up by Flo, but so afraid he'd miss something he could never enjoy what he already had. He said it was because he'd been in a t.b. sanitarium once for six years and always felt he had to make up for lost time. He couldn't say good night to a hat-check girl without getting all messed up in something, though. His friends were always fixing up Flo so she wouldn't walk out whenever she found out things. She never found out anything she didn't want to, though, she knew when to play dumb and get a booby prize of a new car or bracelet. It annoyed Lou for Jay, a pal of his, to never learn any technique, to go on that way, walking into trouble.

"All right, say it, you don't like the idea of Ebie," Jay said when Lou was silent.

Lou shrugged again.

"Ebie's a good egg," said Jay. "I always go back to Ebie. Don't get the idea she's a tramp just because she's an artist. Ebie's all right."

"Ebie's all right, then," said Lou. It was nothing to him what his friends did, but it irritated him to see a smart guy like old Oliver, a guy who pulled down between twenty and forty thousand a year, let any one woman get a hold on him. Ebie was a commercial artist, she hung on to her job, but how, nobody knew, because she skipped all over the country at a telegram from Jay. Jay thought she wasn't a gold-digger because she had gone to Art School and made her own clothes and asked for loans instead of out-and-out presents. You couldn't tell him anything.

"Oh, I admit she's not F.F.V. like your wife," said Jay, a little nastily just because Mary was not friendly with Lou's office connections, "but she's good-hearted. She'd give me the shirt off her back."

"I'll bet," said Lou.

"I think a hell of a lot of Ebie," said Jay. "Ebie's done a lot for me. Ebie's a darn good egg."

No sense in making him touchy.

"Ebie's all right on a party," said Lou. "You can have a good time with Ebie."

He was willing to bet money that *anybody* could have a good time with Ebie, if Jay only knew it.

"Ah, but there's more to Ebie than that," insisted Jay. "Ebie's got a deep side. Everybody sees those blonde curls and gets the idea she's a featherbrain, but I wish I had her mind. The other night we were sitting around listening to

'True or False,' and Ebie could answer four out of every five questions just like that. Reads everything."

"I'm surprised you don't cut loose and marry her," Lou said drily.

Jay Oliver was visibly shocked.

"Marry Ebie? Listen, you can't marry a woman that makes love as well as Ebie," he said. "You know that, Lou."

It was warmish in the little room in spite of air-condition and fans. Lou got up and propped the door open. It was one of those unexpected impulses he often had at certain moments that made him think he was born lucky, for a minute before or a minute later would have been wrong. This was the exact instant that a tall stooped man in loose gray suit was making his way down the corridor and Lou's hand was immediately outstretched.

"Well, Judge Harrod," he saluted him, "I didn't get a chance to speak to you in the club car. Why not come in and have a highball?"

The tall man shook hands without smiling. He was well over six feet and the sagging folds of flesh in his neck as well as the slow careful walk indicated that he was a man used to carrying a great deal more weight. His eyes, gray and almost accusingly penetrating, were deepset under a thick hedge of white tangled eyebrows and these with the high-bridged commanding nose and stern straight lips gave him a dignity that the wide, unmanageable ears and pure bald head bones, as openly marked as for an anatomy lesson, must have enjoyed mocking. His teeth, strong and yellow as field corn, were bared in a momentary smile, none too warm.

"You've heard of Judge Harrod," Lou waved a hand to Oliver. "My wife's uncle. This is Jay Oliver, Judge, Whittleby Cotton, you know."

"I see," nodded Judge Harrod gravely. "How do you do?"

Jay made a reluctant motion to rise but was waved back to ease by the Judge.

"No, I can't join you, Louis," said he. "I have some papers to attend to in my compartment. I didn't know you were going to New York. Mary didn't mention it at lunch."

So Mary had been to the Harrods' for lunch.

"I guess she and Mrs. Harrod were going to a matinee," Lou ventured easily.

"A recital," corrected the Judge. "Myra Hess was the soloist, I believe. I understand she was to be guest of honor at cocktails later at our house."

"Oh, yes," said Lou, reddening, for this was another matter that annoyed him, that Mary should be an integral part of the Harrods' social life except when he, Lou, was home. He didn't really give a damn and, of course, Mary knew how musicales, contract, and formal dinners made him squirm, but he would have liked to have all his customers see him making himself at home in the Judge's pleasant garden, large Tom Collins glass in hand, the Judge's blue ribbon Scottie sleeping trustingly at his feet, the Judge's big shot friends—governors, bank presidents, bishops, all hanging on to Lou Donovan's sound analysis of business conditions. If such pictures could have been distributed without the actual boredom of listening to an evening of musical baloney or highbrow chit-chat, Lou would have been quite happy. But after half a dozen efforts on both Mary's side and the Judge's to include Mary's husband in the Harrod social life with nothing but embarrassment on all sides, the contact dropped back to a family matter between the Harrods and their favorite niece,

Mary. Lou suspected that he was barely mentioned, even, during these family conclaves. He found he could make use of the connection conversationally without the bother of going through the actual meetings, and this suited him fine, except for the increasingly rude attitude of both Judge and Mrs. Harrod when they met him. They knew well enough that Mary was crazy about him, but they acted when they met him alone, as the Judge was acting now, as if Lou Donovan, in speaking of Mary, was presuming upon a very slight acquaintance to refer to this intimate member of the Judge's private family. The fact that he happened to be her husband did not lessen the outrage.

"Sure you won't have a quick one with us, Judge?" Jay Oliver asked hospitably. Jay knew of only one way to dissolve his faint uneasiness with either superiors or servants, and that was to get drunk with them very quickly, and it was this simple formula of his that probably accounted for the hot water he so often found himself in, because it was during these ice-breaking friendly drinks that he was most easily taken advantage of. The Judge did not respond to the friendly offer.

"Hmm, I seldom drink in the afternoon, hmm," said the Judge, and then decided to soften the rebuke with a worse one. "It seems to me unnecessary to my mental processes,—hmm, as well as to my pleasure, hmm. I daresay other men are differently constituted, and possibly depend more, hmm, on, hmm."

His sentence trailed off into a final cough.

"I'll say I depend more," laughed Jay comfortably. "I can't think without a shot first, then I can't relax without another."

Lou was embarrassed by Jay's easy assumption that his

own brain processes and the Judge's belonged in the same conversation, even though in any argument with Mary on Jay Oliver's intelligence he was always quick to say the advantage was Oliver's. Oliver's business took more brains and common sense than the Judge's, Lou always declared.

"I drink to think and think to drink," chuckled Jay.

"I see, hmm," said the Judge. "That, of course, is one way of, hmm."

His voice, earnest, unctuous, and benevolent, was a pat on the head, a well-son-are-we-sorry-now-we-smoked-the-cigarette voice, and his "hmm" was a kindly purring growl that finished off a vague sentence, punctuated a phrase, a stroking soothing lullaby to suspicion; and in sterner, more official conversations it was an official seal on the basic authority of his statement. His voice was always prepared with this apologetic butter, though if it had been unmasked and not keyed to the inferior class or age of his listeners it might have been a harsh whine of intolerance. It was as if his highly exaggerated pharynx, romping up and down his throat like a busy bell-boy, was a jack-in-the-box, and this little lurking demon, as each phrase clicked shut, sprang out with a gurgle of "Yay, bo, amen!"

"Mr. Oliver and I were discussing the opening of my New York office, Judge," Lou said, and as usual when he talked to the Judge he oiled up his own voice.

"A New York office, eh? Ah," said the Judge. "That ought to please Mary. I heard her saying just today how sorry she was to miss the fall concerts again. There's one she spoke of only this week—could it have been the Modern Music one? Something at Carnegie Hall. Too bad she wasn't able to come along with you."

"Oh Mary hears plenty of music right there at home.

We've got the finest radio, she doesn't need to miss anything," Lou assured him confidently. "Naturally on business trips like this I wouldn't have time to take her to any musical affairs. I have to be on the job every minute."

"After all, Judge, you haven't got Mrs. Harrod along, have you?" Jay put in with a guffaw, and was that the wrong tack, for the Judge did not smile.

"I see, hmm," he said. "And of course Mary's having a big dinner party Thursday, that's true. I suppose you have to rush back for that."

"Oh sure," said Lou, who had forgotten all about that party.

"Well, good day, Mr. Oliver, good day, Donovan," said the Judge.

"One of the richest men in the country," said Lou as the door closed. "He could buy out the Gold Coast if he felt like it. Has his own plane, keeps a three hundred acre estate in Maryland, pays three thousand bucks for his hunters, has a bass lake and camp in Wisconsin, Christ, he's rich. Pretty close to the White House, too. Like a father to my wife and me. They brought her up, of course."

"Looks like an old buzzard," observed Jay, yawning. "I wouldn't want him nosing around me, I can tell you, and sounding off to my wife."

That was the kind of dope Jay was; he never took in any connection outside his immediate business that might be needed in some other way.

"I don't need to worry about that," said Lou shortly. "I don't fool around, not in his precinct anyway." Then, as this sounded a little too pious, he added more amiably, "Never do anything you can't deny. That's the old Donovan motto."

"You're a smart guy, Lou," Jay said with a sigh. "You and Ebie ought to like each other more."

Now Lou was willing to go into the club car, feeling that it would give him another chance at the Judge, so they went back presently, but the Judge was not there. Instead a fellow in a threadbare greenish plaid suit got them into a conversation about the difference between English and American business methods. He was a bronzed leathery little fellow with scrappy sandy hair and bleached eyelashes, buck teeth, long humped nose, and tufts of fuzz sprouted out of his ears and nostrils. Lou could not make out from his speech whether he was a genuine limey or just wished he was.

"Take the Duke of Windsor," said the stranger. "A personal friend of mine. My name is Truesdale, here's my card, T. V. Truesdale, originally an old Nebraska family, migrating from South Carolina, and incidentally the present governor is a connection on my mother's side. For the past eighteen years, of coss, I've lived abroad, personally representing the royal families of England and Europe. My wife, of coss, is Eldorana May, the operatic singer, here's a picture of her, a clipping I just chanced to catch in *The London Times* a few days ago. Of coss I read all the foreign papers, German, French, not Russian of coss,—'wife of T. V. Truesdale,' you see the caption there."

Lou examined the clipping, yellowed, with the faded picture of a sumptuous looking brunette of at least a twenty-year ago era, checked on the caption, passed it on to Oliver, who studied it with interest.

"What do you mean you represent the royal families?" he asked.

Mr. Truesdale, who had whipped out the picture like

magic from a bulging scuffed brown briefcase, replaced it now in a large manila envelope which he handled as tenderly as if it was a valuable second mortgage.

"Did represent, did, did," he corrected in his nasal singsong voice. "Europe is to me a dead country. Look at this Spanish situation, that will spread, don't you see, there'll be no business left in Europe. That's why I'm in America once more. America's the only country. And don't think they don't know it over there. I am not a Communist, though I was at one time a member of the Socialist party, voted for Eugene Debs, believe it or not, and personally I feel that there are many things to be said for Joseph Stalin, though I can't say the same for Mr. Chamberlain. Not after what he did to my friend Windsor. One of the nicest fellows you'd hope to meet. I said to him, to Windsor, that is, I said, 'Look here, sir,' I said, 'I don't understand the way half of these Britishers talk, it's not our language at all, do they have to mumble and squeak as if their mouths were full of hot marbles?' and he said 'Truesdale,' he said, 'it's the bunk, they don't have to at all, it's purely an affectation.' "

He paid for his beer very carefully from a frayed ancient pigskin wallet, and this too he fondled as he had his briefcase, as if these were all that had been rescued of his priceless treasures when the palace was destroyed.

Oliver was having a fine time listening to the stranger, winking at Lou over each anecdote. This was the real music of the rails, some eccentric stranger popping up telling his life story, it passed the time while Indiana slid past the window, towns popped up, announced their names with a placarded station momentarily thrown on the screen, then dissolved into fields, forests, hills. The brown stranger swept through a score of countries, his story was mounted on the wind, it sweetened their drinks, it mingled in Lou's mind with a picture of Mary's closed door and the house in Winnetka.

"What was your royal racket, sir?" Lou asked.

The stranger's pale eyes moved suavely from the perfection of Lou's gray suit to the ravelling cuff of his own shirt, and he looked down at this cuff now with astonished concern.

"I must apologize for my shirt," he said. "My laundry did not arrive as I left the coast so I was obliged to borrow from the porter. Disgraceful looking. I hate that sort of thing. I like the best clothes, always have, always will. Well, as I was saying, when I was travelling in Africa I bought for the royal family. If any member of the royal family was about to make a tour of Africa or India or possibly even Canada, I'd go ahead, investigate the private tastes of all the biggies he would be likely to meet, get dossiers on all the leading families, find out maybe that the Chief of the Kenja tribes has a musically inclined daughter, suggest a harmonica as a gift on the royal visit. The man before me, as I happen to know, on a previous royal tour, suggested an accordion as a gift, a tremenjus mistake, of coss, in the tropics, since the thing's nothing but glue, so it fell apart in the heat of the first day, and did not create the right international goodwill intended."

"Pretty smart," said Lou, pleased at such a complicated job. "Look here, maybe I could use you in my business."

He ordered a drink for the man and was even more impressed when the stranger refused, insisting on drinking only his own beer which he paid for himself from his worn wallet. Lou was sorry Oliver was there to hear the guy's story as he would have liked to present him as someone he had long sought for his staff of superspecialists.

"I may look you up sometime," said Truesdale, without eagerness, but efficiently slipping a calling card into Lou's hand. "You can usually get me at the Ellery, in New York, or the Knickerbocker in Los Angeles, or the Lafayette in Havana. I was stabbed in Havana last October. Look."

He was rolling his pants leg above the knee, showing a scar on his knobby calf when Judge Harrod beg—hmm—pardoned himself past them and brought Lou up short. He went back to the compartment, leaving Jay to the stranger, and indeed did not see Jay again till they reached Penn Station, for Ebie had gotten on in Pittsburgh. Ebie was in the corridor beaming when he got out in the morning, and the three of them got together for an eye-opener, Jay, glassy-eyed with a terrific hangover and Ebie still a little tight from all night drinking and inclined to giggles and squeezing both their arms. Lou was more than ready to drop them both when they got to the station but just as they stepped into the waiting room Jay clutched him.

"My God, Lou, look!" And there coming at them out of the crowd was Flo Oliver, no less, laughing triumphantly, and hanging on to some old lady who looked as if she must be her mother.

"I caught the plane to surprise you!" Flo screamed. "Didn't I put one over on you!"

She was upon them before either man could think what to do about Ebie, until Lou was inspired to quietly take Ebie's arm and say, "Well, Jay, so long. Ebie and I have got a day ahead of us. Oh, Flo, this is Miss Vane. Jay, you remember my speaking of Miss Vane—the artist who's going to handle the decorating of my new office."

"I just came down to meet Mr. Donovan," babbled Ebie.

"Just like me," Flo giggled and snatched Jay's arm. "Mama and I couldn't wait to see your face when you saw me here."

"Nothing like a little surprise," Lou said. "Come on, Miss Vane. Good-bye, Flo."

He firmly manipulated Ebie away from the happy little family reunion, leaving Jay still mopping his head in a daze, still paralyzed from the shock of danger. The poor sap just stood there, not having sense enough to make the most of his miraculous escape, gaping after his loyal friend and Ebie as long as they were in sight.

"Now, what, for Christ's sake?" Ebie muttered in disgust as they got into a taxi. "Good Lord, what a squeeze that was."

"Waldorf," said Lou to the driver.

"I'm still shivering from the shock," Ebie confessed. "Honestly, you don't know what a thing like that does to you. So that's his wife."

"That's Flo, all right," said Lou. Ebie really was shivering and Lou put his arm around her shoulders. He hoped to heaven she wasn't going to start his day off with a little womanly hysteria but she soon had herself under control. Looking out through the back of the cab he was suddenly aware of a familiar figure standing by the curb waiting for a cab. It was Judge Harrod and he was looking straight at him with an expression of unveiled contempt.

II

THE stupidity of having a wife who could spring a surprise like Flo's on you! The stupidity, Lou kept repeating to himself, of allowing yourself to be so nearly trapped by her when a few simple precautions in advance would have cleared everything. And above all the stupidity of permitting yourself to be rescued by a business friend who would always have that on you!

Ebie was disgusted, too, that was the first thing she and Lou had ever had in common. They stopped in the New Yorker for a quick shot to brace their nerves after the shock of seeing Flo, then rode uptown in silence since there was only one thing to say and that was what a dope Jay Oliver was, can't he manage anything like a grown man! The picture of his baffled docile face looking pleadingly after them while Flo and her mother encircled him with gay chatter was not an impressive one, but if that was the kind of guy Ebie fell for, all right, so Lou said nothing.

"God-damn fools," Ebie said suddenly with a bitter laugh. "Both of them, I mean. Thanks for pulling us out of that. God knows what Jay would have done if you hadn't stepped in pretending I was with you."

"I'd expect the same thing from Jay in the same situation," said Lou. He was beginning to admire himself for the instinctive good sense he had shown in saving his friend's face. He felt a little fonder of Jay (though still a little contemptuous) for permitting him to give this faultless exhibition of sterling male friendship.

"Ah, he would never have done the same thing," said Ebie. "It would never have even occurred to him."

Of course it wouldn't, Lou reflected; though Ebie looked dizzy she did have sense enough to know that much.

"I'd set aside the next forty-eight hours for him," she said.

"Want to have dinner with me?" Lou asked. Ebie shrugged a might-as-well. He could stop by at her apartment that night around seven. He dropped her at Saks Fifth Avenue and went on to the Waldorf.

When he came back to the hotel that night to wash up, Jay had called twice, and Lou knew what he wanted was for him to fix things up so Ebie wouldn't be sore. There was one urgent message to call Mr. Oliver back at Jack Dempsey's place by six or Suite 26B by seven, but Lou tossed the notes in the wastebasket. If you were signing up for a New York office, seeing bankers and realtors all day—in fact taking one of the biggest steps in your business career, you certainly didn't have time to help some poor dumb-bell out of a wife-trap. Lou felt he had fixed up the front for Flo, now let Oliver do his own fixing with Ebie. He had a laugh when finally a telegram came "Please take Ebie to a show or something and explain situation to her but not to Rainbow Room or Victor Moore show."

Taking a shower Lou thought how well things had gone for him that day. He'd clinched a swell suite of offices on Fifth Avenue in the Fifties, he'd lunched with and made a good impression on one of the biggest hotel men in the country, he'd started a whale of an idea on a kind of hotel survey, and so far as he was concerned, he was J. P. Morgan. He often in the past had dated up a red-headed hostess in a near-by nightclub but tonight he felt more like bragging than he felt like sex, so the date with Ebie was okay. There was no attraction there so it made it sort of homelike. He thought they'd go down to Cella's for a steak and some old-fashioneds, maybe drop in the Plaza later for some highballs and talk. Ebie seemed to have more sense than he'd given her credit for, so it was all in all a rather cheerful prospect. He tried two ties with the newest shirt, finally picked the dark red. Going down in the elevator, he thought it would be funny if he ran into Oliver or Flo in the lobby but he'd brush them off. It was ten to seven, and Ebie's apartment was only a dozen blocks off.

The elegance and respectability of the apartment house when Lou finally reached it stumped him. First there was the Park Avenue address when he had expected some West Forties rooming house, then there was the courtesy of the doorman at mention of her name, a courtesy reserved as he well knew only for the solvent. He found himself vaguely shifting his plans for the evening to something more pretentious—Voisin's, he thought, or the Persian Room, but still he wasn't sure. Once in her apartment he was even more baffled. The fact that Ebie wasn't ready and that a quiet elderly maid had him wait impressed him as favorably as the obvious expensiveness of the apartment. There was a something or other about the place that he could not quite classify or duplicate in his own home though God knows Mary certainly had a better background than Ebie. Maybe it was all the pictures, though he had a half dozen much bigger oil paintings at home that he'd paid at least fifty or sixty dollars apiece for at Marshall Fields. There was her drawing table, easel, and desk that might have looked freakish anyplace else but in this de luxe background, with grand piano, Persian rugs, odd bits of sculpture, these artists' tools seemed a charming decoration since they had so obviously justified their use. Lou sat down and lit a cigarette, oddly pleased with this surprise about Ebie, and still puzzling over the quality in the place he couldn't name. Maybe it was the casualness without disorder of the gadgets lying around, or the aura of good address which gratified his senses like a specially fine cognac, and he kept rolling it over on his tongue in the same sensuous way,—Park Avenue duplex, must be at least four thousand, and for the first time he felt a little jealous of Jay. It made him look at Ebie more closely when she came down from the balcony bedroom. To tell the truth he'd never had a good unprejudiced look at Ebie.

Of course lots of women look better in their own places. Once in a while you get a stunner who knocks them cold in a restaurant but back in her own living room takes on the second-rate lifelessness of her own handpicked ordinary background. Still the majority of women come out better in their own homes, so it wasn't really so surprising that Ebie should look quite dignified, and unusually pretty, coming down the staircase to music, for the radio was playing a Paul Whiteman recording of "Afraid to Dream" as sumptuously soft as the white bear rug in front of the great fireplace. Ebie was a girl who changed at every appearance from pretty to chic to naïve to plain tart, but this was a good night, the socko from Oliver had challenged her. Her hair was reddish gold tonight—Lou dimly recalled it as platinum at one time—and instead of the cutie-pie curls it was arranged in two plaits around her head so that her small naughty face with knowing hazel eyes looked not the least tartish. She wore a long-sleeved brownish-gold dinner dress and the amber jewelry on that with her hair and coloring was something that struck an odd new chord in Lou, something that didn't seem to stem from Ebie herself but from some new force Lou had never struck before.

"I know I'm too dressed up, Lou," she said guiltily, "but that's what I always do when I'm mad."

"You're still mad at Jay?" Lou asked.

"Raging," she said positively and this for some reason struck Lou as extraordinarily amusing for he roared with laughter.

"He's such a fool," she said plaintively, "he never plants anything right."

"He was lucky this time," said Lou.

"Oh, he's always lucky," said Ebie. "Jay always comes out all right except it's always somebody else that has to wangle him out. I'm crazy about Jay, of course, but I do despise a fool. If he wasn't such a natural born genius in business I'd have been through with him ages ago, but he isn't a fool in everything, thank God."

"Jay's a good business man," agreed Lou.

"He ought to save his money, though," said Ebie. "I try to tell him that."

Lou wondered just how much of the grandeur of Ebie's place was due to Jay Oliver's money. Jay would be fool enough to think he had to pay for an apartment, buy the works, when all any intelligent guy needed to do in these cases was to buy dinners and birthday presents. Ebie poured out two highballs.

"Nice place, this," Lou said. "I guess there's some good money in commercial art."

Ebie shrugged.

"I could make more if it wasn't for Jay," she sighed. "I throw up any assignment when he's in town. I'm a fool, you don't need to tell me."

"He don't appreciate it," Lou said. "I doubt if Jay knows what you do for him."

Ebie looked gloomily into her glass.

"I'm always a sap," she said. "I'm a sap for all my friends. I'm a sap for that louse that handles my stuff, too, Rosenbaum. He says to me, 'Do me a favor, Ebie, put up a friend of mine for a few days will you, you got a big place.' So for six weeks I put up his friend. It looks to me like I've got her for life."

"So it's a woman," Lou said.

Ebie tried to look insulted.

"I don't let any men stay here," she said haughtily. "No, this friend of Rosenbaum's is a foreigner. She doesn't want to go back because of war. Rosenbaum can't have her at his house on account of his wife. I'm always being a sucker for somebody."

"German?" asked Lou.

"A little of everything," said Ebie. "White Russian, mostly, I guess. You'll meet her if you stick around. She's always here. Trina's all right, only why is it always me that's got to be the goat?"

"You only got yourself to blame, girlie," said Lou. "Same as Jay. You can't blame anybody else for trouble when you walk right up and shake hands with it."

"I wish I had somebody like you to talk good horse sense to me once in a while, Lou," Ebie said. "As you say Jay's as bad as I am."

It was a surprise to find how really intelligent Ebie was. They had a few highballs and by the time they got out of the apartment it was too late to take in a show so they went over to Leon and Eddie's and ate a steak watching the floor show. They didn't talk about Jay after a while except to wonder where he went and whether Flo was smart enough to catch on. Ebie didn't see why Jay didn't send his wife to Mexico for the fall and Florida for winter like other men did. Then you knew where they were and could relax.

"A fellow doesn't need to do anything that drastic," said Lou, smiling. "A little common sense is all anybody needs."

Ebie was bitter about all of Jay's weaknesses now but Lou didn't say anything because of Jay being his best friend. There was plenty he could complain of but a pal was a pal. Ebie was a good sport, Lou had to admit it. She didn't try to put on a big show of being as smart as a man, the way Flo was always doing, and she didn't put on an act of being a pure young thing before she met Jay. She was on the level, told him about a couple of other affairs she'd had and then she asked him if he'd ever been mixed up with anybody. He was on the verge of telling her about his secret first marriage and about Francie popping up now to hound him, but pulled himself together in time.

"Men don't discuss those things, girlie," he said.

For some reason that made Ebie rather sore.

"Oh, they don't, don't they?" she said. "Then why are they always asking me about things like that? All right, I wish I hadn't confessed anything to you now if you're going to turn into a gentleman."

Lou tried to kid her out of her sulks because he did like her, especially after the apartment had shown him she was no tramp as he had once thought. He took her over to La Conga where they danced, something she said Jay didn't care about but she did. They bumped into a man just leaving the place with a trim-figured little woman who smiled at Ebie.

"My house guest," Ebie whispered to Lou. "The Kameray woman. She's with Rosenbaum."

"Not a bad figure," Lou said looking after the undulating movements of Mrs. Kameray's hips appreciatively.

Ebie turned out to be a good dancer and they danced and drank till the place closed. It had been the best evening Lou had had in New York for years,—friendly, restful, altogether what he needed. He said so to Ebie in the cab.

"I'll bet we had a better time than Jay," she said, her face darkening. "I damn well hope so anyway."

"Listen, don't be so hard on Jay," Lou laughed. "You can't be that mean to a fellow's pal. Have a heart."

He put his arm around her. The sun was shining in her bed-room window when he woke up.

III

"BUT why Maryland?" Jay Oliver wanted to know. He had been summoned to the Waldorf by a phone call from Lou with the insinuation that there might be a nice bit of business waiting there for him. Lou had had luncheon on the roof with Rosenbaum, the advertising and promotion wizard, and then taken him to his suite for completing their deal with Rosenbaum's multi-millionaire backer. The project involved a big order from Whittleby Cotton so Lou was glad to do his friend Oliver a favor. Unfortunately Jay had the shakes so badly from his last night's celebration that he didn't half-appreciate this piece of luck and in fact didn't seem to be able to get anything through his head.

"What's the matter with Maryland?" Rosenbaum asked.

"I don't say anything's the matter with Maryland—I just wonder why Maryland," Jay feebly explained. "You got Virginia—the Carolinas—take Virginia Beach. Ever stay at the Cavalier there? If you want swank, I mean."

"Oh, take another bromo and forget it," Lou called curtly from the serving pantry. "What the hell's biting you today, Jay?"

He came out of the pantry with a bowl of ice-cubes and set it down on the low table before the sofa, where Jay was sitting. Through the windows, curtained in heavy pink toile de Jouy, the afternoon sky seemed marvellously blue, with bubbling clouds stiffly whipped, looking as if the great chef Oscar himself had shot them out with a pastry-gun.

This serene vista seemed to be no comfort to Jay Oliver for he stared out gloomily.

"I hate this damn town," he said. "No offense to you, Rosenbaum. I realize it's your home town."

Rosenbaum shrugged.

"We New Yorkers don't care what anybody says. Maybe we don't have civic pride like other cities. Maybe we're just smug. Anyway go ahead and hate it."

"I don't like Maryland, either," said Jay. "I put in the worst week of my life at the Lord Baltimore one summer. A dame had put detectives on me."

"Will you get over that grouch?" Lou exclaimed. "Maryland or California, what the devil do you care? You're in. It's the sweetest contract you've seen in many a moon, old boy."

"I just don't seem to get the idea," Jay said. "I know it's a big deal or Rosenbaum here wouldn't be in it."

"Call him Syd," said Lou. "We're all friends here."

"If you don't mind I'm going to call him Rosenbaum," said Jay. "I mean if we're going to be personal friends. I always call my personal friends by their last names—first names are just for business purposes."

Jay was getting into one of his nasty moods, as usual at the wrong time and with the wrong people. It was a mystery to Lou how Jay could do the business he did when he was so careless with his contacts. Lou was especially nice to Rosenbaum now to make up for his friend's rudeness. He started to fill his glass but Rosenbaum put a warning hand over the top of it. Drinking was the one feature of business that he heartily disliked. He was a big loose-limbed man with pale gray protuberant eyes, gnarled heavy features, loose mouth and curly graying brown hair. His big shoulders and build made him appear athletic which was far from the truth, just as the humorous curve of his lips and the alert twinkle in his eye libelled his somber brooding nature. If he resented Jay's irritability he did not show it.

"Mr. Oliver missed the Major's explanation," he said.

"Call me Jay," Jay said.

"The property we're dealing with is that big stretch of woodland along the Chesapeake that the Van Duzers started to develop in 1928 then lost to the Chemical Bank. Well, the Chemical Bank is the Major. What we're doing now is building it up into one of the most exclusive resorts in the country. Stables, fox-hunting, health baths, thirty beautiful manors serviced by one great hotel or club."

"You say you can rent these houses for a week-end or a month," Jay said.

"We want your finest goods, Jay," Lou said. "The Major's crest on all the linen."

"Everybody is the Major's guest, you see," said Rosenbaum.

"Be a millionaire for a week-end, see, that's the idea," said Lou, genially. He clapped Jay on the back for he was in a fine mood. The very air of the room seemed charmingly alive with little floating dollar signs and fat little ciphers, commas, more ciphers, all winging around happily, waiting for a mere scratch of the pen to call them into action. The Major's conversation had left this agreeable effect, and although Lou had put in three hard days in the City to say nothing of his nights, and had, right up to the noon conference today, been worn out with nerves and other complications, the final settling of the proposition had left him miraculously refreshed. Like the colored porter on the Pullman, too tired to do anything till the five dollar bill galvanized him into a perfect frenzy of efficiency. "Thought you were tired, George," Lou had teased him. "Nothin' rests me like money, suh," George had grinned back.

"Sounds like a big job," Jay admitted.

"There's a fortune in it for all of us," said Rosenbaum. "If you knew the Major like I do you'd know he's a cautious bastard. He won't put a nickel into anything unless he's going to get fifty back."

"I suppose we'll have to put a lot of time from now on sticking around Baltimore," Jay said. "Baltimore or Washington. You can have them both."

"Don't kid yourself, this place is one of the best locations in the country," said Lou. "Look. Catch a plane at two-thirty—you're in Baltimore at 4:15. Car meets you and takes you straight to Castles-in-the-Woods. You meet the richest men in the country. The cream of society. You're the Major's personal guest. Don't tell me that isn't good stuff."

Rosenbaum went to the table and opened up his brief-case, fumbling in it for photographs which he silently passed to Jay.

"We're going to modernize the whole place," said Lou. "Wait till the natives see what we make of that state."

The pictures reminded Lou that he had not showed Rosenbaum the photographs of his house in Winnetka, so he went in the bedroom and brought back the snapshots of the place, the picture of the kid playing with her poodle in the backyard, and the snapshot of Mary in her sable coat standing beside the Packard.

"My wife," he said.

Rosenbaum glanced politely at the pictures, made appropriately flattering comments.

"I'll bet Mary's sore you're not home for that dinner she's giving tonight," Jay observed.

Lou looked at his watch.

"I'd better call her," he said. He had gotten over his disturbance over her strange behavior at parting and in the exultation of his unexpected good fortune today remembered only how proud he was of his high-bred wife and the excellent way their marriage was conducted. He remembered he had not told Rosenbaum about his wife's connections yet, though he had mentioned them casually to the Major. Both their wives were from the Lucerne convent, then a year at the Boston Conservatory, the Major's father-in-law was a judge, Lou's uncle-in-law was a judge. These little coincidences had been mentioned casually by Lou, that was all, but they had helped. No less a private authority than the recent train acquaintance, Mr. Truesdale himself, had furnished Lou with these little personality tidbits about the Major, at eleven o'clock that very morning, by telephone.

"Speaking of Maryland," said Lou, "did I tell you my wife's uncle has a big show-place down there, not far from your spot? Judge Minor B. Harrod."

"Oh, yes," said Rosenbaum, impressed. "I know of him, of course. Your wife a Harrod?"

"Mary Harrod, she was," said Lou, "Boston originally. Are you married, Rosenbaum? I'd like Mary to meet Mrs. Rosenbaum."

Rosenbaum smoked a cigar impassively.

"If they meet it will not be in the Castles-in-the-Woods," he observed, sardonically. "Part of my job is to protect the guests from non-Aryan intruders."

"Well, if you're ever in Chicago, then," said Lou. He went in the bedroom and called up for more seltzer and put in his call to Mary. He had left word with the operator not to disturb him for the last two hours and now she told him that Ebie had called twice. He had figured out Ebie as good enough sport not to regard last night as anything but a momentary lapse, but he might be mistaken. Sometimes these girls that talked like such good sports were more trouble than the other kind. Even while he had the receiver to his ear the operator said, "Will you take Miss Vane's call now?" and there was nothing to do but say yes. He went to the living room door and nodded to Jay.

"Long distance," he said and closed the door between the two rooms.

"Listen," said Ebie's voice, "do me a favor, will you?"

All right, now it was coming. Buy me some Tidewater stock, please, and I'll send you a check later. Lou braced himself.

"Rosenbaum's there with you, isn't he?" she asked. "Don't be so damned cagey, this isn't going to hurt you. The point is that he's going to suggest my little permanent guest to you for some promotion work and for God's sake say yes to it, will you?"

Lou was slow getting it.

"Who? What do you mean promotion work?"

Ebie was impatient.

"This Kameray dame I have on my neck. She knows too damn much—especially after last night."

"Oh."

"She doesn't know it was you. She only knows it wasn't Jay. Anyway it's getting me. You know. Not knowing when she's going to pop out with something when he comes in."

That was easy. Lou was relieved.

"What do you want me to do?"

"Get her out of town, keep her in the West, I don't care. Rosenbaum's sort of afraid to push her into something for fear you'll catch on to his position, so you help him out."

"That's a cinch," said Lou. He was glad of the tip. Some way to please Rosenbaum, who after all, represented the Major. "How do you feel today?"

Ebie groaned.

"Awful. Butterflies in my stomach, you know. I had to turn in two drawings to the agency this morning. That's where I saw Rosenbaum. I shook so I could hardly hold a pencil. We drank a whole bottle of Hennessey after we got back here, you know."

Lou hadn't remembered that.

"You kept telephoning everybody," Ebie said. "God knows who. Then you passed out."

The operator cut in and told him his call to Chicago was ready so he told Ebie he'd call her back and waited.

"Hello, Mary," he said briskly, "I thought I'd better let you know I'm tied up here. Some things have turned up and it will take me a few more days to get them cleaned up."

"Yes?" Mary said coldly.

It reminded Lou they were not on warm terms, so he tried to think of something personal to tell her, the sort of thing he seldom told her but which she loved to hear.

"Oh, by the by, I had a nice talk with your uncle on the train," he said. "He was on the same car."

There was a silence and he rattled the receiver.

"Mary, are you there?"

"This is the third time you've called me and told me all that in the last twelve hours," she said quietly.

This stunned Lou.

"You called me twice last night," she said. "Once at four o'clock and again at four thirty. It seems to have left no impression on you."

Lou mopped his brow. That was something he had never done before. Must have had his conscience working overtime.

"I forgot to tell you about seeing the Judge," he said.

"The conversation has been exactly the same all three times," said Mary.

Lou pulled himself together. If she was trying to get his goat he'd show her.

"Supposing I call you when I get back in town, then," he said coolly. "No use my wasting long-distance dough. So long."

At that he'd forgotten to ask after the kid. That would burn her up. It was funny, too, because he was fond of the kid. The only thing was that Mary had sort of taken it over from the minute it was born and made it her special personal property, none of his, until he had gotten out of the habit of even taking it on his knee. He occasionally surprised himself wishing he had a child of his own, and then he'd remember why he really had one, only it was Mary's and he didn't dare touch it. Some women took their children that way. It didn't matter, really, and it filled her life all the time he was on the road.

He was about to call Ebie back and get more dope on Rosenbaum when Jay opened the door.

"Flo and her mother went to Atlantic City," said Jay.

Who the hell cared?

"Nice for you," said Lou.

"I didn't have a chance to thank you for pulling me out of the jam there at the station," said Jay. "I sure appreciated it. Flo didn't bat an eye."

"Flo know's what's good for her," said Lou. "I'll bet if she didn't know what was up yesterday she did today when you handed her that hundred dollar fitted bag."

"She didn't say so," said Jay and then astonishment lit up his ruddy tan face. "How'd you know I gave her a fitted bag?"

Lou laughed.

"A shot in the dark," he said. "I ought to know how you work by this time. A woman would have to be mighty dumb not to notice your tracks."

Jay sat down on the bed, and lit a cigarette.

"Bring your drink in, Rosenbaum," Lou called. "We're holing in, in here."

"Listen, Lou, you didn't pull a fast one on me with Ebie, did you?" Jay muttered in an undertone.

Lou was hunting for a fallen cigarette and did not answer at first.

"She said you took her out, and I was wondering," Jay said slowly.

"What the hell are you getting at?" Lou exclaimed, and then Rosenbaum came in.

"I was just wondering if a good smart girl couldn't help us interest the right people in the Castles," Lou said. "Not just the pushing average looker, you know, somebody a little different, higher class, maybe, different."

Rosenbaum went over to the window and looked out.

"I could get you a very competent young woman who answers your description," he said. "Part German, part

Russian. Exiled here. She brought my cousin's little girl over from Germany last year and we feel grateful and of course very responsible for her. As I think of it she would give the right continental class to the thing. Discreet, smart —a very unusual personality."

"Sounds perfect," said Lou easily. "Let's hire her. What's her name?"

"Mrs. Kameray," said Rosenbaum, still not looking around. "I'll have my office get in touch with her and send her here."

It struck Lou as funny that Jay Oliver sat there, knowing who the woman was but not speaking up for fear Rosenbaum would then know about him and Ebie, and Rosenbaum, who knew perfectly well through Mrs. Kameray all about Jay Oliver and Ebie, did not dare mention where Mrs. Kameray was staying for the same cock-eyed reason.

Jay lay back on the bed smoking, shading his eyes with his hand.

"What's eating you?" Lou upbraided him. "Here I give you a nice bit of business and you act as if you'd just lost it."

"I feel lousy, that's all," said Jay. "Can't a guy feel lousy?"

Rosenbaum picked his hat and stick from the dresser-top.

"You people will want to celebrate at some hot spot, I suppose," he said with a sigh. "I'm a family man. I stay home tonight with my family and my little Hilda, and listen to the Jello hour."

Lou saw him to the elevator. When he came back he winked at Jay.

"Family man, oh, yeah," he said. "You should have

seen him doing the rhumba up at La Conga last night."

"Oh, was that where you and Ebie went?" Jay asked.

"It's a good orchestra," Lou said lightly.

"I should take Ebie dancing more, I suppose," said Jay. His tone was so mournful that Lou was annoyed.

"Go ahead, but don't act as if it was such a chore," he said. "After all I see you dancing with every other chippy in town."

"So Ebie's a chippy," said Jay.

"I never said any such thing," said Lou, and that was the way it went on till finally Lou called up Ebie to show how much he respected her and he asked her and Mrs. Kameray to come out and have a cocktail with Jay Oliver and himself.

"Wherever you want to go," he added.

"Trina would like to go to the Rainbow Room," Ebie said with a patient air. "She says she's never seen twilight come over the Rainbow Room."

"For Christ's sake, isn't that too bad?" said Jay, when this message was relayed to him. "Tell her to hustle herself up there then right now before it's too late."

Jay took a shower and borrowed one of Lou's ties and they were pals again.

"We can shake 'em at eight or so and go have a good time," said Lou. "We don't want to get into anything."

IV

The Kameray woman wasn't bad. She wasn't bad at all, Lou told Jay in the men's room.

"That phoney accent throws me," said Jay.

"I think it's cute," Lou said.

"Sure, that's why she hangs on to it," Jay said. "She's a liability if you ask me."

Jay was still worried because he hadn't been able to get back on Ebie's good side. Just as she was beginning to mellow and was hinting at lunching with him tomorrow, Jay recollected that Flo would probably be back by then and he didn't dare commit himself. So that made it worse. It was the longest Ebie had ever been mad with him. All through the cocktails at the Rainbow Room and the dinner at the Trouville she had been high-spirited and charming, always a bad sign in a woman who has every reason to be sulky. She had been brightly interested in everything Jay said, exclaimed "How amusing!" after his anecdotes, and all in all showed such a pointedly polite, agreeable side of her nature that Jay feared the worst. As a feeler he made some remark about wives popping up in unexpected places, but Ebie merely laughed gayly and said, "My dear man, if you'd known as many married men as I have you'd know they all have to jump when the little woman appears." And she added parenthetically to Mrs. Kameray, "After all, you can't blame the wives—it's not their fault they're always getting left at home."

"I'll bet Rosenbaum would do a burn if he knew we

had the Kameray woman out tonight," Jay said to Lou in the johnny. "He was saving her to spring on you tomorrow, wasn't he? Poor leetle Meester Rosenbaum."

"Her accent isn't phony," said Lou. "She's foreign, isn't she?"

Jay made a face.

"Nuts, she spoke English perfectly when she got here," he said. "Then she caught on to this accent business and how it gets the guys. So she's been doing this-how-you-say-in-English, and-eet-ees-zo-how-you-say stuff ever since."

"She's got a right to an accent if she is foreign, hasn't she?" Lou said. "Anyway, she's a darn smart little dame, if you ask me."

Jay brushed his hands over his coat.

"What she says with that cute accent would sound dumb if she said it straight," he said. "Don't be a goddam fool. The dame's a phony of the first water."

"Phony or not she'll be okay working on Castles-in-the-Woods," said Lou. "Snap out of this, will you? I throw a nice bit of business your way, and here you are, griping."

Jay did not smile.

"I got worries, Lou. Flo popping up all over the place. If it was anybody but a wife it would be blackmail, because she never comes right out and accuses me, she just sort of hints until I give her a check to shut her up. And now Ebie's sore. I know you don't like Ebie but——"

"All I got against Ebie is that she's too good for you," Lou interrupted. "What do you want to mess around with somebody like Ebie for?"

"I don't know," said Jay, dolefully. "I'm not messing. It's just that I like to go back to Ebie, that's all."

"That's the trouble with you, Jay," Lou told him frankly.

"You're always getting into fly-paper. Take me. I drop in the Spinning Top, pick up Tessie or Fifi, slip them a fifty-dollar bill and that's the end of it. I can meet them on the street with my wife, they never bat an eye."

"Ah, they got no feelings," Jay argued. "What's the fun of sleeping with some little tart with no feelings?"

"Once you got feelings you're in trouble," Lou warned him. "Those girls are all right. No talk. Nothing. But what do you do? You get some dame that's restless, mad at her husband, maybe, too high-class for a fifty-dollar bill so you got to give 'em a diamond pin. Then the trouble begins. Oh, Jay, this is Mrs. Friedman——"

"That's all washed up," Jay said.

"Never mind, it's always somebody like her. Oh, Jay, she says, I'm here at the fur storage and I'm so embarrassed, I'm short a hundred dollars cash for the alterations on my mink. Do be a lamb and loan me a couple hundred —send it over, will you? . . ."

"Ah, shut up," said Jay.

"Or else she has to get her car out of hock, or she wants to pay her dues at the Golf Club," Lou went on relentlessly. "Too high-class for fifty bucks a night. It's just five hundred a shot, that's all. And then she talks, and her friends are your wife's friends and then you're in. Don't you ever learn anything, Jay, for God's sake?"

Jay looked sorrowfully in the mirror at his brown face, now a little haggard from a combination of hangovers and woes.

"Can I help it if I like high-class women?" he asked. "I like a looker, sure, but I like a little class to them, a little intelligence. To me it's no fun unless the woman has a little intelligence."

"They got more than you can use, believe me," said Lou. "It's that intelligence that costs you money, boy."

When they got back to their table Ebie and Mrs. Kameray had their heads together whispering about something furiously, but drew apart when the men sat down.

"How you women dish!" said Jay. "Clothes and men, that's all you women think of."

"I suppose the subject of clothes and sex never came up in the forty minutes you two have been in the little boys' room," said Ebie snippily.

Lou took charge of that one.

"Men don't have the time to discuss sex when they're alone, I assure you," he said.

"Well, then, I don't know where they picked it up," Ebie said. She turned to Mrs. Kameray. "Wonderful, isn't it? They never talk sex and they never listen to sex talk. They just learn it by Braille."

Ebie getting nasty was a good sign, so Jay cheered up. No man was more miserable in the doghouse, than Jay, Lou reflected, and no man in the world did more to get himself into the doghouse. Figure that one out. They danced a little more happily together this time, but Mrs. Kameray was too tired so Lou sat with her, wondering what to talk about that would keep her seductive accent going. He couldn't imagine why that got him so, but it did, just like Ebie's apartment had got him. Some quality there he had never encountered.

"We were talking about our fren' Meester Rosenbaum," Mrs. Kameray explained. "The feeling about Jews is so strong I say he should make his name Gentile, like Rosetree or Rosebush."

Lou laughed loudly.

"Is it fonny?" Mrs. Kameray inquired innocently. "Meester Rosebush, he laughed too, but I say I am going to make the start until everyone will think he is a good Meester Rosebush and not a bad Meester Rosenbaum."

Lou laughed until the tears came to his eyes. He looked around for Jay and Ebie to come back so he could repeat the story but could not spot them on the floor. They must have gone out to the bar for a private quickie. It was just like Jay Oliver,—here he could easily seize this momentary break in his relations with Ebie to cut it off for good, but no he had to get his head back under the axe again, in a good position so that Flo or Ebie could take turns whacking.

He looked at Mrs. Kameray and wondered curiously why Ebie disliked her so much. Here was a lady, definitely a lady, you could tell that, nobody to be a nuisance around the place, yet Ebie was catty about her. She was different from American women he had known, about twenty-eight, he thought, or less, but tricked out to look like a dainty little woman instead of the youthful college girl type that the twenty-eight-year-old American girls tried to imitate. She had brown sleek fine hair parted in the middle with a little bun at the back, a fine bust, tiny waist, rounded thighs and slender legs, like old-fashioned women, he thought, and small in stature like old-fashioned women. Her little flowered hat dripped a silvery veil over her smooth white forehead and even over the nose—a strong New England nose like his mother's with the same full high cheeks and rich full lips, pouting a little but all the more provocative. He liked her slender sloping shoulders, the long slim forearms, he liked her slim ankles with their slow breath-taking ascent into plumpness, and more seductive than that was her poise, her calm acceptance of her own charms, the cool glaze over her dark brown eyes. He had been a long time trying to figure out what gave the piquantly artificial air to her person, and decided it must be the foreign flavor of her clothes, smart with lacy jabots, and the painted ivory ear-rings must help, for to his surprise she wore no make-up at all.

"Don't you wear lipstick?" he was impelled to ask.

She smiled deprecatingly.

"Everyone looks at me so when I wear leepsteek," she said. "I don't like it when everyone looks at me so. And my eyes are so beeg I cannot put on the stuff they put on."

"Ebie certainly lays it on," said Lou.

Mrs. Kameray lowered her eyes.

"Ebie is so nice," she said. "Ebie is a very nice person."

Lou couldn't help thinking how decent this girl was, nothing catty about her, when Ebie had put *her* on the pan all right behind her back. You didn't often run into women with any loyalty to each other. He saw Ebie and Jay standing out by the bar talking earnestly. They were getting along now, he could tell by their faces.

"Ebie's all right," he said, "when she isn't drinking."

Mrs. Kameray did not reply.

"I wonder what Rosebush would say if he knew you were out with Jay and me tonight," Lou kidded her. "He's arranged for me to meet you tomorrow, you know."

Mrs. Kameray's eyes danced.

"We wouldn't want to disappoint Mr. Rosebush, then, if he's made himself so much trouble about the introduction. Let's pretend tomorrow we don't know each other," she suggested.

Lou laughed again and agreed. He could see Jay and

Ebie craning their necks to look at him and thought they were probably surprised to see him laughing so much. He was usually pretty deadpan, but then he didn't get a girl with such a dandy sense of humor often.

"What's your business like, Mr. Lou?" asked Mrs. Kameray, earnestly, hands locked beneath her chin. "I so want to know."

"Take a hotel," said Lou. "Or take a tavern or a resort. It's got to have equipment, hasn't it—furniture, orchestra, cigarette girls, maybe palm trees? And it's got to have good roads leading to it, good neighborhood around it. All right, I'm the man they consult."

"You do all that?" she was wide-eyed.

"I have small office staffs, sure, but I got investigators all over the world, people making maps, people shopping for equipment, people wangling local politics to clean up bad sections around a hotel,—they report to me. I keep a finger on everything, I'm the works."

"Like an emperor," sighed Mrs. Kameray wonderingly. "Oh, how you must be a genius! Yes, like a czar!"

Jay and Ebie had disappeared for a long time before Lou realized it and even then, he went on explaining his business to Mrs. Kameray for hours, sipping brandies to her Rhine wine and seltzer, glowing in the unexpected pleasure of talking business to a woman, and though he did not even touch her hand he felt more disloyal to Mary than he had ever felt in his six years' married life.

V

ON SUNDAYS Ebie lay in bed and thought what a mess she'd made of her life. She had been in the habit of thinking this every Sunday for years and it struck her that she hadn't run through these Sabbath meditations for weeks. Why was that? By Sunday she still had done enough things to be sorry for, she hadn't stopped making a mess of things, that much was certain. It must be she had turned off the routine during Trina Kameray's long stay. That was it. All during Mrs. Kameray's stay she had waked up, at first irritated and finally furious at the mere sound of somebody breathing in the next room. The shower running made her think jealously—"my new red-and-silver shower curtains, damn her hide!" The smell of coffee reminded her that it would be made in Trina's way with a twist of lemon peel which Ebie loathed. The phone ringing made her snatch the receiver and snap "Wrong number" before the person had a chance to ask the infinitely grating question, "Is this Mrs. Kameray's apartment?" All these little things had made Ebie irritable and continuously filled with Christian intolerance. No one could have been more unobtrusive than Mrs. Kameray around the house, and after all it wasn't as if it was a tiny apartment, there really was room and to spare for two people. Nor was Ebie a selfish person, she told herself, she was perfectly candid with herself, if she'd been a selfish person she would have been the first to admit it. It was just that what was hers was hers.

All right, she'd brushed the woman off. There wasn't a shred of her around, she had been shipped off on a three months' tour of the country for Castles-in-the-Woods, representing the Louis Donovan Service. Therefore now Ebie hadn't any hates and Sunday rages. She had doldrums. The same set of doldrums she'd had for ten years,—ever since she had started being twenty-four, in fact, an age she had loyally stuck to socially for these ten winters. Professionally she admitted twenty-eight, and a maidenly fear of thirty. No reason why not, she looked better than she ever did, that is, dressed up. A commercial artist got a lot of graft, especially when she did clothes, as Ebie did. So even if her income hadn't been enough to dress her handsomely her graft would have. And presents. One thing and another.

The chimes from St. Thomas' told her it must be around eleven so she rolled over and checked this with her little musical alarm clock which had been tinkling "Lazy Mary" for the last half hour. It was the chimes' fault she had such bad Sundays, Ebie decided. They nipped into her sleep, dimly reproaching her for being late to Sunday school at the M. P. Church on Elm Avenue, Greenpoint, Iowa. She would struggle to wake up because although she didn't care about Sunday school she did want to wear her new pink dotted Swiss with the toast-colored straw hat so that the little boy who played in the yard next to the church would see her. Finally she would manage to wake up. And here she'd be in New York and not Greenpoint, and then she'd think of what a perfect mess she'd made of everything since those dotted Swiss Sundays, and that had been, roughly speaking, ever since she'd been ten. No sir, she thought mournfully, she hadn't had a pink dotted Swiss since her tenth birthday, unless you counted that dotted

Swiss kimono with the china blue silk lining. Nothing Sunday school about that, of course. Still, it was dotted Swiss.

She threw off the cover—it had been a warm night but there had been a little cool breeze with a pleasant hint of autumn and burning leaves. The kids in Greenpoint used to burn leaves on September evenings, she recalled. On Sundays, too. She wondered why anybody wanted to burn leaves but anyway it was fun and smelled wonderful. She must tell that perfume company to put out a Burnt Leaf fragrance. They'd say women didn't want to smell like a small-town bonfire, but she would say look at Russian Leather. People had said women didn't want to smell like Russian Leather but it turned out they did. Well, there was a constructive thought. Burnt Leaf Parfum. Only you couldn't say "parfum" any more unless it was made in France, because of that new law. All right, call it Burnt Leaf Smell and see where you got. She got out of bed and walked into the adjoining room, barefooted in her new high-necked nightgown, the one with the train, the one she had been presented with after drawing it for the manufacturer. She wanted to see what the work-room looked like, being a work-room again and not a guest-room. It looked wonderful, the couch a couch again instead of a bed, the table a desk instead of a dressing-table.

"My God, I really am getting selfish," she admitted, and then she decided this joy in the house to yourself was not selfishness but just pleasure in self-preservation, a New York characteristic. In a town full of people the New Yorker's only haven was home, she thought, pleased at being so clever and philosophical with just her own thoughts, and then she wondered if that was what she really thought. That was another angle to her Sunday soliloquies, this thinking things then wondering if that was what she really thought or what she had made up her mind to think, and if so, what was she really thinking behind her thoughts.

Ebie had two small rooms, the bed-room and the work-room, opening on the balcony over the living-room, but the work-room was so dark she usually worked in the sunny living-room below and used the upstairs room just for storing and filing. She had had this apartment for five years and was still amazed and delighted with its magnificence. A woman cover-designer had first had the place, it was a co-operative apartment, and it was still filled with the little touches that had finally bankrupted her,—the concealed lighting, the built-in cozy corners and trick bookshelves on the balcony, the specially made door-knobs, wall fixtures, ventilating gadgets, all things the poor owner could not take with her or resell. Moving in here had represented a big change in Ebie's life, a definite decision to play the commercial game, drop the old artistic crowd downtown and the Village nonsense. She'd spent enough time sitting at the feet of somber soon-to-be-great painters having them lecture her about taking her talent seriously, urging her to make good the promise of her Art League days, and decrying the advertising art she was making a living at and incidentally which they couldn't do. She was a sap for some of those boys, no doubt about that. She used to cook midnight supper for them while they kept her up all night talking art and she was flattered that they allowed her around. Then she met Jay Oliver with one of the advertising men she knew at an Illustrators' Ball and it was a moment in her life all right. The change from art talk to hard-boiled Middlewestern business talk seemed marvellously refreshing. Her ten years with Art seemed a long expedition into a foreign, fuzzy, phony world,—it was fine stepping out of it into straight commercial world, hearing Jay's straight talk. Money. Money. All right, there it was, the thing everybody wanted, artists, too, only it was wonderful to have people come right out and say so. It was like the simple dotted Swiss days, all one, two, three.

Ebie reflected now that she had begun thinking life was a mess ever since she'd made up her mind not to be kidded any more about life or to kid herself about it, for that matter. So here she was, not knowing when she was kidding herself and when not, whether she liked this handsome independent plush life her income brought her or whether she had had more fun, while she had it, out of the old rowdy-serious Bohemian life. The thing she had decided was that a girl alone had to have an above-reproach background in which to be Bohemian. You could slide down banisters yelling "Whoopee" in a palace and you might and could be a gay visiting duchess, but a little gay solo dance in a Greenwich Village basement made a girl out either a nut or a tramp. A good address was a girl's best mother in New York. A man saw a place like this and thoughts of marriage came out on him as obviously as freckles.

Not that Ebie wanted marriage. She'd had chances enough but where would she get off, marrying somebody and then scramming out every time Jay Oliver called up? Still she'd like a little affection, she thought with a modest dab at her eyes with her kerchief, maybe you didn't want a husband or a mother or a father or a child or a dog but you did have to have something. You did really have a right to have something belonging to you, something you could kick around and say, now that, that is definitely mine and nobody else's, and nobody has the right to kick it around but me, and that's security. What did she have secure in her life? I mean tender, true security, not financial security. That set her thinking some more.

Ebie put on the taffeta housecoat and slippers that Hannah had laid out for her and turned on the radio. She felt like a little companionship. If you could only skip Sundays! Her bed-room was rather bare in comparison to the heavy-carpeted luxury of the living-room and it was not so much that she had run out of money by the time she had furnished the downstairs as that she did not like to wake up in a clutter of ruffles. She couldn't quite explain this but if you waked up to bare walls, uncurtained windows, Venetian shades of course but no drapes, you could map out the day's work with no interfering images. The little white radio on the night-table bleated out a sonorous sermon and again Ebie shivered and turned it off. She might as well go down and get breakfast. Hannah never came on Sundays so she got her own.

In the kitchenette off the living-room, shelves were prettily stacked with black-and-white checkered canisters, a glass cabinet of all manner of goblets, tumblers, ballons, liqueur glasses, all betraying the old Southern hospitality standards, and the shelf of fancy canned goods, pickled walnuts, brandied peaches, smoked salmon, pickled mussels, shredded cocoanut, black and red caviar, teas—oolong, jasmine, mate, revealed a nice imagination in food.

"And to think," Ebie reflected, "I'm the girl that used to eat sugar and vinegar on my lettuce."

As a matter of fact Ebie, when she cared to, could whip up a nice little dinner, a gift that had made her quite popular as a Sunday night hostess for her father back in

Greenpoint, and later on as an art student living on Washington Square. She wondered now, as she plugged in the percolator, whether Lou Donovan ever let on to Jay what had happened the other night. Men were always such gentlemen with each other that any dope could tell what they were hiding. She wasn't mad at Jay, as he thought, for the stupid mess about his wife,—though she had let him think she was still mad. She was really mad at herself. There was the telegram on the table cancelling one job, all because she'd delayed it by rushing out to Pittsburgh to meet Jay. She could blame Jay for that if she wanted to be unfair but of course it was all her own fault for being such a fool about him. Here she deliberately sets out to be a success instead of an artist and then lets a married man make a mess of both things! All right, that was bad enough, but then she ought to keep the love part secure, since she messed up her life for it, but no, she had to make even a mess of that by letting the man's best friend stay all night.

"How did I get to be such a louse?" she wondered out loud. "If it had to be somebody why did it have to be his best friend?"

So she decided to blame it on the brandy, but then there were more self-reproaches there. That meant she was making a mess of her life by drinking too much. Drink ruined a girl's looks in short order, Rosenbaum had told her that much. On the other hand, as she had pointed out to him, she could show him girls who had never had a drink in their lives and yet were no balls of fire so far as looks were concerned. She turned the downstairs radio on to WQXR and got the Fifth Symphony. She always got the Fifth Symphony. She could almost write it herself now,—boom boom boom, begin the beginning over and over till every instrument has got in a few well-chosen remarks, then begin again, and again, ah now we're getting into it. But no, just where the middle should be the end begins with each little instrument saying a few last words, then altogether, amen, amen, good-bye,—ah but wait a minute, just a last minute suggestion, then good-bye, but wait, one more final nightcap of finales, boom da da boom, then another (now I really mean it this time, we really must go after this last one). That was the Fifth Symphony and that was what art and culture finally rattled down to—too much spinach, take it all and say you like it, or else throw your weight with people like Lou Donovan and Jay Oliver who made fun of culture because they didn't have any. She had kidded the pair of them the other night at dinner, the night she brushed off Mrs. Kameray.

"What'll you have, baby, a steak?" Jay had asked.

"A steak for God's sake," she had mocked. "These two bums clean up a fortune today and they can't think of anything better than a steak to buy for us."

"Anything you say, baby," Jay said. "You can have quails on toast just by lifting a finger."

"That deal today is nothing," Lou said. "By the time we're through, old dear, we'll be buying you angels on toast."

The waiter stood at attention and Jay looked up.

"Four angels on toast, waiter," he said, "nothing too good for us."

Angels on toast, my eye. Ebie sat eating toast and sausages with sliced pineapple, listening to WQXR and looking over the Art Section of the *Sunday Tribune*. Whenever she got disgusted with her affair with Jay she cried a little over the art columns. That helped along her Sunday doldrums as much as anything. Here was Royal Cortissoz or Jewell approving "Dunes," "Kansas Dirt Farmer," "Apples and Bible," "The Old Captain," "Upstate White Church"—(as if she hadn't practiced them all herself ages ago)—by her former art school colleagues. She too might be in that blessed company—"heavily influenced by Kenneth Hayes Miller," or "under the domination of the Midwest School," or "reminiscent of Cézanne but lacking of course both his gusto and his inspiration." Yes she could be among those contemporary immortals instead of here in this elegant apartment, last night's orchids and tomorrow's breakfast all on ice, her life a mess,—yes there could be no doubt of that, though her gift for prostituting her art had always made those old companions strangely jealous. She dried a tear again, and turned to the society page, for no reason, except that there could be nothing certainly in those small periodic sentences to make her think of either the futility of love or of art. Or so she thought until she was idly glancing down "News of Resorts" and after "White Sulphur Springs" came to the first item under "Atlantic City":

"Mr. and Mrs. Jay Oliver and her mother Mrs. MacAlister are at the Hotel Traymore."

Ebie put the paper down and lit a cigarette. After the way he had tried to make it up with her. After the way she had almost forgiven him and really intended to at the right moment. Then he goes down to Atlantic City with his wife and mother-in-law of all people. No reason why not. A wife was a wife. She shouldn't flare up at Jay. The fault was her own for giving up her simple old life as a real artist—(work away at it even if it takes years! That's what she should have done)—and started distorting all the decent·things in life with commercial art, married men, Rainbow Rooms. Hopping all over the country at a word from the man. Kicking her work over. Kicking over her ideals. Her little old dotted Swiss ideals, she thought sadly. Served her right that he should pass her up now for his wife and a little family stroll down the old Boardwalk. Served her right for picking up with a fellow like Jay. Visiting fireman. That's what fellows like Jay and Lou were called. Fellows the old crowd would have laughed at. Fellows you took to Luchow's for dinner then to Jimmy Kelly's for the midnight floorshow and they shouted "Greenwich Village—whoopee!" And your crowd sneered at them and didn't appreciate that they might be smart in their own line to make all that money, and the visiting firemen looked at your friends' and your own art works and said, "How long did it take you to copy a picture that big?"

You fell for them for a while of course, the firemen, because maybe you got a little too much art talk, a little too much literary conversation, a little too much brain work instead of dancing and fun. But a person was a fool to let them get you. Here Ebie pulled up the shades and saw that the day was fine, it was wearing its finest Sunday clouds, white, calm, substantial, and a stern blue sky, and the sun was all polished up and glittering, throwing eye-stabbing reflections on windows across the court, shining away fiercely, working hard to make a good impression so that it needn't come back after lunch. No, nothing to prevent her picking up her old life, she could always go back to it, just as Jay and Lou could always go back to their wives. Jay and Lou with their big respect for marriage. Doing anything they pleased on the side but keeping up the great marriage front. The Show Must Go On. That was the phony part of the visiting firemen. And just as Ebie had gotten very suddenly fed up one day with artists' life in Greenwich Village she now got fed up with her present. She dialed the garage for her car and then raced upstairs to dress. She rummaged through a drawer till she came upon a dotted Swiss dance set with blue ribbon bows. If you couldn't wear it outside you could at least wear it next you. Then she turned on the radio full blast to a recorded program and sang with it, "I Can Dream, Can't I?" softly along with Bing Crosby while she hurried into a suit. She suddenly felt like kicking over every trace of the present.

"I'd almost go back to Greenpoint," she thought, "only it wouldn't work out because I'm not ten years old any more."

Outside the apartment the doorman opened the door of her little blue Plymouth for her.

"Glad to see you can get away such a fine day," he said heartily. "Sure fine weather for getting out in the country."

She must certainly have had the look of going some place all right.

The little blue Plymouth with the red wheels rolled down Park and over the Grand Central ramp and down Fourth. On Sundays Fourth Avenue below Murray Hill was a deserted street except for the little comings and goings of the Vanderbilt Hotel. There was a nice hotel, Ebie thought, it had Wedgwood medallions all over the doors and a dark mezzanine where you could lunch with one man and see over the balcony rail the man you were going to dine with that night being a big shot with the boys—(cigars, brandy, do-you-know-the-one-about-the-derby-hat-and-the-plumber)—at a table down in the dining-room below. A nice hotel, the Vanderbilt. Caruso had a floor there once, but there were other things about the place, too, Ebie recalled with a reminiscent smile. She had forgotten to salute the old Murray Hill Hotel a few blocks back, but there were memories of that, too. Brass beds, for instance. Bay windows. In the dining-room, publishers, agents, travelling salesmen, and Hartz Mountain canaries, a pleasantly out-of-town flavor to it that made you able to guess the type of man he was if he suggested this restaurant.

A little blue car is very becoming to a young woman as every young woman knows, so the casual pedestrian today turned to look after Ebie as she drove on down and over to Irving Place where the Sunday hush fell on old well-kept brownstones, handsome old apartment houses;—people really lived here, there was even a father out wheeling a baby, a rare spectacle in Ebie's life so she leaned out to see whether the pram really contained a baby or a publicity stunt. Now the lights changed and stopped her directly in front of the house she had once roomed in with her girl friend from the League named Honey. Ebie was surprised to see the house still there, an old brownstone, one of Stanford White's designs (she remembered the landlady pointing out the house around the corner on Gramercy Park where Mr. White had lived before his murder),—oh, yes, and it was there that young musician had shot down the author, David Graham Phillips. It was a romantic murder belt, this section, sometimes famed as the home of Washington Irving though he had never been murdered so far as she knew.

From a fine old mansion this house Ebie once knew had deteriorated into "Furnished Rooms" with an Armenian restaurant in its basement. Odd spacious black walnutty rooms, Ebie recalled, with dark mahogany stairs up and down from one wing to the other, elaborate balustrades, little balconies in the great foyer as if for a small orchestra, so that the bleak rooming-house atmosphere blended with the dim fragrance of long-ago balls. You could almost shake out echoes of "Kiss Me Again" from the dark velvet hangings. Oh, yes, it was an old waltz house, Ebie thought, definitely that. She wondered if Honey still lived there and looked at the door intently, half expecting the old girl friend to walk out as big as life, but there was no sign of her. Just as well since they had parted on very chilly terms for no reason at all except that they either disliked each other's men friends or else liked them too much. At any rate they had a habit of spending the last hour before retiring, the Stocking-washing and Cold Cream Hour, in snarling at each other over each other's dates. Honey was a virgin (at least you couldn't prove she wasn't), and was as proud as punch of it. You would have thought it was something that had been in the family for generations so that no matter what the circumstances she could never quite bring herself to hock it. Honey took courses in oil at the League and modelled for a commercial photographer for money, and Ebie took black-and-white courses and did fashions and illustrating for money. They had a living-room with quite nice furniture, at least like Honey's virtue you couldn't prove it wasn't, since it was always encased in bright chintz slip covers. There was a fireplace with fires forbidden, a little bedroom and bath and kitchenette, all for eighteen a week. Since all they ever cooked in was breakfast or a canned hash supper their expenses were very little, unless they were being rushed by League boy friends at their own expense since the boys there were usually poor. Ebie and Honey used to try to break even by taking out a Visiting Fireman one night and a League boy the next. They even had their moments when they had no dates at all but just went on a girls-together-spree. They'd wait around till almost eight pretending they wanted to finish a detective story, or that they weren't hungry really, then face the fact that there was no dinner date coming up tonight, so they would go round the corner to a tavern where O. Henry used to go, and they'd sit in the dark smoked-wood booth drinking old-fashioneds and telling each other things they certainly wished later they had never told, and bragging about their families, sometimes making them very hot stuff socially back home and the next time making them romantically on the wrong side of the tracks. The families must have been on wheels back in the Midwest, whizzing back and forth across the tracks at a mere word from the New York daughters. The thing about this restaurant, too, was that there was nothing tea-roomy about it, so they felt very sophisticated being the only women in it often. Honey loved literary men so other times they went to a literary hangout on Eighth Street where you could see your favorite author in the sidewalk café. Honey usually carried a magazine with her "work" in it to impress the strangers who usually barged up trying to promote a date. They drank Planters Punches here, a specialty of the place, one that usually brought all the men's eyes to their table, and eventually the "Pardon me, I hope I'm not a nuisance, but would you mind telling me what the name of that wonderful drink is? . . . Planters Punch? . . . Thank you. Look, you won't think I'm fresh I hope, if I suggest buying a round of them. Seriously, I'm just curious about them."

What a drink! The waiter bore the glass with snow a foot thick all around the glass and a mountain above it topped by a miniature fir tree of mint, and extra long straws through which you drilled for rum, and it seemed to come up from the damp bowels of the very earth, you could almost get Floyd Collins on a clear day as somebody had once remarked. After things got going Honey would whip out the magazines and show her Work. She was the girl on page 98 in the nightgown holding her hands to her head and remarking in capital letters right beneath the picture, "Oh, why didn't I take a Selzamint and Wake up Happy?"

"There," Honey would cry, "would you believe that's me? My other profile is much better—the right side of my face, I mean, but they liked this side for a change."

Then she'd eagerly leaf through the next magazine. There she was on the back of the cover page in three colors in three different poses. ONE: Ball gown. Dancing with white-tie man who averts his face. Balloon coming out of her mouth saying, *Let's go home, dear, no one will dance with me, yet I look every bit as nice as Emily.* Balloon from white-tie man says, *Yes, dear, but why not see our family doctor?* TWO: Doctor Troutman's office. Honey in street clothes. Balloon coming out of Honey's mouth saying, *But, Doctor, is there nothing I can do about Body Aroma?* Doctor balloons back, *Fortunately, Mrs. Flashman, there is a secret formula known to physicians for many years but only recently made available to the public. It is ——"* THREE: The Ball. Different ball dress for Honey and this time surrounded by half a dozen men all holding out their hands as she is wafted triumphantly into the dance by her proud husband. *Well, dear,* he balloons at her, *I notice you had every dance tonight. What has changed you? Bodyjoy,* she radiantly balloons right back. *Ever since using Bodyjoy my pores have been breathing properly and I am once again the girl you used to know.*

The strangers were always impressed and usually told Honey that her acting in these three little vignettes from real life was so good she ought to be in pictures, and she always had the snapper ready, "But I AM in pictures, only not the kind you mean. I'm an artist."

Honey was such a feeb Ebie couldn't understand how she'd stuck it out with her those two years. It got so just the sight of Honey on a Sunday sitting around painting her toenails and brushing her red hair one hundred strokes was enough to drive her crazy. When the hairdresser burnt off a big hank of this prized hair in a permanent wave, Ebie did feel sorry for her and tried to comfort the poor girl as she lay sobbing on the bed, the handmirror face down beside her.

"Never mind, Honey," Ebie had said, "you never were the conventional type of model anyway, you're not dependent on a glamor-girl haircut. You've got a different style, see, not the regular model type of face."

At this Honey sat up and looked eagerly into her mirror again.

"I know," she agreed with satisfaction. "I'm more the elfin type. My face is a perfect heart-shape, isn't it?"

Even if it was kidney-shaped Ebie didn't want to hear about it and she moved out almost at once before she started screaming. She took a place then on Washington Square North East with a back door on the Mews. An enormous, high-ceilinged room it was, panelled walls, great windows through whose perennially dirt-stained panes the sun threw a stingy little light. There was an oil-heater to combat the strange blasts and drafts that wolfed around the baronial room on winter nights, whistled through locked doors, walls, closed windows, barred fireplaces. But a great cathedral chair, a vast sofa all bought at auction around the corner and ready to crumble at a glance, and her easel, drawing board, and reproductions of Daumier, Steinlen, Breughel, Grosz, and a few of her own sketches, pinned on the wall, gave the place quite an atmosphere. In fact the studio was so romantically Bohemian, so much the artist's dream, that Ebie did less and less serious art here and more and more discussion of it. The more commercial work she did the more of her old studies did she pin up with pride, and the more money she made the more she enjoyed the company of the arty boys and girls. "My God, but I was bright then," she reflected now with astonishment, "I certainly threw away a good brain when I started up with Jay and Lou's crowd." But of course it was her own fault, she knew that.

Further down the street the blue Plymouth drew up before an entrance labelled simply "BAR and GRILL." It was the tavern entrance to a somewhat mediæval looking hotel, whose time-and-soot-blackened façade was frittered with fire-escapes racing the dingy windows up to the ugly gargoyles on the roof. For Ebie this hotel too held certain associations and for a minute she looked out of the car thoughtfully at it, wondering whether to rouse these sleeping memories. Even on a bright noon like this the BAR and GRILL was a sunless cavern, its dark oak wainscoting rising high to meet grimy black walls, its ship-windows covered with heavy pumpkin-colored chintz, so that entering the room you seemed at first in a cellar fog till a feeble ray of gray light from a window above the door permitted you to grope your way down the long somber bar. Once in you were in for no mere moment, and Ebie, aware of this legend as she was, gave a slight start on seeing that same ruddy but glum man in the derby at the foot of the bar who had been there five years ago day and night, his coat always over his arm as if in the act of flight, a flight that never took place.

It was after twelve, the hour when the bar opened on Sundays, and the elderly lady residents of the hotel were without too much obvious haste taking their places in the grill-room, nodding and smiling to the waitresses, carrying their knitting and a slender volume of some English bard, anything to prop against their first Manhattan. If you ever had asked yourself "What ever became of that famous old suffragette who chained herself to the San Francisco courthouse? What ever became of that lawyer who saved Killer Mackay? What ever became of the girl who survived Niagara Falls? What became of the author whose one book sold so many million copies he never wrote again? What became of the first wives of these now famous men?" the answer would be—"Look at the BAR and GRILL." Here they dwell, as remote from life as if they were in Bali. Coming out at noon to the Grill they retreat at dusk into the even dingier caverns of the upstairs, grope their way through narrow silent hallways to their small dark respectable rooms. Seldom speaking to each other they are comforted by each other's presence and if in the night the lady who had once sung with Caruso should feel once and for good that wild pain in her left auricle she could always rap on the wall and thus summon the ex-eminent architect who had been freed of the charge of strangling a whole family twenty years ago near Albany.

A stained-glass window behind the bar gave a saintly glow to these resident lunchers as they sipped their drinks and dipped into literature. It was sip and dip, sip and dip, until cocktail time was proclaimed by the arrival of the little cocktail sausage wagon, and by that time the barriers that prevailed at noon would be brushed aside, privacies violated, discreet bits of personal information exchanged, letters from absent nephews or far-off celebrated friends read out loud while Music by Muzak played Songs From Cole Porter Hits. Another curious thing about these small, venerable, respectable hotels, there seemed no appeal here to the average customer. BAR and GRILL for instance, appealed to seemingly genteel widows and spinsters of small incomes because there was an air of musty piety about the management, a lady could be a dipsomaniac here under the most genteel conditions,—very quiet, very hushed, this place; then there were these tired flashes in the pan, the one-shot celebrities, and on the other hand there was a gayer younger group whose loyalty to the BAR and GRILL was based on the cheapness of its martinis. Over their simple dollar lunches (four martinis and a sandwich) this livelier set snickered at the old residents, whispered nifties to each other when the small very, very fat little old resident waddled in and was assisted with great dignity to a bar stool by two courtly gentlemen near-by who appeared unable to get a real hold on the gelatinous little creature and must scoop her up by handfuls.

The sight of the smart little blue car drawn up outside joined all groups in a common excitement, heightened by the unusual spectacle of such an uptownish and well-turned-out specimen as Ebie Vane coming in to this ancient cavern. Not that many of the residents did not have friends as splendid as this in other quarters of the city, but these friends were understandably loath to contact them in this dark hole. Who was she meeting—what brought her here instead of to the Lafayette, the Fifth Avenue, the Brevoort or one of the other more expensive and certainly more suitable rendezvous?

Ebie, after a brief glance around, took a stool at the bar and ordered a Dubonnet with a dash of brandy by way of eye-opener.

"What happened to Willie?" she asked the bartender, a beaming rosy young man, a chain grocery store clerk, she thought.

"Willie? Willie's been gone these five years," he said in a pleasant Scotch brogue.

The glum man in the derby with his cane hooked over the bar-rail, the fat lady, and the two gray-haired men drinking Scotch silently at the other end of the bar all were eyeing Ebie in the bar-mirror. She saw their eyes reflected between the mirrored stacks of bottles, their quietly questioning faces. She certainly must look out of place, there, the only normal-looking visitor in the whole joint. She looked around more carefully and then saw in the dim little stall in the corner where the livelier set was lunching the person she was seeking. She paid for her drink and walked over.

"Hello, mama," she said.

"Why hello, Ebie," said her mother pleasantly. "Sit down—these are friends of mine—I didn't catch their names. I was just telling them how perfectly ridiculous this article on Edgar Arlington Robinson was, so don't interrupt."

Ebie nodded to the others and sat down on the end of the bench beside her mother. The others, who had been sitting with resigned, unhappy faces, exchanging hopeless looks with each other, up to this point, now brightened. No good deed of hers was ever more appreciated than this simple appearance at the table, for her natty plaid suit and simple good looks gave point to her mother's endless anecdote as well as excuse to her mother's mere existence, something the group she was now entertaining had doubted could be done. To tell the truth the lively set had just about decided to give up Ye Bar, in spite of its twenty-cent drinks, because of Mrs. Vane. The three of them, two men and a girl, had been hilariously comparing notes on last night's party, burying their heads in their hands as they were reminded of the perfectly awful things they had said and done, and to so-and-so of all people; they had reassured each other that it didn't really matter since the so-and-sos had been known to misbehave themselves on occasion.

"But at Mrs. Whitney's!" the girl kept exclaiming. "At Mrs. Whitney's of all places! Oh, Foster, you shouldn't have! After all, you can't go around tweaking every Van Dyke you see."

"How did I know it was General Vanderbilt?" complained the young man, and then he sighed. "But what hospitality! Two footmen to each guest, pouring up your glass as fast as you could down it till finally they kicked us out. Why aren't there more homes like that?"

"You can't say anything, my dear," the other young man chided the girl, "after you pushed that dealer into the chocolate cake."

They buried their faces again, roared with laughter, reproached themselves, roared, and then Mrs. Vane appeared, as indeed, she appeared to almost every guest in the Bar and Grill at some inopportune moment, and for this reason was known as The Haunt. A tall gaunt woman of sixty, she looked like a witch, black eyes, dyed oily black hair, and strange drapes pinned together somehow on her person with little oddments of jingling jewelry and bracelets which served to set off her amazingly long fingernails. As a wit-butt Mrs. Vane had served her purpose more than well in Ye Bar and Grill, but it was her flair for society that was ruining her and in fact almost ruining the hotel. Mrs. Vane loathed the lonely women of the hotel and yet a literary woman of violent opinions has to have someone to talk to, and frequently Albert, the bartender, was too busy to listen. At those times she would raise her lorgnette and examine the room for suitable companionship. Today she spotted the intelligent young group in the end stall and at once descended upon them.

"I love laughter," she said by way of introduction. "May I join you? I am so outraged by this article on Robinson, Robinson, the poet, you know—let me read you what this absolute fool has to say about him—hmm . . . let's see—here . . . listen to this."

She was in, the young lively set was crushed, and there she sat, ordering her dry sherry, very very dry please, Albert, one after the other because she was not a drinking woman and could only take a dash of sherry or in cold weather a medicinal dose of brandy. Of both these liquors she drank very little but all the time. Her companions were imprisoned, their laughter stopped, gloomily they foresaw hours passing with this sort of thing and no decent escape. Ebie's entrance at least permitted them to watch curiously the smart stranger at the bar, without having to fasten their eyes on Mrs. Vane's witch-face. Then to their amazement the handsome stranger walked up to their very table and was Mrs. Vane's own kin and they respected Mrs. Vane, then, and listened eagerly to her, lest she take their pretty guest away. In a pause during which Mrs. Vane lifted her glass to drink, one of the young men said, "Are you and your mother in town for long?" hoping to draw Ebie in and freeze mother out but it proved to be the opposite, for Mrs. Vane hastily set down her drink and switched at once from reminiscences of Robinson to her own life story.

"Goodness me, young man, I've lived in New York ever since I found I couldn't get a decent psychoanalyst in Iowa. I've been here since 1924, off and on. A few years in Europe, of course. I met Freud. Speaking of Freud, Ebie, what do you hear from your father?"

"I got a Christmas card," said Ebie. "Nothing since then. It was just signed Father and Daisy."

"Probably married again," mused Mrs. Vane but the subject did not seem to interest her for she immediately launched into her life up to a treasured evening she had spent with Gogarty, the great Irish writer, who, she stated, definitely was the wittiest man she had ever had the pleasure of meeting. The young people looked curiously at Ebie, trying to fathom her connection with the weird old bore, and Ebie looked at her watch. Mrs. Vane described in detail the violent prejudices she had mentioned about George Moore, James Joyce, Bernard Shaw, and other great figures to the sparkling Mr. Gogarty on her great evening with him.

"What did he say?" politely inquired the girl.

Mrs. Vane's yellow face lit up.

"Gogarty? He didn't say a thing," she exclaimed triumphantly. "Not a damned thing all evening! Where was the card from, Ebie?"

"Greenpoint," said Ebie. "He still lives in Greenpoint. He still has the store, you know. Look, mama, how would you like to take a house in Connecticut with me?"

The inquiry served to silence Mrs. Vane's monologue as nothing else could. She lifted her lorgnette and frowned intently through it at Ebie.

"Connecticut? A house?" She was suddenly aware of the amenities for she turned to the three now embarrassed young people and said graciously, "I don't believe I introduced myself. My name is Mrs. Vane. You must excuse my daughter for bringing up personal matters at a public luncheon. What kind of a house, Ebie, do you mean a boarding house?"

"No, not a boarding house, nor a bawdy house, either," Ebie exclaimed, exasperated. "A house."

Mrs. Vane now rested her chin on her hand and studied Ebie seriously.

"I suppose you mean a salt-box. That's the kind of houses they have in Connecticut. Salt-boxes. No, Ebie. I don't see why I should have to live in a salt-box. Not at my age."

The girl saw an opportunity now to escape and nodded significantly to her companions.

"Mrs. Vane and her daughter want to talk family matters, boys," she said. "They don't want us intruding."

"No, no," protested Mrs. Vane reaching across the table toward her escaping companion, "it's my daughter who is the intruder. I had no idea she was coming in. Why didn't you telephone me, Ebie? After all, one doesn't just drop in on a person."

"I've left messages," Ebie answered, "but you never called back."

"Probably had nothing to say," said Mrs. Vane. "I see no reason for using the telephone just because there's one handy. If I had had something to say, naturally I would have called. Don't go."

She urged this last in a most hospitable voice as if it was she who had arrived early to snatch this prize corner and had graciously permitted these strangers to join her. The Lively Set, however, climbed over her draped knees with alacrity, the men with a last wistful glance at Ebie. As they hurried out into the little oblong of light that revealed the mouth of the cave Ebie heard the girl say clearly, in answer to some murmured comment from the man, "Yes, but don't you think a little too, too Harper's Bazaar?" All you needed to be Harper's Bazaarish down here was a tweed suit and a loud muffler, she thought.

"Who were they, mama?" Ebie asked.

"I don't know their names," said Mrs. Vane, with controlled ill-nature regretting her loss of public, "After all, Ebie, I have lived around here for some time. It's natural that a great many people should know me without my knowing them. Now what is this about a salt-box?"

"I was just thinking today," Ebie explained patiently, "that here we are, the only two Vanes in New York and we ought to see something of each other. I thought we might have a house in some little village the way we used to out in Greenpoint, and go there when we're sick of New York."

It sounded so perfectly foolish after she said it that Ebie

was not surprised to see her mother twist her mouth into a wry grimace and examine her sidewise, with head cocked, like some curious old barn-fowl.

"I'm sick of New York, right now," Ebie added.

"I'm not," said Mrs. Vane. "I'm not a bit sick of it. Why should I want to live in a house again? I was analyzed out of a house once, I don't want to get back in one. Do you realize what a house means, Ebie?"

"I've got some money, that's all right."

"It isn't money," said Mrs. Vane with a certain amount of passion, "it's the grocery list, the bread-man, the coal-man, the garbage-man, the children."

"I haven't any children," Ebie said desperately.

"There are always children," said Mrs. Vane. "I've never seen a house that children didn't get into sometime or other. A salt-box. That's characteristic of you, Ebie. Typically, typically Vane."

As Ebie had never made any suggestion in her life that even approached the fantastic normality of this one, she let her mother's remark pass.

"We could have a station wagon and on a Sunday like this we could even go to one of those little churches, the kind you used to make me go to when I was little," Ebie said.

Her mother was still looking at her as if expecting a more actively violent evidence of insanity.

"The only reason I sent you to church was to have a little quiet in the house," she said. "That's the only reason people send their children to church. Besides, my property's here in New York. I take a great deal of interest in my property."

Mrs. Vane had used "the property" years ago as an excuse to stay in New York and Ebie recognized the argument now. She had in fact traded her house out in Iowa for first payment on a made-over tenement in New York, and this deal had obliged her to make her first trip to New York, a trip which turned out to be one-way. The "property" was in back of a bakery in the Italian quarter and was tenanted by impoverished artists and writers who seldom paid rent and who left word constantly at the BAR and GRILL for Mrs. Vane to please fix the hole in the roof, the rats in the wall, the boiling water in the toilet-bowl, the two old panhandlers who slept on a newspaper every night in the vestibule, the explosions in the furnace, the roaches, the bugs, the boys playing baseball in the court, and other minor matters. These little messages, written on the hotel's pink memorandum slips as the calls came in to the operator, were brought one by one by the lone hotel bellboy, an elderly negro of sixty, to Mrs. Vane every day at twelve when she reported for her first sherry in the bar.

"Goodness me, Albert," she would say, examining these pink slips with the complacency of a star looking over fan mail, "Two B says the girls up in Four A are streetwalkers and wants them either thrown out or a carpet put on the stairs so the tramping up and down all night is hushed."

"Better throw them out," Albert advised at this point.

Mrs. Vane was astonished.

"Indeed not, I shall throw out Two B instead. They're the ones that are always complaining."

"You can't throw 'em out if they paid their rent," Albert said.

"That's the nice part," Mrs. Vane responded. "They

haven't. I can always throw anybody out I want to because nobody ever pays their rent. Except Four A."

Even Four A complained one day. They wanted Mrs. Vane to come over right away and see about the roof. They did not so much object to the hole in it as to the bricks falling through it. God knows whom they might hit. Mrs. Vane decided to regard this summons and, arrayed in her most splendid vestiges of rabbit and imitation leopard with a green scarf wound round her head to set off her long hooped ear-rings, she went over to her Property and rang Four A's bell. But every time the door opened a crack and a girl peeped out she cried out, "Go way, go way." Mrs. Vane, mystified, finally went downstairs into the little courtyard between the bakery and her house and made noises till the girl looked out the window and again made frantic gesticulations of dismissal. Mrs. Vane shrugged and went home, found a call waiting to come over to see Four A's room at once.

"I was just there, my dear girl," she said. "You wouldn't permit me to enter."

"Oh," said the girl weakly, "we thought you were a gypsy."

It was this very property that was now holding Mrs. Vane in the city and keeping Ebie from living a fresh wholesome family life in a simple village far from Jay Olivers and commercial art. It was not the first time her mother had disappointed her, but Ebie was still able to be surprised.

"My life is here, my dear child," said Mrs. Vane. She tapped her magazine pointedly. "I was just reading this article when you interrupted with this salt-box notion. I like to keep up. I read everything, no matter how mad it makes me. You ought to read more. You're always chasing about. You ought to read and find out what life is all about."

There didn't seem to be much more to say. Every few years Ebie remembered her mother and tried to revive the acquaintance but it was always the same. There was nothing to say to each other, and definitely no need of each other any more than there had been years ago when Mrs. Vane was the leading clubwoman of Greenpoint.

"Now, why," asked her mother, suddenly interested in Ebie's fingernails, "would anybody have fingernails like that?"

"Because I like them, that's why," snapped Ebie.

"I'm glad it's a matter of choice, then," said Mrs. Vane. "For a moment I thought it was doctor's orders. I must go upstairs and see if that little snip that does my hair has come. Good-bye, my dear."

"Are you having your hair dyed again?" asked Ebie.

Mrs. Vane looked pained.

"Not dyed, Ebie, restored. There's a great difference."

She rose and wafted away, her magazine under her arm, and Ebie gave up. She thought she might as well have a drink to revive her spirits and stood at the bar after her mother had floated into the hall.

"We met on the General out of Chicago," a voice said at her elbow. "I believe we have a mutual friend in Mr. Donovan, Mr. Louis Donovan."

Ebie started and drew back. Beside her at the bar was a middle-aged gentleman in the newest-looking suit imaginable, soft gray hat pulled jauntily down over a weather-beaten face now illuminated by an ingratiating toothy smile. Ebie didn't remember ever having seen him before.

"My name is Truesdale," he said, and lifted his hat briefly. "Here's my card."

Bewildered, Ebie looked at the card thrust into her hand.

"T. V. Truesdale," it said, and down in the lower left-hand corner, "Personally representing Louis Donovan, Pres. of the Louis Donovan Service."

"Well, for God's sake," said Ebie. It was quite true as her mother had pointed out, you never knew who knew you until it was too late.

VI

Mr. Truesdale had been nipping in and out of the Hotel Ellery for many years without attracting either the respect or the interest of the management. He had a seventy-five-cent room on the first floor, that is the floor above the Bar and Grill, and since this was the only seventy-five-cent room in the whole place and was originally intended for the colored elevator boy, its possession by Truesdale did not automatically endow him with great prestige. He knew this, of course, and did not draw the manager's contemptuous eye by entering the palm-riddled lobby, but instead scuttled in and out by the delivery entrance in back, over ashcans and stray cats, and whisked through the court up the back stairs to the little dark hole over the kitchen. Steerage, that was what it was, and he was used to it, you could hear the hotel machinery throbbing all night, dishes rhythmically clattering, cooks fighting, ashcans rolling about, milk bottles clanking, delivery trucks backfiring, trunks galumphing up and down stairs, and hearing this you felt you were really going some place, if only into another tomorrow.

The fact that Mr. Truesdale was not a drunkard or woman-chaser or a noisy guest with pets or violins, that sort of thing, did not particularly enhance his position. Sometimes those abstinences from the ordinary vices merely indicated the man was a pauper or possibly a law-avoider for obscure and sinister reasons. Honest, yes. But even this was not too much respected ever since the time he had doled out his two-nights' bill with a dollar in dimes, thirty-eight pennies and twelve cents in postage stamps. The dollar and a half was paid, all right, but supposing one of the fancier guests had seen the exchange offered! It would make the Ellery seem like a flophouse, and decent guests would run like mad.

The manager of the Ellery had a selection of greetings for his customers. For the old gentlemen permanents he had a gravely respectful, "Good day, sir. How's the arthritis today, sir?" Usually he leaped ahead of them to hold open a door and on icy winter days looked out the door after them, calling out "Are you all right, sir?" and none of the old gentlemen permanents thanked him for this apprehension that they would drop dead any minute. With the old lady permanents he was fatherly, humorous, kidding them about their flirtatiousness, complimenting them on their spryness, patting them a good deal, scolding them lightly for not wearing their mufflers, and pleasing them mightily by his assumption they were all feeble-minded. He was especially concerned over his old ladies, though they were a niggardly lot and wanted everything for their money, but he had sense enough to know that women were the ones with the money, old women, anyway, and nobody minds miserliness in guests that have it tucked away in a sock. It's when they don't have another cent that stinginess is a vice. The manager—his name was Mr. Lowry, —had another greeting for the neighborhood husbands who put up at the Ellery when their wives were away or their apartments being done over; these were business men, family men, with daughters in college, and Mr. Lowry treated them as equals; shaking his head over business, the fate of the Dodgers, European conditions, the damn Reds, and gravely making it clear that he too had a home, a family, a Buick, and a cocker spaniel like any other law-abiding citizen, he was not to be mistaken for a fly-by-night whippersnapper just because he was in the hotel business; with these equals Mr. Lowry often had a beer or two in the bar, and if they were really solid men he occasionally got drunk with them on a summer night; you could safely bet on his companions' good bank standing if you ever saw Mr. Lowry weaving about in glorious abandon; with such good men Mr. Lowry even permitted himself to get drunk in his own bar, but he never drank with a drunkard, that is an ordinary drunkard, and he made it a rule never to drink for pleasure. For Mr. Truesdale, who was relentlessly remembered as having paid his bill in three-cent postage stamps once, Mr. Lowry had a democratic nod, or more exactly a half-nod, unaccompanied by a smile or direct gaze, a preoccupied busyman's nod, but at least it was something, better than his brusque half-nod to debtors. Mr. Truesdale, however, stalwartly refused to accept any nod, marching past the manager when they did meet, with a stony face, though afterwards in the hall or in the privacy of his room his lips moved soundlessly in a brief imprecation. "Bastards! I'll get the bastards!" Mr. Truesdale, by throwing Mr. Lowry in the plural, indicated that he was not so much a solitary enemy as a mere private in an army of enemies.

The Hotel lobby was even darker and drearier than the Bar and Grill, not a whit brightened by its palms or circulating library stand that was rarely open for business and when it was only had twenty or less books. A stand of picture postcards, five cents each, showing the Hotel

Ellery did not require any attendant inasmuch as the Ellery residents obviously were never tempted to advertise to the folks back home their present fortunes. Through an avenue of palms the guest strode or crawled to the desk for mail or bills, and here Mr. Lowry usually stood checking on the work of his employees, or handling the guest himself. For ordinary routine he placed himself behind the mail-boxes and frowned out at his telephone operator or the room clerk as if it was his frown that did the work, not the assistants at all. Occasionally Mr. Lowry laughed, a booming fine laugh that made everyone feel better. He had his fond chuckle for the old residents, his good sport laugh for equals, but these were nothing to his laughter when he heard a genuine bit of wit, a good story or a snappy come-back. People were often telling him anecdotes or some merry fellow would toss out a good crack and Mr. Lowry laughed and laughed, that is if the guest had paid or was paying his bill. If the fellow was in arrears Mr. Lowry shrugged at the jest and muttered "Hmm. A wisecracker" sarcastically after him. But what could be wittier or more refreshing than the remarks made by a man paying his bill? Mr. Lowry had a dandy sense of humor and did not consider it his fault that nothing witty was ever said by a party that owed you money, or passed out a rubber check.

In Mr. Truesdale's scuffed Gladstone bag under his bed there was—and this would have astounded Mr. Lowry—a large index card with brief bits of information about Mr. Lowry and indeed in the same package of cards were snip-pets of news about other figures in the hotel, about Mrs. Vane, for instance. Mrs. Vane was listed, with a few per-sonal remarks about her tastes, under "Automobile Prospects." Mr. Truesdale had been able, on occasion, to turn an honest dollar by selling a list of "Interested" Prospects to an auto company salesman. Mr. Lowry, it would have embarrassed him to know, was a potential toupée customer, being a self-conscious bald man instead of a debonair one. Under "Suggested Approach" Mr. Truesdale had jotted "Toupée would add dignity necessary to hotel manager besides making youthful appearance attracting younger clients, also relieve L.'s tendency to head colds." It can be seen that Mr. Truesdale, even when seeming to be unemployed, was in reality never idle, profiting by any overheard conversations as well as by his own sharp little eyes. Mr. Truesdale never forgot a face nor anything about its owner that he'd ever known. This was not really so remarkable since his bread and butter so often depended on this memory, aided by his dossier of tidbits. It was not that Mr. Truesdale was a lover of humanity or an observer of the contemporary scene, either. If he ever got two cents he could rub together, he often mused, he would rejoice in never speaking to anybody, he would shrug his shoulders when anyone asked for recognition and say, "I meet so many people!" He'd have the great pleasure of minding his own business and telling everybody else to go mind theirs. However, he was fifty now, and the chances of ever having two pennies to rub together were less and less. Twenty years ago he might have been optimistic over his little finger-hold on Lou Donovan. Now he accepted it as a bit of luck for today but tomorrow it might vanish. While it lasted he was playing it for all it was worth, never mind about that. There was always a chance of a bit of permanent luck. Within the last three days he'd made more money than he had in the last two months. He'd had a couple of tens and three fives in his worn wallet—in fact he'd gotten a new genuine pigskin wallet at a chain drugstore for ninety-seven cents, ten cents more with his initials. Lou had prescribed a decent suit of clothes, advanced forty bucks on it. Forty bucks for a suit of clothes! Truesdale hated to spend money on clothes, but it was an absolute fact that the trouser seat of his present suit was worn to such gossamer thinness that he had to rise with the utmost caution. So he went down to Division Street and selected a natty extraordinarily aquamarine-colored suit for fourteen-fifty.

"I wouldn't pay a penny more than twelve for this quality suit any other time," he told the salesman sternly, "of coss, as you see my bucket's out in my old suit so I can't bargain with you."

He bought a Paisley-patterned shirt, ninety-four cents with tab collar and came across a rare bargain in bow ties, three for fifty-nine, blue polka dot, green polka dot, and a more severe black polka dot, all absolute rayon. Shopping further at a "PRICES SMASHED! BUILDING COMING DOWN! FORCED OUT OF BUSINESS!" place down by Brooklyn Bridge he was able to pick up half a dozen colored handkerchiefs with "Lawrence" embroidered in the corner for nineteen cents. He could have gotten three with his own initials for the same money, but economy prevailed over egotism. Very few people looked at the name on your handkerchief, and if a manufacturer's mistake about the popularity of the name "Lawrence" could be profited upon, then by all means proceed to profit.

No doubt about it, the new outfit did give him quite a kick. He went to the stationers on Fourteenth Street and bought a new brief case, eighty-nine cents, a beauty, zipper style; he also bought a handsome fountain pen and pencil combination, one buck, a brand new set of index cards, and four bottles of ink named "Aztec Brown," "Patrician Purple," "South Sea Blue" and "Spanish Tile." These were business improvements, for he had decided to use each color on a person's dossier to denote certain things, the blue, say for automobile prospects, the purple for piano or radio possibilities and so on. He placed the ink bottles in a neat little quartette on his dresser-top and laid the two ties with his old one in the top drawer, and felt the first genuine thrill of possession he'd had in years.

"Of coss, it's only a beginning," he reminded himself.

On the Sunday he met Ebie Vane he paid his week's bill with a twenty and was rewarded by Mr. Lowry telling him a joke. He rewarded Mr. Lowry by saying calmly, as he picked up his change, "Yes, as I recall it that anecdote was quite a favorite with the old Maharajah—quite a favorite, as a matter of fact. He's told it for years."

He left while the manager muttered "So. A wiscracker, eh!" quite disgruntled at the rejection of his good-will offer. The good-will was not offered solely because of the new show of affluence on Truesdale's part, it was due also to the sudden series of phone calls, telegrams, incidental indications of a guest's rise in the world. Mr. Lowry was even willing to suspect that the three-cent stamps episode was the gesture of an eccentric rather than a pauper. But if he was prepared with friendly overtures, Mr. Truesdale on the other hand was not, stalking into the Bar and Grill with head high quite as if Mr. Lowry was merely a servant of the hotel, as was indeed the case, not the owner as he liked to imagine himself.

In the Bar and Grill this Sunday Mr. Truesdale found

the conversation between Albert and the glum man in the derby going on about houses in the country, a conversation which Mrs. Vane's raised voice on salt-boxes had given the cue. The glum man wished to God he could get rid of his farm near Danbury, Connecticut, speaking of farms, and this one only raised chickens and taxes. If he could get rid of the place he'd take the dough and buy a forty-foot tub, a sea-goer, and by golly, he'd never get off it. He'd fish from Newfoundland to Bimini and the Keys, he'd go after every damn fish there was. He'd never do a stroke of work, he'd call in his insurance policies, he'd lie on every beach from here to hell-and-gone, and for food he'd eat fish, it wasn't bad, and he'd wash it down with beer, or, if he had it, some plain old Dago red. Albert, the bartender, however, never could see a thing in fishing. So far as he was concerned fish was only something that came in cans and could stay there. He had a lot at Northern Beach, Long Island, bought with newspaper subscriptions and a hundred bucks down, and if he saved some more he'd turn that over with his old Chevy and buy a double house in Bensonhurst, rent out the top floor, keep the bottom, make it pay for itself. Mr. Truesdale made a note of these two desires for his dossiers on each of the men, exchanged cards with the glum man, who was a Tompkins of some paper manufacturing company. Even while his ears were picking up this information his eyes observed Ebie Vane, the lady he spotted on the train with Lou Donovan, and the other fellow. She looked a darn sight better than she had the morning he saw her get off the train; he had marked her then as a high-class tart. Maybe he was wrong. She looked fresh as paint today. What she was to Donovan he could not figure out, whether a train pick-up, a regular secretary, an accidental encounter, or an old friend. Being in the Ellery Bar made the pick-up theory seem the strongest, since Donovan was certainly not the kind of man to park a genuine lady friend in such a dump. After a few minutes' observation, however, Truesdale marked the car, the mother, and the comments of the other customers indicating that Ebie was a stranger here. The old dame was her mother, that was made clear. Mr. Truesdale, always loyal to his many employers, observed everything with the greatest care in case there might be something here Mr. Donovan might care to know. No matter what her connection was with Donovan, friend or employee, there might some day be some complication that a word or two of straight data might clear up. No harm, certainly, in speaking up to her. His new turn of luck gave him confidence, for he was not one ordinarily to accost strange young ladies; on the other hand Ebie's gloom made her more receptive than was usual for her. She looked at his card and then looked over the man curiously. Lou's promotion activities she knew had strange wires out all over so this man was probably all right. Not that she cared much about the references of men she met in public places. The world after all was not a private club, thank God. You could talk or not as you liked with any stranger unless they started making passes or being a pest.

"I didn't know Mr. Donovan had a representative in this hotel," she said.

"I'm in and out here," said Mr. Truesdale. "The cuisine, of coss, is not of the best."

"What is the cuisine?" Ebie idly asked. "I don't eat here, thank heaven."

Mr. Truesdale pondered this only a minute.

"Irish," he stated finally. "Personally, I find East Indian cooking the finest in the world."

He signalled Albert for a beer.

"You're having Dubonnet, I see. May I suggest another with this time a dash of Campari bitters, a favorite of my old friend, the Duke of Malleywell, at one time a resident of Calcutta?"

"I'll chance it," said Ebie, with a shrug.

It struck her that the man might be a detective. He might be a detective for Jay's wife, using Lou as an opening wedge. That was it, of course. The wife flying to New York with her mother, trying to get the goods on Jay, planting this fellow on the train even, so as to have further evidence. Probably right now he was checking up on Lou's alibi that she was an interior decorator doing his office, no connection of Jay's at all. She tried to remember what else Lou had said that day in the crisis. That she'd met him at the train. Well, this man knew differently so she'd have to fix that up a little if he should ask any questions.

"I dassay most of you New Yorkers think you know curry," said Mr. Truesdale. "But what do you get for curry here? A cream sauce with a sprinkle of the powder! No Bombay duck. No shredded cocoanut. A touch of Major Grey, perhaps, perhaps not. Depending. Have you known Mr. Donovan long?"

Ebie braced herself for the witness stand. She was, she decided, a very old friend of Lou's. She had gotten on the train in Pittsburgh, since he must have checked that. She was a commercial artist, since he must have checked that also, but was hoping to branch out in decorating, hence the opportunity to do Mr. Donovan's New York office. She had met Mr. Oliver for the first time on the train with her very dear friend, Mr. Donovan. She was now calling on her mother at the Ellery to discuss settling in the country.

"But why is it me that has to be on the spot?" Ebie's resentful second thought came. "Why don't I get the goods on Jay's wife, instead? But oh, no, it's me that's the criminal. It's me that has to save the home for Jay. Lou Donovan and me. The old marines."

Mr. Truesdale, using a little running sideline of comments on Siamese versus Ceylon dishes, as a siphon, managed to painlessly draw off Ebie's prepared information. The declaration of her friendship for Lou verified his feeling that she was the girl-friend, her mother explained her connection with the Ellery. The matter that interested him most, however, was the desire for a farm. It was a long shot that the lady who wanted to buy a farm would want to buy the very thing the glum man wanted to get rid of and indeed Mr. Truesdale had never known of a case where such a pat deal ever came through. But it was worth a gamble. A word here, a private tip to Tompkins, and there might be ten or twenty bucks in it for the informant. Mr. Truesdale had no lofty notions of his value, a few dollars picked up here and there, no responsibility about further complications, no duties, no ties. Pick up any time and move on to the West or East, unless he had something that looked pretty steady like his Lou Donovan contact.

"A commercial artist makes a lot of money," said Mr. Truesdale, eyeing Ebie thoughtfully. "Maybe more than a decorator."

"It's too high-pressure," Ebie said. "You can't ever catch up. And I never save. No matter what I make."

"Best thing for a type like you, then, is to put it in possessions," advised her new companion, authoritatively.

"Cars. Diamonds. Of coss, you ought to safeguard your future, roof over the head, and all that. It's a tremenjus comfort to a New Yorker to know he's got a little place out somewhere he can retire to if bad times come."

"It sure is," said Ebie. She looked at him suspiciously. Was this a quiet warning for her to get out of town? Maybe Jay's wife was out with a gun. Sometimes wives did get hold of a gun and the first thing they wanted to do was shoot down all the other women, never the guy that needed shooting. Maybe this little dick was tipping her off. Of course she had given him that lead about wanting to settle down somewhere in the country with her mother. He certainly picked it up fast, though. There was some reason for that. Calling her bluff, maybe.

"Of coss, it's a matter of finding the right place," said Mr. Truesdale judiciously. "You might want a showplace —or you might want a self-supporting sort of place. Of coss, if you aren't dependent on your own salary, if you have other resources to count on——"

"I haven't," Ebie nipped that one in the bud. Jay's wife wanted to see if Jay was passing out any of the family silver, evidently.

"I happen to know Mr. Donovan's business is very good so the decorating of his office is bound to be well paid," said Mr. Truesdale with a large gesture, as if the emolument was to come from his own pocket.

"If I should take the job," Ebie said cautiously, "I know Mr. Donovan would be generous. Particularly to such an old friend as I am."

She thought she'd better clear up everything now so she added, "Perhaps all Chicago people are generous, I don't know. Lou is the only person I know really well out there."

Mr. Truesdale blinked and then recovered himself. Ebie thought it was from surprise that she only knew Lou, but then reflected that he might assume she was out to get Lou. It struck her as funny. One on Jay and the little woman. She would not let Truesdale pay for her drink, which she gulped with considerable distaste for the overdose of bitters. She was relieved when the old bellboy came in with a message that if Mrs. Vane's daughter was still there her mother would like her to step upstairs and see her for a moment.

"If I should hear of a place in the country, I'll get in touch with you," Mr. Truesdale offered, affably. "Sometimes I hear things. Not my business, of coss. But sometimes I hear of things. I dassay I can always contact you through Mr. Donovan's office. That is, if you're seriously in the market."

"Oh, I am," Ebie assured him. "Indeed, I am."

"A genuine pleasure to meet you again," Mr. Truesdale said, bowing. "It would be a privilege to be of any assistance."

Ebie gave him a friendly nod and departed into the interior lobby. Mr. Truesdale paid for his beer and glanced around alertly to see what had become of his other friend with the boating desires. Mr. Thompson was at that moment seated in a booth having the dollar steak luncheon. He did not encourage Mr. Truesdale since it is one thing to mix at a bar and another thing at one's board.

"Just a word about that property of yours, friend," said Mr. Truesdale. "Is it in good condition?"

"Forty run-down acres, house leaks, garden gone to pot, chickens dying off," said Mr. Thompson readily, without slowing up the terrific eating pace he had set for himself, eating being merely a necessary stoking of the body to strengthen it for further drinking. "My wife sold all the decent furniture in it before we separated and the rest my daughter took when she got married so it's half-bare. Damned uncomfortable. I stay here mostly but there's the place. Yelling for repairs. Got a nigger out there, shiftless cuss, but he half-tends to it and makes a little, gardening."

"How much would you sell it for?" asked Mr. Truesdale.

Thompson looked more friendly. He thought a minute.

"Four thousand five," he said. "It would cost me that much to fix it up. I'd rather get rid of it."

Mr. Truesdale looked around.

"How much would it be worth to you to know of a good prospect?" he asked in a low voice.

"Not a damn cent," said his friend readily. "Unless they bought it."

"Supposing they bought it?" asked Mr. Truesdale.

"Sit down," said Thompson. "Have a beer."

VII

Mrs. Vane had a seventeen-dollar-a-week room and bath at the Ellery. It was a fair-sized room on the fourth floor front with two big windows and a respectable bath. Through these great windows the sun, at certain glorious moments around noon on certain days in December and late in the afternoon during the summer solstice, flooded the apartment across the street with its radiance and the grateful house at once flung the radiance back by reflection into Mrs. Vane's fortunate chamber. It was a time worth looking forward to, and the lady was always disappointed if a little errand kept her out during this magic interval.

"Oh, dearie!" she'd exclaim poignantly. "I've missed the sun today!"

The furniture was imitation maple, with a day-bed to give a sitting-room effect. This desirable effect, however, was at once offset by the piles of hat-boxes, bulging battered suitcases, and one open wardrobe trunk which took up most of the room and the huge Victorian walnut dresser with pier glass mirror, and marble top, an item Mrs. Vane had salvaged from a country auction somewhere and which she said was worth a perfect fortune if the right person came along. It had cost a small fortune already to have it crated and delivered and hauled to her room at the Ellery, that much Ebie knew.

"Is that you, Ebie?" called her mother. "Come in."

The old lady was in the bathroom, draped in Turkish towels, seated before the washbowl while the "little snip" from the next-door beauty shop worked the dye into the ancient scalp, with dabs of cotton. The snip nodded to Ebie and winked.

"This ain't a dye, you know," she said naughtily, "it's just a tint, if you please."

Ebie pulled up a chair to the bathroom door and lit a cigarette.

"Why don't you have it brown, mom?" she suggested, "it's more softening. I mean, if you must dye it."

"What do I want to look softened for?" irritably asked her mother.

"See?" said the snip.

The snip was a wiry little Irish girl with a big pretty doll's head, blue-eyed and curly-haired, attached to her small, tough little body.

"The old lady's got a bee, today," she whispered to Ebie. "Look out."

"I feel low, mom," said Ebie, "got any brandy around?"

"Now, Ebie!" upbraided her mother. "How did you know I had any? Besides I'm saving it."

"I sent you some not long ago," Ebie said defensively. "Where is it?"

Her mother heaved a sigh.

"I can't keep a thing," she said. "Look in the closet behind the shoe cabinet."

Ebie found the bottle and some glasses.

"Want some?" she offered the girl.

"A half one," said the snip. "I learned that in Ireland. I went back last year, and my dad thought it was awful I didn't drink. 'Come on, Maureen,' he'd say, 'a drop'd do you good, just a half one.' He'd put away a dozen half ones. I'd say, 'Why don't you take a full one, pop, you want it, and he'd say, 'No Maureen, I only take a half one, I'm no drunkard, my girl.' "

"So long as you're passing it out, I'd better have a touch," said Mrs. Vane. "After all it's my brandy."

"Soon as the old boy'd get a snoot full he'd start telling me the stories," said the snip, smacking her lips with pleasure over her glass. "All about the little people, not like your fairies, but little people with beards, dressed up with red shoes, all cocked up. There's a little man dressed up like that in Queenstown in the church, a real little one, he plays the chimes."

"Yes, and you never brought me back the colleen cape," Mrs. Vane remembered reproachfully.

"Your ma's always asking for a colleen cape like she seen once in the pictures. No good telling her the colleens don't dress that way. Like dad wanting me to bring him over an Uncle Sam suit, like the Americans wear."

"Never mind, get busy on my hair," Mrs. Vane ordered peremptorily. "I want to speak to my daughter."

"Fire away," said the snip.

"What's on your mind, mom?" Ebie asked.

"It's that antique," said her mother. "Look at that, Ebie. That's a beautiful thing, isn't it? You ought to know, getting around, what a thing like that is worth. It's genuine antique."

"It's old, but that doesn't keep it from being a pain," said Ebie. "What do you want with a thing like that? It looks like a ferryboat, all bulging out on the sides that way. All it needs is a whistle."

"That's the God's truth," agreed the snip.

"How do you know about antiques, my dear girl?" coldly asked Mrs. Vane, as the snip wrapped a towel around her head.

"My boy friend," said the snip.

"That upholsterer?" Mrs. Vane inquired, then added sternly. "I should think he would have asked you to marry him by this time, Maureen."

"Now, mama!" Ebie scolded. "Girls don't have to be getting married every minute. Times are different."

"I'm not an octogenarian, my dear," Mrs. Vane snapped.

"Sure, my boy friend and I figured we'd just live together," the snip giggled, with a wink at Ebie.

Mrs. Vane struggled to turn around and wither the girl with a look but it was too much with the firm hands now holding her head in a vise.

"A nice Catholic girl like you!" she exclaimed, outraged.

"What's the harm?" innocently asked the snip.

"I wouldn't do it, that's all," Mrs. Vane said, trapped. "I wouldn't do it. He'll leave you, sure as fate. And what if you have a baby?"

"I won't," said the snip.

"Leave her alone," said Ebie to her mother. "I'm the person to worry about. I'm your daughter."

"I hate young people," said Mrs. Vane sincerely. "You two seem to think any older person is someone to be mocked, and ridiculed. Neither one of you has a dime's worth of intellect. Ebie, about that tea-room you were planning . . ."

"Not a tea-room, mom," Ebie protested, now beginning to feel tired of the whole idea of the country what with everyone pressing her about it.

"Whatever it is, I begin to think it's the best idea you

ever had," Mrs. Vane went on, surprisingly. "I'm only surprised it didn't occur to you before."

"You kicked it out when I suggested it downstairs," Ebie said.

Her mother dismissed ,this.

"I've thought it over. I think it could be a gold mine."

"A gold mine?" Ebie was startled at this angle.

"Certainly. Take that beautiful old dresser there. I have a flair for that sort of thing. I'd like nothing better than whipping about the country picking up a piece here and there. I'd make a mint."

"Like you do on your apartment house," jeered Ebie.

"Never mind about that," said Mrs. Vane. "I can do two things at once. Or I might even sell the place and put it into antiques. You run the tea-room, say by some old mill stream, and I handle the antiques."

Ebie got up.

"That's a perfect whiz of an idea," she said, "and I can see right off where you make a million, but skip the tea-room part. The place I want to get is to use for a home, see, a home."

"A home," Mrs. Vane repeated, puzzled.

"Well, skip that part, too, then," Ebie said with resignation. "I just made the suggestion because I'm fed up with New York. I'm tired of the works. I want to lie around the porch all day like decent folks and dig in the garden and read serials in the *Cosmopolitan."*

"Ebie, you're not yourself," said her mother, shaking her head. "But I'm serious. We'll find a place and I'll take the piece out as a starter and snap up a few bargains here and there and make a profit."

"Isn't she a one?" the snip marvelled, working away at

the old head as if her manual operations over the brain centers were helping this wave of inspiration.

"It's the first genuine inspiration I've had in years," stated Mrs. Vane proudly. "I'm really excited for once."

"I guess the Ellery'll be glad to get that thing out of the hotel," said the snip with a nod toward the dresser. "You don't need a house, Miss Vane. Just park that thing on a lot somewhere and move in."

"When will you find out more?" eagerly Mrs. Vane inquired, ignoring the girl. "I'm really intensely serious about this venture."

Ebie felt weak and as if fate was pushing her into something she had no right to fight. Once, in her early days with Jay Oliver, she felt like slashing up her wrists and ending the whole mess. Since then worse things had happened than mere lovers' quarrels, and she only felt now like running away, not poking her head in an oven or anything like that, just walking out of her present life quietly with no fuss, no good-byes, no quarrels. First her mother hadn't liked the country idea, all right, then, that was out. Then that funny little man at the bar, undoubtedly somebody hired by Mrs. Jay Oliver to watch her, challenged her about the country idea again, as if it was either that, or else. She didn't much care. But now her mother was hopping on the idea. The antique gag would occupy the old lady, maybe, but she'd get over it when it was time to really work on it.

"Don't let this old girl bully you into buying her a house," advised the snip jocularly. "I know how your folks are. Believe me, I stopped mine. They write me from the old country and they say, 'Maureen, we miss you, send us your picture and p.s. you might put a bit with it as times is hard here.' So I send 'em pictures of breadlines here in New York and I say, 'There's me, third from the end, with the tin cup up high.' That stops 'em."

"I don't blame you, Maureen," Mrs. Vane said. "You'll need every cent you make for your baby. But Ebie here——"

Ebie and the snip laughed.

"Okay, mom, I'll look around," said Ebie. "We'll see about the antique business when we get the place. I don't care what you sell so long as I'm not in it."

"You'll miss New York, believe me," said the snip.

"The hell with New York," said Ebie and went away, even more depressed than when she had come.

VIII

What a week, what a week, Lou thought, yodelling "ya-ya-ya-ya-dee-die-dee-ya" in the shower bath, what a perfect honey of a week he'd had. What a town, New York, he thought, lathering his head with the piny-scented suds, what a beautiful, big-hearted honey of a town. No place in the world like New York. Everything had gone tick-tock, not a hitch. Call it the town, call it maybe a little bit Lou Donovan knowing how to handle it, too. That was the kind of guy he was, big town stuff. Little things floored him, but give him a big problem, give him a big town, the biggest, and he could swing it with his hands tied. People, for instance, the same. Little people, small fry, they only got in his hair, but give him the presidents, the managers, the thoroughbred women—(take Mary, for instance, his own wife)—and he knew just where to scratch.

He stepped out of the shower and doused himself with cologne. He had decided to plane out at one but first there were some matters of office equipment to settle (the receptionist really did turn out to have white hair, premature, sure, but it did give a high-class touch to the place) and arrangements had to be made to send Truesdale down to Maryland to look things over for him, quite sub rosa. The man could be valuable to him. Then there was the luncheon Florabella Cosmetics, Inc., was throwing for its officials and the press at the Ritz, at twelve. He promised to take a peek in and say hello to the boys before he took the car to the airport. Florabella was in the class with Elizabeth Arden and Rubenstein, and Lou was happy at being able to recommend such high-priced products to his clients. Most of them couldn't afford the prices wholesale but for Castles-in-the-Woods nothing was too good. Florabella Arbutus Soap and Florabella Arbutus Bathsalts in every bathroom, Florabella Make-up and Arbutus Tissue in every powder room, a fountain of Florabella cologne in the Tea Garden of the hotel. He'd already signed the order and it was a pip. A joy indeed on such a fine September day to have an unlimited treasury to dip into, not your own.

He whistled as he selected a gray tie with a small yellow dot, eight-fifty, a gray suit with the merest flicker of a darker stripe, one forty he paid for that suit, gray silk socks, —he looked all right, maybe a little tell-tale crinkling around the eyes, still he looked better than the run of men you'd meet. Nothing flashy, just quiet good taste. Mary had taught him that, she hated loud clothes, it was all he could do to sneak in an occasional pin-stripe.

"I don't know why it is," she said once, shaking her head humorously, "Lou always *looks* as if he had on a plaid suit even if it's the plainest dark blue."

He knew what she meant,—that he could give anything a certain air as soon as he put it on his back. Even in the old days when he paid twenty-two fifty for a suit he could wear it as if it was something.

In the florist's downstairs he selected a neat freesia for his buttonhole, ordered a batch of chrysanthemums, twenty dollars' worth, sent to the Major's wife with his card—ah, those were the touches that counted!—whom he hadn't met but who had just arrived on the *Normandie* according to his informers. He went to the telephone operator's desk to put in a call to Jay Oliver, find out if he was back yet from Atlantic City but he wasn't, so he called his Chicago office and told Miss Frye out there what to do and what to say.

"I'll be back tonight, but better tell Mrs. Donovan I'm not expected till tomorrow," he said, thinking ahead that he might want to date up Mrs. Kameray when he got in town, since she was already in Chicago. There it was, he thought, the difference between him and Jay Oliver,—he paved his way in advance for any little adventure, so he always had an out.

"The first Mrs. Donovan came in again," said Miss Frye over the phone. "She's still on your tail."

Francie again. You'd think you could brush somebody off after fifteen years, and true enough she hadn't crossed his path for ten years till this last month when she and her consumptive husband had hit Chicago. He had nothing against Fran, she was all right, only she made him feel so damned uncomfortable, always reminding him that once they did this and that, and there was always the danger of her spilling the beans to Mary. Why couldn't the past stay in the past quietly?

"What did she want?" he asked.

"Said she was broke," said Miss Frye. "You know. Wants to take the husband to Arizona. Hocked the car here for hotel rent."

"Arizona, hell, I'll bet he wants to get to Santa Anita," Lou growled. "That guy never learns. Dropped all his bonus money at Hialeah in two days, all right, so now he's set for Tia Juana and the West Coast tracks. No wonder he's broke."

"Well, she said she wanted to get him to Arizona for

his health," Miss Frye said non-committally, "I don't know what's on the level with her. She's coming back in later."

"How much she want?"

"Enough to get the car out and a couple weeks' board. Sixty—seventy bucks."

"Seventy bucks is a lot of dough," said Lou. "Give her twenty and tell her I said scram. I'm no Rockefeller."

He was feeling too good this morning to be bothered by Francie still hanging around. He remembered there was a hotel men's convention at the Stevens this week and some business friends might be around.

"Line up whoever calls up for a little party tonight," he said. "I'll be in late this afternoon. Open house. You might check up on the Scotch."

"Mr. Oliver was in," she said. So Jay was home already. "He helped himself to the bar a while ago and left on a high note."

"If he calls again tell him to drop in around sixish," he said.

"He will," said Miss Frye. "He says he's got to check stories with you as soon as he gets in. What goes on there in New York anyway?"

"Never you mind," Lou laughed. Smart kid, Miss Frye.

He paid the telephone operator, a cute trick with bangs. On her mark every minute, too. A kidder, but no funny business. At least that was Jay Oliver's report. Jay never could see a telephone operator without trying to promote.

"Don't you look grand with the posy!" she said. "You certainly do look happy. Is it the flower?"

"Sure, it's the flower," he said. "What else would I have to be happy about?"

"If that's all it takes!" she sighed. "Maybe I ought to

wear a flower myself if that's all it takes to be happy."

Smiling, Lou went back to the flower shop and ordered ten dollars' worth of red roses and a spray of gardenias sent to the hotel telephone operator.

"Not the blonde one," he specified, "the one with the bangs and the Southern accent."

"That's the one that likes sweetheart roses," said the boy wrapping a corsage in waxed paper standing near.

"All right, send her sweetheart roses, too," said Lou. "Let the girl be satisfied, by all means."

He wrote "Now, will you be happy?" on a card, signed it with his room number and "Donovan" and slipped it in the envelope. On second thought he slid a twenty into the envelope, too. That kind of thing gave him a big kick. He could never understand stinginess. These fellows that figured out ten per cent for tips, never tip unless you have to, and all that. All right, he had to figure close that way twenty, even fifteen years ago, but Christ, he was only making fifty or sixty bucks a week then. He was playing the horses then, too, and they certainly were doing him dirt all right. That was another thing. Some men never learned. Some men, like the punk Francie was living with right now, went on following the races year in, year out, losing and never knew when to stop. After three or four years of bad breaks he pulled out. Give him a wheel, the birdcage, roulette, or even poker, at least there was some fun in the game itself. He usually managed to walk out with a little more dough than he went in with. But the horses—well, horses just didn't like him. The hell with them.

He walked up Park, holding his stomach in, feeling so fine that he was surprised to see so many glum faces about, glum-faced doormen in uniform walking tenants' obstinate little dogs on leash, grim nursemaids holding yelling little boys in sailor suits and little girls with a mere ruffle for a dress above little knock-knees, holding them by the hands but plainly wishing it was by the necks. What was the matter with people all so glum today?

He felt fine all morning, approved his receptionist, approved the rug, sofa and chairs that had come for the inner office. Not much was really needed,—just a front, an address. He probably wouldn't see it more than two or three days a month, if that. Unless the Castles-in-the-Wood thing took more time than he expected. He thought he'd drop in the Florabella Show Room over on Madison and pick up old Florabella himself, otherwise Bill Massey, and go on to the lunch from there. The Florabella Show Room was a sweetheart all right, you had to hand it to these guys, they knew how to dress up a cake of soap till it looked like the Hope diamond, all encased in jewelled tinsel paper in a satin box, and the rest of the stuff the same, all displayed in a satin-walled scented showroom with beautiful girls in different flower-colored satin play-suits making you order more than you ever intended. Lou sat down on a dainty pink sofa while Florabella products, exquisitely mounted on little gold stairs, revolved slowly under a glass bell in the middle of the room. Bill Massey came in from the rear offices, which were a far cry from the elegance of the front, but nobody cared. The pretty girl who had summoned him for Lou smiled at them both and departed gracefully. Massey, a big Irishman built like a prizefighter, thick neck, big nose, red curly hair, looked after the girl frowning.

"Was she giving you the eye?" he asked.

"Why the hell not?" Lou wanted to know. "I'm a customer, ain't I? Doesn't the customer get any breaks around here?"

Massey sighed.

"I hire these girls for their sex appeal but I'll be goddamned if I'm going to let them use it," he said. "I got a problem on my hands, believe me. They make the business, but they aren't supposed to make the customer. After all some customers got women in the family. It wouldn't be the first time if a wife walked in right now and started bawling hell out of me for selling her husband a bill of goods. That was Nettie, I'll tell her to lay off, you got a wife."

"Ah, leave her be, she didn't give me the eye," Lou said.

"It was a double take if I ever saw a double take," Massey said firmly. He sighed and rumpled his red hair. "I give 'em a pep talk every morning. Just gave 'em one now. 'Get in there and fight,' I said to 'em. 'It's for Florabella, your old alma mater. But for God's sake, kids,' I said to 'em, 'slow up the hips once in a while.' I said, 'Can't you take your mind off it for say just an hour a day?' "

He went back to get his hat and Lou started talking to the girl who had now come back and was going through her little routine of passing around a silver tray of samples, prettily boxed, stepping about prettily with the rhythm of the professional model, carefully toasted legs very appetizing against her aquamarine satin play-suit with its advantageous little flare-ups at front and back.

"Too bad you've only got two legs," said Lou.

"Thank you," she said courteously with a little bow.

"Don't thank me, thank God," said Lou. "Would you mind loaning me the pair of 'em to pin up in my office?"

She giggled, and wriggled her foot in its silver sandal.

"Yes, sir," said Lou, "if you were a centipede, by golly, I'd marry you."

"Don't be silly, I *am* married," she giggled.

Lou shrugged.

"Okay, you turn me down. How old are you?"

"Nineteen," she said.

"Hell, what would I be doing with an old hag of nineteen?" he wanted to know. "You'd only be good for a couple more years. I'd be out time and money. Make out I didn't say anything."

"All right, Mr. Donovan," she tittered. "I didn't know you were looking for a wife."

"I'm always looking for a wife," he insisted. "I'm fresh out of wives today. Too bad you're not my type."

Massey came back, hat on the back of his head.

"We're early for the banquet," he said, looking at his watch. "Let's drop in the Men's Bar and I'll match you for drinks. I could use a whiskey sour after the helling I did around town last night. Remind me to bump myself off next time I go up to Harlem, will you? Make a note of that, Nettie."

"All right, Mr. Massey," she obediently said.

Lou tucked a ten on her tray and lightly flicked her chin with his forefinger.

"You're in," he said. "Next time I'm in town I'll shoot it out with your husband. How big is he?"

"Six feet," she said, "he was a fullback at Dartmouth."

"Six feet? Then I'd better make friends with him," Lou said. "The way I pictured him was about four feet two. You can tell him it's all right. Come on, Florabella."

"You slay 'em, don't you?" jeered Massey. "A killer-diller. If you had as many of them around as I have day and night you'd be so sick of glamour girls you'd hunt down the plainest fattest woman in the world just for a thrill. Or turn nance. Why, I heard a story just the other day that I—me—mind you, was supposed to be a queen."

"Well?" Lou asked. Massey banged him on the shoulder.

"That'll be enough," he said.

"I don't have to flatter you, boy," Lou said. "I threw you an order, now I can sit back and insult you all I damn please."

In the Men's Bar at the Ritz they ran into Rosenbaum reading the *Journal* and waiting for some client of his. He offered to buy a round but Florabella insisted on matching for it.

"Christ, the match game is the only exercise I ever get," he pleaded.

Rosenbaum shrugged. He didn't know the match game so Florabella patiently explained it, you guessed how many matches the other guy had in his hand and if you were right it was a horse and when you got three horses you won the round.

"Listen," said Rosenbaum, "do you mind if I just buy the drinks and save us all that trouble?"

Lou and Florabella wouldn't let him, however, so he regretfully won and it was Florabella's check. When Florabella went out to see if the guests were coming to the luncheon yet, Rosenbaum drew Lou aside.

"I want to thank you for giving our family friend, Mrs. Kameray, that job," he said in an undertone. "She was very happy about it, and I think will be darn good at promoting. I was especially flattered that you took my recommendation without even bothering to interview her. That's confidence, all right."

"If you say somebody's all right, they're all right," said Lou heartily. "That's how much I think of your opinion, Rosenbaum."

The little rascal! She'd never even peeped to Rosenbaum about being out all hours with him that night.

"I think you would have been very satisfied with her if you had met her," Rosenbaum continued. "She has poise and charm—all the stuff."

"Hell, fella, I can't meet everybody that's recommended," Lou said heartily. "She may be Helen of Troy but when a guy's only got four or five days in New York he doesn't have time to meet all the people he'd like. You say she's okay—all right, then, she's okay."

Florabella came back and said they had to go in to their luncheon party. Nobody was there yet but as host he had to be there. And if Lou could only stay a few minutes he'd better come in now.

"Wish you could join us, Rosenberg," said Florabella.

"Rosenbaum," corrected Rosenbaum.

Florabella waved his hand carelessly.

"Rosenberg, Rosenstein, Rosenbaum—it's all the same, pal, so long as the old heart's in the right place."

"Call him Rosebush the way I do," Lou chuckled, but he ended his guffaw by clearing his throat for a sudden startled expression had come to Rosenbaum's face. Lou was uneasily aware of Rosenbaum's eyes following him thoughtfully as he went out with Florabella. He could have kicked himself for the break. It was just the kind of fool break a fellow like Jay Oliver might make, a dead give-away if the other man was even half-smart. From the reflective look in his eye Lou was rather afraid Rosenbaum was more than half-smart.

"Now why did I have to pull that Rosebush gag?" he lamented. A fine crack to set a guy thinking, all right. As bad as being too quick knowing a wrong telephone number. Lou was so annoyed with himself for spilling Mrs. Kameray's little Rosebush joke that he did himself no credit with Florabella's early guests. He stood around for a few minutes with the bunch, laughing perfunctorily as Florabella wowed them with anecdote after anecdote, shady limerick after shady limerick. Usually Lou jotted down any new gags in his notebook for future edification of clients, but today he only half-heard. Later, on the plane, he tried to remember some of them but couldn't think of a single one.

IX

IN THE dead of night wives talked to their husbands, in the dark they talked and talked while the clock on the bureau ticked sleep away, and the last street cars clanged off on distant streets to remoter suburbs, where in new houses bursting with mortgages and the latest conveniences wives talked in the dark, and talked and talked. All over the country the wives' voices droned on and on about the bridge prizes, the luncheon, the hollandaise sauce, the walnut surprise, the little defeats, the little jealousies, the children, the grocer, the neighbor, and husbands might put pillows over their heads or stuff their ears with cotton, pretend to snore, sigh loudly with fatigue, no matter, the voices went on and on, riveting the darkness, hammering into the night hush, as ceaselessly and as involuntarily as cricket noises.

Jay Oliver sometimes comforted himself with the thought of all those other husbands, and he forced himself to admit in all fairness that perhaps he would not be so dead tired when he spent a night at home if he hadn't been up to plenty mischief elsewhere lately, so that listening was a just penance for past defections. Flo's nasal voice went on in the dark from her bed on the other side of the night-table while she worked Helena Rubenstein's tissue cream into her relaxed pores and laughter lines; Jay could almost tell now by the changes in her tone whether she was working on chin or nose or throat. Tonight through his dozing there ran something about a Tossed Salad. Eleanor, it seemed, whoever Eleanor was, and God knows he'd heard enough about her so he should know by this time, Eleanor had insisted on a Tossed Salad. Everyone else had wanted Waldorf at the club luncheon but Eleanor had absolutely insisted on a Tossed Salad. Sleepily Jay pictured this Eleanor Whosis stamping her feet in the middle of the dining-room, throwing the Waldorf apple-and-nut concoction smack on the floor and screaming, "A tossed salad, or else! I insist on a tossed salad!" He pursued this melodramatic scene in dreamy fancy, half-asleep so that the images changed from normal size to dream proportions and just as Eleanor herself had become a Statue of Liberty in a dining-room as big as the Grand Central Station, in fact a dining-room that was exactly that with trains shooting around under the table on two levels, just then he heard another familiar cue, a phrase that on innumerable other occasions had threaded Flo's bedtime monologues.

"If I could just set foot in that house, just once," she was saying. So then he knew she was on her perpetual grievance about the Lou Donovans, and the cool way Mary Donovan kept her at a polite distance, and of course there's never anything a husband can do about this, even though he harbors the same secret grudge himself.

"Oh, I've passed the place plenty of times, I know the outside," Flo went on mournfully. "It's all right, it's a nice house, if you like Normandy Cottage style. Personally, I think Southern Colonial like ours is a lot prettier and more American looking. And even if this neighborhood is falling off a little at least it's nearer town and that's what I like. I mean I've seen the place outside, but I just want to know for curiosity's sake how she's fixed it inside. She's supposed to be so darned cultured and have such wonderful good taste and being a Harrod, my goodness, you'd think it was royalty the way Lou goes on about 'My wife, of course, is a Harrod.' I guess my folks are just as good as anybody's. My grandfather owned the biggest store in Taylorville, I could have gone to Vassar if I hadn't been fool enough to fall for you. I could have gone to Europe. What I mean is that it seems funny that all of your business friends have had us at their homes for dinner or cards except the Donovans, and here he is supposed to be such a pal of yours. I'd just like to set foot in that house, see what's so wonderful about it that they won't let anybody in. Not that she snubs me, she was just as nice as pie today at Eleanor's, and she asked me all about the petit point I made for Eleanor's dining-room chairs. I must say it is unusual, whether Eleanor appreciates it or not, so we talked about that, I mean Mary Donovan and I, and then I told her all about our trip, and do you know she didn't know a thing about Lou having an interior decorator to do his New York office? I said, 'My yes, she met him at the train in New York,' you know, that hard-looking girl with the pink veil over her hat, that Miss Vance or Vane or something."

Jay's eyes and ears opened so sharply at this last name that he felt as if they must have made a terrific noise. He was suddenly wide awake, and gripping the covers.

"Vance?" he said hoarsely.

"Well, Vance or Vane, anyway, believe me, Lou is in bad about that, I could tell by her expression," Flo went on complacently. "As soon as I mentioned her and how Lou said she was decorating the New York office for Lou, Mary Donovan pricked up her ears, so I knew something was up, and then she said, 'Oh, yes, that must be the one Uncle mentioned meeting with Lou. I'm sure I hope she does as nice a job on the New York office as Marshall Field did on his Chicago office.' Just like that, you know, very smooth, very easy, only you can't kid me. I could tell right away that I'd spilled something that was on her mind already. I could tell something was up right there at the station. So could Mama. Mama said the same thing, when she saw how funny Lou acted. She said, 'That girl's no decorator, she's Lou's girl friend.' "

"Oh, I don't think so," Jay's voice sounded so faint that Flo said, "What?" and he said, "I just said you might be right but I hardly think so."

This irritated Flo so much she sat right up in bed and raised her voice.

"You don't think so, oh, no, of course you don't think so, you men always stick together, you stick together instead of sticking to your wives, you know damn well Lou has a girl friend in New York, you're just afraid to tell me. Well, you don't need to, Mama and I are smart enough, we caught on. An interior decorator doesn't have to meet the customer's train, does she, if you ask me I'll bet she was on the train all along, probably came all the way from Chicago with him. Lou gets away with murder just because Mary is too refined to keep her eyes open. But you wouldn't admit it. You men are so darned afraid to tell anything about each other. Believe me, you don't even need to. Mary Donovan's no fool, though, she's on to him."

Jay lay very still, afraid to trust his voice, wondering irritably what was the matter with him that he couldn't stand up for Lou and defend him the way Lou had for him, and he felt mad at Lou for showing such superior guts in a crisis.

"You won't admit she's his girl friend," Flo said resentfully, "because you do the same thing, probably, and you're afraid I'll find out. Well, listen, old thing, you don't hide anything from me, at all, at all. I have a pretty good hunch about things like that. Now what's the matter? Where are you going? What are you getting out of bed for?"

"I'm going to get a drink," Jay said patiently, sliding his feet into bedroom slippers. "I'm thirsty, that's all."

"It's that ham we had," said Flo. "We had ham at Eleanor's for lunch, too. Baked with pineapple, like a casserole, and mashed sweet potatoes with marshmallow whip along the edges. And then the tossed salad and banana-almond ice cream with strawberry sauce and fudge cake. I was so nervous when one of the girls dropped some sauce and it nearly stained the petit point seat but fortunately it went on her dress instead. Eleanor says when she has men for dinner she protects the petit point on the dining-room chairs by putting an oilized napkin over the seats the men use so they can't drop stuff on the petit point between their legs; of course with the women their skirts protect the petit point. Mary Donovan said they were the most attractive chairs she's seen, and I offered to show her how to work them, so maybe she'll ask me over there sometime. I feel kinda sorry for her, so big as you please and so darned sure of herself, and all the time Lou keeping that Vance girl in New York and pretending it's business. Believe me, if I was in her shoes I'd have it out with him, I'd march myself right along to New York next time he went and I'd follow him wherever he went till I got the goods on him. I'm going to tell her so, too, if she asks me."

"I wouldn't," Jay wanted to say but no sound came

from his lips so he gave it up and pattered out the bedroom door, relieved to stumble over a hooked rug in the doorway so that he could relieve his feelings by cursing and upbraiding the stupidity of the maid, and even the mistress for overwaxing floors and having rugs skating all over the place. The counterattack successfully silenced Flo.

"I'm too tired to argue with you, Jay," she complained. "I've been flying all over the country for the last four days and then the lunch today and I'm honestly dead. It's just mean of you to start something when I'm trying to get a little rest. Go on, get a drink, if you can't sleep, but let me get a little rest, for a change."

He heard her turn over and he drew a breath of relief. In the sunroom he found the drink he was looking for and it was not water either. He sat in the wicker chaise longue, smoking and sipping a brandy for an hour or two, gloomily reflecting on how miserably he was repaying Lou for saving his life. All right, he was a bastard, but what could a man do once his wife sets out to make a bastard of him? God damn fool, that's all he was, he muttered to himself a dozen times, fool of the world, ought to have a rousing good kick in the pants, serve him right. Lou, though, was the regular fellow, a real friend, a pal, the man who saved him when he was on the spot. Well, the least he could do was to tip him off about what Flo and Judge Harrod had told Mary. In a way, though, he didn't see any real reason why Lou Donovan shouldn't get in a little hot water now and then. Other men did. Other men got caught every time they tweaked a stenographer's chin or snatched a kiss behind a kitchen door. A fellow—even a smart one like Lou Donovan—couldn't expect to have everything work out like velvet every minute. It wasn't normal to go through life with never a slip-up in the arrangements. Lou was a fool to expect his luck to always hold. Still, he'd tip him off to watch his step as soon as he got back in town. He owed him that much.

X

At six o'clock who should show up but old Francie. She would! Lou, back in Chicago, was in the "office bar" shaving himself and getting a kick, as he always did, out of the elegant little hideout he had created out of a dirty old fileroom. One of these days he'd put a bartender on the payroll, boy would that be something! More like a yacht than a business office! He had a small handmirror rigged up against a highball glass on a card-table; his coat and vest and gray shirt hung over the chromium chair-back. He was in his stocking feet, because he'd handed his shoes over to Mike the building bootblack so he wouldn't lose any time.

"Well, she's in again," said Miss Frye, closing the door to the office behind her. "What do I say now?"

What could anybody say?

"Now, how did she know I just got in town?" asked Lou. "I get off the plane at five forty and in fifteen minutes she's right on my tail."

"I told you," said Miss Frye. "I warned you."

"Did you give her the check I told you?"

"She wouldn't take it," said Miss Frye. "She said she had to see you personally. I couldn't say anything."

"What she want to hang around Chicago for?" groaned Lou.

"You men," said Miss Frye. "You want to step out of your past as if it was an old pair of pants."

"I wish it was that easy," Lou sighed. In a way it was

a relief to have Miss Frye know about all his private affairs, even to that old marriage. She knew how to ward off trouble, then, and she was dependable. No sex there, nothing but hardboiled efficiency. If he ever got into trouble, he could count on Miss Frye all right. It was worth sixty a week to him to know that.

"Anybody with her? What was the situation, anyway?"

"Well," said Frye, "she's still got the Ford; that means she's not so hard up. I saw her parking it across the street."

"How's she looking—the old girl, I mean?"

Miss Frye's sharp little pixie face went up, sniffing the air, hunting the right word.

"Tacky?" prompted Lou. "Weepy?"

"No," said Miss Frye. "On the make."

On the make. Worse yet. Miss Frye seemed to think so too for she shook her head sympathetically.

"I'll give her ten minutes," said Lou. "She can see I'm rushed, and then when the fellas come in it'll be easy to brush her off. That convention crowd will scare her off."

"Are you sticking around here all evening?" Miss Frye asked.

Lou shrugged. One thing Miss Frye didn't know and wouldn't if he could help it, was that he had fixed up a date with Mrs. Kameray for that evening. Let the fellows use the bar, let them have a good time there, do as they pleased with nobody in town to spy on them. He'd give them the keys, let Jay Oliver be host, and he'd slip off to the Stevens and pick up Mrs. Kameray, get acquainted.

"Maybe, maybe not," he said. "Anyway, if my house calls up I'm not back yet. Give me some cash, too, before you go. Get it in fifties."

As soon as Francie came in, Lou saw what Miss Frye meant. She had taken off ten or fifteen pounds since the last meeting ten years ago, and had a bunch of cornsilk curls sticking out of a black satin lid that looked like an opera hat with an extravagant veil floating around it. Her flaring plaid skirt was way up to here (her legs stayed good and did she know it, for she took one of the bar stools right away where she could swing them to good advantage) and if the swirl of her skirt showed more knee than was necessary they were good enough knees to justify it. A chiffon scarf was tucked around the neck of her black velvet jacket with polka dots to match her poppy-red lips and fingertips. She must have put in some stiff work on her face because it did not look old, not even thirty, only it had that desperate set look that a woman's face always gets when she's decided to show the world she's not afraid of it. It was a brave thing to see, but pretty grim as an invitation to the male. Or maybe he just felt that way, knowing Francie so well. It was a blind spot. Maybe she'd never look or be anything but five hand-to-mouth years, 1920-to-1925, Newark, N. J., to Coral Gables, to Coney. God, he almost forgot that Coney Island rooming house! Maybe to him Francie would never be anything but Lady Bad Luck. Even if she hadn't had a thing to do with his bad luck he still thought of her that way because as soon as he broke with her his luck sprang high. Not her fault. Couldn't really blame old Fran. Still she was always Friday the thirteenth to him, and you couldn't laugh her off.

"Excuse the undress, Francie," he said, deciding to take it very natural. "Just got off the New York plane and rushing right into conference with some big restaurant men."

"Never mind the undress," said Francie, laughing. "An old married couple like us!"

Socko. Just like that. Always bringing up that they used to be married, that so far as that went they still were. Lou couldn't help shooting a look around the room as if Mary or the Harrods might be somewhere behind a curtain, listening, horrified. You'd think he and Francie had never even had the divorce to hear her talk. Just as if he didn't have Mary and the kid now and Francie herself had the punk, but Francie had always managed to take a line somehow that would embarrass him. He really had nothing against Francie—they'd had a couple of good years and three bad ones, but why in the name of heaven did she have to pop up right now in his life? Why did she have to take in Chicago after all these years? Why did she have to walk across his path like some black cat just as he was having the biggest break of his life? Sure, he felt sorry for her, his luck coming and hers going as soon as they broke up, but he'd been decent enough there for a while, sending her a check once in a while when she wrote, not as much as she wanted, maybe, but hell's bells, what was the matter with the punk supporting her?

It would have made him more comfortable if she raised the roof or bawled him out now, but instead she just sat staring at him, smiling and managing to remind him of old intimate things. It was indecent and he could feel his neck getting red. Undressing him with her memory, that's what it amounted to. He wished she would get down to brass tacks and say what she'd come to say—that she was broke again and she hated terribly to ask but this was just a loan, she'd get it back to him the tenth of some month or other. He braced himself for defense against this, he braced himself to remind her that he'd handed out a check twice in the last month to her, after all he'd better make it clear he was no sucker. He knew damn well it was the punk putting her up to put the bee on him.

"This is a new angle," she said, looking around the cozy little lounge. "Bar right next the office. What's the idea? Can't you wait to get to the one downstairs?"

Lou looked at his lathered face in the mirror.

"This is a convention town," he said. "Visitors like a little hideaway where they can drink and talk deals over privately. Have some fun without some big customer watching them. It's all good business for me. I had it fixed up last year."

Francie walked around and looked over the tables.

"Roulette, even," she said. "And look at those bottles!"

She pointed to the glistening array behind the Chinese-red bar.

"Reminds me of the time we had getting enough dough to buy brandy for that Senator who was going to let you in on a deal. He never came through, anyway, that was the joke. I knew he wouldn't all the time."

"Yes," said Lou quietly. "You always knew they'd never come through, didn't you, Francie?"

That stopped her. Without turning his head he felt her grow very still.

"I know what you mean, Lou," she said in a low voice. "If I'd had sense enough to believe in those wild schemes of yours we'd be together right now and I wouldn't be broke while you're riding high. We'd both be in the money. And we'd be—together. Like we ought to be."

Lou finished his shaving, folded up the mirror and put it in his bag on the chair. He didn't look at her because he knew well enough she had her handkerchief to her eyes.

"Still shave twice a day?" she said a little shakily.

"I got up early," he said coldly. The only way to stop this sentiment-fest was to get tough right away and he did. "O.K., let's hear it," he said. "What's the punk let you in for this time? I told you I got big expenses on my hands, the kid's got mastoid trouble, Mary's had to cut short her cruise, the income tax people are after me. Money's mighty scarce."

He saw her stiffen and turn her head away. She was trying to pretend this was just a social call for old-times' sake, and if money came into it the idea was just casual, on the spur of the moment.

"Too bad about the kid," she said, and there was that again. All the time they had been together, he recalled now, she had wanted children—one, anyway,—and they used to fight about it. If he could put two hundred down on a car he could afford to pay for a baby, that was always her argument. His line was that he couldn't stand kids, they'd break up the marriage. And the crazy life they lived, rooming houses, a jump ahead of the sheriff or the landlady,—no, he said, no kids for him. So now he was crazy about the little girl Mary had presented him with. What was wrong with that? Was it his fault he had human nature?

"Like a drink?" he said. "Oh, no, that's so, you never could take it, could you?"

He was glad he could remember something that wasn't too personal.

"One drink and you hit the ceiling, remember?"

"I'm different, now," she said. "Sure I'll have a highball."

He went behind the bar and mixed her one. Where the hell was Jay Oliver or somebody, somebody to break this thing up?

"Look, do you mind not saying anything about being my ex?" he asked, trying to act offhand about it as if it hadn't been on his mind ever since she blew in to town. "I mean there's no point in bringing it up now. You're Mrs. Thomson now and there's a new Mrs. Donovan. You know. Might look funny."

She nodded slowly. Her eyes travelled around the room, studying the silver Venetian shades, and the nudes outlined in silver on the scarlet walls. Through the gleaming silvery curtains you could see the lake, blue and cold and smooth as metal.

"Pretty swell place," she said. "It's a wonder you don't stay here every night instead of going home."

"Lots of times I do," he said. "The out-of-town fellas are keen about it, naturally. Gives 'em a sort of private spot to drop in between trains, put in some phone calls, catch a few drinks, do business or line up a hot date. Like an old-time speakeasy, that's the charm of it. I had a crowd of advertising men here couple weeks ago and they were shooting craps up here till Sunday afternoon. Never left the place. Boy, was it a shambles! Shooting for five hundred a throw. I won three grand but I was the host so I had to let 'em take it off me."

She was sipping her drink and he could tell the way she went at it that she still didn't know how to handle it. Small-town, that was Francie, even to the devilish way she smoked a cigarette, little finger crooked, head cocked, like a stock-company vamp. The Girl from Rector's—that was Francie with a drink and a cigarette and her legs crossed. It had once rather tickled him, he recalled now with amazement. Maybe it was because he could in those early days measure how much he was learning in the world by what Francie was; she stayed exactly where he started, and once this had pleased his ego, now it embarrassed him to think he was ever that much of a hick.

"I'm planning to do a little branching out on my own," she said. "It's this way, Lou. I know you don't think much of Frank——"

"Right!" Frank was the punk she married.

"But honestly, Lou, he isn't well! He's got that bad lung and there isn't much work a guy with a bad lung can do. A little cold and he's laid up all winter. The climate's bad."

Now it was coming.

"Why didn't he go out West with his bonus money instead of dropping it all at Hialeah?" barked Lou. This was the same old fight. "I got no sympathy."

"Listen, Lou, the race track is all he knows. He can lie in bed and study it, and that's all he can do. Gee, that boy knows all there is to know about horses and tracks. You did once, but, honest, you'd have to take your hat off to him, if you could hear him. He knows every stable, he knows which horse likes mud and which likes sand; he has everything figured out. Everybody in the neighborhood comes around wherever we are to hear what he has to say."

"Maybe they didn't hear how he come out at Hialeah," said Lou sarcastically. "Seven hundred bucks in two days."

"Lou, you know you can't do much with seven hundred," said Francie plaintively. "You got to have something to play with. If he'd had a thousand now——"

Lou laughed harshly.

"Seven hundred bucks is a lot of money, baby," he said.

"Can I have another drink?" Francie asked suddenly.

Lou looked at his wrist watch.

"These fellas ought to be here any minute, but O.K. Same?"

"Maybe I'd like it better straight," said Francie. "Or look, maybe you got some absinthe. I got crazy about absinthe in New Orleans. And then in Havana I always drank ojen."

"Been around a lot, haven't you?" said Lou. "You'd better stick to Scotch."

He poured two fingers in a glass. Every minute seemed torture. He didn't want to see her, no reason why he should have to, it downed him, somehow, brought back every bit of the old desperation under which they had lived. If she just would stand up, act as if she was going. Anything. And it made him suddenly see the perfect awfulness of Mary or the Harrods suddenly finding out about a previous marriage. Nothing criminal in it. But why in God's name hadn't he ever mentioned it? How would he ever be able to explain that?

"So your marriage turned out all right, then," Francie said slowly. "I read about it in the papers, of course. She was a somebody, I guess. What'd it say—adopted by her uncle, old Judge Whosis? Anyway I got the idea that you'd married into some class."

Lou started talking hastily, trying to keep her off this tack. He talked about the new house in Winnetka, how the decorator soaked him, how the electrical fixtures alone cost ten thousand, it was criminal, but in this business you had to make a show, entertain the boys, put up a front. You had to look like big money to make it, a funny thing that was, and besides he dealt direct with the big shots, the presidents, the general managers, why only yesterday he lunched in New York with Major– well, not to mention names, but later on the world would be hearing about Castles-in-the-Woods, one of the biggest– Lou stopped as suddenly as he had begun, for in his anxiety to get away from personal matters into business he was making his business so prosperous that he was letting himself in for a bigger touch than ever. Francie, however, did not press it then.

"I should think those convention boys would go some place where they could get girls instead of just drinking here with no fun."

"I get girls for them all right, never mind about that," said Lou shortly. "Never let it be said! I date up a half dozen live numbers from the Spinning Top down the street or a couple of dancers from Giulio's Grotto. They drop in between floor shows over there and keep things moving. Most of them leave with a hundred-dollar bill stuck in their pocket. These guys are the real thing, you know, and do the babes know it!"

Talk to her as if she was a man, that was it! Forget the personal thing entirely. Don't let it get you!

Francie kicked her slippers off.

"I don't know why liquor always makes me do that," she said laughing. "All of a sudden I got to take my shoes off."

Miss Frye opened the door and Lou jumped.

"I'll betcha it looks funny coming in and finding us both with our shoes off," Francie giggled.

Miss Frye smiled uncertainly. Lou tried to signal her to try getting rid of Francie but Francie kept her eyes on him so he dared not try anything.

"Mike brought your shoes back, Mr. Donovan," said Miss Frye, and the dwarfed old bootblack crept in behind her and set the shoes down on the chair.

"Is there anything else before I go?" she asked.

"Can't let you go yet, Miss Frye, sorry," Lou said hastily. Good heavens! Leave him alone with Francie? God knows what she'd do. Cry. Scream. Anything was possible. "See if Mr. Oliver's left his office. Or try him at the store. Or the Drake. That's right. He might be at the Drake with old Whittleby. Tell him I'm waiting. And phone the café to send over canapés, olives, chips—get plenty of everything. There may only be half a dozen of us and there may be twenty."

"Some conference," said Francie.

Lou shrugged.

"Just a routine, that's all. All right, now, what's on your mind?"

And Francie plunged.

"I was figuring if you could let me have sixty-two dollars we could get the car out of hock and drive to Arizona next week," said Francie, all in a breath. "Don't say no, Lou. I know you've been good to me and I realize how you feel about Frank, but this time it'll work out. I'll leave him in Arizona with his aunt and maybe he'll get his health back. Then I'll go on to Los Angeles to pick up a job—I don't mean pictures, I realize I'm too old for that, but maybe in some church or something. They must use organists somewhere; you hear 'em all the time on the radio. After all, when you knew me first I was getting seventy-five a week there in the picture show—more than you made taking tickets."

If there was one stage of his life he wanted to forget

it was his ticket-taking days in that lousy movie house in Jersey. Next she'd ring in the stuff about his being pin boy at the bowling alley when he was a kid, all the stuff he wanted to forget—not because he was ashamed of it, hell, anybody might have to work their way up the ladder, but the days it brought back were so wretched, days of being kicked around, days when he was dumb, too, afraid to speak out, even, just remembering them gave him an inferiority. Oh, sure, she'd have to bring all that up. She couldn't let a fellow be happy in his present. That was Francie for you.

"I was a darn good organist," said Francie. "You said yourself I could get more out of 'I Love You Truly' than anybody you ever heard."

Now the old organ stuff was going to come out, about how long she studied to be a movie organist and had that swell job just a year when sound came in and threw everybody out. It was too bad, sure it was too bad, he'd said so then over and over, day in, day out, but women and elephants never forget anything.

"I hear that in some of the high-class restaurants they've started using organists," she said. "So far as that goes I got my figure back now and might get a hostess job some place. Maybe in a night club."

Lou didn't say anything. If she thought she could compete with the glamour girls he wouldn't remind her how old she was. Two years older than he was.

"How do you make it sixty-two bucks exactly?" he asked. "Why does it have to be sixty-two?"

He was being nasty, all right, he knew it, but there was something about her coming in and hanging around this way that made him feel that way. Coming in, spoiling his wonderful week, his top moment, reminding him that once he was a small-town dumb-bell, taking the rap from everybody, afraid to call his fritter his own.

Francie fidgeted with the chiffon scarf.

"I figure a dollar fifty a day for food for the two of us, forty to get the car out of hock and we're set for about two weeks, long enough to get West. Something'll turn up in Santa Fe, maybe."

"You just might drive on to Santa Anita or Caliente, too, mightn't you?" Lou inquired softly. "Race tracks handy there, for the punk. And supposing you didn't have the car in hock at all, supposing you had it parked around the corner right this minute, you could put that forty bucks on a horse, couldn't you?"

She was trapped and she knew it.

"Okay, I lied about that," she said, looking down at the floor. "A person's got to lie about things once in a while. God knows you ought to admit that. Anyway, you're so down on Frank I can't talk straight to you. Honest, Lou, I can't be mean to a guy that's only got a year or two to live. If talking track makes him feel like a big he-man when I know damn well he isn't one—well, gee, I can't explain, but if you heard him crying sometime because he can't take care of me right——"

"You can't expect me to keep some guy just because you happen to be crazy about him," said Lou, and was sorry he said it right away.

Francie looked straight at him, very solemn.

"You know I was never crazy about anybody but you," she said. "You knew it when you walked out. You'll always know it. Frank was sick in the house and I was low—well, that was all there was to it. You got to have somebody.

Look, Lou, take it this way. If it hadn't been for my marrying him, you'd have had to put up alimony. I ain't ever bothered you much, you got to admit that, I never let out a peep since you been married, not till now. I ain't bothered you."

Those "ain'ts" made him squirm as much as her sorrowful eyes. You'd think women would get over a thing after a while, but no, by God, they hang on to every damn thing in their lives, hoard every little ancient romance as if it was a Liberty Bond. He tried not to see how her eyes followed his hands as he buttoned up his shirt, and he reddened, knowing what she was thinking, that this was like old times, old times she was always remembering, and he was always trying to pretend never had happened. It was funny how a man was so ashamed of having cared for somebody once and funny how a woman never got tired talking about it.

"Sixty-two dollars is a lot of money, Francie," he said briskly. "Maybe not if you don't have to slave for it, the way I do. You can just go back and tell the White Man that Red Feather says if he had to pay the government what I do he wouldn't be shelling out sixty-two bucks to every mug that wants to put the bee on him."

Yes, and that was another thing that made him detest this whole scene, himself, and Francie and everything about it. The little reminder that he had ever had anything to do with a dame that could go for a down-at-heels mug like that dope she finally married. That was the kind of thing that got a man down.

Francie stopped swinging her legs and wriggled the toes in her stockings. Her silence rattled him. Then she spoke in a very low voice.

"You talk about your house," she said. "I've been past

there lots of times. I've seen the baby. I've seen her, too. Mary."

Lou's blood ran cold. Had she talked to Mary? And the thought of the eyes watching him, watching him and Mary when they didn't know they were being observed. The sad jealous eyes of old Francie.

"Oh, I never went in," Francie said bitterly, as if sensing his uneasiness. "I never said anything to her. I just wanted to see, that was all."

Lou suddenly felt he could endure no more.

"Miss Frye!" he bellowed. "Miss Frye, where the hell are those things from the café?"

Miss Frye hastily opened the door and the boy from the restaurant was right behind her with a great tray of hors d'œuvres and a basket of tidbits to spread out in little silver dishes along the bar. Lou mopped his brow.

"Your house just called," said Miss Frye.

"Call back and say I'm expected on tomorrow's plane," said Lou. "And call the Colony. Maybe Mr. Oliver dropped in there."

"Okay," said Miss Frye and again Lou could not give her a signal because of Fran's watchful eyes.

The door to the office closed.

"So you're brushing Mary off, now," said Francie. "Through with her, eh, through with her, too."

Lou gave his necktie a furious jerk.

"Certainly I'm not through with Mary, too," he snapped. "What put that in that little pin head?"

"Staying here nights with all those girls," said Francie. "What kind of woman is she, allowing you to do that?"

"Allowing me!" Lou shouted. "How would she know about it?"

"Lying to her," said Francie. "That's one thing you never did with me. You thought too much of me for that, I'll say that for you."

Lou gripped the table with both hands.

"I'm not lying to her," he expostulated. "I'm merely saving myself explanations, that's all. Explanations take time and I'm a very busy man."

"You never did that when *we* were together," said Francie. She said "together" as if it meant everything. "Honest, Lou, you were happy with me, then, you got to admit that much, you really were happy. I used to call you 'pussy,' remember?"

"Every man that's called 'pussy' isn't the happiest man in the world," muttered Lou. "Can't you drop this, Francie, for God's sake?"

"We were never even separated," went on Francie dreamily, looking out the window over the lake, "except the time you went to Toronto about that advertising job and the time you and your brother went to Texas for that oil deal."

"I've never been in Toronto in my life," said Lou grimly. "And this is the first time I ever heard of my having a brother."

He realized what he had done the next minute, but it was too late.

"Oh!" gasped Francie, clutching her heart. She looked straight ahead for a second then carefully stooped over and picked up her shoes. She wiggled her feet into them silently. She looked pinched and stricken.

"Good Lord, everybody has to alibi once in a while just to save a lot of talk, that's all it means," Lou bumbled along.

Francie straightened her skirt out now and fussed with her scarf. She gave a little laugh that was like cracked ice in a glass.

"I don't know what could have been eating me," she said. "I knew you did a lot of things I didn't like, but I was perfectly certain you never two-timed me. That was the nice thing. I just *knew.* I used to say to myself, never mind how things turned out in the end, at least when they were right, they *were* right. A person has to have something to kinda go on, you know, especially. . . . The brother in Texas. . . . How dumb I must have been. It's a laugh. It was right when we were really crazy about each other, too. I—I—I mean. . . . Funny how you hang on to some things no matter what happens, then it turns out those are just the things you should have skipped."

So now she'd have to cry a little.

Lou scowled and folded his arms. Where were these fellows that should have come in now to save him?

"Snap out of it, Francie," he growled.

"Oh, it isn't that I care so much about that forty dollars," she sniffled into her handkerchief. "Maybe he would lose it right away like he did at Hialeah, but in a way it's your fault. I keep remembering that if I had believed all your talk about buying up hotel concessions, then selling them, and all those other wild notions of yours, you and I would never have split. Now I make it up, see, by believing what Frank tells me. I think maybe if I walked out on him it would be just the time for him to strike big dough just the way it was with you. I don't want to make the same mistake twice."

"You would compare a business genius with a turf tramp," said Lou sarcastically.

He kept himself from screaming at her to get the hell out and stop making his insides squirm this way. He felt like half a cent. He might as well never have made good since the movie house days. Francie could do that to him in just ten minutes.

"Here," he said, inspired, and rummaged through his pockets. "This is all the cash I can spare right now. The checkbook's in the safe for the night. This will help."

He put three tens on the table. Francie looked at it a minute without touching it, then suddenly brushed it on the floor and stamped on it.

"Say!" he blazed at her.

He was so surprised and indignant that he could say no more.

Just as unexpectedly Francie the next moment bent over and picked up the three bills, straightened them out carefully and put them in her pocketbook. He saw a nickel and an aspirin and two one-cent stamps in the coin department.

"Even if it was only a penny," Francie said wearily, "I'd have to end up scrambling for it."

She powdered her nose and fluffed the new blonde curls over her ear. At least she was going. At least that. Thirty bucks was enough to get her out of town. He could have given her more, he would have only she made him so boiling mad the way she got his ego down. It was a gift with some women. But he shouldn't get mad, not show it, anyway.

"So long, Francie," he said. "I'm sorry about things, but you can't blame me, considering everything. It's a tough world, some of us got the touch and some haven't, that's the way I see it."

"Got it all figured out, haven't you?" said Francie. "Mr. Dale Carnegie."

He saw she was looking at him in a sorrowful, still way, and he might have guessed something was coming, but somehow he didn't expect her to do this, fling her arms around his neck and kiss him wildly. It was the worst thing that had happened so far, and of course that was the exact moment Miss Frye chose to open the door and let some men barge in.

"Hot dog!" yelled Jay Oliver.

Lou pushed Francie away from him and tried to grin, wiping lipstick off his face.

"Will you look at old Lou," jubilantly cried Jay. "Damned if he isn't in conference!"

There were the two promotion men from Denver and the Canadian whiskey baron. They beamed and waited for introductions which Lou mumbled through, conscious of Jay's gleeful enjoyment of his embarrassment. Francie quietly picked her bag up.

"I'll be with you fellows in a sec," Lou said, trying to act casual. "I got to see this lady to the elevator."

"Thought you were having some babes in," said the Canadian.

"Oh, the babes will be along any minute," Lou reassured him. "Come on, Francie."

"Why do we lose this little lady?" Jay demanded genially. "What's the matter with keeping her here for a little drinkie or two? Or is she your private property, Lou you old rascal?"

"No," said Lou, "only she's got to——"

His eyes fell before Francie's sardonic smile.

"Look, you can stick around, can't you, Halfpint?" Jay

caught Francie's arm jovially. "What's the matter with playing around for a while? We're all good guys. You tell her, Lou."

"Sure they are," said Lou with a sickening sense of defeat. Outside he heard the shrill giggles and scampering of the girls from the Grotto just getting out of the elevator and it sounded to him like the marines coming. He breathed a sigh.

"Ah, here they come. Here come the babes, now, no need holding you any longer, Francie, if you've got to go. The lads will have company."

"Ah, come on, anyway, and stay," urged Jay, thoroughly happy now that he sensed Lou's uneasiness. "Can't you stay?"

"Sure, I'm staying," said Francie. She yanked off the opera-hat lid and threw it playfully at the big Canadian. "I'd like to play with a good guy for once in my life. Set 'em up, Lou, let's get going!"

Friday the thirteenth, Lou thought numbly, trying to smile, black cat cross your path, new moon over wrong shoulder. Lady Luck. Lady Bad Luck. Okay, shrug your shoulders, take it on the chin.

"Don't I get any caviar?" complained Francie reaching for the tray. Lou passed her the caviar canapés.

"Angels on toast if you ask for them, sweetheart," he said easily. That was the way. Chin up. Always leave 'em laughing.

XI

In the middle of the morning after a party Lou always got a craving for creamed marinierte herring and breakfasted on it at the Old Heidelberg, with a glass of beer. He felt depressed and it wasn't just the hangover, either. A little ammoniated bromoseltzer had fixed that an hour ago over at the Stevens Hotel where he had spent the night. Little things, little things again. He'd muffed the date with Mrs. Kameray last night, simply because, believe it or not, he was afraid to leave the office party last night for fear Francie would tell something she shouldn't. She'd been all right about not mentioning their old marriage, but what was so good about that discretion, after all? Her doting glances and embraces, the little clubby cracks about past intimacies, made the thing look even worse. They all ended up at Giulio's, but it was too late then to meet the little Kameray. When he called her up to explain she was sore as the dickens. That was all right, when he had time he'd smooth her down. She wasn't the type, as he figured her out, to stay mad. But it was simply plans going wrong that irritated him. And old Francie. She'd gone off finally with Jay Oliver and that was safe enough, he thought he could count on Jay even if she told him the whole business. Jay wouldn't tell, but the mere fact that he even knew was disagreeable enough. Well, he'd just have to keep reminding Jay of how he fixed up the Ebie business for him. On days like this the least little thing could set him up or throw him. The waiter fussing around, giving him the "Mr. Donovan" this and "Mr. Donovan" that, was soothingly satisfactory, but then there was the little encounter with old Grahame, the head of a hotel chain and friend of Judge Harrod. Lou had waved genially to him as he passed him.

Grahame, who was about to squeeze his two hundred and seventy-five pounds behind the wheel of a Packard coupé, actually got out of the car and waddled back to the restaurant door to shake hands with Lou. It was the warmest greeting he had ever given Lou and Lou's flagging spirits soared.

"Great seeing you, Mr. Grahame!" Lou said happily.

"Great seeing you, too," said Grahame in his panting breathless squeaky little voice, "and doing fine, now, I can tell by your looks."

"Thanks, Mr. Grahame," said Lou. "Nice of you to say so."

"Always glad to see one of our old bellboys make good in the world," said Grahame, still pumping his hand. "Good luck, Cassidy, and if you're ever around the hotel look in and say hello to the old crowd."

He had waddled back to his car, happy in his democratic little interview, before Lou could think of anything to say. Of course he really had only seen Grahame a couple times at the Harrods' and the old boy was over sixty and probably stone blind. Still that "Cassidy" was a burn. He was glad to see one of Grahame's managers, a fellow named Pritchard, having a late breakfast at the next table, so he could take out his wounded feelings. Pritchard was all right, he thought a lot of Lou and they'd had some deals together.

Today Pritchard, too, was gloomy.

"How do I know what makes the old boy say things like that?" he said, when Lou complained. "Imagine you or me being able to get away with a crack like that! 'One of our bellboys'—can you imagine it! The only thing is that he isn't smart enough to have meant it as an insult."

"He's not so dumb," said Lou. "You don't pile up four million by being dumb."

"The hell you don't," said Pritchard. "Old Grahame's typical old-time success. When he was twenty-five his old man handed him the business. He married dough, and so now he gives a sales talk once a week on how kind hearts and coronets are all you need to get to the top. It's a pain."

"He could have been an ambassador," said Lou, still smarting. "He's travelled all over."

"Not all over. Only where there's a Ritz," said Pritchard sourly. "Why, that old bastard hasn't been off his fritter in twenty years. When he goes to Paris he drives straight to the Ritz and then he has his meals sent to his room till it's time to go to London. Same there. 'Where's the Ritz?,' he says when he comes out of his stateroom, and then they shoot him there and he says, 'Where's my suite?' and then he's done London. Why, he won't go any place there isn't a Ritz. 'Where's the Ritz?,' he says when he gets off the boat or the plane, 'take me straight to the Ritz.' If there isn't any he climbs back on the plane. Oh, sure. The brains of the business and all that. From the bottom up and bottoms up and all that."

"What's wrong with the Ritz?" said Lou. "It's a good hotel. Or wouldn't a bellboy know?"

It seemed funny now, or sort of funny.

"What's on your mind now?" Pritchard asked when Lou was silent.

"I was just thinking I might move to New York," Lou said reflectively. "I don't know. As soon as I get back home here something comes up, some little thing, that throws me. I'm not the small-town type. I'm at home in New York or travelling around."

"Chicago's a small town, then, all of a sudden," Pritchard mocked.

"I mean I care about things here, as soon as I get off a train, that don't matter any place else," Lou explained.

"Nuts, it's just your conscience," Pritchard said. He sighed. "Nobody has their conscience around much away from home. It's like a garage. It ought to be handy to your house. Believe me, I know."

Lou didn't encourage the confession he was pretty sure was coming up for the simple reason that it was his experience that men were always sore at you after they opened up their hearts. As if you'd asked them. He didn't want to find out. He never asked. But try and stop them telling you.

"Last night, for instance," said Pritchard, true to form. "What a mess that turned out to be."

"Yeah?"

"I took my wife and daughter, you know Barbara Lucy, you met her at the races, well," Pritchard took a gulp of beer, scowling, "here it was Barbara Lucy's sixteenth birthday so we took her down to the Chez Paris. I was dancing with the kid or trying to, I'm no dancer, and who should I bump into on the floor but Jay Oliver with a floozy."

Francie, thought Lou. So that's where they went.

"I was kind of high, you know how you have to brace

yourself for the old family outing," continued Pritchard, wiping his moustache, "I'd have one with the little woman —the kid only has sherry—then I'd have a couple of quick ones at the bar. So Jay and I make a few cracks, just good-natured you know, on the floor, and end up switching partners, Jay with Barbara Lucy and me squeezing up the floozy."

So Jay didn't even have sense enough to take Francie to a little out-of-the-way spot. No, it had to be Chez Paris. Why he might even have had Mary there—that is, if Mary would ever have been willing to go out to nightclubs or for that matter, if he himself had been anywhere near her last night.

"Well, of course the wife was sore at Jay, because she knows Flo, and she thought it was laying it on for him to bring a floozy out in public like that. I was too high to care, and the kid got a kick out of changing partners on the floor that way, so I was squeezing up the floozy—I can't dance worth a damn, all I do is sort of march around and love 'em up a little if they're the type, and all of a sudden my wife prances up to the dance floor and calls Barbara Lucy off first, then she tries to catch me by the arm as I'm floating past with the floozy. Well, you know me. I was feeling no pain by that time, so the upshot was that the wife took Barbara Lucy home and left me with Jay and the floozy, and when I got out to Evanston I was locked out. So I spent the night at the Stevens. What the hell I do next I don't know."

Lou lit a cigarette, admiring the way his fingers hardly shook at all. Two up for old Francie, then.

"Wonder where old Oliver stands now at his house," was all he said.

Pritchard shook his head sorrowfully.

"He hasn't got a chance. Not if Eleanor has anything to do with it. I said, soon as we spot the floozy, I said, look, now Eleanor, I know you know Flo and I know how women stick together so far as telling each other any bad news goes, but skip it this once. Let's have a gentleman's agreement, that you don't tell Flo. So she said okay, I'm mad, she says, but at least I'm no troublemaker. So we had a gentleman's agreement she shouldn't say anything."

"Think she said anything?" Lou asked.

This was all old Francie's fault. Typhoid Mary if there ever was one.

"Listen, the thing was all over town by ten o'clock this morning," said Pritchard gloomily. "That's what comes of my wife not being a gentleman."

"I'll hear more about it from Jay, then," Lou said. You bet he would. He'd have to fix it up with Flo again. And Flo would bully Jay until he'd say he was only taking one of the girls home from a party at Lou Donovan's office, and then Flo would say, why I understood Mrs. Donovan to say he wasn't home yet. Or no. There was one salvation. Mary, his dear, dear wife, snooted Flo, thank God. Mary snooted all his business friends, Mary was too high-class to be a little helper to her husband and what could be sweeter than that? She never saw Flo except at some card club they all belonged to, thanks be to good breeding. He suddenly felt safe again and it was all because of Mary. He was glad now that things had turned out so he hadn't had the date with Mrs. Kameray last night. At least that was one thing he needn't feel guilty about. He thought now he'd better fix up the whole business before he went out to the house that night.

"I got a man from New York coming in at twelve," he said. "If you see your boss tell him his bellboy wants a new uniform, will you?"

"Ah, don't mind what that old fathead says," said Pritchard. "I swear to God I've worked for him fifteen years and he still calls me Mitchell. Listen, I was out taking some visitors through my brother's paper mill one day, by accident, when who should I see sweeping through the place but a Chamber of Commerce delegation led by old man Grahame. He didn't even know me. I spoke. He gives me the old handshake and then he says, 'Well, Mitchell,' he says, 'the working man has a better time today than when I was a young man.' I burbled something or other and then he says, 'Are you satisfied with your work here, Mitchell? Have you got a good foreman?' Hells bells, you're bellboy crack is nothing new. Forget it. You're in."

Lou laughed. The hell with Grahame. Next time he ran into him he'd let him have a little bit of the old stuff right back.

"If you see old Oliver tell him we're not friends any more," Pritchard called after him.

Back at the office the sun was pouring in the great windows as if nothing had happened. The false book-cases that formed the door to the bar looked innocent as could be, never for an instant hinting that a mere push of the button could make them swing open into a world of unlettered temptation. Miss Frye was busily typing at her huge oak desk, reading goggles perched on the tip of her sharp nose. Lou tossed his hat in the closet and got on the phone. He got the Building Superintendent.

"What's the matter with this water cooler? Get more ice in it, will you? Right away. Donovan's office."

"How do you know?" Miss Frye queried, looking up from her typewriter. "You haven't even tried it yet."

"Never mind, I go by hunches," Lou said.

Miss Frye looked him over thoughtfully.

"So that's the way it is," she said. "Maybe you should have gone to a Turkish bath."

Lou made an impatient gesture.

"Don't argue with me, Miss Frye," he begged. "I got things on my mind. What's new?"

He went to his own desk, a large kidney-shaped handsome affair in the corner, set between two long windows hung with heavy blue. This blue frame against the oak-panelled walls was a fine spot for a blonde, Miss Frye had often remarked, and had prophesied that one of these days that was just what would happen. Lou picked up the telegrams. One from Rosenbaum advising him to check up at once on Mrs. Kameray, one from the New York office girl advising that the office furniture was now in. Telegrams from his personal scout, old T. V. Truesdale, Personal Representative of Louis Donovan Service.

"PERSONALLY INVESTIGATED MARYLAND VENTURE STOP WHOLE COUNTRYSIDE ANTAGONISTIC STOP FEEL TOO COMMERCIAL VIOLATING SOUTHERN IDEALISM JEOPARDIZING EXCLUSIVENESS OF LOCAL CLUBS AND RESIDENCES STOP ALREADY LOCAL MERCHANTS PREPARING RESISTANCE BY RAISING ALL COMMODITY PRICES STOP PARTICULARLY HOSTILE TO ROSENBAUM STOP WOULD SUGGEST HE LEARN TO RIDE OR DRINK BEFORE FURTHER SOUTHERN PROMOTION WORK COUNTRYSIDE FEARS CASTLES WILL CHEAPEN LOCAL

REAL ESTATE STOP WOULD SUGGEST GOOD WILL SWING THROUGH THIS REGION. SIGNED T. V. TRUESDALE."

"Sweet," said Lou and tore open the next one.

"HOW ABOUT DREAM ANALYZER AS FEATURE OF CASTLES COCKTAIL ROOM? JUST MET UNUSUALLY GIFTED ARMENIAN PRINCESS HALF EGYPTIAN ADAPTABLE TO SOUTHERN SOCIAL LIFE ALSO READS CARDS HANDS AND STARS AND DOES CLASSICAL DANCING AS POSSIBLE DINNER FEATURE IN GRAND HOTEL BALLROOM. JUST A SUGGESTION. SIGNED T. V. TRUESDALE."

"Isn't that just ducky?" Lou exclaimed. The old boy was jumping right into it. And still another one.

"RELIABLY INFORMED MAJOR AND WIFE TIFFED OVER SECRET ADMIRER SENDING TERRIFIC FLORAL GIFTS WIFE MOVING TO AMBASSADOR GO SLOW IN CASE OF DOMESTIC RIFT. SIGNED T. V. TRUESDALE."

"Would you mind telling me who that screwball is that you took on in New York?" inquired Miss Frye, observing Lou as he read the Truesdale works.

"He may turn out handy," Lou answered judiciously. "Right now he's just found out about Western Union."

"They've been coming in every ten minutes," said Miss Frye. "They don't make sense to me. Not unless you've got a syndicate gossip column that I don't know about."

"I got no secrets from you, honey," said Lou, "except a few little things I keep to myself."

There were three phone calls from Mary. That was funny since she'd been told he wouldn't be in town till this afternoon. Somebody must have told her something. Something had slipped up.

"Did my wife say anything about what she wanted?" he asked.

She hadn't. But she must be worried about something to have made three calls in one morning. Mrs. Donovan wasn't one to call up the office much. Lou frowned. A horrid suspicion crossed his mind.

"Look, Miss Frye, do you think Francie might have called up my wife? I'd like your guess on that."

Miss Frye gave a whistle, screwed up her little face in an intense effort at concentration, then shook her head.

"I doubt it," she decided. "She was feeling too good last I saw her."

"Where'd you see her? You left here before seven and she wasn't off the ground till around nine."

Miss Frye tossed her head.

"Listen, I go places like anybody else. Boy friend and I dropped in Chez Paris after the movies and there was the old girl with Mr. Oliver."

"What was she doing?" asked Lou.

"They were trying out a new kind of rhumba, looked like," said Miss Frye. "Mr. Oliver stood still and clapped his hands up over his head and she was doing the bumps."

Why in heaven's name hadn't he given her a couple hundred and told her to leave town? Lou groaned. He called the house. Better not experiment with any fancy lies if Mary was worried. He wouldn't tell the exact truth, of course, but he would shoot around it.

Whenever he heard Mary's cool agreeable voice on the telephone he had an exultant pride in having won her. There it was, sheer class and no mistake about it. It was in the way she walked into a room, in the clothes she wore, in her simple reserve, a man didn't need to say a thing, just "This is my wife" and his stock went straight up.

"Hello dear," he said briskly before she could say anything. "Got in so late last night didn't want to disturb you, so I parked at the Stevens. How's the kid?"

"That's what I wanted to ask you about, Lou," Mary said. "The doctor says she's perfectly well but a little rest would help her. So Aunt Felicia wants to take her with her to Arizona next week."

There it was, as usual. His wife and his daughter belonged to the Harrod family. Aunt Felicia and the Judge were in charge of them. He, Lou, was just a sort of chauffeur, so far as they knew his name was Cassidy. If he hadn't shelled out so much on his home and family it would be different. Then they could rightfully step in and say, "That bastard husband of yours doesn't treat you right, he's not taking care of you, but we'll see that you and the kid get three meals a day." Sure, then it would be all right. He'd still be mad, but at least they'd have a right. But no, they have to nose into a perfectly well-to-do happy family that he's looking after up to the hilt. But there was never any use talking to Mary this way. She never understood or, when she did, understood wrong, thinking he didn't appreciate family feeling because he himself never had any. She sympathized with him but said he must learn that other people did have strong family feelings reaching out even to fourth cousins and even to old servants of fourth cousins. He must recognize his narrow-mindedness there as a forgivable fault but nevertheless a fault.

"What does the doctor say?" he asked after a pause.

"The doctor thinks it would be splendid. He thinks it will build her up."

"Too bad he couldn't have suggested it to me, then, when I paid the bill," snapped Lou, but never mind that, he mustn't get mad. "How long will you be gone?"

"Not more than three or four weeks," said Mary. "Of course Baby is perfectly happy with Aunt Felicia if you think I'd better stay here. I'll send the nurse along, of course, and she won't miss me at all, really."

"Oh, no," Lou said. "You'd be worried without her. I wouldn't want you to stay home and be worried."

"You're sure you'll be all right?" Mary asked.

"Oh, sure. I may not go out to the house. I may stay at a hotel in town."

There was a pause and then Mary said, "Oh."

"When do you want to go? I'll get tickets and make arrangements."

"No no, dear, it won't be necessary. Uncle will attend to everything."

The usual brushoff. Old Cassidy, the bellboy, mustn't try to muscle in on the Harrods' exclusive family affairs.

"You're quite sure you'll manage all right alone?" Mary asked.

"Oh, sure. You do when I'm away, don't you?"

"Of course, dear."

There seemed to be something else she wanted to say but whatever it was she hesitated. Lou was afraid to ask, for it might be something he didn't want to hear. She might explain what troublesome news had made her so unusually cold to him when he left town. It was better for both of them not to have these things out in the open.

He admired her far too much to give her direct lies and it was not becoming in a person like Mary to descend to the nagging, niggling questions that wives like Flo were always putting to their husbands.

"That all?" he asked.

"Yes. . . . You had a nice time in New York?"

"Nice time? Listen, do you think I go to New York for a nice time? My dear girl, I'm on my toes every minute there. I've been working like a dog. New things in the fire. I'm dead tired."

"We'll have a quiet evening tonight, then. It's Aunt Felicia's Chamber Music night but I'll stay home with you instead."

Ordinarily Lou would have taken the opportunity to line up a date on the side since his wife was going to be busy. But now he thought it would be a good thing for the Harrods to know that when he was home Mary preferred his company to theirs. Let them know who was running the Donovans.

"Want some people in for cards?" he asked.

"No," said Mary. "I'd rather we talked. I'd like to talk to you alone. Some things that are on my mind. You know."

So there was something. So now it was coming. He stared out the window after she hung up, beating the desk with his fingers.

"Miss Frye," he called out finally, "I want you to get out all the Castles-in-the-Woods material, pictures, everything, and order all the Florabella samples you can get, and give me copies of the orders we've given out in the last month."

Miss Frye looked up surprised.

"I want to take them out to the house tonight to show Mary," he explained.

"I didn't know you talked business with your wife," she exclaimed.

"Tonight I will," said Lou.

XII

Lately Mary had thought more and more about going to a psychoanalyst. Something was going queer in her mind, but the trouble was she was not having hallucinations, she was having facts. What could the doctors do about that? Well, doctor, she would say if she went to one of Them—(she always thought of the psychoanalysts as Them) I was perfectly normal for the first twenty-nine years of my life, I lived on a normal diet of hallucinations; an unusually intelligent and cultured upbringing enabled me to conduct my life decently blindfolded, but lately my mind seems to be shaking. Doctor, I think I'm going sane. Then the doctor, of course, would say, Nonsense, Mrs. Donovan, you can't tell me that an intelligent woman like you is beginning to doubt your insanity. Why, Mrs. Donovan, he would say, smiling indulgently, I assure you on my word of honor as a medical man you are as insane as anybody in this room. Forget it. You're tired, perhaps, you've been worried about your child's illness, that mastoid operation, natural, perfectly natural, you've overdone your music, gotten yourself in an emotional stage about it, that's all. These Truths, which you describe as disturbing your night dreams and your day thoughts, will soon pass. Why not go to New York on a shopping binge?—forget yourself, don't think about your husband for a few days, don't wonder about these problems; I'll guarantee you'll be your happy smiling insane self in no time.

The difficult thing about Truths was that, unlike Hallucinations, they could not be shared with anyone else. Truth came in little individual portions and that was all there was to it. For instance she had always been able to talk to people about her husband's shrewd business genius, his great reserve of wisdom, his generous heart, but there was absolutely no one with whom she could discuss the sudden blow of doubt, of genuine distrust, that had come to her. Doctor, she would say, though of course she would never in the world dare go to a psychoanalyst, Lou would be horrified, but just supposing she did, Doctor, she would say, can you suggest some harmless powder to restore Hallucinations? Is there some dietary cure for loss of complacency, is there some hypodermic needle to inject self-deception?

For the life of her, Mary could not understand exactly what moment had brought this unwelcome blaze of perceptiveness to her life. It may have been a glance intercepted, a word overheard, but whatever the starting point was it had happened and now everything she heard or saw in her day's routine had significance. There was his calmness, of course, in leaving her for a week or two weeks, any time business called. She was calm, too, about those absences, but she had thought till recently that they were calm in the same way, with their unhappiness locked up inside. Well, his was calmness inside, too, it seemed. There was his lack of responsiveness, the cool kisses, the casual love-making. She was not responsive exactly, perhaps, she too gave cool kisses, but then that was all an impetuous man demanded. It was when he was no longer impetuous that the anemia in their relationship became apparent. Certainly both could not be passive. But what else could she be? It would be more than she could do to confess that she could never sleep when he was away and that she often got up in the night, quite lost without him, and played phonograph records till daylight. And she could never say love-words the way other wives did or hold hands, but it seemed to her Lou would not have liked that anyway. It had always seemed perfectly suitable to her and she had assumed—to him—the man to be the lover and to voice their love, the lady to be acquiescent and shyly passive. But what did you do when there was nothing to acquiesce to, no stormy advances to be passive about? Well, she would never know, for she would never dare ask. Maybe someone could teach her how to kick down her own reserve. Maybe, instead of the psychoanalyst, she should go to a School for Etiquette. Professor, she would say, I should like to know how to forget good breeding. Is there a short summer course in forgetting the gentlewoman's code? Is there a little home study extension course in how to operate like a human being instead of a lady? But then she did not *want* to shout her feelings to the housetops. That was the trouble.

Perhaps it was a surgeon she should consult. Surgeon, she would say, how long would I have to be in the hospital for a minor mental operation? How serious is it to cut out that little section behind the brow that separates what a Nice Girl Sees and Hears from What Really Happens? The night that the woman called up for Lou, for instance, and left word for Mr. Donovan to call her.

"Is this his mother?" the lady had inquired in a foreign accent.

"This is his wife," Mary had answered. "Is there anything I can do?"

There was a brief pause and then a "No, thank you" that sounded almost embarrassed. That was how she guessed he was already in town, though he had said he would not be in till next day. But she could not for the life of her bring herself to mention this, no, you could not deliberately accuse someone of deceiving you. She had wanted him to insist on her staying home and letting the baby go West alone with Aunt Felicia, but she could not propose it herself. And he had merely said, "How long will you be gone?" Then one of the women at a bridge party had declared Jay Oliver had a mistress in New York, and in a flash she was certain this was true of Lou too. But she knew she would never mention it, she could never ask him, she could never spy, whatever suspicions she might have would have to freeze up inside her along with the evidence.

Now that everything about him had new meaning Mary was astonished to realize that her aunt and uncle had never for a moment liked or trusted Lou. She knew they had reservations about him, but she had thought it was merely their disappointment that he was not their sort. She did not dream it was active dislike. He had been new to Chicago and no part of Aunt Felicia's Eastern background, either. He had seemed to Mary just the rugged hearty salt-of-the-earth American that her uncle had always publicly praised and privately patronized. She had discounted their coolness to Lou as just the natural jealousy of the man who took their darling niece away from them. And Lou's loud pooh-poohing of the Judge and Aunt Felicia she took with loyal understanding, as his perfectly unnecessary feeling of social inferiority. She assured him over and over that he was more brilliant, more admirable in every way than anyone in the Harrod circle, he mustn't have a chip on his shoulder about them, he must only understand that they were spoiled, fortunate people who could never match his self-promoted achievements. Now, suddenly, she saw how genuinely they despised him, when Aunt Felicia said, "Your uncle doesn't encourage divorce, my dear, but he often says that if you suffer too much from your mistake he would do anything in his power to get you free."

Mary was too surprised to be angry. It happened the very day after Lou had told her about the friendly meeting with the Judge on the train. She mildly spoke of this now to her aunt.

"Oh, then he told you about that," said Aunt Felicia with a peculiar smile. "The Judge didn't think he would want it mentioned."

Aunt Felicia meant something, and the obvious implication was that Lou was in company he should not have been. Mary dared not ask. Her aunt would have said no more, anyway. Instead they listened to the Simon Barer records that had just come from England, until time for Aunt Felicia to go to her fitting.

When Lou called up later in the afternoon to ask if she wouldn't like a little company for dinner, she did not remind him that they were to have a talk alone that night. It was another mark of change in him that he disregarded their old taboo against unprepared entertainment, at home. Unexpected social demands on him he nearly always took care of by staying downtown and excusing Mary from the picture. She had always taken this as consideration for her shyness and dislike of crowds. Now, he was considering only his uneasiness at being alone with her.

"If you like company, by all means let's have it," she said.

"It's the Olivers," he said. "You know. He's Whittleby Cotton. I do a lot of business with them. You've met her. Sure it's all right?"

"Perfectly," she said.

It was the night of Aunt Felicia's Chamber Music group, which she loved but always gave up when Lou was home. She knew she would be thinking of this and the peace of music all the evening when she would be straining to be gay or merely friendly with Lou's friends. Already her head began to pound with its constant ache of thoughts, feelings repressed. Sometimes she thought she would like to take off the top of her own head just to see what was really in it. All she was certain of was her own trained reactions.

"Everything all right, then," Lou said, with the faintest doubt in his voice. It was almost, she thought, as if she was expected to ask him the questions that bothered her.

"Oh, quite," she said.

XIII

THE house at Winnetka was really Lou's house more than Mary's. He had spent a great deal of time and money on planning it and furnishing it, and once done, he forgot about it and left it up to Mary to finish. First he wanted a bigger house than Judge Harrod's, where Mary had made her home before. Since the Judge, in spite of his superior fortune, was not a showy spender, it was fairly easy to get a bigger house. Next, he wanted a larger living-room, since the Judge prided himself on his large living-room, so Lou's was two feet longer. The extra floor used for Aunt Felicia's little concerts did not interest Lou so he skipped that. The Judge's fresh-air obsession with sleeping porches all over the back of the house, also did not excite Lou's envy. However, the Judge's bar and game room in the cellar was only half as well equipped as Lou's and had but one ping pong table, whereas Lou had two, both usually ignored for the bar. Lou, through his wholesale rug connections, had fine Orientals through the house instead of the worn carpeting the Judge deemed sufficient. And if the Harrods prided themselves on the thick stone walls that made their house so cool in summer, Lou countered this with air-conditioning. At least his wife was not going to complain of being deprived of former comforts, nor could she boast of having left a more expensive home. Lou saw to that.

There was a quiet and bare peace about the house that

seemed to Lou, always happy in his connection with the Harrods, the very epitome of class. Mary loved her music room and the baby's sleeping and play quarters and whatever whimsicalities of taste she possessed were expressed here. The rest of the house was as impersonally well-done as any other interior-decorating professional display. Mary bowed to Lou on this as she had bowed to Aunt Felicia before on home decorating. She did like flowers and collected beautiful vases wherever she could and on drives with the nurse and baby through the country she would often stop to gather appleblossoms, pussywillows, or other decorative branches for the house.

Lou was almost prouder of Mary's lack than he was of her virtues. The thing he admired most in her and counted on the most for his own happiness was her reserve. He never had to listen to what went on in her little mind, and she never asked him what went on in his. If she cried about little things now and then, and he supposed she did, he did not know what it was and certainly did not want to find out. If he himself felt sunk he didn't want anybody asking what was the matter with him, and Mary, even if she noticed, did not ask questions. If he suspected she disapproved of something he said or did—he was forever doing something wrong about her aunt and uncle—all she did was to stay in her room with a headache for a couple of days. It couldn't have been a more agreeable relationship.

Another thing that had won Lou, besides her good breeding, her name, and her discreet passivity, a quality he'd never found in any other woman, was her youth. She was twelve years younger than he and it seemed to give an added piquant flavor to the conquest, as if her youth was a rare diamond that he was able to buy and show off. He spoke of her youth oftener than necessary because, to tell the truth, she seemed older than himself with her restraint and dignity, qualities he was still struggling to master. At twenty-one, when he met her, she even looked a good deal older. She was no beauty, even then, unless fragility could be considered a beauty. Whatever was pleasing about her appearance was certainly nothing he had ever admired before as seductive. Hers was no full luscious body, radiating tropic passion or even the natural vitality of youth. Instead her tall frail frame radiated nothing more than an ingrown anemic sickly spirituality. She had grown too fast as a girl, everyone said, but it was fortunate that her motions were sufficiently graceful to give an air to her lanky limbs. Her face was full, however, and her slender bones seemed well-enough covered. She had heavy drooping eyelids, enormous gray eyes, full wide mouth with fine teeth, an appealing quite angelic face, the luminous dead white skin striking against the short coppery curls. Her face and the mat of casual curls was so pure and childish it was always a shock to see her standing, see the long thin body, too long and too thin, the delicate neck, the incredibly thin wrists, the almost papery white fingers. The upper arm was rounded enough as were the hips and thighs, but the ankles again were unbelievably delicate. Up to the time he met Mary, seven years ago, Lou had been attracted by the very opposite of every one of Mary's bodily characteristics, it seemed to him. But then he fell for her and he found something quite devastating in her dreamy sexless charm. One thing he had guessed—was that here was a woman he would never tire of, because there was not enough of her to tire of. Nor would he ever leave a mark on her, so that would make him keep trying. That pale virginal quality would remain, and even after he had slept with her for six years —a not too satisfactory business because he was still afraid of her—he never felt that he had really made the complete conquest. Her eyes had no different glow than before. He learned something, and that was that while he had dismissed much more satisfying women from his life, the challenge of the too cool woman went on forever with him, as it did with many men, the virgin challenge, and sometimes he reflected that the great courtesans of the ages must have been like that,—cool, unmoved, perpetually unawakened, giving less than nothing to tease the lover into further bondage, instead of being the hot babies history assumed they were.

He came home about six, his brief case full of the material Miss Frye had gotten together for him. Mary was in the bed-room dressing and he went in and kissed her. As soon as he saw her sitting in her slip, thin shoulders bare, brushing her hair before the vanity-table, he realized with a shock how lost he would be without Mary. He still wondered how he had ever had the courage to go after her, how he had ever braved that other world for even a little while, but here was permanent evidence of his bravery, he still did not understand just how or why unless his very effrontery had pleased her. It gave him new confidence in himself just to see her, part of his home, like this. Whatever had been on her mind these last few weeks he was determined to override. This was not so difficult for him, because as soon as he came in the room Mary's doubts lightened, his vigorous presence threw such a dust of general confusion in the air that it was hard to remember what little headaches his absence had caused.

"So you're walking out on me," he said, grinning at her

in the mirror. "Leaving me to shift for myself while you run around with those dude cowboys."

The little reproach showed that he really did mind her going so her face lit up eagerly.

"It's only for Baby, dear," she said, "and even now I wouldn't go if you wanted me badly—I mean——"

"The kid comes first," he said firmly. "You and I don't count. It's the youngster. Wait a minute—I haven't seen her for a month—is it all right to go in?"

This, too, lifted a burden from Mary's soul, for it showed he was interested in the baby, and words of her aunt had insinuated that Lou was an indifferent father. She slipped on her robe and followed him down the hall to the nursery.

Baby was sitting at her small table on the porch eating her supper in the company of her two favorite friends, an enormous Easter rabbit on one small chair, and a black and gold Krazy Kat in the doll high chair. The nurse was straightening the bed in the nursery.

"She's still a little pale," Mary said, though the little girl was like her mother, naturally pale and underweight.

"Well, how's daddy's girl?" Lou asked and lifted her up.

"Please don't disturb her supper, dear," Mary protested, "and it always frightens her to be lifted up."

Lou put her down.

"I don't mind," said the child politely, "if daddy wants to play that way."

Lou laughed, embarrassed. Baby was a Harrod just as Mary was and even though she was only four Lou felt afraid of her quiet, gray eyes, he was uncertain what the Judge and Aunt Felicia may have taught the child, at any rate it was completely theirs, not his. Mary stroked her head, copper-curled like her own.

"Perhaps daddy had better visit you in the morning when it won't make the little head ache," she said tenderly. "Nurse says company at night always gives her a headache."

Lou left the room while Mary gave some instructions to the nurse. That was the way it had been from the time the baby was born, there was no beating that situation, he knew that. Baby was Mary's, just as his business was his. All right, if it made her happy. But he was glad that none of his business friends saw how badly a good mixer came off in his own child's nursery.

"What about dressing?" Mary asked him.

Lou shook his head.

"No, hell, this is just a little home evening, we want Jay and Flo to feel at home, friendly, you know," he said.

Nothing could have alarmed Mary more than the thought of a friendly get-together with Flo Oliver, but she braced herself.

"I thought we'd have mint juleps," Lou said. "It's late for them but there's nothing like them for icebreakers. Have them down in the game room, see."

The new set of silver mint julep mugs was a Christmas gift from the Judge and always made a good anecdote, would show Jay Oliver that the old boy was friendlier to Lou than his attitude on the train would indicate.

"It's all right for me to wear a long dress, isn't it, dear?" Mary asked.

Lou was firm about that, though. It had been an informal invitation, Flo was scared to death of Mary anyway, and the only way to handle that was to show that although the Donovans had a little more dough they were not putting on any dog about it.

"I suppose bridge would be the best thing later," Mary said with resignation.

"No bridge," said Lou. "I've got a little surprise for the evening's entertainment. Leave it to me."

Mary was glad to. It was such a relief to see Lou bustling noisily all over the place again that she began to think perhaps the evening would not be so hopeless after all.

XIV

THE Olivers had started their fight at a brisk tempo at four-thirty—the hour when Flo had summoned Jay to Marshall Field's for ominous reasons—but by six-thirty they were running out of material and on the ride to the Donovans it looked as if there would be no photofinish at all, merely whimpers and "Oh, is that so?"s, and "That's what *you* think!"s, and "Oh, for crying out loud!"s. As the Donovan house hove into view there was one brief moment of complete rapport when both Olivers joined in a vast rage at the Donovans and a mutual silent vow to get stinking as fast as possible. Flo was looking singularly warlike in the brand-new gold-embroidered red evening dress she had bought that very day for the occasion, and had smartened herself up with one of the grimmest permanents her beautyshop had ever turned out, every curl seemingly made of purest iron. She was in the habit of using more rouge than was advisable and had gone to town this evening with a brand new shade, which Jay sorrowfully begged her to wipe off.

"Listen, everyone wears rouge," Flo had snapped back. "You don't like me in red, you don't like me in jewels, listen, I'm not an old lady, yet, I got a right to a little gayety."

The little ermine jacket Flo had purchased at the last minute had started the fight, since the Oliver bill at the store was already steep enough, and Jay didn't see why a little family dinner at the Donovans' should cost him three hundred dollars. Besides Lou had said nothing about dressing. He kept protesting about this point all the while he was putting on his dinner coat.

"Listen, dope, people like Mary Donovan always dress," Flo expostulated. "They don't say anything about it because they take it for granted. Or else maybe they think we're the type that wouldn't know anything about that. They give me a pain."

"Keep your shirt on," Jay said. "Wait till you're insulted, for God's sake."

"What's so special about that house, I'd like to know," Flo sourly observed as they approached the driveway. "I suppose they thought it would be a real treat for us to see their lousy place."

"You asked for it," Jay grumbled. "You've been bellyaching about it from the first time you met them."

"Oh, is that so?" Flo said.

"Oh, for crying out loud," said Jay. "You jump on me every minute I'm home, is it any wonder I hate coming home? I'll betcha there isn't another married man in town that has to put up with what I do every damn minute."

"That's what *you* think," said Flo and permitted herself to be helped out of the car. "You don't know how lucky you are."

The ice was not immediately broken by the homey spectacle of Mary Donovan in a knitted sportdress and Lou in loose collar and sport jacket of vivid green. Lou had spotted the magnificent spectacle of Flo in trailing red taffeta and ermine as she got out of the car and he groaned.

"How nice of you to dress!" Mary said. "You needn't have, of course, but——"

"Well, we did," said Jay. He avoided the lightning look from his wife's eye, for even though it was she who had insisted on dressing he knew that would not save him from blistering reproaches for her own error.

"It's just us, you know," Mary said desperately as she took Flo into the powder room.

"Not really!" Flo said in such frank dismay that Mary was even more confused.

Downstairs in the game room Lou was having no better time of it, for Jay was in a state of profound gloom. If he had ever been a man to admit defeat Lou would have confessed that even a straight heart-to-heart talk alone with Mary about all of his past sins would have been easier than this craftily planned evasion of such privacy.

"What's Flo beefing about?" Lou jovially asked. He was getting out the handsome mint julep service and carefully making his preparations with the help of the fat black maid, Annie, who knew better than to volunteer too much help on this sacred chore of Mr. Donovan's.

"Nothing the matter with Flo," Jay said testily. "What's *your* wife beefing about?"

This was going a little too far, and Lou almost lost his temper. Mentioning his Mary and a battleaxe like Flo in the same breath.

"I was just wondering if anything came up about Ebie," Lou said.

"No, that's all right," Jay said guiltily, wondering just how soon Flo would be tight enough to say something about her own misconception of whose girl Ebie was.

"I was going to get her to do a little mural for the New York office," Lou said. "Not her line but no reason why she shouldn't take a whirl at it. Called her couple of times but Rosenbaum's office says they haven't been able to locate her for two days."

"Can you blame her?" Jay queried indifferently. The wives came in then, Mary looking unusually pale and skeletonic compared with Flo's flamboyant aggressiveness.

Lou hastened his julep ritual, keeping up a genial flow of conversation, all about how the Judge had paid a small fortune for the julep set and had taught him his own special way of making the drink, inverting the glass first over the powdered sugar, and so on, till Flo, said, "Isn't it too bad your uncle couldn't be here to make them personally!"

"That's an idea," said Lou. "We may give him a call on that."

"We were hoping we'd have a chance to meet them tonight," said Flo.

"Do you mind making mine just plain Scotch, old man?" Jay asked. "I started on that and I'm afraid to switch."

"That's a good idea," said Flo. "I always get sick on juleps. They look wonderful, too, but I think it's the Bourbon. I never can take Bourbon."

Silently Lou nodded toward the Scotch decanter on the bar, and Jay happily poured a couple of drinks for himself and Flo. Mary was about to ask for her usual sherry but the collapse of the mint julep experiment was too much for her and to Lou's gratification she took a julep.

"I thought Lou was lying when he said you didn't drink, Mrs. Donovan," laughed Flo. "I guess you're one of those women who just drinks in the home."

"Oh, sure," Lou said. "Mary can carry quite a little package with nobody noticing a thing. You ought to get her to teach you, Flo."

Cooled her off with that one, he thought with satisfaction. He thought no wonder Jay goes for a swell girl like Ebie, anybody would with a hellion like Flo swinging the axe around every minute. He had thought this little friendly dinner would fix up the whole little unpleasantness between himself and Mary and between Flo and Mary, for Flo's wound at being so consistently snubbed by Mary was no secret. Instead it looked as if they were all going to end up in a free-for-all.

Jay and Flo helped themselves to the Scotch again, Jay getting gloomier and gloomier and Flo gayer and gayer. They seemed bent upon outdoing each other and in showing their host and hostess that so far as they were concerned the party, the house and everything in it was no treat to them.

"Go on, show Flo the upstairs," Lou urged. "Show her that mirror we got for the blue Bed-room."

"Is it an antique?" asked Flo.

"Antique, nothing," said Lou. "That antique stuff is nothing but a fad anyway. That's the trouble we had with Castles-in-the-Woods, Jay. Got a man down there, friend of the Major's, wants to load the whole place up with antiques. Bought out the neighborhood, I guess. I put my foot down. Modernistic, I say. Stream-line. Stick to your period."

"I think antiques are such good taste," said Flo, to Mary.

"Yes," said Mary helplessly.

"What's Castles-in-the-Woods?" asked Flo.

"Now you're asking something," said Lou. "After dinner tonight I'm going to show films our Baltimore man took of the whole property, then I've got colored pictures of our plans, the whole proposition. That's what Jay and I have been working over in New York when you girls thought we were playing around."

"I didn't hear anything about it," said Flo.

"I never ask about Lou's business because I know I shouldn't understand it," Mary said apologetically.

"Well, this will give you an idea," Lou said.

Dinner improved Jay's spirits slightly and when the wine came out Jay decided to make amends to Lou for his former rudeness by asking for one of those old mint juleps. Flo decided she would change her mind and try one herself. Lou no longer cared what happened and left the soup course to go downstairs again and throw a few juleps together, not such a delicate operation when performed without an audience, chipped ice, a couple slugs of Bourbon in each glass and some mint poked around in it for a second.

In the dining-room Flo complimented Mary on her china service, her linen, her cook and her complexion and Mary squirmed in her seat unhappily, not having the faintest idea whether Mrs. Oliver was mocking her or flattering her. Flo adjusted each compliment so that it would have a boomerang effect and fly back and hit Jay. All of the things she admired were things she too would have if it were not for Jay's indifference to nice things, his inferior business head which prevented him from making the money Lou did, and his never listening to his wife. If Jay had listened to his wife they would be living in a house bigger and better than the Donovans' and instead of Jay coming to Lou that time for the loan it would be the other way round. But oh, no, Jay was just like his whole family, a good-for-nothing don't-care lot, you couldn't blame them, it ran in the family.

"Oh, is that so?" Jay asked.

"You bet it's so," said Flo.

"That's what *you* think," said Jay.

They were really having a splendid time, but Mary could not know that and looked helplessly from one to the other, smiling politely till the full import of the remark would hit her, then looking with wide grieved bewildered eyes down at her plate. Lou, coming back bearing the mint juleps, saw that Jay and Flo were rattling down to their usual act, no harm in it, and was only annoyed that Mary seemed to be giving them the freeze. He thought resentfully that it wouldn't hurt once in a while for her to loosen up for his friends, God knows he loosened up to her crowd when he saw them; the only thing was he probably loosened up too much with them judging by the way they snubbed him. He was annoyed at her, too, for not mentioning the friends he wanted her to mention, so it left him with the clumsy task of working her contacts into the conversation.

"I read that speech your uncle gave at the college festival," Flo said to Mary. "Believe me I think that old boy knows what he's talking about. These foreigners trying to run this country. I could tell him some things about that."

"Why don't you give him a call, Lou?" Jay asked.

Lou looked him in the eye.

"All right, why not? Go ahead, honey, call up the Judge. He'd be interested in the Castles-in-the-Woods pictures. We're showing the models at the World's Fair next year, Jay."

"No kidding!"

"Why not?" Lou begged to know. "Jay, you old buzzard, you don't seem to realize this Castles-in-the-Woods is the biggest thing since Boulder Dam. For anybody that's getting as nice a cut as your company is out of it——"

"Maybe I'm not getting as big a cut as I should," said Jay, which was not quite cricket, as the little extra cut he turned back to Lou on these deals was strictly confidential.

"There's other firms, my lad," said Lou, dead pan. "There's Cannon. There's Lady Pepperell."

The gentle little threat straightened Jay out and he shrugged.

"When did the World's Fair thing come through?"

"I started it before I left New York," Lou said airily. "Put it up to the Major and Rosenbaum and now it's practically in. The hotel itself, in miniature, serving nothing but Chicken Maryland and coffee. And mint juleps. Then the working models of the whole project with leaflets and photographs. An agent in charge."

"You're a fast worker, all right," said Jay.

"It'll take a few more weeks to get set, of course," Lou said. "I'll have to run back to New York oftener."

"Oh," said Mary involuntarily.

"I guess you don't care much about Lou's work, do you?" Flo laughed. "I was in business myself once in New York, so I understand. I ran a tea-room."

"For six months," said Jay. "Lucky I came along and bailed her out."

"That's all right, I know what business men do in New York," Flo said roguishly.

"For crying out loud, you'd think all we did was chase, from the minute we leave this town," Jay said indignantly.

"That's all right, I can see where Flo might get that impression from some of these fellas," Lou said judiciously. "Take some of these fellas, they get to New York and make fools of themselves."

"It's the high buildings," said Jay. "You got your neck out from the time you leave the station."

"The point is that it's tough on the rest of us," Lou said earnestly. "We got a job to do, we haven't the time to play around."

"Oh, oh," said Flo. "I could tell Mrs. Donovan something about that."

Jay gave her a quick kick under the table.

"Do that, will you?" Lou said. "Give her an angle."

The loud voices, the wrangling, and the new doubts she had of Lou, made every moment seem intolerable to Mary. She had wanted to please Lou but she did not know how, and Lou with these friends was not the Lou she knew. The allusions they made to their common interests made her feel desolately left out and again filled with the odd fears Aunt Felicia had started. She made a desperate try to salvage the evening, when they started in to the huge living-room for their coffee.

"It's Aunt Felicia's night for Chamber Music, Lou," she suggested. "Perhaps the Olivers would like to go over there and listen to some Haydn."

"Say, now, doesn't that sound ducky?" Jay said.

"Shut up, dope," reproved Flo. "A little music wouldn't hurt you. You might learn a little something."

"It's all right with me," said Jay. "I can take it or leave it alone."

It was Flo's turn to give him a nudge.

"If you folks don't appreciate an invitation to one of the most high-class homes in Chicago, then the hell with you," Lou flared up. "If my wife's willing to take you into her Aunt's private musicale, by golly, you ought to be proud to go."

"I thought we were asked here," said Jay. "What's the idea? Trying to brush us off?"

"Now, Jay," Flo complained, "I don't see why we can't drop in the Harrods' for a while. I've never been there. I'd like to see the house even if there is music."

The fat colored maid produced brandy and benedictine, and Lou poured them out.

"Pardon me, just a minute," he said, suddenly. "Is there anything you have against my showing my friends the Castles-in-the-Woods films? That was my original suggestion. Apparently the idea bores you, my dear."

Mary blushed.

"No, no, I—I mean, of course, I'd like to, but——"

"That's all right," he said with elaborate indifference. "We'll go to your uncle's. A little music at your uncle's would be so much finer than your husband's business pictures. Oh, sure."

"It's all right with me," said Jay. "I can take anything."

Mary rose quietly.

"I'll call and tell them we're coming," she said. "I'm sure Mrs. Oliver would enjoy it."

"You bet your life I would," said Flo, loyally. "Personally, I'd rather listen to some good music right now than anything in the world."

"Personally, I'd rather sit around and get cock-eyed," stated her husband. "That's the way it is with me."

Lou was still looking with silent anger after Mary's proud exit when the maid called him to the extension in the hall.

"You didn't call me back," said a charming voice. "I am so cross. You're a naughty boy."

It was Mrs. Kameray. Lou was delighted.

"You don't like me," she pouted. "Here I am, a stranger, and you are too busy to see me."

Lou closed the door and talked to her in a low voice. When he came back he was beaming.

"Hold your hats, kids," he cried. "We're going back to town and fix up the Spinning Top."

"Thank God," said Jay.

Mary came back in.

"Aunt Felicia will expect us in about half an hour," she said. "She says it's always a pleasure to have guests who really enjoy music."

"That's off," said Lou briskly, still angry with her. "The Donovans have to meet some friends at a restaurant downtown. We can drop you at the folks', since that was your suggestion. I'll show the pictures to Jay and Flo at the office sometime where it won't bother you."

"Isn't he mean?" exclaimed Flo, happy always in a little misunderstanding.

"Excuse me while I change," Mary murmured, flushed and head bowed.

"Oho, she changes for the Harrods, then," Flo said triumphantly. "I knew that was how it was."

No one said anything while Mary was gone. Flo tinkered with the piano, playing "Begin the Beguine" with one hand. Jay tossed off a couple of brandies silently. They were sorry for him, Lou thought indignantly. They had stopped kidding him because now they saw how it was about his wife waving her fine family over him all the time, freezing all his business friends and brushing off his business interests, making a cheap tramp out of him by showing off her superior taste. Barely saying ten words during the evening. Making him a laughing stock before Jay and Flo.

"Doesn't Mrs. Donovan care for nightclubs?" Jay asked.

"They give her a headache," said Lou, and then as she came in he thought he'd add for good measure, "just the way my business does. And the way the Harrod family does me."

Everyone laughed.

"Jay, you drop Mary in your car and I'll take Flo on down," said Lou, as they got out to the driveway.

"Oh, but I'm going on down to the Spinning Top with you," Mary said in a low voice. Lou glanced quickly at her but her eyes were staring straight ahead. It suddenly struck him that she had been on the music-room extension when Mrs. Kameray had called and had not hung up.

"That's great," he said. Never let them get you. Ride it through.

XV

"MAYBE we'd better go to the Colony," Flo suggested to Lou. "Maybe the Top is too rough for Mary. Maybe the Chez Paris."

"The Top's all right," Lou said easily. Flo was trying to be a pal, show how well she understood a man's problems. The trouble with a "good egg" was that you had to talk to them all the time, you couldn't just drive along, thinking your own thoughts in silence, the way you could with a girl like Mary who wasn't and never could be a pal. Flo squirmed around in the seat to see if Jay's car was following.

"I wonder what Jay's talking to her about," she mused aloud and then chuckled, as if she and Lou and Jay were one kind and Mary another, instead of Lou and Mary being of a piece. Even if they weren't Lou preferred to keep the knowledge to himself.

"I sure feel sorry for her," said Flo sympathetically.

"Just why?" Lou asked, but getting it just the same.

"Oh, I don't know," Flo said. "She doesn't understand you at all. She doesn't get one thing about you."

"Maybe I don't want to be got," Lou said, sore, but trying not to show it. He wished it had been possible to ride with his own wife but of course that was out of the question. Even mad at each other and the slip-up on the Kameray dame's call he was sure they wouldn't have had to talk it out, anyway. Talking things out was what made people so sore at each other. They were madder at the things they said talking it out than they were over the original misunderstanding. He and Mary, thank God, could misunderstand each other and never have to speak of it. Right now he was appalled at the idea of Mary in the Spinning Top, but he certainly was not going to talk it over with Flo. Flo was the type that fifteen years ago after a few drinks would have welcomed a pass driving out like this with the other guy. Now that she was forty and bulging in the wrong places she took it out in a good heart-to-heart pal talk. Lou stepped on the gas to shorten this intimate little chat.

"No, seriously, Lou, you've never had a woman who really understood you," Flo went right to it. "I mean, you're ambitious, you've got a lot more guts than Jay, you get an idea and go right to town on it. Jay never has any ideas. He just does his job and sells Whittleby Cotton."

This was all okay with Lou but it made him mad to hear it from Flo, especially with the little sideswipe at Mary.

"I don't blame a man like you—I mean I *wouldn't* blame you if you had a little hideout in New York," Flo went on knowingly. "You're too big a man to be tied to one woman."

"I'm satisfied, never mind about that," Lou cut in.

"I mean your wife doesn't understand you the way I understand Jay," Flo explained. "There's no excuse for a man running around when his wife understands him like I do Jay, but in your case——"

"Why should I want a woman to understand me? Just to have the b'jesus balled out of me all the time?" Lou asked. He gave a short laugh. "That's why a fellow runs out; so he won't be understood."

"Well, if you're going to be that way," said Flo. "That's the way I'm going to be," said Lou, and that cooled her off till they got to the Spinning Top.

If Jay and Flo thought there was anything funny in Mary deciding to come along, as indeed there was, Lou was determined not to show it. He wanted to show Flo, damn her hide, just how Mary could be a good egg without making a fool of herself. A woman didn't need to get so fried she had to be carried home in order to be a good egg. She could be a good egg by just keeping her trap shut and letting other people enjoy themselves. She could be a good egg by meeting the husband's girl friends and not throwing a plate at them.

The Spinning Top was not one of Chicago's better spots; its chief charm for its customers was that it was not popular and was no place to take a wife. It was a jolly combination of seedy Hollywood glitter and old-time honkytonk. It was near enough to the station so that a busy man could nip over for a drink and the show between trains, say hello to the girls, maybe, and then, after he missed his train, could even be put up in the little adjoining hotel. The girls were good-natured, not bad-looking graduates of various exclusive burlesque wheels, and they sat around at the bar in little fig-leaf costumes, fluttering their blue-greased eyelids at strangers, and on dull nights at least keeping up a semblance of gayety by their perpetual squeals and chatter. It was said, with authority, that a favored customer could toss his coat to Marie, the hat-check girl, for repairs while he drank, and he could even send her out to do his wife's shopping, if necessary, while he downed a few at the bar. Homey, that was the way a traveller described the Spinning Top, and it was fine dropping in a place where they didn't snub you, a place where the waiters all called you by your first name, and the girls kidded and scolded you and took care of you, and took every nickel you had. All right, it was a clip-joint, but if you passed out the manager himself took all your valuables out of your pocket to look after till you came to, so that at least nobody else would steal them. It was your own fault if you forgot next day where you'd been.

It was a dull evening tonight and the girls had listlessly walked through the dinner-show with little more than the orchestra and waiters for audience. Since their gifts were little more than walking under any circumstances the performance was not too much worse than usual. As soon as the Olivers and Donovans arrived, however, the place sprang into action. Two girls who had been slumping at the bar wrangling with the bartender now rushed to attach a cigarette tray and flower tray respectively to their persons; Tessie, the accordionist, struck up "Give My Regards to Broadway," a roguish reminder that on Mr. Oliver's last appearance at "The Top" he had obliged with a simple timestep to that tune. The head-waiter, a punch-drunk ex-fighter, who was making himself feel like a crowd with a series of short brandies, snapped to his heels, with an almost reverential bow.

"Good evening, Mr. Donovan," he said. "And Mr. Oliver. Well, well!"

He had fortunately learned to take no chances on calling the ladies by name, but men customers sometimes wondered whether the flattery to their ego of the bow and their names remembered was really worth while, since the lady was often not impressed so much with the regard in which her husband or boy-friend was held as by the deduction that he must spend a lot of money here.

Lou saw that Mrs. Kameray had not arrived yet and he had a moment to plan. It was foolish, he thought, to be alarmed at any meeting between Mrs. Kameray and Mary, since there was nothing between him and Mrs. Kameray. That is, nothing as yet. Nothing but a level look exchanged at their last meeting and her eyes dropping, an electric hint that when the time was right would be time enough. It was these little promises without words, not the conquests, that gave zest to a man's life.

"My goodness, those girls don't have much clothes on," whispered Flo.

"Some women get along better without clothes," said her husband.

Lou could tell by the lift of Mary's head and the cool look in her eyes that she was hanging on to herself, she hated the place, the noise, the gaudiness, the company she was in. But he was not sympathetic. She asked for it. When she got that frozen Harrod look he felt either hopelessly inferior or mad as hops. Tonight he was mad. He could do a freeze, too, in his own way. They didn't bicker like the Olivers but they knew how to give it to each other without an unpleasant word. She was continuing to be graciously attentive to the Olivers, with dampening effects on their spirits. When Jay used a bad word or Flo passed out an off-color joke Mary's polite laugh was worse than a rebuke. She had decided now to show Lou that these people were really not her sort and so she was giving an exhibition of correct, thoroughly irreproachable behavior that was more disagreeable than anything that could happen in "The Top." To punish her Lou motioned Jay to come over to the bar. More people were coming in and the girls' voices keyed a little higher with expectation, Tessie started moving around kidding the newcomers and the orchestra took over with a deafening, drum-thumping rendition of "Oh, Mama, please get that man for me," which the leader sang through an amplifier and his own nose.

"The Kameray's coming in later," Lou notified Jay.

Jay whistled.

"Boy, are you in a jam!" he exclaimed with delight.

Lou took a pack of Luckies from the girl, waved away the change for a dollar, offered Jay one.

"What do you mean—jam?" he said. "I got nothing to worry about. Just an extra woman, that's all."

Jay shook his head.

"I wouldn't trust that little baggage," he said. "She's looking for trouble and not for herself, either."

"She's working for me, that's all."

"I hope," said Jay.

"I was just thinking we'll have to look out for her, on Rosenbaum's account," said Lou. "Don't let the women ride her too hard. You know how they go for a new dame."

"Oh, sure," said Jay. "Only hang on to your watch, fella."

"Never let it be said," said Lou, and then he saw Francie and the punk walk in. He might have known that a fourth-rate joint like the Top would be about the punk's speed. He might have known, too, that they'd hang around town till they made trouble. Francie was dolled up to the gills in an olive green fall suit with a pair of supercolossal silver foxes swinging to her knees and a green Robin Hood cap jauntily tilted over the doll-hair. If you hadn't known her of old she wouldn't have looked bad.

"The little floozy's back in," Jay muttered to Lou. "Don't let her speak to me, for God's sake, or Flo will start throwing."

"Is that all?" asked Lou. "I would have said Flo was about ripe for a good hammer murder right now."

"Well, Mr. Thompson," said the bartender and reached in his pocket for some bills. "You're in luck again. She came in third today."

"Better than nothing," said the punk and took it. Thirty bucks.

So he was playing the Pimlico races from here. He glanced up while he was counting it and caught Lou's sardonic eye. Francie followed the quick flush on Thompson's face back to Lou and she gave a little gasp. It was the time to clear up this headache, for good, Lou thought. He would never be in a better position to do it, even with Mary and Flo watching, they could not hear the conversation above the orchestra din. Jay had quietly slipped out to the john.

"Hello, Francie," said Lou quietly. "Glad to see you're in the dough again." He looked over the foxes thoughtfully. "Spend much time at the Top?"

Francie was flustered, looking from Lou's impassive ruddy face to Thompson's pale sullen one.

"Frank won about forty dollars in bar checks here the first night we came here," she explained breathlessly. "We sort of stayed in town to spend them. No good any place else, of course. And then we got a little extra——"

"So I see," sad Lou. "Well, I was glad to be of help."

He nodded to Thompson and started away but Francie grabbed his arm.

"Give me that thirty, Frank," she commanded the punk, and as he reluctantly drew it out of his pocket, she pressed it into Lou's hands. "Here's the thirty you gave me. Thanks."

"Wait a minute——"

"No, no, take it. Take it, Lou, you've got to. Feeling the way you do about it—no, no——"

He managed a laugh, for the sake of the ones watching, and took the money to keep her from yelling any louder. Thompson looked down into his drink and didn't speak to him at all. Lou wasn't jealous of him, how could he be when he hadn't the faintest feeling left for Francie except annoyance, but somehow every time he saw the haggard, weak little blonde face of his successor he wanted to take a poke at it. He did the next best thing.

"What kind of a gambler do you call yourself, Thompson?" he called over to him with an attempt at a grin. "With all your expert information I should think you could play more than two bucks. No use being a piker. Why don't you branch out?"

"I bite," said the punk bitterly. "Why don't I?"

"Lou, please—" Francie pleaded.

Lou brushed her aside and walked over to Thompson.

"Tell you what I'll do," he said. "Here's a hundred. If you can make that pay fifty to one, it's yours. If you can't you owe me a hundred. Of course if you're out of town there's no way I can collect. But——"

"Don't take it, Frank," Francie begged. "Don't take it, honey, he just wants to humiliate you."

"Nuts," said Lou, "he'll take it."

He did, too, slowly, but he took it without a word, Just stuffed the bill in his pocket with a queer look.

Lou started back to his table, with Francie still tugging at his sleeve, and to make it look better he swung her into the dance floor, pretending that was what she had asked him.

"All right, he took it," Francie whispered. "I know you've got that on him just like you wanted, but honest, Lou, the reason he acts so terrible with you is he's so jealous——"

"What for?"

"Oh, Lou, you know. He loves me, don't you see, and it hurts him to know I stay crazy about you, he's not a fool, he knows, I can't hide it, I'm so happy just this minute with your arms——"

Lou stopped.

"Thanks for the dance," he said. "As for the hundred nothing would please me more than to hear I lost it. Night."

He managed a big laugh again, as if they were kidding, but Francie's yearning look after him was no corroboration.

"What a pretty girl!" Mary said when he sat down.

"He can pick 'em," agreed Flo. "If he can't, Jay can. Kinda hard boiled, though, I would say, and certainly no chicken."

"I wouldn't know," said Lou. "Women nowadays can trick themselves out any age at all."

More people were coming in and the orchestra was playing louder, the crooner was going to town on "Tonight We Love" and Flo was blowing the little whistle the waiter left as favors to the ladies. Francie and the boy-friend were doing some fancy steps and whirls that would have finished off a healthy man let alone a guy supposed to have only one lung. Jay came back with an uneasy glance at Francie but she seemed bent on drowning her sorrows in the dance so he got back safely.

"Too bad you can't find a girl-friend like Lou's," Flo shrilly cried. "Then Mary and I can go home and leave you to your fun."

"How do you like the place, Mrs. Donovan?" Jay politely asked.

Mary turned a pale bright face toward him.

"Oh, terribly amusing," she said. "I had no idea there were places like this."

"I knew it, all right," said Flo. "The only thing is try and get your husband to take you to one."

Ha ha ha, laughed everyone, and then the drinks came, and Lou saw that Mary was having plain soda, and to add to this exhibition of good sportsmanship she was taking a couple of aspirin with it to help endure the pain of having a good time. She looked at him apologetically but got no sympathy from his hard smile. It was really the worst thing that could have happened to either of them, this little introduction into his business life, for he could feel not the faintest remnant now of his old-time pride in her. If she had only gone to the Harrods', as he had thought she would, then he could have excused her chilling out the dinner guests by the thought of her later being at ease with much bigger shots. It was the thought of her, that he loved, and how can you have the thought of anyone if they're around your neck at the moment complicating everything? He would have liked to sit here with the Olivers—yes and maybe even with Mrs. Kameray—and brag about how his wife never went to nightclubs, never drank, loved music and culture and riding, that sort of thing, a real lady, and talking he would have sold himself all over on her. But here she was being a lady in person, and away from her own background, a lady was just a dud on a party, a liability, a wet blanket. He could not feel even the slightest admiration at this moment for her wide gray eyes and the gray dinner suit, all he thought was that every aspirin she took was a martyr's silent but public reproach to her brute husband for bringing her out with such people to such a place, and he felt an icy indifference to whatever torment her suspicions of him must be causing her.

"What's the woman's name?" Flo teased. "I mean the blonde. Jay, do you know?"

"Me? Why should I?" Jay asked.

"I thought she kind of looked at you," Flo said, and Jay slid further down in his seat.

"I believe it's Kameray, isn't it, dear?" Mary said, but Lou did not bat an eye.

"No, dear, this is Mrs. Kameray coming in," he said. "The other lady is Mrs. Thompson. I used to know her in Dayton."

Mrs. Kameray looked wonderful to him, coming in at that minute. Her trim little black suit, the simple fur bow at her neck, the charming calm face, not childishly sweet like Mary's, no, this was young but dignified. Lou and Jay got up and brought her to their table. No give-away here, either, thank God, Lou thought, for her little handclasp to each man was accompanied only by the most gracious little smile, any watching wife could see it without a flutter. Lou, without looking at her, could see Mary preparing herself.

"My husband has often spoken of you, Mrs. Kameray," she said.

Mrs. Kameray looked in pretty amazement at her.

"But Mrs. Donovan, how could he?" she said. "It is true I work for him, yes, for him and Mr. Rosenbaum, but even though I call up and call up, Mr. Donovan will not let me see him in person until tonight. Isn't he naughty?"

Lou mentally doffed his hat to this superb job of fixing. It was as if she sensed the telephone extension eavesdropping and was covering every angle. Mrs. Kameray looked appealingly from Flo to Mary.

"But it is naughty, isn't it? I have to see the man, I call up, I tease, I flirt, and when Mr. Rosenbaum calls me up long distance to ask, I say, I cannot talk until I have seen Mr. Donovan and that naughty Mr. Donovan will not meet me. Tonight, I caught him, yes?"

Mary, drawing a long breath at this unexpected solution of her fears, looked at Lou, wanting him to forgive her her suspicions, wishing she had never doubted, longing for the old look of admiration, but Lou, cleared, at least momentarily, was arrogant. He must take Mrs. Kameray to another table for a little talk on Castles-in-the-Woods, a matter which had proved so boring to the others at dinner that he was sure they would be glad not to hear it mentioned again. Mrs. Kameray obligingly drew notes and pencil from her bag and gave every indication of being nothing more than a dutiful, attentive secretary, and her little bottle of white wine was further proof that she was only here in the line of duty. Proof, that is, to Mary. To Flo it was a case for exchanging winks behind Mary's back with Jay, and to Francie, watching from the bar, it was cause to down half a dozen drinks quickly and insist on playing the drums with the orchestra, her hat on the saxophonist's head, her husband Mr. Thompson passed out slumping over on a corner table. The spectacle of Francie at the drums was too much for Flo, and in a huff at Jay for not dancing with her, she joined a lone wolf at the bar, a swarthy Spaniard, and cajoled him into doing a tango. Mary looked at Lou, then at these women he knew and it seemed to her her head would split with the din and the strangeness of this side of his life, the effort of understanding him. She knew that to leave was another hideously wrong step, but tonight had been full of wrong steps anyway.

"Mr. Oliver," she said, "I mean Jay—would you mind taking me to a cab? I feel—I've got to have air. I'd like to go home, so much."

"Cab, nothing, I'll drive you home," Jay said. There was nothing here for him. He'd had the good luck to miss the floozy's recognition but the way she was acting up there with the orchestra it wouldn't be long now before she started the stuff on him, and then Flo would take over. Flo came dancing past with the Spaniard, showing off. She could take care of herself all right. Or Lou could. He got Mary's cloak, and piloted her past Lou.

"We're driving out for some air," he said, and Lou nodded. Mary smiled a little too eagerly at Mrs. Kameray and Mrs. Kameray smiled a little too sweetly back. Jay was glad to get out before anything started. At least Flo was busy with the stranger and she wouldn't be jealous of Mary.

But that was just exactly what Flo was. In fact Flo never took a chance on anything. It was no fun showing off her powers with other men without Jay to see it so she snatched her ermine cloak and ran after them.

Lou and Mrs. Kameray were so busy going over their data, scribbling addresses and other inspirations in their little notebooks, that they were remarkably oblivious to this last departure. All the more wonder then that they stopped talking at exactly the minute the door closed on Flo and looked at each other. It was the same look that Lou had remembered with heightened excitement, the slow measuring promise of complete surrender. He quietly signalled for the check and when they got up they did not even bother to collect the valuable data they had been so busily exchanging. They did not speak as they got in Lou's car and they did not even hear the special drum roll from the Spinning Top orchestra as they left.

XVI

"YOU'RE sure Mr. Donovan's coming back today?" Jay asked.

He sat at Lou's desk drumming on it till Miss Frye thought she'd go nuts. She looked up from her typing.

"Look," she said. "Would I tell a lie?"

"I don't know, sister," said Jay. "All I know is you said he'd be back last week, then you said Monday, then Tuesday, now today. Where'd he go anyway?"

Miss Frye had only told him that about five times, too.

"He's been making a swing through the West," she said. "The way I told you before. Do you want his itinerary?"

Jay saw his persistence was getting on the busy woman's nerves.

"That puts me in mind of my old man," he said. "He was a regular old-time travelling salesman, quit school in the eighth grade and started canvassing right outside Taylorville here. Got to be head of his own business and put me on the road soon as I got out of school. Called me in one day when I got back and he says, 'What's this here?' and I said, 'Why, dad, that's my itinerary.' 'The hell with this itinerary stuff,' he says, 'after this you send us in your route.' That was the old man for you."

"That's darned interesting," said Miss Frye.

"Do you want me to tell more?" asked Jay. "I got a million of 'em."

"Put 'em in a book," said Miss Frye.

"Hell, money means nothing to me," said Jay. "I'm glad to give you a little family history free of charge. You can mull over it while wrassling with the boy-friend."

"I don't 'wrassle,' " said Miss Frye.

"Fine!" said Jay. "That's the kind I like."

Miss Frye got up and giving her caller a measured look, laid a sheet of paper before him.

"There," she said, "is Mr. Donovan's itinerary."

"What's he doing at the Knickerbocker in Los Angeles?" read off Jay. "I thought he stayed at the Ambassador. And what's this about the Park Plaza in St. Louis? I thought he used the Statler."

"Look, Mr. Oliver," said Miss Frye, patiently. "Would you like to wait in the bar? I'm sure Mr. Donovan would rather you made yourself at home."

"I'm at home anywhere," said Jay. "Any old place I can hang my head is home sweet home to me."

"I know," said Miss Frye. "I heard that one."

"I never promised my script was new," said Jay. "All I said was I'd keep sending."

He looked over a stack of telegrams idly.

"All this on Castles-in-the-Woods?" he inquired but Miss Frye pretended the noise of her typewriter deafened her. "Did he put it through with the Frisco Fair people, too? He did! Well, well. And here it says the station wagons are to be maple with a Dubonnet trim, hospitality lights flood every driveway leading to the Castle Hotel, male help is Filipino—what does he want down there—race riots?—wearing white silk blouses with red sashes, pardon me, Dubonnet sashes."

"I know," said Miss Frye patiently.

Jay picked up another piece of paper.

"What was he doing at the St. Francis in San Francisco?" he inquired. "He's a Mark Hopkins customer."

"Mr. Oliver, I don't think Mr. Donovan wants you going over his mail," said Miss Frye. "There's a lot of stuff there in the bar. You look as if you needed something."

Jay got up with a sigh and strolled over to the bookcases which swung open showing the bar.

"In case Mr. Donovan wants my itinerary," he said, "put down that I'm going from Canadian Club to Ballantine's and will spend a short time in Martel. How come the boss stayed so long?"

"It's a big country," said Miss Frye. "It takes three weeks for that Western trip. I admit he's delayed, though."

"Maybe he's having trouble with Indians," said Jay.

Lou walked in and threw his hat on top of the safe.

"Well, son," he said to Jay, and shook hands. "Let's see your report card."

"Thank God, you're back," cried Miss Frye. "Everybody's calling. Mrs. Donovan has called from Arizona a half dozen times, that Mr. Truesdale has telegraphed for all kinds of information, Mr. Oliver here——"

Lou started leafing over the stack of mail.

"Lou, I got to see you," said Jay. "I got to. Just a minute. It's——"

Lou looked up, surprised at the odd tone in Jay's voice. Jay looked terrible. Hollow-eyed, miserable. Lou, staring, walked into the bar behind Jay and closed the door, leaving Miss Frye to throw up her hands in despair.

"It's Ebie," said Jay. "I can't find her. I put in a couple of calls to her apartment and no answer. I called Rosenbaum about something else and slipped in a little inquiry about Miss Vane. No Miss Vane. Severed her contracts. Can't be located."

"That's ridiculous," said Lou.

"Wait. I flew to New York two days ago. No Ebie. And not a word anywhere about where she is. God, Lou,—what am I going to do?"

Lou lit a cigarette.

"Just have to replace her, that's all," he said.

"Lou, this isn't funny, supposing something's happened to her, maybe she's another Dorothy Arnold——"

"Sure, maybe I'm another Charlie Ross, too. I'll bet I can locate her in ten minutes."

Jay poured a small brandy. He was torn between genuine anxiety and his natural desire to believe in Lou's ability to fix everything.

"Lou, I'm crazy about Ebie. It's been going on for years. You know, I chase, and I keep Flo going, but it's always been Ebie with me. And mind you, not a note, not a letter, not a call. It's not like her." Jay saw he was beginning to impress Lou. "Ebie tells me everything she's doing. And if she was mad she'd want to fight, she isn't one to pick up and walk out, without a fight-talk. I thought of everything. I thought—well, she was sort of worried last month, maybe she went to a bad doctor, maybe she passed out and he stuffed her in a furnace—you know those guys are liable to twenty years if they're caught——"

"Good God, Jay, pull yourself together!" Lou exclaimed. "Now, sit down. Let's look this thing over. Last time I saw Ebie was—well, the time Flo pulled the cute trick and beat you to New York. All right, Ebie was sore as the devil at that."

"I know," groaned Jay. "And if I had the guts I would have kicked Flo out as soon as I met Ebie. That's when I should have done it. First time I ever laid eyes on Ebie, I should have broken with Flo. Ebie's worth ten of Flo."

"Check," said Lou. "All right, Ebie isn't the type to walk out, you say. Look. There's the type that walks out and walks out and walks out, know what I mean, round the corner and back, it's a habit. Then there's the type that walks out. That's how I classify Ebie. Just once she walks out."

"But why this time?" said Jay. "She's caught me fussing with other women, and I'm always dropping her as soon as Flo gets in the picture, not because I like Flo better but because Flo raises such hell."

"This was just once too often," said Lou. "You know how it is. You excuse a fellow putting the bee on you a dozen times but all of a sudden it's that one time too often. And you're through. Maybe Ebie's through."

"I got to get her back," said Jay. "I mean I can't get along without Ebie."

"Don't talk like a fool," Lou expostulated. "There's a dozen Ebies in every block. Nobody has to have just one particular dame, you know that. But we'll track her down."

He stepped to the door.

"Get me Truesdale at the Hotel Ellery, New York," he said to Miss Frye, and closed the door. "I'll put my man on her trail."

Jay drew a breath of relief.

"Gee, old boy, you take a load off my mind. It was getting me. Couldn't talk about it, of course."

"We'll find out what there is to know," said Lou. "Now, if you don't mind, I've got a month's stuff to clear up out here."

"What was the idea your changing hotels?" Jay asked.

"Don't you ever change hotels?" Lou growled.

Jay whistled.

"I get it."

Lou scowled.

"Nothing to get. Just trying out different services. I can't be too partial to one place, in my business."

"You put on some weight, too," said Jay, looking him over. "You must have about ten pounds more on you. Must have had a good trip."

"I did," said Lou.

"You old son of a gun," said Jay. "That's one thing I never could get away with—taking a woman along on a business trip."

"I never tried it myself," said Lou, offhanded. "If you want to know I was so damned busy this trip building up the Castles-in-the-Woods I wouldn't have had time for any women."

"I saw Rosenbaum in New York," said Jay. "He said the Kameray was working out all right at the job. I had to laugh. She called him up while I was there."

"Oh, she did?" Lou exclaimed.

"The secretary had given it away, so he couldn't gloss it over much, just said she made a daily report to him from wherever she was, by phone or wire. I got her little phony voice squealing, oh Wosebush, darling——"

"Where was she talking from?" Lou asked.

"St. Louis," said Jay. "Old Rosebush went into his other office to give her the babytalk back. How was she in St. Louis, old boy?"

"Mrs. Kameray is a wonderful person," said Lou sternly.

"If you make any more cracks about her I'll have to poke you right in that mush of yours."

"She's a two-timer, pal," said Jay. "I'm warning you. Old Rosebush has ten times the dough you've got."

Lou was irritated at having betrayed himself.

"Mr. Truesdale can't be located," Miss Frye came in to say. "The Ellery is leaving him a message."

"Go on, now, worry about Ebie," Lou recommended Jay with a nod. "I'll worry about me getting two-timed."

XVII

Your lives, said the analyst to Mary Donovan, are drifting apart, it is up to you to join them again. Make an effort, he said, to draw your husband into your life, above all do not show him you can have a perfectly pleasant life without him; make him feel that your social and musical life is flavorless without him. And in the relations between your family life and your husband do not act as if it was you and your family versus a stranger husband, but you and your husband against even your own family. An egotist like your husband demands this assurance.

So here they were at the Harrods' intimate little dinner party where for two hours Lou had been glancing at his watch and wondering how long it had taken these people to get this way. The ladies were fluttering about the fireplace in the great living-room while the gentlemen dallied over coffee and brandy in the dining-room, chewing at their cigars and their memories. There were Grahame, the big hotel man, Carver, an ex-governor, Sweeney, the old banker, the Judge, and Mr. Donovan, promoter. Mrs. Harrod had sent the butler down four times to get the gentlemen upstairs, but old Mr. Grahame always had one more story to tell, and after he finished that Governor Carter had a now-defunct state secret to reveal, and Mr. Sweeney, a stern gentleman with a trim Vandyke, threw out some secret statistics on world affairs with prophecies on how these figures would affect the war in Spain and the progress of Russia.

"Do you realize," said Mr. Sweeney, turning to Lou on his right, "that in the city of San Francisco there are over two hundred thousand Chinese, a city in itself, with its own telephone exchange? Now what would you say would happen there in the event of the Japanese and Hitler forces combining?"

"I don't bother much with Chinatown there," said Lou. "I usually stay at the Mark Hopkins."

"No prettier spot in the world than the roof of the Mark Hopkins," said Mr. Grahame, sucking at a cigar. "Look right out over the prison across the bay. Top of the Mark, they call it."

"I know," said Lou and thought of Trina Kameray and wondered how long before he could get away. He had assured her he would be out by ten-thirty since he was known to be a busy man and had half a dozen sound alibis at his disposal. Besides, there would be music and Mary knew how he felt about that, she would excuse him and come home later herself in her uncle's car. He nodded to have his brandy glass refilled and looked glumly down the long table to where the Judge was benignly puffing away at a cigar, a large glass of water in front of him with a small vial of his after-dinner medicine beside it. The dinner had been distinguished, as many of the Judge's dinners were, not only by the powerful names of the guests but by the display of medication. Both the Judge and Mrs. Harrod had small medicine bottles beside their plates and Mr. Grahame, before gorging himself on the roast beef, popped two large alka-seltzer tablets in his glass. Mrs. Sweeney, an angry gray woman of sixty, had denied herself every course but the salad which she attacked with the grim determination of a person finishing once and for all a persistent old enemy.

It rather surprised Lou to find himself noticing all these disagreeable features of the occasion. Usually he was so impressed with the magnitude of the combined fortunes and power present in the Judge's house that he noticed little else, and there were always his untiring efforts to show them that he was as good as they were, a conversational effort that took up so much of his time and energy that he had little opportunity to observe anything else. Tonight Mary had told him that if he didn't go, she wouldn't; she had added that her uncle was very eager to hear more about that new project of his on Chesapeake Bay, and that Aunt Felicia particularly had asked for him.

"No kidding," he had said, not really believing it, but half-pleased at the same time. In the veiled arguments he and Mary had been having ever since her return from the Southwest he had for the first time hinted that she had allowed her family to snub him, that they had used his indifference to music as an excuse not to ask him to their most publicized entertainments, and it was very nice, very nice indeed, that in guest lists in the society columns she was referred to as Mary Harrod Donovan, instead of Mrs. Louis Donovan. It was very nice, too, that Mary never had the Harrods to dinner except when Lou was out of town, very much as if he wasn't quite good enough for them. It was odd that at the time these points had mattered most to him he never allowed himself to even think of them, let alone mention them. Now he had it right out, and to tell the truth, it hardly bothered him at all any more. The only thing that had been on his mind lately was what was Trina Kameray doing when out of his sight, and how soon could he get out of whatever he was doing and join her. A woman on your mind did have its advantages that way, he had to admit it, you might not sleep and you might lose your grip on some things because of it, but at least it wiped out a lot of more important worries.

Having made his complaint there wasn't any way of backing out when Mary produced the dinner invitation with personal messages from the Judge and Aunt Felicia. It was something he could mention next week in New York when he saw the Major. He had that to think of. Over the martinis (with tomato juice for the Judge. Aunt Felicia, Mary, and Mrs. Sweeney)—Lou had launched into the Castles-in-the-Woods project, since Mary had told him the Judge wanted to hear.

"The land is right near our place," the Judge explained to the others, "so that the project is of peculiar interest to, hmm, yes, hmm."

"But surely, Mr. Donovan," said Mrs. Sweeney with a menacing smile, "you can't mean you're having neon lights all through that lovely woods and all down the roads!"

"That's just one of the improvements," said Lou. "We're going to put that place on the map as the last word in modernity."

"But I thought the people there had been petitioning the government to make the town into another Williamsburg," said Mrs. Sweeney, looking to Mrs. Harrod for confirmation. "I thought there was an old tavern there with historical relics and a whole group of Revolutionary buildings. It was to be like Williamsburg, wasn't it?"

"Nothing about that in our contract," said Lou.

"Neon lights!" murmured Mrs. Sweeney.

"Same thing happened to us," said Mrs. Sweeney. "Last year I went downstate to visit the old Sweeney homestead. Nephew lives there now. Imagine how I felt when instead of the old rolling acres with cows and horse grazing there were derricks. Oil there now."

"We just wept, literally," said Mrs. Sweeney. "And the young people just sitting around the porch, rocking, watching the oil-drilling."

"How awful!" sympathized Aunt Felicia.

"You mean you didn't have any interest in the property any more?" Lou inquired. "All that oil going to your nephew?"

"Very good," politely laughed Mr. Sweeney. "Incidentally, do you realize that Illinois ranks ninth in petroleum production this year?"

All right, there was something about the Castles business that rubbed these people the wrong way, and as usual they were brushing him off. Lou was about to crash right through again but there was no loophole. Aunt Felicia was giving out an ecstatic description of the gardens at Williamsburg, aided by Mary's memory, and they were getting into the Revolutionary chamber music revivals and how perfectly enchanting they were. Mary actually got excited over this subject, and Lou, rebuffed, watched her with hostile curiosity. He saw how much she looked like Aunt Felicia and it was funny he never noticed that before. Old Felicia was a lean old giraffe, her smiling, smug blonde pinhead stuck on a lean old neck with attached arms and legs. What was she doing with that old diamond dog-collar, when with a neck like that she needed a giraffe collar? Her eyes were still wide and dewy like Mary's and had never seen anything they didn't want to see, you could tell that. Watching them together, Mary's strained eager face a young replica of her aunt's, Lou couldn't understand how the resemblance had not frightened him before, had not, indeed, scared him off when he first met Mary.

It was after Aunt Felicia had assiduously devoted herself to him during the shrimps and soup that the suspicion struck Lou that this evening was all framed up by the Harrod family to make him more tractable. Mary had spent her time in the Southwest confiding in Aunt Felicia all of the little things that had been giving her headaches lately, and Aunt Felicia was doing her best to patch it all up for her little pet niece. Or did those two congenitally cold women confide in each other actually? Probably they had some silent wigwagging signals of distress, understood only by each other and unaccompanied by any indecent revelation of emotion. Whatever it was, old Felicia, instead of the sour reflective smile with which she usually listened to her nephew-in-law's conversation, was giving him the full battery of her graciousness. This obvious resolution to pacify him with undivided attention did not include listening to what he said, so that he had to answer the same question half a dozen times, finally noting the eager glassy old eye shifting around the table during his answers, and noting, also, Mary's anxious gaze on him from time to time as if to see if this attention didn't make him happy.

"I had no idea you were a university man, Louis," said Aunt Felicia. "Princeton, you say?"

"I said Michigan," Lou repeated for the third time, "and just for the football season, if you call four months being a university man. I guess I learned as much as most of them did."

"I had a nephew who went to Princeton," said Aunt

Felicia, with the gusty intensity with which she rode all conversation. "Perhaps you knew him when you were there. Farwell Lease, Junior."

Lou gave up.

"No," he said. "He wasn't there when I was there."

He sank into gloomy silence while Mrs. Carver, the ex-governor's third wife, a little bird-woman with darting head and bright little robin-eyes, twittered about life in Washington and how, really, there was nothing to compare with it in America. Oh the cherry-blossoms, cried Aunt Felicia and Mary in a breath, the wonderful Japanese cherry-blossoms! And Arlington! Perfectly beautiful! Lou looked at Mary's and old Felicia's suddenly animated faces and wondered again at what brought that quick rapture to their eyes—cherry-blossoms, music, a view. His lips curled. That was supposed to be culture, maybe that was supposed to be "sensitivity." Give him the sudden narrowing of the eyes, the intent frown, the suspended breath, that marked Trina Kameray when his hand sought her knee under a table. His glance travelled around the table and he thought of how little they knew of real magic, all this talk of stars over Mexico, fog over the Potomac, tunes from a harpsichord.

Mary must have observed his restlessness for she bent and whispered something to her uncle. Lou shrugged. So now the shoe was on the other foot. Instead of Mary whispering him to please ask uncle this or that, please be nice to Aunt Felicia, please don't monopolize the conversation, here she was urging them all to be nice to her husband. Well, he wasn't sure he liked it any better this way.

"Ah, um, Louis, hmm, I understand the New York office is a great step forward," said the Judge. "I understand you have contracts for the New York Fair and the San Francisco as well. It's not quite clear to me what your particular contribution, hmm, I should say, hmm."

"It's the Castles-in-the-Woods," Lou said. "I've been in business for ten years and I swear this is the most interesting proposition I ever came up against. You take the property itself, now——

"Supposing we ladies go up to the living-room for our coffee," suggested Aunt Felicia, and in the little flurry of exits Mr. Sweeney took charge of the conversation, and Lou gloomily retreated into his own thoughts, emerging only now and then to say, "Yes, sir, that's about right, sir," and "That's about the size of it," and other vague disgruntled little comments. Mr. Grahame, wedging his vast bulk against the table, his watch-chain resting almost horizontally on his bay-window, dozed happily over his cigar; the Judge chewed at his cigar without smoking it, as per health regime, Mr. Sweeney was reminded of a dozen and one anecdotes peppered with statistics and spiced with the great names of banking and international politics. The ex-Governor of the nearby state came in with his war prophecies and went to the trouble of demonstrating on the tablecloth with the handle of his coffee spoon possible military maneuvers for the Spanish war-lords. By this time Aunt Felicia upstairs was peremptorily tapping on the floor with some weapon or other, and the Judge signalled the butler.

"Tell Mother we'll be up directly," he said. "Go on, Sweeney."

Mr. Sweeney did not need to be told to go on, having gone on so long now that nothing short of a stroke would stop him. Lou, on whom he turned the full battery of his well-informed mind, had long since stopped worrying whether his face looked interested, since the tribute was not necessary at all.

"Mind you, two hundred thousand Chinese in San Francisco," repeated Mr. Sweeney, "one third of the population of Nanking, China. An unassimilated foreign group, you see."

"Is that a fact?" said Lou, and quietly noted that it was now ten-ten. It was funny he had made such a fuss all these years about the privilege of being bored by his wife's family. What was the matter with him, anyway, boasting of having been kicked around by these old big shots? Like saying, "Believe it or not, I had my evening spoiled last night by a personal friend of J. P. Morgan!" Or "I was fortunate enough to have a second cousin of the President bore me to death last night."

There was another message from the ladies. Mrs. Harrod was impatiently waiting to regale the gentlemen with a recorded concert beginning with Stravinsky's "Peter and the Wolf" which Mr. Grahame had never heard. Mr. Grahame, roused from his spasmodic napping by hearing his name, pushed the table away from his stomach and extracted his body from the chair.

"Come on, old boy," he urged Sweeney. "Mustn't inconvenience our hostess. You and Cassidy can have this out some other time."

On the way upstairs Lou figured what he would say. He had to get out quick because he could never tell what Trina Kameray was likely to do. She could be brilliantly discreet in public, sometimes, but on the other hand she could be alarmingly high-handed if her little caprices were not given proper consideration. She called up his house whenever she pleased, she wrote whatever she felt like, often quite naughty little notes, and when Lou tactfully tried to correct this sort of mischief, she shrugged.

"Either you are a man or you are not a man," she said. "Either you are afraid of our friendship or you are unafraid. If it is an inconvenience to you I have many other friends."

She never said it but he knew what she meant. It was that there was always Mr. Rosebush. Such a dear, such a valued friend, and she had been so unkind to him, giving him up for Lou, who wished she would not telephone him or speak to him in public, or show her friendship for him. It made one sad to think of giving up a loyal friend like Mr. Rosebush for a man who found her preference merely an embarrassment. In fact, she really ought to be meeting Mr. Rosebush in Baltimore this very minute instead of loitering around the West this way, within meeting distance of such an unappreciative man as Louis.

That persistent little threat usually brought Lou desperately out in the open, and unable to say more about the danger to his home life. They would have a home together some day, Trina said, so what did it matter how soon his present arrangements were blasted? Lou never answered this, for the immediate urgency of being with her always blinded him to future complications.

"Sorry, but I have to see a party from Rochester at ten thirty," Lou said to Aunt Felicia, upstairs, while Mary looked at him questioningly.

"Yes," said Aunt Felicia graciously, "I believe someone did call a few minutes ago inquiring if you had left."

Can you imagine that? That little Kameray had even had the nerve to call him at his wife's old home. That was the sort of arrogance that left a man breathless.

Lou got into his coat and hat in the hall, trying to act pained at this business intrusion of his social life. In the living-room Mr. Grahame settled in the largest chair with a loud creaking of indignant springs, the Judge adjusted the great phonograph, Mrs. Sweeney and Mrs. Carver arranged their velvet skirts on a small loveseat in reverent silence, the ex-Governor stood gazing gloomily into the fire, and Mr. Sweeney took up a safe position in a corner retreat where he adjusted his reading glasses for a refreshing glance through the *World Almanac,* handily placed in a magazine rack.

"You'll be back for me, dear?" Mary asked in a low voice. She knew he wouldn't. She knew he was meeting a woman at the Evanshire bar in Evanston because the operator had called from the Evanshire first. She only wished she had the courage to say she knew. The psychoanalyst—as she had justly feared—had done nothing to give her the simple everyday courage to make a scene. He had done nothing for her with this suggestion to draw Lou into her family's life. And when she had told him, with bursting temples and trembling hands, about the unmistakable evidence of another woman in her very bed during her Southwest trip, the stupid man had merely given her sedatives, and told her such a tiny catastophe was not the end of the world.

"I'm sure the Carvers can drop you," Lou said to her. "And by the by, there's a chance I may not drive back out tonight. Have to meet an early train downtown in the morning, so I may stay downtown. Night, dear."

He hurried out. Aunt Felicia and the Judge exchanged a look. Every one knew he was going to meet a woman. It would have been better if he had not come at all, Mary realized. She wished she dared rush out and follow him, see the woman, accuse her, flaunt the hairpins and handkerchief (shamelessly left under the pillow) and the hoop earring. She wished she was as bold as this woman, whoever she was, who brazenly visited her house. She stood waving to Lou in the door for a moment, then came back to take her seat on the sofa beside the fire. The music began. Aunt Felicia and the Judge were looking at her, so she kept her own eyes on the leaping fire, her long thin fingers interlaced in her lap, and in the pause while the records changed she murmured "Isn't it charming?" just like anyone else.

It couldn't have been her fault, Mary thought over and over, it couldn't, it couldn't. All the things he had admired when he first saw her, had shown so clearly how much he admired them, were still hers, she had not changed, even her feeling for Lou had not changed, her appearance had not changed, nothing was any different from the moment he met her on the ship coming from Honolulu when the Captain gave her a birthday dance. And Lou had made her uncle and aunt furious by taking her away from the dance out on the rainy deck where they sat not saying much, not even holding hands, but when she rose to go back to the others he said, "Believe it or not, I'm going to marry you or your sister." "I haven't any sister," she said, laughing. "Then it's going to be you," he said. So that was her love affair, her only one, the only one she ever wanted—six years of having someone demand more than she could give, of having him look steadily at her when they were out together until her gaze fluttered to meet his, of having her own happiness consist in curbing his desire, in finding that her protests could control his impetuosity. It was the way she was, it was her own version of passion, denying more than she gave, for the charm of her love was what she withheld, just as the basic force of Lou's love was in demanding what would be denied, wanting more, no matter what, than would be given. It was all part of their own special love that she should want him to make approaches so that she could say, "Oh no, no, Lou, you mustn't, you mustn't," and so keep the process within the strictest bounds, no intimate fumbling over her body, which after all was her own, and no reason why marriage in spite of its implicit obligations should give the lover complete and outright ownership to it. That was the sort of quaint daintiness which Lou had found intriguing from the very first, and nothing had happened since to make her bolder or more adventurous in sex. What made her head spin now with curious indignation was the faint suspicion that other women allowed and even encouraged this worst side of him; there might be dreadful creatures like the naked girls at the Spinning Top, like the woman he must have in New York, like the one he was meeting tonight in Evanston, dreadful women who pretended to like it just to trap him and so betray her, make her refusals seem wrong, his cajoling demands right. Puzzling over these doubts Mary cried all night, and she didn't know which was her greatest woe—his probable unfaithfulness, or the possibility that these other women were right to surrender completely and she was wrong. Even so she knew that what she wanted was for him to go through life wresting love from her, and being perpetually denied full abandonment.

It was frightening to wake up in the morning and know that love did not last, no matter how it was treated. Even a shrew, nagging, ragging, bullying and deprecating the husband out of sheer discontent with her own dream of him, must believe it can go on forever, and must be bewildered when, at a kind glance from some gentler woman, he leaves. People think relationships are made of rubber and stretch and give to every crisis, and it is a shock to find they can snap in two like a glass thermometer. Why should anyone feel that a great truth is hidden from him when it is written all over the sky that nothing is permanent? Mary reasoned it all out, rationalized the way the doctor had told her, but what good is reason when the heart is out of order? Just so many sheep to count till the brain got numb, that was all, and then the old heart could go ahead hurting, even exploding, for all the good reason could do.

The worst part was the half-dream before waking, the half-dream that everything was the same as it used to be. She could see herself and Lou dancing, walking, dining in little lovely corners, the way it was when he told her every day he was going to marry her, whether she liked it or not, and whether Aunt Felicia liked it or not. She thought of the way he kept looking at her until she was forced to look up and see the shock of desire in his eyes, and the way in a little while he would be striving for some excuse to touch her, to put her coat on for her, to help her get into her car. And then when she was home, undressing for bed and thinking of this resolute suitor, the phone would ring and he would say, "Mary? All right? I just wanted to make sure. Sweet dreams." And now Lou was calling up someone else, waiting for someone else to look up and meet his eye, calling up someone else to make sure she was all right. And there was no reason for it, no right to it, but there was nothing to be done.

No, there was nothing to be done, no questions to be asked and answered. She tried to do what the doctor had suggested, to think of the man's side, to realize that it is as sad to stop loving as it is to stop being loved. Sad to look at the back of a neck, the slope of a cheek that once gave quick pleasure, and here was the same curve, the same gesture—no change except that no joy, no love was inspired, object and eye were two unconnected telephones. Poor curve, sad gesture, void of all magic, powerless to convey life to expired love. The way she rumpled the back of her hair, once so dear to him, was just the way she rumpled her hair and no more. Her slender foot squirming around when she was embarrassed was just an annoying habit, not an endearingly childish trick. His looking at the menu to see if her favorite duck was on it, not because he wanted to give her pleasure, but to see if there wasn't something he could find to mollify her outside of a caress. Oh, of course, it was a sad role, the lover no longer loving. But once the perfunctory sympathy was given him the heart went out fully to oneself, the real victim, the unloved.

If she was at fault, and she might be, then the fault had been with her at the very start. If all the things he first loved were still there and he no longer loved, then these must now be all the things he hated. She would have to be different, she would be like Flo Oliver, like the women at that nightclub, she would get up with the orchestra and beat the drums, she would talk to strange men, she would drop in at bars by herself the way that Mrs. Kameray did, and ask other women's escorts to join her at her own table. Those were all the things she was *not* and therefore they must be the things he wanted of women since those other women seemed to know him better than she did.

She knew, of course, that he wouldn't come home that night. She knew that Aunt Felicia thought the same. That was the drawback to confession. After the consolation of confessing, the confessor knows the facts and can offer no blind consolations. Mary slowly undressed, knowing he would not come back and knowing she would not sleep. Knowing that if and when he came home tomorrow she would not ask.

The telephone rang suddenly, unbelievably. Mary picked it up with trembling fingers.

"Hello, Mary? All right?"

It was Aunt Felicia.

"Of course," she said. Aunt Felicia didn't ask if Lou was home but that was what she meant.

"Sweet dreams, child," said Aunt Felicia.

"Bless you," said Mary, but after she got into bed she lay there hating Aunt Felicia for thinking, indeed for knowing, that Lou was not home.

XVIII

Mrs. Kameray lay on her stomach in the hot white sand and shaded her eyes with her hand to squint up at Lou.

"You have a very pretty figure," she said. "I don't know why it is you are always so cross."

Lou would not be flattered.

"What do you mean, a pretty figure?" he said. "I'm getting a pot like that old boy over there in the water."

"I like a pot," said Mrs. Kameray. "I think a pot is very nice for a man. A man at forty should have a pot. How old are you?"

"Forty-one," said Lou.

"Seventeen years older than me?" Mrs. Kameray sighed. "You forty-one and me twenty-four!"

Lou didn't answer. She was twenty-eight, he knew. She had started being twenty-four a week or two ago and he suspected it had something to do with the young Cuban band-leader she had found in Havana. He was still mad about it, mad especially that she had flown to Havana without telling him, so that when he arrived in Miami, and with considerable trouble about arrangements, too, he had to wait two days for her to come back. Two days when you worked on a high pressure basis such as Lou did meant a lot of explaining, to the different clients he was supposed to be seeing in New York and Washington. But he didn't dare scold Trina or she would quietly pack up and leave. He had gotten rooms for them at one of the town hotels, but as soon as Trina arrived she had announced they must stay at one of the Beach hotels. So they were at the Roney Plaza, and, awkwardly enough for Lou, as Mr. and Mrs. Donovan, since Trina declared she was not to be regarded as a mistress but as a wife. It was not nice, she said, tiptoeing back and forth across halls in the night. They should have a nice little suite together like a honeymoon couple, and if she wanted to scold a waiter or maid she could do so with perfect freedom and not have them give her that insulting "mistress" look.

"Besides I am your true wife," she stated. "I am the one who should be Mrs. Donôvan. What are you doing about that, Louie? You promised me you would fix it all up."

Lou avoided her earnest inquiring gaze. God knows what he said in the tantalizing circumstances under which Trina extorted promises. It was unwise of him not to have handled the marriage thing better, however, because that came up all the time and she was getting very insistent about it.

"Don't let her tie up all your money, Louie," warned Trina. "You must let me help you with the settlement or she will want to take it all."

"You can't hurry those things," Lou mumbled.

"No? Not even for me? Not even to keep me from going back to Europe?" Trina raised her voice and Lou looked uneasily around them to see who might be listening. "You mean you would like me to go back into a burning building? That's how much you love me?"

For the first time Lou was glad to see the beautiful young Cuban lad coming up to them, for Trina at once was all smiles and demure charm. He was a slight, bronzed young Latin Apollo with little black moustache and sleek black hair. Mrs. Kameray swore that she had been instructed by the Major himself to find a suitable band-leader for the Castles-in-the-Woods ballroom orchestra and Tommy Padilla was one of the very first names she had been told to investigate. It was fortunate that, popular as he was in Cuba and Palm Beach, he still was able to spend all the time in the world at Miami getting acquainted with Mr. Donovan and talking things over so they could make a nice start that very summer. As soon as the young man joined them, Lou became acutely conscious of the brazenness of Trina's white bathing suit, the mere figment of a halter over the fine little bosom, a scant frill for a skirt, the pretty little navel all but out. Since she never under any circumstances went in the water she permitted herself quite an elaborate beach get-up, with a garland of red flowers in her flowing long brown hair, and a little red parasol.

"I love that little mole!" said Tommy gazing at the little brown flaw on Trina's bare diaphragm.

"Naughty!" said Trina primly. "Run along now, Tommy, let us see how beautifully you swim."

Tommy sprinted out to the water and flashed into the waves. Lou watched stonily. This was supposed to be the happy life, having your sweetheart on the beach of some tropic paradise, lolling in the sand, idling away the late winter days, not a care in the world but trying to hold on to your houri and watching other younger men exhibit their superior strength and beauty before her far too appreciative eyes.

"I still don't see why you had to stay a week in Havana just to get a bandleader, "Lou said.

Trina reached out a small hand to clasp his. This was another gesture that made him uncomfortable in public, but when he rebuffed it she revenged herself by rebuffing his private advances. So he returned the pressure of her little fingers.

"I like Havana," said Trina dreamily. "It is like a little live heart beating away in the ocean. How it sways and beats with the maraccas and the dancing feet. Like a little live heart."

"No town for a woman, alone," said Lou sternly.

"I have friends," said Trina. "I have a great many friends all over. There are many Russians in Havana. If there were no Russians there would still be the friends from Berlin and Vienna. You have friends I do not know. I have friends you do not know. Why not?"

Trina, pouting, was as irresistible to him as Trina, smiling, and he always felt a wave of frantic love for her when she made him feel guilty. She was reminding him now of the many times they had encountered business friends of his in the West and even these few days in Florida when he was obliged to pretend he was not with her. He knew that it was a scurvy thing to do, especially with a high class girl like Trina, but in every friend's eye he saw the image of Mary and for the life of him he could not ignore that image. It was thoroughly stupid of him, too, since on other occasions with other casual ladies he had arrogantly brazened it through. It was because this was different, that he had to mess it up. He knew Trina would behave with the most exquisite discretion before strangers—that is almost always—but she never failed to reproach him afterwards. He was ashamed of her? He was sorry he had made her love him? Very well, she would go back when the government made her. She was not a citizen, anyway. She would have to go unless some American man married her. No one would. So she would go back and very likely be killed. Certainly she would be killed. In Russia she was not a Communist. In Germany she was not a Gentile. Very well, she would be killed. It did not matter. Her poor little life meant nothing to no one, no one—expect Mr. Rosebush. Dear Mr. Rosebush. How wickedly she had treated him! He had been so good to her, had paid her whole passage back and forth to America two or three times. Such a good friend. Until Louie had made her fall in love with him and forget all her loyalty. For Louie's sake she must give up all her friends and her loyalties and for Louie's sake she must be treated like some bad common woman, someone not to be introduced to one's friends. Of course she could go back to Paris, but then her old husband Kameray would try to get her to come back to him, and then she would starve for he had no money.

"I thought you said he had money in a New York bank," said Lou. He hated to have her talk of other men, other husbands, other friends.

"A few thousand dollars," shrugged Trina. "It was really mine anyway because he had never made any divorce settlement. And if I had sent it to him in Europe Hitler would have taken it away from him. It could do him no good."

"I guess he's not starving," said Lou, uncomfortably. Trina's little allusions to the discomforts of her friends and relatives still in Europe made him bad-humored. Friends in concentration camps, grandfathers chased across Siberia by bloodhounds for all he knew, an ex-husband living like a rat in a Paris cellar, none of these seemed to stir Trina's emotion so much as the fact that European difficulties made her allowance from her grandpa in Geneva so slow in coming. Lou wanted to write out a check to end his pangs of conscience over the little pictures Trina's occasional remarks evoked in him. Why it should bother him, he didn't know, since she seemed philosophical about it. It bothered him, though, that it didn't seem to affect her. Or maybe it did. She was so mature, not like the American women he knew, she disguised her feelings since there was nothing to be gained by showing them. She was really braver than she seemed. Thinking this made Lou feel better.

"You've seen a lot of trouble, haven't you, Trina?" he said, moved.

Trina's hand gripped his.

"Some people are born for trouble," she sighed. "All my mother's people have had trouble in Russia, so why not me? And a little drop of the wrong blood in my husband causes us both more suffering! I am not born to be happy, Louie. Do you blame me I want everything, everything, quick, before it is too late?"

Her dark brown eyes welling with sudden tears had their usual effect on Lou. He would, that minute, have made a fine clean break with Mary, told her in ringing language that although she could get along beautifully, even better, without him in her life, there were other women who could not, women, or rather *a* woman, who had been through enough hell in her life to appreciate the protection of a man like Lou Donovan. He had one of his secret tempting visions of how sweet it would be to possess once and for all the charming little creature, to have this secret pleasure permanently instead of spasmodically and uncertainly. The image of Mary and the pride in the Harrod connection vanished with his quick longing to take Trina in his arms and hold her forever. These fleeting resolutions were lost, usually, in his sound later reflection that with Trina as his wife, who would there be for the little secret outings that were so much a part of his zest in life? A wife on a business trip, for instance, was just a wife, a poor piece of business, a dangerous exhibition of fatuity, very different indeed from the favorable impression of being independent.

"Tommy is not married," said Trina, sitting up and hugging her knees. The young man was still flashing sinewy brown arms through the sparkling water, occasionally pausing to wave to Trina.

"At twenty-one that shouldn't bother him," said Lou. "What I want to know is how he can spend thirty dollars a day for his room when he hasn't had a regular job for a year? I don't see how he can afford to stay in this hotel."

"He is like me," said Trina. "He likes the peacocks and the flamingoes. And the pretty fish in the dining-room. Everyone is not like you, Louie, seeing only the beefsteaks and the turtle soup."

It was a blonde day on the hotel beach and it may have been a surfeit of blondes in ice-blue bathing suits, or white shorts, that caused eyes to turn to Trina's flowing brown hair and swaggering little figure when she walked down to the water's edge to meet Tommy. Lou's appreciation of her curves was marred by his knowledge that it was shared by many. Trina used very little make-up and her public conduct was elaborately discreet; she never permitted her eyes to roam, and lowered them rebukingly when some crass stranger tried to stare her down. Her modesty and seeming fear of masculine attack gave an added piquancy to her merely average good looks, so that Lou was frequently disturbed by finding that her appeal was so general. For a man like Lou who did not like to be tied in any affair, it was harassing to realize that his little friend could not safely be neglected. Right this minute if he had to leave her Tommy would probably take over, or at least try to. Just as he was savoring this irritating thought a hotel boy came out on the beach and handed him a telegram.

"CAN YOU MEET ME HOTEL MAYFLOWER WASHINGTON TUESDAY CASTLES COMPLICATIONS CONFERENCE NEW YORK THURSDAY STOP ROSENBAUM."

The wire was forwarded from the Lord Baltimore in Baltimore where he was scheduled to be. Trina, coming up with Tommy, looked at him inquiringly.

"Have to fly north right away," Lou said briefly.

Trina's face fell.

"Can't we wait till tomorrow?" she begged. "It's our only really true vacation, Louie, you and me. Like a honeymoon. Don't you like to be on a honeymoon with me, Louie?"

"Yes," Lou said.

Trina took his arm.

"Our real one will be much better, you wait," she said. "We must go talk it over, Tommy. When you are dressed come and have champagne with us."

Back in their room Lou tried to be peremptory with her. Rosenbaum said he should be in Washington at a certain time and it was his duty to be there. He sat on the edge of the bed waggling the telephone receiver to convey that very message, but Trina flung herself down on the bed and wriggling on his lap took away the telephone.

"If you have to see him anyway in New York on Thursday, why must you go to Washington first?" she pouted.

There was something in what she said but in business you cannot point out the customer's mistake, just for your own convenience. However, what the customer doesn't know won't hurt him and Mrs. Kameray persuaded him to spend the hour pleasantly enough, both of them laughing at the idea of the Cuban Apollo patiently waiting for them below.

"Poor Tommy," sighed Mrs. Kameray, her eyes dancing. "He will be so worried about us."

The telephone rang.

"If that's Rosenbaum, I'll say I can't get out till tomorrow," Lou said, but the call was not from Rosenbaum at all. It was from Mrs. Donovan in Chicago. She wanted to speak directly to Mr. Donovan and, said the operator, *not* to Mrs. Donovan. This message, overheard by Trina Kameray, amused her almost as much as the idea of Tommy waiting. It alarmed Lou enough to make him decide to leave at once. For all he knew Mary might pull a 'Flo' on him and descend in Miami to meet this false Mrs. Donovan. He knew Trina was coldly unsympathetic about his alarm over Mary.

"Tell her at once you want a divorce to marry me," she said. "Do you want me to get another husband? If I don't have a husband I must go back to Europe. You want me to be killed, Louie, or is it you want me to make love to another husband?"

"Tell Chicago Mr. Donovan has left," Lou told the operator.

They went downstairs in silence, Lou stony-faced, Trina's cameo skin dewy, and looking fresh and smart in her trim little white flannel suit, her brown eyes sad, the full lips tremulous. The young Cuban did not find his friends very gay even over the champagne. He wanted to know why.

"It is because Louie's wife makes so much trouble for us," Trina explained gravely. "She does not want him to be happy one minute. I'll bet she would be nicer if you took her a present sometime, Louie, eh?"

"Oh, sure," Lou said gloomily. It did not make him happy to hear Trina talk, as she constantly did, about Mary. He had no intention of having anything out with Mary, but on the other hand he had not dared face her for weeks alone. All you could do in complications like this was to mark time. The hint about presents gave him a thought.

"Tell you what, I'll ship you on to New York and I'd better stop off in Washington," he suggested. "You can do a little shopping in New York."

"What kind of presents do you give your sweethearts, Tommy?" Trina gayly asked the young bandman, whose adoring gaze never left her face. He seemed astonished at the question.

"But what would the man give presents for?" he exclaimed. "It should be the lady who gives the presents. The lady always gives the present. It is much better that way."

The waiter brought the timetable and Lou glanced through it. Trina was content, now, to have him plan whatever he wished for them. She could go to New York and report directly to Lou's office on the result of her tour. She might well contact the Major himself, Lou thought. Meantime he, Lou, would see Rosenbaum in Washington and find out what was what; he would even, he graciously told Tommy, discuss the importance of having Tommy Padilla's Band. Tommy was delighted.

"Tell Mr. Rosenbaum it was my band he liked so much at El Dorado last Monday," he said. "Tell Mr. Rosenbaum that."

Lou did not flicker an eyelash.

"I will," he said.

He did not look at Mrs. Kameray, and she went on sipping her champagne unconcernedly.

"So old Rosebush was in Havana last week, too," he muttered.

"Didn't I mention it?" Trina lifted pretty brown eyes frankly. "But then I told you I had so many friends in Havana. In Porto Rico I have friends, too. But I love Cuba best. I like the way the airplanes swoop down flying over the city, like in a circus when the rider swoops down to pick up the handkerchief in his teeth, oh, it is thrilling!"

"Threeling?" Lou mocked her.

"And the cars that go so fast, whiz, whiz, coasting so fast down hill, and guns and masquerades with fighting, always, I love it."

"Life is cheap with Cubans," admitted Tommy, beaming.

"I could leeve forever in Cuba," sighed Trina. "To me it is like a little live heart, you know, beating and dancing like a little heart."

"Exactly!" exclaimed Tommy. "That is Havana to me, too."

To Lou, Havana was a place where Trina Kameray had casually spent a week with Rosenbaum and kept Lou waiting for her in Miami. The only way he could ever keep her away from Rosenbaum was to marry her, and he knew the reason she was not the least disturbed by his finding out was that she knew far too well that this would serve her purpose better than anything else. He wanted to upbraid her, but he had no threats to offer. It was she who held the whip, talking so affectingly with Tommy about the simple joys of swimming at La Playa, and dancing in the peaceful tropic night at Sans Souci. Dancing with Rosebush? Swimming with Rosebush? Lou dared not even ask.

XIX

Lou had dinner in Rosenbaum's suite at the Mayflower with Mrs. Rosenbaum, Rosenbaum, and their little niece, Hilda, and a dark, pinched, intense spinster sister of Mrs. Rosenbaum's, named Liza. In the course of the dinner a thin spectacled student at medical college, the Rosenbaum heir, paid a short visit and at his mother's earnest behest, ate her banana cream pie dessert, then departed. That was Everett. The entire Rosenbaum family seemed to have transported itself to Washington from Park Avenue for the purpose of attending some school function in which Everett was taking a proud part. Mrs. Rosenbaum was a fading Valkyrie, large, blonde, and domineering, with very little conversation, achieving her points by a commanding gesture, or merely by calling out a name as if the duties of each member of her group were so automatic that the sound of his or her name released a set program of action.

"Hilda!" she called out and the plain little ten-year-old with sandy pigtails immediately finished up her vegetables.

"Liza!" she called. "Liza!"

And poor Liza, who was called most often, rushed to pull down the shades, answer the door, pick up Hilda's napkin, answer Mr. Donovan's question, pass the butter, or show Everett the congratulatory telegrams from other relatives. Most of these brief commands seemed to be not for her own satisfaction but to save annoyance to her husband who broodingly sat through the five courses, making very little effort to draw out his guest, and crumbling his rolls into little balls on the tablecloth, an annoying gesture which Mrs. Rosenbaum's attentive blue eye caught.

"My husband is very tired," she said to Lou. "He has no appetite. He gives his life's blood for the Major. He's a family man and it's hard for him to spend so much time away from us."

"He sees more of Everett than he does of us," said Liza. Her thin dried face glowed with worship when she looked at Rosenbaum, as indeed it had glowed for the twenty-five years she had been privileged to assist her brother's wife in making him comfortable.

"Well, an only son, of course," said Rosenbaum.

"Our two daughters are on a cruise for the spring holidays," explained Mrs. Rosenbaum. "They are sixteen and eighteen. To Central America. They wanted to postpone it till summer and go abroad, but Father says Europe is too unsettled."

There was no mention of Castles-in-the-Woods and Lou grew restless. The waiters removed the dinner, Rosenbaum offered him a cigar, Hilda and Liza turned on the radio in the corner of the living-room and listened with somber unsmiling attention to Major Bowes' Amateur Hour. Mrs. Rosenbaum got out her knitting bag and sat down on the sofa beside Lou.

"Everett has to prepare an article tonight, so he couldn't stay with us," she said. "He'll take us to his fraternity house to tea tomorrow and then we won't see him again till he comes home in June."

"We're comfortable here," her husband reminded her. "It's a nice change for you. I wish I could stay over tomorrow night myself."

"If this is your last night," Lou made a stab at escape, "supposing we go downstairs and have a brandy, listen to the orchestra. Or we might drive down and catch part of the show at the National."

Mrs. Rosenbaum shook her head, smiling, her needles flying.

"We don't like public dining-rooms," she said. "We always like to have it seem like home. After all we came down here to see our son, not the city. You go out with him, Father, go ahead."

Lou was relieved to see that this suggestion was approved by the master. He went into his bedroom for a hat.

"Liza! Hilda!" commanded Mrs. Rosenbaum, and the two hurriedly came out to say good night to the guest. The little girl curtsied.

"She can speak English when she wants to," said Liza fondly, "but she is shy. She is so glad to be over here."

Lou didn't know what to say.

"Somebody ought to blast that guy, Hitler," he said. "He's a bad man, eh, girlie?"

Hilda burst into tears and hid her face behind her aunt Liza.

"She can't stand to have anyone say anything bad about anyone," explained Liza, apologetically. "She doesn't want anyone to be unkind to anyone, she says. It makes her cry."

"I'm sorry," said Lou, awkwardly.

Something in the little girl's brown eyes reminded him of Trina and they both seemed sad figures, sad kind figures, for Trina did not like any unkindness either, it seemed to him. Yes, that was what made her different from a fleeting affair, Trina was sad and kind and lonely, just like little

Hilda. Maybe Rosenbaum noticed that, too. It reminded Lou that Trina had other characteristics that did not exactly apply to Hilda and doubtless never would, but now they were mixed up in his mind, and he thought he would make up to Hilda for making her cry by buying Trina a bracelet.

The World's Fair deal was off on Castles, Rosenbaum told Lou in the Occidental, where they went for a highball. The San Francisco contract hinged on the New York one, so that too was off.

"But it was all settled," said Lou. "What went wrong?"

Rosenbaum shrugged.

"The world," he said. "You can't pin down parties to contracts when politics get into it. Besides both ventures were prestige more than profit. We lose nothing."

"We?" Lou laughed mirthlessly. "You mean you and the Major lose nothing. I lose. The firms I contracted for lose. Whittleby Cotton, for instance, loses."

Rosenbaum smoked quietly. The fellow got on Lou's nerves. Getting him to jump to Washington just to let him have the bad news. As easy as that, it was. The World's Fair deal off, he says, and smokes his cigar and looks down at the table, dead-pan, nobody could tell what he was thinking, but you knew he was in the clear all right, the Major's old right-hand man didn't have any worries.

"How does the Major take it?" Lou asked.

He wouldn't give the fellow the satisfaction of showing how much the loss meant to him, personally, the little slices here and there he'd cut for himself that were now shrunk or out of the picture.

"The Major doesn't know, yet," said Rosenbaum gravely. "As a matter of fact the Major is a very sick man. We've kept it out of the papers and it would be bad policy to let it go further—all of his commitments, you see—but the Major suffered a stroke two days ago."

"But he couldn't have—he can't do that!" Lou cried out in frank indignation. "Where are we going to be without the Major?"

That damn cigar of Rosenbaum's. He sucked away on it as if it was piping him the right answers.

"It was wife trouble, mostly," Rosenbaum said, after a proper consultation with his cigar, "The Major's not too self-controlled in the home, and moreover he's a very jealous man. His wife usually leaves him after a row, they divorce or separate, then remarry, then he has a jealous fit again, and the same thing over. Last time was too much for the heart."

"That's too bad," said Lou bitterly. "That's just too damn bad."

All right, what if the World's Fair was out, that wasn't the biggest thing on their programs. It had helped publicize the idea of the Castles, and had been a feather in their cap, but hell, it wasn't everything. What made him sore, though, was that a millionaire, just because he has the world by the tail, could just calmly step out of the picture and say, "Things are getting a little complicated around here, boys, I guess I'll treat myself to a little stroke."

"You have a tan since I last saw you," Rosenbaum said, suddenly looking straight at Lou.

Lou gave it straight back.

"So have you," he said.

"I didn't realize you were spending that much time in the South," Rosenbaum said. "You were lucky to be able to play a little."

"I've always been lucky," said Lou and knocked wood.

"Perhaps opening your New York office is what has brought you luck," said Rosenbaum. "I understand this has been your most successful year."

"I'll make enough to pay my last year's income tax," said Lou, watching him, not knowing what jump was coming next. "That's all I can ask."

"So last year was good, too." Rosenbaum nodded thoughtfully.

"You're damn right last year was good," said Lou. "After all, I do know my business, old fellow."

"You're a clever man, Donovan," Rosenbaum agreed. "You've got a lot on the ball."

But—? Lou waited.

"All right, what's the tag?" he asked, smiling.

Rosenbaum studied the photographs on the wall beside them thoughtfully. Maybe they worked with the cigar to feed him his answers. Lou couldn't figure out what he was getting at, half friendly, half sinister, and so oppressively gloomy, like some big operator waiting for the D. A. to catch up with him.

"You give me the tag," said Rosenbaum. "I mean, where you heading for? What's next? Do you vision a chain of branch offices all over the country, thousands of people working for you, consultants for hotels on a big scale, investigating, even buying and selling instead of just recommending?"

"Not for me," said Lou. "I go faster travelling light. I got to be flexible, change my position at a minute's notice. I'm doing all right handling a half dozen big outfits. You can't delegate my kind of work. Small but personal and selective, that's my angle."

"That's right," Rosenbaum approved. "It's your personality, of course. You're a lucky guy, Donovan."

"I never trust to luck," said Lou. "I work hard and use the bean every minute. You can't go wrong on that formula. It's these fellows that trust to luck that lose out. Me, I'm studying all the time. New angles. New twists. You got to keep at it."

"I wouldn't play down luck," said Rosenbaum. "You can work hard and use the bean and still lose."

"Not the way I work," Lou grinned. "I take no chances."

"Take the war in Spain, the hurricane, the political purges," Rosenbaum went on reflectively. God knows what he was getting at, but Lou kept his eye on the ball. "There must have been plenty of clever business men whose brains didn't help them there. The Major's brains didn't keep him from blowing up over a little wife trouble. No, you need luck. Maybe that's all anybody does need."

A crack in there somewhere, all right, but Lou didn't pick it up. If Rosenbaum wanted to insinuate that his success in business was pure luck, no brains, okay, there were other times for a comeback. You have to wait for a really good comeback. Keep 'em wondering when it's coming.

"I don't know, I don't know," Rosenbaum shook his head wearily. Liver, thought Lou, it must be a bad liver that made a man as glum as Rosenbaum. "For instance, supposing the Major should die. It turns out the entire Maryland estate goes to the Government for retired army men and their families. The Major was sentimental about the army."

"If the Major dies—what?"

Lou stared at him in blank consternation.

Rosenbaum nodded.

"That's the will. I didn't know it myself till I talked to his lawyers yesterday."

Lou drummed on the table, thinking.

"Then the Castles work would all be scrapped the minute he conks out?"

"If he conks out," assented Rosenbaum. "He probably won't. But we might as well know where we stand. It's all luck now."

"You're a cheerful bastard," Lou said. "After all the work we've put in on that job. You've seen my reports. You've seen the plans."

"I know. You get your fee just the same," Rosenbaum said. "The estate will have to settle the contracts broken as best it can."

Lou smiled wryly. Rosenbaum must know perfectly well that the fee was the least part of the Donovan profits. It was the side bets that made him the dough.

"It's going to help me a lot on new business with a lot of litigation about broken contracts hanging over," he said. "That's going to be just great."

"Adjustments can be made," Rosenbaum said. "You won't lose."

You bet he wouldn't. He'd stick a price on wasted services that would make them wince, all right.

"Did Mrs. Kameray's work seem satisfactory?" Rosenbaum asked. He didn't look at Lou, just kept his eyes on the tablecloth.

"Perfectly. Mrs. Kameray is a very intelligent woman, and made a very good impression. So far as her work went, it couldn't have been improved upon. Made some excellent contacts and did some very good field work."

All right, how do you like that? If you want to find out

something, Lou thought, go ahead, you won't get anywhere beating around the bush. The same thought must have struck Rosenbaum for he suddenly clasped his hands together and looked at Lou directly for a minute in silence.

"I know all about you and Mrs. Kameray," he said. "I knew she was probably going to meet you in Miami, just as she met you in St. Louis and on the coast. I don't know you, but I do know Trina. Trina's out to get married. Trina's out for safety and security, and she's going to get an American husband. You can't blame her. A person that's been kicked around, one country to another, through revolution, politics, war—that kind of thing makes a person determined to save his own hide at any cost. Security, that's all. You can't blame Trina."

It was Lou, now, who looked down at the table and then at the photographs on the wall hunting for answers.

"No one could blame her," was all he could get out.

Rosenbaum didn't care about answers, anyway. He seemed to know them.

"I've known Trina off and on for five years. In London, Paris. Her visits here. I've done more for her than anyone else. I can always do more for her than anyone else. All right, the one thing I can't do is marry her."

Lou busied himself with his drink. It was the last kind of conversation he liked. If Rosenbaum wanted to show his cards, go ahead, but he'd be damned if he, Donovan, would. He wasn't sure what they were himself, anyway. He was marking time, that was all.

"You saw my situation, tonight. I'm a family man. I have feelings. I love my wife and my girls, my son. Even if I didn't— . . . You don't have my feelings. You can walk out of your marriage and take Trina without a pang. I can't stop you."

"There's nothing the matter with my marriage, either," Lou said slowly. "It's not as easy as that."

Rosenbaum threw out his hands.

"Talk about happy marriages! It's the man with wife troubles that is the luckiest. He can walk out, with justice. But what about the rest of us with the wives that stood by us when we got started, and then we change, we grow, and they don't, they just go along, bewildered, watching us change, get rich, get smart, and they're hurt and puzzled and even angry that they can no longer name our favorite dishes, even, we don't eat the jelly rolls they make, but they can't see why our taste should have changed. And we feel sorry because we loved them once so we must go on. We don't like to cut off our own memories, and our habits, the habits we don't know we have till they're disturbed."

It was not especially pleasant to know that Mrs. Kameray had been heckling Rosenbaum to marry her, too, all these years. Somehow Lou had gathered from her that he had offered to do this himself, but that she had thrown away this opportunity for Lou Donovan. She had indeed given up everyone for him because, she said, her little tiny love affairs had been so unsatisfactory up till the moment she met him. There was no doubt about her double-crossing, maybe, a little bit with Rosenbaum, but it was not really double-crossing, it was a little show of power, to make him do what she wanted. Well, it worked.

"But you are getting a divorce, I understand," said Rosenbaum. "I can't. You saw that I couldn't. I wanted you to see my situation, so you would see that it wasn't just that I didn't care enough about Trina. It's—well, you saw."

So that was what was weighing him down all this time, trying to make up his mind to meet Trina's terms. And she had given him the "or else." The "or else" was Lou. Well, it must have given the old boy a kick to knock the bottom out of his business while he was handing over his former love. That must have been a compensation to him. No wonder he wasn't worried about the Major dying and leaving Castles up in the air.

"You'll marry her, I can't meet that," Rosenbaum mused. "Maybe you don't want to cut up your home, either, but you will to keep hold of Trina."

"Maybe," said Lou. "I'm not sure."

Rosenbaum signalled the waiter for the check.

"If you're catching that plane we'd better leave," he suggested. They got their hats, both of them somber-faced, unsure of each other. Lou got a cab but Rosenbaum decided to walk a while before he went back to his hotel.

"I might as well tell you that marrying Trina won't settle your future," Rosenbaum said quietly. "Trina never gives up anything. And even married to you, she won't be able to do without me. Good night."

XX

What a lousy town, what a two-timing, ungrateful, ugly, crooked, stinking town New York was, Lou thought, on his way to meet Jay Oliver at the Biltmore. You spend your life, the best years, working to help New York get richer, yes, that's what it amounts to, and as soon as you decide to put your stakes in and stay, then it turns on you. You could almost say that as soon as he got his name in the New York phone book with that good address and the Fifth Avenue office the city put the Indian sign on him. The contacts that he had worked so easily from the Chicago office melted away as soon as he was right around the corner, or at least his office was. It made no sense. The big hotel chain that he had been consultant for these ten years got cagey and talked about paying out too many commissions, their new general manager could handle everything, thank you. The New York receptionist was no Miss Frye, she kept her own hours and if the office was instituted just for the prestige of a New York address the whole point was worse than lost when occasional callers found nobody in, implying vaguely that Louis Donovan Service was out of business. What made Lou sore was that he was working as hard as he ever was, he knew his job even better, he was trimming for the shifts in European affairs, working ahead on propositions for railroad lines and continental air lines to build American playgrounds to take the place of the now problematical foreign resorts, places like Sun Valley to keep the traveller's dough at home instead of Mexico and South America where the trend now was. It made him boil, now that the Major had deliberately gone and died, to think of the winter wasted on Castles-in-the-Woods. He had his fee, all right, but that was only a drop in the bucket to what he had expected to make. And these New York business men. Fine fellows, till it came to a little need for co-operation, and then it was them against the out-of-town fellows, like himself. Rosenbaum, for instance. Nothing hostile, nothing you could object to, all on the level, but just a calm cool brush-off. No chance of even a show-down. "You have your fee," he says. "Your contracts will be settled by the estate with the firms involved. Present your statements. Too bad. Regrets."

He had not run into Jay Oliver recently and he didn't know what had happened since Truesdale had located Ebie for him. There was some talk of Whittleby Cotton merging with a Delaware firm and that might leave Jay out on a limb. All right, they'd have a hard times session. That was one thing about a pal like Jay, you didn't have to put up a front with him.

Jay was in the bar working on a Scotch and soda.

"When did you start?" Lou asked, taking the seat beside him.

"Did I ever stop?" Jay countered. "Hi ya, Lou."

"God, how I hate this town," said Lou and signalled the bartender for the same.

"What about coming out to Ebie's with me on the two ten?" Jay suggested. "Do you good to get out in the country."

"I'd like to see Ebie," said Lou, "even in the country, but I got to see Bill Massey up at Florabella at three. Every god dam thing has gone wrong since I landed in this lousy town."

"What you needed is to relax," Jay counselled. "I been meaning to speak to you, Lou. You act as if everything stops when you stop and it just doesn't. Why, they tell me you been jumping all over the country like a Mexican bean this last year, and look where it gets you."

"That's right," said Lou. "Where?"

"Still you look good, Lou." Jay looked him over approvingly. "That suit must have set you back some."

It was a brown worsted with a faintly shaded darker stripe. Mrs. Kameray liked him in stripes. He wore a mahoghany tie with it, a beauty, that Jay eyed enviously.

"I got a new tailor," said Lou. "I'll send you there."

"The hell with it," said Jay. "What good is a suit when you've lost your shirt? What a fellow needs then is a drink."

It was as good an idea as any and they had a lot of things to talk over. The cancellation of the Castles order, Jay thought, was too bad, but only too bad. The merging of his company with the Delaware firm was ominous, sure, but there were other firms. He was thinking of getting in the hat business. He'd had some propositions. He'd rather make less money and live in the East. Anyway he wasn't going to worry now about anything but catching the two-ten to Danbury.

"I got to take a dog out to Ebie," he said. "I bought her a pup."

"Where is it?" Lou asked, looking around.

"I got a Western Union boy walking him around," Jay said, "I got him at eleven o'clock and I can't get in anywhere with him, so I got this lad to walk him. He'll be back."

"See Rosenbaum?"

"Sure I saw him," said Jay candidly. "He was playing footy-footy with little Kameray in the Versailles last night. The Major checking out didn't seem to upset his plans any."

Lou thought of Mrs. Kameray's tremulous voice on the phone yesterday, saying that such a nice man as the Major dying made her feel too too bad, Louie, she must cry and cry, her nose was red, she could not let him see her. It must have been just the right color for old Rosebush. Lou had suspected something but dared not accuse, instead he took out one of the Florabella show-room girls, but he was blue, it wasn't any fun. He knew Rosenbaum hated to go out to night places, so the price Mrs. Kameray was demanding of him was that, if he didn't marry her, at least he must take her out to nice places, he must not act so ashamed of her that it made her feel bad. And she was a stranger, she wanted to get acquainted with her new country, it was her own dear country, yes it was, even if she did have to go back quick because no American man would marry her and the nasty government wanted her to go back to burning Europe. Lou could hear her coaxing Rosenbaum, and it didn't make him feel any better. It was no comfort to think Rosenbaum being out celebrating the night his boss died wouldn't look good to people. Rosenbaum could look after that part all right. Nobody needed to worry about Rosebush.

He ordered a double Scotch and knew that he was on his way to pinning one on, but Jay was right, there were complications that only a drink could straighten out.

"Tell you what, Lou," said Jay, "I'd like to have you look over this pup of Ebie's. I don't know. I may be wrong."

They had a couple for the road and then went out to

look for the pup. The Western Union boy was returning him from Central Park and Jay waved to him. It was an English shepherd dog, enormous and unwieldy.

"You call that a dog?" Lou demanded. It looked as if two men were working it, like a vaudeville act. That was the pup Jay was taking out to Ebie. It struck Lou as funny and the two of them went down to Grand Central Station, laughing, the dog pulling them along. There was difficulty getting the dog on the train but with a drawing room it was arranged and they sneaked him in. The dog sat with an enormous mournful gray face looking from one to the other. It was the best time they'd had since they'd gotten into the Castles' big money, and they slapped each other on the back and shouted with laughter.

Lou took his coat off and carefully hung it in the closet and Jay kicked his shoes off and they ordered three rounds of highballs so they wouldn't have to wait. It was like old times. When the train started Jay rang for the porter.

"Who's the engineer on this train?" he demanded.

The porter shook his head.

"Tell him I'd like to drive the engine from Stamford on," said Jay. "Here's my card."

The porter took it doubtfully.

"You tell him," urged Jay. "Tell him I'll call the General Passenger Agent if he doesn't. It's Mr. Oliver."

The porter was still doubtful.

"Before you put Mr. Oliver in the engine will you send back a pair of medium sized blondes from Car Number 856?" Lou asked seriously. "Here's my card."

The porter, for another dollar, was willing to be amazed and after he left Lou and Jay laughed again. The dog looked anxiously from one to the other. It was funny thinking of Ebie's face when she saw the pony-sized puppy that Jay was bringing her.

"No kidding, how did Truesdale find Ebie?" Lou asked.

"He sold her a farm," said Jay. "It was easy. Then she got sick and was stuck there. Ebie's all right. Ebie doesn't give a damn where she is so long as I get there once in a while."

"Where's Flo?" asked Lou and then chuckled. "Or do you know?"

"Sure I know," said Jay. "When Whittleby got shaky so did Flo. Seemed to think it was my fault. Christ, nothing I could do. So she kept reminding me everything was in her name, God knows she had me there, and I'd better not count on her, so by the time Whittleby went under there were no surprises. She threw a fit and I walked out."

"Jesus, Jay, she's got everything sewed up," Lou exclaimed.

"That's the nice part," Jay chuckled. "She can't complain. She was so scared of being left out that she hung herself. Told me she'd been putting everything away in her own name for years. Her mother told her. Her mother says, on her wedding day, 'Looky, Flo, you're very happily married, but you must learn to put all the savings in your name against the day he runs out on you, the bastard.' Something like that. So she did. So I says, 'Okay, then you're all right,' and then I says, 'Could you loan me fifty thousand to get back on my feet?' and she says, 'You don't get any of my savings, don't kid yourself, they're mine' so I says, 'All right, then, I'm a bum, I'd only be using up your money' and I walked out. It's a wonderful thing, having a smart wife."

"You mean you're living with Ebie?"

"Sure, I'm living with Ebie," said Jay. "Ebie doesn't care whether we eat or not so long as I'm there. Those two play right into each other's hands."

Lou thought of Mary and of Mrs. Kameray and how they would never play into each other's hands. He was irritated at Jay for thinking that the answer to everything was just throwing the pot of gold to the injured party and walking out. All right with Flo, but what did you do with a wife like Mary? And what did you do when you didn't want to leave her, when she was the kind of wife you knew you wanted, the kind you should have, and you didn't know what to do about it?

"What'll you bet you're in the same old noose?" he said.

Jay didn't get mad.

"Listen," he said. "A noose is what everybody goes for. Soon as they get out of one they look around. 'Where's my new noose,' they say, and nobody's happy till they got the new one, love, business, it's all the same; everybody's got to have the neck in the old noose, it's better than nothing. They call it a place to rest their neck. Everybody's got to have a place to rest their neck, so long as it's always out, anyway."

The dog knocked over two of the waiting highballs lined up on the the windowsill, so they rang again for the porter.

"How big is Danbury when we get there?" asked Lou.

"It's a hat town," said Jay. "They make hats."

"I don't give a damn what they make," said Lou, "I'm just getting information. How big is the place?"

"All right," said Jay. "It's about seven and three-quarters."

"I'm sorry, sir," said the porter, "but the conductor says you got to wire New York for permission to run the engine."

"Did you tell him it was Mr. Oliver?" asked Jay.

"Did you tell him he was with Mr. Donovan?" asked Lou.

"Are you the Lou Donovan that used to manage the Olympia Motion Picture Theatre in Rahway?" asked the porter.

He was. He was indeed. And the porter was the very same porter.

"How's Mrs. Donovan?" asked the porter. "She sure used to play the organ nice. I certainly enjoyed Mrs. Donovan playing that there organ. The only high class feature we had."

"That's right," said Lou, and suddenly it all came back, the old days in the afternoon, the run through of the film of the evening, Francie playing the organ to feel out what pieces to play, the colored porter pausing in his scrubbing to say how good it was, and Francie afterward in the beer place remembering that the porter had said he liked 'I Loved You Truly' particularly. And it made him feel very old to suddenly think of Francie with kindness, it made him feel old to want to remind her of those days, days she was always reminding him of, it was queer being in the other position. He thought, maybe that's all Francie wants, not to sleep with me, just to talk over the same things, on the other hand he never had wanted to even talk over the same memories before this very instant.

"You sure put that movie house on the map," said the porter fondly. "Don't you remember how you used to always be yelling out for William, Mr. Lou?"

"I certainly do," said Lou and slipped him a bill, feeling queer. It was the first and only time he had ever thought of any part of his past before Chicago as if it was a normal pleasant past, and a wave of surprise came over him that it hadn't been a bad past at all. He'd had fun there in little towns with Francie, they hadn't made a lot of dough, but when they did they enjoyed it. He couldn't, at this moment, figure out just when he stepped out of his past and became a different man, despising his past and everything connected with it, but he would remember this moment as the time he went back and looked at his past freely, and saw it was as good as anybody else's. Sure it was. Maybe it was in this present insecure period he was trying to catch on to anything that was solid, and if your past wasn't solid, what was? Maybe that was all it was, but suddenly he felt that it was nothing to be ashamed of, years of scramming in and out of boarding houses, bills half-paid, jobs not paid for, no, it was part of something. And there was old Francie, sticking by like mad. Now that he thought of it he'd never had anybody stick to him like that. When he got going good that was what threw him, it made him feel as if he *needed* someone sticking to him. Well. . . .

"Tell the conductor to go ahead with the same engineer," he said to the porter. "Act like nothing has happened."

Jay looked at him.

"So the fluzy was your wife," he said.

"Any objection?" said Lou.

Jay whistled.

"I'm just beginning to get you, pal," he said. "You're smarter than I thought. You know when I saw you going under for that Kameray phony I began thinking you were not so bright. I see now it was a gag to get Rosenbaum."

Lou lit a cigarete. The big dog came over and put his feet on Lou's lap. He had to laugh.

"I was going to give you a piece of advice," said Jay. "I

was going to tell you to stick to the gals at the Spinning Top or the hostesses there on Fifty-fourth Street. Same as you told me. The Kameray is a phoney. She even gets a per cent on the suit you just bought. She calls up the store every time you buy anything and gets her per cent. Ebie told me."

Lou drank the second drink from the end. The dog watched him anxiously.

"Ebie's a great girl," said Lou, sore.

"Ebie's crazy about you, too," said Jay, pleased. "I used to wonder if you pulled anything on me when I was away, but I guess I was too suspicious."

"I hope, I hope," said Lou.

That was the way to look at it. Everybody was phoney, it made it better that way. The unbearable ache at the things he kept hearing about Trina was nothing but growing pains. You had to be a phoney to get anywhere in this world. Trina had to step faster than some because she'd had it tougher, that was all. You had to feel sorry for somebody like that, somebody that had to keep playing a game every minute just to get along.

"William," Jay opened the door and yelled out, "bring me the funnies, will you, Mr. Donovan wants to see where Lil Abner is today."

Ebie's pup looked worriedly from one man to the other. It had a naturally woebegone face, its drooping whiskers adding to the funereal effect. Jay sprawled out on the seat and chuckled.

"Look at Handsome, will you? No kidding, Lou, did you ever see a dog with as much on his mind as old Handsome, here? Listen, Handsome, while you're on your feet, hand me that last drink over there, will you? Might as well train you while I got this time on my hands."

The porter came in with the papers which Jay decided to read aloud. Every time the porter came in Lou was reminded of some long forgotten remnant of his past. Come to think of it he and Francie had had a hell of a good time bumming around the country in those days. If anybody had any better time they hadn't known about it. Tiptoeing out of that rooming house in Albany at two A.M. wearing all the belongings they could get on since the installment people had taken the wardrobe trunk back that day anyway; having to take the car going north instead of the one going south because they were afraid to wait. Breakfasting in the next town, worn out and punch drunk from all night riding and no sleep, and reading the ad in the paper that landed them his best job, the management of a Newark hotel. Then the fire that wiped out that job, then the free rent somebody gave them way out in the Jersey wilds and Francie got a job in some roadhouse, and some guy, maybe it was the manager, kept trying to make her, and one night Lou was waiting for her out in the dump where they lived, miles from nowhere, and when she was late, he got jealous, imagine that, jealous over old Francie, yes, jealous as all get-out, and what does he do but start walking the ten miles to the roadhouse just to see if that guy is keeping her there, and all of a sudden he remembers some kid down the road with a bicycle and he steals it and rides to the roadhouse, pedalling away against a wind for an hour and a half, his calves hurt still just remembering it, and when he got there he saw Francie playing for a big crowd of customers and like a fool he'd forgotten it was the night of some firemen's banquet and the place was keeping open all night, and he felt like such a fool he didn't even let her know he was there, but turned around and wheeled back home. She was there when he got home, the boss' bus took all the help home, and she was worried sick not finding him, and they had a fight because he wouldn't tell her where he'd been, and by God he never did, either.

"William," Jay called the porter, "will you step up to the engine again and say Mr. Oliver will take over as soon as we pass South Norwalk?"

"William," said Lou," will you furbish up these glasses? There are four of us here."

"Sure is good to see you again, Mr. Lou," said William.

"I got held up here last fall in the hurricane," said Jay. "Train from Boston got stuck just ahead of Providence and by golly we sat there for hours. Ferry boat sailed right up past the window. A couple of old bags and I got out and hired a brokendown taxi to drive us to South Norwalk. Fifty bucks. Took all day, what with roads washed up, trees floating around."

"I was in the Biltmore in Providence afterward," said Lou. "They showed me where the water came up in the Falstaff Room there."

The porter brought the fresh supply of drinks and lined them up on the windowsill. The dog immediately knocked one over, and this set Jay off into roars of laughter.

"Look at that face, Lou. Won't Ebie die when she sees him? Looks like my old man, I mean that. By God the old man used to come home from the road on four legs, too, just the same as Handsome here. Used to hear him coming up the steps on his hands and knees, fried to the gills, and the old lady right behind him giving it to him. 'So that's what you do with your expense account? So that's where the money goes? So that's how you wear out your new clothes!' and 'Where'd you get that carnation in your buttonhole, you old bastard?' I used to lie in bed, scared stiff, sorry for the old boy, you know. I was just a kid."

"My old man was in insurance," said Lou. "We used to move every spring. Akron, Erie, Buffalo, Evansville, Lansing—big houses, little houses, boarding houses, mansions—we never knew how we'd land."

Lou looked at his watch. It was four o'clock.

"Say, what am I doing on this train?" he wanted to know. "I had a date with Florabella an hour ago. Where we going?"

"Take it easy, Lou," Jay soothed him, "you got to relax, now, I mean that. We're just running out to say hello to Ebie. You like Ebie. Ebie likes you. Then there's Handsome. I couldn't very well take an animal that size out there alone, could I?"

"Why me?" Lou asked. "Why didn't you get Frank Buck?"

Jay yawned and pulled a newspaper over his face.

"Do me a favor, Handsome," he instructed the dog, with a weary sigh, "entertain Donovan while I catch a nap."

"How'm I going to get back?" Lou asked. "I can't take time out like this with things the way they are."

"Relax, Lou, for Christ's sake. You got nothing to worry about but money and that'll be gone in no time. Relax, old man."

Resigned, Lou stretched out on his seat. He pulled the funnies over his eyes, and the old days, the old hard luck days came dancing past like an old flicker, and for some reason they didn't seem bad at all, they seemed real, even fun, the panics and the triumphs seemed realer now than anything else, he couldn't understand why that was unless it was age, with all its sentimental fog, creeping up on him,

Or maybe it was just his brain trying to keep from thinking about Trina and Rosenbaum and Mary and the kid back in Chicago, and a winter's work gone to pieces. Maybe that was it. Anyway, the whirring of the wheels was soothing. The dog, Handsome, looked anxiously from one paper-covered face to the other, then back to the remaining high-balls poised on the window-sill and moaned lugubriously.

XXI

Ebie was in her studio over the garage, having such breakfast as Buck Kinley, her colored handy man, was in the mood to serve. There was only warmed-over biscuits, bacon and coffee, so Ebie judged that neither Buck nor his wife Minelda was feeling very well this morning after their night in town.

"Where's the cream?" she asked, not caring much.

"Minelda used it up this mawning," Buck said, yawning. "She say she jes' felt like drinkin' some cream this mawning."

Nothing to be done about that. Minelda was boss of this place. If something didn't suit Minelda she was likely to take Buck and march right back to Asheville, leaving Ebie all alone on this godforsaken farm. Serve her right, too. You ought to be satisfied to let little-gray-home-down-by-the-old-millstream-and-so-on be a tenor solo, your own fault if you bought the property. Your own fault, too, if you were fool enough to try to live in it and prove something or other about yourself that didn't matter to anyone but you, and besides you got sick proving it. She couldn't complain, really, about the getting sick part, because that was where Jay had suddenly showed up as the big protector. You'd think that finding her in bed with pneumonia was all he'd ever been waiting for. Now she was well and sick of the place, but it was Jay's dream home, now, and she had to stay and be part of the song, me-and-you-in-the-little-home-down-by-the-old-millstream. That was what she always wanted, all right, then, what was she kicking about?

"Mis' Vane, where'd you put that gin?" Buck asked.

"Buck, you're not going to have gin before breakfast?" Ebie protested.

"Yessum," said Buck, "that's what I'm gonna have. Where is it?"

Ebie, resigned, motioned to the cupboard beside the stove and Buck hastened to help himself. He poured out a tumblerful and started downstairs with it.

"I better take some to Minelda, she don't feel so hot," he explained. "The way she's feelin' this mawning she's ready to pick up and go. Say she's got on her travellin' shoes, heels afore and heels behind."

"What's the trouble now?" Ebie asked.

"Minelda's settin' to retire," Buck said, "She say she's gonna get outa the washin' and ironin' racket."

"Better hustle over with that gin," Ebie advised.

After he went she sat by the stove with her coffee, her back to the work-in-progress on the easel, said work being a "Haunted House" item that after three weeks fussing still looked like an ad for a new residental section, just as the "Old White Church" canvas in the corner looked like a bride's silverware ad, and the "Old Village Character" portrait would be well set-off by a caption "What This Fellow Needs is a Knox Hat." They didn't look so much worse than anyone's else, if she weren't so darned realistic she could believe they were even better than average. That was what you needed to be a genuine artist, vanity, and vanity on a terrific scale. You could talk all you wanted about the virtues of stick-to-it-iveness, faith-in-yourself, but nobody but an egotistical dumb-bell would have such blind faith in himself that he'd stick to it for years, not noticing he was no better than anybody else. Well, she was good in her own line. She could get an odd job now and then if she went back to town. Rosenbaum had called her on a couple. But Jay liked her better out here, waiting for him to show up. He had called her up last night from some tavern around town, she couldn't make out where, and she didn't ask or demand that he come right out, because you can't do that when you're trying to show how much more understanding you are than the other woman. You're on a spot, there. It's no wonder a man takes advantage of it. On the other hand, Jay wasn't required to understand or forgive anything. He'd walked out on a wife for her sake, so now he had permanent privileges to do as he liked and be forgiven.

"Never mind where I am," he kidded her over the phone, "the point is, where are you?" So he was on a bender. All right, then, he was on a bender. "I want you to tell me and tell me right, what the hell are you doing?"

"I'm listening to the radio, darling," Ebie said. "I've listened to Fibber and Molly and I'm almost ready for Raymond Gram Swing. Any objections?"

"I get it, you're in no condition to see Lou and me, then," Jay said. She could tell he must have spent the day on this one, and she could hear dance music behind him so he was still having fun. If Lou was with him they had some girls, too, those two never wasted their time running around alone. Jay would tell her all about it, they would laugh together about it later, and he would say how well she understood him. Well, she had to. "Sure, I run around," he'd tell her, "it's my nature, but you know you're the one I always come back to, you're the one I have to have, you understand that, Ebie."

"I know, darling," she would say.

The trouble was she had too much time to think out here in the country, waiting for him to pop in and out. It was a little scary getting your heart's desire after getting used to a life of just wishing for it. Here was Jay, all set to marry her as soon as he got his divorce, and also all set for her to forgive him legally the rest of his life. Any fool could see that was no improvement over their old situation, so far as she was concerned. She'd just have to sit home waiting to hear his confessions and forgive him. That was the trap she had been begging for. That was all everybody fought for, worked for, demanded as their right—traps. There was Lou Donovan, getting along fine, free, arrogant, sitting pretty, when he notices he has no trap so he hunts around for a super-duper-trap, little Trina Kameray. And here was she, Ebie, smart girl, for ten years chasing after a man who was pure poison to her career, to any career, made her business success seem silly because *he* was all she wanted, made this whim of hers for a farm a permanent cage for herself because it suddenly struck *him* just right. Talk about learning through your own mistakes, all you ever learned was, "This thing I'm after, this thing I'm going to do is a mistake and I'll always regret it, but that isn't going to stop me now." That was the value of experience. Experience told you not to lose your temper when the man you'd been wanting for ten years called up for the third time long after midnight and cordially invited you to hop in a car and bring Fibber and Molly and Swing over to Billy's Back Room somewhere on the road between Danbury and Brewster. Experience told you that was where the other woman lost out, nagging him to death, accusing, raising Cain, so it was up to you to be sweet, so what do you do? You lose your temper.

"But I tell you we can't leave now, Ebie," Jay patiently explained. "Listen, honey, will you just keep your trousers on while I explain? I'm in a game, I tell you, I just got a dream hand, I can't leave. I——"

So she hung up. Sweet, that was what she was. Now she was sorry, because there it was, she'd rather have Jay driving her crazy the rest of her life, than anything else. She put on the sweater hanging on the hook under the eaves and went downstairs, through the dark garage into the bright April sun. There was the old red barn where her mother was always storing her auction treasures, there was the elegant chicken house, the only modern, well-heated, well-roofed building on the place, now made available to Buck and Minelda by the fortuitous demise of the last chicken. Ebie crossed the road and opened the little white gate to the house proper, a jolly enough little house except that the roof leaked and it was cold as Greenland in every room but the kitchen. Minelda was in the kitchen, large, black and bossy, whipping up a cake, and plainly benefitted by the potion Buck had brought her.

"Mr. Oliver coming out today, Miss Vane?" she asked. "I thought he was bringing you a dawg this week."

Ebie was just explaining that Mr. Oliver must have forgotten about the dog when there was a loud honk-honking out in front from a yellow taxicab, an unfamiliar sight on these deserted roads. Ebie went out, with Buck running behind her, and saw a large gray doleful face peering out the window. It was Handsome, unhappy beneath a pink paper hat. The driver leaned out to ask if this was Miss Vane.

"The gentlemen kept me waiting all night there and then

they thought the dog had better come home," he explained. "Get out, there, Handsome."

It was such an unhappy, dignified beast, that Ebie began to laugh, as she patted him. It was plain to see that being sent home from a bar at this hour in the morning was a mortifying experience for him. A Scottie was what she'd asked for.

"Would you mind telling me what happened to the gentlemen?" she inquired.

The driver was willing to tell anything he knew. The two gentlemen had asked him to summon two other cabs, one to take one of the gentlemen out here later on presumably, the other to drive the other gentleman to New York. Personally he had no idea when they were leaving Bill's Back Room, but maybe they had started right after he left.

"Tell Minelda to feed him, will you, Buck?" Ebie ordered.

She was sick with disappointment. That was the way it would be, she'd be stuck out here waiting for him, and he'd be some place else having a good time, forgetting to let her know, just being sure that anything was all right with old Ebie. She'd just like to show him. She thought she had when she came out here but it hadn't worked out that way. It would be just like him to go back to New York with Lou, without even coming out to the farm. She ought to be braced for anything after all these years. Well, she had her work. She'd just put him out of her mind, forget about him till he walked in, paint like mad, bad or good, and just show that women could forget the same as men. She started back to the studio, while Handsome loped into the kitchen with Buck. At the bottom of the studio stairs she turned and came back. She looked down the road after the vanishing taxi, and after a moment's hesitation started walking rapidly in that direction. If Jay *had* started—and the taxi man said he might have—he'd come this way. She'd walk along to meet him and—if he *did* come, if he *hadn't* gone on to New York with Lou, she could ride back with him.

That was the kind of sap she was.

XXII

Mr. Lowry paused on the way to the bar to cast a furtive look of admiration at himself in the mirror, observing once again how exquisitely his beige shirt set off the rich chestnut waves of his toupée. Two young ladies, emerging from the elevator, bowed to him with what he felt was more than their customary warmth and he thought that next time he saw them having a drink in the bar it would do no harm, as manager, to suggest their having a drink on the house. He smiled gently picturing their astonished, happy faces, their grateful cries of joy, and he was mentally offering them a second round and what-about-dashing down to Barney's for a third (the dark one decided to go home here and he was left with the red-haired one, who made no bones about the terrific physical pull he had for her) when he actually did get to the bar and had to readjust to the somewhat drab reality of old Mrs. Vane.

"Well, well, my dear child," he said in the fatherly tone he used with the old ladies, "you're looking fifteen years younger today."

Mrs. Vane, who was going over some pink slips at the bar, and lecturing Albert, the bartender, on the outrageous indifference of America to the poetry of Emily Dickinson, looked sharply at Mr. Lowry through her lorgnette.

"Nonsense," she stated, "that toupée seems to have gone to your head, Mr. Lowry. Here's a message from Four A.

Says the butterfly sofa I brought her from Pittsfield was filled with baby mice. Ridiculous on the face of it."

"Must have been a mother mouse there somewhere," agreed Albert.

"Sit down, Mr. Lowry," commanded Mrs. Vane. "I was just telling Albert that Emily Dickinson used to carry a little scrap of poem in her apron pocket for days, days, mind you."

"Absent-minded, I guess," Albert said understandingly, and swiped up the bar before placing Mrs. Vane's brandy before her.

Mrs. Vane leafed over her pink telephone slips, studied them through her lorgnette, finally straightened them out fondly and with a deep sigh of responsibility tucked them away in a special corner of her large plaid handbag. Since the maw of the bag revealed a delirious tangle of goggles, cough-drops, aspirin, bank-books, post-cards, timetables, road-maps, memorandum pads, and spirits of ammonia, the careful consideration Mrs. Vane gave to the correct filing of her telephone slip seemed, even to the amiable Albert, a perfectly unreasonable waste of time.

"How's the antique business?" inquired Mr. Lowry, now studying his image in the mirror behind the bar. "Our little manicurist tells me you're branching out wonderfully."

Mrs. Vane nodded with a preoccupied air, then fixed the eagle eye intently on Mr. Lowry.

"Mr. Lowry," she asked. "How would you like a gun?"

Mr. Lowry blinked, and stammered that it was not his heart's desire that moment, but——

"We have a beautiful piece," she interrupted, "a Revolutionary musket that was used by General Washington. The thing for you to do is to put it on the wall in the lobby, with a photograph of Washington."

"Ah, yes," said Mr. Lowry, looking vague, "That might be a good suggestion. Still——"

"Listen to this, Albert," said Mrs. Vane, and held a small volume close to her nose, "this is the stanza I was telling you about yesterday——"

Albert, drawing a beer for the glum man in the derby at the end of the bar, hastily delivered same and leaned on his elbows respectfully, but Mr. Lowry escaped to the doorway, where suddenly a smile of visible ecstasy came over his face. He opened the door and held it open with something approaching a salaam, while a sharp draft whizzed in and enlivened the customers at the bar, indeed obliging Mrs. Vane's camphorated velvet drapes to flutter about her shoulders. The cause of Mr. Lowry's pleasure was soon evident. A shining new station wagon with a slight dusting of snow on the roof to testify to its voyaging had stopped in front of the Ellery, and from this emerged a middle-aged figure in checked brown trousers and swaggering polo coat, brief-case in hand. He was about to pull another bit of luggage from the car, but Mr. Lowry anticipated this by snapping his fingers at the venerable porter now delivering a fresh pink slip to Mrs. Vane.

"Get that luggage, there, boy," ordered Mr. Lowry, and then called out the door, "The boy will take it in, don't trouble about it, Mr. Truesdale."

Mr. Truesdale nodded briefly, acknowledging this, and came in the bar pulling off great woolen mittens so busily he ignored the manager's outstretched hand.

"Howja do, Lowry," he murmured, glancing around the bar.

"Well, well, well, Mr. Truesdale," boomed Lowry, beaming. "Hope your trip was successful."

"Get that front suite for me, Lowry?" Truesdale demanded. "I'm too exhausted to put up with that noisy hole you gave me last month."

"Everything's arranged, Mr. Truesdale," said Lowry, happily. "We moved the Peppers out of the corner suite and it's yours. That back suite was a mistake, very regrettable, I had no idea those people in the next room were so undesirable."

"Hope you put 'em out," said Truesdale. "Can't have that sort of thing in here."

"Exactly," agreed Lowry, tiptoeing behind Truesdale to the bar. "I said to them, 'See here,' I said, 'Mr. Truesdale is one of our oldest and most valued guests. Anyone he complains of in this hotel must go,' so—they went. I said, 'The Prince George or the Seville are up the street or the Lafayette further down,' I said——"

Truesdale waved his hand, frowning.

"Never mind, never mind, Lowry," he said. "I have to talk to Mrs. Vane here, no time for horseplay."

Mrs. Vane tucked away her reading glass and book in her bag at sight of Truesdale.

"We'd better take the booth," she said significantly. "Did you look at the choir-pew?"

Truesdale nodded.

"Beautiful piece," he informed Mr. Lowry. "Victorian pew, you see. Found it in an old barn outside Pawtucket. Ideal piece for the bar here, as a matter of fact, unique doncha know, especially with the stained glass window."

"He wouldn't take the gun," Mrs. Vane accused.

"I have to consider," Mr. Lowry protested, "I'm only the manager."

Mr. Truesdale took out a pencil and envelope and scribbled something.

"I'll speak to one of the better places, if you like, Mrs. Vane," he said patronizingly. "Of coss, only a rally fust claws place would be interested in a choir-pew bar corner."

Mr. Lowry looked unhappily down at his nails. He was not comforted by the appearance of the two pretty girls in the bar-room who this time definitely gave him the eye.

"I'm sorry you don't consider the Ellery a first class hotel, Mr. Truesdale," he said. "We're not big, we're not the newest hotel in the world, but we try to keep up our own little standard."

"I dassay, I dassay," impatiently retorted Truesdale. "Come, Mrs. Vane, let's take the booth where we won't be annoyed."

Mr. Lowry hastened ahead to the corner booth and flicked his handkerchief over the table, lifted the ashtray and set it down again, stepped aside with a bow after these preparations to allow the seating of the couple. Mr. Truesdale looked over the manager, frowning. The manager smiled, waiting for the comment, and finally ventured it himself.

"I know what you mean," he giggled, "It's the toupée. Do you notice it? It does take a little off the age, doesn't it?"

"Maybe so," conceded Truesdale, and added reminiscently to Mrs. Vane, "I recall the same remark was made to me at one time by the late Lord Hawkins, personal friend, of coss, we'd been to India together, Tanganyka, too, for that matter, great hunter, of coss, but bald as an owl. 'Truesdale,' he said, 'do you think a toupée of some sort would make me look a bit younger?' and I said, 'Hawkins, does a baby need a toupée to look younger?' "

"Ha, ha," guffawed Mr. Lowry. "That's good, that's damn good. Ha ha ha!"

He went away, wiping tears of laughter from his eyes, and was still shaking his head at the irresponsible wit of Mr. Truesdale as he passed the two young ladies smiling at him from the bar. He was not too overcome to note their eager eyes and reflected that if they thought their youth and looks entitled them to any extra favors from the manager they had another guess coming. If he looked as good as that to them he must look good enough to get younger and prettier women than they, by Gad, no use fussing around your own territory, getting into trouble, getting the other guests talking. In the hotel lobby, behind the desk, he adjusted his face into its normal gravity, picked up some letters for Mr. Truesdale in the "To Be Held" compartment of the mailbox, weighed them thoughtfully, and muttered, "The bastard! Wouldn't you know a little pipsqueak like that would come out on top while hardworking people like me are always in the hole?"

The ancient bellboy shuffled up to the desk.

"Now, what?" snapped Mr. Lowry.

"Everybody keeps asking me when the new management starts," apologetically explained the fellow. "They keeps sending me down to find out. I don't know what to tell them."

"Everything will go on as usual," said Mr. Lowry with restrained annoyance. "The raise in rates is effective next week. Guests will be notified of further changes as they take place."

"Some of them wants to know if the rates will go down after the World's Fair closes," the fellow went on inquiringly.

"How do I know?" barked Mr. Lowry. "Everything possible will be done to keep our standard the same as always, even if we have to double our prices to accomplish this. Everything!"

The sale of the Ellery Hotel had been a shock to Mr. Lowry, but nothing like the shock it had been to discover that Mr. Vernon Truesdale had been the guiding spirit in this transaction. In pointing out the possibilities of the Hotel Ellery to Lou Donovan as a quick profit-maker, Mr. Truesdale had noted the convenience of the hotel to World's Fair bus and subway facilities, the cheapness with which the place was run, and the ease with which a Guest Shopping Service could modestly capitalize on the needs of guests, even to World's Fair escort facilities. Mr. Donovan had, with no trouble at all, persuaded Mr. Grahame, head of the midwestern hotel chain, that this modest little New York hotel could be utilized as an adjunct to his more elaborate western establishments, be exploited, as a club, for the New York use of all of these western hotel customers. Vernon Truesdale was now Mr. Grahame's direct representative at the Ellery Hotel (through the Louis Donovan Service) and it was only a matter of days before he recommended that Mr. Lowry be thrown out on his ear as too snobbishly eastern and—as he expressed it in his last report to the Chicago office— "a genuine Midwestern type of man be placed in charge here with a staff of same types, in order to inspire feeling of homeyness and trust."

Mr. Truesdale, thinking of this surprise in store for Mr. Lowry, permitted himself a slight wry smile as he seated himself in the corner booth opposite Mrs. Vane. Mrs. Vane, with an air of tremendous importance, adjusted her flowing drapes, recaptured from the floor the decayed morsel of imitation leopard which she wore as ornament more than protection against drafts, and after a sharp glance around for possible spies, leaned toward Mr. Truesdale and hissed, "Must have some advice, that's why I sent word to you. It's about my property."

"My advice is to sell it," said Mr. Truesdale with conviction. "Run down neighborhood, repairs required, money in the bank a much better proposition right now, my dear woman."

Mrs. Vane's eyes glistened with approval at this advice which fortunately coincided with the action she had just taken. She opened her bag, a dreamy expression playing about her otherwise ferocious old face, and produced a folded paper which she put in front of Mr. Truesdale. She looked around cautiously again and then spoke in the reverent, loving murmur with which young mothers speak of their new-born and old women speak of money.

"The money's already in the bank," she confided. "Plus the deed stock and collateral. What do you think of Eastman Kodak as my next buy?"

It is amazing how those three little words, "money in bank" can bring the dewy sparkle of first love to old ladies' eyes. Little voices crying "grandma" do not tug at the old heart-strings as do those sweet words "collateral," "stocks and bonds," "piece of property" and dearest of all "money in the bank," and no one who has seen a woman over sixty dress up to whisper these soft words to her banker or broker can doubt that woman's final love must be negotiable. Mrs.

Vane, having passed through her affairs with woman suffrage, poetry, social work and current events, had arrived at the usual triangle, her passion for food and her true love for the Guarantee Trust. It did not matter how small the sums were that passed through her hands, the point was that sums were passing, the little things piled up in the cunningest way imaginable, and what could be more heartwarming than talking about them in rapt murmurs over a glass of brandy? Mrs. Vane had flirted with "property" and "profits" for years without ever being sure whether she was ahead or behind, the main thing was the sense of power, but in the last winter her resolute forays into the old barns and chickenhouses of the Eastern seaboard had unearthed unexpected little profits. Tenants in her "property" were bullied into buying these treasures, and if these deals were merely spasmodic adventures there was a healthy honest satisfaction in getting paid even a modest sum for something quite worthless. It had thoroughly revitalized Mrs. Vane, and while her literary prejudices were as vigorous as ever she was not blind to the even fresher thrills Mr. Truesdale had brought into her life in assisting her "antique" business. Mr. Truesdale had sold Ebie the house in Connecticut which had set off Mrs. Vane, he had tipped her on how to get the customer first before the object, if possible. Mr. Truesdale would long since have wriggled out of Mrs. Vane's clutches except for an exaggerated conception of the old lady's finances, and a pride in her resorting to him for final judgments on matters her bank and broker had already advised her. It was astounding to Mr. Truesdale to find his authoritative words to Mrs. Vane often turn out perfectly sound, and thinking of the profit some word of his had brought her he would mutter to himself, "Well, I'll be damned, what do you know? It really worked, by Gad, it really did. Well, I'll be damned."

"Have you consulted your daughter?" he now remembered to ask.

Mrs. Vane looked pained.

"Vernon, you know perfectly well I never consult any one but you. Ebie doesn't have a brain in her head, and besides I never see her."

"She's still on the farm, of coss," Mr. Truesdale said tentatively.

"I haven't the faintest idea," said Mrs. Vane with candid indifference. "Very likely so. Ebie's just like her father, no spirit of adventure at all. Wanted me to stay out there in that godforsaken place. Ridiculous. I have to be in touch with affairs. Let the young people stay out in the country and rot their brains, if that's all they ask. Personally, a woman of my intelligence has to be right here in the center of things, looking after my affairs. You know that, Vernon."

"The art work," said Mr. Truesdale, "does she continue with it?"

The subject plainly bored Mrs. Vane for she tapped the table nervously, impatient to get back to her romance with property.

"Ebie's throwing herself away," she said. "She doesn't make a cent—just paints around the place. Then she cries. Absolutely ridiculous. I can't be around people crying, I told her. No go. I have my own life to live."

"I understand she was sick quite a while," ventured Mr. Truesdale.

"Is that so?" Mrs. Vane rattled the paper in front of him.

"See if that sounds legal to you, Vernon. I don't trust any one but you."

"Hmm, let's see," Mr. Truesdale stroked his chin. "Hmmm. Yes. Hmm. I see."

He was about ready to make a stab in the dark, having no knowledge of deeds or mortgages, and okay the paper, when he was relieved to be called to the telephone by the bellboy. It was a call from Lou Donovan, asking if he could locate Mrs. Kameray for him, who should be at the office that afternoon. Mr. Truesdale had not been keeping his eyes and ears open for fifty years for nothing and he could have given a fairly sound guess on Mrs. Kameray's whereabouts, if not the exact place at least the company in which she could be found most any time she was not with Mr. Donovan; it seemed more professional, however, to merely accept the duty and say nothing. It was a good way to clear himself of an evening listening to Mrs. Vane so he went back to the bar with a lighter heart. She was frowning over her volume of Emily Dickinson when he got back with his excuses.

"I'm sorry you have to go, Vernon," she said. "You're the only intelligent person I know, the only person I can discuss poetry with."

XXIII

"Do YOU want me to call the house?" Miss Frye asked.

She stood in the door of the office bar, looking at him curiously. Her hat was on, ready to go.

"I know, I heard you before," Lou muttered, just sitting there staring out the window at the summer sun glittering on the blue lake beyond. His bag was on the chromium-trimmed bar chair just as he had left it, half-opened, the new dull rose shirt on top. He knew Miss Frye was giving him those funny looks just as she had ever since he came in, and it got on his nerves. You can't keep up a front every minute, and Frye ought to be smart enough by this time not to show surprise when things seemed a little unusual.

"I checked over the liquor supply last week," said Miss Frye, finally getting the idea that routine details of the business were all the boss cared to hear at this minute. "We're low on Ballantines and Black and White and I reordered. Short on brandy, too, but I didn't know what kind you wanted. What's that stuff on the end there?"

"Sloe gin," said Lou. "It's the old honkytonk dish."

"You'd know," said Miss Frye, and he grinned. That was a little more like it, she thought, but she still hated to leave him there without doing something for him.

"How many you got coming in?" she asked.

"There's two or three hundred of them over at the Blackstone," he said. "The Western hotel men. They're all looking for something for tonight and without wanting to brag about my city I think, by God, they'll find it. So probably only a dozen or so will turn up here."

"I guess there's plenty for that many, then," she said. "They couldn't have used up that six thousand dollars worth of liquor here in just a year. Look, Mr. Donovan, do you want me to say anything to Mrs. Donovan? Tell her you're not back yet or something like that?"

Lou whirled around at her.

"Miss Frye, for God's sake what do you want to know? I'm here. You got your salary. It's six o'clock. Why don't you go home?"

Miss Frye's mouth opened.

"All right, all right," Lou shouted, "if you want to know, I've already been home. I saw my wife. I saw my wife's room, too, with some guy's fifty-cent necktie hanging up over the dresser, and a bottle of ten-cent-store hair grease in the bathroom, a lousy bottle of hair grease in my bathroom! Carnation Hair Oil! That was the kind of guy my wife picked to put her to bed! A five- and ten-cent store gigolo!"

"I know," Miss Frye murmured, "it was that Spaniard she picked up the night she showed up at the Spinning Top! It was awful."

"You know so much, what do you hang around asking questions for?" Lou snarled. "I suppose you know all about her showing up there that night, plastered, all alone, playing the drums with the orchestra, asking this lousy foreigner to dance with her, taking him home——"

"Listen, Mr. Donovan, she wasn't herself, she was just getting even," Miss Frye cried out, "honestly, Mr. Donovan, you can't blame a woman, when you never are home any more and you do have somebody else——"

"Shut up!"

Miss Frye shut up. Lou was ashamed.

"All right, I was a bastard, myself. All right. But when a man's wife, the woman he has a right to expect something from, maybe not faithfulness but at least good taste, breeding, for Christ's sake, when she takes on a phoney with a fifty-cent tie and Carnation Hair Oil—even the pajamas, mind you, were there—imitation black silk pajamas, this sheik, this phoney Valentino——"

"Maybe you left some imitation lace panties around her room yourself once," Miss Frye, nettled, rose to defend her sex. "I don't notice you men always picking your social equals for bed, either."

It was ridiculous taking it out on Miss Frye. Old Frye, the only woman he could ever really count on, so far as that went. She would do anything for him, he knew that. Loyal. Still, there was nothing like loyalty to get on a person's nerves. Funny, but there it was.

"Frankly, Miss Frye, if you want to know the truth, I think my wife is going nuts," Lou said, more calmly. "That's all I can figure out. Takes this guy out to the black and tan every night, flaunts him in front of my business friends——"

"I know," said Miss Frye, "I didn't want to tell you before. That's why the Harrods kept trying to find you. The idea is it's all your fault starting her off with your divorce talk."

"Oh, sure," said Lou. "Everything's my fault. Oh, sure."

"Well, if you wanted to get out, now's your chance," Miss Frye said hopefully. "At least everybody knows now you got a reason. Everybody's seen her tooting around town with that heel."

"Oh, sure, it's all simple as that," Lou said bitterly. "I can walk out and leave a wife that's going nuts, sure, that's easy. What kind of piker would that look like? How long do you think I would be in business when that little news got around?"

"Lots of women doing what she's doing," Miss Frye said. "They're not nuts, either."

Lou didn't answer. He wasn't going to tell about Mary taking her clothes off the minute he got in the house and imitating the Spinning Top hootch dancer, yelling out, "This is what you like, isn't it? This is why you always leave me. This is what you're crazy about, all right, give me time, I'll be the kind of woman you like. Why don't you kiss me? Make love to me, go on, show me how the other woman does, I'll learn—" Lou had backed out of the room, his blood congealing, he had run down the hall to get the baby's nurse. The nurse only looked at him with cold hostile eyes.

"Mrs. Donovan's perfectly all right. She drinks by herself now, that's all," said the nurse. "It's your fault, Mr. Donovan. I don't need to tell you that."

"Well, go look after her, anyway," Lou had ordered. "Call her aunt. Call a doctor."

"Mrs. Donovan doesn't need a doctor," the nurse said harshly. "I'll give her a sedative myself. A doctor can't do anything about a woman being so unhappy she don't know what she's doing."

Lou had quietly picked up his bag and driven back to town. No point in telling these things to Miss Frye. No point in even thinking about them. No point in remembering that cheap perfume smell, that lousy hair-oil—that sheik, that dime-a-dancer——

"I'll stay at the Stevens till things settle," he said to Miss Frye. "Stock up the cognac tomorrow. And don't say anything."

Jay Oliver stuck his head in the door.

"What—no dames?" he exclaimed. "I was told you'd ordered a fresh lot from the Spinning Top for six o'clock maneuvers."

"What are you doing in town?" Lou demanded. "You old son-of-a-gun, they told me you never gave us a tumble since you switched to the Eastern office."

It was fine seeing Jay again. You got so used to getting Jay out of hot water that you missed him more than anybody else when he wasn't around needing help.

Jay threw an arm over Lou's shoulder.

"I sneak in," he whispered in his ear, mysteriously. "I creep in in the middle of the night and creep out. But I heard the gang was coming in over here so I thought I'd drop around."

"Flo still raising Cain?" Lou asked.

Jay nodded sorrowfully.

"When I don't catch it from Flo I get it from Ebie," he confided. "I just choose which hell I want to take. I usually take Ebie's but I get Flo's long distance, then."

"Why don't you hang up?"

Jay looked grieved.

"Listen, can't I catch hell if I want to? Anyway, with Ebie I like it because then we make up. Make a note of that, will you, Miss Frye? You got to fight to make-up."

"Tell our friend here about Mrs. Oliver," Lou urged Miss Frye. "It's a panic."

"She calls up here all the time," Miss Frye obediently revealed. "She says 'You can just tell Lou Donovan I hope he's good and satisfied now that he's ruined a home.' "

"Can you beat it?" Lou exclaimed. "Can you beat that, no kidding? A woman spends a lifetime ruining her own home and then blames it on somebody else. Me. Old Lou Donovan."

"She blames everything on you, Mr. Donovan," Miss Frye giggled. "You're the boy that taught Mr. Oliver to drink, you forced his first drop down his throat, you're the one that made him gamble and chase skirts and be a bum."

"That's right," Lou admitted. "I remember the trouble I had teaching Jay to like women. We had to tie him, he was that wild, but by God, we drove the lesson home."

"I'll leave you to give him another lesson," said Miss Frye. "I'll leave the door open for those little tramps."

"Tessie and Marie and Bobby tramps?" Lou reproached her indignantly. "Hell, they all live with their mothers."

"Then I'll leave it wide open," said Miss Frye, "in case they bring the mothers."

After she went Jay pulled a chair up beside Lou.

"What burns Flo up is that she can't get me back to give me hell to my face," he explained. "That's all a wife wants a guy to come back for. Either that or she wants to remind him all the rest of his life of how she forgave him that time. Flo's got everything sewed up in her name and it makes her boil that Ebie doesn't give a whoop. It makes her sore that she can't say the other woman is after my money."

"She got me on the phone once," Lou said. "She says, 'If you happen to see that so-and-so husband of mine you can just tell him I'm suing for plenty alimony, and what's more I'm taking a trip to Hawaii after I leave Reno. You can just tell him I'm the one that's got the pocketbook, and don't he wish he could take that woman of his some place.' " I said, 'O.K., Flo, if I see him I'll tell him.' "

"That mother of hers!" Jay shook his head in gloomy recollection. " 'That's right, Florence,' she'd say to Flo, 'go ahead and make him give it to you. If you don't get it, Number Two will.' Not much left for Number Two when those two harpies get through with a fellow. Not that Flo hasn't got some good qualities."

"Doesn't Ebie get sore at all you got to pay out to Flo?"

"Ebie don't care about anything but having me around," Jay said complacently. "She says, 'Go ahead, give her everything, we'll get along. I can always go back to work. Give her all the alimony she wants. All I want is you.' That's the way Ebie feels."

Give her time, Lou thought, give her five, ten years and then ask her how she feels about Number One getting all the money, while Number Two has to do her own housework. Give her time.

"I hope marrying Ebie won't spoil things," Jay meditated, frowning. "I kinda hate to get hooked again. This way suits me, but you know women."

Maybe, Lou granted.

"Jesus, Lou, you're too damn smart, that's what makes me mad," Jay said. "You chase but you never get caught. I thought for a while you were letting the Kameray dame play you against Rosenbaum but I guess you didn't let yourself get in as deep there as I thought."

"That's how much you know," Lou commented silently.

"I used to see that little devil putting the screws on you, flashing Rosenbaum's bracelet around, asking your advice in that little phoney shy way she had about going back to her husband or marrying some band leader since she couldn't get any extension on her passport, and I'd think, well, look at old Lou squirming around in the old trap, old Wise Guy Donovan right on the old hook." Jay smiled at the idea of his own mistake. "I might have known you'd get out of that one if any man could. Stringing her along, letting her give you a little more line, and then getting away. Old son of a gun, I wish I had your technic."

Technic. That must be what it was to lie awake nights wondering how soon you could see her again, wondering how to keep from killing the men you knew she slept with, wondering how to give her more than Rosenbaum could give her, Rosenbaum who was so crazy about her he'd give her anything but marriage, but that was the thing she wanted most, and if Lou could only manage it– Now his back was to the wall. How much longer he could mark time with her he didn't know, the game had been getting sharper and sharper lately. Then just as he was giving in, this thing about Mary throws everything out. He couldn't tell that to Trina. Trina had had enough excuses. You couldn't blame Trina.

"I don't know whether it's brains or just fool luck that you never run into trouble," Jay sighed. "I sure envy you, though, old boy."

"I'll change spots with you any day you say," Lou offered.

There was the sound of voices in the adjoining office. It was no treat, in his present mood, for Lou to recognize old man Grahame coming in, and in a condition that his great friend Judge Harrod would not approve. The old boy was tacking in the wind like an old sailboat and a smile of vast good will illuminated his moon face. It was the first time he'd ever done Lou the honor of a social call, but it took more than that to cheer up Lou this day. Pritchard was with him and to add the last touch to a fine day who should be hanging on his arm but old Francie, all dressed up in white with a big straw hat that gave her more than she was entitled to in the way of looks.

"I brought my friend," Pritchard said. "This is Mrs. Thompson, Lou. Have you met?"

"Oh, sure," Lou said. Francie kept looking at him warily as if she thought he was going to bawl her out for coming along, but that was all right. She hadn't bothered him since the night at the Spinning Top months ago, and even though Mary had found out about the first marriage it wasn't Francie but Flo that had told her. You had to be fair, even if it didn't get you anywhere.

"How long do we wait for a drink in this joint?" Jay complained. He got behind the bar with Lou and they fixed up a round. Some more of the men came in and Lou was busy filling glasses. Keep busy, that was the trick, keep doing something, if it was only drinking, till the old brain quieted down. Noise was good, too, noise was wonderful, and there was so much noise in the place suddenly that Lou didn't hear Francie call him, just saw the hundred dollar bill she slid across the bar to him.

"That's the lucky hundred, Lou," she said. "It brought us luck. Frank never had such a run of luck. He's in Saratoga now, waiting for the track to open there. He told me to give you this and gee, Lou, he's so grateful."

"Ah, keep it, Francie," Lou said, but she shook her head and pushed it toward him. If it made her feel better, okay. Nothing could make him feel better, one way or the other.

"I understand you been doing a lot of running around, Francie," he said, in an undertone. "What's the idea? You got a good guy now, why don't you stick to him? You liked him well enough to marry him."

Francie's eyes filled.

"You're the only person for me, Lou," she whispered. "You know that's the only reason I'm running around. Just so damned miserable that's all, ever since you left. It's always you, Lou. I just happen to stay crazy about you."

It was too bad. You can't go around making a fellow feel like hell for not loving you any more. It isn't right. It isn't fair. When Lou didn't say anything Francie dashed a handkerchief across her eyes and turned abruptly to old Grahame who was hanging on to the bar to keep from tipping over like a leaded inkstand.

"Can a fellow get a little drinkie here?" Grahame asked with a little difficulty, then he rather adventurely let go of the bar and thrust his hand across it at Lou. "Great seeing you, old man. Shake hands. Always glad to see you, Donovan, my boy."

Now wasn't that a break for you!

"Thanks," said Lou, "but Cassidy's the name."

THE WICKED PAVILION

◆

". . . oh this wicked Pavilion! We were kept there till half-past one this morning waiting for the Prince, and it has kept me in bed with the head-ache till twelve to-day. . . ."

Mrs. Creevey to Mr. Creevey
from *The Creevey Papers*

Contents

Part One

. . . *entrance* . . .

• Shortly after two a sandy-haired gentleman in the middle years hurried into the Café Julien, sat down at Alexander's table as he always did, ordered coffee and cognac as he always did, asked for stationery as he always did, shook out a fountain pen and proceeded to write. Considering that this was the very same man who spent each morning staring, motionless, before a typewriter in a midtown hotel, it was surprising how swiftly his pen moved over the pages at the café table. At five, just as the first cocktail customers were arriving, he paid his check, pocketed his papers and went to the desk in the lobby.

"Keep this for me," he said to the clerk, handing over the manuscript.

"Okay, Mr. Orphen," said the clerk, and opened the safe to put it with Mr. Orphen's other papers.

The sandy-haired man went out, buttoning up his overcoat in the flurry of snow over Washington Square, hailed a taxi and drove back to the hotel room where he sat for a while staring at the empty page in the typewriter until he decided it was time to get drunk.

That was the day he had written on the Julien stationery:

There was nothing unusual about that New York winter of 1948 for the unusual was now the usual. Elderly ladies died of starvation in shabby hotels leaving boxes full of rags and hundred-dollar bills; bands of children robbed and raped through the city streets, lovers could find no beds, hamburgers were forty cents at lunch counters, truck drivers demanded double wages to properly educate their young in the starving high-class professions; aged spinsters, brides and mothers were shot by demented youths, frightened girls screamed for help in the night while police, in pairs for safety's sake, pinned tickets on parked automobiles. Citizens harassed by Internal Revenue hounds jumped out of windows for want of forty dollars, families on relief bought bigger televisions sets to match the new time-bought furniture. The Friendly Loan agent, the Smiling Banker, the Laughing Financial Aid lurked in dark alleys to terrorize the innocent; baby sitters received a dollar an hour with torture concessions; universities dynamited acres of historic mansions and playgrounds to build halls for teaching history and child psychology. Men of education were allowed to make enough at their jobs to defray the cost of going to an office; parents were able, by patriotic investment in the world's largest munitions plant, to send their sons to the fine college next door to it, though time and labor would have been saved by whizzing the sons direct from home to factory to have their heads blown off at once.

It was an old man's decade.

Geriatricians, endowed by the richest octogenarians, experimented on ways of prolonging the reign of the

Old and keeping the enemy, Youth, from coming into its own. Pediatricians were subsidized to strengthen, heighten and toughen the young for soldiering; the eighteenth-birthday banquets were already being planned, the festive maypoles of ticker tape set up, the drummers hired, the invitations with government seals sent out, the marching songs rehearsed. The venerable statesmen and bankers were generously taking time off from their golfing, yachting and money-changing for the bang-up affair that would clear the earth once again of these intruders on old-men pleasures and profits. Some who had triumphed too long were deviled by fear of a turn of fortune and besieged their psychoanalysts for the expensive reassurance that they were after all boss-men, superior to their victims and the ordinary rules. When the stifled conscience croaked of justice to come they scuttled feverishly to the Church and clutched their winnings behind the King's X of the sacred robes.

In the great libraries professors studied ways of doing away with books; politicians proclaimed reading and writing unnecessary and therefore illegal, for the action of written words on the human brain might induce thought, a subversive process certain to incite rebellion at robot leadership. All the knowledge required for the soldier generation could be pumped in by loudspeaker; eyes must be saved for target practice, hands preserved for bayonets. Why allow an enemy bomb to blast our accumulated culture when we can do it ourselves by government process?

In the city the elements themselves were money: air

was money, fire was money, water was money, the need of, the quest for, the greed for. Love was money. There was money or death.

But there were many who were bewildered by the moral mechanics of the age just as there are those who can never learn a game no matter how long they've been obliged to play it or how many times they've read the rules and paid the forfeits. If this is the way the world is turning around, they say, then by all means let it stop turning, let us get off the cosmic Ferris wheel into space. Allow us the boon of standing still till the vertigo passes, give us a respite to gather together the scraps of what was once *us*—the old longings for what? for whom? that gave us our wings and the chart for our tomorrows.

There must be some place along the route, a halfway house in time where the runners may pause and ask themselves why they run, what is the prize and is it the prize they really want? What became of Beauty, where went Love? There must be havens where they may be at least remembered.

The shadow that lay over the land was growing mightily and no one escaped it. As in countries ruled by the Gestapo or the guillotine one must only whisper truths, bribe or be bribed, ask no questions, give no answers, police or be policed, run in fear and silence ahead of the shadow.

. . . *a young man against the city* . . .

• At half past nine that February evening the Café Julien around the corner from Washington Square was almost deserted. Solitary gentlemen on the prowl strolled in expectantly, ready to crowd into any corner if the place was jammed, but horrified into quick retreat at sight of the empty tables. Three young teachers, briefed by *Cue* Magazine on how to have a typically French evening in New York, had cast a stricken glance into the bleak expanse of marble tables and mirror walls, then backed out.

"This can't be the place," one cried out. "It looks like a mausoleum."

The remark brought complacent smiles to the grim-faced old waiters, guarding their tables with folded arms like shepherds of old. The Julien waiters were forthright self-respecting individuals who felt their first duty was to protect the café from customers, their second to keep customers and employers in their proper places. The fact that only two of the marble-topped tables were occupied was a state of business perversely satisfactory to these waiters, who had the more leisure for meditation and the exchange of private insults. A young Jersey-looking couple peered curiously in the doorway looking for some spectacular rout that would explain the place's cosmopolitan reputation, then drew back puzzled at seeing only two patrons. Karl, the Alsatian with the piratical mustaches, turned down a chair at each of his three empty tables, indicating mythical reservations, folded his arms again and stared contentedly at the chipped cupids on the ceiling. The more excitable Guillaume, given to muttering personal comments behind his patrons' backs, flapped his napkin busily as if shooing out flies, and shouted after the innocent little couple, "Kitchen closed now, nothing to eat, kitchen closed."

The two solitary diners who remained at their tables after the dinner crowd had departed smiled with the smug pleasure of insiders at such a typical demonstration of the café's quixotic hospitality. The plump monkish little waiter, Philippe (said by many old-timers to resemble Dubois, the celebrated waiter of Mouquin's where the artist Pennell, you may recall, hung a plaque in his honor, "*A boire — Dubois*") turned from his peaceful contemplation of the old fencing studio across the way to twinkle merrily down at his favorite patron, Monsieur Prescott. He liked Monsieur Prescott first because he loved youth and beauty, seldom found in this rendezvous dedicated to testy old gourmets, miserly world travelers, battered bon vivants and escapees from behind the frank-and-apple-pie curtain. Philippe liked Monsieur Prescott above all because he had the grace to appear only every two or three years, while other customers were exasperatingly regular. Philippe felt young and refreshed just looking at Ricky Prescott, a young man built for the gridiron, wide of shoulder, strong white teeth flashing above square pugnacious jaw, long legs sprawling under the table, hard black eyes ever looking for and receiving friendship and approbation. Other Julien visitors were always asking Philippe who was this breezy young man, so obviously from the wide-open spaces, and what did he do.

"It is Monsieur Prescott, a very good friend of mine," Philippe always replied with dignity, as if this covered everything. Hundreds of people all over the world would have given the same answer, for Rick had the knack of getting on with all classes and all ages, ruling out all barriers, loving good people wherever he found them. Stray dogs followed him, office boys called him by his first name; cops, taxi drivers, bootblacks never forgot him, nor he them. He had been back in New York for several weeks and had been popping into the Julien almost everyday. Tonight he and Philippe had gone through their usual little game of ordering the dinner.

"What do I want tonight, Philippe?" Rick had asked.

"Blue points in *sauce mignonne*, *pommes soufflées*, squab *sous cloche*," Philippe had said, straight-faced.

"Fine, I'll have pork chops and Schaeffer's light," Rick had answered, and as always during this routine Philippe had demanded to know why a strapping fellow with the appetite of a bear and no taste for good food should ever leave those big steak-and-pie places on Broadway. Why did he choose to come to the Julien anyway?

"Why does anybody come here?" countered Ricky.

Philippe gave this question some judicious thought.

"They come because they have always come here," he said.

"Why did they come here the first time, then?"

"Nobody ever comes to the Julien for the first time," Philippe said, and as this was a thought that appealed to him hugely, his plump little body shook with noiseless chuckles. Recovering his gravity he leaned toward Ricky's ear and asked, "You tell me why you come here."

Rick frowned.

"I guess because something happened to me once here and

I keep thinking it might happen again, I don't know what, but — well I'm always expecting something I don't expect."

He grinned with a confidential wink that captivated Philippe, whose inner chuckles began all over, this time ending in a little toy squeak.

"Maybe you expect Miss Cars, hey?" he said slyly.

Miss "Cars" (and Philippe was tickled to see that the young man flushed at the name) was a young lady romantically identified with Monsieur Prescott, indeed the real reason for Prescott's devotion to the Julien as both of them well knew. It was on Prescott's first visit to the café that he had met Miss Cars, it was Miss Cars he sought in the café every time he returned to New York. It was here they quarreled and said good-bye for ever, it was here they made up after long separations, here they misunderstood each other again, and here Prescott once again was seeking the lost love.

"Oh, Miss Carsdale," Ricky said. "How is Miss Carsdale, Philippe?"

"I no see Miss Cars, like I told you," Philippe sighed. His feet were too tired after a lifetime of carrying trays to and from the distant kitchen to tramp out the final syllables of long words. He would have liked to be able to produce Monsieur Prescott's little lady or at least to give him advice on how to find her again. He had a vague recollection of some scene last time the two had been there and of Miss Cars running out of the café alone.

"Maybe Miss Cars think you not nice to her," he ventured vaguely.

The young man was righteously offended.

"Me not nice to her?" he repeated bitterly. "After all she got me into?"

He was about to recite his grievances to Philippe, decided they were too complicated, and allowed Philippe to waddle away for another beer while he sat brooding. It was undeniably Miss Cars who had made him reject the fine job in Calcutta after World War II for the simple reason that he was wild to get back to her. It was Miss Cars's fault he had got tangled up with three other women just because of her maddening virtue. Yes, there was no question but that Miss Cars, fragile and sweet as she was, had precipitated Rick Prescott from one mistake into another. It was her fault entirely, and this was how it had happened.

Seven years ago in the excitement of our-regiment-sails-at-dawn, Monsieur Prescott had made a heavy-handed attack on Miss Carsdale's virtue on the spittle-and-sawdust-strewn staircase of an old loft building on East Eighth Street where she rented a work studio for her photography. Whenever he remembered that night Rick cursed the mischievous jinx that had twisted the most magical day of his life into a sordid memory. It was the first time he'd ever been in New York, the city of his dreams, the first time he'd worn his officer's uniform, the first time he'd been drunk on champagne. New York loved him as it loved no other young man, and he embraced the city, impulsively discarding everything he had hitherto cherished of his Michigan boyhood loyalties. In Radio City Gardens he looked up at the colossal Prometheus commanding the city's very heart and thought, Me! He wandered up and down in a kind of smiling daze, slipped away from the buddies and home-town friends supervising his departure, and strolled happily down Fifth Avenue, finding all faces beautiful and wondrously kind, the lacy fragility of the city trees incomparably superior to his huge native forests. Under the giant diesel hum of street and harbor traffic he caught the sweet music of danger, the voices of deathless love and magic adventure.

My city, he had exulted, mine for these few hours at least, no matter what comes after. He wanted to embrace the Library lions, follow each softly smiling girl to the ends of the earth, bellow his joy from the top of the Empire State building. Wandering on foot or bus in a joyous daze he suddenly came at evening upon the treasure itself, a softly lit quiet park into which the avenue itself disappeared. Bewildered, breathless, as if he had come upon Lhasa, he walked around the little park, seeing couples strolling, arms about each other, windows of vine-covered houses lighting up, hearing church chimes, as if the city outside this was only a dream. The sign on the canopy of a corner mansion, CAFE JULIEN, told him he was in Greenwich Village and this café was the very place he was to meet his friends for dinner. And here they were waiting for him, not believing that he had stumbled there by chance, not even believing his day's adventure had been with a city and not a girl.

He kissed all the girls enthusiastically, regardless of the men in the party who were all spending the war comfortably in Washington or at 90 Church Street. He was handsomer and younger than they, and grateful for his departure they sang his praises while the girls found patriotic excuse to stroke his black hair or urge soft thighs against his. Rick loved them all, loved the café, loved even war since it had brought him here. With each fresh champagne he looked for the wonderful surprise, the special adventure that the city had surely promised him.

All around the café he could see little groups chattering happily, new arrivals being joyously welcomed, tables joining other tables, and though eyes strayed to the good-looking young soldier, Rick had a pang of knowing they were complete without him, they would be complete long after he had left on his unknown journey. Tomorrow night these very friends of his would celebrate without him; even Maidie Rennels, who felt she had home-town rights to him, was already planning a theatre party with someone else. The city he had fallen in love with would carry no mark from him, this café would not know he was gone. Impatient with these glimpses of future loneliness he suggested going to other spots, gayer and louder, where tomorrows could be drowned out in music.

"But we have to wait for Ellenora," Maidie Rennels kept explaining. "Don't you remember I wrote you all about Ellenora, the girl I met when I was studying at the League? She has a studio around the corner and we told her we'd be here."

"You mean Rick doesn't know Ellenora?" someone else asked, and shook her head pityingly.

You may have observed that whenever you enter a new group there is apt to be constant allusion to some fabulous character who is not present, someone whose opinions are quoted on all subjects, someone so witty or unique that you find yourself apologizing for not having met him or her. You may think you are having a perfectly good time, but how can you when this marvelous creature is not present? The name "Ellenora" was dangled before Rick until he began working up a foggy hostility to the absent one. Ellenora was everyone's darling, all painters wanted to capture her charm on canvas, and she herself, a child of artists, was wonderfully gifted, studying art on money she earned as a photographer. How exciting for her to be engaged to marry Bob Huron who had proper security to give an artist wife, and who adored her as she deserved. What a pity Ricky might never be privileged to meet her! Ricky began to feel that her absence was a subtle snub to him, and her being engaged to another man without even waiting to meet Richard Prescott was an insult. Then the sudden arrival of Ellenora in person changed everything.

"Darling — you did come after all — Look, here's Ellenora. See, Ricky, here's Ellenora, the girl we've been telling you about —"

"Just for a minute," Ellenora had said, as they pulled out a chair for her. "I'm on my way to the studio to pick up some proofs but I had to stop in to say hello."

Ricky's unreasoning prejudice wavered at first sight of her radiant little face. He had braced himself for a blasé beauty from a Hollywood picture of artists' life, a too clever poseur, full of arty talk and sophisticated repartee. This girl was nothing like that nor was she like any girl Rick had ever known. She had a delicate, quaint femininity that belonged to the past and seemed all the more striking in the New York setting. All in a moment the others seemed blowzy, their gaiety heavy-handed, their friendliness aggressive, their flattery obvious. He marveled that he had ever found hearty Maidie Rennels even mildly desirable. Ellenora had the teasing fascination of a light perfume, hovering in a room long after the unknown visitor has vanished.

She disarmed him by being no beauty, yet he couldn't keep his eyes away from the luminous pallor of her face, the delicate, humorously tilted nose, the tender, voluptuous coral mouth, the wide-apart eager hazel eyes with the soft babyish shadows beneath and the fine silky blond hair drawn sleekly up from the pretty ears, from which hung heavy topaz earrings. Whatever it was she wore — the tiny brown chiffon hat with its scarf falling over the shoulder of the cinnamon wool dress, the unexpected glimpses of bright emerald green silk somewhere in the lining of her brown cape — seemed special to Rick and made the other women appear drab. Whatever it was she said made the others seem stupid. They sounded shrill beside her soft breathless voice that seemed to quiver on the verge of either tears or laughter, just as the gentle comments she made seemed halfway dolorous and halfway comical but always miraculously right to him. At that time there was a special vocabulary college girls used as a precaution, it would seem, against communication. But Ellenora talked, as many articulate artists do, in terms of visual imagery and it was new to Rick. Even her long narrow hand fluttering to secure a stray lock of hair or to stamp out a cigarette in the ashtray bewitched him, hinting of the sweet helplessness of long-ago ladies.

He felt himself back again in his schooldays, a halfback when he wanted to be a bookworm, always too big for his age, clumsy and oafish, hands and feet all over the place. It angered him that she should have this effect on him, reducing him to the old boyish sense of inadequacy. He felt rebuffed when she took a seat on the other side of the table, and to show how little her presence affected him he found himself directing idiotic taunts at her, which she received with polite indifference. There was a lacy unreality about her that reminded him of the ailanthus branches or the Chrysler Tower he had admired. He suspected she must be amused by his too obvious subjugation, and he tried to restore his happy self-assurance by challenging every remark she made until the others cried out, "Rick, stop picking on Ellenora, she's such a darling!"

Any person experienced in love recognizes these outwardly hostile first encounters between a man and woman as the storm signal of immediate attraction, but fortunately for the two, the ordinary bystander reads only the exterior antagonism. Ellenora, only recently engaged to her nice young broker, was immediately conscious of the electric bond between her and this soldier and it frightened her that whatever this new feeling was — reckless, dizzy, ecstatic — she had never had it for Bob Huron, the man she was going to marry. Even when each of them spoke to someone else they were saying something wild and dangerous to each other. Ellenora tried to tell herself that it was the young man's situation, not the man himself, which was shaking her emotions as they had never been shaken before. He was going away to war, that was all. She hated the other men, her friends, for their safe jobs. She hated the tenderness with which the gods protect mediocrity while the rare irreplacable specimens must be tossed into danger. She wished it was Bob Huron who was saying good-bye and as soon as she found herself thinking this she knew she could never marry Bob, never, never, not even if she never saw this soldier again. These strange sensations and thoughts filled her with terror. She did not know what she was saying, when she spoke, except it must be something he willed her to say. She kept her eyes from him lest they fill with frightened, revealing tears, and it relieved her that he construed this as a snub. Let him think she disapproved of him rather than guess that her lips must be guarded to keep the word "Love!" from flying out to him. The more he mocked at her sobriety in contrast to the merry party the more shaken and foolishly bewitched she felt. Nothing like this had ever happened to her in her twenty years and surely this kind of sudden sickness must betray itself to everyone else if not to him. Bob Huron, she thought, appalled, how could I ever have thought of marrying him when I know there is this man somewhere in the world? She would have to leave, before whatever in the air swelled into an explosion.

"I have an early appointment tomorrow and have to leave," she said, rising. "You know I told you I had to pick up some work at my studio and couldn't come along. But I couldn't resist saying hello — "

"See what you've done, Rick," the Barnard girl exclaimed. "You've teased her so much she's going."

"I told you I had to leave early," Ellenora said almost sharply.

Rick's face looked suddenly desolate.

"I won't have it said I drove away a lady," he said and pushed back his own chair. "I'll walk her to her door to make up for it."

Going out the café door they had walked along in a tense silence that was like a fierce embrace. These things did happen, one did meet the one love, knew it at once, fought it, surrendered to it, stayed forever true.

"Where have you been all my life?" he finally asked and the question seemed brilliantly original to the bemused girl.

"Nowhere, I guess," she answered helplessly.

"What will you be doing until I get back?" he asked.

"Nothing," she murmured and they were hushed as if they had just exchanged solemn vows. They walked slowly along Eighth Street, hand in hand, and the silence seemed to fill in everything that Ellenora wanted said. She was beginning to wonder if she dared risk asking him up to the studio, for legally the students and artists were not allowed at night in these condemned old buildings except for emergencies. If they did manage to creep up there, if she could manage to build a fire in the fireplace — for really this was an emergency, once in a lifetime you might say —

"Here we are," she whispered at the entrance to the bleak loft building where she had her studio. At that instant, without warning, Rick made a wild predatory lunge toward her. When she pushed him away he backed into an ashcan that tipped over in the gutter with a tremendous clatter and suddenly the spell was broken and Rick was roaring with laughter.

"Please be quiet, Rick, or I'll lose my studio!" she cried.

The humiliation of his chasing her up the dirty staircase where any passer-by could see the clumsy struggle, her shame at her own sentimental expectations when all of their friends back at the café must have anticipated just such shenanigans made Ellenora give a heartbroken sob and a slap that sent him off balance tumbling down smack into the ashheap. She bolted the door behind her and stood there trembling, afraid to go on upstairs now and afraid to go out and back home to her apartment on Irving Place until he had gone. Everything that had seemed true between them now seemed a romantic schoolgirl distortion. He was just a soldier on leave, nothing more. She should have expected nothing more. He must have thought she was a complete fool. And she was, she was! She would never forgive him, but now she would never marry anyone else, never.

Prescott, for his part, was furiously disgusted with himself. The moment she had said "Here we are" he realized this was the end and he had swooped on her like some cave man, fully as astonished at himself as Ellenora had been. The ashcan episode restored him to his senses but then in his disappointment and embarrassment he had worked up a rage at the girl who had led him on to believe she had the understanding of angels. Didn't she realize that finding the city of his dreams and dream girl to match on the very night he plunged into nowhere was a miracle no man could handle? He was twenty-six, decent, already an officer, and if he was good enough to be killed for his country he deserved some help in his emotional crises even if he had acted like a lumberjack. More unfair still was the fact that he, a prize marksman and athletic champion, should be sent hurtling down ten dirty steps into a garbage pile, forced to spend his precious hours before sailing in a doctor's office having three stitches taken in his head, all caused by a feeble little tap from a small white hand.

So this was Love at First Sight. So this was what happened when you met the dream girl. Brooding over this with mounting indignation on the flight to England, Ricky had celebrated his first night there by gallantly getting engaged to a Liverpool barmaid, also disappointed in love, who had listened sympathetically to him and who did him the inestimable favor of eloping with a corporal before he had his first leave. Three years later the armistice brought him back to New York and since New York was Ellenora he was in a fever to find her again, past error forgotten. He was so sure she had not married, so sure his own mark was on her, that it did not even seem chance to find her in the little art shop near the Julien. Of course he would find her. Of course she had not married. Of course she would meet him whenever he asked. And of course everything would be the same as before.

They met every day at five at Philippe's table in the Café Julien — same place, same waiter, same table as their first meeting, for they must start all over from scratch they tacitly agreed. They laughed a great deal, spoke very warily of personal matters, maintaining the gay exterior intimacy possible only in café relationships, where a man is as rich as his credit and a lady is as glamorous as her hat. Ricky, reduced again to being overgrown boy with tiny dainty woman of the world, knowing too well the sudden wild impulses that carried him away, tried to maintain his masculine poise by cagily indicating that this relationship was only a delightful oasis in his otherwise full life. Ellenora, being all loving and as dangerously bemused by the young man as before, guarded her susceptibilities by behaving archly worldly and mysterious. The very violence of their attraction for each other put them fiercely on guard, as often happens to people who use up their resistance on one great desire and have none left for the mildest of future temptations. They skipped gracefully around the edge of love, retreated when it compelled them to look into its blinding face. Avoiding major issues they found minor ones turned major wherever they turned. How strange that they had both read *The Life of the Bee*, odd that they both knew Cummings' poetry by heart, rather uncanny that they preferred the bare charm of the Café Julien to uptown gayer spots. Prescott had a dim idea that Ellenora had come to New York to study art from somewhere in New England; Ellenora gathered that Prescott stemmed from Michigan, and that he had studied some kind of engineering.

They asked no questions of each other, barely mentioning other names or other places in their lives but finding each other out in a kind of breathless, intoxicating hide-and-seek. And the truth was that everything else faded away in the excitement of each other's presence. They would have forgotten to eat or drink if Philippe's affectionate supervision had not nudged them. Wary of allowing strong drink to betray his emotions as it had at their first meeting, Rick suggested vermouth cassis for the first week of their postwar cocktail meetings, and they parted discreetly at seven with great checking of wrist watches to imply other important claims. The second week, confident of their civilized control, they graduated to the pernod that was just coming back on the market, and though this heightened their pleasure in each other they still pretended that their daily meetings were accidental, a continuous lark maintained as a joke on the friends who thought they hated each other. A little more lax under pernod they did not look at the clock until the tables were filling with diners, tablecloths being whisked over marbletops. Then with little exclamations of alarm each must rush out to the hall to telephone explanations to importunate dinner companions waiting elsewhere. The third week they did not even try to part but stayed until the café closed and then Ellenora allowed him to take her to her door.

Ellenora's feminine pride made her take pains to indicate that though she enjoyed his company, her availability was purely accidental; she was by no means a girl to be forgotten for three years (war or no war) and then picked up at a moment's notice. She hoped he would never find out that the day after he had sailed she had broken her engagement to Bob Huron. She hoped he would not hear about the young doctor she had been on the verge of engaging herself to just at the moment Rick next came into her life, changing everything. She was afraid to risk seeing him alone in her studio, not for fear he would take advantage of her, but for fear this time she would surrender too easily. Rick was smart enough to make no demand, his own pride (as long as he could hold on to it) was in demonstrating that he never made the same mistake twice. The fourth week they discovered French Seventy-fives, a seasonal favorite concocted of brandy and champagne which made them laugh long and loud at their newfound wit, reach across the table for each other's hands over some delectable comment, find each other's eyes suddenly and stop laughing for a breathless moment. By this time Ellenora was recklessly putting all her eggs in one basket, refusing dates with nice fellows who adored her, and arranging for special permission from the landlord to live in her work studio since the apartment she shared with two other girls left no privacy for love. She intended to resist stalwartly of course, but she was desperately eager for the opportunity to show her strength.

One night they were in the café dawdling over French Seventy-fives, putting off the moment of parting, when some army pals of Rick joined them. Ellenora hoped they would go for she had decided this was to be the night, but Rick kept urging them to stay. Their drinks were two dollars apiece and the check was bound to be big enough to send an ordinary young couple on a week-end honeymoon (for Ellenora was ridiculously thinking on those lines), but what really stabbed her was hearing Rick, who had told her nothing of this, carelessly mention to his friends that he expected to take a job in Chicago next week. Stunned at the foolish dreams she had been building on this man for a second heartbreak, mortified at the thought of how close her surrender had been, Ellenora sipped her drink, smiling stiffly at the loud jokes about other girls in other places, Rick's record as a wolf, and how they might have known he would hide a creature as lovely as Ellenora in some out-of-the-way place like this where no one else could have a chance at her. It was then that Rick, a little disturbed perhaps by his friends' obvious interest in Ellenora, took it into his head to relate the story of their ashcan romance, embellishing it to his advantage, declaring that he had noticed this kid had had One Too Many and had gallantly offered to take her home from the restaurant.

"I was drinking Coca-cola that night," Ellenora had protested, but the men paid no attention and she realized that every one of the warriors would have told the same story in the same way so she couldn't really blame Ricky too much. But when it came to the payoff, the part where one little tap from her sent him sprawling, Ricky's version for the boys was that this poor sweet kid couldn't make it up the stairs and he had tried to carry her upstairs so her folks wouldn't be worried —

"My folks!" Ellenora had interrupted in indignation. "They weren't even living there!"

— then the girl, whose name, mind you, he had not even caught, took her purse trimmed in heavy gold and slugged him with it so he had to have eighteen stitches taken, all because these New York girls insisted on mistaking simple kindness as attacks on their honor. The loud laughter of the men, Rick's humorous admission of getting his only war wounds from a five-foot virgin infuriated Ellenora, fearful as she was that Rick might guess the thought of him was all that had kept her a virgin in his absence.

"At least he came out alive," she said, managing a sweet smile. "What Rick never knew was that I was trying to save him from getting killed by the man waiting for me upstairs."

With these words, which she noted had the effect of turning the laughter on Rick, she picked up her coat and said, "That reminds me, somebody might kill me right now if I don't get home. Good night, everybody. And incidentally, Ricky, I'm five-feet-five."

It was such a mean trick to humiliate him in front of his pals, implying that he wasn't getting anywhere with her and had been so naïve as to think her a virgin, that Rick did not even rise for her departure, merely saluting her with smiling fury.

"A second round for you, my dear," he said. "I assure you there won't be a third."

Having successfully ruined her own good name and future

happiness Ellenora marched out victorious, all ready to embark on months of weeping nightmares over her insane act. That was what happened when you held on to your normal impulses so rigidly, your whole being got deranged and trained for every other kind of self-destruction. They had ruined the reality with their foolish little game. Grimly flinging himself into a two-day binge Rick took one buddy's drunken challenge to fly to Texas next day. There he signed up with the fellow's oil company, and generously married his sister, a good-natured big girl who had tearfully confided men didn't like her because she had no mystery and didn't play little games. In another year she was no longer good-natured (having been praised for that alone too often) and he was a free man again, celebrating the annulment in New Orleans during Mardi gras, when the desire came over him for Ellenora. He was in his room at the St. Charles, drinking sloe gin with a lot of fine strangers in masquerade costumes, when his forgotten long-distance call came through, and when Ellenora heard all the babes giggling she hung up, thinking it was one more cruel joke. This time he didn't come to his senses till a month later in St. Croix with a girl he had taken along for a Mardi gras gag (after Ellenora's brush-off), and it took plenty of time and legal business, for this babe was no fool, to get rid of her and then, happily, a transfer to the New York office. He was still with the Glistro Oil Company, doing very well, though he knew and had in fact known for some time that the job bored him, and each unasked for promotion depressed him. His friends and family irritated him by their praise of his success with Glistro Oil as if this was a loftier career than they had ever dreamed of for him. In these moments of unreasonable dissatisfaction he longed for Ellenora, as if Ellenora and New York would resolve his future, Ellenora would somehow illuminate the wonderful road he was destined to follow. Until then he must mark time, venting his unrest in wild ruinous ways, and someday they could not be undone. Ellenora was his future, his dream, his harbor.

He still hated to admit her spell over him, and he put off surrendering to it, certain she would be around and available, and he could save his vanity by letting her make the first steps. Again he would make it a casual reunion, he thought, strolling into the old Julien café and running into her. Only this time it didn't happen.

At first in this 1948 winter he didn't even ask for her, just took to occasionally dropping into the café, then daily as his stubbornness got aroused. Finally he asked a question idly here and there, and at last he made a definite quest. From a walk down Eighth Street he saw that her old studio was torn down, from the janitor of her old apartment house on Irving Place he found that her two roommates had married without leaving their new names, from a telephone call to her old fiancé, Bob Huron, he received the chilly news that neither Mr. Huron nor his new wife had kept in touch with Miss Carsdale. From the corner florist he learned that flowers had been sent to her at some uptown address a year ago but he could not discover by whom. Nor was their mutual friend, Maidie Rennels, to be found at her apartment. By this time Rick was leaving messages, in case anyone met her, to call him at his office or leave word in care of the Café Julien. He moved from his hotel to a furnished apartment near the Julien, not admitting to himself that he proposed to trap her in there before she could get away next time.

"You're sure you haven't heard anything about her?" Rick asked Philippe, the waiter.

Philippe shook his head.

"Maybe she got consump," he ventured politely.

"Funny she should stop coming here," Prescott said.

"I no see Miss Cars for maybe two year," Philippe told him as he had several times before. "Maybe she come on my day off. Maybe she got married. Hah. Monsieur Prescott married, no?"

"No," Prescott said impatiently. "I got enough wives already."

"Maybe Miss Cars got husband and big family, too," Philippe suggested mischievously.

Prescott gave a short laugh. He was not worried about her being either dead or married because he simply would not have it so. He was not unfeeling in his conviction that she was in no trouble, he was merely showing his profound faith in Ellenora's powers over destiny. That little slap that had felled him had left an enduring respect for Ellenora's might. He could tease her with his anecdotes of other women, leave her, but she would always be the winner, and while this angered him it also continued to fascinate him. It bewildered him, too, that he could not settle down to the flirtations and pleasures of his New York life until he had got Ellenora pinned down. A fancier of beauty, wit and flamboyance in women, he could never understand why he had pegged Ellenora as his special property from the minute he laid eyes on her. He never could remember her features and sometimes thought perhaps she hadn't any—just a couple of smoky eyeholes in that sort of luminous Laurencin mask. She was taller than you thought and plumper than you thought; he had reason to know she was stronger than you thought. He had a couple of photographs of her but they didn't look anything like his inner picture of her. He knew he laughed most of the time he was with her but for the life of him he couldn't remember a single funny thing she ever said. He liked a sleek flawlessly tailored woman and it was strange he was so amused and delighted by Ellenora's penchant for feathers, ruffles, tinkling jewelry, softly swishing silks. They were so definitely and ridiculously ladylike in an age of crisp business girl ensembles. Like a peacock, he thought, silly and lovely; she walked like a bird, too, fluttering along the street helplessly and prettily as if her feet were made for perching on high branches and not for walking.

In distant places it disturbed him that he had so little to remember about Ellenora, for after all he knew little about her. She was homesickness, he knew that much, though God knows she represented nothing secure or known. It was New York he loved and he guessed Ellenora represented New York or his idea of New York the way the mind arbitrarily elects some unsuspecting cruise acquaintance to embody the hopes and glamorous expectations of a Caribbean trip. He would be in some deadly dull little southern town or on some desolate ranch and suddenly he would ache for Ellenora — not Ellenora as a body, mind you, but Ellenora complete with name band, Blue Angel, Eddie Condon's, El Morocco, Chinatown, Park Avenue cocktail party, hansom ride in the Park, theatrical lobby chatter between the acts, champagne buckets beside the table, keep-the-change, taxicab characters, and ha-ha-ha, ho-ho-ho, kiss-kiss, bang-bang, tomorrow same place. This was Ellenora, who, as a matter of actual fact, was not tied with any of these memories. He had never even danced with Ellenora and if he had been to any nightclub with her would certainly have been too polite to leave his drink sitting alone at the table while he whizzed Ellenora around the floor. Very likely the reason she represented this fictional and legendary Manhattan to him was that they had spent too many hours in one spot postponing going someplace else until what they had not seen together was more real than what they had.

The Ellenora who figured in his dreams knew everything about him, for he had long soul-satisfying conversations with her, telling her everything and being understood completely. She knew that he was meant to do something finer than just bury himself in business. He'd even told her — in these imaginary conferences — the dreadful way his mother had let him down, doting as she had been, too, on his twelfth birthday when she asked him what he intended to be when he grew up.

"A foreign correspondent," he had whispered almost choked up with the awe of putting it into words. It was the year he was reading Vincent Sheean and Walter Duranty, and besides he had been made sports editor of the school paper. His mother had burst into spontaneous, crushing laughter, and then explained to him fondly. "But Ricky, darling, nobody in our family is ever a journalist. We've never been the least bit clever that way. We're always lawyers."

"What about Grandpa Weaver?" he had shouted furiously, angry at her laughter after he had opened his heart so foolishly.

"He wasn't able to finish law so he went into business," his mother said. "And that's lucky for us, because now he can see you through law school."

"He doesn't need to," young Ricky had said, obstreperously, "I'll go in business myself since you think I couldn't do anything else."

But Ellenora knew he could have done anything, this Ellenora he always carried with him. Later whenever he found the real one it was a surprise to have her not know, for it was fixed in his mind that his thousand mental confessions had miraculously reached her and most of the time it really seemed as if they had. But what had gone wrong with the connection now? He had to find her. She *must* know that.

On this February eve Prescott had been drifting in and out of the Julien since five, sitting down for a while, then wandering up University Place to the stationer's, glancing over the magazines, exchanging track news with a messenger boy, getting his shoes shined across the street, anything to pass the time till he might enter the café again, all primed to see Ellenora seated at a table. He would act as if he didn't know her at first, he decided, one of the harmless jokes they used to have; pretending the other one had made a mistake, summoning Philippe, always in on the joke, to please remove this presumptuous stranger.

But Ellenora never came, and disturbed by this defection Rick drank fast. A person traveled, knocked around, liked to see new places and make new friends, certain that the harbor was always there safe and sure whenever the mood came to return. It was outrageous to find the shore line changing behind one, no lamps waiting in windows for the returned wayfarer. Let everyplace else in the world change but let Manhattan stay the way it was, his dream city, Rick insisted in his thoughts, the way it had been that first day, the day he met Ellenora, the way he pictured it in far places. He was not a man to admit things could be other than he wished, and now, he thought, let other lovers default as they would, if he sat tight and willed it the world would stop at the spot he insisted — *here, now,* with Ellenora smiling across the table.

He would give chance a little more time, he decided, and summoned Philippe.

"Save our — my table," he said. "I'll be back."

Outside once more for the restless stroll down the block, a peep into the Brevoort, a look into the Grosvenor, then back to the Julien stubbornly hopeful. She wasn't there, and he wavered between childish resentment that he couldn't *make* the wish come true (this was Ellenora's fault and if she walked in this minute he would not even look up, just to punish her) and the uneasy suspicion that he was making a fool of himself. He ought to shrug his shoulders and call up Maidie — there were dozens of girls, thousands! Still, now he was here, no reason why he shouldn't stay on and have dinner, and after that wait just a little longer. He knew this was only an excuse; he was chagrined to find himself still dawdling there hopefully at half past ten. For a full hour there had been nothing worth observing in the place except the patron at the opposite end of the room whose beard showed above his French newspaper. Earlier in the evening the relief telephone operator, a majestic blonde, had been emerging from her switchboard every half hour with the regularity of a cuckoo clock to stand at the café door and cluck "McGrew? McGrew? A call for Mr. McGrew." Each time Prescott was hopeful that one of his messages left in every possible place, from delicatessen shop to Art Students League, had reached Ellenora. But each time the lady's eyes rejected him, traveled thoroughly up and down the room again, not at all convinced by the bareness of the room. Each time she raised her hand to her eyes and peered at the red velvet curtains, the cuspidors, the cupid-strewn ceiling, as if clues were concealed there by mischievous colleagues. At ten-thirty she appeared again, but this time she stood in the doorway quietly scratching her blond chignon with a pencil and staring intently at Rick Prescott. Hopeful and happy he started to rise.

"A call for Prescott?" he asked.

"No," she said haughtily, "Mr. McGrew."

It was too much. Rick sent her a look of deep reproach followed by a burst of plain fury, as if the poor woman was personally responsible for telephones refusing to ring for him. Whoever McGrew was he hated him, too, for it seemed to him they all must have guessed the depth of his infatuation; they must have sensed that his desire was now so violent he would have begged Ellenora to marry and stay with him forever if only she would walk in the café door this instant. They thought he was making a fool of himself once again, and they all knew Ellenora was deliberately teasing him, trying to see to what lengths he would go to catch her again. How they would laugh when she came into the café with her fine New York boy friend and there would be the old Middle Western yokel waiting at the same old table with his silly heart on his sleeve!

All right, let them laugh! He would laugh, too. Fully as outraged as if Ellenora had publicly mocked at his honorable offer of love everlasting, Ricky leaped to his feet and followed the operator back to the switchboard.

"Is the same lady calling McGrew who called before?" he inquired.

The girl nodded, and he said briskly, "I'll take the call and tell her where she can find him."

A lady disappointed in not finding a McGrew might be in the same reckless mood as a man disappointed in an Ellenora. He was in Booth One speaking into the telephone before the operator could make up her mind whether this was permissible.

. . . *the man behind the beard* . . .

• It was a matter of supreme indifference to the tall Catalan waiter at the opposite end of the café that his lone customer, Dalzell Sloane, was making the decision of a lifetime. For the Catalan every hour of his life had held a problem of terrific moment, whether to punch a fellow worker, throw a plate at a customer, resign his job, present all of his possessions to a daughter momentarily the favorite, enter a monastery, return to Spain, go west, east, north; all problems ending in the decision to have another cup of coffee in the kitchen.

But Sloane, so it seemed to him now, had never had to make a decision before in his life. There were always two paths, and if you stood long enough at the crossroads, one of them proved impassable. There were always two women, but one of them wouldn't have you or one of them kidnaped you. There were two careers but at the crucial moment one of them dropped out, something happened, somebody made an appointment, and there you were. For Dalzell, destiny had shaped itself only through his hesitation. But though he had hesitated over this one problem, waiting for chance to decide, it would not solve itself. Something must be done, once and for all, and tonight. This necessity had produced in his head nothing more constructive than a kind of perpetual buzz that was like a telephone ringing in some neighbor's apartment. He tried to draw counsel by detaching himself from his body, watching the bearded stranger in the mirrors across and beyond, assuring himself that such a calm, distinguished-looking citizen could have no real worry. He knew the beard made him look older than his fifty years, but at least it made him look successful, and after half a century one has the right to at least the appearance of success. If someone were to ask, "What have you done with your fifty years, Dalzell Sloane?" he could answer, "I have failed in love and in art, but I have raised a beard." The beard had given him credit and character references, for people assumed in a vague way that a man with a beard had traveled everywhere, knew all about art and science, had influential friends and doting ladies tucked away all over the world, and was securely solvent. Dalzell had only to look at himself in the mirror to be almost convinced this was all true. "Thank you, beard," he saluted it silently, marking that the gray was beginning to dominate the brown as it did in his thick hair, though his brows were still as dark as his eyes.

The beard, like everything else in his life, owed itself to no decision of his, but had grown of its own accord during a long illness, and all that had been demanded of him was to select a cut from the page of style offered by a Parisian barber. Later his fellow painters, Marius and Ben, took turns cutting it during their merry parties, shouting hilariously all the while. Old Marius and Ben, Dalzell thought, the three of them always together then, and now Marius dead, Ben lost for years.

A group of diners emerging from the large dining room beyond the café paused to stare in the door, pleased to discover a bearded bohemian philosophizing over his glass, even though it was not absinthe, and he wore no smock or beret. Dalzell looked steadily into his glass, trained to tourist curiosity. He had noticed them earlier in the evening when they came in, the pouting, red-mouthed, bare-shouldered young girl in blue taffeta with the white camellias in her blue-black hair, the tipsy, pink-faced fiancé, the two busty, gray matrons in their mighty silver fox capes, the large, purple-faced, responsible men of affairs. Thirty years ago he would have noted it as an effective idea for a canvas. Family Outing, Engagement Dinner. Now he had learned to reject such inspirations on the spot as he rejected any flare of desire, thus protecting himself against the certain failure. Family parties such as this were familiar to the big dining room, usually chosen by the host as a place where the appetite was king, undisturbed by music, glamour or youthful pleasures. The young were inevitably bewildered and disappointed as they discovered that the excited clamor of happy voices did not mean gaiety and dancing but sheer middle-aged joy over bouillabaisse, venison, or *cassoulet Toulousaine* with its own wedded wine. Dalzell was sympathetically amused at the youthful impatience with stomachic ecstasy, and it amused him, too, that the naughty word "café" made responsible men herd their families into the respectable safety of the dining room. Where did they get the money to feed Julien dinners so casually to five mouths? Thirty dollars at the least, more than he spent for food in six weeks, Dalzell thought.

There were people, and Dalzell was one of them, who were born café people, claustrophobes unable to endure a definite place or plan. The café was a sort of union station where they might loiter, missing trains and boats as they liked, postponing the final decision to go anyplace or do anything until there was no longer need for decision. One came here because one couldn't decide where to dine, whom to telephone, what to do. At least one had not yet committed oneself to one parlor or one group for the evening; the door of freedom was still open. One might be lonely, frustrated or heartbroken, but at least one wasn't sewed up. Someone barely known might come into the café bringing marvelous strangers from Rome, London, Hollywood, anyplace at all, and one joined forces, went places after the café closed that one had never heard of before and never would again, talked strange talk, perhaps kissed strange lips to be forgotten next day. Here was haven for those who craved privacy in the midst of sociability, for those whose hearts sank with fear as the door of a charming home (their own or anyone's) closed them in with a known intimate little group; here might be the chance companion for the lonely one who shuddered at the fixed engagement, ever dodging the little red book as a trap for the unwary. Here, in this café, were blessed doors strategically placed so that flight was always possible at first glimpse of an undesired friend or foe's approach. Here was procrastinator's paradise, the spot for homehaters to hang their hats, here was the stationary cruise ship into which the hunted family man might leap without passport or visa. Here in the Julien it was possible to maintain heavenly anonymity if one chose, here was the spot where nothing beyond good behavior was expected of one, here was safety from the final decision, but since the doors closed at midnight sharply, a bare two hours from now, Dalzell began wondering from where his solution would come. At this very moment in the dining room there might be someone he had known and forgotten years ago, now risen to great consequence in the world, and this person would pause at the café entrance to cry out, "Dalzell Sloane, as I live and breathe, the very person I'm looking for!" Or a theatre party, dropping in at the last minute for a nightcap, would carry him off to someone's apartment for midnight music, and one 'clock would pass, two o'clock, three o'clock — he would have missed the train, not the first time his future had been determined by negatives. But then what about tomorow? Ah well, even if nothing else would be accomplished, at least he would have closed a door.

Dalzell had been sipping *mazagran*, for the strong coffee with the twist of lemon served in a goblet for twenty-five cents seemed less odiously economical than the same brew in a cup, but now he remembered that the last time he had been at the Julien with Ben and Marius they had drunk *amer picon citron*, and just as Marius had insisted, it had had a curiously magical effect on him, alcosomatic perhaps. It seemed to seep delicately through his bones, detaching his mind from his body, transforming him into a cool, wise observer of himself. Since he wished to observe instead of to be, he recklessly decided to spend eighty cents on a glass of the magic potion. He would step outside himself, perhaps change into Marius watching from the other world. Almost with the first sip his mood changed into a Marius-like desire for genial companionship. He was lonely. He'd been lonely for months, years. He regretted that he had been systematically avoiding people for so long, afraid they might guess his circumstances, or that he might be foolish enough to confide in someone. He had taken the back corner in the café to hide from possible discovery, but now that he was changing into the boisterous Marius he wanted to be found. He didn't want just anybody — the gray little half-people resigned to failure and poverty who had been creeping through his life all too long, demanding nothing, giving nothing. He wanted the bright beautiful wonderful ones, the stars in his dark sky whose fleeting presence raised him to their firmament. He thought of Andy Callingham, photographed only last week on arriving at the Ambassador. "Dalzell, you old son-of-a-gun, I'll join you in fifteen minutes," he pictured Andy as saying over the telephone, but that was nonsense. Andy would never go anyplace where there were no columnists, no gaping admirers, no publicity for his last novel. He wouldn't even pick up the phone except for Zanuck or a Rockefeller. Dennis Orphen, then, but this would be what Dennis called his "drunk time" and he'd bring all of his convivial cronies. Dalzell began berating himself for his folly in keeping up with his valuable friendships only when he was in the chips and didn't need such support, then scuttling down to Skid Row at the first drop in fortune, cowering under cover guiltily as if bad luck was a crime or contagion that must isolate one from all humanity. If the bad luck stayed on, as it usually did with him, you cut off all bridges back to civilized living and the chance of revival.

How long had it been, Dalzell pondered, was it months or years, that he had kept his door locked to his old friends as if Despair was a lady of the streets hiding in his room? A familiar voice on the telephone, a glimpse of an old friend on the street, was like a dun; the simple words "Let's get together" filled him with panic, as if "hello" committed him to horrifying expenditures — twenty cents worth of cigarettes, a beer, a cup of coffee — all these were obligations he could not face. After his emergence from his underground hiding — and how could he explain what had brought about his release? — the habit of friendship was hard to regain. The connection could not be won back with a simple phone call, the loving path was now overgrown with thistles and angry brush. Forget the solace of the old, then. Dalzell decided whatever was to save him must come from the new and unpredictable.

With a vague idea of tempting the unknown, Dalzell rose and strolled out into the little lobby that was now as deserted as the café. He observed the café's other customer emerging from the first phone booth. The other stood for a moment at the café door hitching his belt around his middle with the nonchalant pride of a big guy who knows how to keep in trim, knows what he wants, goes after it, gets it. There was something familiar-looking about him, and it struck Dalzell that he might be a film actor choosing this spot to get away from fans. Yes, he looked like that star Monty Douglass, and Dalzell was warmed by his grin, envisaging a quick friendship over a nightcap, an impulsive putting of cards on the table, a miraculous solution to everything. Childish dreaming, Dalzell scolded himself, and he went on his way down the stairs to the men's room.

He was slightly bewildered to find there a tall bushy-browed beagle-nosed man, coatless in a fancy mauve shirt and scarlet suspenders, his pinstriped gray jacket dangling from the doorknob, solemnly flexing his right arm with a regular rhythm before the mirror.

"Feel those muscles," commanded this gentleman, without taking his eye from the mirror, apparently not at all perturbed by an audience.

"Like iron," said Dalzell obediently.

"Of course they're like iron, because I keep them that way. Golf. Tennis. Sixty years old. I just put my arm through the door. Take a look at the other side. Right through. Wanted to see if I could still do it."

"You must be a professional athlete," Dalzell said, properly awed by the jagged hole in the door.

"Think so?" beamed the man. "Believe it or not, I'm in the advertising business."

"No!"

"I'm telling you. Here's my card, Hastings Hardy of Hardy, Long, and Love. I just don't let myself get soft, that's all."

It was the name of a leading advertising firm, one that had saved the lives of many a struggling artist by its sweet temptations. Dalzell himself in a low moment had offered to be corrupted there, but with no success. Maybe this was the time and this the opportunity, if only he knew how to make it work.

"Another thing, I eat right," said the tall man, patting his stomach. "The best food and not too much of it, three times a day, or don't you agree?"

"I do, indeed," said Dalzell.

"By best foods I do not mean health foods, understand," said Mr. Hardy, looking at him sternly. "Do you think I could have busted that door with my fist on a diet of health foods? I've always had the best food and liquor, and as a result how old would you say I am, sir?"

"Forty-four," Dalzell said, and was rewarded by a handclasp of deepest affection.

"Sixty next month," said Mr. Hardy, pleased to see Dalzell's expression of suitable astonishment. He took his coat from the door knob. With considerable care he managed to get the right arms into the right sleeves. After a complacent glance in the mirror again he looked at Dalzell.

"You look to me like a mighty intelligent fellow," he said. "I like a man who *looks* intelligent. What do you do?"

The beard again, Dalzell thought.

"My name's Dalzell Sloane. I paint."

This seemed to strike Mr. Hardy with tremendous force for he took a step back to stare at Dalzell.

"An artist? What do you know? As a matter of fact I'm talking to somebody right now about having my portrait done."

He seized Dalzell's hands and shook it vigorously, and then Dalzell saw that his eyes were brightly glazed like gray marbles staring straight past him.

"Look here, what do you say to joining my wife and me for a brandy when you come back up? We're with my daughter and her fiancé's family and we're arguing about the portrait right now. I'm going to tell them you're the man to do it. Sloane, eh? Frankly Sloane, I like you. I'd like to regard you as a friend. And what's the use of old friends if you can't do 'em a favor? We'd just about decided on some little chap I forget, oh yes, Whitfield. He did the president of Bailey Stodder, our biggest client. Did vice-president of General Flexmetals, too, hangs right there in the bastard's private office. Whitfield, that's this artist's name. Know him?"

The artists who make the most money from the bourgeoisie are usually never even heard of in the art world, and this name was unknown to Dalzell.

"I suppose he's good on tweed," Dalzell said, tentatively.

"The best in the field," declared Hardy. "On the Bailey Stodder job you can almost spot the tailor's name, it's that good. But why shouldn't I have a man of my own, why should I have to have Stodder's fellow? Come on back and join us and we'll talk it over. By George, I like to make my own decisions."

"That's mighty nice of you," Dalzell said, and again they shook hands. "I'll settle up first in the café and then join you in the dining room."

This was it, then, Dalzell thought with a deep breath, this was the crazy chance that was going to settle everything. After all these years Fate had decided to make him a portrait painter. Okay, Fate, this time he'd take whatever came. He washed his hands, turned back his frayed cuffs, flicked tentatively at his suit and decided he'd look better covered in topcoat, and then he followed his new friend back upstairs. The clerk was back at the desk in the lobby and the telephone girl was at the switchboard. Dalzell looked at the clock. Eleven. He tried not to let his hopes rise too insanely.

In the café he settled his bill, six eighty-five, as much as he had spent all last week. In his wallet there was still the eighty dollars he had reserved for his ticket from his — well, call it stolen profits—and it struck him that under the circumstances Alex deserved a larger tip so he drew out a dollar bill and left it in place of the seventy-five cents, but habit was so strong he could not leave the cigarette pack even if there was only one smoke left in it. Matches, too, went in pocket. He put on his loose brown topcoat, its shabbiness forgiven, he thought, by its English cut and the wide white scarf around his neck. He strolled through the center hall back into the dining room, surprised to find that in spite of all his experience hope was rising once again. The conviction that this-is-it was so strong that already he could visualize the rich portrait of Hastings Hardy, the belligerent marble blue eyes, the grasshopper jaws about to clench the biggest steak *Chateaubriand* or the biggest contract, the three-hundred-dollar suit, the twenty-dollar necktie (flight of ducks, black, *à la* Frank Benson in formation on a blue and white ground), the thirty-dollar fountain pen in hand signing the million-dollar contract nattily unscrolled to look like the Magna Carta—Oh no, not that way, Dalzell caught himself hastily, and altered the picture in an instant to a stern but wise executive, the mandibles parted in a paternal smile, the eyes and forehead Jovelike.

Hastings Hardy Hastings Hardy, he repeated to himself like a charm as he looked over the dining room, searching the small inside banquet room, then with mounting apprehension, the inner alcoves.

Every table was deserted.

He realized how firmly he had fastened on this last fantastic hope, because it took so long for his mind to admit that there were only waiters left in the darkened room.

"Mr. Hardy's party?" he asked incredulously of the waiter who was busily pushing a wagon of dishes toward the kitchen.

"But the dining room has closed," replied the waiter, as the last lights dimmed on the ceiling. "Everyone has left, as you can see."

Dalzell stood for a minute, a kind of panic coming over him. If Fate was sending him perfect strangers to play jokes on him at this late hour, then he would be compelled to make some move for his own preservation. He would go back to the café and summon enough assurance to invite the other lone customer for a final drink. In the café he looked all around but the other table was deserted.

"Has Monty Douglass left?" he asked Philippe who was going through the unmistakable signs of clearing up the table for the next customer.

"My gentleman?" countered Philippe. "That's not Mr. Douglass."

Now there was no one who might rescue him, and his fear returned. It might mean that at twelve o'clock, the very minute the last chair was piled on the last table, Dalzell Sloane must take a train to a lonely far western village perhaps for ever, perhaps to die and drop like a dried apple into the family graveyard, or — and the dread of making a choice brought a dizzy seasickness over him — go back to the lie that would eventually devour him.

Quite pale, Dalzell sat down abruptly at Karl's table by the door. There was something ominous, he thought, in the mockery of last-minute hopes being raised only to be dashed. The furies indeed must be after him. He raised his hand to signal Karl for another drink but Karl, his arms folded majestically over his little chest, was staring fixedly at a poster advertising the skiing pleasures of the Bavarian Alps which hung above his table, and he made no move to ask the patron's pleasure. He was, in fact, asleep, in the manner he had perfected after forty years of avoiding the customer's eye. He was startled into attention by a sudden shout of laughter and blast of cold air from the outer hall as a clutch of ladies and men in dinner clothes plunged in, the valiant survivors of some party who must make a merry night of it now that they were in Greenwich Village.

"Dalzell Sloane, as I live!" boomed a male voice that could belong, as Dalzell knew, to no one but Okie, the indefatigable, omnipresent, indestructible publisher, refugee from half a dozen bankruptcies, perennial Extra Man at the best dinners, relentless raconteur, and known far and wide as The Bore That Walks Like a Man. "I've been trying to get hold of you for months."

Wonderful Okie, Dalzell thought joyously, dear, deadly, boring Okie, the friend in need! Fantastic that the day should ever have come when the sight of old Okie would make his heart swell with fond affection. And the beaming lady with him was none other than Cynthia Earle, Cynthia with new short ash-blond curls clustering around her narrow once brunette head, which swiveled, snakewise, in a nest of glittering jewelry. As her arms reached out eagerly to embrace him the thought leapt between them that he still owed her six hundred dollars.

"Darling!" she cried, flinging her arms about him. "We've come to this place dozens of times hoping we'd find you. Where on earth have you been all these years?"

"I've telephoned," said Dalzell evasively.

Her friends were busily drawing up chairs, tossing their

wraps on neighboring tables, pushing Dalzell back into his seat against the wall until he felt himself plunged straight through the mirror, saved only by Cynthia's purposeful grasp on his arm.

"We've just escaped from a funny little dinner and I brought everybody here for a nightcap, only I haven't any money," Cynthia burbled on. "Do tell the waiter I want to cash a check. Waiter!"

But Karl was rudely obstinate about cashing Cynthia's check. He insisted that the Julien would cash checks only when sponsored by a trustworthy customer such as Monsieur Sloane. Cynthia's face reddened at this insult to her credit, and she looked on incredulously as Dalzell, equally appalled and embarrassed, wrote his utterly worthless name on the back of her check. It was such a typically Julien incident, so endearingly French-foxy, that he would have burst out laughing if he had dared. Cynthia, worth millions, whose mere name gave her credit any other place, must have her check certified by a man who owed not only her but the Julien itself for years past, and who could not even afford a bank account! He saw Cynthia looking at him half mockingly, her lips curled tightly to keep back some taunting query. She must be thinking he had had a great windfall and had been neglecting her, as other favorites had, because of brighter opportunities. He was on the verge of setting her right but if he said he was no better off than ever, then she would be on guard against impositions. People like Cynthia enjoyed observing the ups and downs of artists' lives but they became bored and irritated when it was all *downs*. One could not blame them. Dalzell himself was bored by the monotony and shame of always needing fifty dollars, forever needing fifty dollars, fifty dollars to go, fifty dollars to stay, fifty dollars to pay back some other fifty dollars. Cynthia's eyes were covering him sharply after Karl's rebuff to her and he fancied she recognized the topcoat as the one he'd worn in London fifteen years ago. The sudden withdrawal of her radiant emanations told him — how well he knew the signals! — that she regretted mentioning "checkbook," cautiously anticipated a request from him, and a minimum sum had already lit up in the cash register of her mind. You didn't have to be a mind reader to know the reasoning of the rich.

No, he couldn't endure it, Dalzell thought angrily. Better be considered ungrateful, forgetting true old friends in his heartless climbing, rather than be found beaten, tired and afraid. Let them think he dined regularly on Julien squab and Moselle with only the richest and noblest. To confirm their suspicions he smiled vaguely across the room at new groups of visitors crowding into the café.

"How are things going, old man?" Okie asked, throwing an arm around Cynthia's slim shoulder as if to protect her from contagious poverty.

"Very well indeed, judging by his credit here at Julien's," Cynthia said dryly.

"When you never hear from a fellow, you can figure he's in the chips, ha ha," Okie told her.

"I did have rather a run of luck in Brazil," Dalzell said.

He had always found it saved pride, on emerging from retreat forced by poverty, to claim in London great success in Hollywood, in New York to boast of Continental favor, and in Paris or Rome to ascribe his disappearance to ethnological pioneering in unknown isles. Better to have people jealous and skeptical than pitying or scornful.

"I thought you looked disgustingly cocky," Cynthia answered. "No wonder your real friends never hear from you."

There, he congratulated himself bitterly, he had delivered himself into their hands. They could blame him now for chronic ingratitude but not for chronic poverty.

"Wouldn't you know it?" Cynthia exclaimed petulantly. "I never see them when they're having their success. Okie, you are so right. About them."

Them, of course, meant the artists she had "subsidized" in the past, the subsidy consisting, as Dalzell well knew, of never more than a hundred dollars a month for a year or two, which gave her a fine philanthropic reputation, dictator rights and the privileges of the artist's bed and time. He himself had been a bargain, having been young and naïve enough to think he was really in love with her and that she really admired his talent. Later, of course, he and Ben had laughed over the printed interviews in which Cynthia had modestly excused her largesse to artists: "I don't want to spoil them, really. I just think a little security doesn't hurt real genius."

Security! As if even Cynthia herself had ever had it! She kept her iron fingers on his arm possessively, and he recalled an old trick of hers of fondling one man publicly while planning to sleep with someone else. He wondered which one of these others was her present lover and was surprised to discover he was still capable of a twinge of jealousy.

"You might at least have answered my letters!" she reproachfully hissed in his ear.

What would he have said in answer to that last letter of

hers six years ago? *I am not pretending that I need the money, Dalzell, but if you are in the chips now, as someone who saw you in Paris was telling me, why not return at least part of the loan so I can pass it on to some young artist who really needs it?*

"Order up, everybody," Okie roared genially. "Cynthia Earle's money is no good here, but Dalzell Sloane's is, ho ho."

"Allow me," Dalzell said calmly and motioned to the waiter.

Now he was in for it. He was into his ticket money already just because he couldn't stand Okie's needling. It was going to be Okie, then, who decided his future and he resented this intrusion even though it was all his own fault. He could see that Okie was showing off his intimacy with Cynthia, reveling in his new eminence as right-hand man to rich lady, a role that allowed him to regard the rest of mankind as beggars, borrowers, swindlers, pennypinchers and imposters.

Okie had become important through the passage of years merely by never changing, loyally preserving every trait, however disagreeable, of his youth, adjusting them to his spreading figure and whitening hair until he exuded the mellow dignity of an ivy-covered outhouse. For years he had been a last minute telephone call, an emergency escort, for Cynthia in bleak periods between her lovers and marriages, until finally these caesurae in Cynthia's life totted up to more than the big moments and here was Okie at long last Cynthia's Man — not lover, scarcely friend, but reliable old Stand-In, glorified by garlands of snubs from the best people and bearing his scars from Cynthia's whip as saber cuts from royal duels.

His bulging frog eyes were beamed at Dalzell and then at

Cynthia with the permanent anxiety for her approval. Do we insult him or is he going to insult me? Do we like this person or should we put him in his place? Do Cynthia and he gang up against me? Dare I count on Cynthia to gang up with me against him or may I have the delicious relief of ganging up with him just for a moment against dear Cynthia? Who moves first? Do I jump on his lap or at his throat? The throat is always the most fun, but what if the mistress's whim was the opposite?

Dalzell was sensing Okie's problem when Cynthia's lips tickled his ear once more.

"Talk to Severgny," she whispered urgently. "He's been trying to find you for weeks."

A dealer looking for him? Dalzell's heart beat faster.

"We talked about you all evening," Cynthia said mysteriously. "Wait, I'll tell you about him, while they're yakking about the drinks."

The sudden influx of last minute customers created a din outside the din at his own table and Cynthia was obliged to shout introductions. No one heard or paid any heed to the names and all Dalzell could hear was the loud buzz of Cynthia's voice in his ear sometimes punctuated and sometimes obscured by a wild squeal from one of the ladies or a bellow from Okie. It was easier to study them in the looking glass in tableaux whose titles were zealously furnished by Cynthia.

It was the looking-glass world, at that, he thought dazedly, and it must be that he was the rabbit.

"Severgny is the new proprietor of the Menton Studio, getting a terrific reputation in moderns and everyone thinks he's French but of course he's just Swiss," Cynthia buzzed in Dalzell's ear, "and he would never have been anything but an interior decorator except for the war, and he spent that in Hollywood painting monster murals over those monster beds, but it's all paid off as you know. The woman beside him talking about this café's Old World charm — " she nodded toward a gaunt spinster in bony but dauntless décolletage — "is Iona Hollis, steel mills and Picassos, you know, and that egghead is Larry Whitfield, the portrait painter — Laidlaw Whitfield, that is — "

"Indeed," murmured Dalzell. The tweed specialist himself, no less.

" — and the little cotton-haired dried-up doll is Mrs. Whitfield. He had to marry her in order to meet the right people, of course, but the joke was the Social Register dropped her right afterward." A sudden lull in which Mrs. Whitfield bent toward her made Cynthia continue shamelessly, "As I was saying, there we were at this strange little dinner tonight."

"I've barely met Jerry Dulaine and I can't imagine why she asked me to dinner," Iona Hollis' deep voice sounded, "or why I went."

"Come now, we went because we wanted to meet Collier McGrew," Okie said benignly. "It was a damn fine dinner even if he didn't show up, but Elsie Hookley drove us out, that's all."

"I was positive that any party a girl like Jerry Dulaine would give would be really wild, in a chic way of course," Cynthia complained. "But it was as stuffy and correct as one of Mother's own dinners. I wouldn't want her to know I said so but she must be disgustingly respectable at heart."

"Do you suppose she or Elsie had something up their

sleeve?" Miss Hollis pondered. "Why should anybody throw a party like that for nothing?"

"I'm sure there was some reason we were asked and some reason McGrew backed out," Cynthia said. "He's no fool. I'm sure we were about to be tapped to back a play or a little magazine or adopt some refugees. I noticed Elsie's brother wasn't there, whatever that meant. Anyway it was worth coming down for just to run into Dalzell here at the old Julien."

"I've been most anxious to see you." Severgny leaned across the table toward Dalzell and Dalzell's heart missed a beat. A Fifth Avenue dealer anxious to meet him? More people arrived with more introductions and Cynthia's documentary going on and on in his ear, but Dalzell was thinking only about Severgny, waiting for the moment to resume conversation with him, wondering if this was the chance he had known was coming to him. Feverishly he tried to think of plausible excuses for being without a dealer at present. He could do himself no good by confessing he'd broken with the Kreuber Gallery because Kreuber insisted on charging him storage rates for holding his canvases, so dim was his faith in them. In his mind he began sorting out pictures suitable for his first one-man show in fifteen years. There would be the terrible cost of framing, at the outset. . . .

Cynthia's elbow dug into his ribs.

"Severgny is asking you a question," she said.

Dalzell made the effort of jumping back through the looking glass and directing himself toward the trim little mustached gentleman leaning across the table towards him.

"Could I count on having some of your time very soon,

Mr. Sloane?" Severgny repeated, and before Dalzell could answer he went on, "I understand you and Ben Forrester knew more about Marius than anyone else."

Marius? Dalzell came down to earth.

"Severgny's working on a big memorial show for Marius," Cynthia explained. "It's to be the same month Okie's definitive biography of Marius comes out."

"We need your help in tracking down certain canvases we know existed," Severgny pursued while Dalzell arranged a smile to conceal his stricken hopes. "Did he leave a large body of work in Rome, for instance, or where would you say he left most of his paintings?"

"Ask Household Finance," Dalzell replied grimly. "Ask the Morris Plan. Ask the warehouses and landladies all over the world who sold it as junk to pay storage rent, or else took it along with his furniture and clothes to auction off when he couldn't pay."

"Not literally!" Okie laughed. "He's joking, of course, Severgny. Dalzell, surely you have an idea of where his stuff is. You have some yourself, I know. If Marius had only been like Whitfield here, who keeps a record of every scrap of work he ever did!" Okie exclaimed.

"Can you imagine anybody ever caring?" Cynthia whispered in Dalzell's ear maliciously, though she might have shouted without giving offense, for two new young men were crowding around the table exchanging shrill introductions, more chairs were being drawn up until Dalzell, squeezed against the mirror, was dizzy with claustrophobia. Severgny was trying to tell him something and Okie was obliged to relay the words.

"Severgny got hold of Ben Forrester," Okie said. "He reached him through a San Francisco dealer, and he's promised to help us with the Marius show."

Dalzell's first thought was of the burst of new hopes that must have flared in Ben's breast at the urgent summons from any dealer, and the double disappointment on finding the call was not for Forrester, the artist, but for Forrester, bosom friend of Marius! How well he knew that hurt flash of jealousy on learning that Marius had been the one to win the Grand Immortal Prize of death which opened the gates closed in life to all of them! Marius is my dear friend, Ben must have said just as Dalzell had, and he is a fine painter, but what has he got that I haven't got except a coffin? The feeling had lasted with Dalzell for days after the first funeral fanfare in the papers, a perfectly ridiculous resentment at Marius for "selling out," quite as if he had started toadying to patrons and critics, dropping his old friends merely for the publicity and success of death. Then reason had set in, and as the definitive articles and kiting of Marius prices grew, the affair became a wonderful joke, something Marius himself would have loved. Ben must have gone through all these stages, too, thought Dalzell, for in the old days Ben had more intermittent bouts with success than any of them. If they could only meet, check the comedy step by step, wipe out all the bitterness with wild laughter! If Ben were really in New York —

"Remember when Marius would have been glad to take a thousand dollars for everything he had in the studio?" Okie was shouting. "Yet that little oil we saw tonight in Miss Dulaine's — just a boy's head looking up at clouds — would bring five thousand. Remember? The brown eyes, torn blue shirt, the clothesline — "

Did he remember? Dalzell gulped down his drink.

"Marius had his different periods, too," Okie was pontificating, waving a cigar at Severgny, "but as I point out in my book, they were not right-about changes, they were logical transitions and all consistent with his marvelous gusto and what I refer to as his greed for beauty, that is to say beauty complete — to be *completely* drunk, *completely* mad, and that reminds me I want you to give me a few of those wonderful anecdotes about him, those bawdy — ha ha ha — Rabelaisian, ha ha, sayings of his we all used to love."

In his ears Dalzell could hear again Marius mockingly mimicking Okie, *My sense of humor is as good as the next one but I find nothing funny in bawdiness for the sake of bawdiness, after all, Marius, one is a gentleman first and a clown last and I must ask you to leave my room if you will not be a gentleman.*

"My theory on Marius' final use of white — " said Okie, and suddenly Dalzell felt that he must get out of here, he must find Ben and laugh before the joke became too ugly for laughter. What did these people know of old Marius? The mere circumstance of Okie knowing a woman rich enough to back a magazine for him made him a mighty critic of all the arts with trespasser rights to all of them. The fact that Severgny knew how to bargain (it might have been real estate or canned beans for all he cared except that he liked the social advantages of more elevated wares) gave him the right to encourage or discourage Titian himself. Cynthia Earle's ability to buy a porkchop for an artist or writer when they were hungry endowed her with the most exquisite perceptivity and the right to judge their work. Marius was dead and these were the people who had killed him, these were the demons who had destroyed him as they were destroying himself, too, Dalzell thought. These were the embalmers, the coffin salesmen, the cemetery landlords who carved up the artist. There was some consolation, though, that had Marius's success come during his lifetime he would have had to play the idiot success game with these buzzards. He would have been obliged to listen to Okie's asinine pronouncements on technique, he would have had to defer to Severgny and to Cynthia; the stench of success would have risen higher than that of his moldering carcass. Still, let's face it, he would have had the satisfaction of knowing he was good, his talent would not have been corroded and crippled with doubt.

Or would success have corroded and crippled, too, as some said it did? It was a risk he himself was willing to take, Dalzell reflected. If his integrity, morals and whole spirit were to be corrupted, why then let it be by Success for a change.

"Think about it and make memoranda of canvases you remember and where he did them," Severgny said. "Ben Forrester is doing the same thing."

"Funny Ben hasn't looked you up yet, now he's here," Okie remarked. "Such old pals." Ben here? A quick apprehension struck Dalzell.

"I'm not surprised he didn't look me up," Cynthia said plaintively. "I know artists better than you do, Okie, and they never look anybody up unless they need them. And when you need *them* you can never find them, because they're always hiding out someplace from creditors or wives or something. And lies! Once I gave a marvelous party for Dalzell and Marius when they were going to Spain, and then they told me the wrong ship so I couldn't find them to see them off!"

Dalzell suppressed a faint grin, remembering that the name of the ship had been that of a Staten Island ferry and their Pyrenees had been the hills around Tottenville. It was one of their jokes that whenever the going was too tough they could discover havens within subway or ferry fare from Manhattan. Rooming houses in the Bronx, abandoned beach cottages, river barges, the wastelands of Queens — how often they had announced some proud foreign destination and then merely disappeared in a subway kiosk until luck turned!

"Ben didn't give us his address," Okie said. "I sort of gathered there was a lady friend. All I know is he took the Queens subway at Fifty-Ninth."

"I'll bet Dalzell knows perfectly well where Ben is," Cynthia said. "They always covered for each other. You do know, don't you, Dalzell?"

Why then, perhaps I do, Dalzell thought with a sudden glimmer of light. Perhaps . . . Before Cynthia could tease him further a new couple entered the café and there were screams of recognition, more introductions, more chairs pulled up at Cynthia's insistent invitation. Guillaume crossly insisted the place would close in ten minutes, but even with this repeated warning, the same three young teachers were in again, pushing past him purposefully, convinced that the mounting uproar indicated something exciting was surely about to happen.

"We'll all go up to Cynthia's," Okie shouted. "Dalzell, you'll come."

"Later," Dalzell said.

In fifteen minutes his train would leave, but for him it had already left. Through his mind raced a series of pictures, the closing gate to the Sunflower Special in the Station, the certain desolation in his heart as the train sped westward to that old attic bedroom looking out over the peaceful prairie, the burned church with the ruined cemetery (the painting that had won him the prize money to leave home) and his sister's face smiling a tired welcome to the prodigal, home at last in final defeat. Dalzell shivered. In the confusion of last minute noise he rose and slipped out to the hall.

The porter was talking excitedly to the clerk at the desk. "I tell you, someone has broken the door downstairs! Ah, Monsieur Sloane, you were downstairs, yes, did you see what had happened?"

"No," said Dalzell, and went out the door. He had to move fast before his courage failed him, but whether it was the *amer picons*, the idea of having escaped Cynthia and Okie, the thought that soon the train would be moving westward without him, liberating him, as it were, for whatever might happen, or whether it was the thought of having at last made a decision, feverish elation possessed him. It carried him along East Eighth to the B.M.T. station where he had to compose himself for a moment, trying to bring back that long ago — had it been ten or twenty years? — address. Uptown, under the river in the subway, or over the Queensboro bridge on the bus, the last stop, then the local bus — no by George, he'd take a taxicab to — where? Keane, wasn't it, but what number?

"Something about the Battle of Hastings," he remembered, and then laughed aloud triumphantly. "Ten Sixty-Six Keane Place."

Unexpectedly for this hour and this neighborhood a taxi's lights came toward him from downtown, and taking it as a sign Dalzell hailed it. At least a three-dollar tariff but magic was brewing—that is, if the driver happened to be in the mood to transport anyone to another borough.

He was. He happened to live in Queens and was on his way home.

It was his lucky night, just as Dalzell had known it would be. He would have thought so even if he had known that Mr. Hastings Hardy at that moment was back in the Julien looking for him.

. . . *ladies of the town* . . .

• In the living room of a charming made-over brownstone house four blocks north of the Café Julien and one block west of Fifth Avenue there sat this very evening two ladies in the most festive of evening dresses in the most profound of melancholies. The scattering of half-filled coffee cups and liqueur glasses about the little tables, the atmosphere of mingled perfumes and cigar smoke, the grouping of the chairs hinted of recently departed dinner guests; the gloomy faces of the ladies, the earliness of the hour—it was not yet eleven—and the visible signs of elaborate expectations indicated all too clearly that the party had not "come off." The dresses and even the living room had the look of stage properties about to be packed off to the warehouse now that the play had failed.

Whatever had gone wrong, the fault had certainly not been with the *mise en scène*, though the eyes of the hostess had traveled anxiously over every inch of the room, looking for some guilty flaw. The wallpaper was the correct silvery-patterned green; the crystal-beaded lamps glittered with suitable discretion; the shining striped satin of the sofa and chairs, the unworn blond rugs, the cautious blend of antique and modern furniture all murmured of "taste" or that decorator's strait-jacketing of personal revelations that is accepted as taste. Through an arched door could be seen a dining room, china cabinet, chandeliers and all, a daring gesture toward formal tradition for such a small apartment, and a soft coral light on the opposite side of the entry hall led not to the wings but really and truly to a white and gold little gem of a bedroom.

"When you think of how long it took us to cook up this party," mused Elsie Hookley bitterly, "then to have us right back where we started in just three hours! Look at the place! You wouldn't know anybody'd been here, even!"

"Did you expect them to wreck the place?" inquired the other tartly.

Of the two ladies you might have surmised that the older, ferocious-looking one was chaperon, singing teacher or stage mother for the other, but then Miss Dulaine looked far too glossily self-sufficient to need such protection, and Elsie Hookley (she had dropped the "Baroness" along with the Baron Humfert himself) was the merest babe in the wood, as she admiringly confessed, before the younger woman's knowledge of the world. Consider them as bosom friends by necessity in spite of the twenty years difference in their ages, bound together by a common foe and at the moment by defeat. They had known each other hardly two years, they had nothing in common but a profound distaste for women friends and a passion for private life, but friendship had spread under them like an invisible net waiting for the certain catch. Both had moved from more fashionable sections of New York into the Washington Square quarter at the same time, with identical motives for marshaling their resources while unobtrusively retrenching. Being the only solitary ladies in the Twelfth Street house they spent months fending off possible neighborly advances from the other. Finding themselves on the same bus they carefully hid behind their newspapers, bumping their carts into each other in the A. & P. Supermarket with identical cocktail crackers, club soda and red caviar, they looked carefully past each other; hands touching at the Sixth Avenue newsstand as they reached for the same columnist's newspaper they did not exchange a single smile.

Months of this wary circling finally persuaded them that they had nothing to fear from each other, and extravagantly relieved, they backed into a minuet of neighborliness, courting the casual encounters and excuses for the very conversational exchange they had formerly spent so much time in avoiding. Elsie looked for her neighbor's name or picture in gossip columns; Jerry was impressed by society page references to Elsie's family. Without being aware of it they fell into a companionship that on the surface made no demands or encroachments but consisted of confidences over nightcaps when they arrived home at the same hour, intimate revelations one makes to someone safely in another world or in another country. They felt completely safe with each other; neither could conceive of the possible intrusion of the other in her own sphere. They could tell about their own sins or those of their dearest friends with all the pleasure of spilling the beans and without the attendant fear of just reprisals. Never going to the same places they exchanged little worlds like party favors whenever they met, cheered and amazed that their offerings were so highly prized, their discarded and discounted currency so valuable. Each was fascinated by the vice the other wished most to hide; in Elsie it was her respectability; in Jerry it was her lawlessness. They had never known anyone like each other, but in their blind progress towards opposite goals they had reached a simultaneous stalemate, and the temporary collision seemed a rare union of minds. Whatever it was they wanted in life, they were confident it was not the same thing; they would never be rivals, but between them they might play a winning hand.

Like shipboard acquaintances they confided freely everything about themselves except what they did last night or were going to do tomorrow. Elsie talked about Boston, to Jerry's great delight, for Elsie was an escaped Bostonian, in perpetual and futile flight from everything that city represented, as obsessed with it as any excommunicated Catholic with the Vatican. She derided her brother Wharton for being a proper Bostonian, horrified by the democratic waywardness of his sister, and she chose to fancy herself voluntary renegade instead of involuntary exile.

"Boston is supposed to be the center of culture, but there's no place on earth where money is so much worshiped. Talk about Chicago or the oil cities! Good God!" Elsie was wont to rant. "In Boston a family is supposed to be distinguished if some scalawag ancestor socked away enough loot to keep the next five generations in feeble-minded homes and keep their lawyers in yachts. Nobody's ever read a book in Boston, they just have libraries. Nobody likes paintings, they just buy them. They go for concerts in a big way because all real Bostonians are deaf as posts so music doesn't give them any pain. I tell you in Boston the word "ignorance" just means no money in the family. That's the way my brother Wharton thinks. Boston! Ugh! I'm ashamed to admit the twenty-five years I spent there trying to conform. But give me credit for pulling out finally, even if I had to marry a European crook to do it."

Elsie could not understand that the more elegantly eccentric she made her family out to be the more delighted Jerry became. The running stock of tidbits about family quarrels, scandals, lawsuits, feuds and hidden passions opened a curious world to Jerry and she followed it, fitting pieces together as she might have a jigsaw puzzle. It seemed that after Elsie's marital debacle brother Wharton felt it was her duty to stay with Mother in the great house on Marlborough Street, but Elsie absolutely refused, so Wharton and his family had to live there and of course simply ROBBED dotty old Mama. Finally Mama, with her last shred of intelligence, had put the house up for sale and went to live in happy senility at the Hotel Vendome with an ancient dependent. Brother and sister continued to accuse each other of filial neglect but Elsie didn't feel a bit guilty because Mama had never forgiven her for the scandal about the Baron. And Mama and Wharton had been so gaga about him at first, so dumbfounded that it should be Elsie the barbarian who had brought the Almanach de Gotha into the family and vice versa. And even after the Baron von Humfert had gotten into that swindling jam and had to be bought out, brother Wharton still enjoyed baronessing his sister in public until Elsie, just for pure spite, had dropped the title.

"Of course the man was a crook," she quoted Wharton as fuming, "but the title left us a little dignity. But oh no, Elsie won't leave us even that little shred of pride!"

Elsie swore that wild horses would not drag her into her brother's stuffy clutches now that he had taken up residence in New York on Gracie Square. But after a few months when it became apparent that the Wharton Hookleys were in no way importuning her to be one of them, Elsie began to worry. Perhaps she had been too blunt. She heard everywhere of their social activities, so evidently they did not need her introductions. A furtive familiar that she usually took to be her conscience reminded her that blood was thicker than water, a brother was a brother and then there were the children, her nieces. God forbid that she should ever be the snob her brother was, but the fact was those girls soon to enter society needed the experience and guidance of an aunt who was a woman of the world. Nita, their mother, was nothing but a child herself.

So Elsie had nobly decided to make the overtures and sacrifice herself. She called and magnanimously offered herself as chaperon for the older girl who had just come out.

"I would be perfectly willing to take Isabella shopping or driving," she reported to Jerry she had told Wharton. "I have lived in New York for years and therefore know everyone and would see that Isabella got to know them too. I could arrange little parties for her — take her to the right galleries, the right plays, the proper restaurants, in a word prepare her for a successful marriage."

And what do you think Wharton, the stinker, had said?

"My dear Elsie," he had said, and in repeating her brother's incredible words Elsie gave him a quavering sort of village idiot voice just as in quoting herself she used an ineffably dulcet, benevolent whinny, "what in the world would it do to my daughter's future to be seen about with your sort of friends? I'm sure they're the most interesting people in the world to you but what would it do to little Isabella's reputation?"

Those were her brother's very words.

This absolutely killed Jerry, though Elsie thought the story merited indignation rather than laughter. On second thoughts she decided it made her feel better to be amused by Wharton rather than insulted so she joined heartily in the laughter.

"But believe me, my dear," Elsie sighed, "these are the moments I just wish I'd kept the Baron."

She said this as if the Baron was a wool hat she'd given away not knowing a blizzard was coming.

From Elsie Jerry got the general impression that the best Bostonians rattled their family skeletons at each other as proudly as Texans flashed their jumbo diamonds. She concluded that Elsie's whimsicalities were a proof that the Hookleys were gloriously rich.

But if Jerry was spellbound by Elsie's Boston legends, Elsie was even more entranced by her peep into Jerry's world — a world without trust funds, no windfalls from forgotten relatives, no estates to be settled, no wills to fight, no salary, no family, yet a world illuminated with vague opulence. How on earth did a girl without a boat, so to speak, sail triumphantly through life, knowing the best people and the best places? It couldn't be that Jerry was merely a shrewd manager for she was always tipping grocery boys in dollar bills for bringing up a quart of milk, or handing out five dollars to a taxi driver and saying to keep the change. When Elsie rebuked her for this folly Jerry shrugged.

"I just remember what a thrill it was when some uncle gave me a buck when I was a kid," she explained. "And then I figure that anybody in a three-thousand-dollar mink coat hasn't got any right to be waiting around for eighty-five cents change from a cabby."

No, Jerry was certainly not the shrewd type. Of course a good-looking girl with a figure for clothes and a model's opportunities (for that's how Jerry had started) could always assemble a fine wardrobe on credit or gravy, and have unlimited dates, but how had Jerry managed to collect so many important men as close friends? Gossip columnists never seemed able to link her name in shady romances, her escorts varied from Cabinet members to industrialists, bankers, yachtsmen, and for bohemian relief older editors of *Fortune*, *Life* or play angels. How could a girl without family or social sponsors acquire such a circle? Elsie could not rest until Jerry would consent to clear up this mystery. It took Jerry a little time to figure it out herself.

"I guess I learned a lot watching the other girls make mistakes," she finally confessed, rather enjoying the luxury of being candid about herself. "I'd see how some of the girls scared men, big men, I mean. I knew big shots want to have fun the same as anybody but they're awfully skittish. They're afraid of their jobs and publicity and their wives and their children, and of being used. If a new girl flatters a man too much he's afraid she's going to move in. If she finagles a couple of drinks out of him he's scared she's going to stick him for a sable coat. You've got to calm him down right away like you would a nervous virgin. He feels easier if he finds out right away that you know bigger shots than he is and could introduce him to them, or tell him about them. You ask his advice about business. You show him you're not on the make, you're just trying to make friends with him because you admire him. Maybe you surprise him by buying him a tie or a book. Look, he says, here's somebody doing something for me at last, instead of me having to do something for her. After that he relaxes with you — and he can't do that with many people, see."

From a sharp little lawyer Elsie sometimes consulted and whose work gave him the opportunity to observe Jerry Dulaine's rise, Elsie heard another angle.

"Jerry's antecedents and background are so hopelessly low grade she's never had anything to lose," he explained. "Nothing surprises her, nothing awes her, and never having made any particular class in society she's at home in all of them. Like genuine royalty, you might say — or the oldest peasantry."

Elsie congratulated herself on providing herself with such juicy nourishment for she had devoured most of her old friends, her enthusiasms were thinning out, and she had reached a time of life when the zest for adventure properly takes itself out in belaboring a daughter-in-law, ruining a grandchild or defending a worthless son. Having been denied these natural channels for her robust energy she had satisfied herself in years past by feeding on younger people who had talent, or a capacity for unique mischief. She liked to be in the midst of uproar without leaving her rocking chair, and for her chosen ones she was always ready with a shoulder to cry upon even though it was often she who had to make them cry. Certain disappointments in the last few years had made her more cautious but had not lessened her appetite, and after her preliminary reserve she plunged into Jerry's private career with the single-minded gusto of a folio collector. It delighted Elsie that there should be individuals like Jerry, wild cards, you might say, being anything the dealer named, anything that was needed for winning.

It was the first time she had encountered one of these girls so inexplicably in the city spotlight, girls everybody seems to know or ought to know, whose names invariably euphonious or amusing, ring a very faint bell, and rather than admit ignorance the businessman assumes she is a débutante, the débutante guesses she is an actress, the actor deduces she must be rich, all credit her with distinction in some field of which they are ignorant. With no letters of introduction she builds a kind of social security for herself simply on the importance and dignity of her escorts. Here was democracy, Elsie thought, a joke on the bourgeoisie, particularly a joke on her brother, who for all his position and influence, could not know half the great names in Jerry's date book. She chuckled to think of the elaborate hocus-pocus he would have to go through to get suitable matches for his daughters when little

Jerry Dulaine, runaway girl from a Kansas small town, could know anyone she wanted. It was a pleasure, at those times when Wharton used the outrageous excuse of having some very important visitor, too important to risk meeting his sister, for Elsie to mention that she had just met that very gentleman on her doorstep escorting her dearest friend home from the races. Wharton could not disguise his helpless irritation that a sister he liked to reproach as surrounding herself with cheap wastrels and Bowery bums should have contacts he himself had made with difficulty.

"He's always knocked his brains out for something you take right in your stride," Elsie chortled privately to Jerry.

It was just as well that Elsie was completely in the dark as to how her young friend had gotten her start "taking everything in her stride," miraculously keeping her name above water at the same time. Jerry herself could not disentangle that first introduction from the chain of subsequent introductions that had been her staircase. The fact was, her success, such as it was, stemmed from an error made fifteen years ago.

This was what had happened, only a few months after Jerry had landed in New York.

A young couple of some social distinction, pondering their financial woes in the bar of a midtown hotel, remembered that an elderly uncle, high in government affairs and rich in oil, usually kept a suite at this hotel. Brave with double Manhattans and last hopes of fortunes, they rushed up to his suite to surprise him, which they did indeed, for they found him entertaining a personable young woman, two gay goblets on the coffee table, a serious-looking bucket of champagne on the floor. In the ensuing embarrassment the young couple hastily stated that their visit was for the purpose of inviting Uncle George to Oyster Bay for the week end with some marvelous people, and of course they would be delighted if Miss Dulaine would come too. Miss Dulaine went, and since her appearance and deportment were perfectly acceptable, the girl wearing the proper clothes, saying the proper things, playing tennis and swimming well, she interested influential men who issued invitations to places where she met higher figures who moved her further along, and no one ever discovered that Uncle had picked her up in the lobby of his hotel a bare thirty minutes before his nephew's call. Even if they had discovered this, it would have been too late to matter, for Jerry was already being mentioned in gossip columns on the fringes of both glamour and fashion.

A likable, good-looking young woman without affectations, on speaking terms with the leading names, can always get along in New York, and Jerry got along. She was blessed with that easy confidence that all men are men and everybody's only human that often induces the world to behave as if this was true. She had quit high school in her Kansas home to come to New York on her father's railroad pass (he was a fireman on the Southern Pacific Railroad), met another girl in the Grand Central Station ladies' room who got her a job in a wholesale garment house where she modeled. Tessie also took her to her rooming house on West Fifty-Fifth, invited her on a couple of double dates with a press agent boy friend and a photographer, and Jerry was started. She made enough money, had a good time, and was happy enough for a few months.

But the social popularity she began enjoying after her successful début in the Biltmore lobby made the demands of her job seem increasingly oppressive. Staying up all night in the best nightclubs with the easiest spenders, who themselves need not get up next day till dark, made Jerry's own alarm clock seem a cruel dictator. She had quickly picked up the standards and patter of the garment trade, could appraise within a dollar every rag on every back, see through fur and leather to the designer's label, nose out makeshifts and imitations until her tastes and needs were elevated hopelessly beyond her ability to satisfy them. Her modeling job, well paid as it first had seemed, became merely a means of meeting spenders, and the truth was that as a model Jerry was not as pretty as others at that time (that radiant sheen of youth came to her much later) and she was much too grateful. Older men liked to take her out, because a more conspicuous beauty would have caused gossip. Jerry looked like just a nice girl. She had the clean healthy look of a Western niece or the suburban bride of some junior associate. Her friend Tessie and other play girls in her shop and hotel called on her when the party required another girl who could be trusted not to encroach on their special game. Wives did not bristle jealously at her presence, or if they did they were reassured when some respectable older citizen spoke to her. Older men were flattered that she seemed to prefer them to younger, hotter blood, and Jerry really did. Younger men demanded too much, drank too much, cost too much, and got you nowhere, as Jerry had seen by watching her friend Tessie's occasional lapses into love. A floater herself, and from a family of floaters, Jerry reacted to a man of fifty or more, of established reputation in business or public life, securely solvent, the way most women react to a fine masculine physique. She cut out pictures of such men of affairs from *Time* and *Newsweek*, pinned them on her mirror, and if opportunity came to acquire a personally autographed photograph she framed it in silver for her dresser.

But the camera lens was cruel to sleepy eyes and her modeling jobs dwindled as more and more men depended on her ready assent to last minute calls, "Come on over to the Stork and help me get rid of a branch manager, Jerry, atta girl." What had first seemed her chief asset turned out to be her misfortune: looking like a nice girl who would never accept diamonds or foreign cars, these were seldom offered. Even the ordinary negotiable loot of a popular girl got less and less. Open-handed men of substance, half tempted to settle a good sum on her, looked into her clear, honest blue eyes and switched to vague offers of marriage (with a big home and ready-made family out in Nebraska) or else proposed a regular job with fine opportunities for a girl with personality. Her girl friend, Tessie, who had launched her so kindly, was no longer her friend for Tessie had counted on some gratifying male skepticism at her loyal claims for Jerry's beauty, brains and wit. It was a betrayal of confidence, Tessie indignantly felt, that her men friends were taken in by her praise and soon went so far as to prefer Jerry to her prettier self. Jerry had naïvely thought her sponsor would be proud to see her accepted, but to her surprise she soon saw Tessie's eyes fixed on her with unmistakable hostility, lip curled in accusing scorn; and presently Jerry realized that Tessie's fondness had been based on her unflattering faith that Jerry was merely a good foil, and could never make out without Tessie. There were bitter words. No, Jerry discovered, you could not depend on girl friends in this little world, not after you moved up into their class. Just remember not to grieve over them, but save your tears for that ominous twilight when their flattering jealousy turns to kindness.

The girls separated, Tessie to marry a natty-looking promoter named Walton simply to stop him making passes at Jerry, who honestly detested him and had not wanted to offend Tessie by rebuffing him. They knew too much about each other to dare be enemies outright but each felt, when they divided their joint possessions, that she had been robbed. They spoke to each other only when they chanced to meet head on, once or twice a year. Catching a glimpse of each other in a crowd they made a swift estimate of the other's appearance, saw that muskrat had replaced mink or vice versa, wondered a little, and ducked out of sight.

Jerry who had moved to the Pierre slid back to Lexington Avenue hotels. She took to leaving the receiver off the hook mornings to block early assignments for work. The simple truth was that with her increasingly extravagant tastes she really could not afford to work. A miserable hundred or so a week (taxes and social security deducted), did not pay the upkeep of a job like hers. As for settling for the safety of marriage, that seemed the final defeat, synonymous in Jerry's mind with asking for the last rites. Then suddenly — all in a day, it seemed — men friends were looking at the girl next to her instead of at her, and were saying, "Who was that attractive girl in your party at the Café Julien the other night?" or "What a little beauty over there at the corner table!" Not daring to analyze these warning signals Jerry was only conscious of a growing desperation, hidden and solitary, a desperation never to be faced openly but nevertheless lurking for her in mirrors and in men's eyes. She found herself hiding iodine and sleeping pills from herself, avoiding edges of penthouse roofs, afraid.

It was Uncle Sam, the one with the red, white and blue pants, who eventually cornered Jerry. One of the pleasanter tasks he had assigned his internal revenue men was a secret investigation of the patrons of expensive restaurants, shops and entertainments. The larger spenders were, of course, able to come to a gentleman's agreement, or else were lavishly protected by distinguished lawyers or politicians, so the industrious officers must make up their records with names of minor lone unfortunates whose clothes, companions, residences and checks were out of all proportion to their avowed incomes. Jerry Dulaine was one of these, and like a sporting fish showed such guilt, terror and impudence as to guarantee her constant persecution with fines, threats, warrants, superfines for not paying fines. In particular there was a cadaverous Mr. Prince in the Empire State head offices who had made Miss Dulaine's tax deficiencies a gruesome case for the government far more evil than the million-dollar lapses of mighty corporations. Nothing less than a small fortune was needed to appease these bloodhounds, and Jerry had observed that nobody reaps a fortune nowadays from working union hours or even double-paid overtime. As for saving for these quarterly raids, if such a thing were possible any more, the slogan of the new economy was "Save the pennies and the bank will charge you double to take care of them." Luckless citizens with no genius for major crime were obliged to apply themselves to figuring out quick-profit schemes unique and complicated enough to elude tax classification. There must be a Gimmick, they told themselves, and toiled night and day to find how to make the quick dollar without toil. They were constantly goaded onward by news of a lady relaxing in her bubble bath who thought up a perfumed chewing gum and made a fortune; a retired but restless black marketeer bronzing his pot on Miami Beach thought of a dolls' roller derby and was back in big business; a radio bit-player, between shots, thought of a sound-skip device that would eliminate all voices but the one desired; a bartender on Rubberleg Square thought up the idea of a juke-box psychoanalyst, two backward students at Penn State thought of a Baby-Naming Personal Service. All through the night and all through the land the geniuses, the bums, the experts and the birdbrains were pecking away for the golden gimmick that would fell the great enemy, Taxes.

Jerry Dulaine, who knew everyone, learned by listening, introduced Ideas to Capital, shuffled contacts personal with contacts professional, joined the quest for the Gimmick. She got a bank ten good clearing-house days away from her New York bank, took a $500 option on a $100,000 business block, "sold it," "bought" a suburban movie theatre, borrowed on it, "bought" a textile works, traded it for a piece of a musical show, wangled advances to pay past losses, her distant checks passing her local checks on slow trains, one deal juggling the other, all maneuvered so swiftly that the eyes never quite caught up with the prestidigitator's hands.

For the past five years — Jerry was not thirty-four — she

had lived perilously on the brink of disaster, but she had lived well and still clung to the brink. It was still a good show, Elsie Hookley declared, mystified and admiring. But Jerry was beginning to wonder. How much longer could she keep it up and where was it leading? Instead of the game being easier it was getting tougher. She was calling up more men than called her up and, worse yet, some of these gentlemen belonged to the older and lower part of her ladder. And there were the lunches every day with other girls whose luck was running out except for restaurant credit.

Elsie, once Jerry's apprehensions had penetrated her consciousness, was far more disturbed than Jerry. Taxis, instead of private cars, were bringing Jerry home, and earlier besides. Jerry's doings had filled Elsie's life and made her forget her uneasiness about her own. She had countered Wharton's victories with Jerry's and if the show was not to go on forever then she must see that the curtain came down on a triumphant finale that would pay off both star and audience. Elsie made wild plans in her worried sleep to rent a bigger, finer house than her brother's where she would bombard his finest guest list with royal dinners at which Jerry would shine. She would pick up the old exclusive club memberships gaily discarded decades ago and install Jerry in the inner circle. She would rent a palace in Capri or Rome where Jerry would preside over international royalty.

"It wouldn't do," she always had to sigh before resigning herself to sleep. "I'm too old and too tired."

The great inspiration came at last on the morning she had carried Jerry's mail up to her from the hall table and found the young lady sitting cross-legged in bed absorbed in scissoring a photograph out of *City Life*. The sight of the worldling's tousled head bent over her paper-doll cuttings, shining black locks loose, brow knit, pajama coat carelessly unbuttoned down to the twinkling childish navel, charmed Elsie. An innocent little devil-child, she thought, her innate generalissimo instincts deeply touched. Oh yes, she vowed, she would fight to protect this happy picture. Who would dream that this dear child, so simple and guileless-looking without make-up, pretty mouth puckered in concentration, small pink bare foot peeping out of blankets, had been probably nightclubbing all over town most of the night?

Elsie looked fondly about the room. There always seemed such order in its disorder, the dresser drawers always half open, the satin puff always sliding to floor, coffee cup with cigarette butts always on night table, a book always face-open on the floor where it had slid, mottoes and cartoons that had appealed to Jerry pasted on the mirror. ("It's just our club motto," Jerry explained, seeing Elsie puzzling over one card: The Lady Flounderers Club. *They said* I *couldn't do it so* I *didn't even try;* Fishback, Elsie read, and saw pasted below this inspirational thought, *Better half-done today than not at all tomorrow.*) These touches, with the jet slippers toppled wearily in a corner where dance-tired feet had kicked them, gave the place a jolly, inviting air, as cozy as a kitchen fireplace.

At the moment Jerry was carefully inserting the clipped photograph into the silver frame that always contained her Man of the Week. Elsie dropped the letters on the bed, noting from the corner of her eye that the envelopes had ominous cellophane windows, and then looked at the latest idol, relieved that this ones' face didn't look like a trail map through the Badlands as the *Time* cover men always did.

"Collier McGrew?" she exclaimed and took a second look.

"Isn't he a dream?" Jerry demanded happily. "The most marvelous man I ever met in my life."

Elsie sat down, shaking her head in speechless amazement.

"I knew you got around," she finally sighed, "but Collier McGrew! Where on earth did you meet him — the White House?"

"Why shouldn't I meet him?" Jerry asked, squirming off the bed and sliding her feet into rabbit-furred mules. "He's in public domain. Let's have some coffee."

"But he doesn't go to nightclubs or any gay spots. How did you meet him?" Elsie eagerly followed Jerry into the kitchen and took two cups out of the cupboard as Jerry adjusted the Chemex.

"I had lunch at the Julien the other day with Judge Brockner and he was there with some Congressman Brockie knew," Jerry explained. "Brockie and the Congressman had to go to some meeting and McGrew and I had a brandy and he walked me home. Then there was that benefit fashion show. I was with the fashion people and he was bored with his benefit people so he took me out for dinner. Just a quiet little steak house. He hates crowds he said. Then last night a drip I knew took me to a newspaper party and there was McGrew with some Washington big-shot and bored stiff. I was the only person there he knew, he said, so he and I slipped out and had a quiet snack, then he drove me home."

"Well!" Elsie exclaimed. "When I think of everybody in the Pentagon and U.N. after him, my brother Wharton quoting him on everything and bragging about how close they are, and then you walk away with him just because everybody else bores him!"

"The most attractive man I ever met," Jerry declared with such an unwonted dewy look that Elsie gave her an approving thump on the back. They carried their cups to the living room and Jerry dropped on the sofa.

"I could marry a man like that," Jerry said, dreamily stirring her coffee. "I swear I could."

Much to her surprise Elsie did not take this as a joke.

"Now this is something I'll buy!" Elsie shouted, and clapped her hands as the idea began burgeoning in her brain. "Don't you see it? You've been wasting your time on small stakes, but this is the time for the big kill. You're thirty-four and still gorgeous. You've got a chance at the biggest man you've ever met and you ought to play it big. How would you like to be an ambassador's wife?"

Jerry's answer was to burst out laughing. How would Elsie herself like to be Pope, she countered. Who wanted to get married, for heaven's sake? All anybody asked was some ready cash and a good time, and besides McGrew wasn't any ambassador.

"Everybody says he will be," Elsie insisted, her eyes beginning to glitter and her nostrils dilate at the whiff of the marvelous mischief she was about to launch. In her excitement she began to stride about the room, holding her cigarette aloft like a torch and waving it about as she swooped back and forth until it seemed to Jerry the room could not possibly contain this mobile statue of Liberty. "And let me tell you something about marriage, my dear girl."

"Now Elsie!" Jerry cried in alarm. "Not the facts of life!"

"You don't realize what a future there is in marriage," Elsie said, ignoring the interruption. "Why, I've seen women without looks and no talent for anything else be perfect geniuses at marriage. They really clean up. You marry your man, pop a baby right off the reel, enter it in Groton or Spence on its christening day, have the father set up a trust fund for it right off with you as guardian, get your divorce, marry the next guy, pop another baby with trust fund, repeat divorce and same deal all over. Finally you're living high on the income from four or five trust funds, without lifting a finger."

"Like a prize stud," Jerry observed. "Frankly I don't see myself as a breeder, old girl."

Elsie was obliged to admit that it might be a little late for Jerry to get into that field, but there were other ways of making a business out of marriage.

"You work it out like a big merger," she said with a large gesture. "After all a girl like you has a lot to offer and you expect top price. A man like McGrew needs a woman like you and you need a man like him."

"He's done all right for himself all these years without a wife," Jerry objected. "Why should he need one now?"

Elsie could answer that one. First, everybody said he should marry and mothers all over the world were throwing their daughters at him. He had been so busy dodging daughters ever since the New Deal had flushed him out of an aristocratic private life into public service that he'd been afraid to marry. But now that he was rising in importance, honored from the Pentagon to United Nations and Wall Street, he needed a hostess to help share his tremendous social obligations. Brother Wharton said so and Elsie was positive he was grooming his eldest daughter for the job, a little goon like that, mind you! When obviously the one woman in the world equipped to handle such a man of affairs was Jerry. And the great part of it was that evidently McGrew himself had recognized this.

"Tell me again just what he said," she urged.

Jerry looked dreamily at the photograph.

"He said I was the first woman he'd met in years he could talk to without feeling she was either a competitor or a responsibility," she said in a faraway voice, and then remembered something fresh. "He said I was plastic, that's it."

"Plastic?" Elsie queried doubtfully.

"Not like Dupont products, silly," Jerry said, impatiently. "He said he was frightfully tired and bored and I had a plastic charm that gave to any mood. He thanked me for refreshing him, he said."

"That does it!" Elsie cried. "He admits you've got the quality he needs. If we follow this up right you'll be Mrs. McGrew and all your future will be solved."

"What do you want me to do — blackmail him into it?" giggled Jerry. "Elsie, darling, don't be an idiot."

"There you are!" Elsie exclaimed. "You just don't know your own value. Believe me, I've been around enough to know how high you could go if the right person handled you. Why, I could put this across myself if you'd let me handle you and do just as I said."

Jerry's continued amusement made Elsie the more resolute. She swore she was going to study this problem and map out a campaign that Jerry would have to follow. The idea of Elsie as marriage broker and talent manager kept Jerry in hysterics for several days, but she stopped laughing when she had to buy her own dinner two nights in a row and another envelope frank-stamped from the Collector of Internal Revenue arrived. This letter turned out to be a warrant form with penciled-in threats and rebukes by the clerk. Hopelessly Jerry tore up the letter and turned to Elsie. The hour had come for her to put her destiny in someone else's hands.

Elsie, seeing that she had made her impression, set to work. She devoted herself to planning her strategy with the thoroughness of a long pent-up housewife going after a belated college degree. She pried all the information about McGrew she could get out of her brother by the ancient technique of disparaging the man so that Wharton would angrily blurt out everything he knew. By poking around she ascertained that little Isabella was studying cooking at a fashionable cooking school (McGrew was a Chevalier du Tastvins); little Isabella was also boning up furiously with tutors in French, Spanish, and Persian (there was a rumor that McGrew might be sent to Iran on a government mission); little Isabella was having a second début in Washington, D.C., on the excuse that Hookley cousins there demanded it. Obviously Wharton was doing his best to land McGrew and Elsie's nostrils quivered happily at this familiar challenge.

McGrew was to leave that week for Florida, Elsie learned, for conferences with certain politicos there and best of all he was to spend some time, at Wharton's insistence, with some Palm Beach Hookleys. They were her cousins, too, Elsie joyously cried, and they could just as well sponsor *her* friend as they could Wharton's. Jerry would meet McGrew under finer auspices than she ever had in New York and a different background often acted as a forcing spot for romance. A long-distance call arranged for ten days at the cousins' estate and after that Jerry could bide her time at a hotel—McGrew's hotel, if possible.

"My cousin's set is the last word in stuffiness," Elsie said. "I want McGrew to see that you can handle a stuffy set as well as you can a party crowd. A diplomat's wife has to know all kinds. But above everything else she has to know food and wines. I'll teach you."

"Nobody has ever complained that I didn't know how to order a fine dinner," Jerry laughed.

"I mean to serve it in your own home," Elsie said. "Why else do you think Wharton and Nita are forcing their poor daughter to study gourmet cooking when all she knows is chocolate malties? But leave this to me. I'll arrange everything."

While Jerry was away Elsie was to have decorators do over her helter-skelter apartment into a tasteful background for a lady of discrimination. Good books, a fine modern painting or two, and the ultimate in equipment for serving such dinners as would melt away all barriers of class and race in any capital where a diplomat might be sent.

"I'll loan you my Iola to cook for you," Elsie said. "We will stage a marvelous demonstration dinner for McGrew the minute you get back just to sew him up if Florida hasn't already done it."

Jerry was ready to do anything or go anywhere that was financed. Cheered by Elsie's generosity, she set out with a fine southern wardrobe privately sure she could get McGrew one way or another. Hadn't he refrained from making any passes at her? Wasn't that how you knew a man had seriously fallen for you? At her door he had kissed her good night, a sweet, warm, sexless sort of kiss that had left Jerry absolutely dewy-eyed, knocked for a loop as she admitted dizzily to herself afterward. This must be It. No groping, no clutches, just a boy-girl kiss. Jerry was thankful she hadn't been in the least tight or she might have been fool enough to make a pass or two herself. But McGrew or no McGrew she had a few private ideas for making the most of a Florida trip, though Elsie, suspecting that in her present state Jerry might give up the game at the drop of a hat, gave her last minute warnings.

"Don't you dare forget this deal isn't just a flop in the hay," Elsie said severely. "It's a roll in the orange blossoms. So don't get mixed up with any fly-by-nights down there, don't get plastered except with the best people, don't forget you're not there to have yourself a good time but to build a respectable marrying background for yourself. You've still got a good reputation, God knows why. You've had sense enough to know you can have more fun with better people that way, but that Irish in you is beginning to come out more and more so watch out for it. You be working on being top drawer down there while I get the nest all ready. When you get back you're going to start making your name as hostess in your own home instead of party girl."

"But I hate staying home," Jerry complained. "I hate ending up in the same place I started out and with the same people."

"There you are!" Elsie exclaimed, quite shocked. "Don't

you know that no matter how many men you get by being seen around all the spots with all the big shots you only get a husband by having him see you in your own home? You've got to give dinners — fine dinners. Once you've got people at your own table you've got the edge on them. They've as good as admitted they're your friends and are committed to stand by you. Wait till you get back and see all the things I've planned for you. It's a new life, my chick."

So off Jerry went, glad to be away from creditors, returning weeks later radiantly bronzed, confessing to many happy hours with McGrew and allowing Elsie to deduce she had practically won her game when the truth was she had, to her own bewilderment, merely been playing McGrew's. He was too experienced a bachelor to permit any pressure, and she sensed soon enough that her appeal for him was in her demanding nothing but being *there* when he chose to see her. No use hoping to rouse his interest by her popularity with other men of his rank, for he would not compete. If he was so delighted to find her alone with no plans, then she would be that, like a back-street mistress, she thought, without the romance. He was a new kind of fish to her, and for the life of her she couldn't understand why she would feel so flattered and elated after a perfectly harmless swim or ride with him. She knew most men would class her as desirable but McGrew gave her the dizzy delusion that she must be intellectual, and that was a new sensation indeed.

Just as she persuaded herself she was getting someplace she found that the gentleman had left for New York without so much as a good-bye. A curious man, she reflected, slightly chilled by his efficient use of her for exactly what and when he liked, with no loose ends or wasted time, just as he dropped being charming to order the dinner, then resumed charm the minute the headwaiter left. She did not betray her doubts to Elsie when Elsie suggested she give a dinner for McGrew as soon as she got back to town. It gave her an excuse to telephone him, and he was in the mood to find it amusing to be invited to "test her new cook." Happily relieved, Jerry made out a guest list but Elsie immediately crossed off all Hollywood or Broadway names and substituted more worthy ones.

"I hardly know these people," Jerry protested at Elsie's list. "Why should they accept any dinner invitation from me?"

"On account of the guest of honor, silly," Elsie said. "You'll see."

Indeed it had been funny, Jerry admitted, the way people hemmed and made excuses till the McGrew name was mentioned and how fast they accepted then. But now the masterly plan had been tested, the dinner was over, and at eleven o'clock the two ladies, deserted, knew they had failed. Jerry had known it was a flop for hours but Elsie refused to admit it till the last guest had fled. Then she decided to be philosophical about it, for she feasted on catastrophe, and there had been so many subtle angles to the evening's failure that she anticipated a whole season of warming over tidbits, souping and hashing. She enjoyed her power as secret entrepreneur of a grand comedy. She was not vain enough to expect gratitude from Jerry or personal applause if the game had succeeded; all she had dreamed was a slow trickle of fury through her brother's future thoughts. She did not think yet about the financial loss to herself, not because she was generous but because she was vague about money, blind in arithmetic and only spasmodically foxy. For her it was chiefly a dazzling, amusing scheme that had missed fire. It had occupied her energies for a while very nicely, and she did not realize how serious it was for Jerry. Her young friend's gloom gave her the opportunity for a few cheerful words on errors in strategy. She felt there might be consolation in analyzing the whole situation, now that the show was over.

Which Elsie proceeded to do.

. . . *evening at home* . . .

• "At least my husband was a gentleman," Elsie Hookley suddenly announced, helping herself from a decanter of Jamieson's Irish which she had drawn within cuddling distance. "What if he did ruin my life, the bastard? He had a great many women, true enough, but he was a gentleman and he treated them like ladies. He paid them and he paid them well. All right, what if it was my money? The way he put it was that a real gentleman expected to pay and a real lady expected to be taken care of. That's your European aristocrat for you."

"So McGrew isn't a European aristocrat," Jerry Dulaine replied crossly. "So I don't get paid. It still doesn't explain why he didn't show up."

"And not one word out of him," Elsie said happily, for she

was beginning to enjoy the enormity of the catastrophe. "Not a telegram. You're sure he understood he was to be guest of honor?"

"He's known it for two weeks," Jerry said wearily, for they'd been all over this a dozen times. "You know perfectly well he told me his favorite dishes and you had Iola make them especially for him."

Elsie nodded sadly.

"Guinea hen, broccoli in creamed chestnuts, wild rice — my God, my brother would do murder for a dinner like that! And Iola all gussied up in turquoise corduroy uniform from Clyde's! I had counted on McGrew telling Wharton all about it just so he'd burn up." She thought of something new. "You're sure he never came to your apartment before we fixed it up? He's such a wine and food man he might have been afraid your dinner would be a weenie roast."

"He brought me home but he never came up," Jerry said.

"You're sure you remembered not to sleep with him?" Elsie asked with a meditative glance at her friend.

Jerry had a flash of righteous indignation at this insult.

"I told you this was *serious*, Elsie," she exclaimed. "I told you it was his never making any pass, just saying little things to me — never anything personal, too — that made me know he meant something serious."

"You mean nothing really happened when you were with him so much in Florida?" Elsie asked as reproachfully as any designing mother. "For goodness sake, what did you do when you were alone?"

"Talked, like I told you," Jerry muttered.

"What about, for God's sake?" Elsie demanded.

Jerry shrugged and lit a cigarette.

"Art," she admitted defensively. "He buys paintings, doesn't he? And I asked his advice a lot about investments and — oh, things. He liked my ideas, he said."

She lit a cigarette and looked at herself in the mirrored wall, thinking back ruefully of how important it had seemed to get exactly the right white taffeta to show off her tanned shoulders and enhance her cloudy hair. Every square inch of that sleek bronze skin cost a good fifty dollars if you measured it in Florida hotel rates, and when you considered that this gilding encompassed her whole body you realized that here was indeed complete folly. Staying on down there week after week just because McGrew was there, borrowing and charging right and left to anybody she could think of (particularly Elsie), writing post-dated checks on bank accounts she'd long outspent, counting on one big throw of the dice to recoup. Even so, she wouldn't have got in so deep if she hadn't been carried out of her depth by Elsie's enthusiastic urging. Elsie had really shoved her into this mess, and God knows Elsie had certainly made the whole evening a hundred times worse, but you couldn't say that.

"I know you wish I'd go home," Elsie said, kicking off her slippers and stretching out her long bony legs in their stockinged feet to the fender, her skirt pulled up above her knobby knees in the careless sexless way that always obliged people to look studiously away. "You wish I'd gotten out sooner, so you could have gone out with the others. They wouldn't invite me of course, because they couldn't stand me. I don't care. Right now, I feel like a little cozy post-mortem. A party that's a flop is more fun to talk over than a good party.

Now get yourself a drink and sit down."

She wants me to drink with her so I'll blubber out more troubles and it'll cheer her up, Jerry thought. She knew Elsie loved her best when she played her cards badly and any other time she would have humored her by reporting a whole book of errors, the way pretty women mollify their enemies by stories of childhood freckles and miseries. But tonight she could not bear consolation or advice. She wanted Elsie to go home, for the sight of the gaunt, brassy-haired confidante of her misadventures, like the half-filled glasses left about, the inordinately festive profusion of fresh flowers (forty dollars' worth) smote her with the grim evidence of the evening's disaster. She didn't even dare put her fears into words; she could say it, but if she ever *heard* it she would surely gobble her bottle of Nembutal on the spot. It wasn't that she had counted too much on this dinner party to which the guest of honor had failed to come. It was the hint that her luck had run out and would never come back, that this was the beginning of worse disasters to come, of situations her blind knack could not manage. Already she could see the sunken black eyes of the dreadful Mr. Prince of Internal Revenue, wagging his bony finger at her and thundering, "If I can't afford to buy my wife or girl friend dresses like yours, then you ought to be in jail!"

In another minute she might burst into tears, Jerry thought with horror, and then where would she be? You didn't start sniveling until you'd given up hope of getting anything out of life but pity. Hastily she poured herself a stiff highball and sat down on the rug, doing her best to suppress her ungrateful exasperation with her friend. It was turning out to be exactly as she had always feared intimacy with a neighbor would turn out — and she should be kicking herself instead of blaming Elsie.

The trouble with accepting Elsie's devotion in an off-guard moment of need was that she moved in on you, so to speak. You should have been prepared for that. It was only reasonable. You thought it was fine that you knew how to spend beautifully without knowing where your money was coming from, but unfortunately Elsie, who had it and was willing to back your imagination, had to have an orchestra seat at the show. Elsie saw no unfair irony in herself wearing a ten ninety-five rayon crepe from Klein's-on-the-Square while Jerry wore a two-hundred-dollar dress she'd charged to her account at Bergdorf's. That was perfectly natural, Elsie thought. Pantry and cellar were her only indulgences, her sole requirement of clothes being that they should either be or at least look like basement bargains, but she placed no limit on what Jerry demanded for her proper setting.

"I should be grateful," Jerry reproached herself.

Of course it had to be a boomerang. Elsie financed you to a party designed to settle your whole future, then she queered everything by attending it. It was the first time they had attempted to fit together the odd sections of their social jigsaw, and in spite of all the knowledge they had of each other through after-hours confidences, they appeared to each other before an audience in a completely new light, like summer lovers suddenly popping up in winter clothes. Elsie, for her part, was more than satisfied with Jerry's easy manner in handling a large dinner party, and her loud compliments with hearty pats on the back made guests and Jerry wonder just what vulgar hi-jinks she had anticipated.

"Would you have dreamed that Jerry Dulaine could have

managed a thing like this?" Elsie crowed again and again. "Isn't she marvelous? Just see what Colly McGrew is missing!"

Even if he had come, Elsie would have bollixed everything, Jerry knew. The more Jerry tried to pass off the slight from her missing guest the more Elsie insisted everyone should be mortally insulted. McGrew had decided they were none of them worth his while, Elsie reminded them again and again, and she just wondered what lies her own dear brother Wharton had said about Jerry Dulaine to keep McGrew from coming.

Jerry was accustomed to making a party go under the most trying handicaps, and after the hour's delaying of dinner, beautifully prepared and served by Elsie's precious Iola, she expected to salvage a pleasant enough evening for the others, with no further reference to the truant guest, loss though it was to herself. But she had never bucked against Elsie Hookley, and seeing her on show, so to speak, for the first time, Jerry thanked her stars that Prince Charming had not come, for if he had, Elsie would have driven him off forever. In those friendly hours when they had let down their hair, Jerry had taken for granted that Elsie, like herself, put the locks up in public. The picture Elsie had given of herself was of a worldly-wise gentlewoman, obliged by her station to put up with certain silly conventionalities, carrying on properly with straight face, but all the time saving up her real democratic feelings for the private orgy of honesty. Now Jerry saw that Elsie not only let her hair down in public but pulled out everybody else's hairpins as well. The spectacle of a few people dressed up to go through the motions of a genteel social routine inflamed Elsie, as she saw in it a masquerading dragon sent by her enemy, Boston, which she must attack with fiendish vigor. No simple exchange of amenities could pass without suspicion, the merest mouse of a polite compliment to the hostess must be harpooned and held up as deadly rodent. *Don't believe him when he says this is the finest Montrachet he's ever tasted, Jerry, he's got too good a cellar himself to kid anybody, though fat chance anybody ever gets of sampling it these days.* . . . An escape of talk into general fields while Elsie enjoyed a bite of fowl had her stopped only momentarily and then she was loudly declaring that were she the hostess, God forbid, she would never speak to anybody present for their neglecting to appreciate the marvel of the cooking, the equal of which she defied them to find short of Julien's, the *old* Julien's of course, not the new one her dear, dear brother Wharton continued to be so devoted to.

The fact was that Elsie was being herself, never less than overwhelming. Youthful years of excessive shyness, awkwardness and suppressed desires had fitted her out with a perfect treasure chest of home-truths conceived too late for their original cues but all waiting for some victorious day when they could be uttered. There was something pernicious, she felt, in the efforts of the others to pretend the party was a success; she felt she must prove her contempt for society's emptiness by emptying it before Jerry's very eyes. By the time they had arrived at dessert general conversation had been pretty well blocked, Elsie tackling, single-handed, every sentence that ventured down the field. The withdrawal to the living room for coffee offered a dim hope of loosening Elsie's grip.

"By George, that's an early Marius," Okie, the publisher of *Hemisphere*, had exclaimed, studying the painting above the fireplace. He had been invited as the last of a vanishing race, the Extra Men, and moreover Cynthia Earle, whose family background paralleled McGrew's, was using him these days as escort. Jerry nodded modestly to him, hoping Elsie had not overhead his remark for she would certainly declare that the picture was hers and that she knew more about it than Okie.

"An early Marius, at that," Okie went on. "You are lucky, Miss Dulaine."

"You must come in the gallery sometime and talk to me about it," murmured Severgny, the art dealer who sometimes employed Jerry as decoy to bring into his place certain rich collectors. "I am extremely interested in Marius right now."

"Let me tell you what Marius said the time I bumped into him at the Whitney — " Cynthia Earle began.

"But Marius is dead!" Elsie Hookley had boomed.

"This," Cynthia had patiently conceded, "was *before* he was dead. I mentioned his Paris show and you know how terribly, terribly funny Marius always was — "

"But Marius hasn't had a show in Paris for years!" shouted Elsie.

"This was 1939," Cynthia continued graciously. "The year before I met him at the Whitney as I was saying — "

"I can't understand why the Whitney didn't buy more of Marius," Elsie said. "They overdid on Ben Forrester, if you ask my opinion, and then only one little Dalzell Sloane. And speaking of Dalzell — "

"So you met Marius." Jerry raised her voice pointedly to

Cynthia, not only to get the ball away from Elsie but because a certain idea for a profitable deal with Severgny had just occurred to her.

"Oh I wish I could remember the exact words. It was so — so *Marius.*" Cynthia's little-girl Tinker Bell laugh at this moment was a tactical error for she had barely got on to her story again before Elsie charged.

"Oh I admit Marius was funny, oh screamingly funny. But Dalzell Sloane was a genius and a gentleman." Elsie placed one hand on the tense knee of Park Avenue's pet portrait painter and fixed the others with a beady blue eye. "I know geniuses aren't supposed to have any decency, they're supposed to be just sexy and funny like Marius, but let me tell you, Dalzell could paint rings around all of them. Just because he was too much of a gentleman to *use* people, the way you have to do, Mr. Whitfield —"

"Cynthia is telling a story about Marius," Jerry chided without conviction, and then since everything was already lost she gave up to a mild speculating on whether Cynthia could ever get the ball any nearer goal against Elsie's overpowering tactics. Cynthia had resolutely started her anecdote all over again when suddenly Elsie snatched the Whitney Museum from her lips and whooped down the field scoring a touchdown with a big inside story about a Hookley ancestral connection with the museum in Boston, a city where Collier McGrew's great-great-grandfather's South Boston wife had been unable to write her own name, and how do you like that, you people who think he's so perfect. Cynthia gave up, as indeed did everyone else, for Elsie was trimmed to take on every verbal offering, shaking an argument out of the merest name, questioning the pronunciation of a word before the speaker had gotten out the last syllable, finding political affronts in the first sentence of some attempted joke, pouncing on some orphan cause barely mentioned as needing noble defense, cutting through whispered asides like a school monitor, finally managing to keep the conversational ball on her big nose and batting it up and down like a trained seal. No use, Jerry thought, almost admiringly. No use, concluded the guests, and surrendered to glazed apathy as Elsie triumphantly regaled them with detailed grudges she had had for years against characters they had never known and never wished to know, delicately prefacing her remarks with a "Jerry's heard me say this before but since I'm on the subject — " convinced she was making the talk general by keeping one hand on Whitfield's knee, the other on Cynthia's back and addressing herself across the room to Jerry as if she was in a distant cornfield.

Yes, Elsie had been in great form and the guests had fled as from a tornado at half past ten, and not one of them had invited Jerry to come along with them for a store nightcap for fear Elsie would come too. Let them go and the hell with everything, Jerry thought, she was a gone goose now, anyway.

Being sorry for herself Jerry spared some morose speculations on poor Elsie, who, it was evident, was a comforting flannel nightgown for lonely winter nights but not to be worn in public. There were people like that whose shoulder-chips, spiritual ulcers or painful vanities were fluoroscoped by a party, though the weaknesses never came out in everyday life. A kind of disease, really, and you simply ought to make allowances. It couldn't be any fun being fifty-four years old with no men left in your life, being sore at the world for the mistakes you had made in it, feuding forever with your ancestors while you boasted of them, sitting up there in your family tree dropping coconuts on yourself.

Poor, angry, honest, openhearted old Elsie, lavishing love and gifts on chronically unworthy, ungrateful wastrels! ("I'm as bad as the rest of them," Jerry guiltily admitted, "but how can I help myself and anyway if it wasn't me it would be somebody else"), then shrieking for vengeance when they behaved as she had so wonderfully predicted. Poor old Elsie, Jerry thought, she's so proud of having kicked over that fine old family and being so democratic, yet every time she meets a title or a millionaire she wishes she could mow them down with superior lineage. Instead all she can do is to bellow at them. And it was funny to see her heckle everybody like an old eagle, sort of brave, really, poor mad creature. They said she had once been rather striking, in that old Boston war-horse way, six feet tall with flame-red hair and legs right up to her shoulder blades as some contemporary had remarked. Her hair was now on the pink side, frizzed in front and looped into a limp bun on top. Her eyes were brilliantly blue and if she would use creams instead of a careless washrag her skin might have been more human-looking. As it was, her striding walk, her great height, her icy glare and booming voice quite terrified people and it was always necessary to reassure those who were backing away —"You know she comes from a very old family, the Boston Hookleys, you know, her brother's Wharton Hookley—he got the mother to do poor Elsie out of her proper place in the old Marlborough Street home just because Elsie refused to live in Boston — some legal twist, and of course she could call herself Baroness but she's so democratic — "

Good old Elsie, indeed, but that didn't give her the right to ruin everybody's evening and a great deal more than that. Now that it was all over there was no point in regrets or reproaches. Besides Elsie seemed blissfully unaware that she herself was responsible for anything going wrong. She sat there wiggling her toes before the fireplace and sipping her drink with the pleased expression of a day's wrecking well done.

"Did you hear me take down that little museum monster when he said, 'I had no idea Miss Dulaine did herself so well!'?" Elsie asked. "I simply looked him in the eye and said, 'Just what kind of an evening *did* you expect from Miss Dulaine, may I inquire?' and of course he was on a spot. And as for Okie — "

"You made him mad, too," Jerry acknowledged. "You told him he knew nothing about art."

Elsie's blue eyes widened in honest astonishment.

"Why should that make him mad? God knows Okie has always been the dumbest man on earth but at least I gave him credit for *knowing* it. Now *really!* Look, do you think I should telephone around some more for McGrew? Just in case — "

"No, no," Jerry hastily protested, for one of Elsie's tricks had been to keep telephoning various clubs and restaurants during the evening to track down the missing guest so that all present should realize all was lost without him. It might be funny someday but right now and tomorrow it was serious, so that Elsie's sudden chuckle as she comfortably poured herself a dividend made Jerry's kindlier thoughts switch to resentment that a girl of her own looks and capacities should have to sit around in a handsome new evening dress with a noisy old girl just because she owed her a fortune. The favors weren't all on Elsie's side. She had been bored and lonely for years until her frustrated appetite for holocausts had been gratified by Jerry's magnanimous sharing of her ups and downs. It was just as she was thinking this that Jerry's downstairs bell rang.

"I knew he'd come!" cried Elsie clapping her hands. "Just let me give him a piece of my mind."

But suddenly Jerry's cheeks flushed and her eyes began to glow.

"Pull your dress down, Elsie," she commanded briskly, giving herself a quick glance in the mirror. "This may be somebody else."

"But who — ?" Elsie began, bewildered, and then she stared at her friend with dawning suspicion. "You telephoned somebody a few minutes ago, didn't you?"

"I told you," Jerry said evasively. "I called the Julien Café again just as you suggested and talked to a man who said he was looking for McGrew, too. He asked where I was — "

Elsie threw up her hands.

"And you invited him up," she accused incredulously. "Good Heavens, Jerry, what's the matter with you? He might be a ripper or a lunatic. I can't understand you."

For no matter how thoroughly she approved and felt she understood her young friend there was always more to be found out. It was her turn to look with bewilderment at the change coming over the other, for if an audience brought out Elsie's disease the prospect of a strange man brought out Jerry's.

In any great crisis, financial or emotional, that would send most persons to the bottle or out the window, it had long been Jerry's habit to turn to a new man as restorative, someone unknown, hazardous, unique. She took care to maintain most circumspect relations with any man whose valuable friendship she knew was an important asset, not to be traded for a transient affair with awkward aftermaths. But a moment of pique, a broken date, a lost earring, an unpleasant interview brought out a wild lust for compensating abandon, the more fantastic the better. Elsie had her own outlets which she kept to herself, and she had gathered from cryptic references to "characters" and low barroom types that Jerry, too, favored piquant contrast in her conquests. All very well and a woman's only human, but tonight was more than a mere broken date, it was a whole future, and weren't they in it together? But Jerry seemed slipping from her grasp, needing neither her sympathy nor her company. She tried to make Jerry meet her reproachful eyes but the young lady was busily spraying *L'Amour L'Amour* on her hair and wrists and humming happily.

"I always can tell you're up to something when you start singing 'Where or When,'" Elsie accused her. "I just wish you'd learn the rest of the words."

"There aren't any other words but where or when," Jerry said, and then exclaimed impatiently, "Listen, Elsie, this night has sunk me. But I'm going to have one good time before I give up and maybe this is it."

"With a total stranger!" Elsie gasped. "Don't you know this sort of caper will finish you with McGrew? You can't play high and low."

"That's how I play, old dear," Jerry said.

"I will not be called old dear, not by anybody," Elsie said as she stalked proudly out the door, a little miffed not to be called back.

The hall light was out and it was too bad she could not get a good look at the stranger as she passed him on the stairs. She stood outside her own apartment door listening for a moment as Jerry opened the door to him. Prescott was his name, Elsie overheard him announce.

"At least he sounds human this time," she reflected. "No *deses* and *doses*."

That the late guest must look as satisfactory as his accent Elsie could deduce from the sudden dovelike flutiness in Jerry's voice, a change she had observed before when her companion would be interrupted mid-sentence by a husky delivery boy or dreamy solicitor. The change in voice was accompanied, in these moments of fleeting lust, by a telltale glitter in the gray-green eyes that made the pupils tiny pinpoints of desire and the color go hard and unrevealing.

"The little devil," Elsie marveled with a chuckle. "I wonder how much longer she can get away with it."

The old great Dane, whose fur had a pinkish tinge similar to his mistress's hair, was waiting inside Elsie's door, and he rose with arthritic chivalry when she entered. Her living room looked small and untidy after Jerry's brand-new grandeur. Still, it was a cozy dump, Elsie thought, with the garden outside and the jolly little dining corner where Iola daily displayed her priceless culinary treasures. Elsie strode into the kitchen, which was larger than the living room, indeed had to be to house the extraordinary collection of copper and clay utensils, graduated pots and weapons and lordly equipment of herbs, groceries and general fodder sufficient to pacify the fussiest chef and feed a tribe of gourmets. Elsie opened the huge icebox with a fond pat on its belly as if it was the favorite stud in a fine stable, and reached in for her inevitable nightcap of beer — this time a good Danish brand — and a prize hoard of chicken livers for Brucie.

"What'll you bet!" Elsie mused aloud with a reflective glance upward, another shake of the head. But it wasn't funny, come to think of it, it was downright asinine for a girl of Jerry's potentialities and opportunities to throw her body and brains around as if there were plenty more where those came from. Elsie had always muffed her own chances and took for granted that she always would, but it angered her now that Jerry was bent on doing the same thing, no matter how a person tried to help her.

Now what satisfaction is that going to be for her to wind up this mess in bed with a strange man? Elsie thought, exasperated. How is that going to fix up everything? If she'd only have let me stay and thrash out things we might have figured out something.

She picked the *Evening Post* out of the wastebasket to read Leonard Lyons' column in bed and her eye caught the pile of unopened bills she had thrown there earlier. It was an outrage to have to think about money. It crossed her mind that her quixotic vanity would ruin her some day, that idiotic pride she took in being regarded as a woman of unlimited means. Whatever they might criticize in her looks or brains she would not have it that anyone dared be superior to her financially. Even with her brother Wharton, who was supposed to be guardian of the family fortunes, Elsie had all sorts of little dodges to make him think she had mysterious other sources of revenue of which he could not guess. She switched off the kitchen lights and carried beer and paper into the bedroom. The fine glow she had experienced in carrying off the evening in such bold style, delivering so many good punches at possible detractors of her protégée, faded and she felt rebuffed for a moment. Brucie followed her to the dresser where he stood beside her like a watchful valet while she skinned off the blue rayon satin dress, the pinned-up magenta slip — imagine anybody paying more than two ninety-eight for a slip, though come to think of it a Hattie Carnegie slip for Jerry had cost thirty-odd dollars — the elastic girdle, the incredibly long nylons. It occurred to Elsie to study her naked length in the dresser mirror thoughtfully as if she was viewing it for the first time. The truth was she thought of herself seldom in physical terms, and even soaping herself absently in the shower she was as likely to wash Brucie's curious snout thrust through the shower curtains as her own bottom. She shook her head now in quizzical dismay over the roll of fat over her stomach and the lack of padding in proper places. No one can remain dissatisfied completely with one's body even if all one can honestly boast is a rare birthmark. So it presently struck Elsie that her upper thighs were evenly matched, her knees if knobby were knobbed in the right direction, and even if dressmakers did complain that her behind seemed to slope down all the way to her knees, still her shoulders were quite remarkable for her age, not too bony and certainly not flabby.

"Not so bad, eh Brucie," she asked her dog complacently.

Maybe she had given up too soon, she reflected. Maybe instead of fixing up Jerry Dulaine's lovelife she should have another go at her own. Maybe she could have hung on to that Portuguese lad on the Cape a little longer, maybe she should have given him the car he kept pestering her for. She'd gotten him away from her mulatto maid by promising him a secondhand motor bike with a fire horn but of course that was when the little bounder was in oilskins and before she'd put him into a Tuxedo and taught him to carry fancy canes. Yes, she could have kept him from that Gloucester widow if she'd given in about the car. Not a Buick, of course, but say a used Chevy.

"I'm just too damned Yankee, that's my trouble," Elsie sighed giving her hair a couple of licks with the brush. "I could have strung along that little monkey another summer or two just buying him a couple of flashy shirts and a Tattersall vest. I always get stingy at the wrong time. Darned if I wouldn't like to have the little rat around right this minute."

Musing on love, Elsie gave another deep sigh and hopped into bed, thrusting her long bony feet over the edge to make room beside her for Brucie.

. . . *the telephone date* . . .

• Rick hurried purposefully up Fifth Avenue, savagely proud of having conquered his weakness for Ellenora. It was no good telling himself that she had no way of knowing he had been waiting for her; he felt as righteously injured as if she had deliberately stood him up to make a fool out of him. At the corner he hesitated just a fraction of a minute, half turned to catch a dim glimpse of some people getting out of a cab in front of Longchamps, firmly dismissed the wild idea that the girl might be Ellenora (which indeed it was) and pushed onward. He knew perfectly well he was about to get into trouble, the way he always did, as if spiting himself would make everybody else sorry. Chasing up some unknown dame from a phone call like a dumb freshman, he mocked himself, but nothing could ever stop him in these stubborn moods. You had to see these blind adventures through to the bitter end, though they were never worth the trouble and could ruin your life. Still anything was better than sitting on in the Julien waiting for someone who would never come.

When he saw the handsome girl who opened the door of her apartment he knew he was having the luck he didn't deserve. Jerry was congratulating herself along the same lines.

"Looks like a party," he said. "How nice."

"How do you do," Jerry said with a shrug. "It's all over and it was not at all nice."

"Then I'm sorry I missed it," Rick said. "I see McGrew isn't here yet. I was expecting him at the Julien, myself. That was why I suggested we might as well wait for him together."

"Of course," Jerry agreed.

Eying her new guest with increasing appreciation she felt cheered and elated. If she could produce a beauty like this out of thin air in her very darkest hour, then she was certainly not done for. The hell with McGrew, she thought.

"I gather you had important business to discuss with him," she said politely. "Will I be in the way?"

Rick hesitated and then grinned at her.

"Not as much as he will be," he said, and then they both laughed shamelessly, understanding each other.

"You never even heard of him," Jerry accused.

"I've heard of nothing but McGrew all evening," Rick defended himself. "Everytime the phone rang at the Julien it wasn't for me, always for McGrew. I answered it to put a stop to it, that's all. A man like that can get dangerous. I only wanted to warn you in case he is really a friend of yours. By the way, is he?"

"Of course he is," Jerry said. "Friend enough to stand me up."

"So that was it," Rick said. "I thought you were making it too easy for me, telling me to come on over. But I was getting tired of being stood up myself."

"Not you too!"

"Every night for two months," Rick said. "I'm damn sick of it."

"I'm sick of everything myself," Jerry said. "I was trying to get rid of the last guest so I could put my head in the oven."

"Could I help?" Rick asked. "Just show me the oven."

"It would have to be the pressure cooker," Jerry said. "Mostly I was considering pills, being a lazy girl. Then I rather hoped you'd turn out to be the killer type and save me the trouble."

"No, I'm just as lazy as you are," Rick confessed. His experienced eyes had taken in the carefully decorated look of the place, the kind of impeccable taste often used to mask the dweller's secret life. Kept, he thought.

"I wouldn't want to mess up such a pretty room," he said.

"Oh it's not paid for," Jerry said, and then to her surprise tears came to her eyes, and suddenly she was gulping and choking away like any Southern belle with the vapors. She snatched at the handkerchief her guest quietly handed her and would have started to bawl in earnest except for the curious fact that the young man showed no disposition to stop her. Indeed he was looking over a book casually as if the lady had asked him to look away while she fixed a garter.

"Thanks for not saying anything," Jerry said, surprised. "How nice of you not to say it will make me feel better to cry because it never does."

"I could have said things can't be as bad as all that," Rick admitted, putting the book aside to look at her. "But probably they're worse. I warn you, though, if you tell me anything I'm likely as not to blab it."

"If I did tell you anything I'd make out I'm just crying over a broken heart," Jerry admitted, "but it's much more important than that. To tell the truth — "

Rick put up a protesting hand.

"Can't we be strangers?" he asked.

"Then let's get out of here," Jerry said.

"Back to the Julien?" Rick asked.

"Too chummy," Jerry said. "I feel like loud company. Dingy bars with fine low types who could never do me any good. I know a few spots."

"I know a few myself," Rick said. "Better change your costume."

Jerry started for the bedroom door but turned to look at him.

"Do you always know the right way to handle people's troubles?" she asked curiously.

"That's what they tell me," he said. "Trouble is just what I'm good at. I have a feeling I see it coming at me right now."

"Let's not look, then," Jerry suggested. "Let's get even with everybody and have one good time before we die."

"Hurry up, then," Rick said. "We've only got all night."

This was the way it always ended up, he thought, resigned. Every time he tried to blot out Ellenora he wound up blotting out himself. He wanted to have a light gay adventure to make up for his romantic wounds but it always bogged down into his feeling sorry for somebody and getting himself in a mess trying to help them out. As if he was God's gamekeeper, his mother used to scold him.

Gourd's grimekipper, Geep's Godkimer, Gam's keep — he was muttering it angrily to himself hours later.

. . . *one good time before we die* . . .

• The electric light in the middle of the ceiling sent a steady unrelenting warning and it was this, more than the rhythmic moaning sound, that finally opened Jerry's eyes. What she saw was a dream, she knew, and closed her eyes again, reaching out an arm to the light she knew was by her bed but which somehow now was not there so she slowly opened her eyes once more. Her room would be a mess, she knew that from the fierce throbbing in her head which meant that she had drunk too much of something terrible, and of course her clothes would be thrown all over the place and probably the lamp turned over. But this bulb in the ceiling? The pale woman with long red braids lying in the other bed? The funny-looking windows with no curtains — dungeonlike windows — yes, with bars.

Suddenly it struck her that she must have done it — taken poison or dope pills just as she had been afraid she might. This was no dream, this was a hospital.

How had it happened, how long ago, and where? Frightened, she sat up in bed abruptly and the sudden motion made her sick. She leaped up to go to the bathroom but the door was shut.

"There's not even a doorknob," she gasped, and then saw the little pane of glass on a level with her own eye in the top of the door. It was a hospital corridor outside but she saw no one pass until a young mulatto nurse hurried by, paying no heed to Jerry's pounding on the door and outcries. Frantically Jerry looked around for a basin or sink but there was nothing in the room but the two beds and only one sheet. She was stark naked and there was no sign of her clothes. Her hands were bruised and she realized that her rings had been torn off.

"What kind of hospital is this?" she cried out.

The girl in the other bed, with the sheet pulled up to her chin and her braids lying on it, turned quiet empty eyes on her.

What had happened? Where had it happened and with whom? Another stab of pain in her head made her snatch the sheet and vomit into it. She rolled it up and sat on the bed-ticking, shivering. Think, she commanded herself, think hard. There had been the dinner party and Elsie's voice booming in the dining room, Elsie's voice booming in the living room, people sitting around, but clearer than anything else she remembered the sick desperation in her heart, a feeling that this was a wake for her because this was the end. She remembered being alone with Elsie, slipping to her medicine cabinet to count her sleeping pills, praying that Elsie would get out. Well, had she gone and was this waking up in hell? No, there was something else. Then she remembered the door-bell, the arrival of the angel, it seemed at the time, named Ricky, a crazy good-looking stranger who made her forget the medicine cabinet. They had compared notes — each was in a mood to kick over the traces, each was ready to trust the first passing stranger or, if requested, take a rocket to the moon. Oh, they had met at the precisely right moment for anything to happen. They had decided to go out on the town — not to the uptown places but to all the dives — Monty's on Houston Street, the Grotto down by the bridge, the Sink, the Bowery Lido —

The Bowery Lido. Suddenly Jerry saw it again.

The band was booming out "Rose of Washington Square," the grizzled chorus boys in straw hats were shuffling-off to Buffalo, arms around each other's shoulders, the Lido Ladies, old variety hoofers and stompers and ripe young strippers, were prancing off the stage, the mission derelicts were peering in the windows at the uptown slummers whooping it up inside, the cops were getting their handouts at the bar — this was the real New York, the real people, the good people, the bitter salt of the earth. None of the phoniness of Fifty-Second Street, or the fancy spots. "Isn't it wonderful? Isn't it fun?" That was what she and Rick kept saying to each other and whatever strangers they invited to join them, the Chinaman, the old streetwalker they prevailed upon the waiter not to throw out, the old hunchback. And then she remembered Tessie. That must have been when it started, she thought, pressing her hands to her head. Imagine seeing Tessie in a G-string and transparent fan marching along in the Lido chorus line, Tessie, her old roommate who had married a respectable customer's man and moved to Mount Kisco! Tessie, who had advised her ten years ago to give up the gay life and settle down before it was too late. Tessie, obviously fifteen pounds over model size sixteen and with the silveriest blond dye job on her too long flowing locks, strutting past the customers and so flabbergasted at sight of Jerry she had forgotten their past differences and shouted, "My God, Jerry!"

"Tessie!"

Next Tessie was sitting at their table and they were hugging and kissing each other like long-lost sisters, so Rick could never have dreamed that they hadn't been speaking to each other for a good ten years, and the waiter was bringing round after round of whiskey and fizz with Tessie sending drinks to all her buddies in the floor show and inviting them all to join them. What happened then? Was Tessie here, too? What had become of Ricky?

Jerry ran to the barred window and shouted their names into the stone-gray daybreak. A great animal roar answered her, lunatic laughter and a sustained inhuman moan that seemed to come from the stone walls shuddering into the new day. Jerry ran back to the door and peered out the aperture, pounding on it furiously. This time she saw two eyes in a dark face in the peephole of the door opposite. Whoever it was shook her head as if in warning and then lifted dark wrinkled hands to the peephole, spelling out in sign language "W A I T." The eyes appeared again and the head nodded. At least someone was a friend, Jerry thought. The mulatto nurse hurried down the hall and this time she came in the room.

"Shame on you, dirtying your bed, I'll teach you," she cried out, and smacked Jerry smartly. "Shouting and carrying on, you dirty thing, running around naked, disturbing everybody."

"I want a nightgown, I want to go to the bathroom," Jerry said carefully.

"Oh yes, a private bathroom and a lace nightie, oh sure," the nurse smacked her again. "When it's time to go to the bathroom I'll let you know, you filthy little tramp, you."

This is a dream, Jerry said out loud over and over, this is a dream but why don't I wake up?

"Shut up," said the girl. "If you behaved right you wouldn't be here, you tramp."

"Can't we please have the light out?" Jerry begged.

The girl gave a jeering laugh.

"That light stays on, so if one of you gets killed I can look in and see which one did it."

The door closed behind her.

A dream, a dream, Jerry chanted, pulling a corner of the wet sheet across her nakedness, a dream, only all she could think of now was of how to choke the nurse to death. She went to the peephole again and her friend across the hall winked this time and again spelled out "wait" with her hands.

The stone walls were still moaning; it was a hollow, beyond-pain baying noise like beasts at the water hole, but now the sky was a lighter gray and there was the croaking of river tugs, the clatter of delivery trucks, and garbage cans. Out the window she could see the stone court surrounded by bigger gray stone buildings with barred windows, and there was a smell now of dead river rats, sour coffee grounds, boiling hay or mush, and Jerry vomited again into the sheet. No, this was not a dream, but what was it? She felt a little better now, except for the pain in her head and the sudden piercing desire to kill the nurse.

Back to Tessie and the Bowery Lido she pushed her thoughts. They had talked about what wonderful times they used to have, the limousines sent to take them to house parties in Bucks County, Saratoga, Montauk Point, New Haven — anywhere, private planes toting them to masked balls in Palm

Beach, Hollywood, New Orleans, Texas, the big spending gentleman buying a name band to amuse them on his Miami-bound yacht, champagne raining all the time, oh the happy, carefree, days of old, the dear wonderful good good friends whose names were either forgotten or never known, ah those pure, unclouded happy times! And those two loyal, devoted, true-unto-death friends Tessie Baxter and Jerry Dulaine, such friends as neither had ever had before or since, all of which made this chance meeting here in the Bowery an occasion for unlimited celebration and hosannas.

"I'm just working here for laughs," Tessie said. "I wanted to get in off the road, no matter what I had to do. I've got the most marvelous midget, a real clown. You'll die."

Jerry tried to concentrate on what happened after Tessie's midget brought up the two punks who wanted to dance with her. Then Tessie took her backstage and they sat there gabbing, not listening to each other, until she remembered to go back in and look for Rick. But the place was suddenly in an uproar, full of cops and shouting. Someone snatched her arm and somebody else grabbed her when she struggled — that was as far as she could remember.

The door of her room opened and the nurse stood there.

"Well, get out to the washroom and on the double. Throw that sheet over you, you can't be running around here naked, you dirty tramp!"

Jerry's fists clenched but the open door was there and she ran out, the soiled sheet bunched in front of her, joining the sudden horde of half-naked women running down the hall, her red-haired roommate being shoved and yanked by the mulatto nurse. They were nearly all youngish women except for the tiny dark Porto Rican called Maria who Jerry realized must be her friend from across the hall. It was so wonderful to be in the washroom, able to wash and have a turn at the comb with the others that Jerry's murderous rage changed to the humblest gratitude for this privilege.

"That nurse wouldn't give me a sheet or open the door last night," she murmured, waiting behind her friend who was combing her short shaggy gray hair.

The little woman smiled.

"If she open door maybe you try to run out of place naked," she explained. "Maybe you get to next floor then they lock you up for crazy and maybe long time before you get out, like happen to me here once."

Jerry shivered, knowing it would have happened just like that because now she knew anything could happen. Everybody else seemed to be old hands here, calling each other by name — Babe, Chick, Bonny, Bobby, Flossie, Sally — taunting each other with having boasted that last time was to have been the last time and now look. It was amazing how quickly the human mind adjusted, she thought, for she felt more bound to these women than to any other group she'd ever known. When the day attendant, a hard-faced white woman, came in with a clean sheet for her to wear she surprised her with her burst of gratitude. And when the woman put down a cardboard box of used lipsticks, Jerry's joy equaled that of the others.

"Doctor says you tramps can put on lipstick this morning," the nurse shouted out. "But don't forget where you are and start making passes at him or it's the lockup for the lot of you."

"Where are we?" Jerry asked Maria.

"What's the matter, you forget?" said Maria. "City hospital."

"I never was here — " Jerry started to say but from the mocking smiles around her knew no one would believe her. What frightened her most was the curious way she felt in the wrong, as if the mulatto girl's cruelty must not be questioned, nor did she have any right to a gown, or any right to be anyplace else but here. She saw that there was a bump on her temple and remembered something.

"The policeman hit me, he hit me with his club," she exclaimed, and there was a titter from the others.

"They always do," said Maria. "The bump will go away before you get out."

"What do you mean?" Jerry asked. "I'm going home as soon as they give me my clothes."

"That'll be when," said the tall sixteen-year-old named Bobby with the translucent white skin. "Where'd they pick you up?"

"The Bowery Lido," Jerry said. "I don't know what happened, if I got sick and doctors brought me here or — "

"What are you talking about? The cops brought you, girl," Bobby laughed scornfully. "Same as they brought all of us. For cripes sake, what made you try anything in the Bowery anyway?"

"I wasn't trying anything."

"Break it up, you tramps, and come and get it!" the nurse yelled through the door, and again they ran down the hall, some in hospital shirts, bare-bottomed and barefooted, some, like Jerry, with sheets held in front of them or dragging behind. They slid onto benches at a bare table at the end of the hall, a bowl of watery farina and a cup of cold tea in front of each. The nurse and a new attendant went from one to the next, popping pills in each mouth. Bobby resisted hers and was slapped. Jerry held hers in her mouth, and slid it out on her cereal spoon.

"They have no right to hit us," she said.

Maria shook her head at her.

"They got all the right they want," she whispered. "There's nothing anybody can do."

"When do the newspapers come?" Jerry asked, thinking that there might be some explanation in the news, but all heads turned to her again with a mocking smile.

"No reading's allowed here," Bobby said. "That's why they take away everybody's glasses. No radio either. They always take away Sally's hearing aid, too, and then when she doesn't hear what they say they let her have a good wallop."

"I like to read," stated the quiet, waxen-faced woman about Jerry's age with the chrysanthemum bob of black hair and the carefully manicured white hands. "I went to school when I was a kid and I was always reading."

"I know the school you went to, Bonny," jeered the nurse.

"Shut up, you creeps," said Bonny quietly, as everyone hooted with laughter.

"Some school," taunted the one named Chick. "Sunday school."

"I taught Sunday school class once, damn you," shouted Bonny, rising.

"Break it up, girls," the day nurse ordered. "The doctor's here. Good heavens, Bobby, this is the third time you've been in since Christmas."

"I had a fit in a subway station," Bobby said.

"She had a fit in the Hotel St. George, don't let her kid you," said Chick, winking at Jerry. "It scared this sailor she was shacking up with and he got the cops."

"Men are all jerks," said Bobby. "A girl has a simple everyday fit and they start screaming for the cops. A fellow I knew had a fit once, we were sitting on a bench in Prospect Park, and I was only a kid fourteen years old and did I call the cops? No, I stuck my handbag in his jaw so he wouldn't bite off his tongue, and the dumb cluck bit through the bag and got pieces of my mirror in his windpipe and darn near killed himself. But it was the right thing to do."

"How do I telephone?" Jerry asked.

"Are you kidding?"

"But people will be looking for me," Jerry said, and then stopped. Who would be looking for her? Creditors, maybe. Rick Prescott must have thought she had skipped out of the Lido when she stayed out so long with Tessie. What had happened to Tessie?

She could tell that some of the guests or patients or prisoners were locked in their rooms for the attendant was carrying trays in and out.

"Can you find out if my friend, Tessie Baxter, came in with me last night?" Jerry asked the nurse. "Is she here now?"

"That's none of your business, miss," said the nurse coolly, and everyone laughed. Obviously this nurse was regarded as a wag. "If your friend is the same kind as you she'll be here sooner or later, I can tell you that much."

"Are we allowed to telephone?" Jerry asked meekly.

"Sure, we all have private wires," said the one called Chick.

She sat on the bench beside Jerry and suddenly patted her on the cheek. "I like you, kid. When we get out let's see what we can do together. Where'd you get your hair done?"

"Elizabeth Arden's," said Jerry and realized it was the wrong thing to say for there was a silence till Bobby said, "She had Elizabeth Arden fix her up so she could go down to the Bowery and get herself a man."

"I was kidding," said Jerry.

"There's a phone booth in the hall but your pocketbook's in the office safe so you won't have a dime to call, anyway," volunteered Maria. "Maybe somebody will call and leave a message for you. Whatever name you told them when you were brought in."

Jerry knew it was no use trying to remember how she had come in or what she had said.

"Anybody want me to do any phoning for them when I leave this morning?" she asked.

"Who told you you were getting out?" asked Chick. "Tell me the truth, where'd you get your hair done like that? I like your fingernails. What shade is that?"

"Opalescent," said Jerry.

"You certainly did a job on yourself just to work the Bowery," said Bobby, admiringly. "Look, girls, the toenails yet!"

"Opalescent," repeated Chick, giggling. "Opalescent toenails!"

"It's nice." Maria nodded to her kindly, and Jerry felt a wave of love for her, as if here was the dearest friend she had ever had, one she would cherish forever.

"Would you like me to tell your family where you are?"

Jerry asked her, wanting to do something wonderful for her.

Maria looked alarmed.

"No no, please," she said. "My husband will come wait for me outside and beat me up."

"Maria's old man gets drunk on Porto Rican rum and starts whamming the kids around and Maria clobbers him with everything she can lay her hands on," explained Bobby, while Maria smiled apologetically. "The neighbors call the police and they cart off Maria yelling her head off so they bring her here. Then her old man lays for her to get out so she doesn't care how long she stays here."

"I don't know maybe this time I killed him," Maria said thoughtfully. "Better for me maybe to stay crazy."

The girl with the red braids who had shared Jerry's room was standing in the hall facing the open door of the bathroom. The day nurse had stood her there like a window dummy and she had not moved.

"She's making up her mind to take a bath," explained Bobby. "She'll stand there maybe all day and all night unless somebody lifts her in."

"The doctor's ready, girls," shouted the nurse, and the mere thought of a man around excited everyone to fever pitch. "Come on, you, he wants to see you first, miss."

Jerry got up, trying to cover herself with the sheet, and made for the office. The doctor was a young man, disguising his youth behind a short black Van Dyke. He had a card in front of him and looked at her over this briefly.

"Well?" he asked crisply.

"I want to know how I got here," Jerry asked quietly. It was funny how fast you learned. Any protest of injustice brought on more injustice, so you must be quiet, accept outwardly whatever punishment the powers give, and wait, as Maria had told her, just wait.

"You don't remember?" the doctor said skeptically, then nodded. "That's right, you were in such a state the cops said they had to give you a shot to quiet you. The report says you and some other prostitutes were picked up in a Bowery joint with a hunchback who peddles reefers which you were smoking — "

The blood swam in Jerry's head.

"He passed us cigarettes, I didn't know they were reefers," she said faintly.

"You gave him a five-dollar bill, they said," said the doctor. "You wouldn't give that for a pack of Camels."

"I thought he was poor, that's all," Jerry said.

The doctor looked at her still skeptically.

"Are you so rich? Anyway there was a clean-up all over town last night. Some of the girls went to jail and the ones that were hysterical were taken to alcoholic or psycho wards in the city hospitals."

"What made them think I was a prostitute?" Jerry asked evenly.

The doctor looked at her again and then shrugged.

"The place you were, the people you were with, the reefers," he answered. "The hunchback is a procurer in that section and you gave him money."

"I told you I was sorry for him being a hunchback," Jerry repeated. "Was he arrested?"

The doctor gave a short laugh.

"I doubt it. Those places always pay protection for their regulars. When there's word of a clean-up the cops go after the strangers."

"Is that how those other girls out there were brought here — just to cover for the really guilty ones?" Jerry asked, trying to keep her voice steady, concealing the anger with which she was filled.

"That's not my business," said the doctor. "I'm the doctor, not the law. I can tell you that most of the girls out there today are brought in regularly — usually drunk or hopped up, either a little weak in the head like Bobby, or so long in prostitution that they don't even know it's a bad word and knowing no other life and not learning it's considered a sin they go right back in it."

"Those aren't bad women," Jerry said. "I'll bet you always get the wrong ones and they are too scared to say so."

The doctor was annoyed, and tapped his pencil on the card.

"It's not my business to prove their innocence or guilt," he said.

"Oh we're all guilty, I know that," Jerry said bitterly. "I know now that you become guilty and you feel guilty as soon as someone treats you as guilty. The only innocent ones are the accusers so all of you try to accuse the other person before you're found out yourself. You know it will *make* him guilty."

"I can't give you more time, Miss — " he referred to the card, "Dulaine. I agree with some things you are saying, but I advise you to take care where you say them. You made the office downstairs very angry last night screaming accusations at them and at the police, and threatening to report them all to your fiancé, Collier McGrew, who would order a big investigation. He's on our board, of course."

Jerry drew a long breath.

"I said that?" she murmured. "I can't remember."

"Reefer smokers think it's funny sometimes to pass their cigarettes to greenhorns. They get a kick watching their reactions," the doctor said. "I'm surprised you didn't suspect that. It usually creates delusions of grandeur. Maybe that's what made you boast of all the important people you thought you knew."

"Yes," said Jerry. There were evidently a lot of things she had said and done that it would be better not to know. But bringing in McGrew's name! Her fiancé! She felt weak with shame.

"I'll see if we can get you out of here as soon as possible," said the doctor. "That's all for now."

His phone rang and he picked up the receiver. He motioned Jerry to wait as he answered and when he hung up he smiled at her.

"Well, that's one on me," he said. "It seems you did know Collier McGrew. You insisted on his being notified last night, and he has sent his car for you and arranged for your release. The nurse will bring you your clothes, and your valuables are down in the office. I can only advise you to stay in your own class after this, Miss Dulaine. Stick with the people you know."

"Thank you," gasped Jerry, plunging out the door, tears in her eyes thinking of how good everyone was, how incredibly kind people were. The other women were standing in line outside the door waiting their turn with the doctor and the nurse stood by with her clothes over her arm.

"I'm going, I'm getting out!" Jerry cried out to the others. "Tell me what I can get for you outside, whoever you want me to see. I'll telephone your office and say you're sick or maybe there's somebody you want to come get you."

"Listen, those tramps got no offices," muttered the nurse.

"You're all right, Jerry," Chick called to her.

"Send me a newspaper or something," said the quiet-looking one named Bonny. "I'd like to do a little reading instead of sitting around yakking with these creeps."

The pale girl was still standing looking into the bathing room, her red braids over her shoulder, the slender legs bare from the thigh down posed in an arrested step like the statues of Diana. Jerry hesitated beside her, wanting to do something.

"Your hair is lovely," she said but the blue eyes looked calmly, patiently off as if waiting for a magic word to waken her.

"She's all right, she feels no pain," the nurse said impatiently. "Here's your clothes, now get into them, you're so anxious to get out."

She tossed the clothes on the bed, frowning, not wanting to show her curiosity and respect for someone able to escape so quickly into a world outside her authority. Jerry hurried into her clothes, overwhelmed with the privilege of wearing stockings and shoes, powder, her own comb. It was a dream that she was really getting out — she must make the most of it before she wakened and found herself back in this room with no doorknob on the door. She was glad she had changed from party clothes to street wear before she went out for that good time last night with Rick Prescott.

The girls were lined up outside the doctor's office as she passed and Bobby ran up to her, her sheet dragging behind her thin bare childish body.

"Got any rouge?" she whispered.

Jerry took out her compact and gave it to her, and handed the others her comb, lipstick, perfume vial, handkerchief.

"She'll take them all away tonight but we can hold them till then," said Maria, nodding toward the nurse down the hall.

Jerry followed the attendant down the corridors and out, thinking of the doctor's advice to stick to her own class and with the people she knew, and she thought these were the people she knew, this was her class.

A chauffeur in livery was standing in the office waiting for her.

"Mr. McGrew's car is outside," he said. "I'm to drive you to your home. He asked me to give you this note."

She opened the note, sitting in the back of the car.

> I could not reach you last night as my plane from Texas grounded in the desert and the relief didn't get me in till this morning. My secretary took the hospital's message and tried to straighten out what seems to be some fantastic error, or was it a joke? It will be amusing to hear all about it from you. Can I make amends for failing you at dinner last night by having Swanson pick you up at seven tonight?
>
> As ever,
> McGrew

Jerry smiled faintly as she crumpled the note. Elsie would certainly get a bang out of that, she thought, though it seemed a long time ago and of no matter to herself. She caught a glimpse of a man standing in front of her apartment. A process server, she thought, and decided to ask McGrew's chauffeur to drive on but it was too late. He had already stopped and opened the car door for her.

"Any message for Mr. McGrew, Miss Dulaine?" he asked, as she got out. "He thought you might want me to call for you later."

Jerry hesitated. It was too late, she thought. Everything happened too late. There wasn't anything she wanted of McGrew now.

"Thank him and tell him I'm not free tonight," she said and walked bravely up the steps. But it wasn't a process server at all, she realized, just her good friend of last night.

"I was just about to dredge the river," Rick said to her, taking her keys from her hand. "I've been chasing all over trying to find out what happened to you. I went backstage hunting for you and Tessie. Then there was that raid on the place and they shooed everybody out of the joint. All of a sudden I sobered up and remembered you said you were going to jump in the river."

"Me?" Jerry asked with a tired grimace. "I thought I said I was too lazy."

"You look pretty rocky," he said, surveying her doubtfully.

"Someday I'll tell you about it," Jerry said.

"Don't," he said. "I could guess when I saw the limousine."

"It wasn't that way at all," Jerry said. "That was just the happy ending that happens a day too late, at least that's the way I always fix it."

"That's the way I fix it, too," Rick said. "Born that way. Has something to do with the middle ear. Can't change it."

"Don't look so scared," Jerry laughed. "I won't faint."

"Sure you're all right?" He hesitated, about to go.

"Now I am," she said. She saw her mail on the hall table, topped by the long envelope from the collector of internal revenue, and sat down on the bottom stair suddenly, her head in her hands.

"Ever play crack the whip?" she asked, quite dizzy. "I feel like the one on the end that gets whirled off the faster they go."

Ricky turned and helped her to her feet.

"We'd better go make some coffee," he suggested. "We need a bracer. Let's face it, we had one hell of a good time even if it kills both of us."

He had intended to go back to his apartment, shower and shave, and get to the office around noon. But she was a nice kid and he couldn't leave her like this, half in a daze. It was just another one of those things he had started and had to see through.

Waking up in Jerry's bed later on, much refreshed, he asked Jerry why she was smiling.

"I can't get over that doctor taking me for a prostitute," she said.

Part Two

. . . *gentleman against women* . . .

• Wharton Hookley had the most profound admiration for his sister Elsie's incorruptible character, and he often dreamed of the monuments and even scholarships he would institute in her name when she died, the Elsie Hookley Club for Art Students, the Elsie Hookley Orphanage, the Elsie Hookley Woman Travelers' Aid (all inspired by his sister's latest vagary and worked out in systematic detail by his insomnia), but the trouble was that Elsie never would die. This put her brother into a most exasperating position, for almost every time he saw her or heard about her he got into such a sweat that he was bound to betray the very opposite of those emotions he wished to have. How could he eulogize his sister's classic candor until it was conveniently silenced once and for all? How could he state that no matter how unconventionally Elsie had lived and through whatever gaudy gutters she had trailed the Hookley traditions, she herself was the soul of honor when he was forever hearing that Elsie bore him no ill will for doing her out of her rightful inheritance? "Wharton really *cares* about possessions and I don't," she had generously said — no sense in doubting this report for she often made the same statement in his presence — "Grandmother's diamonds and the Maryland and Boston homesteads really mean something to Wharton, and I don't deserve them since I don't appreciate them, so let him keep my share, I have all I need in my little income."

The fact was that Elsie's outspokenness was Wharton's hair shirt, or rather one of his hair shirts as he had rather a full wardrobe of them, mostly the gifts of women as such unnecessary sartorial luxuries are apt to be. For most of his lifetime he had been able to maintain a Christian forbearance in the face of such vague aspersions from his sister's bohemian adherents, the kind of gentlemanly poise possible when one is sure the world is wise enough to wink at these fabrications. Wharton had been so confident that everyone agreed with his own exaggerated admiration for himself that he felt he could afford to excuse, even publicly defend his sister's eccentric doubts about his honesty. Elsie had never been well as a child, Elsie had been taken in by an early marriage to a titled foreigner, Elsie had been a child beauty and then, at the age of twelve, shot up to a grotesque six feet and been obliged to compensate.

But too late it was borne in on Wharton that the world secretly believed Elsie. Who put on the big social show in Boston and New York, after all, and how was it Wharton, with four expensive daughters, could live and travel in grandeur, fling around pews, stained glass windows and cemetery lots in endless memoriams to related Hookleys, unless he was nibbling away at Elsie's proper funds? Wharton, who had always been fiendishly meticulous and efficient in money matters, rued the day he had inherited the management of the family estate (though he would have cut his throat if anyone else had been given the nerve-racking privilege). Elsie, caring little as she did about diamonds, forgot she had casually changed them into bonds on which she now drew interest, and all that her loyal supporters saw was that Wharton's girls wore the diamonds. So many people felt guilty for finding Elsie Hookley's excessive heartiness and belligerent bohemianism almost intolerable that they pounced gratefully on any chance to prove they were not snobs, and after being chased into the most queasily genteel position by her excessive earthiness they were happy to proclaim their essential democracy by denouncing her brother for lack of it. Often Wharton found himself waking in the middle of the night accusing himself of dishonesty, remembering that he had forgotten to notify Elsie of the sale of five acres of timberland in northern Maine, and he would get up and paddle to his desk in his bare feet to jot it down right then and there at his desk. These careful notes referring to the sum of $304.64 being deposited to her account only made Elsie, who hadn't even known of any timberland, speculate sarcastically on how much Wharton was holding back from her on the deal. The more Wharton heard of Elsie's reflections on him the more slips he made, like a child who's been told it's clumsy, until he sometimes wondered if he was not being slowly tortured into unconscious chicanery, and at these moments he fiercely cursed his sister for puncturing his good conscience. A fine head for figures and careful bookkeeping being his particular vanity, slurs on these were all that worried him; like someone so absorbed in boasting of his abstinence he doesn't know he's sipped away a pint of bourbon, Wharton was so engrossed in his careful bookkeeping accounts and business management that he never seemed to notice that all the family furniture, silver, china and other accouterments of solid living unobtrusively found their way into his possession. In all her life Elsie had never noticed whether she was eating off a gold plate or a picnic pasteboard and besides, with the hit-or-miss life she led, what would she do with things?

That was why her request for the cane was so astounding.

It was one of the days when Wharton Hookley felt he owed it to his peace of mind to sojourn down to the Café Julien to lunch alone in state, for Elsie's note about the cane had been the last straw. The only thing that soothed him in moments of stress was to buy himself and nobody else a lavish lunch in an expensive restaurant, and look about him at all the people buying expensive lunches with money they were obliged to earn themselves, whereas he did not have to work for his lunch money and therefore must represent a superior order of mankind. It always surprised him that acquaintances, seeing him exhibiting his superiority in this fashion, did not envy him but often attempted to join him under the fantastic impression that he was lonesome. He ordered with the loving care he always bestowed on his stomach, starting off with a solitary Gibson, and a green turtle soup with Madeira. Sipping his wine with a complacent survey of an adjoining table where three businessmen were feasting on what must have taken them a good half day's work to earn, he felt sufficiently composed to take out his sister's note.

"I hate to have to keep after you about Uncle Carpenter's ram's-head cane," the large flowing handwriting said — now why must she dot her r's and h's, he wondered pettishly — "but honestly, Wharton, this must be the tenth time I've asked you for it during the last few years, and why on earth you hang on to it when you know what it means to me on account of Uncle Carpenter being my favorite relative — etcetera, etcetera."

The fact was that every time Elsie remembered Uncle Carpenter's ram's-head cane, Wharton knew something nasty was in the wind. He and his older sister were poles apart, had never understood one thing about each other's nature, lived completely different lives that crossed only occasionally, on the surface of things meant nothing to each other, but somehow had never been able to make a single move unless they were convinced it was the exact opposite of what the other would do. Even when they were not in the same country they had some kind of radar that told them what the other was up to, always something extraordinarily wrong and inducive to a countermove carefully planned to cause equal irritation on the other side.

Take the matter of Uncle Carpenter. For several summers, Wharton had sent his younger daughters up to Uncle Carpenter's big place at Narragansett, and once in a while Wharton would have a faint twinge thinking that Uncle Carpenter was half his sister's property, too, but still if she didn't have sense enough to feather her nest he wasn't going to do it for her. On the old man's death the place, technically, was half Elsie's, but since she showed no interest — of course if it was ever sold, Wharton always said, she would get her half — he continued using it for family purposes, carefully deducting repairs and general upkeep from Elsie's as well as his own estates, fifty-fifty fair and square. Then — just as he was vaguely expecting some much more justifiable alarming demand—he received Elsie's request for Uncle Carpenter's cane. In his relief he was about to send it to her post-haste when a shrewd second thought came to him. Just what was there about that cane, one, incidentally, which he had never even remembered? He went through a hundred ancestral canes in the Narragansett attic until he found the one with the little ugly jade ram's-head. The eyes and horns were studded with emerald and diamond chips and it was made of some perhaps remarkable Malaysian wood, the head unscrewed for a dagger, but it was an ugly thing at best and certainly of no great value. Wharton did not remember ever having seen his uncle use it, and at first he just sat there looking at the damn cane shaking his head and thinking what a fool Elsie was. Why on earth did Elsie want it? Was it a museum piece, was there something about it that made it worth a king's ransom, and what mysterious enemies were behind Elsie in this strange request? Wharton hung on to the cane, reading up about cane collections, asking questions here and there, with Elsie making repeated demands. Something more important always came up and the cane would be forgotten, but maybe after two years of silence up popped the matter of the cane again. The worst thing was that he couldn't think of any reason for not giving it to her so he always promised to hunt it up. He went to Uncle Sam's Cane Shop on Forty-Sixth Street with it and they said it might be worth something as a curio, the ram's horns were remarkably carved and the end capped with a miniature hoof was a quaint conceit, but even though it might be worth five hundred dollars to some collector the cane shop would not offer more than two hundred at most.

"Why should Elsie have Uncle's cane?" fretted Wharton, and looking around at the bustling lunchers who surely could not enjoy their armagnac when they knew it was the sweat off their own brows, it seemed to him they were all his enemies, all of them knew what there was about the cane that made Elsie want it and they were all laughing at him. Well, she wouldn't get it this time, either, he vowed, and see how they liked *that!* He saw that everyone was laughing today and he wondered if maybe it wasn't the cane, but something else, something somebody might have said about him in Boston, for instance, or something about Nita, his wife —

The thought of Nita popped up like a jack-in-the-box from the bottom of his conscious mind, the way it had been doing lately, and it would not go away no matter how he tried to remind himself that it was not Nita but Uncle Carpenter's cane that was bothering him.

At the age of thirty-five (having lived dutifully with his mother in the Boston house during all of her strokes, pursuing his private eccentricities with the utmost discretion) Wharton had found exactly the right bride and had married her. She was the sixteen-year-old daughter of a Peruvian dignitary, so the step had none of the hazards of a union with some overeducated, wilful American woman but was like taking on a sweet, dutiful daughter with none of the inconvenience of creating her. Wharton was a frustrated mother, and far from having a mother complex, had only enjoyed his own mother when she was too feeble to resist his maternal care and dictatorship. Mother now retired, Wharton found Nita gloriously childlike, a blank page as so many carefully reared and protected South American young girls are. She had been an obedient daughter and except for occasional wayward weeping fits of nostalgia for tropic skies and convent playmates, tried hard to be an obedient bride. Wharton had never been nor wished to be a ladies' favorite, for the young ones were like his sister, arrogant and superior, and moreover he had constantly before him that particularly terrifying breed of Boston women, unsexed by age and ugliness, hairy with old family fortunes, the spayed witches of subterranean bank vaults, perpetual demonstrations of the Horror of Femaleness.

Wharton himself had been no beauty, licked at the start by a nose that did seem an outrage, a mongrel affair beginning as the Hookley Roman then spreading into Egyptian, and possessing a perverse talent for collecting lumps, iridescent scales, ridges and spots so that it seemed to reflect half a dozen colors simultaneously, ranging through bruise-purple, cabbage green, mulberry red, baby-bottom pink and chalk white. Wharton had such a terrific reputation for efficiency that many friends swore that the reason his nose changed colors before your very eyes was because of an elaborate Rimbaud color code, indicating varied reactions to his surroundings. But middle age had been kind to him, for nose, mottled skin, prim mouth, grim chin and irritable grape-green eyes were blessedly dominated and softened by luxuriant, wavy iron-gray hair and eyebrows. "Distinguished" was the word for Wharton at fifty-five at exactly the time in his life when the overpowering egotism built up by his marriage was being dangerously punctured. Ah, what a stroke of genius it had been for him to have found Nita! How happy he had been on his honeymoon and for years afterward basking in the safety of Nita's childish innocence where his intellectual shortcomings, sexual coldness and caprices — indeed his basic ignorance — would not be discovered. He corrected her language, manners, dress, aired his opinions on all subjects as simple gospel, but particularly he enjoyed her gasps of bewilderment when he lectured her on some new angle of art, literature, psychoanalysis, or perversion that had secretly shocked him. He was well aware that many men of his quixotic moods preferred young boys, but he dreaded to expose his inexperience to one of his own sex, and after certain cautious experiments realized that his anemic lusts were canceled by his overpowering fear of gossip.

Marrying Nita was the perfect answer, just at the moment when Boston had formed its own opinion of him. Against the flattering background of Nita's delectable purity he blossomed forth as the all-round-He-man, the Husband who knows everything, the reformed rake (as Nita's tradition informed her all husbands were) who was generously patient with her backwardness. He soon taught her that snuggling, hand-holding and similar affectionate demonstrations were kittenish and vulgar. He had read somewhere, however, that breathing into a woman's ear or scratching her at the nape of the neck drove her into complete ecstasy, and this was something he did not mind doing, lecturing her at the same time on the purpose of this diablerie so that the dear gullible child did a great deal of dutiful squealing. This success led him into reading many frank handbooks on the subject of sharing one's sex with women, his own instinctive revulsion neutralized by Nita's disapproval. In due course Nita bore him four daughters, a sort of door prize for each time he had attended. This was again fortunate since any male infant would surely have terrified him with the hint of future knowledge surpassing his. Nita allowed him to assume the position of hen mother, clucking and clacking rules for their every moment, herself in the role of conscientious older sister. But when the youngest turned six and Nita herself was thirty-two, looking, to tell the truth, a bare nineteen, she suddenly blossomed out before Wharton's horrified eyes as the complete American girl.

Wharton had grown so complacent in his role of tutor that it never occurred to him that his pupil might graduate. Nor had it ever struck him that the ideas he pronounced purely for dramatic effect would really take root in virgin soil. Suddenly he found his wife utterly changed, as if seduced by his worst enemy. The charming little doll wife was his Frankenstein monster confronting him with all the sawdust with which he himself had stuffed her. He groaned now at the idiotic satisfaction he used to take in nagging her for her convent shyness (he being a very shy man himself), telling her that now she was an American and must learn American confidence. He dared not remind himself of the daring new books, plays, pictures, philosophies which secretly appalled him that he maintained (against her shocked protestations) were necessary for the modern thinker. "You must learn the ways of the world, my dear child," he had patronizingly instructed her, smiling kindly at her naïve outcries, "this is the world, this is life. You're no longer a child and you're no longer in Mother Clarissa's convent in Peru. You're a woman of the world, a wife and mother, and an American!"

The first time Elsie had demanded Uncle Carpenter's ram's-head cane was the very year Nita had burgeoned forth with the bombshell that as an American woman of the world she could naturally waste no more time in the wilderness of Uncle Carpenter's Rhode Island estate or the Hookley morguish manor in Boston. A New York establishment was indicated as the suitable headquarters for the midwinter season of an American matron whose four ugly daughters were safely tucked away in boarding school, and in his consternation Wharton found himself doing exactly as Nita directed him, unable to answer her query as to whether he wasn't pleased with his little pupil, now that she had become the kind of wife he wanted.

Nita had learned more than he intended, and in that maddening way women have, had not been content to leave the knowledge in print the way it was supposed to be but must put it into practical use. She was enthusiastically modern now, frighteningly knowledgeable on all the matters he himself had pretended to be, as worldly and bold in her conversation as any American woman he had ever feared. Wasn't he proud, she demanded, that she was no longer the little provincial prude he had so patiently brought up? Now she could carry on the most fashionably free conversation with any man; wasn't he flattered when he saw how his years of patient criticisms had finally taken effect? It must make him laugh to think of the way she used to embarrass him by slipping her hand in his in public as if he was her papa, as he often said in scolding, and the way she had been afraid to talk to men, turning really pale when the conversation turned openly on sex! How sweet and patient he had been, reading to her, explaining and scolding until she was now — as you see — a genuine woman of the world. She no longer drew back in consternation when some male guest kissed her or casually caressed her, for she knew her husband would mock at her foreign backwardness, and if necessity arose she could breathe in their ears and scratch the napes of their necks like any other proper American woman.

Baffled as he was, Wharton was certain she had not gone to any lengths with any other man because if she had — and it tortured him to face it — he had a terrible conviction that she would never have returned to him. With a herculean effort he adjusted himself superficially to the new order, saw with newly opened eyes that his wife was not regarded as an appropriate detail in Wharton Hookley's properly furnished background, but as a powerful little female in her own right, holding sway over a circle of admirers who listened respectfully to her shrewd worldly conversation. Overhearing her at times Wharton groaned inwardly at the world-weary comments on love and sin with which he had often delighted to shock her now being repeated, contrasting so devastatingly with her charmingly childish figure, bright innocent eyes, Latin lisp. People must surely get the wrong idea from her talk, he thought desperately, but there had been too many years of gentle scolding her for prudery, ignorance, and convent-narrowness to start reproaching her for the exact opposite. He dared not remember the evenings in the country when he had read aloud to his four daughters and Nita, carefully explaining all hidden meanings, scatological or sexual (nothing to be afraid of, let us face these matters openly), insisting on his superior masculinity, furious at himself for blushing or stammering when the five female faces remained dutifully blank and unimpressed. Now he found his wife's vocabulary astonishingly racy, and when some involuntary reproach escaped him she would mildly remind him that these were good old Anglo-Saxon words long in use, and he was perforce silenced by this parroting. Sometimes a glib quotation from some radical nincompoop, some facile praise for an anarchistic artist or philosopher exasperated him to the point of screaming protest, his sensitive nose glittered like a rock in Painted Desert and it seemed incredible for Nita to answer, troubled and wide-eyed, "But, Wharton, have you changed your opinions, then, after you worked so hard to make me see things your way?" Every scarecrow that had ever appalled him from his sister Elsie's mental pastures he had held up for Nita's fright, but it turned out his scarecrows scared nobody but himself; they leered at him on all sides, from sister, wife, and even his four little daughters.

You couldn't trust women, Wharton thought, sipping his brandy, moderately soothed to see fellow diners taking out watches and hastily paying their checks to get back to their wretched desks while he, one of the master men, could dawdle all day if he liked without losing a penny. Still, it was his second brandy, a rare indulgence for midday, and with a sigh he signed his check, placed the exact tip on it and strolled to the checkroom. The checkroom girl was helping a young man into his overcoat, the young man, being a little drunk, waved his arms clumsily and winked at Wharton. Wharton allowed himself a discreet flicker of a smile in response and when the lad gave an impatient oath Wharton inclined his head sympathetically. To tell the truth the young man had a sudden and utterly unreasonable appeal for Wharton, perhaps because his thoughts had been so overrun with women. It seemed to Wharton that there was about this young man, as there had been about himself at that age, absolutely nothing that would capture a woman's fancy. He was a swarthy, undersized, wiry little chap with wide ears, a knobby black-thatched head, close-set beady little eyes, a comedy button nose, crooked mouth, and an outthrust impudent chin — a little monkey you might say, and his arms swung about like monkey arms, too long for his body. Wharton wondered how he happened to be in such a place, for he looked as if he belonged on the other side of an all-night lunch counter, maybe in a turtle-necked black sweater with a dirty apron tied around his waist. Here was a young man who must have been born knowing everything; there was nothing you could tell this one, judging by the knowing mockery of the face. You wouldn't catch this one being harassed by the complexities of femaleness, or cornered by his own weaknesses. Here was the kind of son he should have had, Wharton thought, the ugly essence of masculinity itself, arrogant, fearless, raw. There was something familiar about him, and it was as he was smiling involuntarily at the outlandishly big coat the boy was getting into that Wharton realized the familiarity was in the coat itself.

"Why, that's my coat!" he exclaimed, startled out of his good manners.

The young man laughed, shrugged, the girl hastily pulled off the coat and handed it to Wharton, who found himself apologizing ridiculously for claiming his own property, even though there was his name woven in the lining for all to see.

"But you didn't have a coat when you came in, Mr. Hookley, I'm sure," the girl murmured, confused.

"Perhaps I left it here last week," Wharton graciously allowed. "Usually I wear — "

As a matter of fact usually he wore his new topcoat. It came over him that he hadn't worn the one in his hands for at least a year. In fact he could have sworn he'd left it in the country. Mystified and embarrassed he tipped the girl and followed the young man out the hallway to the street. Not at all perturbed by the episode the young man was swinging jauntily down the street, a derby hat on the side of his head, twirling his cane like some old-time vaudevillian.

Wharton's eyes followed the cane. It was a ram's-headed cane capped by a dainty little goat's hoof.

. . . *the animal lovers* . . .

• The enormous portrait of the four Hookley girls which hung in Wharton's library was an unfailing comfort to everyone and well worth the ten thousand dollars extorted by the artist, Laidlaw Whitfield, that charming gentleman-painter whose exhibitions were reviewed in the society columns instead of on the art page. Wharton's plan had been to have the four girls, great galumphing grim replicas of himself, curled, and socked, and pearled, grouped around their mother in the Boston garden. This turned out to be such an ungentlemanly enterprise, the lovely little Nita amid the four gargoyle girls forming a satirical fantasy that would have ruined the artist's social success, that the four girls were done alone, long heavy locks and costumes given especial attention to soften the reality. Visitors, unable to compliment the children, could speak effusively of the beautiful painting, the velvet so "touchable," the lace so *real*, the sunlight on the flowers so charmingly done, Bluebell, the great Dane, so true to life. Wharton could look at this soothing idealization and flatter himself on being superior to all women for he had produced four himself, and could honestly boast, conscientious mother that he was, that he had plotted, planned and guarded every thought and move of their lives. It was he, not Nita, who directed their diet, dentistry, reading, recreations, dress, friends, schools, manners, and when they were at home he was at them indefatigably every minute, so that he seldom heard their own voices except the docile, "Yes, Father," "Thank you, Father," and "Good-morning, Father." Their aunt Elsie, who had heard them conversing beyond this point, loved to report elsewhere the delicious news that these exquisitely trained girls spoke a most regrettable, and probably incurable Brooklynese caught from their first nurse (medically irreproachable), and their riding master (a jewel, also, in his own field). Further reports from Elsie were that her brother could not distinguish between his daughters, so similar were they in appearance and so abysmally ignorant was he of any shades of difference in the female character, anyway.

"Just four junior Whartons in different sizes," she jubilated. "I think he had them by parthenogenesis."

Elsie, teeming with a marvelous new idea, had taken it into her head to drop into her brother's duplex on Gracie Square without warning, quite aware that to have pinned him down to a definite appointment would have put him on his guard. Whenever she popped in like this, Wharton was furious with himself for not forestalling this inconvenient visit for it was always inconvenient, as everything about his sister was and always would be. Nita was never any help in these difficulties, and today she herself was put out. She was expecting guests at six and Wharton was already cross because they were part of the new group he did not know. She was sure Elsie would stay and make everything worse by shouting family matters at Wharton. It was long after five and for special reasons she wanted to spend more time arranging her charming little person to perfection. The maid reported that Elsie had brought her great Dane which had started the dachshund yapping, and it so happened that the children had brought in Bluebell herself, Brucie's mother, to see the vet. Out of sheer high spirits Bluebell had immediately disgraced herself at sight of the new Ispahan in the hall and was at the moment confined upstairs to the children's bathroom, refreshing her fagged old gums with some nubbly bath towels and wet nylons.

"Elsie will have to wait till after my bath," Wharton called out testily from his bedroom. "She knows she should have telephoned me first or come to see me at my office."

"It's *your* sister, Wharton, dear," Nita called back from her mirror-walled dressing room. "The sooner you see her the sooner she'll go away."

"Why couldn't Gladys have told her I was out?" Wharton asked peevishly.

"Darling, you know Gladys is absolutely petrified of her," Nita retorted. "You *must* get down there, and do try to keep her from staying."

Elsie was not at all unconscious of the flutter her calls always occasioned. The instant her firm voice sounded at the door, "Tell Mr. Hookley I'm here, Gladys," there were scampers and scurries and whispers and tiptoeings all over the place as if it was a prohibition raid. Then the cautious stillness, indicating that everyone was in their hiding place holding their breath. Elsie knew something special was afoot by the way the Hookley's ancient retainer Gladys recoiled from the door, palsied hands uplifted as if this was the devil himself.

"And how are you these days, Gladys?" Elsie raised her voice a good octave to the eminence she deemed proper for addressing inferiors. This kind inquiry set Gladys to trembling all over again though she managed a terrified smile even as she backed away, quavering "Q-q-q-q-uite n-n-n-ic-e, madam," her faded blue eyes begging for mercy. Gladys had worked in the Hookley homes for fifty years out of sheer terror. She was afraid of all Hookleys and everything else. She believed the world was a lunatic and she was its trembling nurse. If she only could manage to coax and soothe it it might not leap at her, but on the other hand it might, just as Brucie or Bluebell might. The slightest overture found her backing warily toward any door with a fixed oh-I'm-not-afraid-a-bit smile, wide frightened eyes and little gasps of Yes, please, it is a warm day, oh *please*, yes of course it is, dearie, now, now, of course you know best, and please, oh *please* I'm very well, and there, there, everything's going to be all right, please — oh dear — *Yowie!*

Today's encounter with Elsie and Brucie, coming so soon after the *affaire* Bluebell, left the poor woman shaking like a leaf, knowing she was to blame for everything, even for Brucie's instant recognition of his mother's traces on the rug and dutiful lifting of leg to follow example. Having set the household rocking on its heels Elsie stalked straight into her brother's library, Brucie loping behind with poor Gladys scampering around for mops and Airwick.

Elsie selected a cigarette from Wharton's special hoard and seated herself before the portrait of the Hookley daughters. This never failed to amuse her, and she sat there smiling at it, till it occurred to her to torture Gladys further by shouting for her to bring a bowl of water for Brucie and a double Scotch for herself. Gladys was apparently too spent to accomplish this mission alone and it was Williams, the butler, who bore the tray, obviously resentful of being hurried from his own tea into his party coat.

"Thank you, Williams." Elsie ascended the scale to the master voice again. "Thank you very much. Leave the bottle."

She critically studied the drink Williams had poured and then added a proper amount more and was resuming her artistic pleasure in the Hookley portrait when she realized that she herself was being examined. Eight-year-old Gloria, already five feet tall, Hookley-nosed, baby fangs fearsomely clamped in steel, lanky fair locks dripping about her head like an inadequate fountain, legs bruised, bitten and vaccinated, startlingly bare from ankle socks to bloomered crotch, stood in the doorway.

"Did my mother invite you to her party?" the tot inquired without preamble, her eyes disapproving first of Brucie sitting on the love seat with Aunt Elsie, and then of Aunt Elsie sitting on the love seat with Brucie.

"Not a bit," Elsie answered genially, pulling off her gloves and adjusting her Filene's basement hat with great care at an angle leaving only one eye diabolically visible. "How are you, Gloria?"

"Very well, thank you. Did my father give you that hat?"

"No, dear. Your father did not," Elsie answered, and then,

as she was really sorry for her nieces, foreseeing a grim girlhood for them either under her brother's thumb or on their own sparse merits, she said, "You look very nice today, Gloria."

"Thank you very much, Aunt Elsie," said Gloria, graciously seating herself on the ottoman opposite her aunt. "You have very nice new shoes. Did Father give them to you?"

"Indeed he did not, darling," replied Elsie, thinking the girl has no more business wearing bobby-sox than I have.

"Did my mother say you could have that highball?" Gloria went on politely, her attention focused on Brucie's pursuit of fleas. "Would you like me to bring you something to eat?"

The girl is too damn tall, Elsie thought, you feel like snapping at her as if she was a grownup. She always had to remember not to get angry, for the children always asked these same questions of everybody as a kind of courteous repartee. Where did they learn it? No matter what faults Wharton had, or Nita, either, they certainly never credited themselves publicly or privately with grandiose benevolences, and it was strange where the girls got the idea that their visitors were thanes of the family. Cooling her irritation by trying to figure out the source of this childish obsession Elsie concluded that it was born in them, as it was born in all rich people, excepting, of course, in rogue elephants like herself. All friends and relatives of other rich people are supported by them. ("I met a nice little couple at the Lambreths' the other day; they drove me home in their new Cadillac." "What? So the Lambreths are buying Cadillacs for their protégés now!") The Born Rich eye strips every other guest in a friend's house of talent, beauty, personal ability and independence and makes them at once the dependent of the other Rich — else why should they be there? What other bond is there between human beings? It entertained and soothed Elsie now to reflect on the industrious instruction Wharton had lavished on his wife and children, and how Nita had learned something unforeseen from it, and the daughters had allowed it to roll off their knobby little skulls like tropic rain, leaving the basic I.Q. undisturbed by any philosophy except I-AM-RICH, WE-ARE RICH, YOU-ARE-NOT-RICH.

A strange moaning sound echoed suddenly through the upper hall. Aunt and niece exchanged a nod as Brucie pricked up his ears.

"Bluebell?" asked Elsie.

Gloria nodded with a beam of anticipation.

"She's locked in my bathroom, but she always smells Brucie, doesn't she? Will you let Brucie visit her again this summer, Aunt Elsie?"

"I doubt if your parents will allow it," said Elsie. "You know what always happens."

Aunt and niece were silent, smiling reminiscently, united for the moment in pleasant memories of the glorious days when Brucie visited Bluebell's kennels in the country. The great dogs had to be locked up separately but there was always the day when one or the other broke loose and freed the other and they streaked off to town, rejuvenated, like sailors on leave. They loped joyously down the highway, chasing anything that moved in the bushes, stripping clotheslines of the day's wash in back yards, scattering chickens, detouring traffic, and heading always for Mulligan's Bar at the edge of town where they had once been taken and been made much of by a highly temporary former gardener. Police, state troopers, veterinarians and sundry public officials were alerted by indignant or frightened citizens, the Hookley home was soon called and in a matter of hours the mother and son, tired but triumphant, were back in their reinforced kennels while Wharton furiously wrote checks making amends for lost laundry, broken bottles and glasses in Mulligans', lost chickens, rabbits and sundry properties.

"They have fun together, don't they, Aunt Elsie?" Gloria said dreamily. "Big dogs like to play the same as little ones, don't they, Aunt Elsie?"

"Of course, my dear," Elsie said, looking at her niece more kindly.

Wharton came into the room, cloaked in the manner he reserved for his sister, that of a preoccupied, harassed, weary man of Christian patience and forgiveness, resigned to any personal slurs or impositions, a man not too well and given to pressing a throbbing temple or overworked heart but never mind, it's really not your fault, it will be quite all right if you will not tax him too much with your idiotic demands. He kissed Elsie tenderly on the brim of her fedora, patted Brucie and Gloria twice each on the head and said solicitously, "I hope nothing's wrong, Elsie, to bring you away from your colorful little cocktail bars." Having established his impression of Elsie's slavish devotion to bars and the fact that her visit would have to be a matter of life and death to excuse it, he remained standing with an arm around Gloria's shoulders, smiling carefully at his sister.

"I came for the cane," Elsie said briskly, with the easy confidence of one who has the power of being a nuisance. "You've been so frightfully busy and couldn't get it to me."

The sound of guests arriving in the outer hall saved Wharton, and the next moment a loud wail from upstairs provided distraction. Brucie threw back his head and yowled back.

"My dear Elsie," Wharton exclaimed sharply, "you know how often I've asked you not to bring Brucie when Bluebell is here! There's always bound to be trouble!"

Elsie put a fond restraining hand on Brucie's collar.

"My dear Wharton," she replied easily. "Bluebell is Brucie's mother after all. Can't you ever forgive or understand animals having family feelings even if human beings don't? Brucie and I will be off in a minute, as soon as you give me Uncle Carpenter's cane, there's a dear boy."

More guests were arriving and at last Nita's voice could be heard greeting them in the living room. Wharton threw out his hands in a gesture of polite exasperation.

"Really, Elsie, for someone who has never taken any proper pride in the family and has done her best — yes, I'm going to say it! — to belittle the name, this sudden sentimentality about Uncle Carpenter is too ridiculous. As I recall only too well you were too busy chasing after that phony Count of yours to even come to Uncle's deathbed and now — "

"Phony, Wharton?" Elsie interrupted ominously. "You refer to the Baron Humfert as *phony* in just what sense, may I inquire? I too can recall all too well the offensive way you used to roll out all the Humfert titles and connections to impress your friends. Surely you're not trying to imply his title is phony just because he's no longer in the Hookley family."

Hypertension, watch out for hypertension, Wharton strove to watch himself.

"You know perfectly well what I mean, Elsie, my dear," he said with a steely smile. "He was phony in the sense that he was not a true royalist at all, insisting on giving up his title and joining the underground like any peasant. We've been over this too many times for you to pretend you didn't know he used the money we settled on him to promote all sorts of uprisings."

"I think it was the finest thing he ever did, Wharton," declared Elsie ringingly, who thought no such thing and had a private conviction that her ex-husband would have joined any church or any cause, even a good one, for a price.

Wharton controlled himself with difficulty, maintaining his patient smile which he directed now significantly at the drink in his sister's hand.

"Is that stout you're drinking, my dear?" he asked. "It's very dark for Scotch, isn't it?"

"I like it dark, old boy," Elsie shouted, "just the way your mother always liked it and all the red-blooded women in the family, right back to the original Hookley barmaid in Lancashire. I hope you've told little Gloria here all about that great-great-grandma."

"No, he didn't, Aunt Elsie," Gloria piped up, her beady little eyes leaping hopefully from father to aunt while she stroked Brucie's hide vigorously.

Wharton's emotions were now discoloring his nose just as she feared, and he raised a hand for truce, even though he would have found great relief in a real out-and-out no-holds barred fight with Elsie.

"May I ask you to lower your voice, Elsie?" He was mad enough now to be able to use his most dulcet tone, even though he knew it acted like a red flag to his sister. "We have guests here, nice people if you'll forgive my using such an old-fashioned expression, gentlemen and ladies, if you please, who wouldn't want to be subjected to the inside story of the

Hookley barmaid even by her reincarnated descendant. Now, let us get to the point of this visit, Elsie, as quickly and quietly as possible."

Elsie swallowed her drink and put down the glass.

"Gloria, dear, I know you love Brucie but would you mind not pinching him? He still has his teeth, you know." She spoke very kindly and then composed herself in her chair leisurely before answering her brother. Lighting a fresh cigarette provided a further delay. "I have come to the conclusion, Wharton, that you must have lost Uncle Carpenter's cane and that indicates that perhaps a great many more of his treasures, which, as you know, are half mine, may be lost or misplaced. I'm not accusing you or Nita, of course, but you have had sole use of his house for all these years — "

"I grant you that, Elsie. I've always told you I can't understand why you've chosen to live in comparative squalor instead of in any of the family houses at your disposal," Wharton said impatiently. "If you choose to pass up your legal rights — "

"Don't be so sure of that," Elsie interrupted with a pleasant nod at little Gloria. "Your peculiar attitude in refusing to give me poor Uncle's cane, a simple little memento like that, has made me realize it's about time I should protect my other rights."

Wharton stiffened.

"And might one inquire just what it is you are proposing to do?" he asked with a glacial smile.

Elsie pulled her felt brim further over her right eye and then flung her head back sidewise, in a regal gesture revealing half an eye beamed ominously at her brother.

"I propose to look over the Narragansett property myself

and select what items I wish in order to realize cash on them," she stated. "Moreover I shall then go to Boston and talk to Mother about reopening the Marlborough Street house. I see no reason why I should not spend a season or two in Boston after all my years in squalor as you call it."

Wharton whipped out his kerchief and pressed it to his lips to stifle a scream of rage.

"Elsie! You know Mother's condition!" he shouted. "You know she has a stroke every time she sees you!"

"Nothing major," corrected Elsie calmly. "May I ask you not to raise your voice unless you wish to excite Brucie? As for an only daughter wishing to visit her ailing mother, only a man without human feelings like yourself could regard it with such astonishment. How do I know if Cousin Beals is doing the right thing for her?"

"Cousin Beals is doing everything that can be done for a senile old lady in her eighties," Wharton said, breathing heavily but getting himself under control. "She won't recognize you, and if you attempt to move her from the Vendome you'll kill her."

"It's a chance you yourself have often taken, Wharton, when it suited your book," Elsie said, lowering her head to give him the benefit of the full crown of her hat.

He was outmaneuvered and he knew it. He had been braced years ago for Elsie's illogical brainstorms but today he was prepared only for the silly cane struggle. He dared make no objection to her demand for the Narragansett property, though after exclusive use of it for so long Nita had come to regard it as completely theirs and he knew she would scold him for surrendering anything in it. He was licked, but at least the battle was over temporarily, he did not have to explain the cane mystery, and perhaps she would change her mind about the monstrous Boston plan. At any rate she would go away.

"Why not call at my office and pick up the Narragansett keys?" he suggested, knowing his calm surrender took away part of her pleasure. "Naturally there is nothing I can do to keep you from upsetting Mother if that is your peculiar desire. And now forgive me if I join Nita's guests. I would ask you to meet them but you know how insupportable you always find our friends, my dear. A pity we will have so little time to see you what with this being Isabella's first season out."

"I'll run up and see Isabella now," said Elsie, but Wharton raised his hand hastily in protest.

"The poor girl has worn herself out already," he said. "She has taken to her bed and doesn't even join in our family meals."

"You drove her too hard," Elsie said firmly. "Absolutely barbaric to hound the poor child to land a husband the first year. The whole town's talking about it."

"I can trust you to keep me informed on the town talk," replied Wharton, smiling brilliantly.

Both rose, feeling a little regretful that they could not extend their always bracing quarrels, and though the room still seemed to reek of gunpowder they looked at each other with a kind of fond admiration. Gloria, who had been enjoying the battle, turned away in disappointment and petulantly gave Brucie a good pinch. With a howl Brucie bolted through the door, an echoing howl resounded from the upper floor, and the next moment Gladys could be heard screaming as she streaked, white-faced, down the stairs. The noise had electrified the quiet little group just assembled in the great living room though Nita had laughingly explained it was only the dogs.

"Bluebell and Brucie always have wild reunions," she was saying in her fetching Spanish lisp. "Sit down, everybody, they won't hurt anybody, they just want to get at each other. It is just a little incest like anybody else. Wharton will quiet them."

Fortunately Bluebell had not succeeded in breaking down the bathroom door because Brucie was trying to break it down from the other side. Elsie, with great presence of mind, took a tray of caviar, whipped sour cream and smoked salmon from Williams as he was bearing it to his mistress and took it upstairs as lure for Brucie. The strategy proved effective and the hors d'oeuvres dulled Brucie's filial passion to the point of allowing Elsie to lead him downstairs again with amiable docility. Wharton, mopping his brow wearily, paused at the door of the living room. His bout with Elsie and Brucie left him with little strength to face Nita's guests, for this was one of the newer cultural groups which always had him at a disadvantage anyway. Nita hurried out into the hall, sparkling and happy seeing that her sister-in-law was about to leave with no further disaster. She was looking even prettier than ever, hibiscus in her black hair and a huge cluster of scarlet taffeta flowers at her tiny waist and trailing down the white skirt to her hem. She embraced Elsie tenderly, reproaching her for not staying with them for dinner when there were such nice people here.

"Now, now, darling," Wharton interpolated with a warning look at his wife, "you know Elsie always finds our friends too respectable for her."

"Oh I don't know. I might have one highball," Elsie said

just as he had feared, hooking Brucie's leash on to the newel post with dreadful finality.

As she strode into the living room Wharton transferred his irritation to his wife who should have known this would happen.

"I don't even know some of these people," he muttered crossly.

"Do be nice to Mrs. Grover," Nita whispered to him. "In blue over by the window."

But Wharton had stopped short as Nita went forward with Elsie. A curious puzzled expression came to his face and he did not seem to hear people greeting him, his eyes fixed on a swarthy young man standing by the mantelpiece, thumbs thrust nonchalantly in a fancy waistcoat, short legs spread apart and bowed as if astride a horse, a black lock falling over his low forehead, a crooked smile quivering on his lips.

"This is Elsie, Wharton's sister," Nita was saying, looking very tiny beside Elsie. "Elsie, this is Nigel di Angelo. He was in my art class and we're in the same dianetics group now."

"Pleasure," mumbled the young man.

Elsie blinked. Now really. No, it simply could not be.

"Nigel?" she repeated. "Did you say Nigh-jell?"

The young man returned her stare with a defiant grin.

"Nigel di Angelo," Nita said. "You've no idea how gifted he is."

Elsie nodded with a faint smile.

"I believe I'm familiar with his work," she said musingly. "I think Mrs. Jamieson in Gloucester has his very first oil painting."

The young man tugged at his lock as if it was a bell rope and evidently memory answered the summons.

"That's right," he said. "I remember. Four clams on a green plate. Let's see, this Mrs. Jamieson you mention — "

"Had a Buick," Elsie said, obliging him to meet her significant gaze.

The young man blew a smoke ring at her, unperturbed. "I picked out an M.G. for her later," he said nonchalantly. "I like English cars."

"Of course," Elsie said. English cars! Nigel! "I wish you'd help me pick one out sometime."

It was fun to see the greedy little black eyes sparkle at that.

"Be glad to," he said. "Let me get in touch with you."

An overwhelming desire to laugh came over Elsie and to Wharton's great relief she snatched the drink he offered her and gulped it down.

"Must get Brucie home," she gasped, making for the door.

"I was sure you'd find it too dull for you," he replied. As she untied Brucie's leash from the newel post he glanced around the hall and coatroom, glad to see no sign of the young man's cane, but wondering why he had not carried it today and what this signified. Nita's new interests were increasingly curious, he thought wearily, and this odd young man's presence here was as baffling as his having the damnable cane and his own topcoat.

Elsie managed to get out on the street with Brucie tugging at his leash before the laughter came.

Niggy of all people! And calling himself Nigel, if you please. Memories of that fantastic summer on the Cape came back to Elsie, and since they were naughty memories a fond smile curled her lips. Niggy had been the Portugee of the year, and the summer ladies, always undermanned, had talked of nothing but Niggy. It was Niggy this and Niggy that. They fought over him in bars, they ruined his fishing by following him in their speedboats; they gave up husbands, jobs, reputations, for the Niggy chase. Elsie recalled her disgust at the hysteria, not having yet seen him, and picturing a slumbrous-eyed Latin of incredible beauty and delicious stupidity.

And then her prim, hymn-singing, Baptist Iola, the best cook on the eastern seaboard, had tried to kill herself for love of this hero. Outraged, as well as mightily inconvenienced, Elsie had taken it upon herself to confront the cad and bring him to account. She was astonished to find the heartbreaker one of the ugliest little monkeys she had ever laid eyes on. How did he get away with it? Evidently good girls are forewarned against wickedly handsome males but their guards are down before such disarming ugliness, so before they knew what was happening he had them all — the maids, the arty spinsters, the bored matrons. Elsie well remembered the stern scolding she had given him to leave poor Iola alone if he did not mean marriage, and to protect and console Iola she had sent her, virtue only slightly nicked, flying back to New York City to recover.

The day after she had straightened out Iola's problem, Elsie had strolled down to the docks to watch the fishing boats come in. Intellectual curiosity was what she termed it, as she stood watching the ugly little monkey scrabbling around his wretched little boat, always grinning, always legs sprawled apart astride an invisible beast — porpoise or billygoat, perhaps. He looked scared to death when he spotted Elsie standing there, tall and formidable in her oilskins.

"Want a fish?" he asked tentatively.

"Bring it to the house tonight," Elsie had commanded regally.

He was there, grinning, after dark, amused to be at the front door instead of the back, and just as he had impishly guessed, the fish was not mentioned.

He was impressed with the way this tall lady ordered him around, and he was respectfully awed by her superior gift for mischief on a grand scale. She didn't give a good damn, he marveled! He was glad to give up his fishing future to trot at her heels, cruising around at her expense, learning something all the time.

Elsie chuckled as she remembered how she had arrogantly forced the higher circles of the lower Cape to accept Niggy, and his own delight in her instructions. A real monkey he was, learning the art and music chatter as she fed it to him, learning the book talk, the patter about places. You get a higher type of girl that way, she had explained, and was rewarded by his grateful industry in bed.

He learned too much too fast, Elsie reflected. I'll never forget the day I told him he could have that secondhand motor bike for his birthday. "I want a Buick!" he kept yelling at me, absolutely furious. So I lost him and now it's an M.G. To tell the truth I did a lot better with him than I did with Jerry Dulaine. I wonder if I couldn't —

She was so absorbed in her sentimental meditations that Brucie had dragged her half a dozen blocks down the East River Drive before she remembered she hated this part of town and hailed a cruising cab.

Part Three

. . . *journey over the bridge* . . .

• He should have taken the subway, Dalzell Sloane reflected, watching the taximeter jump with what seemed to him a kind of demoniacal complacency to a new pair of ciphers led by a proud figure three. Still, he might never have found the place at this hour, for once they left the lights of Flushing the road was pitch-dark. It had started to drizzle, too, and the sharp wind coming up from the river reminded Dalzell of the winter he had spent in these very environs with a fearful bronchitis, one that lasted even after he was able to get back to Manhattan, and everyone said, "You have one of those Paris colds, it's those old buildings!" He squinted out the window, rubbed the mist off the glass as they passed a street lamp, and saw the hulk of an old mansion in a tangle of bushes and broken walls, the impressive stone steps and arched entrance still standing proudly, the side walls and chambers scattered about in odd heaps of bricks, tin cans, pipes, rubble. Nothing had been done to it in all these years, indicating a civic reverence for antiquity, Marius used to say, that Europeans don't credit us with having.

"A few yards more," Dalzell instructed the driver, who was twisting his head around to scrutinize his fare suspiciously and who now said, "Say, mister, we're getting into the wilderness here. Have a heart, I gotta get back to the other side of town. I hope you're not counting on my waiting on you if your party ain't here."

"No," said Dalzell, thinking how fantastic of him to count on the party being there. He hadn't been near the place for nearly eight years, and that time it had been Marius who had suddenly walked in the door in the middle of the winter night with a big load of Bohemian rye bread, a blackjack of salami and a bottle of genuine rotgut bourbon. It had been his own fourth week of hiding out, Dalzell recalled, and he was down to a very clever schedule of taking his one meal of a can of beans or chile with a solitary glass of hot wine at midnight so that the gnawing in the stomach was lulled to sleep until time for the next day's pot of coffee and carefully doled out pieces of bread. Marius was down and out then, too, but when two of them were in the same condition it seemed almost like success. Together they had the courage to tap Ben for a touch, and on the twenty-five dollars Ben managed to squeeze out of his wife — this one fortunately had a regular salary as a schoolteacher, owning a cottage in Maine to boot where Ben lived cozily, leaving the Queens dump to whatever hobo cared to fix it up — they roared with laughter and drank and worked and bragged and argued for a good two months, when Marius' dealer came through with the money to buy a suit, pair of shoes and a ticket to some midwestern university where he'd been offered a teaching job. Dalzell had gotten some money from Cynthia Earle — or was it from his brother-in-law? — to go to Arizona, and later, when he tried to find Marius, his only answer was a vituperative letter from Marius' mistress — the German one who produced all the children for him — saying that she was not going to have Marius ruined by his parasitical friends when his children needed care and even if she knew where he was she wouldn't tell his evil companions, particularly Dalzell Sloane or Ben Forrester who were notorious for their devilish attempts to force liquor, naked women and godlessness on a decent family man unable to make a living anyway, what with his obstinate devotion to painting.

"Old Trina," Dalzell murmured aloud, and thought she certainly must be dead, too, or she would have been stampeding around the town, unless she was still afraid of his legitimate wives popping up.

Three dollars and ninety cents, the driver said, stopping the car, and from his voice it was clear that nothing less than a dollar tip would avert the ugly business for which the neighborhood was noted. Dalzell got out in the rain, handing the driver the exact sum with the suitable tip, nothing to elicit a thank you but satisfactory enough to draw a "Some neighborhood you got here, brother, some neighborhood," and the headlights of the taxi swept over the can-strewn lot, past the fallen oak and uprooted dead bushes left from old hurricanes, and recognizing these old landmarks Dalzell would not have been surprised to see the same old goat carcass as of long years ago, but rats or buzzards must have disposed of that, certainly the local authorities could not have done so. The lights, as the taxi turned, covered the big house at the top of the slope, showed the broken windows, the chimney bricks tumbled on the porch roof, the drainpipe dangling uselessly from the eaves.

So the place was still there, Dalzell marveled, his heart beating fast as the vanishing tail lights of the taxi bumping down the road reminded him of past encounters in the night with unsavory derelicts. The wind from the water was brisk, the rain cut like hailstones and he pulled his muffler over his ears and chin, standing still for a moment until he could get his bearings, remembering the unexpected ditches and garbage pits underfoot. He sniffed the old smell of burnt or rotting wood with the whiff of river rats and the drowned, the moldy cemeteries of ancient burghers. "Paris!" Marius had cried out — was it in 1928? — like Columbus discovering America, "this is the smell of Paris, and this will be our Paris!"

There were the soft, furtive sounds of footsteps somewhere nearby, the low growl of night-prowling mongrels, whisperings, and a car without lights slithering by, but these were not the things Dalzell feared, these were not oblivion, disgrace, poverty, loneliness, these were the friendly, human sounds of footpads, burglars, gangsters, killers — these were not *Things*. *Things* were what lay in wait in his familiar places, certainly in that cozy room prepared for him in his sister's midwest home. He stumbled up the pathless bank of weeds and his feet found the remnants of the gravel path, they crunched on broken gin bottles, tripped over tangles of barbed wire and dead bushes where tree-toads yipped rhythmically as if it was their industry that produced the rain. He felt movement under his feet, toads, rats, lizards, snakes, perhaps, and they cheered him as if these materializations exorcised the intangibles. The garage doors that had dangled by a thread for years had finally fallen, he noted, and the roof, too, judging by the rain falling through. There used to be a door from the garage into what had once been used as an office, and if this was still open, a closet would lead to the middle portion of the mansion that had remained solid through decades of fires, bankruptcies, storms, lawsuits, and other scavengers. In the eighteen-nineties this had been Ben's grandfather's home and the seat of his small coal business; when the business went the place was left to neglect and quarrels among the heirs all over the country. As a child Ben remembered playing among the ruins, later on camping out for days there with amiable young women. The city had threatened for years to sell it for taxes but until it did this was the last retreat for the three friends. Evidently the city had still forgotten about it.

He groped his way along the muddy wall, found the step to the old office, and even the door, which pushed open. There was the fireplace wall, more broken glass underfoot, then the place for the closet door—yes, it was there, and Dalzell gave a little laugh of triumph! But it did not push open as of old, and he realized something must be shoved against it on the other side. Someone was there, then. Indeed he could smell coffee boiling. He tried to look out through the paneless french windows to see if some ray of light outside might guide him, and he saw a faint glitter as water dripped from the eaves onto some gleaming metal. He lit his cigarette lighter and peered out, saw that the narrow old porch was still there but the railing had fallen off, dragging down the dead ivy vines. This side of the building faced a dumping lot that stretched through swamps and sewers to the old wharf, and now Dalzell could see the lights on the bay winking throughout the mist, and after a full minute of incredulity he saw that the little pinpoints of glittering reflection he had observed were raindrops on the metal of an automobile parked by the porch. In the late twenties such a sight merely indicated bootleggers or highjackers making use of the place as a temporary hideout, and later it had meant some adventure-loving heiress involved in a temporary amour with Marius or Ben. Dalzell had no idea what it meant now, beyond the fact that somebody was obviously making use of the place. He heard sounds of furniture being moved on the other side of the closet, and quickly collecting his thoughts knocked vigorously on the door, rather than be caught as a snooper suddenly when it opened. The bureau or whatever it was on the other side was being pushed aside and the door opened suddenly. A man stood there and Dalzell put up his hand, shading his eyes from the glare of the flashlight on him. Behind the man a ship's lantern on a charred work bench flickered over a mottled plaster wall and the strips of oilcloth blocking the windows. The fumes of a rusty old oil heater blew out from the room and while Dalzell was blinking the other man reached out to seize his hands and pull him into the room.

"Sloane, you old son of a gun, how did you know I was here?"

"I knew in my bones, I swear!"

The next minute they were roaring with delighted laughter, slapping each other's shoulders, trying to look each other over in the dim light. Then for want of sensible words, bursting into laughter again, and shouting that it was just like it had always been, how one would arrive at the Cavendish not knowing anyone else in London and next day the other breezes in from Marseilles; and the time Marius was being thrown out of his studio on the rue Mazarine, the concierge shoving his easel out the door, when up the stairs comes Ben, pocket full of dollars, just arrived from New York, and two hours later in pops Dalzell, just landed from Rome, innocently looking for the vacancy advertised on the front door. Never needed to write each other, those three, let the years pass without a word between them, then they get a hunch and hit the same spot again — sometimes the three of them, sometimes two.

"I'm not surprised to find you here, not one bit," Dalzell said, looking around. "What does surprise me, though, is that the place hasn't fallen apart."

His eye went from the paint bucket sitting in the fireplace to catch the rain dripping down the chimney to the opened door in the corner hinting of snugger quarters further inside. At least they were still able to patch up a couple of rooms for shelter.

"Wait till you see how fine it is," Ben said, pushing the chest of drawers against the outer door once again. "Marius must have been here since I was last. An old ferry captain shacked up here, they tell me, till his wife found him and dragged him back to the village."

Ben had a bad cough and in spite of his boast that the old dump had never been cozier Dalzell noted that he was in several worn sweaters under the patched jaunty sport jacket. His beard was only a gray stubble, now, and he was bald as an owl, great frame shrunken, worn face with sunken eyes hinting at no cushioned past. He must have had it worse than I did after his spurt of luck, Dalzell thought; at least I didn't have wives and mistresses and children dragging at me along with all the other troubles. Ben was pushing him peremptorily through the corner door into a smaller room, fitted out very handsomely indeed, Dalzell saw with appropriate exclamations, for the walls were soundly weatherproofed with panels of old doors, their hinges neatly dovetailing; the floor's deficiencies were covered by layers of carpets and linoleum. A big four-poster bed, wood blocks taking the place of two missing legs, was in an alcove with a motorboat's tarpaulin draped over it, humorously ribboned as if it were the finest lace canopy. Other loose doors were latched together to make a stout screen around an oil cookstove and it was from this makeshift kitchen the smell of boiling coffee came. On a long oilcloth-covered table were two lanterns illuminating a stack of plates, jelly glasses and mugs of all sizes.

"Looks as if Marius himself might be here," Dalzell exclaimed, pulling out a packing box to sit upon.

"I've been sorting out all the junk and cleaning up," Ben said.

"Must have found traces of Marius," Dalzell said. "He was the one last here."

Ben flashed him a sharp questioning glance.

"He left a batch of work here, yes," he answered curtly.

"As soon as I heard they were having trouble locating his canvases I thought they might be here," Dalzell said. "How do they look — mildewed?"

Ben took the coffeepot off the burner and poured it into two cups.

"Most of it snug as a bug under the tarpaulin up in the dry closet," he answered. "Mucked up here and there but easy enough to touch up. When Marius was alive and getting nowhere, being misunderstood, I thought he was a great painter. But do you know, now that he's dead and so damn well understood I don't find this stuff so wonderful. He must not have been satisfied with it himself," he added defensively, seeing Dalzell's reproachful look, "or he wouldn't have dumped it here, most of it half done. Why, remember that sketching trip we made on Staten Island around Richmond and Tottenville? He's got some half starts on those old taverns and street markets that aren't any better than mine — or yours."

"What are you going to do with them?" Dalzell asked, uncomfortable at the disparagement of their old friend.

"The fact is," Ben said deliberately, "I intend to finish them and touch up the others and tell the blasted dealers Marius left them with me in a trade."

He folded his arms and looked defiantly at Dalzell.

"Go ahead," he urged as Dalzell silently puffed a cigarette. "Tell me I'm taking too big a chance and so I'm a crook, go ahead and say it."

"I was only about to tell you I'd like to help out," Dalzell answered. "That's why I took a chance on finding you here. The two of us together could do better."

"Fine," said Ben. "Pardon my overestimating your scruples."

"A dealer who wouldn't give five bucks for my work bought three thinking they were Marius'," Dalzell said dryly. "I could have gone on, but I decided if the only way I could get by was to pretend to be somebody else I'd better go back where I came from. Now that I've seen you I feel differently."

"It looks like this is the only way out for both of us," Ben said. "I've had nothing but bad breaks for the last couple of years and when I got the message from this guy Severgny I snatched at the chance to clear out. Left a note for Martha and one for my girl friend, then hopped in the jalopy and took off."

"I'm as good as gone myself," Dalzell said. "My trunk's in Grand Central Station. I've got about sixty bucks of my ticket money and that's all."

"You're a godsend," Ben said. "I've got about eight. We can hole in here for almost nothing. We'll work over the stuff and let it leak back little by little. I told Severgny I'm rounding up what canvases I know exist. First cash we get we can move back to Manhattan."

"Marius would think it was a big joke," Dalzell said.

"We're doing him a big favor," Ben declared. "He'd be glad artists were making a living off of him instead of dealers. All we want is enough to give ourselves a new start on our own, isn't it?"

"A fresh start, yes," murmured Dalzell.

He looked around him, filled with incredulous joy that he was here instead of on the train bound for surrender and death. His eyes took in the old rope-bound trunk at the foot of the bed with the same old *De Grasse* stickers on it, the black-painted initials M.M.M., the dangling broken lock. He got up and went to the middle partition, pushed the improvised paneling of doors gently till one of them tipped forward and showed the ladder of boards leading upstairs just as it used to be.

"This section upstairs is still fairly solid," Ben said, "if you're wondering how soon the place falls in on us."

They stood for a moment looking each other over, Ben reading the ups and downs of Dalzell's life in the familiar old topcoat, the souvenir of love in the expensive gaudy muffler, the hope and havoc in the still youthful eyes; Dalzell seeing the challenge still burning in Ben's defiant gaze in spite of the stooped shoulders.

"If we're not too old," Ben murmured, half to himself. "Good God, Sloane, we *are* old!"

Dalzell shrugged.

"We were always old part of the time, Ben," he answered. "Not Marius, of course."

"Never Marius," agreed Ben. He studied Dalzell fondly and silently for a moment, then banged on the table suddenly with his fist until the big lanterns shook. "But now we're beginning all over again, Sloane, my boy, we're young again!"

"Thanks to Marius." Dalzell lifted his glass, and then the memory of Okie's pompous words came to him and he began to laugh, sputtering out the story, all about his ticket money, Cynthia's new blond hair, the chase to ride on Marius' chariot, the five thousand dollars Okie would give for the brown-eyed boy looking at the sky —

"No!" gasped Ben. "The best thing you ever did and he thought Marius did it! That shows how easy it's going to be!"

They began to laugh again, tried to talk but couldn't stop laughing. It was wonderful to have fear and loneliness transformed at last into a great joke between friends.

. . . *the waters under the bridge* . . .

• How Marius would have loved the joke, Dalzell and Ben kept crying out to each other every day! Here was a merry vengeance for everything the world had made him and his two friends suffer, and they could almost hear his deep laughter in the echoes of their own. Camping out in the old Queens property, not an hour from Times Square, they were as safe from invasion as if they were cruising on some yacht in mid-ocean, while they were being sought all over New York. Someday, Dalzell was sure, when they confessed their secret, it wouldn't be funny. But for the first week of their reunion everything was funny.

"Tell me again how Okie claimed he could tell that boy's head of yours was an early Marius," Ben begged. "I can almost hear him."

"First he knew it was a Marius because Marius always got that sense of starry yearning in his children's eyes," Dalzell tried to imitate Okey's pompous lecture-hall voice, "and then there was the quality of the white paint that Marius was using at one time after he thought his old whites were fringing off yellow."

"Very good," approved Ben.

"It never struck him that we used each other's supplies, of course," Dalzell said, "and since I hadn't finished the picture I hadn't signed it. The museum scout who turned it up in that antique shop swore it was Marius and by the time Okie got through describing the special Marius touches to it I almost believed he *had* done it. I certainly would have gotten nowhere trying to prove it was mine."

"Supposing Trina shows up with whatever he left with her," speculated Ben. "She was the only dame shrewd enough to have saved anything. Remember the Sicilian model who ripped up everything in his studio and then set it on fire when she found him in bed with somebody else?"

"If Trina's anywhere in the world where she could have heard about his new reputation she would have been throwing her weight around long before this," Dalzell said. "And if Trina hadn't shoved Anna out of the picture we might look forward to Anna popping up to claim all rewards — that is if she's still alive."

"His women are all dead or they'd be brawling over his grave," Ben said.

It seemed to Dalzell that it was he and Ben who had died and gone to Heaven and not old Marius at all. That night at the Café Julien he had stepped out of his old life completely, and here in this ghost house he felt as if he was preparing for a new birth. To wake to the sound of birds, river tugs, or flapping of loose boards on the roof instead of to the creditor's knock was a kind of heaven. They had stocked up their shelf with groceries and bare necessities, and for Dalzell it was luxury to begin the day with coffee and bread that did not require his shaking out all his pockets for the pennies to buy it. Each day was opened fresh for painting instead of being snarled and gutted by arguments and futile plottings of the mind as to ways and means of getting through this day and tomorrow. For Dalzell this was a security he had not had in years, and for Ben it was the same at first. They worked over the Marius sketches and canvases diligently, planned how they were to be presented, and made notes for their own work. They took long walks along the water's edge, scarcely believing that across the river from the old abandoned ferry slip was New York itself, the city that had rejected them but would sooner or later receive them. At night they relaxed over Chianti or brandy, remembering the past, filling in the lost years. They wondered that they had done without each other so long, and even if they had only troubles to tell each other how much easier they could have borne them together!

Telling Ben about all the promised fellowships that had fallen through, the planned exhibitions that had dissolved at the last minute, the honors and commissions that had inexplicably melted before his grasp, down to the Hastings Harding misadventure, made the disappointments seem comical pranks of Fate. Dalzell dredged his memory to find more hilarious catastrophes to keep them laughing, and now it seemed to him that they were marvelous clowns who had cleverly planned their pratfalls for the grateful amusement of the world.

"Of course I had better luck than you or Marius at the outset." Ben was so cheered up by Dalzell's chronicles of frustration that he began to swell with the feeling of being a child of Fortune himself, only temporarily sidetracked. "Dough in the family, and I knew the right people. The only trouble was that whenever I was on the upgrade Martha would start being the old helpmate, shoving me down people's throats, till I'd get so embarrassed the deal would fall through."

"No!" Dalzell observed, as if he was not well aware of Martha Forrester's reputation as the aggressive agent-wife.

"Marius was the lucky bastard, though," Ben said. "I know, he had to die to make a living, but the fact was he never even tried to get anywhere. He didn't want to be anybody. All he wanted to do was paint what he liked when he liked, have the dames he liked, get as drunk as he liked. You and I tried to act decent once in a while, at least. But Marius just insulting the best people made them think he was a genuine genius. Remember when he threw Piermont Bradley out of his own house and next day Bradley buys one of his pictures?"

They roared with laughter as if their entire lives had been delightfully spiced with mischief instead of spiked with mistakes. They talked of their women, picturing themselves as pursued and bedeviled by avid females who fended off more desirable creatures. It was true that all three had left a trail of shrews, for they were the genial type that makes shrews of the gentlest women anyway in order to have their peccadillos condoned by society. Even if the ladies had been sweet and unreproachful these gentlemen preferred to sit in taverns boasting of angry viragos waiting for them with frying pans lifted, for it made their dawdling in bars and wenching more brave and manly. Dalzell, whose nature had been far from bold, was aglow with the honor of being classed with Ben and Marius.

"You were always pretty sly about your lovelife," Ben accused him now. "Smart, too, keeping from getting hooked."

"I don't call it smart always falling for somebody out of my reach," Dalzell said.

"Now there's the difference between us!" Ben exclaimed,

relaxing in the luxury of candor under alcohol. "You just don't know how to go about it, that's all. I'm a perfectly frank person so let's be honest with each other — "

Dalzell had a momentary impulse to say he'd never seen bold Ben fetch down any birds that weren't already on the ground but he knew that the one thing a perfectly frank person cannot take is frankness, so he allowed Ben to continue unchallenged for a moment.

"You're just too soft, Sloane," said Ben. "When things get tough you just fold up, nary a whimper, as if you had no right to anything better. You're too damn modest, Sloane, and that's no good for an artist."

"Modest!" Dalzell shouted, suddenly outraged. "How can any man who has the gall to put a brush to pure white canvas be called modest?"

Startled by this outburst Ben retracted.

"Anyway you're not egotistical — " he started.

"I am enthusiastically egotistical," Dalzell interrupted hotly. "or else abysmally suicidal. I pride myself most on a kind of oafish stubbornness that gets me from one state to the other."

"All right, you're not modest," Ben conceded. "But you can't say you're a go-getter. Everytime a streak of luck aims at you you have a trick of deflecting it, as if you were some kind of lightning rod, so you end up with nothing but a hole in the ground. Now with me, whenever luck struck I managed to grab it by the horns and ride it till it threw me, at least. With the right breaks I could have been a first-rate businessman."

Dalzell was about to match this but decided it was neither the time nor place to boast to each other of their fine flair for business.

Ben was sick of women, so he claimed, and dismissed his wives and mistresses as such a pack of avaricious, ignorant harridans clamoring for gold, bed and babies that one might marvel how such a strong intelligent man ever fell afoul of them. But after a while a certain wistfulness crept into his voice and Dalzell suspected he was casting about for new chains as soon as he could find some.

"I married Martha because she was educated, a lady, understand, not like the arty bohemian tramps I'd been sleeping around with," Ben explained. "Nice New England family, a little money. How did I know she'd break with them on my account and turn artier than anybody? Finally I had to go on living with her because I was too broke to get away, and she could always get a teaching job. Then, out in Santa Fe, I got this girl Fitzy, a hospital nurse."

A fine, upstanding, simple country girl, Fitzy, Ben said, good drinker, good model — big hips and bosom with tiny waist on the Lachaise style. But the trouble was that after listening to him a few years she started talking art, too, just like your other women, all the stupider for finally knowing the names of all the things to be stupid about. Fitzy and Martha would have a beer and start fighting, not over Ben, but about art.

"All Martha knew about art was what she heard from me when we first married," Ben complained. "All Fitzy knew was what I'd come round to thinking later. I got it on both sides — Martha nagging at me for not being a good enough painter to earn a living, and Fitzy pitying me for being too good to make money. Then that Hoboken scene of mine that I gave Marius on a trade got printed in the papers as his and that did it."

"The girls recognized it as yours?" Dalzell asked.

"Hah!" snorted Ben. "That was the test I gave them. I was sore as the dickens at the mistake and wanted a little loyal sympathy. So, without saying anything, I showed the reproduction to Mart to see if she spotted the mistake. She just bawled me out for not being able to paint a good picture like that and make some money. I didn't say anything, just showed it to Fitzy next day and what does she do but tell me how lousy it is and why should this Marius be so famous when I could do a million times better. That finished me. When Okie started hunting me down I was ready to run out. I had a lot of Marius canvases. I threw them and my own into the old chevvy and started driving East. I'd made up a plan then what I was going to do."

"I didn't plan. It just happened in my case," Dalzell said. "When the demand began after his death I was broke and sold a couple of Marius sketches to a decorator. Then when the guy came in my studio and saw a little water color of mine he said, 'How much for that Marius?' I just swallowed hard, said 'A hundred bucks' and he took it. Next time it happened I got scared. I said to myself if the only way I can get by as an artist is by pretending to be somebody else then I might as well give up and go back where I came from, raise chickens, teach country school, be a grocery clerk. I was scared."

"I'm not a bit scared," Ben answered. "When the idea hit me I thought it came straight from old Marius himself, a kind of bequest. Whatever we get out of it you can be sure the dealers and chiselers will get a hundred times more, but at least it gets us out of the woods and ready for a new start on our own."

"I want to pay back Cynthia Earle, damn it," Dalzell confessed.

"Are you crazy?" Ben asked. "Nobody ever pays back Cynthia. Cynthia's had her money's worth, never fear."

Yes, he would pay back Cynthia, Dalzell thought, every last penny. She had never expected it and would be vexed to have no more excuse to patronize him. Once the debt had been removed between them he might be able to clean her out of his mind. For Cynthia had been his one great love. The flame had stayed alive for years, giving no warmth, merely illuminating the falseness and unworthiness of the beloved, cauterizing him against other surrenders. Knowing all about her, viewing her with cynical detachment as the enemy of everything he believed in, he had still felt slaked in her presence at the Julien the other evening. You lived and learned what a fool you'd been and wise, at last, continued to be a fool.

At twenty-six he had fallen in love at first meeting with Cynthia, braced though he was with warnings and devastating reports of her eccentricities. All the other artists knew her and none spoke well of her, but speak of her they did. She was rich and commanded you to dinner like a princess royal, but expected you to pay. She was a nymphomaniac and could easily have appeased her needs by taking you into her silken sheets, but oh no, her perverse pleasure was in climbing up your dark tenement steps and wallowing in straw ticking and dirty blankets. She could have introduced you into the soft lights of her world but it always ended with her invading yours. She promised fabulous favors but changed her mind at a minute's notice. She inveigled the best pictures out of you as gifts and in return was as likely as not to coyly send you her garter! In spite of all these legends, Dalzell had longed to meet her if only to be in on the joke. It had struck him, too, that her detractors were only too glad to hasten to her parties. Marius knew her, Ben knew her, and it seemed to Dalzell it would be an achievement just to be able to add his own personal criticisms to the common legend.

But he had capitulated at the first meeting. He was prepared for someone thoroughly pretentious, vain, and evil. Her affectations came as no surprise, but what enslaved him were certain mannerisms of which no one had told him and which seemed therefore for him alone. She was not ugly as they said, but handsome in a swarthy, gamy, medieval way. She was overtall but had a coy way of ducking her head to look up at you with a bashful little-girl smile, hands clasped behind her, all but twisting her apron strings, and she spoke in a tiny tinkling Betty Boop voice. To his surprise he found the contrast of her little-girl posturings with her full-bosomed woman's body enticing, and the sophisticated talk in the baby voice curiously piquant. He was convinced she had perfectly good brains but she seemed to make a deliberate effort to keep her conversation on an arch débutante level. Her pet artists, ungrateful by vocation, amused themselves by imitating her gestures and baby-talk. They drew private cartoons of her underlip pulled out in a bad-baby pout, wounded little raisin eyes blinking when someone had crossed her certainly full-grown will. They imitated her arch way of clapping a hand over her mouth after saying a catty or naughty phrase. She was notoriously avid for lovers, aggressive in pursuit of each new flame, primly genteel about other people's morals, but knowing all this, and seeing even more faults than had others, did not save Dalzell. He found her very vanity a virtue, and something magnificent in her never suspecting men's love for her was for anything but her own self. He had the good sense to speak of her half mockingly just as his friends did for he knew to admit anything else would be to expose himself to ridicule. He did not mind what they said about her for he exulted in a secret belief that he alone knew who and what was under this mask.

Perhaps she represented Art itself to him, and her kiss was admission ticket to the world of immortals. She represented the World, too, for he had never before met any millionaires with yachts, castles, ranches and noble kin all over the world. The stories Marius and Ben had told him of her promiscuity did not lessen his triumph when she leaped into his bed, for it seemed a proof that he was at last deemed a real artist. He saw her pretentiousness, her disloyalty and trickery, but when she finally banished him he was so stricken he could not paint for a year. Art had dismissed him. For years and years he had moments of wild thirst for her, and it was no relief to dismiss it as merely a sex need for she had been singularly unsatisfactory in that respect, eager and indefatigable though she was.

It is curious that some men lust all their lives for a woman who leaves them unsated. They are challenged by visions of unexplored delights ahead. Cynthia had obsessed him and always would, but whenever he spoke of her it was with the cool detachment of her other protégés. He had forgiven her other lovers but he had furiously resented her husbands. Why, he often asked himself? Everyone said she only married a man because she didn't want to sleep with him. There was a kind of flaunting of her basic snobbery in her marriages, for she wed only bankers or titles. All very well to amuse oneself with artists, but good heavens, one didn't marry them any more than one marries the grocery boy. Every time Cynthia was divorced Dalzell had a perfectly ridiculous feeling of victory, as if one more banker down the drain was proof of artist superiority. But he had never wished her unhappy, and when other flames of her past chuckled over her growing defeats in love, recounting gleefully some futile campaign, Dalzell felt only a twinge of sadness and reproach for the inconsiderate male who dared deny her. He couldn't be still in love, ever so slightly, with her, but it was odd how old jealousy remained long after the name and face of love have been forgotten. And here he was, bitterly jealous of dull old Okie who had never been either lover or husband and therefore had never been banished! Male vanity at its worst and most unreasonable, Dalzell told himself sternly: he wanted to be succeeded by superior men to make the object of his love more worthy and the reason for his years of desire more justifiable. He certainly didn't want to be in Okie's shoes.

He could still tingle with shame at his obtuseness to what had been transparent to everybody else at the time. Cynthia couldn't abide love in the abjectly adoring form he offered it. She must chase and snatch reluctant men from their wives or mistresses, flaunt her victories before her less powerful rivals, wear a new artist every day as Marius had once said of her. She must have been through with him, Dalzell forced himself to admit, the instant she found he had willingly given up all others for her. How blind and stupid he had been to her persistent efforts to banish him! He managed to smile a little ruefully when Ben reminded him of that moment of cruel revelation.

"Do you remember the time Cynthia summoned her whole stable to bring her that California painter, What's-his-name?" Ben asked one evening. They were drinking strong coffee laced with bourbon while they put finishing touches on two canvases Ben was going to take in to Severgny.

"The blond beast," Dalzell said, laughing as he had trained himself to do at this bitter recollection. He had had no idea at the time why she had been cross with him, picking quarrels on every occasion, accusing him of infidelities and other defections as an excuse to avoid him. Then came the day she had a pang of remorse and allowed him a quick kiss, saying, "Now stop being silly and run along. Of course I'm not angry any more, silly, I'm in a frightful rush to get out to Mother's and you keep bothering me. Now run back to the studio and stay there in case I phone you to come out to the country tomorrow."

He had stayed in the studio dutifully, happy at the reconciliation, not daring to stir outside for fear of missing the call. The next afternoon Ben and Marius had burst in, shouting with laughter. It was a wonderful joke on Cynthia, they said.

"You know that big Swede she's been chasing, the one that paints bridge builders all looking like himself," Ben said. "You know how she's been pestering all of us to bring him up every time she invites us, because he refused to come by himself. Well, she finally beat him down last fall and set him up in a fine studio in Carnegie Hall with the biggest allowance she ever gave any of us — "

"Five hundred a month he held out for," Marius chuckled.

Dalzell remembered still the sickness in his stomach and the terrible effort to laugh.

"The woman's crazy," Ben had gone on. "She got me in a

corner at the Julien the day after she'd managed to make him and you could hear her all over the café bragging about Swedish technique. Her husband, the big stiff, sitting right there all the time, not even knowing what she was talking about."

"All the waiters did," Marius said.

Last fall, Dalzell had thought dumbly, this has been going on for months. So that's the quarrel she has with me.

"She always spent weekends in his studio," Ben went on, and both men shouted again with mirth at what was to come. "Then today they were having breakfast when a big blond girl walked in the room. Asked if Oley had made his proposition yet. Seems she and Oley had gotten married as soon as he started getting the allowance, but it wasn't going to be enough when they had the baby. So Cynthia would have to double it."

"Ha," Dalzell managed to say weakly. "And did she?"

"Cynthia give any money without priority rights?" exclaimed Ben. "Are you kidding? She scrambled out of the place as fast as she could, said she'd have to send the check, and then she marched in on Marius and me at the Julien, mad as hops. Outraged decency. Artist having the gall to marry somebody. Wife having the gall to have baby. Bad manners. Simply frightfully bad manners even for an artist and Swede. Well she blew off steam and we made her all the madder by laughing, then she started bawling and we put her in a cab and sent her home. Marius promised her a new doll, a young Polish sculptor."

"How about you, Dalzell?" Marius had demanded teasingly. "Or have you done your time?"

"I've done my time, thanks," Dalzell had said and he found he could laugh very convincingly. After all these years he could still feel inside his chest how much that laugh had hurt.

"That's right. We used to call him Oley, the blond beast," Ben mused now as they remembered. "He was a pretty fair painter till Cynthia got hold of him. Then he and his bride found out they could get along a lot better just selling his Swedish technique and nobody's ever heard of him since."

"Okie's her consolation prize, now," Dalzell said, casually.

In another week he and Ben were going to take an apartment in town. Gerda Cahill was going to Mexico again and would let them sublet her cold-water flat in the East Thirties. They would have money, this time, they rejoiced. Even so Dalzell dreaded New York and fervently wished he could stay hidden in the safe kindness of the rat-ridden old mansion forever.

. . . *the Marius assignment* . . .

• The greatest favor Marius, the man, had ever done for Marius, the artist, was to die at exactly the right moment. Many men have triumphantly exploited a minuscule talent through life only to ruin themselves by muffing their deaths. Missing their proper exit cues they have hung around like dreary guests at a party, repeating themselves until it is made clear to all how little they ever had to say.

But Marius, bless his heart, had made death his great achievement. He had fumbled gloriously every chance in his lifetime, wantonly antagonized all who could help him, been stubbornly loyal to every outcast or dungheap that enhanced his mischievous nuisance value, stood valiantly in his own light, and then, by wonderfully timing his death, removed the enemy shadow, Marius the man, allowing Marius the artist to step into clear blaze of sun. He had been away from New York so long that journalists and art dealers had stopped smarting from his bawdy insults, husbands had lost the zeal to avenge their honor, harassed old friends once goaded into barricading their doors, beds and cellars when the big man stormed into town with all his bar friends, ladies and lads of the town, with the inevitable disasters ending in hospitals or jails, could breathe easier. Everyone was filled with the Christian pleasure of giving full praise to a man without requiring police protection from him. How considerate of him to die far away in Mexico so no one had to pass the hat for the funeral. How brilliant to choose a month barren of news fit for publication so that editors had to pad their pages with broadsides against the plague of surrealism and existentialism, the sure causes of juvenile delinquency, homosexuality and suicides! The coincidence of a news magazine reprinting Marius' painting of a Hoboken Square the very day Hoboken's oldest building burned down gave feature writers and Sunday critics a nice lead into large thoughts on our American art heritage, the neglect of our native great men, and fulsome appreciation of the true-blue American realism that had been wickedly pushed aside by decadent foreign influences. Checking up on the artist they found that he had just been killed in Mexico. Marius' death was a national catastrophe, they said, and there were suggestions that he be disinterred and given a burial in Arlington. To the very end, they wrote, Marius was an *American* in every sense of the word, regardless of his foreign studies and travels.

It happened that for some reason — perhaps an extraordinarily dry decade creatively — there had sprung up from American university campuses, European pastures for grazing scholars, and other academic preserves a ravening horde of cultural necrophiles. Wars, planetary bombings, invasion by Martians and such fears of premature destruction were driving these opportunists into snatching chargers of long-proven might on which to steal quick rides to glory. Intelligent enough to concede their personal inability to get anywhere without a celebrated mount, and too lazy to take the bellboy's job for which they were fitted, they rushed to stake claims on the great names of the past, boasted with a gènuine sense of a deed accomplished that they were about to write a book on Dostoyevsky, Tolstoy, El Greco, or Bach, and dined out with dignity on nifties panned from the richly plummed legends. Some, who had the chance, stalked aging celebrities who might do them the favor of dropping dead and providing juicy material for future memoirs. Sometimes a subject who had been buying Scotch and steaks for a permanent entourage of doting biographers had the bad taste to live on and on, getting politically or socially *de trop* and allowing the biographers' rightful property, you might say, to deliberately deteriorate in value, making the once prized treasury of private journals and personal anecdote plain rubbish. Worse yet, sometimes the subject lived beyond his bad period and betrayed old followers, who had dropped him, by dying in a blaze of new glory, with new riders in at the death.

Marius, at the last, had proved his worthiness and generosity. Anyone who had once hoped to ride on his name and been brutally thrown, or else had given up, could claim whatever valuable connection he chose, for his long absence equalized all their claims. They could vie with each other without loss of face in anecdotes about long ago days when they, and they alone, had stood by the man against his enemies, heard his secrets, indeed provided him with advice and inspiration.

"You working on Marius?" they cried in astonishment to each other. "I'm working on Marius, too, but of course you knew him at a different period."

The increasing number of those who claimed to have been the dearest friends of the artist was causing a great deal of bewilderment to an honest young man named Alfred Briggs, who knew nothing of either Marius or art till his discharge from the Navy four months before when the news magazine *City Life* hired him to give a "fresh angle" to the traditional neglected-artist story. Briggs had stayed on in the Navy as a warrant officer after World War I for he was having a good time and was not at all sure of where he would fit into civilian life. The decision to be a writer had come over him while the fleet was cruising in the Caribbean, pausing in St. Thomas, Montego Bay, Port-au-Prince and other playlands where he met fellow Americans and British ladies and gentlemen lounging around swimming pools with tall frosted drinks in their hands, being fanned by tireless natives.

"Who are these people?" Briggs had asked, and on being told that these fortunate folk were all writers — novelists, playwrights, journalists — Briggs cried out, "Then that's the life for me! How do I begin?"

With the flattering letters these genial professionals obligingly wrote for someone they felt could never be a rival, Briggs had no trouble in landing the magazine job when he got out of the service. His honest statement that he had never written anything but clear, straightforward reports for superior officers charmed the *City Life* editor. Briggs had hoped for assignments in the field of sports but the editor felt that literary training and education were required for that, whereas art was a department where inexperience and ignorance would not be noticed.

Pleased as he was to have a regular job which would permit him to return soon to the Islands with some dream girl and live like a lord, and flattered as he was at the outspoken envy of free-lance writers, Briggs found himself utterly bewildered by the first assignment. It had seemed like a breeze, at first. Nothing to do but call up or go see a list the editor gave him of people who would tell him about Marius, and all he needed to do was to write it down like a day's report. But no sooner had one person given him a tasty anecdote about Marius than the next person would deny it.

"I can't imagine where you heard such a ridiculous story," one man said on being asked to verify a legend. "From Dennis Orphen? Why, Marius hardly knew the man. I myself knew Marius for years, here and in Paris, and never even heard him mention Dennis Orphen. He must have gotten it from the Barrows and they weren't even there when it happened."

"Then something *did* happen?" Briggs would press patiently.

"If you mean did Marius take a love seat from a house on Gramercy Park and set it up outside the Park gates for some Bowery pals of his to have a bottle party," said the old friend who was named Ainslie Flagg, "something like that did happen in Prohibition days but it wasn't Gramercy Park, it was Gracie Square and he didn't steal it, he simply took it and why should people spread these nasty stories about him just because he drank too much?"

"This happened when he was drunk?" Briggs asked.

"Now don't go making this a big drunken story about Marius," protested Flagg angrily. "He's dead and no reason to drag his name through the dust. Of course he was drunk. When he wasn't painting he was always drunk. Anyhow the next day after this thing happened he got all dressed up and went back and made a beautiful apology, I give him credit for that."

"Then it did happen or he wouldn't have apologized?" craftily pursued Briggs.

"As I say it was a handsome apology only it seems he picked a different house by mistake this time and they thought he was crazy and had him thrown out so he landed up in jail."

"Jail?" Briggs pricked up his ears. "Marius was in jail once?"

"He was always in jail for something or other, how do you think he got those jail pictures?" the loyal friend shouted. "And let me tell you I'm absolutely disgusted with people pretending to be Marius' friends and then rushing to tell you newspapers every scandal about his private life. I refuse to be part of such a dirty deal, I don't care how big your magazine is."

Baffled, Briggs called on the next friend on his list, explained his purpose, said he had just talked to Ainslie Flagg about Marius.

"Ainslie Flagg?" the latter repeated, knitting his brows. "I don't think he was ever a close friend of Marius. Oh yes, he's the rich old crock who tried to have Marius arrested once. I've forgotten what it was about, something about stealing his sofa or some silly thing. No use trying to get any information about Marius from *him*."

Small wonder that young Briggs was beginning to think those hibiscus-wreathed fortunates lolling around tropic swimming pools had betrayed him into a most maddening profession. Marius was supposed to be worth four installments, yet how could you get anywhere forever crossing out? And what could you do when so many times he had barely mentioned the object of his call before the old friend would brush him off hastily with "Frankly we'd done all we ever could for Marius and if his wife told you to ask us for funeral expenses we'll just have to refuse." This sort of answer stopped after the publicity started really rolling, for after that everyone was eager to talk. Briggs knew nothing of the art world so he had to copy down very carefully every phrase he heard and every explanation of Marius' technique, and when the next person contradicted this he crossed it all out with equal care.

"At this rate," he meditated gloomily, "I'll have crossed out all four installments before I've got even one written."

Then came the lucky day he visited the museum which had managed to flush four large Marius canvases out of its basement and was displaying them with proper pomp in its best room, one on each wall. It was the first time he'd ever been in a museum and he was more concerned with how to behave in a big mausoleum than he was with the pictures themselves. Huge clumps of marble in the main hall studded with a recognizable human eye or navel made him glad that at least he was not required as yet to have any dealings with this form of art.

He marveled that the young visitors trudging through could take so calm a view of these amazing creations, which he feared would bring on a fit if he looked twice at them. He was relieved to reach the Marius room without mishap and to be smoothed by the simple, almost photographic pictures. But again he saw how backward he was in his reactions, for here the jaded young visitors suddenly came to life, gazing in incredulous amazement at the walls, seemingly paralyzed by their emotions. He listened to their excited cries, their bewildered comments.

"Look, it's a real room!" one said. "Out the window you can see the bridge so it must be around Fifty-Ninth Street. Look, there's that corner store where my uncle works. Imagine a fellow painting a real room like that in a real place. What do you know?"

"This one called 'Burlesque,' " another young man said. "A naked girl right there. I read somewhere that they used to have these shows right on the stage with live naked girls."

"It looks real, all right," granted another. "It couldn't have been here though. Must have been Paris or Chicago or someplace like that."

Mr. Briggs got out his notebook and jotted down these comments and then sought out the young lady in charge of public relations. She seemed very cross since it was almost six, closing time, and Mr. Briggs had already asked questions of a sort to indicate he would do the cause of art no good whatever he might report.

"All right, all right," she said irritably. "This new generation was brought up on Picasso and Modigliani and they think women have three heads and two guitars. Naturally when they see Marius' paintings they are all bowled over — like people were when moving pictures started talking out loud."

"But look, Essie, this dining-room table has real spaghetti on it!" someone was exclaiming.

"Next they'll be trying to dig it out," muttered the museum girl to Briggs. "You should have been here when we showed Harnett and some early American primitives. We caught a screwball trying to get a revolver out of one painting to shoot himself right here."

"What imagination to have a real little girl with a real doll in a real rocking chair!" another voice exclaimed in awe. "You can almost see it rocking."

"They always go for that one," said the girl, as she turned to leave. "Real chair, real girl. He called it 'Little Ellenora' first, then changed the title to 'The Live Dolls,' I suppose because the doll looks as if it was being squeezed to death. The way it's pushing its arms out as if it was trying to get away."

Studying this picture Briggs felt an almost irresistible temptation to push the child's pale brown hair out of her eyes. He looked around hastily, hoping no one had guessed his naïve reaction but the visitors had marched on and there was only the girl in blue seated on a marble bench in front of the portrait. He looked at her twice, puzzled, for there was something exceedingly familiar about her. She looked away from him and rather self-consciously lifted her hand to push back a stray bang. A light burst on him.

"Why, you're the Live Doll!" he exclaimed. "I know you are."

He was pointing a forefinger at her as accusingly as if he'd caught her red-handed digging out one of Harnett's convincing props.

"Can't I be allowed to look at myself?" the girl inquired. "How did you guess?"

It must have been the gesture of pushing back the hair, Briggs reflected, then he wasn't sure. The girl was now in her twenties but she had the kind of special little-girl face that some women carry from the childhood to the grave. He realized he had been conscious of her sitting there as motionless as the picture, ever since he had come in the hall, and there was the same waiting expectancy in both. He was pleasurably amazed at his new perception. He had actually recognized someone from a painting by detecting an identical inner quality in picture and model. Briggs was thrilled, prouder of his own newborn perception than of the painter's. His eyes behind the thick, black-rimmed spectacles sparkled.

"I didn't know I was that smart," he exclaimed excitedly to her. "It's funny what goes on in the back of your head without your knowing it, I saw you sitting here when I came in, then after I look around you're in the same position and—well, all of a sudden it just hit me. Something said, that's the girl. Isn't it uncanny?"

The girl looked at him with amusement.

"It is, except that after you go to galleries a lot you usually can tell that the person sitting very still in front of a portrait is either the artist's wife, the owner, or the original," she said, and hastened to add kindly. "No, really, it was clever of you and I'm sure no one else ever could have guessed."

"Of course you're wearing the same shade of blue as the child," Briggs acknowledged, peering closer at the portrait, "and the nose is the same, a special kind of little tilt to it—

well, maybe it wasn't so smart of me. Only you see I'm writing a piece about Marius and this is the first time I've gotten hopped up about him. Look. When he paints a room like that one over there you just know the kind of person who lives there. You almost know who's going to come in the door. It's real, but there's something else he gets — like past and future. A sort of magic key."

The girl smiled a little.

"Maybe that's it," she admitted. "Let's see if you can tell the past and future in my picture here. What's my key?"

Briggs looked from her to the picture and back again.

"Believing, that's what it is," he said, and scratched his head. "I mean like always believing in Santa Claus, always believing everything is on the up and up, just — well, just believing."

He was a little disconcerted at her burst of laughter.

"You're absolutely wonderful," she said. "I really believed he was going to change me into a fairy princess, just as he promised. I went on believing it ever since, without ever seeing him again. But I'm glad I got over that."

"Oh no you didn't," Briggs said positively. "You've still got it."

She looked at him, quite startled and he could see he had impressed her.

"Oh dear, I suppose it's true," she said ruefully. "So that's my jinx."

"Don't lose it," Briggs begged her. "Nobody has that look any more. It's beautiful."

He felt unreasonably pleased with himself and intolerably brilliant. He could see by her face that she thought he was brilliant, too, and he wished he could go on shining for her, but she had risen and was pulling on her gloves.

"Good luck with your piece," she said.

"Oh please!" Briggs cried out impulsively. "I mean I was hoping you wouldn't leave me. I don't know much about Marius or art and you clear things up so wonderfully. Couldn't you give me about half an hour — have a drink with me, say?"

Ellenora hesitated.

"It would help so much," he said. "You really must."

"There's a place next door," Ellenora said. She sighed, thinking that here was another example of how easy it was for anybody to bully her. Once you had your feelings hurt badly you couldn't bear to hurt even a passing stranger.

"Let's go to that place Marius used to like," Briggs urged eagerly, hurrying her through the hall. "That will give me the atmosphere don't you see? What's its name — the Café Julien?"

"The Café Julien," Ellenora murmured uneasily. "It's pretty far downtown and I have to be back uptown."

"So do I. I'll bring you back," Briggs promised. "I have to cover a shindig in honor of Marius that a Mrs. Earle is giving so I won't keep you long."

A taxi slid conveniently to the curb beside them and Briggs had firmly helped her in before she could change her mind. He was so pleased with his conquest that it was several blocks before he remembered he was supposed to pick up Janie at six to take her to the Earle party. He could telephone and explain he was detained by an unexpected assignment but he'd have to think up something good. Janie wasn't the believing type herself.

. . . *the portrait found and lost* . . .

• "Maybe you have some objections to the Café Julien," said Briggs tentatively. "Maybe you know some other place he hung out."

"Objections to the Julien? Oh no, of course not," Ellenora feebly assured him.

Unless you counted it as an objection that she had tried to avoid the place ever since she had fled from it that last night with Ricky. Unless it was an objection that she looked upon it as an old friend who had betrayed her. Unless you called it an objection that the mere mention of the café reminded her that here she had all but offered herself to a man who was already planning to leave her. Idiotic to go on blaming places and people for your own weaknesses, she scolded herself. Besides she was cured now. At least, almost. No one could ever know, of course, that once or twice a year in the middle of a gay party she gave in to an insane, uncontrollable impulse to telephone the Café Julien and ask for Mr. Prescott. Luckily he was never there.

"Marius always went to the Julien when he was in town," Ellenora informed the young man. "When I was a student we saved our money to go there just to spot the older artists."

"They told me to hang around there for the right Marius atmosphere," Briggs said. "I tried to get something from the waiters about the good old days. I asked them did Lillian

Russell eat there? Was it true that Scott Fitzgerald and David Belasco and T. S. Eliot and Wendell Willkie used to go there? This one waiter just looks at the other one and shrugs his shoulders. 'Why not?' he says. 'Everybody's gotta eat somewhere, maybe here, I don't care.' "

"That's the way the Julien is," Ellenora laughed.

Briggs shook his head.

"I give up," he said. "I can't picture Marius there, a guy supposed to be full of life. A bleak old dump like that."

"It's the way it strikes you at first," Ellenora said defensively. "Then you find yourself coming back again and again, not quite knowing why. The tables look bare, the lights cold and bright, so the people and the talk become the only furnishings, and you come back to find just that."

"I guess you love the place," Briggs said.

Ellenora was silent, thinking that everything had begun and ended in the Julien. Each time she had started up with Rick she had entered the café an eager, confident woman, and after each breakup she had left it with her pride and love shattered. It did no good to tell herself she had expected something that had never been promised, for then she felt ashamed for assuming he was as caught as she. After each parting she had deliberately set to work to build up a completely new Ellenora. She changed her work, her friends, her neighborhood, her coiffeur, and above all tried to stamp out the damaging softness — yes, the young man was right — the "believing" in her nature. She taught herself to lunch with Maidie Rennels and not wait for mention of the beloved name, not even to ask, because she was foolishly afraid all of his friends must have guessed her infatuation — perhaps he had boasted of it himself so she must babble of serious beaux for them to report back to Rick. This did not work out with good old Maidie who said one day, "I can't understand why none of your love affairs seem to work out, unless you deliberately pick out men you know you'll have to drop. You just don't *want* them to come out right. Like Rick Prescott, always getting mixed up with girls he really doesn't care about, so he can have a free hand."

A form of fidelity for both of them, Ellenora had thought, perilously consoled, and the next instant scolded herself for lapsing into believing again. That was the way it went. As soon as she thought she was safe and strong, happily absorbed in her work either illustrating books or designing screens for a decorating firm, a crazy wire or card would come from across the world, and work, new friends, new self collapsed again. She should have had an affair with him that very first night, she argued sometimes, and then it would be all over and forgotten. It angered her that because she had denied herself to the one man she wanted she should be unable to go through an affair with any other man, as if he had demanded this vow of her. She strove so eagerly to find worthy superiority in her men friends that they could not get out of love with her and Ellenora fervently wished she could surrender to them instead of brewing her fantasy of true love out of nothing.

"Here we are!" Briggs's voice reminded her, and there they were at the Julien.

It was easier than she had imagined. She found she could walk right in the café door without a qualm. She didn't quite dare look around to see if anyone was there she knew, and she hastily ducked past Philippe's tables to the opposite corner in the back. Except for the new waiter at their table the place hadn't changed a bit, there were the same marble tables, the same pleasantly subdued excitement, but evidently she was cured, for her heart didn't turn over nor did she swoon with memories. She was glad this young man had obliged her to make the test.

"I understand pernod is the thing to drink here," he said, beaming. "I've never tried it."

It had turned out that they were almost old friends, having nearly met several times before. Ellenora's decorative screens had been given a nice plug by the household editor of *City Life* whom Briggs sometimes met in the office elevator; Ellenora had illustrated a children's book written in a hangover whimsy mood by one of Briggs's Caribbean author chums. At the *City Life* annual ball Ellenora and escort had left early because it was too rowdy at almost the exact moment when Briggs and Janie had left because it was too stuffy. These remarkable coincidences, patched up in the taxi coming down, served as a splendid background for a warm future friendship.

Briggs was feeling enormously pleased with himself. He looked around hoping someone he knew might be witnessing his arrival in this well-known spot with a beautiful new girl. He wouldn't have cared if even Janie could see him, because she was too smart a girl not to realize that any man would stand her up for a girl like Ellenora Carsdale. At least he thought so. Janie was a good scout, with brains, but the only reason he kept on with her was a lurking fear that he might not be able to do any better. Janie knew quite well where she stood, and as a matter of fact had gotten sore about it last night at the ball. She had made some crack about feeling pretty seedy in her Budget Shop navy blue taffeta in the midst of all the diamond-studded glamour girls with bare suntanned midriffs, but instead of telling her she looked fine Briggs had made the mistake of saying, "What do you care how you look, you've got more brains than any of them. Let's dance."

They had started quarreling about everything else, then, as they rumbaed, and Janie had said she was sick and tired of either getting all dressed up or else all undressed and then having him tell her what a fine brain she had. He tried to say that he wouldn't be offended if she complimented him on *his* brains and she had countered, grimly, "You would if I did it in bed."

After that they gave up trying to have a good time and went to Costello's bar on Third Avenue where he built up a big thing about brains being the only thing in the whole world he cared about next to money and porterhouse steak. Janie was calming down after a few bourbons on the rocks and after his admitting a dozen times that he had always been a dumbbell with a psychopathic worship for a real intellect, but then he overshot himself by leaning across the table to burble, "Why Janie, honest-to-God, if I had your brains you'd never see me again."

Janie's chief from United Nations came up just as she was about to blaze away and that was all that saved him then, but Briggs knew he had a great deal of fixing to do, and tonight he had planned orchids, poetry, diamond fizzes (she had some gin and he would bring some cheap champagne) and lots of talk about her good legs and her dandy complexion and her big old blue eyes.

Yet here he was with another girl a good fifty blocks from where he was supposed to be meeting Janie, and instead of talking about brains he was getting himself all worked up about art. In a minute or two he would telephone Janie, but first he would order drinks and sit for a while just in case this dear girl he had captured might elude him. She had started to tell him how Marius came to paint her, and of course he could not interrupt, so presently he forgot about Janie.

"It was one of those crazy mix-ups Marius was always getting into," Ellenora said, "the sort of thing that drove his friends to distraction. It was that hot, hazy summer my father died and Mrs. Addington, the one that's always the Empress Theodosia on a float for the benefit of blind miners, had given Mother a cottage on her estate near Pawling."

"Two pernods," Briggs murmured to the waiter.

"I'll have a martini," Ellenora said firmly, determined to have no holdovers from the Prescott days. "It was the summer of '36, the summer that Marius' friends had sold Mrs. Addington the idea of his doing a portrait of her. She always had the artist do two portraits of her, one in formal dress for her husband and one thrashing around on a chaise lounge with nothing on for the artist. Like the Duchess of Alba. She'd never seen any of Marius' painting but she'd heard he was a big he-man and that was enough."

"Was he married then?" Briggs asked, taking out his pencil.

"Oh please don't take this down," Ellenora implored hastily, and Briggs obediently put away his pencil. "Mrs. Addington wouldn't stand for any wives. She thought they were sort of obscene and an artist should be dedicated when she herself wasn't around. Anyway it was such a terrible summer that I've never forgotten it, because everything went wrong."

"How?" Briggs's pencil made another appearance and was frowned away.

"First Mother was annoyed because she said we were just to be a cover-up for Mrs. Addington's fun," Ellenora said, "Then Marius kept being delayed and wild wires kept coming from all the taverns along Route 9. After days and days he finally rolled up the driveway, drunk, in an ambulance he'd hired. Mrs. Addington had been told what an amusing character he was so for quite a while she thought it was all great fun. Then he started pouncing on the maids when he was supposed to be pouncing on Mrs. Addington. Then he chased Mother and then he insisted on painting me instead of Mrs. Addington. He was such a great big bear Mother was scared stiff of him, but I adored him. Mrs. Addington got jealous of Mother and told us we must leave, and Marius was so outraged he disappeared. Mrs. Addington sent detectives after him — "

"Poor guy," Briggs murmured. "He was always being hunted down."

" — and she tried to make him give back the two thousand advance. But his other creditors already had it so she took the portrait of me and gave it to the village thrift shop just for spite."

"Are there two *d*'s in Addington?" Briggs asked.

"Oh you couldn't print that," Ellenora cried out.

"No, I suppose not," Briggs sighed.

"You see now she claims to have discovered him," Ellenora said.

"It's tough on a guy being dead so anybody can say what they like about him and he can't deny it," Briggs said. "Everybody seems to have been his best friend but they were perfectly content not to know where he was for the last five or ten years. Nobody would give him a show but now all the dealers are claiming him. Take that picture of you, worth thousands now, and all Marius got out of it was a few weeks' board and a new passel of enemies. What I can't understand is how a man could go through life *always* breaking up his luck, making the same mistakes over and over."

"It's hard to understand," Ellenora agreed, adding half under her breath, "but awfully easy to do."

"Say, this stuff is good," Briggs exclaimed, holding up his glass. "Let's come here again sometime and spend more time on it."

He was nice, Ellenora admitted. Something about his glowing black eyes behind the horn-rimmed spectacles reminded her of Ricky — but as soon as this thought occurred she was disgusted with herself for always comparing, then always discarding some promising future for a past that was little more than a dream.

"I suppose you intend to write other things besides your magazine work," she said flatteringly. "Novels? Plays?"

Briggs's writing ambitions had gone no further than the desire to put off getting fired as long as possible, but Ellenora's words excited his fancy, and before he knew it he heard himself popping away with his thoughts on literature as if he was himself one of the anointed he had admired around the tropic beaches. He did not deny that his brain was teeming with ideas for novels though he managed to hint that his impossibly high literary standards prevented him from actually putting anything on paper. Or to be honest he wasn't really so full of basic plots for novels, it was just that he knew how he was going to go about writing them once the mood did strike him.

"The trouble with most novels is that they don't tell you the things you want to know about people," he said with an involuntary glance over his shoulder to make sure that Janie's sardonic little face was not behind him. "Now the minute I meet a man the first thing I want to know is how much money he makes, what rent he pays, whether his folks have money, whether his wife has a salary or income and if there's any inheritances expected. That's what makes him the way he is. I notice how he tips and what he considers the most important item on his budget. No matter what else we talk about it's a person's financial status that forms his point of view about everything else. I propose to X-ray each character's bankbook as soon as they enter so everything falls into place. Is that so crazy?"

Ellenora resisted a desire to burst out laughing. It wasn't so crazy. She had been vaguely wondering if he knew how expensive the Café Julien was and if he had enough money with him, or if he would appeal to her when the check came, and she would have to fork over her last five dollars.

"I think a character's situation should be clear," she said.

"For instance, here's what has me baffled about Marius," Briggs plunged ahead, earnestly. "They say he was always poor, but how poor is poor? He came to the café here and drank pernod which was eighty-five cents a glass. He went back and forth to Europe and even in those days a round trip would be three hundred dollars or more, wouldn't it? Some of his paintings brought him eight or nine hundred dollars, subtracting a third for his dealer, and he never sold more than one or two a year, but yet he always had women and wives and children and nobody starved to death. He often ate here in the Julien, they say, and even if he only had a beer and one egg it would be over a dollar. But he always had eggs Benedict. How?"

"People loaned him money and he never remembered it," Ellenora answered and went on patiently. "You see you can't figure out some people by arithmetic when they never lived by it themselves."

"Look how much other people are making out of him now, for instance," Briggs went on, tossing down his pernod as if it was a slug of rye and signaling the waiter for another. "Figure out that I've already made sixteen hundred dollars out of him without doing anything, more than he usually made in a year. Figure out the space rates of all the fellows writing articles on him, figure out the price dealers are getting for his stuff, the art teachers sucking out an extra course by lectures on him. Tot up the whole lot against his own figures— Supposing I were to write a novel about him," said Briggs. "First, here's what I do."

He had produced a pencil and an envelope and was busily jotting down figures between gulps of his drink. Ellenora knew it was time for her to go, but her mind had become its usual blank as soon as statistics were mentioned and besides the waiter had brought two pernods again, regardless of her request for a martini. How clever of him, she reflected dreamily, and how pleasant it was to be here again, remembering only the gay moments and that ever present atmosphere of something delightful about to happen.

The café was crowded today, and people kept strolling around looking for tables or else pausing to speak warmly to acquaintances whose appeal was in having empty chairs at their tables. These fortunate table holders, possibly avoided as bores at any other time, could avenge themselves on old snubbers now by withholding invitations to sit; in answer to the eager "May I join you?" they could look coldly toward the door saying "I'm expecting friends" and perhaps win much better company. For his part the visitor never asked to sit unless he had first looked carefully around to see if finer friends were available. Everyone smiled a little, knowing the game so well and experiencing mischievous triumph in outmaneuvering the other.

Out of the corner of her eye Ellenora caught glimpses of Philippe toddling back and forth holding his tray aloft, steering himself by it as if it was an outboard motor that propelled his plump little body. She saw other familiar outposts pegged out across the room, the Van-Dyked old gourmet with the velvet-draped Brunhilde wife laying into an angry-looking lobster about to be drowned in Piper-Heidsieck. She saw the Wall Street Sunday painter who came to the Julien to watch the professional artists, and she saw the pompous painter and his sculptor wife who were Sunday brokers, keeping themselves artistically fit by playing the stock market. There was the savage drama critic, fearless in print but cravenly dragging his palsied old mother wherever he went as bomb shelter from exploding playwrights and actors. There was the voracious columnist who could wedge into any famous group by using his frightened little pregnant wife and golden-haired child to run resistance and was now, Ellenora saw, pushing them masterfully upon the unsuspecting university professor who leered wolfishly across the table at his latest pet pupil. Ellenora thought she detected reproachful glances at her own escort as if she had no right to be in this café without Ricky, and indeed she felt guilty herself. She noted with amusement that Briggs, who had vouchsafed such great curiosity about the Julien, was oblivious to everything but his literary mathematics. He passed his notes across for her inspection.

"Why don't you have your characters all checked by National Credit Association?" she inquired. "Make out a chart, like those maps in historical novels, with their credit ratings."

"Now you're kidding," Briggs accused, disappointed that she should be as skeptical as Janie. A furtive glance at the clock told him it was nearly seven and if he got hold of Janie by phone to head her off he might beguile his new friend into giving up her own date for him. He motioned for more drinks and excused himself to telephone. Ellenora picked up the paper, mystified by Briggs's figures, but then two and two making four had always baffled her. He was a nice young man, though, and she mustn't laugh at him.

"Eggs Benedict, $1.85," she saw had been crossed out, the idea of adding up Marius' own expenses abandoned in favor of assembling the sums other people were making out of him. As these figures were approximations and made no sense to her anyway she took his pencil and wrote down "Legitimate Expenses, Taxi $1.40, E. Carsdale Art School Tuition, $2000, Pen for keeping score $1.95 — Pernods at $.85 each — " giggling.

"Here she is," she heard a voice beside her say and saw Philippe beaming at her. The next moment a mirage of Rick Prescott slipped into Briggs's seat opposite her and speechless, she picked up her glass as he picked up Briggs's. It couldn't be. But it was.

"I see you ordered for me," he said, offering her a cigarette. "Nice of you to hold a table, too."

At first her heart had done a complete flip at the incredible joy of seeing him and she looked around for Philippe to thank him for his demonstration of Julien magic but he had darted back to his own table, his stout little body quivering with suppressed chuckles. Then Rick's triumphant grin filled her with pent-up indignation that he should assume she would always be there, ready to play whatever little games he chose until he tired of it. This time she would show him that she was no more a sitting duck for him. This time there would be no pretty talk around the main issues. If she couldn't keep her nature from always believing, then perhaps she could make it find something worth believing. Don't you dare let him get you again, she commanded herself fiercely, clenching her fist tightly. Don't you dare.

"I'll never forgive you," she burst out.

The smile left Rick's face. She couldn't bear it.

"It's the third time you've forgotten my birthday," she heard herself say. "I'd hoped for a bicycle."

The smile returned.

"Did you really think I'd forgotten that?" Rick asked reproachfully. He put down his glass and came around the table to take her hand. "Just come out and see what's standing out at the hitching post right now a-stomping away."

He reached for her other hand and she let him pull her to her feet.

"With a handlebar basket for my skates?" she asked, letting him lead her unresisting out the café door.

"My skates, too," he said and held open the outer door for her. A cold blast of air came in. "Now shut your eyes and count up to a little drink around the corner."

Here we go again, she sighed inwardly, not even aware that she'd left her scarf in the café and was firmly clutching her drink, as if it was a sure protection against folly. He kept a tight grasp on her arm, hurrying her across the Square, neither of them speaking, and turning the corner to his own apartment.

"But this isn't a bar," she said.

"Of course it isn't, my poor fallen creature," he said unlocking the door. "I have brought you here to reform you if it is not too late. Now, sister, step inside the mission and tell me what brought you to this pass."

It was the little games again, Ellenora thought desperately, when there was so little time; she needed the truth not a paper hat and this time she wouldn't play.

"It was a soldier that set me off, sir," she said as he closed the door behind her. "His regiment was to sail at dawn — ah well, the old, old story."

Part Four

. . . *we'll all go up to Cynthia's house* . . .

• There was no sign of Janie either at her home, Costello's bar, her girl friend's apartment, or in the U. N. lounge, Briggs's telephoning informed him. He was hardly more than an hour and a half late for their date and it made him sore that she should have gone out instead of waiting around like a lady for him to stand her up. He went back in the café and sat down, surmising from Ellenora's absence that she had gone to the powder room, since her gloves and scarf were still on the chair. He sipped his drink thoughtfully, trying to figure out what his approach should be to get her to go to the Earle party with him, and serve Miss Janie right, too.

"You're the new art man on *City Life*, aren't you?" Briggs looked up to find himself surrounded by half a dozen men, all seeming at first glance to be the same Hollywood country squire type in different sizes. The largest, a middle-aged, beery fellow in black beret, black flannel shirt and plaid jacket, was thrusting out his hand. "Saw you in the lobby as we came in. We've met before at the magazine. I'm Hoff Bemans."

"Oh yes," Briggs said, meaning oh no for he could not recall the man at all and he saw they were ready to pounce on his table.

"I spoke to you about appearing on my Fine Arts discussion panel on TV, you remember," Mr. Bemans said, firmly pulling out a chair. "Sit down, fellows. This is Briggs. These fellows were on my show just now. Ever been on TV?"

"No," said Briggs, extending a feeble paw to the bevy of panelists looming behind him, all looking alarmingly like spacemen with their black-rimmed goggles, berets, vast woolly mufflers and briefcases bulging with interplanetary secrets. Desperately he held up Ellenora's scarf to ward them away from his table. "I'm sorry, I'm with a friend — "

"The lady left with Mr. Prescott," the waiter interrupted.

Briggs looked at him blankly.

"I think she left note," the waiter said, pointing to the notepaper, which Briggs picked up, saw his own figures and then Ellenora's postscript about taxi and pernods which he couldn't understand unless somehow she had taken offense at his commercialism.

"They went across the Square," volunteered one of the panelists.

That would be his luck, Briggs thought irritably, and it was all Janie's fault, too. Assuming an air of knowing just what had happened, he paid the check offered by the waiter. He remembered Hoff Bemans very clearly all of a sudden as a fellow reputed to be always joining you with his friends and leaving you with his check.

"I understand you're doing the piece on Marius," Mr. Bemans said. "We talked about him today on the show, and of course you know I've done a biography of him, coming out next month. I knew him in the twenties, of course, and that's one reason I wanted to talk to you. These chaps are all avant-garde critics, teachers, editors. What say to a beer, fellows?"

"I can't," Briggs shouted, for the place was getting crowded and nothing less than a shout would deflect Bemans' chosen course. "If my friend should come back — "

"They won't be back," insisted the youngest space-man, leering.

It was the sort of thing that was always happening in Briggs's life and he wished he had hung on to Janie, now, just to have on hand in such emergencies.

"Anyway I'm due at a party at Mrs. Earle's," he said more feebly.

At this Bemans let out a cry of joy.

"Cynthia? Is Cynthia Earle having a party? Why, that's great. Come on, boys, we'll all go up to Cynthia's house, one of my oldest friends. What a gal!"

"Now wait a minute," Briggs protested, for he hated people who said gal even when it stood for gallon as was too often the case. "It isn't a party, really, it's a sort of symposium of what old friends of Marius remember about him, speeches, letters — "

"Fine! We're all vitally interested in Marius," Bemans said jovially, propelling Briggs outward through the café door while the others looked wistfully back at a passing tray of highballs. "Besides I get these guys to come on my program for no dough and the least I can do is try to give them a little treat afterwards. Always plenty of liquor at Cynthia's. Haven't seen her for years. Great old girl. Understand she's going to do her life story, is that right?"

Briggs muttered that rumors had reached him that the lady

had a terrific book she wanted to write and was looking for a writer, a big name, who would write it for her and leave his big name off of it. Outside the Julien he tried to shake off Bemans' grasp with every intention of plunging back into the café or someplace far from these resolute companions closing around him.

"Scotty's station wagon will take us right there," Bemans said. "Pile in, boys, I'm going to show you one of the splendors of the Prohibition Era."

"I hope there's something to eat there, I'm starved," said the young man, evidently Scotty since he was unlocking the station wagon.

"Don't worry about that, and all free, too," Bemans cried.

"Look here," Briggs said firmly, backing away from the car. "I haven't any business taking all you people. I don't even know the woman. I'm only going because the magazine sent me. How can I show up with all of you bastards?"

"I guess you don't know Cynthia," Bemans said with a patronizing grin, cuddling his pipe in mittened hands. "I guarantee you Cynthia will be okay. Maybe a little beat up by this time, and that reminds me, fellows, a word of warning. Everybody stick together when it's time to go. Lady wolf got no chance if six little pigs stick together."

Everyone guffawed, piling into the car. Six little pigs and the lady wolf, by George, that was good, and they drove away quite overcome with laughter, as if their manly honor was constantly besieged by lecherous heiresses. Anecdotes to that effect were soon forthcoming, chief raconteur being Hoff Bemans who was oldest and loudest of the group and more richly stocked. Briggs could not listen, his mind on the ticklish question of whether bringing six extra guests to a dinner excused your being two hours late.

He recalled that Hoff Bemans was an old rear avant-gardist with an inky finger in all the arts, who had set himself up as general handyman for the twenties, always ready to patch up a red carpet for Millay, Fitzgerald, Hemingway or Anderson, and a fast man with the blurb for anything from pottery exhibits to the new jazz. Years ago he had "returned to the soil" with the compliments of the Farm Home Finance Company, and was now quite the country squire, sprouting children regularly from his sturdy little peasant spouse from Minetta Lane, and singing the joys of the simple life in every bar on Third Avenue. He had a real old red barn on his place richly stocked with enough old *transitions* and his wife's old still lifes to keep their goat happy for years, a quaint old-time kitchen complete with Erector sets, broken toys, diapers, and old Chianti empties, and a fine old piny library stacked with Sears, Roebuck catalogues and bound volumes of *The Swan*, to which he contributed his quarterly tithe of three thousand words illuminating aesthetics. A good life and a good hearty man, Bemans, and it was too bad Briggs detested him so bitterly.

"Hey, where are you going?" he yelled suddenly as the car nipped past another red light up Fifth Avenue. "We've passed it."

"The Earle house is on Sixty-Fourth," Hoff said. "I know."

"But she said the old Beaux Arts studio building," Briggs said.

"What?" roared Hoff. "Turn back to Fortieth, Scotty, it's at her studio!"

The brakes were jammed so hard Hoff's pipe fell out.

"Damn, I wouldn't have come if I'd known that," he shouted angrily, replacing his pipe in his mouth. "Why couldn't she throw her party in the big house the way she used to? Confound these rich girls turning arty so nobody can have any fun any more. There ought to be a law. Studio, my foot! There won't be any place to sit down and we'll have her idea of a simple artist's supper and God knows what to drink."

Briggs felt that since none of them were invited they had small right to set up such a wail of righteous indignation, and as the car turned and sped downward again he had to listen to a chorus of complaints about the hardships wrought on friends by rich girls turning bohemian. They invited you to dinner and you went thinking for once you'd get a bang-up dinner in a fine house but what did you find? The hostess in an ominous-looking apron, the cook and butler dismissed, a great pot of the same old home spaghetti on a burner, a scraggly looking salad and a few knobs of cheese! Just what you would have had every day only you'd have had it better and more of it. It was the limit the way these rich girls tried to be simple and make everybody else suffer for it. But then most of the upper middle class was playing pioneer now, giving the money they saved by having no maid or nurse to their and their children's psychoanalysts, feeling some kind of grisly virtue in banging around Bendix and babies with their own sensitive untrained hands.

"The funny part is that it's now the artists and real poor have turned stuffy," said the driver, who Briggs fervently wished would pay more attention to the red lights than to his cosmic reflections. Back and front seats chimed in agreement to the observation and upbraided the new bohemia for wallowing in its middle-class euphoria of neo-modern furnishings, TV rooms, Sunday roasts, blended Scotch, and Howdy Doody. How different it was in the twenties, Hoff Bemans said, in the days of Marius and Dalzell Sloane and Ben Forrester! He assured his panel companions that in those days he would not have repaid their work with such miserable hospitality as he was now offering them, ah no. Rich people had fine homes in those days, places you were proud to take your friends, great parties it was a pleasure to crash.

Hoff was still puffing somberly at his pipe and shaking his head over the defections of the arty rich when they reached the Beaux Arts. They were soon rising upward in the trembling old elevator. Briggs was so unhappy wondering how to explain his associates that Bemans finally sensed it and patted him soothingly on the back.

"Nobody gets mad when unexpected men come to a party, son," he said kindly. "Especially Cynthia. It's just when you take women that it ain't etiquette."

This statement turned out to be absolutely true, for Cynthia's face on seeing her door full of strange men was a pleasure to see. She was glad to meet Mr. Briggs and as for his being late, why the spaghetti had hardly started to burn yet, though the anchovy sauce had been somewhat charred during the last round of martinis, but come in, come in, and how wonderful of him to bring so many marvelous people! It turned out that like many other well-known characters of the twenties whose friendship Hoff Bemans claimed, she did not recall ever having met him, but was happy to have him none the less. Briggs expected Hoff to be disconcerted by this, but he swaggered into the room, an arm about her shoulder confidently, reminding her of that night at Webster Hall, and those jolly treks up to the Cotton Club in Harlem, the time she came to a New Playwrights party on Cherry Lane with Otto Kahn and Horace Liveright, the time she came to a Salons of America auction ball at Schleffel Hall over on Third Avenue with Marius and got mixed up and bid against herself up to three hundred dollars for a Ben Forrester watercolor tagged at ten bucks. What good times those were and since they sounded perfectly plausible and Cynthia enjoyed hearing about them, Briggs began feeling proud of himself for having brought these fine fellows.

Cynthia was wearing her Tyrolean peasant outfit and everyone was telling her she didn't look a day over ten, a perfect child in fact. This flattery incited Cynthia to skip about and look up roguishly at the boys, all but fluttering her fan, and then look modestly downward with a clatter of eyelids, weighted as they were with layers of iridescent eye shadow and heavily beaded false eyelashes. Her golden hair was flowing freely tonight, bound Alice-in-Wonderland style with a gold ribbon. The large bare studio contained a great square couch on which several men and two women clustered; a dozen ladies in décolletage befitting a coronation party and men in dinner jackets stood in little groups holding warm martinis or New York State sherry. A large lumpy snowy-haired gentleman named Okie welcomed Briggs to the big work table on which the goblets and refreshments were laid out. Through the window could be seen the twinkling lights of Bryant Park and the red glow above Forty-Second Street.

"I understand you're doing the *City* piece on Marius," Okie said affably to Briggs, handing him a cocktail. "I'm doing a book and everybody here is interested in the man, critics, dealers, all friends of his. As a matter of fact this is sort of a belated wake for him, that's why you'll be interested, everybody telling what they remember of Marius and over there we have a tape recorder taking everything down. I think it's a great idea, a thing like this; as a matter of fact I suggested it to Cynthia. A get-together of all his oldest and dearest friends. Dalzell Sloane, the guy over there with the beard, and Ben Forrester, the big fellow with the funny-looking mustache, they just showed up."

"There are folks here that have been dead for twenty years," a wizened pixie-faced, brillo-haired little woman named Lorna Leahy said, giving Briggs a sunny smile. "I'll introduce you."

If he could hold out long enough and keep from getting tight, Briggs told himself, he should get enough material right here to finish up his piece without putting himself out in the least, so it was really a good thing that Janie and Ellenora had failed him after all.

"It's just like old times, by Jove!" Okie kept crying out, and the phrase summoned fatuous simpers to some faces; nostrils quivered sniffing out fragrant old memories, while to others the words brought an expression of helpless alarm as if some pesky visitor routed with desperate strategy had suddenly popped back in for his hat.

"Old times!" Ben Forrester muttered in Dalzell's ear. "Let's hope *they're* not here again."

Dalzell made no answer. He was the one who had dreaded

most coming back into the world, yet here he was happier than he'd been in years. Maybe it was soft, as Ben would surely say, to have present pleasure obliterate years of defeat but the truth was he felt young again, he had money in his pocket, work ahead of him, and Cynthia was being nice to him. Odd, that seeing through her made him feel the more bound to her, as if her transparency was precious and must be protected. He wanted to have her go on thinking she was powerful, beautiful, and that all men were in love with her, because that was the Cynthia around which his youth had revolved; for the capricious vanity that was Cynthia's to be shattered meant the end of hope for him, too.

"What a kick Marius would get out of this!" exclaimed Okie. "I'd give a million dollars to see him walk in right now."

"The trick would be worth it," Ben said sardonically.

"Wouldn't you love to hear him when he saw the prices Severgny is charging for him?" Cynthia cried out.

"She'd ask us to throw him out for using such language," Ben whispered to Dalzell.

Dalzell felt his face reddening and he moved away from Ben imperceptibly. He didn't feel he understood the Ben he had come to know of late. The apparent ease with which dealers accepted their counterfeit Mariuses canceled Dalzell's sense of guilt but inflamed Ben's bitterness all the more. He was jealous of Marius now, as if the dead man had personally defeated him, and he would almost have been glad if some expert had spotted his own characteristic bold brush in a Marius half-finished water color. But none of these fine experts could even tell the break in the originals where Marius, drunk or bored with the picture, had had Trina finish the job, a vandalism obvious to any friend who knew how Marius worked or, for that matter, knew how Trina handled a broom. Dalzell feared that Ben's smoldering rage would boil over into a damaging public outburst and confession, and was glad to have Ben's attention caught by a pretty young art student sitting at his feet.

"Now that everybody's finished eating, let's get down to the business of the evening," Okie shouted, banging on the table with a tray for quiet. "What we're here for, as you know, is to put on record a permanent tribute to Marius. You all know of the books, exhibitions, articles about him and all that, but a few of us hit on the idea of making a Long Playing record of spontaneous reminiscences of Marius, tributes to him as man and as artist, the sort of thing that pops in your head just sitting around like this. We have Mrs. Earle's tape recorder and it will catch everything that's said. Later we cut it down to record size. I'm glad Hoff Bemans came in tonight, as he is familiar with radio discussions and has volunteered to act as sort of m.c. And what a thrill we'll have afterwards with the playback!"

What a perfectly marvelous way of paying tribute to Marius, people exclaimed, filling their glasses to pave the way for spontaneity. Older guests smiled as they recalled old Marius anecdotes they would narrate, and they could not help feeling relieved at the chance to shine in reflected spotlight, so to say, knowing that if the master himself had been present they would not have a chance to open their mouths.

Sitting on the floor beside Lorna Leahy in front of the table on which the recording machine rested young Briggs took out his ball-point pen and a notebook, and being moderately drunk adjusted his reading glasses for better hearing. He squinted intently at the notes he had already jotted down during the evening, and Lorna looked over his shoulder at them with considerable curiosity.

Cynthia's Studio Rent, $150 per mo.

Ford Foundation Grant to Busby—for study of Marius and his Group, $3000.

Guggenheim Fellowship to H. Bemans for Marius Biog., $2000.

Rockefeller Grant (Marsfield)—Color research from Delacroix to Marius, $4000, 2 yrs. travel.

Fulbright award (Canfield) Marius Contribution to American Thinking, $4000.

Last known Marius studio rent, $20. (Possessions seized for $80 unpaid.)

"All set, Charlie!" Okie motioned to the young man delegated to attend to the machine, and Hoff Bemans stepped over the groups clustered on the floor to take a position behind Lorna. But at this moment there was a commotion at the door. Cynthia and Severgny bustled out to the hall and came back leading the new arrival, a faded little woman in the most widowy of widow's weeds.

"Good heavens, it's Anna!" Lorna whispered. "Where did they dig her up? Look, she must have brought in some new pictures."

For Severgny was reverently placing on the table against the wall two small canvases, arranging the table lamps to illuminate the pictures while gasps of appropriate awe swept over the room. Dalzell Sloane felt Ben Forrester's hand suddenly grip his shoulder and their eyes met in something like fear.

"Just a minute while I introduce Anna Marius." Cynthia held the arrival by the arm. "Everybody knows how hard Mr. Severgny and Okie and I have been working all these months to locate traces of Marius' work and his family. We've been scouting all over the globe and now it turns out that Anna, here, Marius' first — ah — wife — was living right over on Staten Island, not even knowing Marius was dead till she read someplace about this meeting tonight. She says she never comes to Manhattan but made the trip just to bring us two of the canvases she still had and here they are and here she is."

There was a round of polite applause and a ripple of excited murmurings as the lady sat down modestly in a corner.

"Was she legally married to him?" Briggs whispered to Lorna Leahy.

"Certainly not," Lorna muttered contemptuously. "Her real name is Anna Segal and she was always hanging around some artist or writer in Provincetown or Woodstock or Bleecker Street, wearing them down by sitting on their stairs till they'd come home and let her in, then running errands for them or begging for them. Marius was always throwing her out but she'd creep back and when he'd wake up with a hangover there she'd be with a pick-me-up and ice bag ready, showing what a good wife she'd make. She was always losing her guys by marriage or death and now I suppose all she has left is Marius' bones. She's a ghoul, that's all."

The young man Okie had invited from CBS to operate the recording machine was testing sounds around the room and in a sudden blast of monkey chatter a cracked voice shouted, "*She's a ghoul, that's all,*" and then the apparatus was subdued.

"Okay, here we go," Hoff Bemans shouted. "Everybody just act natural and forget the record."

. . . *the playback* . . .

• "We should have had a professional regulate the whole thing," complained Cynthia much later, sitting on the floor wedged between Briggs's legs now that the young man had gotten a seat on the couch. He felt trapped and embarrassed by Cynthia's lively squirmings but she seemed quite unconscious of any undue intimacy, throwing a bare, braceleted arm over his knee or resting her sharp chin in deep thought on his thigh. "A professional could have picked up the right sounds instead of having all those whispers come bellowing out."

"It was a mistake letting Hoff Bemans try to m.c. it because he's a chronic air hog," said the young man from CBS. "He has to push in front of everybody the minute he sees a mike or a camera."

"He thinks he was chums with everybody just because he saw them eating in the same restaurant he did," Ben Forrester said. "Twenty years later he thinks he was at the same table, maybe in the same bed."

"I'll run it through again and cut out Hoff," said the young man.

Dalzell Sloane, Ben, Briggs, Okie and Severgny had stayed on for one more run-through although it was after two o'clock. Cynthia had graciously brought out her best brandy when the other guests left, for the evening had proved most unnerving for all. In the first playback private whispers and asides had come booming out drowning proper speeches and a dozen quarrels had started because someone waiting to hear his own pretty speech heard instead malicious remarks about himself made at the same time. Almost everyone had stalked out either wounded to the quick or eager to report the fiasco. Careful editing must be done by a chosen few, Cynthia had declared, and here they were, ears critically cocked, eyes on the Martel bottle. The machine whirred and voices came crackling out like popcorn.

"She's a ghoul —"

"Everybody knew Lorna meant Anna when that came out," Cynthia giggled, digging her elbow into a vulnerable angle of Briggs's lap. "But Anna just gave that patient martyr smile. Did you ever see so many yards of black on anyone in your life? That poor, rusty, humble Christian black! So like Anna! Go ahead, Charlie, skip the preliminaries."

The whirring began again.

"All the newspapers said was that it was an accident on a lonely mountain road in the Mexican interior. Nobody knows who was with him."

"You can bet it was some dame. We ought to demand an investigation and find who collected the accident insurance."

"For heaven's sake don't start anything like an investiga-

tion or we'll all be in trouble just for having known him. Don't you know they've already got him pegged as a Commy just because he was always painting ragged children and slums and beggars and women slaving away?"

"Are they crazy? Marius never sympathized with Commies or workers either. Those ragged kids were his own, the slums were where he lived, the poor women were slaving to support him. He'd a damn sight rather have painted Lord Fauntleroys and well-fed beauties but he had to use what he had."

"Nonsense, Marius just liked to paint muscles and big bottoms and hungry eyes and, boy, that's what he always had around! Don't you remember how he used to say 'Kinetics! there's your secret for you, the hell with the rest.' "

"Wonder how he managed to lose Trina and that brood. Didn't she write everybody a few years back trying to locate him?"

"Trina was a she-devil. She must have eaten her young and passed on or she'd be hounding Marius still, dead or alive. Still she was always faithful, a monstrous faithful woman, he used to say."

"That's just what drove him crazy, the sheer monotony of her faithfulness. If she'd only be faithful once in a while, he always complained, but oh no it was all the time, and it got him down."

"At least he never needed to say that about Anna— "

"Good heavens," gasped Cynthia in alarm, "I had no idea the damn machine was picking me up when I said that!"

"*—One martini and she'd start tearing her clothes off. Then she joined Alcoholics Anonymous, remember, because she* *had waked up one morning in bed with the janitor. From all I heard she enjoyed him all the more sober.*"

"Wait a minute, please," begged Cynthia. "Did Anna hear that on the last playback? I think it's awful for people to listen to what other people say about them and make everybody so uncomfortable."

"She was busy telling what an inspiration she was to Marius about that time," Dalzell reassured her.

"Not that I wasn't telling the truth," Cynthia went on. "Why, I heard she stayed with A.A. right through the Twelve Steps, but one night she got tight and got into a surrealist art class by mistake next door to the Twelve Steps Club and it scared her into beginning all over in A.A. They call the art school the Thirteenth Step now, isn't that a scream?"

"I must say I thought Anna's statements were very interesting," Severgny said.

"Skip to that part, Charlie," said Cynthia, throwing her head back into Briggs's stomach so that he emitted a startled *woop*. "I missed part of that."

" *'Anna,' he used to say to me, 'if it wasn't for you I'd be dead of starvation, Anna my sweets' and I'd always say, 'Now, ducky, you know your old friends don't mean to let you down this way, and if some of those that could help haven't come through, never writing and never putting anything your way, you mustn't be too hard on them, they're just thoughtless and maybe they'd rather have their bellies full of steak and Scotch whiskey at the St. Regis and ride around in their powder-blue Cadillacs than keep a genius from starving.' And Marius would be so darling he'd say, 'Anna, old girl, I can't say I blame them at that.' Why, if Marius would be here right now he wouldn't blame any of you for letting him down, he'd act as if all of you had always been his best friends.'*"

"*Listen here, Anna, don't look at me because I never let Marius down and if you're referring to the time you popped in on me and said Marius had to have eight dollars for his gas bill the reason I didn't give it to you was that I knew Marius was living with Trina up in Peekskill anyway —*"

"*Oh, Ben, I'm not accusing anyone, and as for Marius leaving me for Trina it wasn't because he was in love with her, it was only that she had that shack on the lake and the city was so hot. You know perfectly well he came back to me when the cold weather set in —*"

"Good heavens, is she crying?" burst out Severgny, for unmistakable snuffles were being broadcast.

"Of course she's crying," said Cynthia. "Don't you remember how she always cried when she was trying to wheedle something out of you, saying it was for Marius? Imagine her showing up to play the grieving widow when she didn't even know he was dead till six weeks ago!"

"Has she tried to claim insurance and how much?" Briggs piped up, but the machine drowned out any answers.

"*Now don't say Marius' friends let him down, just look at all of us here honoring him tonight. The thing was Marius never appreciated what his friends did for him anymore than you did, Anna. He's the one who never wrote. Never a word except a card about five years ago from Vancouver asking me to send money to come back east.*"

"*Last I heard from him was from San Francisco saying the same thing. Didn't Cynthia say she got a card from Del Rio?*"

"Wait a minute, what did he do with all that money if he never used it to come back?"

"Nobody ever sent him any money, Mr. Briggs, that's what I mean by letting him down—"

"People, people, we're here to tell stories about Marius not to abuse each other! This record is to be a tribute to Marius, a kind of bringing him to life, as it were—"

"If he was alive he wouldn't be invited here and Severgny and the other dealers wouldn't even handle his pictures because he owed them all, and what's more Marius wouldn't even know half of these people claiming to be his best friends."

"People, please, let's try to remember gay little things—"

"You mean like the time Cynthia Earle took Marius on a cruise, and her hair was black as a witch then and she was awfully yellow and skinny. Ha ha, I'll never forget Marius said it was the longest Hallowe'en he ever had—"

"Whose voice was that?" Cynthia cried out suddenly, leaping up so that Briggs fell backward on the bed, his notebook sliding down the crack next the wall where he rolled over to retrieve it. "Let's stop this right now, Charlie, till I find out who said that."

Nobody knew whose voice it had been, and since Charlie, the expert, had gone into the bathroom the machine was left on sputtering away, ignored by Cynthia who was shouting her indignation, all the angrier for Okie's roaring to her defense. He was accusing everyone of treason to that great benefactor, Mrs. Earle, who had done everything in the world for Marius, a big peasant oaf who didn't even appreciate a fine woman's love, let alone the trouble she had trying to help him make a name. No gratitude—

"Marius had just as much gratitude toward his benefactors as they had toward *their* benefactors," Ben Forrester interrupted. "When someone gave him money left them by their ancestor Marius always said he and the ancestor were the only ones who did anything to earn it."

"When I think of all I did for that swine," Cynthia cried indignantly. "And for all his wives, too. Why I even made him bring back a Spanish shawl for one of them when we came back from Trinidad. I was always decent to them. When I'd invite him to a party I'd always say now don't forget, do bring what's-her-name. No, you can't say I wasn't a real friend to Marius, Ben Forrester."

"Like your old man was a good friend to General Motors," Ben retorted. "You got your dividends. Then when you got through with him you never looked him up even though he was right down on Houston Street. Like everybody else here tonight. If they thought he was still struggling away down there they wouldn't even bother about him."

Ben was working up to something and Dalzell gave him a warning frown, fearing an explosion of Ben's pent-up bitterness. Ben got the signal and rose. Severgny caught the look and followed Ben to the door, picking up the pictures Anna had brought on his way.

"I never claimed to know the man, Ben," he said appeasingly. "I only have the *expertise*. For instance I have a suspicion these two pictures are phonies, and from the way you two looked at them I felt you had the same hunch. What about it?"

Ben busied himself sorting out their hats and coats from the hall.

"Why should you doubt them?" he asked guardedly.

"The background," Severgny said with a quiet smile. "Marius hasn't been east in the last seven years but one picture shows a Staten Island bus that only started running two years ago. I just happened to notice."

And the charred walls of an old brewery that had burned down only last year, Dalzell mentally added, and how could Marius have done that?

"I'd swear it was Marius' work," Dalzell said cautiously.

"Let's discuss them at the gallery when I've studied them longer." Severgny shrugged. "I think I should have a little chat with Anna. She may have talents none of us ever suspected."

Not Anna, Dalzell reflected, but who then? Who could have done that gnarled, tired truck horse like Marius? Not even Ben or himself. And if Severgny was beginning to suspect, where did that leave them?

"That's right, walk out on me!" Cynthia wailed woefully. "Walk out without so much as good-bye!"

Dalzell half-turned, but Ben significantly pushed him out the door.

"I'll call tomorrow, Cynthia dear," Severgny called out tenderly. "Get a good night's sleep. A pity the record was so unsatisfactory. Come on, gentlemen, poor Cynthia is utterly exhausted."

Dalzell hesitated, fancying he detected real woe in Cynthia's voice, but now was not the time to console her.

"Poor Cynthia, my foot! I'm not a bit exhausted," Cynthia wailed as the door closed on the three men. "I'm just the loneliest person in the whole world and everybody leaves me — "

"Cynthia dear, I'm here!" Okie cried out and in the hall

the others heard her irritated retort, "Of course you're here, silly, there's never any getting rid of you."

"Cynthia, now, just a minute — "

"Oh go way, Okie, can't you ever learn when you're not wanted? For God's sake, Okie!"

With a heart-rending sob Cynthia flung herself about on her couch, face-down in the pillows, beating her fists into them with a great jangling of bracelets. Okie had planted himself doggedly in front of her, breathing heavily, his hands clenched at his sides.

"When you wish to apologize to me Cynthia," he said in a choked proud voice, "I am willing to listen."

"Stop being such an ass!" wailed Cynthia. "You just want to stay and finish up my brandy the way you always do. Go way, I say."

She redoubled her sobs and pillow-beatings, kicking up her heels in anguish till a sandal flew off and hit Okie in the eye. It was more than even Okie could bear, especially since the young man named Charlie had come out of the bathroom and was staring at the scene with astonishment. Okie was so humiliated by this audience he could not restrain himself, and pointed a trembling finger at Cynthia's heaving back.

"Yes, you can say 'go way' but you should be glad there is one man left for you to order around because all your other men have run off years ago. I wasn't good enough for you, then, oh no. I never got invited on the big house parties and the cruises, oh no, you just had the big shots, I was always on the outside. But I could take it, just like I took it from everybody else. I knew nobody liked me, but that didn't bother me. I hung around and took all the snubs and insults, because

I knew if I hung around long enough the day would come when none of you would find anybody else to take the dregs, and that's why I've got the last laugh. You've got to have me now because I'm the only one that will take the dregs, the scraps of all of you."

"Go away!"

"All the time you used to kick me around and make fun of me there were plenty others making fun of you, Cynthia, and you can snoot and snub me to your heart's content, I knew who they were really laughing at, and I could laugh too, my girl, only I'm sorry for you, because you got nobody but me and what would you do if you couldn't whistle me back? Think about that, Cynthia, and see how you like being left with nobody — nobody — "

Okie's voice broke with emotion and he gulped, looking hungrily at Cynthia's shaking shoulders but she showed no signs of listening to reason, just letting out little heartbroken gasps as she clutched the velvet spread. Taking a long tremulous breath, Okie cast a yearning look at the brandy bottle, then tossed back his white head, clapped on his Homburg and strode out of the door which the young man named Charlie held open for him as if for a great star and followed him out.

Cynthia's sob stopped the instant the door closed and she sat up, wiping her eyes. Looking around petulantly her gaze fell on the space behind the couch where young Briggs had fallen and was wedged between bed and wall, sleeping peacefully with his mouth wide open.

A triumphant smile lit up Cynthia's face.

"Left with nobody, er? Well, look who's here!" she said and leaned over to yank him back up on the couch. The motion woke Briggs who saw Cynthia's doting face above his and no one else around. Hoff Bemans' warning not to be left alone with the hostess rang an alarm in his brain, and he was out of the door like a flash, almost pushing over Dalzell Sloane who was coming back down the hall.

"Thank Mrs. Earle for the nap, will you?" Briggs shouted, just making the elevator.

Dalzell opened the studio door gently and Cynthia gave a glad cry.

"Oh Dalzell, I knew you wouldn't leave me! I'm so lonely!" she cried, holding out her arms to him. "Promise me you'll never leave me again, never, no matter what! Am I so hideous, Dalzell, am I so old?"

The mascara and purple eyeshadow were streaking down her cheeks and her nose was red. Dalzell took out his handkerchief and carefully repaired her face which she held up to him trustingly.

"You're beautiful, Cynthia," he said. "You'll always be beautiful."

. . . *the bore that walks like a man* . . .

• In the Pink Elephant bar around the corner from Cynthia's studio Okie stood at the bar, or rather rested himself upon it, continuing the long list of grievances that the evening had unleashed. To assure himself of a sympathetic ear he had gone so far as to invite the fellow Charlie What's-his-name for a nightcap. He had a suspicion that Cynthia's ignoring of his accusations had put him in a rather weak position with his audience, and he wanted to go over the whole thing and put it into what he referred to as "proper perspective."

"A gentleman can take only so much, Charlie," he declared, stirring his brandy and soda with a knobby forefinger. "Then the primitive man comes out as it did in me tonight. 'Try and whistle for me,' I said to her. They can all whistle for me — every damn one of the lot — see what good it does them. I took a lot from them."

"Sure you took a lot," agreed Charlie. "They were always trying to shake you."

"They couldn't do it, though," Okie said proudly. "I'll say that for myself, no matter how my feelings might have been hurt I stuck right along. Now I've got them all in my pocket, don't you see?"

"Sure," said Charlie. "You were right, too."

The intelligence of this comment brought an approving look from Okie, who studied his companion gravely.

"Where I made my mistake was not joining the Communist Party when I was your age," he mused.

The young man and bartender looked shocked.

"That would make me an ex-Commy, of course, right now and I could get even with the whole lot of them, Cynthia, Forrester and Sloane, all of them. I'd swear every one of them had a Party card at one time or other, and boy, it would take the rest of their lives to get out of that one. But I was too dumb to see ahead that far."

"You could be an ex-Commy without going to the trouble

of being a Commy, couldn't you?" argued Charlie, rather pleased with this picture. "The real Commies wouldn't dare say you weren't one without giving themselves away. Go ahead, sic the F.B.I. on them, why don't you, and have yourself a ball watching them squirm."

"Other people do it, why shouldn't I?" said Okie reflectively.

"I think this guy really means it," Charlie observed to the bartender. "He's that mad at these characters, he'd turn 'em all in."

Okie shook his head with a sad, noble smile.

"No, my boy, anybody else would but I'm too much of a gentleman." He pounded the bar with his glass and the bartender, at a quick nod from Charlie, construed this as an order for two more drinks and poured them. "That's why I hate everybody, because they're not gentlemen. Do you realize that in all the years I've known Larry Whitfield he has never once invited me to lunch or to visit his big place there in the Berkshires? Do you believe me when I tell you that this dealer, Severgny, never once has taken me to his home or made any effort to know me? The bad manners! The rudeness! Like Ben Forrester, when he was riding high a couple of seasons there in Paris and could have taken me to some fine parties but oh no. I tell you people aren't gentlemen, that's all that hurts me!"

"Maybe they didn't want a Commy around," Charlie suggested, swigging his drink.

Okie whirled on him indignantly.

"How dare you call me a Commy?" he said.

"Wasn't you telling him you was a Commy?" asked the bartender coldly.

"No, he was telling me he was a gentleman," explained Charlie. He gave Okie a nudge. "Drink up, or the bar will close before we can order another. All that wine and sherry made me thirsty for a real drink. You should have saved your quarrel till after we'd finished the brandy."

Okie fixed bulging oyster eyes on his young friend belligerantly.

"What quarrel are you referring to?" he demanded.

Charlie's jaw dropped.

"Well, when Mrs. Earle told you to go away and then you told her what you thought of her and — "

Okie put a hand on the lad's shoulder, groping past the shoulder padding to contact the shoulder proper.

"My dear fellow, can't you tell the difference between quarrels and the simple joking between friends? Cynthia and I enjoy putting on our little acts, but I'm surprised you were taken in by it. The reason I invited you here was that I thought you had a sense of humor. And now — ha ha, so you really didn't know Cynthia was kidding!"

"Were you joking about being a gentleman, too?" Charlie asked, which set the bartender off in silent chuckles of deep appreciation. Okie was looking at the bar check, holding it far away and then drawing it near his eyes.

"One-sixty!" he exclaimed incredulously. "What is this, El Morocco?"

He reached for his wallet cautiously as if it might bite off his hand and having located it in his inside coat pocket tugged away at it, evidently meeting with mighty resistance until his final capture of it almost lost him his balance. He fished some coins from his change pocket, extricated a reluctant one-dollar bill from the wallet, then restored it to its warm nest.

"I must say I don't see the point in paying out good money for drinks when we were having them free at Cynthia's," he grumbled.

Charlie looked at him in astonishment.

"But she ordered you out and you told her off, didn't you? You said what you thought of the whole lousy lot of them — "

"What?" Okie cried out, shocked. "You must have misunderstood the situation, my boy."

"What are you getting sore at me for?" Charlie said, nettled at Okie's reproving tone. "I thought you were a hundred per cent right. What kind of people are they, anyway?"

Okie straightened up, frowning at him beneath proud beetling gray brows.

"They are my friends, young man, friends of a lifetime, and I should think you would regard it an honor to meet them. Instead you stand here in this common saloon making derogatory remarks about your betters, insinuating that I myself behaved badly to our hostess —"

"I said I didn't blame you!" interrupted Charlie.

Okie lifted a forefinger admonishing silence.

"I shall apologize to poor Cynthia in the morning," he stated. "If she misunderstood our little joke as you seem to have done, then of course she will be upset until I make apologies."

"You're always going around apologizing," muttered Charlie, baffled and exasperated, seeing an end to nightcaps in Okie's final gesture of buttoning up his Chesterfield.

"Because I happen to be a gentleman, my dear fellow," Okie said haughtily. "Something you young upstarts know nothing about. Have you so much as uttered one word of thanks for my invitation to a nightcap, for instance? No. There you are."

"Thanks," said Charlie sulkily.

Reluctantly he followed Okie out and stood on the corner watching him swagger proudly eastward toward Fifth Avenue, noting that the Chesterfield was too snug but still seemed the proper armor.

. . . *one has one's own life to live* . . .

• The time had come, Elsie Hookley decided, to drop Jerry Dulaine. You took an interest in someone, knocked yourself out trying to help them get on their feet, defended them against a world of enemies, gave them the shirt off your back, and what thanks did you get? The person didn't want a shirt or to be on her feet. Your money, time and tender sympathy were all down the drain. Once you've made up your mind what a person ought to be you can't go back and be satisfied with them the way they are. Jerry had fascinated her as capable of magic transformation, but now that this had proved a false hope, Elsie felt righteously let down. She found daily justification for her decision to dismiss this friendship. There were the bills for objects Jerry had charged to her accounts all over town; there was the loan company to which Elsie had unwittingly given her name as sponsor now trying to collect from Elsie. There were the neighborhood tradesmen ringing

Elsie's bell to ask for Miss Dulaine. And there was the cruel fact that the young lady herself kept away from Elsie's apartment and was never to be found by phone or knock in her own place. Once you have made up your mind to drop a person it is most inconsiderate of them not to come within dropping distance. Elsie had planned to keep a cool, polite distance, to keep her own counsel about what steps she was going to take in her own life — such as her intention of descending on her mother in Boston to wrest outright cash for splurging on the old family homestead just to show brother Wharton that from now on she was going to live on the same scale as he did.

"I'll simply make it clear to her I'm through trying to help people," Elsie told herself virtuously. "From now on I'm looking out for myself, and I shan't encourage her to tell me any of her troubles, either. When she tries to explain about all these financial mix-ups I will just shrug my shoulders."

There was no use denying that she had twinges of regret for the old happy days of friendship, and perhaps she was being unkind and unfair to her former protégée. But one had one's own life to live, after all. To avoid an open scene Elsie took pains to be out in the hours she thought Jerry would be in, and she had her lights out early at night in case Jerry might be tempted to drop in for a nightcap. But there were no encounters, and after congratulating herself on how well she was handling a rather awkward situation Elsie switched to the suspicion that it was Jerry who was avoiding her. This drove her crazy with curiosity. What was the girl up to? Maybe she was keeping her distance out of shame at the failure of their recent enterprise. Still she'd never known Miss Dulaine to be ashamed of anything.

"The least I can do is to let her know I don't hold anything against her." Elsie relented a little as she helped Brucie locate a tick on his belly. "After all, there's no reason I should go to such extremes to punish her when she couldn't help the way things turned out. Even if she did hurt my feelings — "

Elsie did not try to define exactly how Jerry had hurt her feelings but hurt they were, and it was because Jerry had absolutely refused to cry on her shoulder or accept any consolation. She, Jerry, had shrugged off her benefactor as if their positions were reversed, and Elsie, with her heart full of belligerent defenses and excuses, found her charge rejecting them. Very well, Elsie had found new interests, but she would give her eyeteeth to know what Jerry was doing without her. It seemed hardly fair that Jerry betrayed no equivalent curiosity about her neighbor's new life.

"Haven't you gone yet, Iola?" Elsie called sharply to the kitchen. "I told you to leave as soon as you got things ready and I'll do the *scampi* when I feel like it. Now run along."

"I'm in no hurry, Miss Hookley," Iola whimpered. "I'd just as soon stay and fix 'em when you're ready."

She looked at her mistress dolefully, pale brown face smugly pious with love of duty, or was it, Elsie wondered suspiciously, malicious determination to bedevil her mistress by hanging around to see what was going on?

"Run along, I said," Elsie said firmly, and Iola with an audible sigh took off her apron and put on her coat and hat, looking reproachfully from Elsie to Brucie for being able to do without her.

"I been kinda scared lately, Miss Hookley," she said, standing in the doorway. "Couple times lately I seen somebody round this neighborhood look like that awful Portugee that used to devil me. If he starts bothering me again I just don't know what I'd do."

Elsie found another tick.

"I'd like to know how Brucie can get ticks in a city yard in winter," she said absently. "Good night, Iola. Nobody's going to bother you."

The door closed on another deep sigh. Elsie went to the kitchen and got out the ice bucket, fizz water and the bourbon. The shrimps were in the pan all ready for broiling in garlic butter, the avocados and salad greens waiting in the icebox, the chunk of provalone paired with the half-moon of Gruyère, the rice steaming gently on the stove. Elsie nodded approval and settled down in the living room with a highball.

She had just begun on her second when the door opened quietly and the young man whom Iola feared slipped into the room and grinning, without saying a word, poured himself a fine drink.

"You could at least knock, you little imp," Elsie said, not at all displeased. "I suppose you swiped my key and had a copy made."

He nodded happily.

"I like a lot of keys," he said. He looked around cautiously. "I saw Iola go. She won't come back, will she?"

Elsie laughed.

"You're still afraid of her. Iola can't hurt you."

"You never heard a dame scream like that one." Niggy shuddered. "Makes my blood run cold every time I think about it. I never knew a dame to start yelling when you made a little pass at her. She won't be back, will she?"

"Don't worry," Elsie reassured him. She looked over his suit, a gray with wider pin stripes than she had ever seen, and enough shoulder padding to float him in case of shipwreck. He flickered his sleeve self-consciously, catching her eye.

"Okay, I know. A little loud but that's my style. Nita likes it. Says it make me look like a South American millionaire," he said defensively. "Anyway I'm an intellectual now, I can dress any way I damn please. Look, can we talk or are you expecting somebody?"

Elsie motioned him to a chair.

"I expected you to phone," she said. "What are you up to in New York?"

"Old Brucie looks all right," answered Niggy as Brucie laid his head trustingly on his knees, waiting for the soothing scratch beneath the chin.

"He misses his fresh fish," Elsie said wickedly. Her guest's eyes flashed but he grinned and shrugged as she chuckled.

"Okay, you pulled me out of the fish pile but I wish I was there right now," he said. "At least I'd be making some dough."

He yanked a cigarette savagely out of a pack and lit it, his black eyes on Elsie waiting for her to say something, but Elsie kept her eyes on Brucie.

"Brains cost money," he said. "I was better off when I just had a boat."

He sounded injured and accusing, as if Elsie had made this unfair trade behind his back. Elsie laughed mockingly.

This angered the young man for he jumped up and poured himself another drink, planting himself in front of Elsie.

"All right, laugh, you know I was doing all right when you

got hold of me. I made money on my boat, I played around with the waitresses at the Gull House, or the schoolteachers or the help around town, and it never cost a cent. They paid for everything. Then you fix me up with all the highbrows and rich dames and they want me on tap twenty-four hours a day and I'm lucky if I get a few meals out of it. Sure, I ride around in their cars, I drink their liquor, I sleep with their mothers or their daughters to break the monotony, but no cash, see, never a damn bit of cash."

"What's stopping you from going back to the Cape?" Elsie asked calmly, knowing he wanted something from her and enjoying the sense of power. She had every intention of giving in to his demands but she couldn't resist the desire to make him jump for his sugar.

Pouting sulkily, the lad's blue-shaven face with the snub nose and long upper lip and button eyes looked more than ever like a monkey's. Elsie found the resemblance charming and appealing. She pushed the dish of toasted almonds towards him and the nervous little monkey fingers snatched at them and stuffed them in his mouth as he talked.

"The guys there are all sore at me since I started running around with the summer people," he complained. "That's where you queered me year before last. And now that I've been around I don't want to go back to what I was. You said yourself I could paint as well as those mugs in the art classes. Sure, I can throw a couple of apples on a plate with a clam shell and a pop bottle and call it a still life but what kind of a living is that?"

"Who said it was a living?" Elsie said. "At least you met some new people through it. And now it seems you don't even paint, just go to cocktail parties and pontificate with the fine minds in my sister-in-law's intellectual group. Who pays for that, by the way?"

Niggy smirked annoyingly, and examined his fingernails.

"You've picked up a lot of camping tricks," Elsie said, deciding that she wouldn't give him a thing if he was going to act coy with her. Evidently sensing this Niggy changed his tactics.

"I worked nights in a garage up on the West Side," he said. "But damn it, Elsie, I can't go around with nice people, visit their homes and all that, maybe go on pleasure trips with them, if I have to drudge away in some dirty garage. A fellow's just got to get his hands on cash to keep up. Nita's been nice enough, letting me drive her car, letting me have some of Wharton's clothes — whatever isn't too big for me, passing out a ten-spot now and then, but I got my future to look out for."

"So?" Elsie said, determined to make it as difficult as possible.

Niggy was silent, scratching his crew cut moodily.

"Well, what's your problem?" Elsie persisted. "I take it you're sorry you gave up the fisherman's life but now you're too good for it. You like going around with rich people and highbrows only there's no money in it. You have to jump when they whistle but on the other hand you don't want them to stop whistling. Well?"

The young man took Brucie's head between his knees and gazed moodily into the dog's red-rimmed patient eyes.

"You can kid about the spot I'm in but you know you're the one that set me off," he muttered. "You're the one that told me it was easier to make upstairs than downstairs, the very words you used."

"It does sound like me," Elsie admitted, pleased. "I don't see why you hold it against me, Niggy. You got a summer in Gloucester out of it, you learned to talk Tanglewood, you helped make sets for summer arena theatres, you sat around the best beaches, then you jump into philosophy and literature and end up with my brother's wife. What more do you want?"

"Cash, like I told you," Niggy said. "So it looks like I've got to marry Isabella."

Elsie sat up straight, staring at him.

"Isabella?" she cried. "You're not referring to my niece, by any chance?"

Niggy nodded gloomily.

"What on earth is Nita thinking of to let you marry Isabella?" Elsie exclaimed indignantly. "My poor brother knocks himself out grooming the girl for a big marriage and then you step in and ruin everything, just because you've got Nita interested in you! What are you thinking of?"

The young man pushed Brucie aside and got to his feet. He downed another whiskey neat and this inspired Elsie to pour herself a revivifying swig. They banged their glasses down on the table at the same moment and looked at each other for a moment in silence.

"Look," Niggy said patiently. "When a fellow like myself gets mixed up with people like you he can't call the turns any more. He gets a lot of breaks, sure, but he has to take a lot of kicking around too, never knowing how soon the show is over. I got good and sick of that Gloucester setup, believe me, but I had to keep on till I was sure of what was next. I didn't even know what I was getting into with Nita, because we met first in the New School. It turns out she's your brother's wife, so most of the time she's busy doing the family social stuff and I'm hanging around somewhere waiting for a call. Then she thinks up a deal for me to teach Isabella art, and keeps me around, but it's a dog's life. Isabella has a dog's life, too, let me tell you."

"I shouldn't be surprised," Elsie murmured.

"Her father has her doing this, her mother has her doing that, and she can't do anything to suit them so she just sits in the Park all day or goes to double features with me, both of us in a jam, see, only she doesn't know about mine."

"She's no beauty, of course," Elsie observed.

Niggy shrugged.

"I don't care about women's looks," he said. "They all look the same to me in the long run. Anyway Isabella's got herself set on running away with me and getting married."

Elsie was aghast.

"I always knew you were a little devil, Niggy, but I must say I never dreamed you were capable of such a dirty trick as that! Marrying that poor girl just to get a living!"

"As if it was going to be any picnic for me!" Niggy retorted angrily. "She's the one that gets the bargain. She told me she never had any fun in her life till I came along. Does that mean I have any fun? I should say not! The whole damn family bores the living daylights out of me, especially that brother of yours, and Nita being so darn cutie all the time, pretending she doesn't know what the deal is because she's such a itty-bitty. The whole bunch makes me sick but I can't go back where I used to be, so I'm stuck."

Elsie pondered for a moment and an amusing idea struck

her. Wharton had never tired of reminding her how much it cost the family to pay off her Baron and how he alone had saved the family honor. Someday she might be able to reply that the sacrifice was not all his.

"How much cash do you want and what would you do with it?" she asked.

The young man brightened.

"I could get by with a few hundred," he said eagerly. "I just want to clear out of town for a few months till I get some dames out of my hair. That jam between Nita and the kid is the toughest one but there's an old movie queen at the St. Moritz, too. I want some new territory. I'd like some fun, not this rat race."

"I went to the bank today so I've got some cash," Elsie said. "Maybe two hundred and some. And I'll give you a check."

Niggy was so excited he threw his arms around Brucie's neck and kissed him, an attention that made Brucie rise and draw back, growling ominously. Elsie went to the bedroom and got her wallet from the hatbox where she kept it. Two hundred and thirty, she counted out, and then carefully wrote out a check for three hundred. She always hated to give away cash outright, and on second thought took back three tens. Then she went back out and presented the money to her visitor. As soon as it touched his hands his cockiness returned.

"You're a good egg, Elsie," he stated. "I figured you wouldn't let me down, especially since you got me into this mess."

Little bastard, Elsie thought, highly delighted, reproaching her for giving him a leg up just as if she'd ruined his life! She decided she would invite him to share her *scampi* now that his business seemed settled, but she should have remembered that money in his hand always meant he would be out the door like a shot.

"You ought to be glad you have so many nice people as friends," she said primly.

"I only hope they lay off me for a while," Niggy said with his most impudent grin. "I'm fed up with nice people."

Elsie straightened up with a shocked expression.

"Ah, don't look so insulted, you know you're not nice people," Niggy exclaimed. For some reason, even though he had his money he was lingering by the door with a preoccupied air. What else did he want? Whatever it was she knew he wouldn't be long in telling her.

"I know a boat I could get for three thousand dollars," he announced. "Fellow in Boston. Wants me to come in with him taking fishing parties out, around Hyannis, summers, then take her down to the Keys winters. I'd be set for life, see."

Elsie saw. She sipped her drink reflectively, Niggy watching her out of the corner of his eye.

"Why not?" she said. "I'm going up to Boston tomorrow to settle some business with my mother. Meet me there and show me the boat. I'll be at her hotel."

Niggy jumped over a footstool to embrace her.

"Elsie, you're wonderful," he cried excitedly. "By George, if you were just a foot shorter I'd marry you tomorrow. Bye, now, till Boston."

He was gone, the door banged behind him. Elsie sat musing with a wry, doleful half smile that disturbed Brucie for he shook himself and ambled over to her, stood up and placed forepaws on her shoulders and licked her ear sympathetically.

"Dear Brucie, good old boy," Elsie said tenderly.

When she got up to put the shrimps in the broiler she saw that in his haste to leave the young man had left his cane. She looked at it incredulously and picked it up. It was Uncle's ram's-head cane, the very one she had feuded about with Wharton for so long, the one she had wanted for the express purpose of giving to Niggy.

"He got it anyway," Elsie marveled. Nita? Or Isabella? Whichever one had given it to him the idea struck Elsie as delicious and she felt more lonely than ever because there was no one with whom she dared share the joke. Presently she made up her mind and marched out to the hall and upstairs where she knocked on Jerry's door firmly. Getting no answer she knocked again and rang the buzzer. Then she tried the knob and to her surprise found the door was unlocked. She stepped inside and switched on the light.

The apartment was completely bare except for a barrel of junk in the middle of the bedroom. A pair of jet evening slippers were on top of the barrel and a crumpled magazine photograph of Collier McGrew.

. . . *everybody needs a boat* . . .

• "I ought to get in touch with Elsie," Jerry was admitting to her old friend Tessie over a jolly lunch at Louis and Armand's. "But I can't think of any way to make her understand."

"You can't even make me understand," Tessie said, shaking

her head. "You say he never makes a pass?"

"Not what I'd call one," Jerry said. "A little kiss on the forehead, a little squeeze of the hand."

"He's not married, he's not queer, and he isn't a cripple, you say," pondered Tessie. "But he has you moved into his hotel, sets up your charge accounts again, gets you set with this TV job, and lets you have me stay with you. Crazy?"

Jerry laughed.

"No other signs of it," she said. "I thought when he had me meet his aunt that maybe he meant marriage but I count that out now. Sometimes I think he's rehabilitating me."

"I wouldn't stand for anybody doing social work on me," Tessie said. "Don't he ever say anything to give you a clue?"

"He likes me to tell him things about people," Jerry said. "I don't think he knows much about people, he's got such good manners he doesn't notice anything. But he gets a kick out of hearing inside stories about them. I guess I'm his court jester."

"What do you care so long as you've got no money worries?" Tessie said unconvincingly.

"Well he's managed to get me so hopped up about him that I don't know where I am," Jerry sighed. "I don't think he'd mind if I went out with other men but he has me so baffled I just stay home and wonder if he'll show up or telephone. How did I get into a fix like this?"

"You call this a fix," muttered Tessie. "There's just no limit to the kind of fixes a man can think up. Someday I'll tell you about my marriage."

Now that they were friends again they lunched together almost every day and reminded each other of old shared experiences, more fascinating now that they had nothing to lose by telling the truth. Tessie had quit the Lido and had dieted herself back into a modeling job with Jerry as her trainer. For the time being she was following Jerry's advice in everything just as Jerry had done with her when they first met. They needed each other again and after fifteen years of experience they could admit the need. Tessie had jumped from her play-girl career straight into a kind of super-respectable suburban life. It had to be super because $15,000-a-year husbands must live religiously on $25,000 in the excessively conventional manner demanded by wives who had been models, receptionists, or hat-check girls. After a few years of this struggle Tessie had run away with a jazz drummer, worked in the chorus line of whatever nightclub he played in, working her way down to the Lido in a determined effort to go to hell, after he left her. She was glad to start over again, however, after she and Jerry had compared notes, and she was shopping around now for a glossier respectability all over again.

"I never got over the kick of calling myself Mrs.," Tessie confessed. "Bill used to tell me I Missused myself so much everybody in Mount Kisco thought we couldn't possibly be married. I passed as Missus with Hotsy, too, of course, but it wasn't the same, not being on the level. Believe me, that's what I'm after now. Big church wedding, real wedding dress, big wedding ring, calling cards with a big Mrs. Somebody Junior the Fourth."

Jerry shook her head doubtfully.

"I can see the bridal suite on the *Ile de France* and the Do Not Disturb sign on the hotel-room door," she said, "but the rest of it looks like a big bear trap to me. If you liked the life so much why did you knock yourself out to quit it?"

"I liked everything about it but Bill," Tessie said. "Him I just couldn't take. You don't know what it is to know everything a man's going to say. You get so you move heaven and earth to get the conversation around to where he won't have a chance to say it. That's marriage."

"Can we stand another brandy without falling on our facials?" Jerry asked, and answered the query by signaling the waiter for two more.

"You liked Bill well enough at first," Jerry said.

"Ever go out with a fellow who pretends he's conducting an orchestra every time any music plays?" Tessie demanded. "That was just one thing Bill did. When he was driving a car, making love, eating a steak — let him hear music and he's got to pretend he's Toscanini. It just embarrassed me to death. Maybe that's why I ran off with a drummer. At least Hotsy was a real drummer. But the real reason I left Bill was his damned boat."

It seemed that every time Bill met somebody he considered a valuable contact he got the conversation around to boats. Sailboats, motorboats, cabin cruisers, any kind of boat was his meat and he was always telling people if he had to choose between his old cruiser and Tessie he'd take the cruiser. The boredom, Tessie declared, of listening to him brag about his old *Bucephalus*, as he called her, and his troubles with the Miami Yacht Club and all the stuff about tides and bottom-scraping. If she was drinking it always ended with her making a scene and there was always somebody to take sides with Bill and say, "Aha, so the little lady is jealous of *Bucephalus*. No sporting blood, eh."

"I still don't see why you worked up such a grudge against his boat," Jerry said.

"His boat!" Tessie exclaimed scornfully. "He didn't have any boat, that was the whole trouble. Same as the orchestra. It was a pretend boat. Wait till you're married to a congenital liar and see what happens. Nobody else knows he's lying, so they end up hating you for trying to keep him off his favorite subject. I just hate boats, I'd have to say, and Bill would just give that jolly laugh of his and say, 'Believe it or not, Tess won't set foot on that boat to this day.' Funny thing, that was the only thing he ever bragged about, the dope."

It was fun having Tesise to go around with and it was fun being back uptown, safe in a beautifully impersonal hotel suite with a magic pencil that could buy anything from a hat to a Carey limousine. It was a more discreet, more cushioned life than that they had ever known together before but it was otherwise the same, and what Experience had taught them was that they liked it.

"You swear you won't ever tell anybody I was in the Lido line?" Tessie anxiously begged Jerry for the hundredth time. "I may tell a guy if I get matey with him but I don't want you to tell."

"I promise," Jerry said, "only you've got to promise not to tell that Collier McGrew isn't sleeping with me."

"I won't," Tessie said sympathetically. "I must say I simply don't dig it, though. He must like you, he does all this for you, he's not ashamed to take you places when he does come to town, he doesn't mind people talking — "

"Do they talk?" Jerry interrupted, startled.

"A big shot like that? Sure they do," Tessie said. "Everybody in the hotel and in the Fifth Avenue Credit Association knows who pays the bills even if he doesn't have a bed in your apartment. What's bad is that when a man doesn't put you to bed right at first he's likely to get over the urge."

"It kind of scares me," Jerry reflected. She wished she dared ask Elsie Hookley's advice but she couldn't get over the feeling that Elsie was bad luck for her. Just seeing Elsie would bring back the tense sick desperation of those days, the frantic hopes and fears, the daily failures, not to mention the danger of Elsie camping around her new home and scaring off McGrew. No, it had to be good-bye, Elsie, old dear.

"Why don't you go to an analyst about him?" Tessie suggested.

Jerry gave a short laugh.

"I'd feel like a fool showing up for psychoanalysis at this late date," she said. "I can save money by worrying. I figure it this way. He's a smart man, always too smart for the people he has to work with or for the people in his class, so he's always played a lone hand. He's like those birds, falcons, I guess, that peck out gazelle's eyes and throw the rest away. He pecks out just what he wants in people and throws the rest away. He likes my company when and where he likes it and he likes knowing he's trading that for something I want."

"Maybe he's got somebody else for the hay," Tessie said.

It was a disagreeable idea and Jerry winced.

"That would be my luck to get crazy over a man who's only crazy about my wizard brain," she said gloomily. "The gazelle's eyes falling in love with the hawk, that's about it."

They swirled their brandy glasses thoughtfully.

"How long do you give it, Jerry?" Tessie softly asked.

"I give myself forever, since I never felt like this before," Jerry said. "As for him — well, he might run for his life if I started something myself. Or maybe he expects me to. One of these days I'm afraid I'll take the chance."

"You've got that TV job, anyway," Tessie said. "What do you have to do, just line up celebrities for the show? Brother, who's that good-looking man looking at you?"

It was the producer of Jerry's show and he was only too eager to bring his good looks up for closer inspection. He had all sorts of program details to discuss with Jerry, including another drink around, and how about using this delightful young lady —

"Miss — I mean Mrs. Walton," Jerry said.

— in the fashion show. He had been admiring her carriage as she had darted in and out of the powder room and was sure she must have had show girl training. No? Well, it didn't matter. All he really wanted was her particular kind of statuesque beauty. He seemed so taken with Tessie and she with him that Jerry joined some friends at another table. In her absence the producer told Tessie he had heard Miss Dulaine was kept in great style by no less than Collier McGrew, and he wouldn't have dreamed she was the type, but maybe it was just Platonic. Tessie loyally assured him it was far from Platonic. They discovered they had both lived in Mount Kisco once, been married and divorced, and when Jerry rejoined them Tessie was telling all about the good times they used to have on her husband's cabin cruiser, the *Bucephalus*.

Part Five

. . . *view of the harbor* . . .

• Somebody had to take care of Marius' women before she went stark mad, Cynthia Earle declared passionately. It was true she had rashly opened the gates to trouble by sounding off in print and on the air as a Marius collector, friend and chief authority, but everybody else was doing the same. She was better placed, however, so her telephone and doorbell rang night and day with female supplicants. Gracie, Hedwig, Jeannette, Natasha, Moira, Babsie —

Marius was the father of their children, their common-law husband, their legal groom, their fiancé, anything that gave them the right to protection or support from Marius admirers. Sometimes they even brought babies, and swore they had made the trip on foot from suburban jungles or farther to share in the great man's success, and nothing less than railroad fare home would budge them from Cynthia's handsome home.

"Not a one of them attractive," Cynthia complained. "You know how Marius used to sleep with people just out of morbid curiousity. And then Anna — my God — how was I to know she was going to do a Rip Van Winkle? I admit I encouraged her at first — I was so shocked she was still around — but I never dreamed she'd come creeping up with her hat out every time I turn around! Somebody's got to do something."

This was unfair, for Anna's technique had never been open begging. She was a born poor relation and would not have been a rich relation if she could because that would mean she might have to do something for somebody else. No, in her sweet, humble way she merely rang the doorbell of the big house and collapsed on the doorstep, only sorry that it wasn't snowing and that she didn't have her newborn babe in her arms. As poor artist's neglected mate she followed these tactics shamelessly, according to Cynthia, and she had a way of getting herself up in dusty, rusty clothes, with moldy fur collars than which nothing looks poorer, and she would do this no matter how many dresses you sent her, a deliberate trick so that the mere sight of her was a reproach to you. Here I am in rags, her pious smile said, and though I am not one to blame anyone I am sure you must be ashamed of that fine coat you're wearing.

Severgny, too, was regretting that the memorial exhibition was receiving so much publicity, for he too suffered from Anna and the increasing horde of Marius' avowed connections. Lawyers must be retained to investigate claims, bouncers must be placed strategically in the gallery to dispose of weird characters eager to make scenes. A long lost brother turned up on the West Coast smelling money from Marius' name in the papers, and was only brushed off by newspaper men discovering Marius' father living alone on a New Hampshire farm.

"Neither of those boys was any doggone good," said the old man. "Both of 'em run away from home soon as they was old enough to run, wild as they come, just like the Purvises, that's their mother's folks. Willard, he's the oldest, run off with a carnival one day at milking time, the way he would, that one, and Marius was always fooling around with his paints even after he was a big boy, anything to get out of work. I knowed they'd end up in trouble, but nobody's going to take my little farm away from me now to pay for their funerals or bail or whatever it is."

Nothing would convince the old man that Marius' new fame was on the up and up.

"Those New Yorkers wouldn't stop at anything," he said dourly. "It's some trick to make me look after his family. I told that woman of his to stop pestering me years ago and this is her way of getting back at me. I won't have any part of it and you can tell that good-for-nothing Willard for me to keep his nose out of it too, if he don't want to get in the same fix as his brother."

From a San Antonio art dealer who had made the trip to Marius' last known home in Mexico had come a small package of all his landlady there could find of his belongings, at least all that she had been unable to sell or find use for. These consisted of a notebook in which recipes, restaurant addresses hither and yon, telephone numbers, notes for future sketching grounds, bus schedules, and other odds and ends were jotted down; a dozen dunning letters forwarded from as many other addresses; some snapshots of children, probably his, in varying stages of growth; a roll of used film that the landlady had been too thrifty either to throw away or have developed. The letters were from Trina and her lawyer, all written after Marius' death and obviously unaware of it. They indicated that Trina had taken the children and walked out in a huff three years before in Vancouver, returned soon afterward repentant only to find Marius gone. The letters swung from her begging to be allowed to follow him and look after him wherever he was to wild denunciations and threats. The lawyer Trina had managed to hire as tracer and his stern promises of punishments to be visited as soon as the lost one returned to his family were certainly enough to keep a man on the run. At any rate it established that Trina was still on earth somewhere far away, or had been three months ago, and was likely to loom on the scene one of these days.

Something would certainly have to be done, Dalzell Sloane had agreed, but it took a lot of arguing to get Ben to see it that way.

"We've got to do it before Severgny or Cynthia start something," Dalzell kept insisting, and finally Ben assented.

He was still grousing about giving up a date with the young art student he had collected at Cynthia's party when they took off on the ferry from the Battery.

"Whatever we find out from Anna will make things worse," he prophesied.

"Not if we find it out before the others," Dalzell said. "Whatever it is we can put the lid on it — and her — before Trina shows up and blows up the whole apple cart."

"Women are bloodhounds," Ben said moodily. "Once they get their hooks in a man they can sniff him out the rest of his life across oceans and graves. Those old hooks have just got to get back in. You don't understand that because you always managed to clear out before they got their hooks into you."

Dalzell didn't say anything. There had been hooks all right, but emotional ones only that hurt the more for not hanging on. As for women sniffing out their prey it struck him that Ben himself had been offering his own persecutors the scent whenever they withdrew the hooks. Certainly the letters coming to Ben from his Southwestern ladies couldn't have found him so easily at Gerda Cahill's apartment, where he and Dalzell were staying, without being led. Ever since their fortunes had picked up, Ben had been restless, homesick Dalzell suspected, for his old familiar ties. We get sick of our clinging vines, he thought, but the day comes when we suspect that the vines are all that hold our rotting branches together. One without vines, like himself, knew all too well one's dry rot and longed for the old parasitical leaves to mask and bind it.

"What say we stay on the ferry and go right back to Manhattan?" Ben proposed as the boat bumped into the St. George slip. "What do you expect to find out anyway?"

"We'd just be thrashing the whole thing over every day till we found out the truth — or it found us out," Dalzell said doggedly, aware that he was irritating Ben with his obstinacy, but then Ben was constantly disappointing him, too, by his belligerent self-interest. They had expected each other to be not so much the friend they remembered as the creature made up of parts they needed most and it seemed unfair that the person had developed quite differently. Their first joy in discovering bonds of mutual necessity had changed subtly to an aggrieved surprise that their aims were so different. Their disappointment in each other was the familiar discovery of age: the old friend of his youth has failed him because he fails to give him back his youth.

At the St. George station Ben followed Dalzell to the Tottenville train which was waiting. It was midday, a time evidently not popular with Tottenville travelers for the only other passengers were a stout old German-looking couple laden with bundles, and a harassed young mother in a fishy-looking leopard coat with many glittering ornaments, twin girls in pink-flowered Easter outfits clinging to her knees and a fat little Hopalong Cassidy asleep in her arms, one boot hooked into the stirrup made by her purse handle.

"I hate this island," Ben said, looking out the window as the sleepy little villages slipped by like pictures through an ancient stereoscope, ivy-grown station shanties, old corner taverns with pointed roofs, winding roads with weather-beaten houses whose gardens were already turning green, the meadows and village four corners seeming unchanged through the centuries. "I know we used to claim this trip reminded us of the one from Paris out to St. Germain-en-Laye — but I only came here when I was dead broke or in trouble, and you know how you blame a place for that."

Dalzell was beginning to feel excited and a little afraid. He would not admit that the expedition might be a mistake for no matter what trouble came of it the risk must be taken. Now that they were nearing Prince's Bay where the old German couple were getting off, he allowed himself to think of the possible consequences to himself and Ben.

"I agree that Anna has something up her sleeve all right," Ben said. "Anybody could tell that, but is it something we want to find out? We certainly don't want anybody shaking our sleeves, either."

"I don't think Cynthia suspects Anna. She hates her too much to give her any credit for mischief," Dalzell said. "But Severgny does. We've got to check before he does."

"I'd rather have Trina to deal with than Anna," Ben said. "At least there was never any doubt about where she stood, roaring all over the place like a storm trooper. But Anna was always changing her style, laying low and biding her time, sneaking up on you, sniveling and whining till she got what she was after. You can't lick the Anna type and we're fools to even tangle with her."

The young mother and her little family and the German couple had gotten off and they were the only passengers left by the time they got to Tottenville, the end of the line.

"The end of the world!" Ben muttered, looking around the station platform, but Dalzell felt a wave of old affection for this quaint remnant of a long-ago America. The Jersey shore was hardly a ferry's length away and the old roofless ferry was waiting to cross just as it always was while to his left the cobbled street led up the hill and around and the peaceful old houses followed the curve of the bay, their wide lawns sprawling down to water's edge. If the old Queens house had given them shelter and hiding in their bad times, the Island hereabouts had offered a healing vision of long ago to wipe out today. On summer days Dalzell had wandered through these roads, reminded of the old midwest lanes of his boyhood and the little foreign villages of now. For a moment of grateful memories he forgot Anna and their mission till Ben reminded him.

"I can't figure out how Anna happened to land in this territory," Ben pondered. "Sure, she used to hear Marius and the rest of us talk about it but what tidal wave threw her up here at this late date?"

A laundry truck from the Jersey ferry came up the hill and Dalzell flagged it as it turned, saving them the hour's walk to the old brewery where they were heading. It had gone out of business years ago but the building had stayed and only burned down last year, the driver informed them. Yet one of the pictures Anna had produced of Marius' had been of an old brewery horse grazing around the charred remains of the old brewery. "Home," the picture was titled in Marius' hand. The sight of this picture, offered by Anna as an old Marius that night at Cynthia's studio, was what had shocked Dalzell into action. He and Ben had the same sudden suspicion but Ben, aware of where it might lead, had wanted to forget it.

"All right, let's say Marius couldn't paint that picture unless he'd seen the place within the last year and that means he's still alive and maybe Anna's hiding him out here," Ben had said. "It also means he doesn't want to be found out. Why should we be the ones to track him down if he wants to be dead — that is, if he really isn't dead?"

Dalzell struggled to find a logical answer. All he knew was that for a cherished old friend to wish to be dead meant an unbearable wretchedness that must be alleviated. He had been lonely himself and he couldn't let old Marius suffer the same quiet terror if he could help it.

"It isn't just that he wants to be considered dead," Ben had argued. "It's that a whole industry has been piling up on his death. All these Marius worshippers only love a dead Marius and if it turns out he's alive they not only will lose money but will make his life worse than ever. And what about you and me? Do we confess to fixing up and painting a few bogus

Mariuses, then bow out into Sing Sing? or maybe they have worse dungeons for artists than for axe killers."

"That's what we may be able to head off," Dalzell had said. "You know how Anna roused Severgny's suspicions right off claiming those new canvases were old ones from twenty years back. Then she gets Cynthia's back up. So both Severgny and Cynthia are going to check up on Anna and they're likely to find out more than they even dreamed of."

Ben reluctantly conceded the danger of this. But supposing Marius was still alive, what made Dalzell think he would not resent his old friends tracking him down?

Because, Dalzell said, of that one picture he had sent in by Anna, of the tired old brewery horse back on the ruins of his old stable.

"Marius called it 'Home,'" Dalzell said, "and I had the feeling that he meant it as a message to us."

The house was the only one for miles on the weed-grown road off the highway from the old brewery. It was that gaunt unpainted shingle house, barest symbol of home, often found on acres given over to truck farming, chickens, or temporary money-making where all funds go into the produce, not the worker. The project, long abandoned, left the husks of failure scattered over the field—unfinished sheds piled with rusted machine parts, post holes dug, broken-down chicken coops, empty paint buckets, scraps of tar paper. A few scraggly hens fluttered through the bushes and a collie was chasing a squawking rooster around the house. The mailbox at the head of the long lane was marked "Jensen," Anna's latest married name.

"Cut it out, Davey," a man's voice called out as the collie

dropped his rooster chase to lunge vociferously toward the intruders.

"Marius," Dalzell breathed. "Ben, it *is* Marius."

"Either he doesn't know us or he isn't very glad to see us," Ben muttered.

"Come around the back way," Marius' voice came out.

The weary tone dampened their sudden excitement and they walked on hesitantly, wondering why they were here, frightened of what they might find. They saw him sitting in a low armchair by the kitchen stove, a blanket over his lap, a man indeed back from the grave. In the first shock of seeing him no one spoke. All that was left of the great ruddy-faced Marius was a gray skeleton with sunken blue eyes, deep lines rutting the hollow cheeks, the wide mouth drawn back in a bleak effort to smile, the hands, deeply veined, clutching the arms of his chair as if bracing against an expected attack. Dalzell's heart turned, thinking of what Marius must have been through to drain him of everything but fear.

"We got you!" Dalzell cried out, but he felt the trembling fear still in Marius' handclasp.

"You bastards!" Marius laughed weakly. "I should have known better than to trust Anna."

The kitchen was almost bare but they found a stool and chair and drew them up to the stove.

"It wasn't Anna. It was the brewery horse," Dalzell eagerly explained. "It worried us. If those last pictures were yours then we knew you had been in this section within the last year. And if somebody else had imitated you they were doing a better job than Ben and I have been doing and that worried us even more."

"What?" shouted Marius, and his laughter relieved the tension between them. "You rascals. Can't a man trust anybody even here in heaven?"

"At least you admit you're dead," Ben said. "Dalzell and I were afraid you'd try to palm yourself off as alive and bring your prices down. If you do I warn you it won't be worth our while doing any more of your work."

Marius was laughing weakly, brushing the tears from his gaunt cheeks.

"No sir, by God, I'm dead and I'm going to stay dead!" he declared and motioned Dalzell to bring out the bottle of bourbon handily sitting by the pump in the kitchen sink. "I never had it so good. But I can't trust anybody for long — Anna — even you fellows. Right now I'd like to just be an old brewery horse jogging home to graze till I hit the glue works, but it seems I'm a highwayman with a price on my head."

"How long had you been dead before you found out about it?" Ben asked.

"A good six months," Marius answered. He lit a cigarette Ben offered and looked for a moment from one to the other. "I guess I can tell you about it since you got me anyway."

"You've got us, too, don't forget," Dalzell reminded him. "We're all three in this together."

"I'd been living one jump ahead of the sheriff for years," Marius said. "Creditors, fights, dames, then borrowing this guy's car — that is, without his knowing it — Well, I had about every bone in my body broken when I wrecked it. The Indians that found me dosed me with every herb and poison known to man until all my livers and lights damn near blew up, but I was afraid to go near any villages for fear I'd get arrested for stealing the car or maybe some more of Trina's bloodhounds might catch me. The Indians looked after me but I got stir-crazy, sick of Mexico. I would have given my soul for one hour at the Café Julien. An oil truck came along bound for Acapulco and I hitched on and shipped out for New York on a freighter as dishwasher. I'd heard from Anna a while back that she'd got a farm here on insurance from some merchant marine husband and I figured she'd take me in. I'd planned before that to hide out in Rio but I thought Tottenville is further from civilization than Rio. I headed out here as soon as the ship got in and sure enough there was old Anna, sweet and silly as ever, broke and full of crazy ideas for making a fortune — dog kennels, chickens, tearooms, you know."

"Did she know you were supposed to be dead?" Dalzell asked.

"Sure, she was the one that told me. Seems she'd been trying to figure out some way of making something out of it, if Trina wasn't going to beat her to it, and she was a little put out when I showed up," he said. "I'd had pneumonia and flu and malaria and everything else with the Indians and my lungs and heart were pretty well shot, so I told her I wouldn't last long and if she'd let me stay here I'd play dead for her. No skin off her bottom. I did some pictures she could take in and sell. Lousy. I've lost the touch somehow. It made me sore she sold them so fast. But she saw being dead made me worth a hell of a lot more to her so she managed to keep quiet. But you know Anna. She'll botch it up. What I want to know is what do I do next?"

"What do you do? Why, you come right back to New York with Ben and me," Dalzell cried out impetuously. "Everybody will be so glad to have you back you'll get well in no time. You stay with us in Gerda's apartment and we'll all work together. We'll have a big celebration at the Julien."

"If I could sneak into the Julien for just one drink — " Marius said. And then he was shaking his head. He sighed, mopped his forehead with his handkerchief, then reached for his whiskey glass with trembling fingers.

"I can't risk it," he said. "I don't think I can take it any more." He grinned wryly. "Being dead has spoiled me. Gone soft."

"You're safe now, Marius, don't you see? You're a great man," Dalzell argued earnestly. "You've got the world on your side at last, and nothing to worry about. You should hear how they talk. Why, I promise you — "

He stopped at the skeptical expression on Ben's face and Marius' quizzical smile.

"You can't promise me anything and Ben knows it if you don't," Marius said quietly. "The minute I come to life I'm in trouble again."

"How about the rest of us?" Ben asked Dalzell. "People will think you and I cooked up the whole trick just to make money. They won't just accuse us of passing off bogus Marius for our own profits, they'll get us for hiding a fugitive — if Marius still is in trouble with police."

"I'm always in trouble with police." Marius shrugged. "But don't worry about signing my stuff because I'll stand up for it if the pinch comes. Just let's leave things the way they are."

"How?" Dalzell pondered.

"The most wonderful thing that ever happened to me was finding out I was dead that morning," Marius said. "No troubles, nothing to worry about but the cost of living. Damn it, why did you fellows have to spoil it? I always knew Trina and bill collectors would manage to drill a pipeline straight into my grave but I did think my old pals would respect the sleep of the dead."

"What did I tell you, Dalzell?" Ben nodded toward Dalzell, who felt helpless and defeated. Ben had been right, maybe, that they were safer to leave things as they were but when a lie was involved there was never any safety. Certainly with Anna as sole protector of the secret there was none. Through his mind there flitted all the possible reactions to the news that Marius was returned from the dead and right back in New York. There would be the initial amazement, the cries of joy, the eager questions, and then the slow mounting sense of outrage.

"If that isn't exactly like Marius!" he could hear Cynthia, Okie, Elsie Hookley, the dealers, all the old friends cry out indignantly. "That *would* be his idea of a fine practical joke, letting us go out on a limb for him, making fools of ourselves, while he has a good time laughing at us! How dare he! Here we are, knocking ourselves out to make him immortal and trying to forget what a big nuisance he always was, always broke, always in trouble, always having to be bailed out or nursed or helped! And now he pulls this! Believe me, I don't want to even see the man again."

In the silence he knew that this was in Ben's mind, too, and maybe in Marius'. Marius was looking out the window.

"I want you to go before Anna gets back from the city," he said. "She's gone down to New York for supplies for me, if I can ever get to working right again. I won't tell her you were here or that you know."

"You've seen the stuff they're writing about you, of course," Ben said. "Right up there with Titian and the old masters, my boy."

Marius threw up his hands.

"If I hadn't known it before I would have known I was dead when I read some of that bilge!" he said, and then shrugged. "What am I talking about? It was what I believed about myself. It was what made life worth living until—well, all of a sudden it—whatever it is—was gone. I was dead, all right. I couldn't figure it out. I couldn't paint. Me! Thought at first the damn harpies had killed it."

"Maybe too much liquor," Ben said.

Marius looked at him, astonished, and poured himself a new drink.

"There *can't* be too much liquor!" he said. "I decided maybe I was just under-drunk. And under-womanned. You know how a new dame can give you a fresh start. As soon as I'm well enough to light out I'll get a new one. Maybe that'll do it."

Ben and Dalzell exchanged an uneasy look.

"We've got some money for you," Dalzell said. "It's yours."

"Anna's brought me more than I ever had in my life," Marius said. "I've got it stashed away. In a couple of days I'll get the hell out of here, take the ferry to Perth Amboy and get a ship out of Hoboken for Greece, maybe Corsica.

I got friends there. Always could work there, remember? If I don't get myself back there then count me out for good."

He threw off the blanket and got to his feet.

"See, I can get around," he said. "Damn it, now I've got to. I'll leave Anna some stuff to sell and she'll send me some dough. I'll be staying with Sophie, if she's still there and still loves me."

Dalzell pulled his wallet out with the last sixty dollars he had gotten for a Marius sketch.

"Here's a part payment," he said. "You let us know where to send any more we get."

"*If* we get — " Ben amended under his breath. "Look, Marius, do you mean you're going to let those dealers clean up over your dead body?"

"Looks like that's the only way they can do it," Marius said. He drummed on the table restlessly. "Now will you do something for me? Beat it and forget you saw me."

"Marius, couldn't you — couldn't we — " Dalzell began but with Marius and Ben looking at him whatever he wanted to offer fled from his brain. He felt angry that the love and warmth he felt for both his friends could not even reach them or do them any good, only the sixty dollars could help. He was bitterly disappointed that Marius alive, should destroy his dream of him, and he was angry with Ben for having been right.

"Come on, Sloane," Ben said. "Marius will let us know when he needs us. Let him stay dead now."

"Thanks, Ben," Marius said. "I'll do the same for you."

They heard him calling in the dog as they walked down the lane. At the road Dalzell stood still for a moment, looking back. A fog had rolled in from the bay and blurred out the meadow so the house seemed suspended in a ghostly haze, its two upstairs windows bleak eye sockets, its front porch railing the teeth in a death's head.

"What can we do?" Dalzell murmured.

"Nothing," Ben said gloomily. "Go back right where we were when we first heard he was dead. Forget about today. Will you have to tell Cynthia the truth?"

No, Dalzell would not tell Cynthia, he said. He did not intend to tell Cynthia the truth about anything, he thought, for the truth was what she must be protected from.

"Funny, now that we've seen him alive, I'm convinced he really is dead," Ben said, puzzled.

They were silent walking across the meadow to the Hylan Boulevard bus, depressed with the certainty that they would never see Marius again.

. . . *olive branch in family tree* . . .

• Wharton sat stiffly upright in Elsie's cozy-looking club chair whose new slip cover cruelly disguised its broken coil springs all eager to snap at the sitter. He was going crazy. He *was* crazy! The curse of the Hookleys was upon him. He would be put away, probably in the very retreat his uncle and two cousins were patronizing — if that was the word and if they were Hookleys it was indeed the word — at this very minute. Poor Nita! How she would cry at being forced to certify him. Or *would* she cry? How did he know what might go on in that pretty but increasingly foreign little head?

He looked at Elsie, trying to keep his eyes from the corner behind her. Maybe it would be Elsie who would be the one to certify him. He was certain Elsie wouldn't like it one bit. She wouldn't like being deprived of her chief sport. It alarmed him that he could almost hear her forthright voice answering what he was thinking even while she was really saying something quite different.

"Wharton crazy? Nonsense!" It was exactly what she would say, of course. "He is obstinate, selfish, greedy, intolerably snobbish and in almost every way a monster but I will not have my brother called crazy."

"—must say I am immensely flattered at this sudden interest in my little home," Elsie was really saying.

Wharton drew a deep breath for strength and twisted around in his chair so his back would be to the corner, wincing at the punishment from the chair as he did so. No doubt Elsie had had the chair made especially for him. There! he thought in horror, I've got to stop *thinking*, that's all!

"My dear Elsie," he said tenderly, "you seem to regard a simple brotherly visit as an invasion of your privacy. I happened to be lunching at the Café Julien and thought it a good opportunity to see your flat and perhaps hear what news you brought from Boston. Do I really seem like such a *monster* to you?"

The very word popping out of his mouth upset him again and before he could stop himself he had looked at the corner by the fireplace and seen it again, or thought he was seeing it — the damnable ram's-head cane of Uncle Carpenter's. This time he stared at it steadily to make it go away, as you do when seeing double, but the cane would not go away. Impetuously he jumped up and walked over to it, touched it, more frightened than ever to find it real, the emerald eyes leering at him. If Elsie would only say something that would make it real, if it was real, or a hallucination if it was hallucination.

"I see Uncle's cane is in mint condition," he forced himself to say casually.

"Have you any objection?" Elsie snapped. "I suppose you think of me as a complete vandal, unworthy of the family precious treasures."

"No, no," Wharton protested. It was a real cane and he was not crazy but he'd opened himself up for a row and Elsie was raring to get at it so he'd have to find the explanation of how the cane got there in some more devious way.

"What about Mother?" Wharton asked firmly, sitting down in a kinder chair. "How did you find her and did she know you?"

"Of course she knew me," Elsie said coldly. "She simply refused to admit it. Mother is an imbecile, I grant you, but no more so now than she ever was, just more cunning, that's all."

"Perhaps she should be in an institution," Wharton said.

"What would you call that hotel?" Elsie answered sarcastically. "No, Wharton, Mother's act has never fooled me for one minute. She was always bored with her family and the pose of having no memory is very convenient for her, just as it was convenient for Father to pretend to be stone deaf."

This sort of talk from Elsie usually irritated Wharton to distraction but today he decided to be amused instead of getting Elsie's back up before he found out what he wished.

"Perhaps you're right," he conceded graciously. "Childhood is the happiest time, after all, so why shouldn't she want to spend her last years in a return to that happy state?"

"I never found anything happy in childhood and neither did you," Elsie stated pugnaciously. "I don't think I ever saw a smile on your face till the day you were allowed to clip your own coupons."

Wharton counted ten inwardly and went on again.

"I was surprised your visit was so short," he said. "You had told me, you recall, that you were considering opening the old house, and even making it your home again. I made no objections, you know. I didn't think it would be a wise move, for Boston is so changed — "

"Ridiculous!" Elsie said flatly.

"What I mean is that your old friends are scattered and even if you have some I don't know, still Boston does not have the — er — relaxed social life you enjoy here in New York. Besides you used to hate Boston."

That remarkably benign tone made Elsie look fixedly at her brother who was even bestowing a pat on Brucie's head, an unaccustomed compliment that made Brucie look questioningly at his mistress, then withdraw to a spot beside her where he too could watch the caller.

"I don't hate Boston," Elsie explained impatiently. "It's just little things I can't stand. The way the banks and restaurants and department stores are all like nursing homes, the very tone of voice the clerks have is that baby-talk you use on mental cases. 'Oh dear oh dear,' " she mimicked the soothing hushed voice, " 'we've spilled our nice gravy on our nice little jabot,' and 'aren't we the naughty girl overdrawing our nice little checking account.' "

"So you did go to the Trust and see Mr. Wheeling!" Wharton said. She must have got Mother to sign something or give her something, he thought, and in his exasperation he forgot his plan to use the honeyed approach but plunged to the heart of the matter. "I shall have the details of that later on, of course. What I should like explained, however, is just why you should purchase a boat and why you should be brazenly running all over Boston with a man who appears from all reports to be barely half your age. Why must you drag the Hookley name again through the mud — oh you don't care, I know that, — it's my wife and daughters who suffer. Actually bringing this bounder, whoever he may be, into my mother's hotel, foisting him on her as guest —"

"She cried whenever he started to go," Elsie said defensively. "Mother is lonely and she likes new people even if she just babbles."

"Elsie!" Wharton pointed his finger at her so menacingly that Brucie let out a yowl. "Carry on your routs or whatever they are in Greenwich Village where such things are common but I insist that you behave yourself in the places where my poor daughters have to bear the shame. As if poor Isabella's first year out hasn't been difficult enough as it is—"

His sister's voice tried to cut in twice before he would pause.

"Will you please listen to me now?" Elsie haughtily commanded. "It seems my good heart has run away with me again and what I did for you out of pure family pride only makes you abuse me the more."

"Now what?" Wharton exclaimed, knowing too well that no matter what deviltry he might suspect in his sister she was certain to have perpetrated something far worse.

"I merely was buying off a young man to save your daughter's good name, thank you very much," Elsie said, rising with a grand air and pulling her slightly soiled green quilted house robe about her. "You were so busy bullying Isabella about and scolding her for not doing the traditional things you never saw what was under your nose. The poor girl was being driven to running away with one of Nita's admirers."

Wharton's face paled and then the orchard shades came out on his sensitive nose, indicating the emotional confusion her words had aroused. He said nothing and Elsie's momentary glee in her advantage melted into sisterly concern.

"It's all right now, Wharton, dear," she said solicitously. "I saw what was going on and I felt it my duty to handle the situation as I saw best for the honor of the family. You say I have no proper family feeling but I'm very fond of Isabella in spite of your fears of my bad influence. I've had a little more worldly experience than you, Wharton, and I knew the man was not right for her. So — I sent him away. I shan't tell you the sum of money involved but then money doesn't mean as much to me as it does to you."

Wharton sat rigidly, staring at the cane unseeingly. Elsie, a little alarmed at this unprecedented collapse, started to speak again but he rose and lifted his hand wearily.

"Don't tell me any more now, Elsie," he begged. "I can't quite take it all in at once."

He shook out his kerchief and wiped his forehead in silence. Impressed into some sort of first aid Elsie clopped over to the bar in her wooden-soled sandals and poured out a brandy, turned to hand it to Wharton, but on second thought decided she needed one herself and poured another.

Wharton gulped the restorative. Pictures rose in his mind of the monkeylike little dark man at the restaurant wearing his old topcoat, the same little man in Nita's drawing room, the ram's-head cane, Isabella's constantly tear-stained, red-nosed lugubrious face, Nita coming in from one of her confounded culture classes with the "fellow student," the living room doors closing on the cozy laughter of the two scholars, Isabella peering in the library door and excitedly whispering, "Who's in there with Mother, Father? Can I go in?" These were the pictures but he couldn't make them fit together into any kind of meaning, and he knew he didn't want to. It was better to accept Elsie's meaning.

"I'm afraid I haven't been entirely fair to you, Elsie, my dear," he murmured. "I didn't realize that in exposing yourself to all this talk you were only saving Isabella."

"Of course you didn't realize," Elsie readily agreed. "You never do."

But Wharton did not react to the needle. It was no more sport than playing with a dead mouse, Elsie reflected, feeling unjustly deprived. There was something almost obscene, she felt, in Wharton sitting there all slumped over, letting her take cracks at him without striking back. It simply wasn't sporting. Quitting the game with the highest score just as his opponent has gotten warmed up for victory. Tears came to Elsie's eyes, and these Wharton saw. He got to his feet and patted her on the shoulder.

"I appreciate this, Elsie," he said, stiff-upper-lipping. "We'll talk it over another time."

We certainly will, Elsie thought, watching him make his way wearily out the door, we'll talk it over every time you bring up all you ever did for me, and you won't have a word to say.

But it wouldn't be the fun, she sighed, it would be just like losing a brother.

. . . *the café had three exits* . . .

• Dalzell was having a *mazagran* in the Julien. There was small reason for him to be feeling content but he was, and he thought it was probably due to some basic masochism in his character that made surrender a relief if not a pleasure. He was down to his last twenty dollars, he had no idea where the next was coming from, but this was a state of affairs that seemed home to him. It was a pity that Ben was still angry with him, accusing him of messing up their prospects before they had gotten what they might out of them. He thought Ben was probably right: he *was* foolishly romantic and sentimental and it didn't do Marius or anybody else any good. But a person had to do the things he had to do.

"Mind if I join you, Mr. Sloane?"

It was the young fellow from *City Life* standing beside

him. Dalzell motioned to the seat opposite and Briggs sat down heavily, placing a fat briefcase on the chair beside him.

"Don't let me forget that," he said. "Have you ever noticed that you can tell a person's looking for a job because they carry a fat briefcase? Like new wallets. You don't catch a fellow with lots of cash carrying a brand-new wallet."

He threw down a very new leather wallet on the table contemptuously.

"When you see a man trying to build up his morale with that sort of front you can tell his morale is pretty low," he said.

"Yours is low, I take it." Dalzell smiled.

"So-so," said Briggs gloomily. "I suppose you heard I lost my job, right after the Marius piece came out. It seems *City Life* hired me because I didn't know anything about art. Seems they like the simple average citizen approach to everything — science, medicine, books, everything. They only use the intellectual angle on sports and business. Well I started out fine from their point of view, then I had to interview so many artists and museum people that I got too smart. I was using fancy words and technical phrases. Would you believe it that six months ago I thought *gouache* was some sort of Spanish cowboy?"

"You should have kept it that way," Dalzell said sympathetically.

Briggs signaled Karl and ordered Scotch.

"It's not so bad because I had saved some money — four hundred and ten bucks," he said. "I figured that what I learned about painting would have cost me a couple of hundred in school, too, so that's something. And finding out I was really a writer would have cost me maybe a thousand bucks worth of psychoanalysis. Oh, I'm ahead."

"You don't have to take care of a family, then," Dalzell said.

Briggs shook his head.

"I'm not married yet but if things get tough I may have to," he said rather gloomily. "Oh I don't mean I'd marry a rich wife — not that I see anything wrong in your marrying Mrs. Earle as the papers say. I guess you've known her a long time and you aren't doing it for money anyway."

"No," Dalzell answered, embarrassed. "It isn't that."

"That's good, because I've noticed men who marry for money have trouble getting their hands on any cash," Briggs said. "They're always borrowing from fellows like me who have to work. They get a lot of credit on the strength of their wife's credit but that's what hangs them because they can't get their mitts on spending money."

"Thanks for the warning," Dalzell said.

"A girl with a small steady salary is the thing," Briggs said. "This girl I know, Janie. I've moved into her apartment and we can keep going on her paycheck while I work on this novel I'm planning and wait for a job. It works out fine like this. I tell her marriage would only tie her down."

Someone was waving from the doorway and Briggs nudged Dalzell. Okie came toward their table, sweeping a hand over his long white pompadour.

"May I offer good wishes, Sloane?" he said pompously. "I just left Cynthia at the Gallery cocktail party and she was kicking up her heels and acting like a child bride. What in the world made you give in to her?"

"You seem to think I was drugged," Dalzell said, nettled,

even though he had known he would have to grow more armor than ever now.

"You've hardly seen her for years and you hardly know the same people any more," Okie went on pleasantly. "You've never been married and you've no idea how difficult Cynthia makes things for her husbands. I do. I've seen them all. And they were all rich and influential in their own right, too."

"Maybe that was the trouble," Briggs put in.

"If I'd known Cynthia really wanted to get married after being through the mill five times already — " Okie began and paused meditatively.

"Only four," Dalzell corrected him.

Okie looked from Dalzell to Briggs, but Briggs did not take his briefcase off the chair since he wanted Okie to go away and let him continue discussing his own affairs.

"What happened to Ben Forrester?" Okie asked abruptly.

"He went back West," Dalzell said. "He found he hated New York now and he couldn't paint here."

"Was he really good?" Briggs asked.

"Ben Forrester and Dalzell Sloane here paved the way for half the successful young painters today," Okie declared generously. "Maybe they didn't have too much success but what they tried out was the fertilizer for the talent blooming today. How do you like that for appreciation, Sloane?"

"If it's a trade-last I can't think of anything to equal being called fertilizer," Dalzell said.

Okie burst into a loud haw-haw and decided to leave on the note of good humor since neither of them had invited him to sit down. There seemed to be no other table free and he put on his hat.

"This place is getting awfully common," he said fretfully. "No wonder they talk of converting it into apartments. I prefer the Florida Bar nowadays myself."

He clapped his Homburg over his locks and sauntered proudly out.

"I think you're wrong in your figuring, Sloane," he turned to call back from the door. "I think you're Number Six."

. . . *the farewell banquet* . . .

• By eight o'clock it began to be apparent to even the dullest tourist that this was no ordinary night at the Café Julien. Guests who had dropped in for a single apéritif, en route to an inexpensive dinner at San Remo or Grand Ticino's in the Italian quarter, stayed on through curiosity drinking up their dinner money very slowly, ordering a new round just as importunate newcomers were about to snatch their table from under them. They could see important-looking elderly gentlemen in dinner clothes peep in the café door, then proceed onward into the private dining room at the rear. It must be the Silurian annual banquet, someone hinted, the Silurians being newspapermen who had been in the trade twenty-five years.

"How could anybody afford to dine here if he's been in newspaper work that long?" argued others. It was a dinner honoring Romany Marie, or Barney Gallant, or survivors of the Lafayette Escadrille, others said, recalling similar occasions in the past. It was a banquet of real estate men commemorating their grief in selling the Julien to a mysterious concern rumored to be about to change it into apartments. This last theory was gaining credence when the unfamiliar sight of Monsieur Julien himself gave old-timers the clue to what was going on. Yes, it was a dinner of the Friends of Julien, an association of gourmets of great distinction, and what was more sensational was the whisper that this was their farewell dinner. Photographers from newspapers and magazines were setting up impressive-looking apparatus in every corner and mousy little people who inhabited the cheap little rooms upstairs and were never seen in the glamorous café suddenly showed their frightened little faces at the door. Hoff Bemans, leading his guest panelists into the café for a rewarding drink at anybody else's expense, spotted Dalzell Sloane and beckoned his men to crowd around that table, so that when Briggs returned from the men's room he could scarcely squeeze in.

"By George, I've done it again!" Hoff exclaimed proudly. "I didn't even know the Café was going to go out of business and here I stumbled right into the big night. So that's the old master, Julien himself!"

Monsieur Julien was a gay bachelor of sixty who made enough from the café bearing his name to live and usually dine at the Plaza. He was the last of a formidable dynasty of French chefs, inheriting the great reputation without the faintest culinary interest. But after a youthful struggle against the public insistence that all Juliens must be cooks he had surrendered. Very well, he would accept the unearned but profitable mantle. Cooking contests, cook books, food columns, canned dainties, all must have his name as sponsor. Wherever he went he was questioned about this dish or that sauce. At first he had sighed candidly, "I assure you if I had a pair of eggs and a greased griddle on the stove I would still starve to death." Later on in his career he answered more archly, "Ah, if I were to tell you how I make that dish then you would be Julien and what would I be?"

His grandfather had been proprietor of the famous Julien's in Paris and had founded the New York branch early in the century. All over the world there were people who quivered at the name. Even those who had never tasted *escargots Julien* quickly realized they must pretend they knew, and would sniff the air and paw the ground like truffle hounds, sighing, "Ah, Julien's!" Having put by a nice fortune paying French salaries and charging American prices the old gentleman was finally done in by the shrewdness of his equally thrifty employees who sold furniture and dishes under his very nose and found many convenient ways of rewarding themselves. The Paris place vanished in World War One and the New York café had been about to give up in 1929 when a group of wealthy gentlemen from all over the eastern seaboard (and one very proud member from Seattle) decreed that the name of Julien must not perish. All those who had swooned over a Julien lobster bisque or cassoulet of duck Julien-Marie (or said they had) vowed with their hands on their checkbooks that Julien's must go on. The finest lawyers, bankers, jurists, all manner of men of affairs co-operated to insure future security. Monsieur Julien was put on salary and to keep the venture from smacking of Depression opportunism the group called itself simply the Friends of Julien, standing by the thin of the thirties to reap profits in the forties. Self-made men, lacking in clubs and college backgrounds, listed membership in the Friends of Julien beside their names in *Who's Who* for it hinted of world travel and financial standing.

Most of the Friends were by no means habituées but appeared only at the annual dinner where they toasted bygone days, the chef, the wine steward, the bartender, and above all the great Julien. Julien, who appeared in the kitchen only for photographers, always wept over these unearned tributes to his magic touch with a field salad and permitted himself to quote elegies to his skill from old rivals — Moneta, the Ambassador's Sabatini, Henri Charpentier; and he summoned sentimental memories of days when the incomparable Escoffier of London's Carlton called personally on Papa Julien to pay his respects to the only man in the world he deigned to call "Maître," or so Julien *fils* declared. The anecdotes grew more impressive each year and convinced by his own publicity Julien made himself instead of his forebears the hero.

This evening's banquet had finally gotten under way in the private room but the café guests continued to dawdle, sending emissaries back to spy on the feast and report back who was there and what was being said. The waiters' unusual speed in presenting checks as a method of clearing the café only made the guests more obstinately determined to stay on enjoying the splendid affair by proxy. Caught in the spirit of the occasion Hoff Bemans was ordering round after round of highballs, figuring that he might stick Dalzell Sloane with the check by carefully timing his own departure or if Sloane got away first there was a very young first novelist along who had been on his panel and would be too shy to protest. On the program that evening Hoff had made insulting and derogatory remarks concerning the young man's work and youthful pomposity but he vaguely felt letting him buy the drinks would atone for this. For that matter no reason why old Sloane shouldn't have it since he would be getting into Cynthia Earle's pocket any minute.

"Thought your *City Life* piece on Marius didn't quite come off," Hoff said genially to Briggs. "Some good things in it but as a whole it just didn't come off."

"Thanks," Briggs said absently. He was staring at the young novelist wondering what it felt like to have your name on a fat book, and have people talking about it as if it meant something. The novel had worried him because the author's method wasn't like his own at all. Instead of building his characters on a sensible economic structure this fellow built them on what they had to eat and drink from the breast right through Schrafft's and the Grand Central Oyster Bar; whatever they elected to eat was evidently supposed to mean something about their hidden natures. Even their retching was recorded and it didn't indicate they had had a bad oyster but meant they were having an emotional *crise*. When they weren't eating, this author's characters were all put through boarding schools and colleges, all Ivy League, no matter how poor they talked, and Briggs, having worked his way through a minor university, was irritated at having to work his way again through these fictional characters' education. What did people like about that kind of book? Maybe it was the deep sex meaning the fellow gave to those menus, for the hero was always drawing some high-bosomed girl into his arms between courses, the hot oatmeal pounding through his veins.

"I read your book," Briggs roused himself to tell the young man.

"Thanks," said the author gratefully. Briggs noted that whatever fine liquors his characters enjoyed their creator was limiting himself to simple beer, though this economy might later be regretted when he found he had to pay for his comrades' expensive tastes.

Hoff was continuing the discussion on Marius' show, pointing out errors in the critics' reviews due perhaps to their not having consulted Mr. Bemans' recent book on the subject. The *Times* critic, for example, persisted in linking Marius' work with that of Forrester and Sloane which was utterly idiotic because neither Ben nor Dalzell could paint the simplest apple to resemble Marius' touch. Hoff wished Dalzell to tell Cynthia Earle, moreover, that he felt very hurt that his contribution to the Marius Long Playing Record had been cut out and he considered that was probably the real reason the project had been such a flop. Without his key words the thing hadn't jelled, had not, as he liked to put it, "quite come off."

The café had never been noiser or more crowded. Everyone was shouting to be heard and from the private dining room there were periodic roars of applause. As the banquet progressed curious changes were taking place all over the restaurant. Certain of the banqueters were slipping out to the café between their gourmet dishes to freshen up their palates with quick shots of rye or invigorating martinis and later on grew sociable enough to draw up chairs and make acquaintance with the café customers. Some of these truants urged their new friends to return to the banquet with them, gave them their own places and went back to the café for more informal fun. Before the dinner was eve.. nalf over the personnel of the Friends' table had changed in such a surprising fashion that there was a lively sprinkling of sports jackets and dark shirts and these strangers were being served roast duckling with the finest of Chambertin while out in the café their legitimate highballs and rubbery canapés were being finished by distinguished drunken Friends. It was in this interchange that Hastings Hardy wound up at Dalzell's table while Briggs, done out of his rightful place, found himself in the private dining room drinking toasts to personalities he'd never heard of. He had arrived at the moment when Monsieur Julien was making the great salad with his own hands — that is to say he took into his own sacred hands various ingredients deftly offered by assistants and poured them personally into the bowl. In the solemn hush induced by this traditional rite cooks' caps could be seen bobbing around corners as they strained to see; other diners bent their heads reverently, and down in the lower kitchen the seafood chef was sustaining himself with mighty swigs of Martel in his pride that Monsieur Julien had thought his sole good enough to claim as his own handiwork.

Toasts had been made to famous dishes, countries, high-living monarchs and again and again to Monsieur Julien until the master was shaken to tears, and many others were moved to blow their noses heartily. To restore calm the oldest living member rose to propose a health, he said, to that great chef, Henri Charpentier, inventor of the *Crêpe Suzette* which had brought happiness to so many thousands. The applause inspired Monsieur Julien to interpolate that Charpentier, excellent genius though he was, had been surpassed by Sabatini, king of them all, next of course to Escoffier.

" 'Born with the gift of laughter and a sense that the world is mad,' " shouted one of the café intruders joyously, but a neighbor yanked him down by his brown-checked coattail hissing, "You ass, not THAT Sabatini."

"Five generations of kings Sabatini served," Monsieur Julien went on unperturbed, his black eyes flashing proudly around the table, "including Umberto and the Czar of all the Russias. As for Charpentier's *Crêpe Suzette*, can it really compare in delicacy and sheer originality with the *Coeur Flottant* Sabatini created especially for that queen among women, Mary Garden?"

A Friend who had spent the last three courses in the café returned in time to catch the last words and squeezing into the group snatched up Briggs's glass and shouted a ringing toast to Mary Garden, King Umberto and the Czar himself, then sat down on the nonexistent chair dragging napery, silver, dishes and six kinds of greens to the floor with him. It was too bad that the photographer chanced to get a fine shot of this disorderly scene for it spoiled the nostalgic sentimental tone of the accompanying article on "Farewell to the Café Julien" and made many ministers give thanks that this palace of sin was finally to be routed by clean-minded citizens.

It was this picture, showing Briggs wiping salad off the fallen comrade with Monsieur Julien handing him a napkin with Gallic courtesy, that turned out to be lucky for Briggs. The very day the picture appeared he was offered the job of restaurant reporter on a tabloid. It meant postponing his literary career which grieved him but was a great relief to Janie, who loved him devotedly and without illusions.

. . . *the nightcap* . . .

• The café crowd had thinned out a half hour before closing time when Ellenora and Rick Prescott came in for their nightcap. They had been coming in every night again, and tonight's news that the rumors of the Julien's approaching end were all too true filled them with dismay and foreboding. They had fallen in love with what they had seemed to be in these surroundings: these were the selves they knew: when they set foot inside these doors each became again what the other desired. Now that they were together so much elsewhere, their ordinary selves surrendered to each other, they were secretly conscious of a dimension missing. Fulfillment, so long desired, was somehow not enough. They had to have the Julien about them, Philippe beside them, the marble-topped table between them, their reflections in the wall mirrors a supporting chorus.

They had spent nights and days in Ricky's apartment telling each other everything about themselves, listening eagerly, but failing to fit the new portrait to the image of love they had been cherishing. Rick wanted to absolve himself of past follies and errors by confessing everything, recklessly handing over material for an ordinary lifetime of reproaches, for part of his love for Ellenora was his sense of guilt, a comfortable feeling of you-dear-darling-girl-to-forgive-me-for-all-the-ways-I-have-wronged-you. She was never to be spared

Ellenora thought, a little frightened at the role he had given her of forever forgiving him and then consoling him for having hurt her, inviting more hurt by understanding and forgiving it. She would have liked to shut her ears to his admission of other, lesser loves, but he had to know that she understood. She would have liked to know where they were heading for, now that they were lovers, but she understood her part well enough to realize she was to be near when he needed her, accept what he offered, ask no questions. It was enough that there *was* love, and the woman's duty was always to guard it, to have it ready when the man needed it.

"Calling Mr. Prescott!" The telephone operator stood in the café doorway and beckoned Rick. He blinked, puzzled. He had spent hours in this spot waiting for a call from Ellenora that never had come. Now she was here beside him and the call was just catching up.

It was Jerry Dulaine, he found when he went out to the booth. She wanted to tell him about her new job, and maybe get some advice. She was working on a television show about problems of career girls. She had moved to the Hotel Delorme on Park Avenue if he'd like to call on her.

Rick hesitated. In his confessional orgy he hadn't said anything to Ellenora about Jerry, maybe because it didn't matter or maybe because you only tell about the closed episodes. He didn't like refusing Jerry when all she asked was some friendly encouragement. He was glad things were looking up for her, he said, and he'd drop around one of these days. Maybe he would at that, he reflected, going back to the café. His eyes lit up, seeing Ellenora at their table, just as he liked to think of her, sweetly waiting for him. Where would they go to hide from their real selves when the Julien vanished?

"Wrong Prescott," he said, pulling out his chair and sitting down happily as if their feet entwined under the same café table was home enough for him.

. . . *the bird's gone* . . .

• October was as hot as August that year and the wreckers were shirtless under the midday sun, their bare backs glistening with perspiration. Rick Prescott had been leaning against the park fence watching them for a long time, thinking ruefully that of all the happy workers in the world wreckers were undoubtedly the most enthusiastic. The whole back wall of the building was down now, and the top floors, but the handsome Victorian Gothic façade with the imposing marble steps still stood, and it was disconcerting to look through the paneless café windows straight into open garden. Now the crimson entrance canopy was a tumbled pile of rags on the sidewalk, the white letters C A F E J U L I E N almost indiscernible under rubble, and next the thick laurel vines fell in a great heap of gleaming green leaves that seemed to be still breathing and quivering with life.

"That laurel must be near a hundred years old," a workman beside Rick said. "The walls come down easy enough but those vines are strong as iron. You wouldn't think it."

"My poor birds!" quavered a woman's voice behind them.

She was a rouged and dyed old lady elaborately dressed in the fashion of pre-World War One, the low-crowned beaver hat atop her pompadour laden with birds and flowers, long peg-top brown velvet skirt almost concealing her high black kid shoes, a green changeable silk duster floating about her. She was dabbing at her mascaraed eyes with a lacy handkerchief and looked at Rick appealingly. "Their nest was right outside my window and now they're homeless. I used to feed them on the sill every morning for thirty years and more. Oh what will they do now the vine is gone?"

"Don't worry about your birds, lady," the workman said, nudging Rick. "They've gone South by now. Probably got a lot bigger nest down there in Miami."

"Do you really think so? Oh. I'm so glad." The old lady smiled tremulously. "I've cried every night worrying about them ever since they started tearing down the building. My room — right over the café window there — went yesterday. Thank you so much."

She hobbled slowly across the park and the workman winked at Rick.

"Betcha she never came out of her room till they tore the place down," he murmured. "She comes here and watches every day."

"I didn't realize people lived upstairs," Rick said.

"A lot of old-timers lived in those little rooms," the man said. "You see 'em wandering around the Park now, like her, all in kinda mummy clothes. A lot of queer old birds flushed out of their nests. They used that side entrance."

Rick took the cigarette he offered and lit it. He thought, as he walked on, that tonight at midnight he would bring

Ellenora over here and they would sit on the park bench right opposite the old café with a split of champagne. The loving-cup would be the little Venetian glass slipper from Ellenora's dressing table and they would drink it the very minute of the old closing time. In the light of the street lamp at midnight they would see the old entrance steps up to the doorway and shadows would reconstruct the old café. The idea cheered him up and he quickened his steps, smiling a little to himself as he always did when he thought of something to tell Ellenora. He remembered that he hadn't told her yet he was being sent to Peru for six months but the funny thing was he didn't have to tell anything important to Ellenora because he felt she knew, without words. It was like his knowing she would always be waiting, sitting there at the café table, charming extravagant little hat — a "lady" hat as he always called Ellenora's hats — tilted at the chic angle, feathery wisp of veil or scarf making a smoke ring around her eager, radiant little face. Ellenora — keeping beautiful New York for him.

Sitting at the café table? — Rick stopped short, frightened. The nest was gone. He felt a sudden panic at the thought of his dream without the Julien frame. Where would he be sure of her waiting, loving, knowing? He couldn't, wouldn't dare leave her again with no Julien walls to hold her. He hurried frantically across the Park toward his apartment where she would be waiting — where she *had* to be waiting.

Dalzell Sloane looked again at the young man rushing past him, certain that he had seen him somewhere before. He frowned and then it came to him that the familiarity was only in the resemblance to Monty Douglass, the film actor. He walked on to the ruins of the Café Julien and sat down on a park bench opposite. It was odd that he didn't feel sad, he reflected, but then the Café had been gone from him long, long before the building came down. If it had been there in full glory at this very minute he would not have gone in, probably, for his new self might not belong there. He was not accustomed to his new self, yet, the Dalzell Sloane who was painting portraits of Hasting Hardy's entire family, at a fine fee, the Dalzell Sloane who would presently have to report at Elizabeth Arden's as he had promised to pick up Cynthia. He sighed a little, knowing just how it would be.

"Mrs. Sloane wants you to wait here until she's through," he was sure one of the beauteous young ladies would inform him. "She said for you to be sure and wait."

He would stand in a corner, fearful of smashing the jeweled perfume bottles or damaging the elegant, perfumed creatures gliding in and out, and sometimes a honey-voiced young lady would call him Mr. Earle and tell him his wife was almost through. He wondered, idly, if all of Cynthia's husbands had been called Mr. Earle after her first one since none of the other names had stuck, and whether he might not end up signing his paintings Dalzell Earle. It really didn't matter, he thought, any more than anything that happened to his new self mattered, for there was no more Dalzell Sloane than there was any more Marius or Julien. No good looking around the old neighborhood for souvenirs of the vanished past. He went to the curb and flagged a taxi.

The red-haired man sitting on the nearest bench watched him get into the cab, made a move to wave to him but thought better of it and resumed writing in the notebook spread open with his briefcase as desk.

What Dennis Orphen was writing was this:

It must be that the Julien was all that these people really liked about each other for now when they chance across each other in the street they look through each other, unrecognizing, or cross the street quickly with the vague feeling that here was someone identified with unhappy memories — as if the other was responsible for the fall of the Julien. Curious, too, that everyone connected with the café looks so small on the street. The arrogance and dignity of the old waiters is now wrapped up in a bundle under their arms when you catch a glimpse of one of them, shriveled and bent, scuttling down a subway kiosk; the men of affairs who had spent hours sipping their brandy and liqueurs, reading their papers with lordly ease, are suddenly old and harassed-looking, home and family harness collaring them for good, their café egos stowed away in vest pocket pillboxes like morphine grains.

The Café Julien was gone and a reign was over. Those who had been bound by it fell apart like straws when the baling cord is cut and remembered each other's name and face as part of a dream that would never come back.

THE GOLDEN SPUR

◆

For Margaret De Silver

1

THE HOTEL STATIONERY was Wedgwood blue like the wallpaper, delicately embossed with a gold crest and a motto, *In virtu vinci,* a nice thought, whatever it meant, for a hotel. Nice paper, too. Paper like that could make a writer of you, if anything could.

He took the whole pack from the desk and inserted it among his other papers in the briefcase with his pajamas, shirt, the monogrammed Hotel De Long ashtray, hand towels, and dainty lavender soap. Too bad there were only two hotel postcards left. Anyone seeing that view of the De Long lobby, magnified beyond recognition, jeweled with tropic blossoms, oriental rugs, divans, and liveried pages would assume that seductive sirens and fabulous adventurers lurked behind the potted palms. Actually, Jonathan had observed only a few old crones and decrepit gentlemen hobbling or wheeling through the modest halls last evening. He chose, however, to believe the postcards. That was the city as he had pictured it, and he wished he had a stock of them to keep sending out as camouflage for the cheaper quarters he had to find.

He addressed one card to Miss Tessie Birch, R.F.D., Silver City, Ohio.

"Dear Aunt Tessie. No time for good-by. Will write when I get more leads. J."

His window was on a court within hand-shaking distance of other windows, but a wedge of the street below was visible and there rose the contented purr of the city, a blend of bells, whirring motors, whistles, buildings rising, and buildings falling. The stage was set, the orchestra tuning up, and in a moment he would be on, Jonathan thought. Curious he felt no panic, as if his years of waiting in the wings had prepared him to take over the star role. But it was more as if he were released from a long exile in an alien land to come into his own at last. In a window across the court he could glimpse a fair young man seated at a desk, idly smoothing his hair and smiling as if at some happy secret. The figure moved, and it dawned on Jonathan that the window was a mirror, the young man with the secret was himself.

He looked around to see if there was more magic to be discovered in the room. He'd certainly gotten his seven dollars' worth. Last night he had sat up till three, marveling at the new life so suddenly opened to him, trying to organize the plan he had outlined before leaving Silver City. Again he flipped through the fat little red notebook, on the flyleaf of which was written: CONSTANCE BIRCH, NEW YORK CITY, 1927. Beneath his mother's name was written: PROPERTY OF JONATHAN JAIMISON, NEW YORK CITY, 1956. The old names his mother had listed and those he had added from the references in her letters Jonathan had already checked in this year's telephone directory with little success. Beside each name he had jotted the connection with his mother and the last known address. Two names offered possibilities. The first was:

"Claire Van Orphen, author. Typed mss. Last Xmas card 1933. Care Pen and Brush Club."

The Pen and Brush Club, he had found, was right in

the vicinity, and a note might bring results. Second to Miss Van Orphen as a source was another but more famous writer, Alvine Harshawe, whose early work his mother had been privileged to type. She had continued to collect his press notices for years after she had returned to Ohio and married Jaimison, Senior.

"Copied Alvine's last act today and he was so pleased he took me to celebrate at The Golden Spur," she had written in her diary, which Jonathan knew almost by heart.

The Golden Spur still existed, he'd found, and Jonathan planned to ask there for Harshawe.

He knew the "Hazel" mentioned frequently in the diary had shared rooms on Horatio Street with his mother, and "George" had been her fiancé, a rich young lawyer. George's opinions on literature were faithfully quoted. He seemed to awe Jonathan's mother, but then she was awed by everybody she had ever encountered in New York, just as she found all places incredibly charming, such as the Horatio Street rooming house, the Hotel Brevoort (where George and Hazel took her to Sunday breakfast and where the public stenographer graciously gave her some work), the Black Knight, Chumley's (where all the great writers and artists congregated in better style than at The Golden Spur), the Washington Square Bookstore ("Alvine's friend Lois works there"), Romany Marie's, the Café Royale, and other romantic names that Jonathan could not find in the directory.

Tucking the priceless little notebook in his inside coat pocket, Jonathan considered the wisdom of trying to find Miss Van Orphen this very day. The wall clock registered eleven-forty. A printed notice advised that guests would be charged for another day after one o'clock. Better wait until he was settled in permanent quarters, he decided. No use fooling himself that the mystery of these many years could be unraveled in a day. Let's get on with it, then, he told himself, and picked up his briefcase.

The corridor appeared deserted, and he seized the chance to nip in an open door where he could see a stack of postcards on the desk. He had barely time to slip them in his pocket when an ancient hump-backed porter materialized in the doorway. His withered old neck stretched out of the De Long uniform like a turtle's, and the watery eyes under wrinkled lizard lids blinked suspiciously at Jonathan, the old nose sniffing stolen postcards, towels, ashtrays, and precious soap.

"I must have missed him," Jonathan said nervously.

"He checked out an hour ago," said the porter, suspicions allayed. "Maybe you could catch him at the funeral parlor."

"That's so," said Jonathan.

"Or maybe his home," offered the porter. "He was just staying here to fix up the Major's affairs, all that legal stuff. Did you come for the funeral?"

"Yes," said Jonathan. "I—I got the word in Ohio."

"The Major would have appreciated your coming all that way just to bury him," said the porter. "He was a great one for appreciating little favors like that. They don't come any finer than the Major is what we say here."

"That's what I always said," Jonathan agreed, edging out the door past the porter. Lucky to touch hunchbacks, he remembered. "I hope I'm not late for the funeral."

"You'll make it," said his friend with a dry cackle. "The Major wouldn't let anybody hustle him. Things have got to be done just right, you know how he was."

"That's so," said Jonathan and returned the smart salute,

grateful to the dead Major for his unexpected protection. He had one friend in New York, it seemed, even if the bond was a peculiar one. He was still glowing when he came out on the street. It was a wonderful July day created especially to surprise and delight the timid visitor. The street of old brick houses with their fanlights over white doorways, trellised balconies of greenery, magnolia trees, vined walls, cats sunning themselves in windows, was not so different from the residential streets in hundreds of home towns far away. Even little saplings on the sidewalk sprouted leaves, and pigeons strutted along the gutter until routed by a street sprinkler bearing a sign: KEEP NEW YORK CLEAN. A dirty but friendly baptism, Jonathan thought, brushing the mud from his trousers.

"Is this the way to Aunt Nellie's Carolina Tea Room?' a lady in a hatful of violets called out to him, leaning out of a taxicab door.

Jonathan was flattered to be taken for a seasoned New Yorker, and he pointed impulsively to a restaurant sign down the street. The lady beamed gratitude and with a flower-hatted companion clambered out of the cab, backsides first. The sign turned out to advertise MAC'S BAR AND GRILL, Jonathan saw on closer inspection, but maybe the ladies wouldn't know the difference.

Along the way doormen, decked out in more braid than banana generals, were being propelled by clusters of peanut-sized Poms and chows on mighty leashes, braking to allow each hydrant and every passing pooch to be checked. A dog was a necessity in this city, Jonathan deduced, and promised himself that one of these days he would have one, a Great Dane, say, something to give his doorman a real workout, a big-shot dog to show the world. He'd never had a dog, but now he would have everything the old Jonathan had never dared to want, for this was his city, and his mother's secret was the key to its treasure.

"I'm not a Jaimison," he murmured to himself over and over, and his stride grew longer, his head higher. "I could be anybody—*anybody!*"

Before him lay Washington Square.

Only eighteen hours in New York, and he loved everything, every inch of it. Ah, the square! He crossed Waverly and stood at the corner by the playground. He beamed at the ferociously determined child aiming a scooter straight at him, and jumped out of the way of a chain of girl roller-skaters advancing rhythmically toward him. An enormous-busted, green-sweatered girl with a wild bush of hair, black skin-tight pants outlining thick thighs and mighty buttocks, came whooping along, clutching the legs of a screaming bearded young man she bore on her shoulders.

"Let me down, now! Now you let me down!" he yelled, waving his arms. A short muscular girl with ape face and crew-cut, in stained corduroy shorts and red knee socks, ran behind, shouting with laughter.

"Didn't I tell you that Shirley is the strongest dyke in Greenwich Village?"

The big gorilla girl stopped abruptly, letting the young man fall headlong over her shoulders and sprawl crabwise over the green.

"Don't you dare call me a dyke!" she shouted, shaking the smaller girl by the shoulders.

The lad snatched the moment to pick himself up, with a sheepish grin at Jonathan, and tore down the street, combing his long, sleek locks as he ran.

"Go ahead, Shirley, pick up this one, go ahead!" the small girl yelled, pointing at Jonathan while she wriggled neatly out of her attacker's hands. Too startled to move for a few seconds, Jonathan saw the big girl's eye fall on him with a speculative smile. He clutched his briefcase and ran, the girls howling behind him. He made for the fenced-in space where the smallest kiddies, drunk with popsicles, were wobbling on teeter-totters or reeling behind their buggies. He knocked one of these live dolls over and quickly snatched it up in his arms as Big Shirley came toward him.

"Look out, he's going to throw the kid at you, Shirley!" the short girl yelled warning. "Come on, let's go."

They loped away, stopping for the younger ape to leap expertly onto Shirley's back. With a sigh of relief, Jonathan set down the howling child carefully.

"Thank you very much, sir," he said to the child, picking up the raspberry Good Humor his savior had dropped and restoring it to the open red mouth. He remembered that he hadn't had anything to eat since last night's hamburger in the station and he was ravenous. A benign white-haired old gentleman, wide-brimmed black hat on lap, black ribbons fluttering from his spectacles, sat on a bench reading a paperback copy of *The Dance of Life*. Reassured by the title, Jonathan coughed to get his attention.

"Could you tell me where I can get a cup of coffee here?" he asked.

Without looking up from his reading, the gentleman reached in his pocket and handed out a quarter before turning a page. Jonathan stared at the coin in his palm.

"Thank you, sir," he said. "Thank you very much."

How strange New Yorkers were, he marveled, but he would get used to their ways. He crossed the park and wandered up a side street. Golden letters on a window, where a menu was pasted, announced that this was Aunt Nellie's Carolina Tea Room. His two old ladies were several blocks off course, he thought, unless Mac of the Bar and Grill had set them right. Perhaps they were inside right now, jubilantly wolfing the farm-style apple-peanut surprise, home-boiled country eggs, barn-fresh milk, cottage-made cocoa, garden-good lettuce sandwiches. Rejecting these gourmet temptations, Jonathan turned in the other direction.

Lunch hour had filled the streets, and Jonathan studied the people, fearing they were frowning at his best gray tropical tweed because it was last year's style. His confidence melted even more—as his confidence always had a way of doing—after a couple addressed him in Spanish, and a girl asked him directions in Swedish. On second thoughts, he might be too dressed-up to pass as a native New Yorker. The standard costume seemed to be loose sport shirts and slacks, or even shorts proudly exhibiting knobby shins, hairy calves, and gnarled knees. Certainly these people were nothing like those natty cosmopolitans pictured in *Esquire* and the movies. As for the girls, he tried not to notice them. After his encounter in the park he figured that they must be a stronger breed than those back home.

Ah, New York! A flying pebble nicked him in the eye, and as he was blindly trying to shake it out he found he was caught up in a crowd around a demolition operation that took up the whole block. Evidently something dramatic was about to happen, for all eyes stared skyward intently. Maybe the Mayor himself was about to appear on the roofless tower and beg for their ears. Jonathan nudged his way to the front and stared upward too.

A giant crane was the star performer, lifting its neck heavenward, then dropping a great iron ball gently down to a doomed monster clock in the front wall of the structure, tapping it tenderly, like a diagnostician looking for the sore spot. Does it hurt here? here? or here? Wherever it hurts must be target for the wham, and wham comes next, with the rubble hurtling down into the arena with a roar. A pause, and then the eager watchers followed the long neck's purposeful rise again, the rhythmical lowering of the magic ball, the blind grope for the clock face, and then the avalanche once more. The cloud of dust cleared, and a cry went up to see the clock still there, the balcony behind it falling. "They can't get the clock," someone exulted. "Not today! Hooray for the clock!" The spectators smiled and nodded to one another. Good show. Well done, team!

Jonathan returned the congratulatory smile of the fat little man on his right bearing a bag of laundry on his back, and composed a graver expression for the scowling neighbor on his other side. This was a ruddy-faced, agate-eyed man, bare-headed, with gray-streaked pompadour and mustache, carrying an attaché case and a rumpled blue raincoat over his arm.

"Do you realize the bastard who runs that blasted contraption gets sixty dollars an hour?" he asked Jonathan. "Sixty dollars an hour—twenty, thirty times what a college professor makes. And time and a half for overtime. Figure it out for yourself. Seven, eight hundred dollars a day just for sitting on his can in that little box and pressing buttons."

"Is that a fact?" Jonathan asked, feeling richer at the mention of such large sums. He moved closer with the vague hope that money was contagious.

"Destruction is what pays today," said his neighbor, twisting his mustache savagely. "Wreckers, bomb-builders, poison-makers. Who buys creative brains today?"

"Nobody," Jonathan said, glad to know some answers.

"Name me one constructive, intellectual activity that pays a living," pursued the quizmaster.

"You got me," Jonathan said.

He accepted a bent cigarette from the pack offered by the man, who was now brooding silently.

"Can you tell me if there's something special about this particular wrecking to bring out such a crowd?" Jonathan asked.

The gentleman snorted.

"Of course I can tell you. In the first place this was a splendid old landmark and people like to see the old order blown up. Then there is the glorious dirt and uproar which are the vitamins of New York, and of course the secret hope that the street will cave in and swallow us all up."

Jonathan looked down uneasily at the boards underfoot.

"Dear old Wanamaker's." His companion sighed. "If I had paid their nasty little bill, perhaps they would never have come to this. Well, mustn't get sentimental."

Another avalanche of rubble roared into the pit.

"Eight hundred dollars a day is a lot of money for pushing buttons," Jonathan thought aloud.

"Entertainers must be paid," the other man said and walked away.

What a brilliant fellow! Jonathan thought, looking after him regretfully. He remembered that he was hungry and started looking for a lunchroom, rejecting one because it looked too expensive, others because they looked too cheap, too crowded, or too empty. After wandering up and down, he stood still finally in front of an auction gallery he had passed three times, pretending to admire a gold sedan chair. On the other side of the street was a great glass and chromium supermarket advertising its opening with valuable favors to be given away to every customer. He might buy a bun, he thought, thus entitling him to the valuable favor, and come back and eat it in the sedan chair. Or— Then a sign swinging out over a dark doorway next to the auction window caught his eye.

THE GOLDEN SPUR, he read mechanically and stared at the red and gold swinging horseshoe.

The Golden Spur! His mother's Golden Spur, the place she used to go to meet the Man, the place she went with her famous friends, but above all, the place where the great romance had started, the place, indeed, where Jonathan came in.

So the place did exist—not the grand Piranesi palace he had vaguely imagined, with marble stairs leading forever upward to love and fame, but a dingy little dark hole he must have passed before without noticing. He lit a cigarette with trembling fingers. If The Golden Spur was real, then all of it was real. His mother had stood on this very spot, and suddenly her image leaped up, not the pale face on the pillow he remembered from long ago, but the stranger, Connie Birch, the girl who had written the letters, the girl who met her lover in The Golden Spur. He saw her as she looked in the old snapshots, the thin, chiseled face with shining, appealing eyes (*Oh, do like me, do try to like me, please*), the coronet of thick fair braids, the parted lips half-smiling, the eager when-where-who expectant aura that must have attracted its own happy answers. This was the girl whose trail he must find, the girl who had written her sister (he had that letter with him too):

"Oh Tessie, please don't expect me to marry John Jaimison when I come home to visit because I don't care how he hounds me, my life is here. I've told you how lovely all the marvelous people I meet at Miss Van Orphen's are to me when I go there to type her stories. Hazel, the girl I live with, prefers a wild time at cabarets but I'd much rather listen to the important people at Miss Van Orphen's. Then there is the restaurant where the writers and artists go, The Golden Spur, and I've met the most exciting man there and Tessie, he's going to be famous and how could I ever go back to John after being in love with a really great man?"

Jonathan took a step toward the magic door and then stood still, desperately trying to steel himself for the part he had chosen to play and that had seemed so simple, so right, when Aunt Tessie had told him the truth in Silver City just forty-eight hours before.

"Once you get on the track, things will come to you like in a dream," Aunt Tessie had said. "Keep thinking of all those stories your mother used to tell you every night, stories about people and places she knew in New York, like that Golden Spur where she met all those famous ones. Think of the ones she used to find mentioned in the magazines, always cutting out their pictures and all that."

"I remember," Jonathan had said.

"I never got it straight in my own mind," Aunt Tessie had confessed. "Used to go in one ear and out the other like all those stories girls tell about their good times away from home, all those beaux, all fine men, all better than the hometown boys. 'After my time in New York,' your poor mother used to complain to me, 'how can you expect me to marry John Jaimison?' 'You were glad enough to get engaged to him before you went away,' I told her, 'and he did wait for you.' 'But Tessie, you just don't understand,

I see everything different now,' she kept at me, crying her eyes out. 'I'm used to geniuses, men with great minds, now, and John Jaimison doesn't think about anything but selling Silver City flour products. All he reads is sales letters, all he writes is orders. All he does is brag about the Jaimison family, and how they're the biggest old family in middle Ohio and how proud I'll be to be allowed at their family reunions. Oh, Tessie,' your mother says to me, 'you can't see me marrying John Jaimison and going to those awful reunions!' "

"Of course not!" Jonathan had answered Aunt Tessie "Why did you let it happen?"

"I said to her, 'Connie,' I said, 'what you say is true and I do understand how New York City changed your ideas about men, but honey,' I said, 'the point is he's still willing to marry you and in your condition you'd better snap him up, the sooner the quicker!' So!"

"Maybe he did suspect," Jonathan had said. "Maybe that was why he dumped Mother and me on you just three years after they married."

"John Jaimison turned her in just the way he turned in his car when it went bad," Aunt Tessie said. "He didn't suspect, he was just naturally a Jaimison, a small-minded man. He beefed about her turning tubercular on him as if he'd been sold a pig in a poke, and what a tussle it was getting money out of him for the doctors and you! Hard enough to catch him, and when I did he'd complain, 'You can't get blood out of a turnip, Tessie Birch,' and I'd say, 'Out of a Jaimison turnip you can't even get turnip juice.' But there, I never meant to tell you the truth about yourself!"

"I only wish you'd told me years ago," said Jonathan. "I needn't have gone to all those Jaimison reunions, with the old man bawling me out for not getting ahead, telling everybody that the Jaimison genius had skipped a generation. I only wish you could tell me who my true father was."

"I never thought it mattered, Jonny-boy," Aunt Tessie had said. "Connie told so many stories about New York. Don't you remember?"

"The bedtime stories she told got mixed up in my mind," he said. "The Golden Spur people weren't any more real than the King of the Golden River.'

"It'll all fit together," Aunt Tessie consoled him. "You'll find your answer."

"I'll find the answer," Jonathan repeated aloud, as if Aunt Tessie were right there before The Golden Spur urging him on.

Through a gap in the plum velvet café curtains he could see the bar and was heartened to recognize his friend from the excavation standing inside. He breathed deep of the heady New York air, that delirious narcotic of ancient sewer dust, gasoline fumes, roasting coffee beans, and the harsh smell of sea that intoxicates inland nostrils.

Then he pushed open the door.

A long bar stretched before him back to dark stalls with dim stable lanterns perched on their newel posts. Framed photographs of the great horses of old covered the wainscoted walls, horseshoes and golden spurs hung above the bar itself, and photographed clippings of old racing forms. Jonathan examined these souvenirs, noting that all that was left of the sporting past were the bowling alley ads posted on the bulletin board. These were overshadowed by notices of summer art shows, off-Broadway entertainments, jazz concerts, night courses in Method Acting, sketching, folk-singing hootenannies, poetry readings, ballet and language groups. Penciled scraps of paper were Scotch-taped to the wall, advertising cars, scooters, beach shacks, lofts, or furniture for trade or sale. Homesick Californian with driver's license asked for free trip back to North Beach. A new espresso café on Bleecker Street wanted a man to get up a mimeographed Village news sheet in return for "nominal" pay and free cakes and coffee. A Sunday painter offered free dental service in exchange for model. An unemployed illustrator would teach the Chachacha or even the Charleston for her dinners.

"Brother, she's hungry!" Jonathan heard a feminine voice say over his shoulder and turned to see a big girl with shrimp-pink hair laughing at his absorption. He drew away, embarrassed at being caught in tourist innocence.

The girl got her cigarettes from the cigarette machine and sauntered back to the dining booths, throwing him a friendly, mocking smile. He took a stool at the bar and saw, farther down, his neighbor from the excavation applying himself to a highball with deep satisfaction. Near him a man with a skimpy gray goatee, in a plaid shirt and scalp-tight beret, was reading a copy of *Encounter* with a beer in hand. He had a mountain of pennies stacked in front of him, and now he raised his glass for a refill. The bartender silently counted off fifteen coppers. Conscious of Jonathan's interest in this little game, the man looked up from his magazine and stared at Jonathan, frowning.

"Excuse me," he said. "You remind me of somebody."

"I do?" Jonathan asked, well pleased to look like somebody.

The man studied him, frowning, then shook his head. "I can't place it," he said.

"My name's Jaimison," Jonathan offered.

"Don't know any Jaimison," said the man.

He looked like a real Villager, Jonathan thought in deep admiration, ageless, jaunty, wearing his faded bohemian uniform with the calm assurance of the true belonger. (I must scrap this tourist outfit of mine and get one like his, Jonathan thought.) He was somewhere between thirty and sixty; the bags under the eyes and deep furrows between the tangled brows might testify to dissipation instead of years, for the sharp-cut sardonic face was otherwise unlined, the figure trim.

"Two double Bloody Marys on the rocks, Dan," a female voice pleaded from the dark recesses of the dining booths.

"So Lize is back in the Village," said the Villager.

"They always come back," said the bartender. "Will somebody tell me why?"

As no one answered, Jonathan seized the opportunity.

"Alvine Harshawe, for instance," he said boldly. "Has he come back?"

The bartender selected a tomato-juice can from under the counter thoughtfully.

"I'll have one of those too," added Jonathan. "Bloody Mary."

"Harshawe, Harshawe," mused the bartender. "Must be a night customer. Harshawe, eh? Maybe he comes in here and I just don't know him by name. Lots of good customers, my best friends, I don't know the names."

"Dan never heard of Alvine Harshawe!" The shrimp-haired girl was back again, standing by the goateed man, watching her drinks being made. "Don't you love Dan for that, Earl? Imagine not hearing of Alvine Harshawe."

The girl picked up the two drinks the bartender pushed toward her.

"Writers don't come in this bar," she said to Jonathan. "Try the White Horse."

"Just a minute, Lize," said the goateed man reproachfully.

"I forgot about Earl here," the girl amended. "I mean the hardcover big shots—like Harshawe."

She retreated to the dark dining section again with her two gory potions, and Jonathan took the third.

"A writer's got to go where columnists can see him," the goateed Villager stated. "Alvine Harshawe could be dying of thirst in the middle of the Sahara. Suddenly there's an oasis, a regular Howard Johnson job, with fifty-nine flavors bubbling up in all directions. Terrific. But if Lenny Lyons isn't at it, I won't go, Alvine says."

"So he dries up, who cares?" said the bartender.

"Don't be silly, Lyons would be there all right," said the fellow named Earl. "You don't catch Alvine taking a chance on no publicity."

"Outside of this guy Harshawe being a big shot, what else have you got against him, Earl?" inquired the bartender, polishing the rimless spectacles that made him look like a respectable white-collar worker.

"What have I got against him?" mused Earl. "Why, he's my oldest friend, that's all."

"Now we're getting somewhere," said the bartender approvingly.

Jonathan, ears alerted, moved closer.

"Then he did use to come here?" he asked.

"Everybody used to come to the Spur," the man said carelessly, "until they could afford not to."

"Supposing we don't get these writers like Lize says," argued the bartender. "Who needs writers when we're already stinking with painters?"

"Painters have got to drink, especially these days," Earl observed. "A painter can't turn out the stuff they have to do now without being loaded."

The bartender subtracted a fresh supply of pennies from the board and pushed another beer across the counter.

"That's where you're wrong, Earl," he said. "I know more about artists than you do. After all, I'm the bartender here. The way I size it up is that they got to paint sober, then they're so disgusted with what they done they got to get stoned."

"And wreck the joint," said Earl. "Look at the crack in that table where Hugow and Lew Schaffer bashed it."

Jonathan looked admiringly at the damaged table indicated.

"The place sure seems quiet with Hugow out of town." The bartender sighed. "Ah, what the hell, painting's no kind of work for those guys. They got to let off steam, beat up their girl, kick in a door. It's only human nature as I see it."

"Sure," said Jonathan. "Human nature, that's all."

"Artists get away with more human nature than anybody else," Earl muttered morosely to Jonathan.

"Hugow sure gets away with murder," the bartender agreed. "Dames? They're all over him. What's he got?"

"Same thing he always had," Earl said. "Only it works better now that his stuff sells big, now that he's the champ."

"Hugow's a great guy. Why shouldn't he be making up for all his bad times?" The bartender turned to Jonathan for agreement. "Can you blame him? You know Hugow."

"No, I'm afraid I don't know any artists," Jonathan

said, flattered at the assumption. "Is he a great painter?"

The question seemed to require thought.

"He gets away with it," finally said the bartender. "I guess that's great enough."

The gentleman who had spoken to Jonathan at the excavation had kept to himself at the end of the bar but was listening.

"Art is all you hear in this bar nowadays," he explained to Jonathan. "We used to have brains. Real conversation."

"Speakeasy days," said Earl. "Brains, bathtub booze, and blind staggers. We had our champs then, too."

Jonathan longed to have the discussion continue, but Earl had scooped the last few pennies into his pocket and vanished before Jonathan could summon up the courage to ask about the champs of those other days, for one of them must have been his true father. His head throbbed with vague anticipation. He felt as if he had just pushed the magic button that was to open up the gates to his mother's past and his own future.

What and who was waiting to guide him? he wondered. He knew he would follow without any questions, no matter where he was led. His guides were closer than he knew.

2

Lize Britten and Darcy Trent having lunch at the Spur, stuck with each other at last, meant that the season was over, the summer drought was on. It meant that all the men—or the men Darcy and Lize shared—had taken to the hills, gone off on their Guggenheims, off to Rome or Mexico or Greece, off to Yaddo, MacDowell, Huntington Hartford, back to their wives or mothers for a free vacation.

There was nobody left in town except the outsiders, the summer faculties and students of the university, the deserted husbands, the tourists, and the creeps. From Hudson Street to First Avenue, in haunts old and new, Lize and Darcy cruised, pretending not to see each other but finally obliged to exchange a lipstick, borrow a dime to phone, until their year-long feud was crossed off in mutual loneliness. The chances were they would have another big showdown come September—oh, they'd manage to fix each other's wagon somehow during the summer, as they always did, but for the time being hostilities must go in the deep freeze, for they had plenty in common and good reason to unite.

Just two weeks ago that popular artist named Hugow, the Spur's leading attraction, had been whisked off to Cape Cod by that insatiable lady art dealer Cassie Bender. Brazen kidnaping, Darcy called it. Rescue was Lize's private word. Whichever way you looked at it, Darcy was left out in the cold. Deserted. Double-crossed.

"He never said a word!" Darcy kept saying, for good-by was a word Darcy never heard, as Lize and the Spur regulars knew full well. "It's the awful shock that gets me!"

"But he hadn't showed up at the studio for weeks!" Lize reminded her.

"I knew how to find him," Darcy muttered, for she had the same talent Lize herself had for tracking men; their itineraries lit up like the arteries on an anatomy chart the first time she met them. "But now he's really gone, don't you understand?"

Good thing you understand it at last yourself, old thing, Lize wanted to say, but she was not unkind. Darcy's eyes were puffed and her face swollen from weeping bitter brandied tears. She had chosen the darkest booth in the farthest corner of the Spur to wallow in her grief in private, but since she continued to heave and snuffle there could be no secret about her broken heart. This frank exhibition was what had won over Lize. A stiff upper lip would have challenged her, but for her old rival Darcy to make a public show of her defeat brought out the sportsman in Lize.

"Hell, Hugow was always sleeping with Cassie Bender!" she now offered as soothing consolation. "A guy's got to eat."

"I knew he did when he was living with you, Lize." Darcy sniffled into her handkerchief. "But what you don't seem to understand is that our relationship was different. Hugow was absolutely frank with me about everything, that's what I always liked about him. Most men are such liars. But when he went to Chicago that time with her and I hit the ceiling, he said I must be crazy to think of such a thing. 'Cassie Bender is my dealer, you little dope,' he said. 'You don't go around sleeping with your bread and butter. Sure, I go places with her, take her home and all that—I'd do the same for Kootz or Sidney Janis or Pierre Matisse. It's business. I like to make a buck and Cassie sells me, but as for an affair, you must be kidding.' Oh, he was perfectly honest about it."

Lize blinked.

"You knew Hugow before I did, Lize," Darcy said, "and you've got to admit he never lied. He was always honest."

"Maybe he just lied to himself," Lize suggested, a little dazed.

Darcy nodded emphatically.

"That's just it. He was so honest that if he had to lie he'd lie to himself too, don't you see?"

Lize was silent, a feat that took all her strength. It would have been so easy to say, "Yes, Hugow was always honest, as you say. Only last year when *I* was living with him and accused him of sleeping with *you* he burst out laughing. 'That dumb kid,' he says, 'are you out of your mind? Look here,' he says, 'I'll level with you. I've got my share of male egotism, call it plain vanity, so believe me I don't make passes at any dame that asks me why don't I paint like Grandma Moses. I could learn, she tells me. Listen, Lize,' he says, 'you must know how a crack like that would paralyze a man with my ego.' So we both had a good laugh, and a few months later you moved in and I was wondering what hit me. Old honest Hugow."

Anyhow Hugow didn't ever chase a woman, Lize was forced to admit. He was a softhearted fellow, and if a woman climbed into his bed he didn't kick her out. He made a brave stab at being independent, keeping his studio strictly for himself, but Lize had managed to move in, the same as the other girls, and Darcy after her. Poor guy. The technique was so simple you'd think the sap would have learned some defense tricks.

You got into the sacred old studio first with a crowd, after an opening or to see a new picture he might be feeling good about, and then you managed to hang around, helping clean up after the others left. So you stayed that one night and then if he didn't phone you afterward—which he never did, sober—you went back for something you'd left. This time you brought a toothbrush and an office dress, in case you stayed again. Next time you casually left a suitcase, because you'd just lost your apartment and couldn't find a place to move yet, you told him. So there you were, in. Poor old Hugow, it was so easy, but damn his hide, he did always manage to get away, even though he couldn't get you out.

It was a consolation to know he'd walked out on her successor just as he had on her the year before, Lize told herself.

"You might have guessed what you were in for, seeing how he treated everybody else before you," she said.

"But Lize, with me it was *serious!*" Darcy patiently protested. "I don't know how to explain it, but I *understood* Hugow, and none of you others ever had. I just happen to understand the artistic temperament, and that's where you failed him, you see."

Again Lize exercised stern self-control to keep from reminding Darcy that they'd covered the same artists in their time with about the same scores. And as for "failing" Hugow—she'd blow her top if she listened to Darcy go on about why she, Lize, and the others had never been right for Hugow anyway. With Darcy's little voice quavering on and on, Lize found herself brooding all over again about her own season with Hugow. Maybe she would have lasted longer if she'd realized that he took that crazy painting of his seriously. But how could you guess that a grown man thought it mattered whether he made a green or purple blob on the canvas? You could understand his being pleased when people liked it or when he got a big check for it, but to think the stuff mattered all by itself—as if it were a machine that would work, depending on a line being here instead of there. Crazy! Luckily she'd kept her mouth shut when he was in one of his sunk moods, though heaven knows she'd wanted to say, "Why in God's name do you go on with something that makes you so miserable?" She'd just let him fool around with the stuff while she quietly got the studio fixed up with a kitchen unit, a few rugs and chairs from the Salvation Army Furniture Store. She had just gotten to the point where she was inviting other couples in for hamburgers and beer, and the grocer was calling her Mrs. Hugow, when he simply disappeared.

Somebody mentioned something about a shack he used sometimes up in Rockland County and that maybe he'd gone up there to work. His friends didn't seem worried or even surprised. But days passed, and no word from him. Lize would come home from the office and then hang around The Golden Spur, hoping for some news of him. But nobody told her anything. That's the way Hugow always was—his pals shrugged—maybe he'd turn up tomorrow, maybe next week.

If she'd known more about his work she would have soon suspected that he wasn't coming back—at least not to her. She would have noticed that he or one of his cronies was slipping into the studio whenever she wasn't there and taking out stuff he needed. That his newest canvas was gone should have told her something, but she wasn't sure which was the new one because all his pictures looked alike to Lize. Great lozenges of red and white ("I love blood," he always said), black and gray squares ("I love chess," he'd say), long green spikes ("I love asparagus"). All Lize had learned about art from her life with painters was that the big pictures were for museums and the little ones for art.

Lize remembered that the first inkling of real trouble was when she heard that Darcy Trent, who had been at loose ends ever since Lew Schaffer went back to his wife, was commuting to work from Rockland County.

Well!

Lize never allowed two and two to make four until she was good and ready. So she went on hanging around the empty studio for a couple of weeks more, knowing what was up all right, and having it rubbed in whenever she went to The Golden Spur or The Big Hat or The Barrel. Whoever was Hugow's girl was queen of the crowd, in a way, with all the hangers-on clambering to sit with her. But the minute the grapevine had the word that she'd been bounced, the boys who wanted to paint like Hugow and the ones who just wanted to be around a big shot all faded away when she hailed them. Sometimes the whole bar would clear out—a party somewhere, they didn't dare ask her in case Hugow and the new girl (Darcy) would be there. Lize found herself stuck with a moist-eyed Hugow-worshiper, Percy Wright, whom everybody had been ducking for years, but at least he had money enough for them to close the bars together. The poor mug actually got the idea he was *stealing* Hugow's girl, and Lize let him think so.

Percy wasn't as spooky as the crowd thought, even if he did have money (too much to be a respected artist and too little to be a respected snob). He was in some Wall Street office, but his analyst had set him painting, so he had started hanging around the Spur, trying to pin artists down to depth conversations on Old Masters, when the proper thing was to pop off on galleries, dealers, and critics. Lize was bored by his constant boasting to strangers that she had once been Hugow's girlfriend, as if this meant Hugow's talents would automatically rub off on him now.

Still, his spaniel adoration was consoling. He had inherited his mother's old brownstone house in Brooklyn Heights and lived there alone with two floors rented out. He was flattered when Lize started leaving her things there, a make-up kit, douche-bag, then a suitcase "just while she was looking for an apartment." To please her, he let her persuade him to give a couple of big parties, thinking it would establish him with the artist crowd. But, just as Lize had feared, the good guys didn't show up, knowing Hugow wouldn't be there, and the guests were the dregs of all the Left Banks in the world, North Beach, Truro, Paris, or Rome, all knights of the open house, ready to spring at the pop of a cork, ready to stand by through thick of bourbon to thin of wine. Percy didn't mind the expense of these sodden revels that seemed to drag on for days, for he had learned Brooklyn hosts must always be taxed high for wrenching guests from their beloved dingy Manhattan bars, but he resented having their taxi fares back home extorted from him. Lize reproached him for being mean and stingy, but he retorted sulkily that he was *not* stingy, he just didn't like to spend money on other people, that was all. The parties didn't get him anywhere, Lize saw, and she was Indian-marked by her new escort. No use nagging him into buying drinks for the crowd in their own bailiwick, either, for Percy soon set up a squawk. Cash! Money in general was sacred enough, but *cash!*

In spite of these mistakes in adjusting, Percy bloomed under Lize's bullying, as everyone could see. This must have been the same nagging Hugow himself had gotten, he figured, and that set him up as Hugow's equal. He put on some weight, which made him look almost virile. He took to using a sun lamp, grew a little sprig of mustache, wore black-rimmed glasses, tuned his apologetic voice a few notes lower, walked on the balls of his feet, and all in all acted like a man important enough to be kicked around by an ex-girlfriend of Artist Hugow.

Lize had been regarding her time with Percy Wright as a sabbatical year, doing the things outsiders and tourists did—the theater, good restaurants, driving around week ends in Percy's MG, and getting what she could without wounding him in the wallet directly. If a guy could produce enough background, music, and scenery changes, a girl could stand almost anybody. Her pride was saved, too. Some people even thought that orchestra seats at a good show and The Embers afterward was socially a big step up from Hugow's bed in an East Tenth Street dump. And she had a chance to case the field for somebody better. There were fellows in her office—she worked in a printing outfit near Grand Central—who made passes and asked for lunch dates, but they were mostly commuting husbands, scared to miss more than one train, and likely to shout "Yippee!" when they went to a Village spot. Lize had gone for them when she first started working in New York, but after doing the artist bit you couldn't go back to business types, except maybe once in a while. Percy never suspected, being so faithful to Hugow himself that he couldn't imagine a

Hugow woman would go anywhere but back to Hugow, and Darcy Trent had that situation covered. Percy often said how glad he was that the master had consolation for losing Lize.

Lize had a rangy Southwest style and was at her best in trim slacks and sport coats or tailored suits that hung negligently on her lean frame with a fine Bond Street air. Dolled up for a big evening, freckles lightly dusted (those freckles were as good as any collateral for assuring the simple sophisticates of her sterling honesty!), a fillet of rosebuds or butterflies in her close-cropped sorrel hair, a great pouf of satin ribbon on the sleek hips, a dangle of beads at the ears and over the boyish bosom, Lize drew the interest of men of all sexes, but Darcy Trent managed all right too.

Darcy was a wood violet, not as diminutive as she appeared at first glance, but small-boned, small-nosed, small-faced, and given to tiny gestures and a tiny baby voice. She seemed womanly and practical too, and you thought Darcy must be like those small iron pioneer women in the Conestoga wagons, whipping men and children across the prairies, sewing, building, plowing, cooking, nursing, saving her menfolks from their natural folly and improvidence. The fact was that Darcy had never darned a sock, seldom made her own bed, thought coffee was born in delicatessen containers and all food grew in frozen packages. Her practicality exhibited itself in tender little cries of, "But you'll be sick, honey, if you don't eat something after all that bourbon! You must eat! Here, eat this pretzel." In other crises she could figure out efficiently in her head that four people sharing a taxi wouldn't be much more than four subway fares, and that way they could carry their drinks along. She was very firm too in insisting that a man coming out of a week-end binge still reeking of stale smoke and rye should keep away from his job Monday unless he shaved and changed his shirt.

Darcy was delicate in color, almost fading into background, but strong and gamy like those tiny weed-flowers whose roots push up boulders. A man felt that here was a real woman, an old-fashioned girl with her little footsies firmly on the ground, someone to count on, someone always behind you. Darcy's pretty feet were more likely to be on the wall or tangled up in sheets than on the ground, and as for being behind her man, he found out sooner or later she was really on his back. Alas, little women are as hard to throw out as Amazons, especially a confiding little creature like Darcy who had no place to go until there was another back to jump on. Between backs Darcy had no existence, like a hermit crab caught in a shuttle from one stolen shell to another.

Now that Hugow had vanished with Cassie Bender and her damnable station wagon—it was always transporting some artist and his canvases to some place his true mate couldn't get at him—Darcy, the little pioneer woman, had given up completely. She didn't show up at her job in the portrait photographer's studio on West Fifty-Seventh Street for three days on account of her tendency to cry all the time, and after that she was afraid to go in, having a hunch she was automatically fired. She sat around Hugow's studio, hoping there was some mistake, but knowing better. You would have thought she'd stay away from The Golden Spur, where the ritual of brushing off Hugow's cast-off ladies was as rigorously practiced as suttee, but there she was every day or night, getting what Lize had got the year before.

It was "Hello, Al, how's everything? Anybody sitting

here—oh, you're just leaving? . . . Hello, Lester, have a beer with me—oh, you're joining friends? . . . What's that, waiter, you say this booth is reserved? Don't be silly! Reserved booths in the Spur, ha, ha! . . . Oh, you mean because I'm just one person—but supposing somebody else . . . oh, well . . ."

The crushing blow was when some fellow conspirator of Hugow's (probably Lew Schaffer, her old lover) had gotten into the studio when Darcy was out and cleaned out all Hugow's smaller possessions. The stuff, in a cardboard suitcase, was under the bar of The Golden Spur at this very minute, waiting for somebody on the way to Provincetown to pick it up. Hugow was really not to blame, Darcy had been insisting up to this point, everything was the fault of Cassie Bender and his other false friends. But to be deserted like this, left in that rat-ridden old slummy studio with the improvements she had generously installed for his comfort—the makeshift shower, dressing mirror, the wardrobe for her dresses, the cute make-up table—it was as if he was saying, here, take the works, my dear girl, you were so anxious to move in. Oh, that was cruel of Hugow, and so ungrateful.

"I think it was darned decent of him to leave you the place," Lize observed after some thought. "He could have locked you out and changed the key" (as he finally did to me, Lize added privately). "You'd been telling him all along you couldn't get an apartment, remember, so I think he meant to be nice, giving it up to you. After all, he loved that lousy dump."

Darcy was beginning to be sorry she'd bleated all her woes to Lize if they were going to be thrown right back at her. She recalled with relief that she hadn't confessed that Lew Schaffer had treated her the same way—walked out of his place after she'd fixed it up so pretty, walked right back to his wife. She'd been stuck with the rent until she'd unloaded it on some Vassar girls who wanted to Live. She'd found out that Lew had retrieved the place the minute she'd moved out to Nyack after Hugow. Men were sneaky that way. But twice stuck like that! Well, at least Lize didn't know that part.

"I never meant I wanted to live way over in that slum all alone," Darcy said. "Bowery bums sleeping on the doorstep and juvenile delinquents slinking up and down the fire escapes. And fifty dollars a month! Sure, it's cheap when you're dividing it, but all that by yourself for a dump where you're afraid to be alone."

Lize, smitten with a brilliant inspiration, looked meditatively at Darcy.

"Oh, I know I look a wreck," Darcy said defensively. "You don't need to tell me."

"I was just thinking your hair's cute with that lock falling down," Lize said.

For some time Lize had been trying to figure out a way of getting back with the old crowd on her own without losing Percy altogether. He had a big inferiority, with every right to it, and a mean way of getting even when he was wounded. She didn't want to break off till she was sure what came next. This week Percy's sister's family from Buffalo were visiting the Brooklyn house, which gave Lize a good excuse to stay out of the picture in a Village hotel. Whatever came of this Percy would have to admit was largely his fault.

"I was so hurt when you didn't want your family to meet me," she could say to him when the time came.

"I think this is a good chance to break with Percy," Lize said to Darcy.

"I can't understand how you endured him this long, Lize," Darcy said, absorbed in admiring her hair in her pocket mirror. "Hugow couldn't get over it. He just despised Percy, always sidling up to him—'May I join you people? I do hate to miss a word of Hugow's conversation.' Blah blah blah."

"No more blah blah to Percy than Hugow once he gets going," Lize retorted in a burst of obstinate loyalty.

Hugow, Hugow, Hugow—the way damn fool women carried on about him—sometimes not seeing him for years, too—you would think he was the Great Lover of the Ages, a perfect panther of a man, wonderfully equipped, wonderfully insatiable, every nuance at his command. Well, it just wasn't that way at all, and all his men friends, who were sure that was it, were plain stupid. Ask the women (not that they'd admit the truth). There was the big rush at the outset, while he was on a binge between pictures, a hungry-farm-boy technique, that was all; then you could wait for weeks for another pass, living right with him, too. That was what got you,—the cruel, indifferent, teasing withdrawal, all the worse because he had no idea he was being heartless. He could be lying on the bed right beside you, buck naked, absently flipping your eager hands off his body like so many horseflies, till you got so hurt you had to go off to some corner and bawl, with him lying there staring at the ceiling with nothing on his mind but how blue is sky and how black is night. He got under your skin that way, and damn his hide, he could always get any woman back—fifty years from now he could whistle through his old gums and they would all come flying up from hell to warm up his old bones. Other men—like Lew Schaffer and all the artists Lize and Darcy had run through—became just part of the everyday scenery after an affair was over.

Like Lize or Darcy, who never left any trace of their past love.

Oh yes, there was usually a lipstick and a babushka left by Lize in a drawer. And Darcy's potato. ("There's nothing so beautiful in the whole world as a potato, I don't care what you artists say. A potato has everything," was Darcy's very own stand in all aesthetic arguments.) Darcy's potato crept into one painting or another like a Kilroy-was-here mark. Lew Schaffer had done a saint with potato eyes sprouting all over it, for instance, and Mrs. Schaffer had screamed, "So you've been sleeping with Darcy Trent!"

But Hugow got into your blood, kept you itching for him and hanging on shamelessly long after you knew he was through. Lize wondered how long before Darcy would admit it was hopeless.

"How do you mean this is a good chance to break with Percy?" Darcy suddenly asked. "How could you afford to go on staying at the Albert?"

"I could move into the studio with you," Lize said triumphantly.

Darcy's eyes widened.

"Oh no! What would people say, two girls living together! Oh, Lize, we couldn't, we just wouldn't dare!"

"Don't be so old-fashioned, for God's sake!" Lize said impatiently. There was something in what Darcy said, of course. Lize could already anticipate the snickering around The Golden Spur set when the news got out.

"It splits the rent, and you say you're scared alone. Okay, forget it," Lize said, but she had no intention of giving up the idea.

"I'm sorry, I always think of appearances." Darcy was sniveling again, and Lize could have given her a good slap. She looked toward the bar to see if any fresh company had arrived. The young man who had been reading the bulletin board was still there and, meeting his eye, Lize gave him a warm, friendly smile, which she saw had the proper energizing effect, for he started edging down the bar at once, pleased but hesitant.

"I think we can work something out," Lize murmured to Darcy absently, and waited for the right moment.

Jonathan had been stealing curious glances at the two young women in the back, even while his ears were tuned to the bar talk. He wondered if his mother had had just such a girlfriend who could, if he found her now, tell him all the intimate little confidences he longed to know. It was hard to picture his gentle mother in these surroundings, and surely she had never been as sophisticated as these two girls seemed.

The improbable red of the taller one's hair impressed him as stylish, while the smaller one's bright orange skirt lit up the dark corner like a forest blaze—an inviting touch, he thought. (Lize had been thinking that in that brassy hue little Darcy looked like a rather flashy mouse.) Jonathan was heartened to see that these two clean-cut New Yorkers were not above working over a good old American steak, and after Lize's friendly smile he was sure they were not formidable cosmopolitans after all, but simple, foursquare American girls. Never in the world would he have suspected the scrambled montage of bars, beds, and bushes behind their open, homespun faces. They were modern versions of his mother, Jonathan thought. He was considering a move to take the booth next to theirs when he felt a hand on his arm.

It was his companion of the wrecking scene.

"Come have a drink with me, young man," said the gentleman. "I have a class in precisely fifteen minutes and I defy anyone to face that sea of cretin faces without an anesthetic."

As Jonathan hesitated, his new friend went on confidentially, "I overheard you asking about Alvine Harshawe. It so happens that I recall seeing him here many years ago. He was just coming up then—some powerful stories in *The Sphere* and a play in the experimental theater. People used to point him out, that sort of thing."

"What was he like?" Jonathan asked eagerly.

The professor shrugged.

"Too sure of himself for my taste. Of course I was older and had done some writing of my own, but Harshawe was the comer, and the Spur was the writers' speakeasy."

"I'd like to know all I can about the Spur in those days," Jonathan said.

The professor studied him shrewdly.

"Another thesis on the twenties and thirties, eh?" he said. "Just what my colleague in the English Department has been working on for ten years. The Speakeasy as a Forcing Bed for Literature is her angle, I believe. I'm sure she'd be glad to share the background picture with you, because I'm the one who gave it to her, ha, ha."

He signaled for drinks, which Jonathan regarded uneasily.

"Place was horsy at first because the owner was a retired cowboy, got thrown by a wild horse in the rodeo at the old Madison Square Garden and won the place in a roll of dice. Fixed it all up with these racing prints and used to hobble around on crutches in his tight pants and satin shirts, Western style. Fought with a drunk and got thrown right through his own window, there. The place kept the horsy decor after he left, but then the jazz musicians took over till jazz went uptown; then it got the actors from the little theater upstairs, and finally the artists. Harshawe hasn't been even heard of in this place since the abstract wave took over."

"Did you know people who came here, say, around nineteen twenty-eight?" Jonathan asked.

"A few," said the gentleman." I had just started teaching here in the East then, and I used to come in here with a student occasionally, and they would always point out the characters."

"Phone call, Doctor Kellsey," said the bartender. "What do I tell her this time?"

"Damn it, does a light go on all over the city every time I step into a bar?" cried Dr. Kellsey indignantly. "You told her once, didn't you, that Doctor Kellsey hadn't been in for weeks?"

"This is a different lady, Doctor," said the bartender.

"Ah. My wife. In that case tell her you don't know any Doctor Kellsey." He waited till the bartender hung up. "What did she say?"

"Said I was lucky," said the bartender.

"Damn these female bloodhounds," said the professor. He paid his bill and then fished out a card, which he handed to Jonathan.

"Here's where you can reach me if you'd like to get more information. Always glad to talk over the old days with a fellow researcher. Helpful to both of us."

He gave Jonathan a genial handclasp that warmed his heart and hurried out.

DR. WALTER KELLSEY, KNOWLTON ARMS, GRAMERCY PARK, Jonathan read on the card. He copied it carefully in his little red notebook, glowing with the compliment of being taken for a fellow academician.

"Got a light, Buster?"

Startled, Jonathan looked up to see the tall girl with the pink hair beside him. He lit a match for her.

"Come on back and have a drink with us," she said, taking his arm. "No sense in being lonesome. Darcy and I are back here."

"I ought to be out looking for a room," he said, allowing himself to be led into the dark recesses, "and a job."

"It's too nice a day to be outdoors," protested the girl and nudged him gently into the booth. "Isn't that so, Darcy?"

Jonathan saw that the other girl was none too pleased at his intrusion.

"Really, Lize!" she exclaimed reprovingly.

"Okay, I picked him up, so what?" Lize looked him over with obvious satisfation. "Doesn't he look like somebody, Darcy?"

"Doesn't everybody?" snapped Darcy.

She knew Lize had been getting bored with her damp sorrow, finagling for the last half-hour to get the eye of the stranger at the bar. Oh, he was good-looking in a clean, strapping Midwest way, and he did stand out in the Spur's galaxy of battered, beat-up gallants, but personally she preferred that battered, beat look on a man. At least you knew what they must have done to get that way, and what they were likely to go on doing. This eager, dewy-eyed Buster was too healthy to trust, apt to invite you for a chase over the moors, or to romp around a dance floor, clapping his hands over his head or swinging you around by the ponytail. Health was all right for women—God knows they needed it!—but a man ought to have something more special, an eyepatch, a broken nose, a battle scar, or a tired gimp like Hugow's. That was Darcy's theory. But Lize was on the prowl again, ready to snatch up the first thing that came along, now that she'd made up her mind to ditch Percy.

"You one of those college creeps?" Darcy asked Jonathan politely. "Is that why you got stuck with that stuffy professor?"

"Kellsey isn't stuffy except when he's on the wagon," Lize said severely. "Personally I like him. He's just a good-natured old slob that hates everybody, that's all. Be fair."

"He was very kind to me," Jonathan said. "He's going to help me on my research."

"I'm not going back to work this afternoon," Lize stated. "I think we should stick around here and get acquainted. Were you looking for a room on the bulletin board?"

Surprised that she had noticed, Jonathan nodded.

"I thought as much," Lize said. "You can relax, because we've got the place for you."

"Me?"

"Darcy needs a man to stay in Hugow's studio," Lize said, at which Darcy's crumpled little face tried to stiffen into an expression of moral outrage.

"Really, Lize!"

"It's all right, I'll be there too," Lize said. "Get it?"

Darcy looked at her with unwilling admiration.

"There's only the couch in the studio and the broken-down Hi-Riser in the back room," she said. "It has mice in it—just baby mice, though."

"He could have the couch," Lize said, who knew the place as well as Darcy did, after all.

"That's awfully good of you," Jonathan said, startled. "Are you sure you really would like to—I mean—"

"Listen to him," Lize said. "With his looks. Isn't he a beauty?"

She smiled at Jonathan meditatively.

"I love his hair," she mused. "I wonder what a real sharp crew-cut would do for him."

"You're always cutting people's hair," complained Darcy. "I had to cut Hugow's all over again to get it the way I liked it."

"Well, Cassie's probably sent him to a real barber by this time," Lize said maliciously; then, relenting, "Okay, Darcy, you can cut it this time. Can't she, Jack?"

"Jonathan," he said, embarrassed, not sure they were serious about anything.

Lize clapped her hand on his knee affectionately.

"Now I call that cute," she said. "Don't you, Darcy?"

Darcy was sulking, as if a new baby brother had put her nose out of joint.

"What's he doing looking for this Harshawe?" she grumbled. "Is he FBI or something?"

"We can help him get the lowdown on everybody once we get settled, eh, Darcy?" Lize chuckled. "Is that all right with you, Jonathan, moving in with us? We'll all save money by it."

It must be a perfectly ordinary New York custom, Jonathan thought.

"Everything's in a mess over there," Darcy said. "There's only some moldy marmalade and stuffed olives and shaving cream, but you're welcome."

She was cheering up under the prospect of company and taking an interest in the list of needed supplies Lize was jotting down. A little alarmed at the speed with which things were moving, Jonathan suggested he had better spend the rest of the afternoon looking around for a job.

"You sit right here, Bud," Lize commanded. "Everybody gets their jobs right here in the Spur, you might as well learn that right now. Why don't you take that café job up there on the bulletin board?"

"Do you think I could do it?" Jonathan asked.

This question struck both girls as irrelevant. If a job was what you wanted, you took whatever came along and found out later whether you could do it or not. If you got fired you still had your week's pay and came back to the Spur to hang around till another job turned up.

Jonathan was speechless with wonder at the amazing kindness of city women. Not only did the two new friends insist on dividing the check in three equal parts when it came, but they gave him explicit directions for getting to the Then-and-Now Café on Bleecker Street to apply for the job, and further information on getting to the new home he was to share with them. Then they left to do their marketing and to pick up Lize's suitcase at the Albert.

Jonathan took out his little red book after they left and wrote down his new address on the flyleaf. Before he gave up the booth, he wrote a note to the Miss Claire Van Orphen mentioned in his mother's letters, asking for an interview.

That's the way you did things in New York, he said to himself. Go right after 'em before you have time to think.

3

THE NOTE forwarded to her from the Pen and Brush Club had given Claire Van Orphen a full morning of reflections on the past. Some young man—the signature was unknown to her—would like to call on her on purely personal business connected with Constance Birch. He realized, the writer said, that a busy author like Miss Van Orphen must have had a dozen secretaries, and Constance Birch had worked for her less than a year—1928 it had been. But the experience had meant so much to his mother (for he was Constance Birch's son) that he dared to hope Miss Van Orphen might retain some recollections of her. Since his mother's death years ago he had regretted the lost opportunities for not having known her better, and now that he was in New York he was trying to enrich his picture of her by meeting those who had known her during her own New York period.

Constance Birch, Miss Van Orphen mused, putting down the note and frowning into space. What in heaven's name could she remember about her beyond the fact that she'd been the last secretary she had been able to afford? A pale, sweet, quiet little creature, Claire recalled, so shy you thought she'd be afraid to go home at night when she had to type late. Not at all, the girl had assured her. It was true that she had to cross that dark block under the El to get to her room, but she had the habit of stopping in a very nice bar for a sandwich and a beer, and there was always some nice fellow there going in her direction.

Well, I certainly can't tell her son about that, Claire reflected. Nor about the literary tea Claire had given—oh, those were the lavish days—in the Brevoort banquet suite, with Connie helping her in her nice unobtrusive way, and the surprising way the child had passed out in Claire's room later, passed out cold, as if there wasn't enough to do after a party.

"I'd never tasted champagne before, Miss Van Orphen," she had explained when she revived, greatly mortified. "And I'd never met so many famous men. Wasn't it awful?"

For the life of her Claire couldn't remember the girl's face or much of anything except that she was so obliging you couldn't fire her for her inexperience, and she didn't get on your nerves like the more hard-boiled efficient ones did, who charged more, besides. She did remember how anxious the girl was to learn city ways and yet how singularly blind she was to them. For instance, she always wore tennis shoes and simple little cotton dresses she made by hand, oblivious to the stylish touches from the *Vogues* she studied. Her pale cheeks would flush with excitement when she had to type a letter to some well-known editor, and she would stare with wide, eager eyes when Claire was on the telephone, then stammer, "M-Miss Van Orphen, excuse me, I couldn't help overhearing—do you really know Susan Glaspell personally? My!" Yes, her candid naïveté had made Claire feel sinfully worldly, she recalled, though there had been curious features about it. Like the time it had struck Claire that the child was available almost any hour of day or night and therefore must be having a friendless sort of life, so she decided to take her to The Black

Knight for dinner, that being a popular speakeasy below the square where Claire had been taken once by an editor. On the way down Claire had felt a few qualms about introducing the little country girl to the kind of Village life she herself did not know or even wholly approve. It puzzled and amused her that, when they entered, several patrons, and the owner himself, cried out, "Hello, Connie."

"I thought you said you'd never been here," Claire said.

"Oh, I didn't know you meant Sam's," Connie said. "We just call it Sam's, you see."

Aside from those little kinks, Claire remembered nothing remarkable about her except that she had typed a serial Claire had sold to the *Delineator,* almost her last success. Well, all she could do for the young man, Claire thought, was to fill him in on the general background of Greenwich Village in the late twenties, the way biographers did when they ran short of personal facts.

Having so little to tell him, she would have the added embarrassment of disillusioning the lad about his mother's fine connections. Obviously the slight contact with Claire had been built up after the girl had gone back home and married the old steady beau. Claire recalled Christmas cards signed "Connie, with appreciation for all your kindnesses my wonderful year in New York." She would certainly have to do something for the boy, have him come to the cocktail lounge for tea—the canapés were free. Sometimes a talented guest played the old grand piano, and there were young people around once in a while, so the place didn't seem such an elderly retreat.

It had been a long time since any stranger had looked her up, and Claire began to brighten. In the old days people they'd met on trips were always telephoning the Van Orphen girls—"You told us in Florence to be sure and look you up when we got to New York." It used to put the girls on their mettle, trying to put on a good show at home for those fascinating worldly strangers. Bea wasn't on hand for the sister act any more, of course; she had to manage alone now.

Claire pushed aside the avocado plant she was nursing in its glass of water on the window sill, and selected a pen from the glass slipper on her desk. She addressed an envelope to Mr. Jonathan Jaimison at the East Tenth Street address and began writing her note.

One thing Claire had no worry about was her clothes. She might be obliged to live in a cell, uncertain of selling a line she wrote, uncertain of the dear moments she could be granted with Bea, too modest to cling to successful old friends, but at least she need never worry about her appearance. She was happy in that knowledge.

Friends and relatives had scolded her years ago for throwing away all her money on clothes. "You'll have to go into your capital first thing you know," they warned. But in these difficult years Claire was glad of her wardrobe because good, really good clothes never go out of style, she said, and she'd rather feel a good three-hundred-dollar Molyneux dress on her back, even if it was thirty years old, than a brand-new budget-shop print, which she couldn't afford anyway. The ever-rising room rent in her modest hotel took a huge bite out of her vanishing income and dwindling royalties, but the backlog of fine clothes made her feel secure.

She had had to give up her original nice little suite for a bed-sitting-room barely large enough to hold her huge wardrobe trunk and hatboxes. The file cabinet had had to go to the cellar, but that was just as well. Instead of its testifying to her long, honorable professional career as a writer, those drawers full of manuscripts with attached lists of rejections and future publishing possibilities (now largely out of business) were rude reminders of a lifetime of misspent hopes. The simple little desk with its six pigeonholes, tiny Swiss typewriter in the drawer, notebook and vase of pencils on top, were equipment enough for her present literary activities. The published pieces, the travel books and Christmas juveniles, were on the closet shelf, wrapped in cellophane. The stories she was always writing —for she could not stop the silly habit any more than she could stop saying Now-I-lay-me every night—she kept hidden in orderly stacks under the bed.

In the always-open trunk, stuffed closet, and bulging dresser drawers there were enough costumes for Claire to appear in different combinations for years to come. Some of the older creations, dating back to Paquin and Worth, remained in almost mint condition or only "slightly foxed," as the booksellers would say, and some of the post-World War I numbers seemed to be coming back in style. It was a pity that social life had deteriorated to the point where formal evening dress was seldom—indeed, where Claire was concerned, never—required any more. She had wistful moments of shaking out the bouffant rainbow tulle *robe de style,* the jewel-encrusted beige satin, the ruby velvet with richly embroidered panniers, the bronze lamé décolleté with flying wisps of gold-dotted net, and she would vow that if she ever got her hands on a good fat sum again it would pay her to go on an ocean cruise—they still dressed for dinner there, she was sure—just to get the good out of these treasures. She thought of the places where the gowns had appeared—the opera houses, the embassy balls, the garden parties, the state affairs honoring Colonel Van Orphen. All vanished and forgotten, wiped out, it seemed, almost in a day.

Every morning around half past ten, having had her instant coffee and an orange in her room at seven, Claire went to the Planet Drug Store around the corner and had an egg sandwich or Danish and a real coffee. This was the big adventure of the day, for all sorts of people dropped in at the fountain for a cup of coffee and chat with the counterman or with one another. They seldom started conversations with Claire, and although she realized her careful ensembles with matching hats and gloves intimidated them, she simply could not bring herself, a well-bred woman of over sixty, to step outdoors without hat and proper accessories. However, the counterman called her "baby," as he called all the ladies, and she could listen to the chatter, sometimes quite strange, and mull it over in her room later. There was a young man who talked about Shape Notes and the Fa Sol La Singers, from the West Virginia hills, and some television actors who talked about "bennies" and "dexies," and there was talk about show openings, reducing diets (these were always recited over chocolate sodas), new jokes, hospital experiences with explicit details that made Claire wince, and gloomy business talk by neighborhood merchants having a coffee or seltzer break.

"What do you do for a hangover, Jake?" the battered-looking haberdasher from next door begged to know.

"I just don't go there any more," said the counterman, and to his and Claire's amazement this made the gourmets split their sides laughing and became the great goody to be revived every day with wild shouts of joy. After this daily dip into the world, Claire retired to her room to write until her night meal of beans or spaghetti from the Horn & Hardart Retail Store, or, for a change, a tin of corned beef or a chicken leg and a pastry. She allowed herself the hotel dinner once a week. It was not fair that economizing on food should make you put on weight, but it was sadly true, and Claire had the devil's own time squeezing into her old gowns. The young woman at the hotel news stand was always gesturing to her that an under-arm seam had popped or that a top hook wasn't fastened. She further annoyed Claire with her helpful comments that her rouge or lipstick was crooked or too thick, and had she read that rouge wasn't fashionable any more? Claire always thanked her politely and continued making up the same way, placing a circle of fuchsia rouge in the exact center of each cheek and working it up toward the eyes as she had been doing since her first Harriet Hubbard Ayer beauty kit.

Once or twice a week, after she had revised an old love story or sold a little garden piece to a home magazine, she celebrated by walking over to a certain bar out of range of her hotel and treating herself to a Manhattan cocktail, sometimes two. When the frozen faced bartender or one of the oldtimers would spot the somewhat formidable lady in her hat, gloves, and carefully chosen afternoon costume rounding the corner, he would warn, "Here comes Miss Manhattan," and the customers would tip to the end of the bar like the balls on a bagatelle board, leaving one whole row of stools free for the lady.

"Good afternoon, Frank," Claire always said, assuming her place on the stool with dignity and speaking in her clear world-traveler voice, "A Manhattan, if you please. With cherry, thank you." After she had paid her bill, adjusted her veil, and marched out to the street, bartender and oldtimers would shake their heads and declare (as if they were Beau Brummells themselves) that nowhere in the world could there be found any outfits to equal those contrived by Miss Manhattan. In this they were quite wrong.

There was a twin of Claire's trunk in a hotel storage cellar on West Fifty-sixth Street, in which were many duplicates of Claire's collection. This trunk was the long-forgotten property of Mrs. Kingston Ball, née Beatrice Van Orphen, Claire's twin sister. Beatrice and Claire had dressed alike and done everything together until they were twenty-eight, when Bea, always the bolder of the two, declared the end of twinship. They had just lost another lover who, like all his predecessors, couldn't make up his mind which twin he preferred and was intimidated by there being two of everything. If there must be a pair, then he should have both or none; one would only make him feel cheated, as if he'd got only one book-end. Bea prophesied that this vertigo would attack every suitor they ever would get to the end of their days (somehow they got only one beau between them at a time) and they were blocking each other's futures. Claire was shattered and hurt by this proposal, as if she were to be stripped of her very skin, but Beatrice was determined. From now on she would tint her hair lighter and wear it short, and, since Claire loved their former style of dress, she could keep their dressmaker and Bea would buy ready-made. They would begin new, separate lives.

It was a bewildering blow to Claire to realize that this revolt had been simmering in her dear twin's head for years. It embarrassed Claire to think of her fatuous complacency, never dreaming of any divergence in their ideas on any subject. Her sense of humiliation (for she felt she had somehow fallen below Bea's standards) made her accept Bea's program without protest. When Bea burst into contrite tears at the final parting, saying, "It'll be much better for you too, going it alone," Claire gently comforted her with "Of course, dear, we're just standing in each other's way."

So Bea moved to a hotel near Carnegie Hall, for she would concentrate on their musical interests. Claire would pursue her budding literary career and live downtown as before. They would have different social engagements, take trips separately, affect different restaurants. This strategy, murder for poor Claire, worked out well for Bea. When Claire chose a Scandinavian cruise, Bea took Hawaii and there met and wed Mr. Ball, a widower. At his death she returned to her old hotel in New York but never to active twinship again. By that time the wound had been assuaged for Claire by her trickle of literary success—garden and travel articles and love stories for family magazines; she too was content with occasional meetings which usually did nothing but reveal how far apart they had drifted.

When Claire, carefully corseted and squeezed into the plum velvet suit with moleskin toque and scarf, came up to Bea's gloomy hotel for lunch, Bea hastily whisked her through the long lobby, past the overstuffed Gothic sofas where the passé (let's face it) international musical greats sat all day reviewing the American scene. In the coffee shop Bea would pounce on the darkest corner table, half ashamed and half protective, suspecting the quizzical looks from the amusing young men of her present circle, fervently hoping that her current pet would not see her and guess her true age by Claire's costume. She knew that Claire did not look any more of a period piece than the majestic old Brunhildes and Isoldes wafting their moth-eaten velvets through the hotel corridors, but it seemed worse to flaunt your antiquity as Claire did than to be merely eccentric.

On the other hand, when Bea arrived down at Claire's hotel for the Washington Square summer concerts, wearing a jaunty strapless print sundress, gold barefoot sandals exposing red-painted toes, shoulder bones stabbing out behind like stunted wings, arms bare except for the costume jewelry and short white gloves, flowered ribbon bandeau on the close-cut blond hair, large Caribbean straw handbag swinging from her elbow, Claire led her to the very darkest corner of *her* gloomy dining room, feeling the sour glances of the lobby crones, reading bitchy meanings into the remarks of the nasty desk clerk that Bea was so sure she had beguiled.

"She's my sister, my own twin, and I love her, of course," each lady said after these reunions, "but we have nothing in common—nothing!"

All the same Claire longed for the day when Bea would need her and they could be together again.

4

A MAN is lucky if he discovers his true home before it is too late. True mate and true calling are part of this geographical felicity, but they seem to fall magically into place once the home is found. Virtues that have been drying up in the cocoon bloom and flourish, imp becomes saint, oaf becomes knight errant, Pekingese turns lion.

Jonathan recognized New York as home. His whole appearance changed overnight, shoulders broadened, apologetic skulk became swagger; he looked strangers in the eye and found friendship wherever he turned. With the blight of Jaimison heritage removed, his future became marvelously incalculable, the city seemed born fresh for his delight. He took for granted that his mother's little world, into which he had dropped, was the city's very heart.

Within a month he knew more of New York than he had ever known about the whole state of Ohio. True, each day he learned something that upset whatever he'd learned the day before, but after all the world went round, didn't it? He had an address, and he had a job which allowed him time to pursue his private program. The job was collecting historical tidbits about the neighborhood for a giveaway news-sheet in the new espresso café called Then-and-Now. The café was in the basement of a Bleecker

Street real-estate firm that wanted to siphon off excess profits for tax purposes. Jonathan received thirty dollars a week, free sandwiches, cakes, and coffee, a desk, and a percentage of any ads he brought in. His new friend, Dr. Kellsey, adopted the café and furnished him with old Village lore. His other new friend, Earl Turner, was generous with editorial advice too, for he had once edited a glittering magazine called *The Sphere*. Mimeographed copies of *Café News* were stacked on the café's pastry counter, and to make sure the owners would consider it a success Jonathan saw to it that the sheets disappeared with speed.

A safe rule, Jonathan thought, was to assume that whatever would seem amazing in Silver City was the proper thing in New York. In Silver City people fussed over where they lived, the size and number of rooms, the suitable neighborhood, the right furniture. All New Yorkers, however, fell into whatever bed was nearest and called it home. In Silver City you lived with your family. In New York you lived with anybody but your family. The sofa might be full of mice just as the cot was full of rocks and the trundle full of nits, but for all Jonathan cared they could have been jumping with aardvarks. It was New York!

He was fortunate in having as roommates two ladies who were authorities on everything that mattered, and Jonathan listened gratefully to Darcy and Lize. The Golden Spur, they explained, was the cultural and social hub of New York City, which was bounded on the south by the San Remo, on the east by Vasyk's Avenue A bar, on the west by the White Horse, and on the north by Pete's Tavern. Friends who had deserted this area for uptown New York or the suburbs were crossed off as having gone to the bad. All connection with respectable family background had best be kept dark. Anybody with a tube of paint and a board was an artist. But writers were not writers unless decently unpublished or forever muffled by a Foundation placebo. The Word came only through grapevine gossip, never through print. The printed word on any subject was for squares. Although he had not met them, Jonathan felt on intimate terms with all the characters Darcy and Lize discussed, and soon was giving his own opinion on their affairs without hesitation. Hugow, Cassie Bender, Percy, Lew—they were his instant best friends, unseen.

It would take a little time, of course, to get used to living with two girls, having them stumble over his sleeping body in the studio on their way to bed at dawn. He had been gauche enough to propose that he move his bed to the windowless storeroom, a suggestion that brought a look of blank bewilderment to the girls' faces.

"What's the matter with your sleeping right here in the studio?" demanded Lize.

"What's so good about the junkroom?" Darcy pondered, equally baffled.

"I mean I'd be out of your way." Jonathan floundered. "I mean you'd be free to use this room for your dates and if you wanted to cook you could get to the kitchen without falling over me."

"Why would I be bringing a date to *my* place?" Lize asked Darcy in great mystification. "What makes him think we knock ourselves out cooking supper for a date?"

"I think it's kinda sweet of him, Lize," Darcy said tenderly, studying Jonathan with her little head sidewise, like a mother hen. He blushed and wondered whether she was measuring the depths of his naïveté or merely planning a new haircut for him.

"For your information, Buster, and strictly for the records," Lize told him firmly, "any date of mine takes me out, see. Home is for when you don't get a date or want to change your clothes. I've passed the stage where I date a guy just to save him money."

Darcy began to giggle.

"That would be the day," she said.

"Forget moving your bed," Lize said. "What I want to know is whether you can cook."

Jonthan had been used to cooking his own meals at Aunt Tessie's. No trick to it. Put some butter in a pan on the stove, throw in a piece of meat or can of something, and when it starts smoking, eat it.

"Steak? Hamburgers?" Lize asked with a light in her eye.

Especially steak and hamburgers. Ham and eggs.

"Didn't I tell you?" Lize cried triumphantly to Darcy. "I knew he was just the boy for us."

Jonathan was glad they allowed him to prove his helpfulness by fixing hamburgers for them that very night. The kitchen was his, they cried, from now on. Eager as he was to please, it took several days to learn just what was expected of him as cook, since the girls took off for their work before noon and never came home till there was no place else to go. Jonathan could use the kitchen table as a desk with no culinary distractions except at night, or rather at daybreak. The girls, though their programs after office hours seemed identical to him, did not hunt in pairs, but they did come home at approximately the same time, i.e., around four in the morning, after the bars had closed. Jonathan soon adjusted to this schedule, assuming it was typically New York. If he was awake he was glad to fix them bedtime scrambled eggs, but other times they did not disturb him.

Then one night he was roused by a little visitor groping

her way into his bed. In the dim light from the street lamp he saw that it was Darcy, haloed in curlers, garbed in a pajama top, and greased as for the Channel swim, with some pleasant-smelling ointments. Flattered, he made room for her and she snuggled silently into place. The poor girl must be a sleepwalker, he deduced, and he should be ashamed for taking advantage of her infirmity, but, as often happens, his conscience arrived too late. All he could do was mumble, "Darcy, I'm terribly sorry this happened. I promise you I won't let it happen again, if you'll forgive me."

"Now you're waking me up!" wailed Darcy impatiently "Can't you be quiet?"

"I just want to apologize—" But Darcy was fast asleep.

A few nights later he was wakened by Lize's sprawling into bed beside him.

"Just looking for a light," said Lize, extending a cigarette which he drowsily managed to light for her, but it seems she needed other comforts too. Taken off guard, conscience failed to strike, and since Lize had not a stitch on she must have had some dim inkling that the beast might be near. This time Jonathan reflected that an apology was not in order, nor even a thank you, but certain things mystified him. He knew it was his provincialism, and he would soon learn city ways, but—

"Do you always smoke—I mean—in bed?" he asked her cautiously, looking at the cigarette still dangling from her fingers.

"Hell, a girl has to do something." Lize yawned.

He had feared that these episodes, in which he blamed himself for taking advantage of their hospitality, would result in a change of atmosphere, but it finally dawned on him that they were no more important or meaningful than the midnight hamburger. City women were wonderful, he decided, but very strange. He heard them arguing over the comparative merits of their diaphragms and had the good sense to know they were not speaking of singing. In any case he was resolved to dodge further service as diaphragm-tester.

He also had the good sense to keep his private mission a secret from them, hoping they would not ask him about it, but he need not have worried.

The girls never asked questions about a man's private interests or listened when he tried to tell them. For them it was enough that he was a man and that he was there. Who needs a *talking* man?

They were both dear girls, Jonathan thought, looking after his interests and approving of everything he said and did in a way no one in Silver City had ever done. They liked the plaid shirt and moccasins he'd gotten on Eighth Street, just like Earl Turner's, they understood his passion to grow a beard as the flag of his emancipation from Home and Family, and then applauded his change of mind due to the initial itching. It was funny, Jonathan thought, when you considered how constantly these girls disagreed when they were together, how similar their tastes really were when you got one of them alone.

Both girls claimed to be afraid of their Tenth Street slum neighborhood but would spring out at any hour of the night to go any place else fearlessly. Coming *home* was what got them, each said, and maybe this wasn't fear of marauders but a sense of defeat in the evening's operations. In any case, after a while Lize took to dropping into Jonathan's espresso spot before closing time, for his protection going home. As soon as Darcy found this out, she insisted they divide his time equally, night for night. Protecting these young ladies from hoodlums was not just a matter of walking them across town and home, Jonathan discovered. It meant collecting nightcaps along the way, invariably ending up at The Golden Spur to check up on who was there, what they'd missed, and to make sure that home was all there was left of the night.

In spite of their new truce, Darcy was distrustful of Lize. She warned Jonathan of his danger on one of their walks home.

"You've got to watch out for that Lize," Darcy said. "She claims she walked out on Percy, but he told me himself that he's the one that made the break. You can say what you want to about Percy, maybe he is a creep and nobody wants him around, but he's no liar, and he told me she's trying to get him to take her back. Talks about you all the time just to make him jealous. I hate seeing her try to use you the way she does. I try to sleep on the outside so she can't go barging in on you in the night—oh, Lize doesn't stop at anything, you know, where there's a man."

The next night Lize favored him with the same warning about danger from little Darcy, who was really stronger than he guessed. Jonathan thanked them both. He found he could keep them from harping on his danger by introducing Hugow's name, for this was a topic of which they never tired. It was a lesson in female psychology to hear that although Hugow had cruelly deserted each of them they bore him no grudge, for he had more than atoned by treating the other one badly too. The real villain in the case was that gallery woman, Cassie Bender, who was forever swooping down on some unsuspecting artist just as a girl was making out with him. A snob, they pronounced her, forcing Hugow to leave the old bars he loved for great champagne dos uptown with movie stars and Texas millionaires, the sort of thing Hugow detested, downright vulgar really, especially if you weren't invited.

Worse than snob, Lize cried, Cassie Bender was a common whore.

"Slept with every artist she ever handled," affirmed Darcy "They all admit it when you pin them down."

Jonathan noticed that these caddish admissions were "pinned down" in the girls' own beds, but somehow this did not reflect on their own virtue.

"I swear I'm not going to break in any more artists for that old nympho," declared Lize, and both girls looked thoughtfully at Jonathan.

"I guess Hugow is a very fine painter," Jonathan said quickly. "Do you consider him better than Schaffer or the others?"

The girls pondered this for a moment, as if they had not thought of it before. They must have some opinion, he added, since they centered their private lives on painters.

"I don't see that there's much difference." Darcy shrugged. "They just think so because Cassie Bender gives them a line. One is the best one year and another the next. Cassie ruins them."

Jonathan gathered that Cassie Bender's real crime was her connection with that enemy, Art. She created a world of fame for a man and, common whore that she was, could lock other girls out of his life for weeks on end (as she was doing now with Hugow) just to get work out of him! Smart businesswoman, nuts! She'd just been lucky enough to grab a big chunk from some rich old goat years ago. She had started her stable with that and now could buy her own pets.

"Wait till she gets a load of Jonathan here," Lize said.

"Me?" Jonathan was startled.

Darcy clapped her hands and studied him with fresh appreciation.

"Wow," she said. "I never thought of that."

"She'll buy him a box of paints just as an excuse to get her mitts on him too," Lize predicted. "I shouldn't be surprised if she doesn't line him up as a Hugow replacement."

"Wow," Darcy said.

"That's the Bender bitch for you," Lize said. "One of these days we'll come down here and find no pigskin briefcase, no electric razor, no tan raincoat on the hook, no Jonathan, just Cassie Bender's Lincoln streaking up the avenue."

"I'll bet he'd go, too," accused Darcy.

Jonathan wondered wistfully if his ignorance of painting would prevent him from meeting this predatory temptress, but he thanked his friends and said nothing could persuade him to leave his new home.

More important than the finding of a home with experienced guardians was the adoption of The Golden Spur as Jonathan's club. Earl Turner, the world traveler and personal friend of the great Harshawe, was responsible for this move. Before you looked for a job or a home or a girl, Earl instructed Jonathan, you must establish your bar base in a new city, just as you would choose a fraternity on entering a university. Look them all over carefully, he counseled, every bar people mentioned in the Village area—Minetta Tavern, White Horse Inn, San Remo, Leroy, Jumble Shop—all offering their special brands of social security. Compare their advantages and disadvantages. Is this a tourist trap, a "Left Coast" hangout, or is it on the Bird Circuit, a meeting place for queers? Once you've made your choice, you conduct your social and business life there, since your home, mate, and job are bound to switch constantly. Make the owner or bartender your friend, use the place as a mailing and phone address, make your appointments there. Note the hours best suited for confidential talks there, the time for crashing a big party, the days when the roast beef is fresh and when it is hash; learn which barflies to duck.

Even if The Golden Spur had not recommended itself to Jonathan because of his mother's association with it, he would have chosen it. There was, as Earl pointed out, a nice diversity in the patrons. There were the college-faculty types, superior of their kind, for had they been average they would be sucking up to their departmental chiefs over in the Faculty Club or angling for academic advancement and traveling fellowships in stuffier environments. They wouldn't care to be caught bending elbows with the Spur's wild artists. The Spur artists were all "modern" in that they were against the previous generation, though generations in art were not much longer than cat generations.

In season, these individuals flooded the bar Monday nights, flushed down in the preview champagne from the Upper East Side gallery openings, and on Friday nights from the show closings. The star of the occasion, at other times perhaps an inarticulate modest painter, then appeared with his brand-new claque, a tangle of patrons, dealers, and a change of blondes, himself now loud with triumph and ready to lick his weight in wildcats, which often turned out to be necessary. It's a madhouse, everyone cried joyously on these nights, a real madhouse, let's never go home.

Now that it was midsummer, the Spur's daytime character had a more tranquil aspect. Summer bachelors, whose absent wives disapproved of such places, strengthened themselves with a few scotches to face their shrouded rooms in the new luxury apartments nearby. Somber Adult Education students, in town to slurp up enough culture to nourish them through the long dry winter in some Midwest Endsville, sipped beer at the bar and dreamed of a wild Greenwich Village nymphomaniac who would oblige them to forget their careers. Young housewives in pants and sandals, hair in curlers under scarves, dropped in for a beer with their last-minute supermarket purchases and looked wistfully around for the no-good boy friends they'd given up to marry good providers. There were the old-timers, fixed in their own grooves of this drink on this stool at this bar at this time every day, year in, year out, so that they never heeded the changes in patrons from touts and bookies to little-theater people to neighborhood factory- and shop-workers, to whatever there was now.

Since Jonathan had accepted the Spur as the hub of New York life, it was only fitting he should invite Miss Claire Van Orphen to meet him there. It struck him as a favorable omen that chance had made him spend his first night in New York in the Hotel De Long, under the very roof of his mother's old patron. He read encouraging warmth in the note hinting that her memories of his mother were pleasant.

"Claire Van Orphen? Never heard of her," said his literary monitor, Earl Turner. Seeing Jonathan's face fall, Earl added kindly, "She must have been a best-seller in her day, that's why I never knew her."

Claire had dressed herself with care in the rose-spangled chiffon from a 1924 seasonal sale in a Paris boutique. In the hall mirror she saw that the dipping hemline might date it, and she evened it with gold safety pins. In a softly lit tearoom she would pass nicely, she thought, and the beige silk cape would cover any defects.

As with many writers, Claire's powers of observation worked only in unfamiliar territory, being comfortably off-duty on her daily beat. She had passed the Village Barn, Nick's, Ricky's, and a dozen other spots regularly for years without seeing them. The nasty little man at her hotel desk looked surprised when she asked how to get to the Golden Spur, and she thought it must be due to something racy about the place.

"It's right under your nose, Miss Van Orphen," he said with his customary sneer. "Right around the corner next to the auction gallery."

Even so, she would have walked past the place if a young man had not stepped out and called her by name. She could not help smiling back at the engaging face.

"You must be Jonathan," she said. "How did you know me?"

Jonathan could not answer that the regal attire was exactly the costume he expected of a lady author, so he stammered that his mother had described her often. This gave Claire a twinge of uneasiness, for she had so little to tell him about his mother. She could not bear to disappoint him. What a dear young man he was too, with his twinkling brown eyes and quick smile that radiated a warmth uncommon in the world today! The gallant way he urged her to keep on her cape because of the air-conditioning inside moved her almost to tears, so long had it been since any man had been so solicitous.

Gratefully Claire vowed to herself she would do anything to help this dear lad get whatever it was he wanted. He was surprised that she had never been in the Golden Spur, since it was, he understood, the cultural center of Village life. Claire hastily assured him that she had, of course, often heard its praises sung and was happy to be there. She was flattered that he took for granted she would have a cocktail instead of sherry, and when he instructed the waiter to make her Manhattan dry, not sweet, she did not confess that the sweetness and the maraschino were what she liked best in a Manhattan. What a fascinating life she must have led among all the famous characters in this neighborhood, Jonathan said, and Claire nodded and smiled mysteriously into her glass, happier than she had been in years.

But nagging away behind her immense enjoyment of this adventure was the worrisome problem of digging up memories of his mother. For the life of her, Claire could not conjure up any but the palest picture of Connie Birch. A soft voice, yes, a very nice voice, unobtrusive, almost apologetic, she remembered, though the accent was cornbelt with that little bleat over the short "a"s and the resolute pounce on every "r." She must have had something special, though, Claire reflected, or else her mate had had, to produce such a remarkable offspring. It pained Claire to think of how obtuse she had been all her life, never seeing the true nature of those close to her—her own sister, for instance!—and now this boy's mother; granted she had been too much the lady to stare, polite blindness was surely no virtue in a writer. How nice it would be if she could produce a few intimate little vignettes to justify the young man's seeking her out!

Already Claire tingled with possessive pride in him, beaming when other patrons spoke to him, wishing fervently that sister Bea, who had many young men, could witness the way he introduced her, as if she were Edith Wharton. "This is Miss Van Orphen, Claire Van Orphen!"

She laughed at the story of his night in her hotel and of discussing with a porter the funeral of the newly deceased major he'd never known. Claire declared this to be a most amazing coincidence, for this would have been the funeral of her good friend Major Wedburn. Glad to gain time before she must answer questions about his mother, Claire chattered eagerly about the late Major Wedburn, such a distinguished military historian, pompous perhaps, but most impressive. He used to invite her every year to Ladies' Day at the Salmagundi Club and then was so amusingly discreet lest someone gossip about their residing in the same hotel! They exchanged manuscripts for criticism, which was nice, and had other professional contacts.

"Why, Major Wedburn was the one who sent Constance Birch to me for typing!" Claire suddenly interrupted herself, overjoyed to have found one small nugget, and in her relief invented words of admiration the Major had used at the time. Claire was ordinarily truthful, but she did want to prolong the interview. She made a bold decision to invent other little tidbits as coming from the late Major.

"That's the sort of thing I need," Jonathan said gratefully. "Sometimes I have only first names to go by; then my Aunt Tessie remembered others. When a name would be in the news, Mother would tell Aunt Tessie all about meeting the person with you or at your big parties."

Big parties indeed, Claire reflected wistfully, remembering the episode at the Brevoort, almost certain that it was the last time in nearly thirty years that she had entertained over six people at once.

"For instance, she wrote of meeting Alvine Harshawe with you," Jonathan went on, producing his little red notebook, "and there was a famous lawyer, George, who often called on you."

"George?" Claire repeated, her face reddening with embarrassment, for this nice boy's mother had certainly done some exaggerating, to say the least! Alvine Harshawe indeed! Claire found his work much too gamy for her own taste, but she would have been glad to claim his acquaintance. She could not deny knowing the man without calling the lad's mother a liar, so she improvised. "She must have met Harshawe when she was researching for the Major, who knew him well"—it *could* be!—"and the lawyer would have been George Terrence. George handled our family affairs for years."

She saw that the young man had his pencil poised alertly above the little red notebook.

"Of course I don't see much of him nowadays, because we haven't much for him to do any more," Claire said a little uneasily. "And he and Hazel have the place in Stamford, so—"

"Of course that is the George Mother meant!" Jonathan exclaimed. "Terrence, eh? All I knew was that the girl Mother lived with on Horatio Street was named Hazel and that later she married this lawyer named George. How do you spell Terrence?"

Claire spelled it out mechanically for him and gave the address outside Stamford where the Terrences lived. She was thoroughly baffled now. She could have sworn that

Connie Birch had never been around during George's calls. But on the other hand she had not realized that the girl George married had been Connie's roommate. It was hard to believe that stuffy, ambitious Hazel had ever shared bohemian quarters with a colorless little nobody from the Midwest. But, if Connie had lived with Hazel, of course she had met George.

"I will write and ask them for an appointment," Jonathan said, pocketing his book again, beaming. "They're sure to have a lot to tell me."

Thinking of the Terrences' rigidly circumscribed social life of the past fifteen years, Claire wondered, and felt a little sad.

"I'll write them a note too," she said firmly. No matter how stuffy they had become, they surely could not fail to be charmed by Jonathan. Goodness knows, anyone as anxious to play the social game as Hazel Terrence could always use an extra young man, and George had always set himself up as such a liberal (carefully cushioned on a solid old capitalist tradition), which certainly meant being kind to strangers, didn't it? Claire thought, a little ruefully, that, although she was too proud to ask the Terrences any favor for herself, she had no compunction about asking for the young stranger. There was so little she could do for him; she had not really earned a second Manhattan. To deserve it she began improvising compliments that had been paid to Constance Birch. The Major, for instance, often mentioned the girl's outstanding ladylike qualities in a crass age. The Terrences—yes, it must have been the Terrences—often had remarked that little Miss Birch was too fine, her standards too high, for the vulgar struggle of the big city. Indeed—here the dryness of the second Manhattan must have affected Claire's ordinary prudence—she believed it was George Terrence himself who had advised the sweet child to go back to the simple decencies of her Ohio home. " 'Go and marry the boy back home,' " she improvised. "Those were his very words."

"Mr. Terrence advised that!" exclaimed Jonathan. "Then perhaps he was the one—"

"Unless it was Harshawe," Claire amended. "Or someone in the poetry group she attended, I remember—she was so different from the modern girl of the time, you see; we'd gone from the flapper to much worse, and such a plain old-fashioned girl stood out. I do hope you appreciate what a genuine lady your mother was, Jonathan, one of those shy, innocent little creatures everyone tries to protect. We all missed her when she went home, but we were glad for her sake. As George Terrence said—"

She paused, at a loss for more plausible remarks from George, but Jonathan took no notice, for he was consulting his precious notebook.

"Here's what my mother wrote about her friend Hazel's fiancé," he reported. " 'George is practically certain to be a great lawyer, another Clarence Darrow.' "

What a desperately romantic young woman the boy's mother must have been, Claire thought.

"Dear me, George Terrence was much too modest to make a trial lawyer," she corrected him gently. "Very brilliant on briefs, of course, and highly regarded, but—"

"He might be the man!" Jonathan said, pursuing his own thoughts. "He didn't marry Hazel till Mother had gone back to Ohio and gotten married herself, don't you see?"

"No, I don't see," Claire confessed.

"All I have to go on is the fact that my real father was a very famous man," Jonathan explained.

"Mr. Jaimison?"

"No, I mean my *real* father, the man my mother was in love with before she married," Jonathan said. "He might have been a famous lawyer, mightn't he? And George Terrence, as you say, took a great interest in her?"

Claire's mouth fell open.

"You can't mean what you're saying." She choked. "Not that quiet, sweet little girl. My dear boy, you're not going to ask George a question like that!"

"I shan't ask him directly," Jonathan reassured her. "I just want to meet him and find out what he can tell me about my mother, and I can judge from that. If it turns out I'm the heir to a great legal mind, I will know what to expect of myself."

She mustn't spoil this beautiful friendship by behaving in a panicky, spinsterish way, Claire told herself. Be cool, be debonair.

"Of course," she said quite casually. "I felt better about my literary potentialities when I learned a great-grandfather had once published a novel. It's like money in the bank, knowing there are certain genes you can count on."

"I knew you'd understand," Jonathan said. "All my life before this I didn't think I could count on anything but the Jaimison pigheadedness. Now I can be anything. For instance, if my father was a great writer—"

"Like Alvine Harshawe." Claire smiled.

Jonathan blushed, but defensively admitted that it was a possibility. He had taken to keeping an extensive literary journal himself, he said, writing at his espresso shop, which, so far, was pleasantly ignored by the cake-and-ice-and-coffee set.

"I had no idea young people nowadays took anything

but martinis," Claire said. "Do they really go for ice cream?"

"Sometimes they're on 'tea,' or else heroin," Jonathan said. "They keep off alcohol because they don't want to mix their kicks, you see."

Claire nodded approvingly.

"Very sensible, I'm sure," she said, taking a dainty sip of her Manhattan. "I've always felt one gets more out of life by enjoying one pleasure at a time."

There, now! she thought, proud of herself for having smothered her virtuous instinct to warn Jonathan against dope fiends, drunkards, and harlots. But the pitfalls were everywhere, waiting to trip her into some horrid puritanism that would limit the youth's confidence. To be on safe ground she asked about his room and if he found New York lonely.

"I couldn't ever be lonely in this town," Jonathan said dreamily, "even if I lived all alone instead of with these two girls."

"It must be jolly," Claire said, catching her breath. "I mean it must be so much more interesting with two than just living with one."

She was steeled to babble on about the sheer common sense of triangular living or multiple-mistressing, but was saved by a man beckoning to Jonathan from the telephone corner. While Jonathan was gone to confer with his friend, Claire looked about her, filled with the joy of being brought —perhaps shocked—back to life. The hunting prints and racehorse pictures on the wall struck her as masterpieces of art, the flyblown lamps perfect period gems, the stables as booths a most original decorating caprice, and now Jonathan was bringing toward her the stranger with a little goatee and a plaid shirt exactly like Jonathan's.

"This is Earl Turner, Miss Van Orphen," Jonathan said triumphantly, as if he had finally brought the heads of two great nations together. "You're both writers so you must have lots to talk about. Earl tells me I have to go right over to see about a fire in my building—"

"It's all over now," Earl explained. "It's just that Hugow wants Jonathan to let him in and get out some canvases he left in there. Valuable paintings, that sort of thing."

"Earl will look after you," Jonathan assured her. "You've helped me so much, and I'll call you again next week."

He grasped her hand with a radiant, innocent smile, as if illegitimacy, opium-smoking, two mistresses, and a house on fire were all on the good ship *Lollipop*. He dropped a bill on the check. Claire sat back as he hurried out, and his friend in the beret slid into the seat. Claire saw that the friend was a man over fifty, and she knew from experience that there's nothing irks a man over fifty more than being stuck with a woman his own age. Earl's glum expression agreed with her guess.

"It's an interesting little place," she said politely. "Such interesting types, don't you think? Those artists at the bar, for instance."

"They're waiting for their girls to come in from work and buy them a drink," Earl said morosely.

"Interesting!" Claire said firmly, but she felt weak and deserted and knew she should leave.

She could feel the fine self-confidence built up by young Jonathan melting away under the bored expression of her companion. He scarcely glanced at her, classifying her no doubt as a dull family friend of Jonathan's, entitled to the respect due her age but nothing more. He looked beyond her to greet new and young arrivals, drumming on the table as he smoked. Stubbornly Claire took her time finishing her drink.

The Spur was filling up with the pre-dinner crowd now, all races and all costumes, bohemian, white-collar, beach, collegiate, Hollywood. There was an undercurrent of muffled anticipation in the air, and the special timbre in the murmuring voices, the secret knowledge in the gurgling laughter, the searching look in the eyes of everyone seemed faintly sinister to Claire. The revelation of what Jonathan Jaimison was seeking here, his sudden departure, and the letdown after her initial excitement left her frightened and unnerved, as if all this were building up to the real opera, in which there was no part for her. It annoyed her that her hands shook as she drew on her rose-colored gloves and that Jonathan's friend should be watching her now.

"Pretty rough crowd for you, I'm afraid," he said.

"Not for me, Mr. Turner," Claire said with dignity. "I find the people most attractive. The blond girl you bowed to looks fascinating."

"Fascinating indeed!" Earl said. "She just got back from Greece, where she's been living on money she got from selling her baby. Couldn't afford an abortion, you see, so she went ahead and made a nice deal out of the kid, if you call that fascinating. Now she'll make a career out of breeding."

He wanted to shock her, Claire knew, and steeled herself.

"Enterprising, then," she said lightly. "Girls today are so clever. I suppose that nice boy—or is it a girl?—with her is on 'tea.' "

Earl snorted derisively.

"He never made that kind of money," he said. "He's lucky to scrape enough together for Dexedrine and beer."

"A pity," Claire said wildly. "He looks so intelligent, you'd think his habits would be more original."

Earl was looking at her now with puzzled amusement.

"You think he ought to live up to that long hair?" he said.

"Why not?" Claire asked and rose to go. She would be the stately literary figure that Jonathan assumed her to be, she told herself defiantly, not the timid spinster. "At least he looks an artist."

"Trust the buckeye boys to play the tourist's dream," Earl said. "Like the drugstore cowboys."

Maybe he wasn't being deliberately rude, Claire decided.

"I'm sorry I don't know your work, Mr. Turner," she said graciously. "Jonathan said you were a writer. I'm sure I've heard the name."

"Probably from the time when I edited *The Sphere,*" Earl said, mollified. "Of course that was some time ago."

Some time ago indeed, Claire thought, for the magazine had come and gone a good twenty years ago.

"Such a brilliant magazine!" Claire said. "I was so sorry to see it fail. Well, good night, Mr. Turner."

"Wait," said Earl. "I'll walk you to your hotel."

The polite gesture seemed to surprise Mr. Turner himself as much as it did Claire, but it had been a long time since anyone had remembered *The Sphere.*

"No reason you should know my work," he said as they walked up Fifth Avenue. "I haven't published anything recently."

"Nor have I, Mr. Turner," Claire admitted. "There doesn't seem to be the demand, do you think?"

"Certainly not for me." Earl gave a mirthless laugh. "Frankly I never got back in my own stride after rewriting all the world's leading geniuses for *Sphere.*"

"I'm sure you're much too modest," said Claire. "I'm afraid you're being too severe an editor of your own work."

"Well, in a way," Earl conceded, and was moved to tell Claire of his foolish perfectionism that made his stories too good to sell or for that matter even to write. They stood in the lobby of the Hotel De Long, eagerly chattering of literary matters, ignoring the avid eyes and ears of the elderly witches and aging beaux propped along the wall sofas.

"You should make them into a book," Claire advised. "I must remember the name of that editor at Dutton's for you."

The lobby heads swiveled unanimously as the two literary friends moved toward the elevator and were lost, alas. In Miss Van Orphen's tiny room (she was glad her little plants were blooming so nicely) they continued their discussion with great animation over glasses of instant coffee laced with a few drops of Christmas brandy. When Claire reported the delicious recipe the Planet's soda jerk had for hangover ("I just don't go there any more"), Earl declared she had the makings of a perfect little vignette for *The New Yorker.*

Claire promised that she would certainly try to write it, for it had been a long time since she had had any editorial inspiration. Earl acknowledged that it had been a rare pleasure for him, too, to exchange ideas with a fellow writer. They should meet often. As a first step he would call on her this very week and give her his constructive suggestions on whatever manuscripts she had on hand.

A wonderful day, Claire thought, and all due to the invasion of New York by young Jonathan Jaimison. In her gratitude she wrote a note before she went to bed to the George Terrences, urging them to see Connie Birch's son by all means. And then—because it was cruel to have a red-letter day and no one to share it—she had to write a note to sister Bea, imploring her to name a day for lunch, for it had been weeks, months. You just had to have someone, Claire told herself, tears in her eyes. Even when you knew they were bored with you, as Bea was with her, you had to have someone to *tell*.

5

HUGOW SAT on the cracked stone stoop of the brown tenement on East Tenth Street and watched the fire ceremonials going on across the street. He had been so interested in the black and gold medieval-looking firemen's uniforms, the loudspeaker directions from the chief, the beautiful red engines, and the hose snaking in and out of windows that it took a minute to penetrate that the fire was in his own building. It was a small fire, put out almost at once, but he had panicked, thinking of the canvases he had stored in the fourth-floor studio. He was shaken, too, with the evidence that his hunch to rush home had been justified.

Last night, for instance, he had been swigging Tom Collinses on the terrace of Cassie Bender's shore house four hundred miles away when he was suddenly smitten with a passionate, overwhelming hunger. And for what?

For hunger.

He wanted to throw up the whole scene, the fine yellow gin, the perfect studio Cassie had fixed for him, the successful authors and actors and art-lovers and Bennington girls —"the cream of the Cape," as Cassie said—their Good Conversation; Christ, how sick you could get of Good Conversation. "Good Talk." There was no such thing as Good Talk. Talk was Talk and worse than marijuana for getting you high and nowhere. Sure, he talked too much when he was drunk, but he had the sense to be ashamed afterward, ashamed for diluting the pure classic joy of drinking with the cheap vice of yakking. He had wanted to throw up the fine Cape Cod air, the beach, the crystalline sunshine, Cassie's smothering love, and the rooms full of intelligent appreciators, and get back to a slum full of overturned ashcans, Bowery bums sprawling over the doorstep, lousy barflies who insulted him, jerks, Eagle jerks, Cub jerks, people who hated him for himself alone and not just because he was doing all right. He wanted to get back to a studio that had no comforts, just light and nobody in it; he wanted a new girl, someone who didn't understand him and that he couldn't understand, so that they could run through each other fast with no dead vines clinging, as in most of his other affairs. He wanted to *want,* that was it, he wanted to see something far off floating up like a forever-lost kite out of all possible range, something to blind and dazzle him so he could work for it. He wanted dirt, limitless oceans of dirt, so he could have the intense need for clean, he wanted loneliness so he could suffer the old ache of yearning for human contact.

The urge was so overpowering that he had walked past the pretty girl waiting for him to bring her a drink, pushed through the little groups on the terrace, down the sunflower path through the vegetable garden, through the tangle of bayberry bushes down the hill to the highway, the martini glass still in his hand. A butcher's truck stopped for him and turned him over at a gas station to an oil truck headed for Brooklyn. Hugow had to fight carsickness all the way down, but it wasn't the riding or the bumps, it was being fed up with being fed. Fat-cat-sick, that's what it was. Death. He had to get back to the screaming panic of the city. He had to get back to his own Village, to the half-finished canvas he had deserted. He had to find again that green, the wonderful green, the true paint-green, the unearthly sea-bottom moon-green, not the lousy nature-green of trees and grass. He'd almost gotten it once, then Darcy bugged him and he bolted and left everything in the old Tenth Street studio. When he got down there finally and saw the fire, he knew the picture had been calling for him, calling for help, and that had scared him, reminding him once again —as if he needed to be told—that what came from his brush was his own blood.

He could have gotten there earlier, but he had waited to be sure Darcy wouldn't be around, so he could sneak out his canvases without a scene. The crowd collected for the fire had drifted away, the Chinese laundry in the basement had been flooded, Chu Chu was out front, screaming curses at the cops and firemen.

Hugow had rushed up the steps, was putting his key in the lock when a cop's hand closed over it.

"What's your name, bud?"

"Hugow. I want to get into my studio."

"Hugo, eh. So you got a studio here. Funny there ain't no Hugo name here."

"It's the fourth floor rear."

"Fourth floor rear, eh. 'Jaimison, Trent, Britten. Fourth Floor Rear.' No Hugo. Let's have that key, bud, before you go making trouble for yourself."

You can't argue with cops—not when there was a chance of Darcy's popping along to make things worse. Even old Chu's recognizing him did no good, since he shook his fist at Hugow in his crazy-mad way, shouting that those evil artists upstairs must have set the fire in his honest laundry, throwing their turpentine rags around. Hugow had to withdraw, finally having extracted the information that the whole place was under guard until there was no chance that the original blaze would spread upstairs. No one would be admitted without credentials. After a moment's puzzled speculation on what had brought Lize and Darcy under the same roof, Hugow turned his attention to the third name. If he could get hold of this Jaimison he might be able to get in. Somebody at The Golden Spur would know who was staying here with the girls, Hugow was sure—the bartender, Earl Turner, or Lew Schaffer. He went to the candy store on the corner and phoned the Spur. Sure enough, Earl Turner was around and said the fellow Jaimison who was camping out with Lize and Darcy was right there. Earl promised to see that he came over to let Hugow get in and collect his stuff before the girls showed up.

"What goes on here anyway?" Hugow asked as an afterthought. "Is this a design for living?"

"Wasn't it always?" Earl answered.

It had been several weeks since Hugow had been in his old neighborhood, and he walked around Tompkins Square while he waited, dropping into the Czech bar for a beer, buying a bagel at a Polish delicatessen, and thinking that for all its many nationalities and mixed customs it was a mean, thin-spirited, hostile neighborhood. That was the East Side, rich and poor, all the way up till you got to Yorkville. He'd spent three years in the Tenth Street studio and was glad to be out of it, glad he'd lined up a new place way over on the West Side near Houston. The lights coming on around Tompkins Square and the fading daylight gave a romantic glow to the old houses, the "fudge light" that made madonnas out of the fat old shrews yelling out windows for their children or dragging them along the streets with a whack and a cuff; it made kindly peasants out of the suspicious, foxy merchants waiting in the doors of their shops to short-change any crippled blind man, especially if he was a brother. You could live on the East Side all your life and still be a stranger. It must be the Italians who warmed up the West Side, for they laughed and sang and loved their babies: they wore pink shirts and red dresses so their flying clotheslines were really glad rags. The East Side was too near Vermont, maybe that did it, Hugow mused, happy with this fancy, Vermont, where the country itself was always trying to throw off the people, like a beautiful wild horse that will never let itself be conquered by inferior riders.

The bums were the only good thing about the East Side, Hugow thought, getting back to the stoop opposite his studio. At this time of day they had drifted down to the Bowery missions for their handouts, but they'd be back later with their half-pints of muscatel as nightcap before bedding down in the entry halls or stoops along here. The Third Avenue El used to hold them in as much by its safe shadows as by its posts stretched out like a lifeline all the way down to Foley Square. When the structure was torn down, leaving the avenue shorn of shade, bald as the Siberian steppes, the bewildered bums spilled all over to the side streets, rootless and compassless, churning east and west, river to river, still calling the Bowery home, but the Bowery was now an overblown matron without her stays. There was no home except other bums, bottles, empty doorways, a sunny stoop in winter, a shady one in summer. The Bowery was only in the uncaged, prowling, alley-happy heart. Like mine, Hugow thought, always on the prowl for something to louse up his life.

He lit a cigarette and watched for the Jaimison man, wondering if he belonged to Lize or to Darcy. Either one would serve to get himself off the hook. It was a relief to be free of Cassie too, good old Cassie who was always rescuing him and had sustained him during his last work. Funny how a woman and a picture got finished for him at the same time. Funny that, whoever she was, she could never reach him again, her warmth could do nothing for his chill, the empty chill of finished work, the chill that he knew was a piece of dying. For this he could only be revived by a fresh love, simple and childish, or worldly and artificial, or perhaps a wild, nettlesome, raging affair of action, drama, brutal encounters without affection or any plane of communication. No one could say he was unfaithful. The word unfaithful was not for him, nor the word promiscuous, nor the words irresponsible or ungrateful, because a man who has never been chaste, faithful, responsible, or grateful could not become *not* those things. Say he was a person of prodigious needs, using everything and everybody as his personal fuel. Only when he was drained, between pictures as he was now, did he become a human being, simple, lonesome, and sweet, making the friends and loves then that would feed him later.

The blond young man hurrying down the street must be Jaimison, Hugow surmised, and went to meet him. Having heard of the great Hugow, Jonathan was surprised to find him no Viking Apollo with a thundering baritone voice, but a man shorter than himself, with a hesitant apologetic drawl, an indolent way of walking that partly concealed a slight limp, long grayish-brown hair that he shook out of his eyes impatiently, a pointed sort of face, fawnlike when he focused his intense gray eyes on you, through you, perhaps beyond you. He was in slacks and sport shirt and needed a shave. After the brief mutual examination, Hugow took Jonathan's arm.

"So you're the replacement," he said. "You paint?"

"I'd like to," Jonathan said politely.

"Either you paint or you don't paint," Hugow said. "Did Earl tell you what I wanted? I've got to get the rest of my pictures out of the place before Darcy shows up and gives me a bad time. The cop thinks I'm a burglar, so you have to sponsor me."

At the entrance there were now only two cops and Chu, who was angrily boarding up his broken window. Jonathan unlocked the door, and they climbed the three flights to the top floor. Jonathan had gotten used to coming home to a hurricane of feminine disorder, realizing after only a few weeks' training that the trim perfection of two young ladies' working appearance could not be achieved without a wild trail of bath towels, shoes, powder, bobby pins, scattered hose, coffee cups, tousled pajamas, empty milk bottles, and basins of soaking lingerie. Now he felt embarrassed and scooped up a tangle of wet nylons.

"I usually throw everything in a closet," he mumbled apologetically. "I'm the last one out in the morning."

Hugow took a look around the room and threw up his hands.

"They've taken over, I see that much. This is what women mean when they say they want to look after you. How do you manage to fit into this picture?"

"We're in and out at different times," Jonathan said. "We don't interfere with each other."

Hugow went to the kitchen. The dishes from a spaghetti supper of two nights before were in the rusty sink, and a half-gallon chianti bottle with an inch of red in the bottom stood on the floor. Hugow opened the closet door, where a shredded broom and a balding floor mop leaned. He reached up to yank a pulley which brought down from mysterious heights a clutch of canvases strapped together. He handed them to Jonathan. He reached up again and triumphantly fetched down a bottle labeled BURKE SPRINGS BOURBON. He noted that it was almost full and nodded with satisfaction.

"First thing you have to learn about a dame is whether to hide your bottles high or low. You have to hide them high for Darcy," he explained. "I'm surprised Lize didn't spot it, though."

He took a drink from the bottle and handed it to Jonathan.

"Lize and Darcy! How do you like that!" He laughed. "Thank God it's you in the middle and not me this time. I guess I owe you something for taking Darcy off my neck. I suppose they're both sore at me now."

"They blame it all on Cassie Bender," Jonathan said.

Hugow frowned.

"I forgot about Cassie," he said. "She's the one that's cursing me out right now, I suppose. I should have sent a wire or phoned collect or— Oh hell, I can't be apologizing to Cassie all my life, can I?"

"Not for the same thing, I guess," Jonathan said, and this seemed to please Hugow for he slapped him on the back approvingly.

"Too bad you aren't an artist or you could take on Cassie too," he said. "Never mind, you've got your work cut out with Lize and Darcy. How'd you happen to get trapped?"

"We thought it would save money," Jonathan said.

"More power to you, man," Hugow said skeptically. "Maybe you can handle those things better than I can. Let's get a move on before they can jump on us. You and I can cart my stuff over to my new studio. They don't know where this one is, that's a break.'

Hugow opened a closet door, peered under the cot, took a last look around the studio, found a tin can of evident value to him, which he handed to Jonathan with the whisky bottle.

"You take these. Let's go."

There seemed no question that Jonathan would come with him, and Jonathan thrust the bottle into his pocket and followed down the stairs. A bearded old bum, pockets overflowing with rags, grinned and pointed urgently at Jonathan's bottle.

"I'm a Harvard man too," he said. "How about it?"

"Get your own brand," Hugow said, flipping a coin at him.

They walked down First Avenue, down toward Houston, where they would get the Houston Street crosstown, Hugow said, which would let them off near his new studio. He was always so glad to get back to Manhattan, he said, that he started walking as soon as he hit the beloved pavements so as to get the empty, clean smell of the country sunshine out of his system and let God's own dirt back in. He stopped at a pushcart and bought a bag of plum tomatoes. In the shadow of a boarded-up tenement building a group of derelicts were quarreling quietly over a bottle. The light from a basement bar next door shone upon a huge figure of a man blocking the street.

"Doesn't anybody want to buy my blood?" he was saying in a tired singsong. "I have very good blood. Doctors give a hundred dollars a pint for my blood. Don't somebody want to buy?"

Outlined by the traffic lights and lamps above and below, he stood motionless, like a wax display figure on sale, one great hand uplifted, commanding Hugow and Jonathan to stop. He had no dangling rags and bags as the other bums did, but his outfit had a mission-neat, mothball, decayed shabbiness, vest, jacket, pants, shoes in the same varying shades of ghoul green as his skin, and the wide-brimmed moldy old Quaker hat. The large bulbous nose, the greenish-gray hair and lashes, the gray-white eyes, all had the deathly color of leather buried for centuries in Davy Jones's locker, and the neatly rolled cloth bundle under his arm seemed a mariner's kit. His complexion was the curious paste of Dutch blondes mixed with blue-black native, with no gold or glow of tropic sun coming through. He must have been drowned a long time, Jonathan thought.

"Do you wish to buy my blood, sir?" the man murmured.

He was still standing there, motionless, as Hugow and Jonathan got on the bus. Hugow looked back out the window, and Jonathan saw that he was smiling radiantly.

"That's what I've been needing," he said. "God, how I love New York. Did you see that green?"

"Mushroom color, I thought," Jonathan said.

Hugow shook his head dreamily.

"The green I love, the green that is everything but green," he murmured. "I should have bought his blood just to see what makes it."

Jonathan said nothing, afraid he might strike the wrong note and cut off this beautiful new friendship at its very birth. This rare creature, this great god who seemed to be the heart of The Golden Spur circle, had taken him in as one of his own kind without hesitation. Jonathan felt as if a wild bird had flown to his shoulder and one false move would frighten it away. Now *he,* like the others, would be one of Hugow's willing slaves. He forgot about Claire Van

Orphen left in the Spur, he forgot what chores were expected of him at the café, he was in the beatific glow of the master's favor.

At Varick Street, Hugow motioned to him to pick up the canvases and get off the bus. They turned a corner and stopped in an alleyway behind an old wooden warehouse. Hugow unlocked the door and they entered a pitch-black hall and fumbled their way up rickety wooden stairs. At the third flight a skylight let in enough light to show the way, and through a tiny half-moon window Jonathan glimpsed the twinkling lights of the North River craft and the Jersey shore beyond. The loose boards clattered underfoot, and a piece of stair rail broke off in his hand and rattled down the steps.

"I figured if I got a place crummy enough, I could keep out dames for a while," Hugow explained. "A guy's got to have a little time to himself, right?"

"They couldn't find their way here," Jonathan said.

"Women find their way any place," Hugow said. "They know where you're going before you've even made up your mind. But I'm safe for a while here, thank God."

Jonathan lit matches while Hugow fiddled with the latch. It turned out a key wasn't necessary, for the door fell open at the first push.

"Damn those kids," said Hugow.

But the burglar was a female and seemed to have made herself at home.

The girl was sprawled over a battered Victorian sofa, her long legs in black leotards flung up over the back. A pair of candle stumps dripped into saucers on an empty packing crate beside her and cast a glow over a dark face, sullen in sleep, with a tangle of thick black hair falling over it. She opened her eyes as they entered the loft.

"Iris!" Hugow exclaimed. "How'd you find it?"

"Asked around the bars," she said. "Mad?"

"Tickled to death. How'd you get in?"

"Beer opener." She sat up, yawning, and looked at them defiantly. "No use getting excited just because you forgot to invite me. I can't get into my room because the sublet is still there."

"What about your tryout?" he asked.

"Flopped. I flopped, especially. I was run out of Westport."

"So hello," Hugow said and tousled her hair.

She stood up and stretched herself lazily, like an enormous cat. She was taller than Hugow. Jonathan could not take his eyes away from her, fascinated by the tawny sheen of her skin and by her voice, which was rough and dark, with breaks in it like a boy's.

"There's nothing in the icebox but ice," she said.

"Ice is all we need," Hugow said, taking the bottle out of Jonathan's pocket. "This is my best friend. Better ask him his name."

"Jonathan Jaimison," said Jonathan.

"You're a writer?"

"Oh yes," Jonathan said, pleased. "Yes, I think so."

"Isn't this place great, Jonathan, boy?" Hugow demanded. "Look at that window. Look at those rafters."

Jonathan nodded but he could not take his eyes off the girl. Why, this was love at first sight, he thought. It had something to do with Hugow's adopting him and the man selling blood and the half-moon glimpse of river lights and the way the dark girl in the candlelight lit up the room with her voice and flash of laughter. Did she know it was love too? She was staring at him with her thick black brows drawn together.

"You look like someone," she said.

"Who?" Jonathan asked eagerly.

"Maybe somebody in the news," she said. "I'll remember later."

Hugow found jelly glasses and set them out with a tray of ice and his bag of plum tomatoes. He pulled out a lopsided brown leather chair, into which he sank happily.

"Beautiful!" he said, and Jonathan agreed enthusiastically. It was a barn of a place, really, floored only in the middle, with the rafters spreading out under low eaves at both sides. Etched on the big window, the West Side highway strung red and green lights into a dark yonder. A folded cot leaned against the long plank table.

"Wonderful to be back." Hugow sighed, fondling his drink. "Cozy nest, fine drink, fine old friends. Then Iris! My hunches are always good. I got the message about the fire in the studio and then the message that Iris was here. Amazing!"

"I knew if I had sent you a real message you would never show up," Iris said.

Hugow winked at Jonathan.

"Iris is a quick study," he said.

"You taught me," said Iris.

Jonathan looked from one to the other, feeling very much left out. They were a thing, no doubt about it. You could feel the current crackling between them, even though they were half the room's length apart and not looking at each other. He felt miserable and suffocated with love for both of them. If they were lovers, he should have the decency to clear out, but he couldn't bear to leave them, or the beautiful room furnished so sumptuously in shadows, distant lights, and unknown desires.

"Iris is going to be a great actress, Jonathan," Hugow said.

"I know it," Jonathan said sincerely. "You can tell."

"Can you really?" Iris asked eagerly, fixing her eyes on Jonathan. They were great dark eyes that seemed to drink in more darkness, brimming over with night, he thought, orphan eyes, deserted-wife eyes, slave eyes, beggar eyes. Even with her white teeth gleaming in a fleeting smile she seemed utterly dark, only reflecting outside color like the black river yonder. It was a relief to have Hugow break the spell.

"Iris is almost twenty-one, so she thinks she knows what the score is," Hugow said banteringly. "Three years in New York, what the hell? Wait till you're forty-five and doubt sets in."

"Hugow never has had any doubts," Iris said.

He should go now, Jonathan thought, forcing himself to move toward the door. Hugow jumped up and clutched his arm.

"Stick!" Hugow's lips formed the command.

Jonathan sat down again. Hugow was hungry and talked of going to either Ticino's or the Bocce place. Jonathan, mindful that he could get free cakes, sandwiches, and coffee at his place of employment, tentatively suggested the Then-and-Now. Iris said nothing for the simple reason that she had fallen asleep, her dark eyebrows tangled in a frown, but even with the eyes closed a deep black unhappiness clouded her face.

"Iris is my one good deed," Hugow confided. "I broke it up when I saw I was going to louse up her life for her."

"Where does she come from?" Jonathan asked.

Hugow shrugged.

"Middle West, or maybe upstate. Far enough away so she can live her own life. I picked her up when I did a backdrop for a little theater over The Golden Spur. She was in the cast and got some notice. I don't know whether it was because she can really act or because she looks so goddam tragic."

"I'm hungry," Iris said unexpectedly, then sighed. "But I am so tired."

It was agreed that Hugow would run around the corner and bring back pizzas and peperoni and more bourbon.

"You can look after Iris," he said. "Do you mind?"

Mind!

Now he was alone with Iris, here was his opportunity to register, but without Hugow he couldn't think of a word to say. Jonathan could scarcely breathe when she bent forward and put a hand impulsively on his.

"I'm so glad you stayed," she said in an intense whisper. "You see I just did something that scares me terribly and I've got to tell somebody—not Hugow—to make it go away. I mean I came so close to—well, please let me tell you and promise not to mention it again or tell Hugow."

Jonathan could nod at least.

"You see I had this wonderful part, and if the tryout was any good we were to come in to Broadway next month. But I was all wrong for it. Oh, I never dreamed I could be so bad! We flopped and it's my fault. So I got my sleeping pills and came here and—"

"You mean you were going to—" Jonathan choked.

"Please don't tell Hugow," she implored, clasping her hands together. "He's got guts and he thinks I have too.

But I just couldn't stand living if I thought I was no good as an actress. There's just nothing else in life for me."

"Not even—Hugow?" Jonathan ventured.

She smiled at his innocence.

"You mean because he was my first lover. But you see that was all mixed up with my first job in the theater where Hugow was the scene designer, and it was my first year in the Village, and he was my first famous man. Hugow stood for the whole picture, don't you see? That's the way a girl's mind works."

That was the way it must have been with his mother, Jonathan thought.

"Hugow was good for me," Iris acknowledged." I was flattered that the great man liked a kid like me. He thought I was older and when he found out I was just eighteen he panicked. We were shacked up in Rockland County, but he packed me up and sent me back to town. I was so embarrassed to be treated like a child after all. 'Marry some nice guy,' he said, can you imagine? 'Have some kids, live a nice normal life.' "

"Do they always say that?" Jonathan asked, surprised. "That's just what the man said to my mother."

"What man?"

What man, indeed?

"Something like that happened to my mother, that's all," he said. "At least you didn't listen to him. You stuck to your guns."

Forget about his mother, he advised himself sharply, think Iris, Iris, Iris.

"Oh, but do you know what I said to him? You won't believe me!" Iris covered her face with her hands at the memory. "I burst out crying, if you please, and said, 'But

I don't want a normal life. I don't want a nice guy. I just want you!' Oh, I was such a little stupid, Jonathan!"

How in the world could Hugow have resisted such charming naïveté? Jonathan marveled, wishing he had been on hand to console her.

"I thought my heart was broken. Honestly!" Iris's great sooty eyes begged him to forgive her childishness. "I must have been a pest, hanging around the Bender Gallery, phoning Cassie Bender to try to find him, lurking outside the Spur. Wasn't it too silly of me? As if he was Gregory Peck! Not that Hugow isn't a dear, but really!"

"I'm glad you're over it," Jonathan said sincerely.

She flashed him a sad, grateful smile.

"I am too. As soon as I got a job touring in a Chekhov revival I forgot him like that! Awful of me, wasn't it?"

But she was here tonight, Jonathan reflected.

"It might start up again," he suggested.

"You don't know me, Jonathan." She shook her head firmly. "I've grown up. When I close a door I really close it."

He was very pleased to hear this. That was exactly the way he was himself, he said.

"I'm fond of Hugow still," Iris granted. "After all, I admire him as an artist. And we still can laugh over how crazy I was. And I wouldn't hurt him for anything in the world."

"Certainly not," Jonathan said, elated by the faint warning and promise in her voice. "But what about the sleeping pills? Would you have gone through with it?"

"If you hadn't come in?" Iris shook her cloudy hair and considered for an intense moment. "I don't know, Jonathan, I really don't know myself. Maybe if I hadn't fallen asleep first. Then when you said you could tell I would be a great actress I wanted to live, because you made me believe in myself again."

Jonathan glowed with happiness. He had saved this lovely girl without even knowing he was doing so. She was leaning toward him, and he could not keep from kissing her tempestuously. He kissed the tiny mole that finished off the corner of her mouth like a beauty patch, and he looked with delight at the slow smile that transfigured her dark face with light.

"Do you know something, Jonathan?" No, he thought, utterly bemused by the way she murmured his name. "I knew something about you too, the instant we met. I knew you were going to be somebody different and really great. Like me. I could tell."

"You could?"

"I could tell, Jonathan."

It must be the real thing with her as it was with him. But he wouldn't want to hurt Hugow, his new friend. He heard his step on the stairs and went to the door with one of the candles to light the way.

Hugow beckoned him out to the hall and handed him some packages.

"Beer for breakfast too," he said. "Stick around till I get rid of the kid. She's a sweet kid and hasn't many pals, but I don't want to start this up again, you know how it is. Don't want to hurt her, but—"

"She oughtn't to be alone," Jonathan said cautiously. "I shouldn't tell you, but she's got some sleeping pills—"

He was surprised at Hugow's mocking retort.

"Pay no mind to that sleeping-pill bit. She's stagestruck, don't forget. There's always got to be an act."

Unsympathetic, Jonathan thought, but that would make

his own sympathy more welcome to her. Iris made no move to play hostess but lay back regally on the couch, accepting cigarettes and drinks. Jonathan was happier than he'd ever been in his life, he thought, knowing she liked him and that Hugow wanted him there. He suggested warily taking Iris off Hugow's hands by inviting her to the Then-and-Now for a café Saigon.

"Iris thinks that espresso coffee tastes like wet blotters," Hugow said. "You fix us some highballs instead, Jonny-boy."

"Jonny-boy"—just what his mother and Aunt Tessie called him.

Jonathan went into the kitchen, glad to be useful in so many ways. He wondered how he could go about getting Iris to himself, since Hugow had been firm about not wanting her there. Each had made it clear that the last thing they wanted was to reopen their affair. Pondering how to handle the situation, he brought the ice back into the room in time to surprise the two friends locked in a passionate embrace. They sprang apart guiltily, snatching for cigarettes; Hugow lighted them both busily from a candle.

Jonathan stopped in his tracks, baffled. Even though they didn't want to hurt each other—

"I've got the ice," he mumbled idiotically. Then, as neither spoke, he hurried on. "It's a good icebox. Makes a lot, so you don't need to worry about running out of ice. Lots better than the old one over on Tenth Street."

"That so?" said Hugow. He was examining his cigarette intently. So was Iris. They didn't look at him, and he tried not to look at them. He dropped the ice tray on the sofa and backed toward the door.

"I've got to be running along," he said and went on explaining, as if any explaining was needed. "I've got to go to the espresso, see, then it's a long way over to East Tenth—"

"Sure you don't want to stay here?" Hugow murmured absently.

"Couldn't possibly," Jonathan babbled, burning with embarrassment. "Lize and Darcy expecting me, see, and I—see, I wouldn't want to hurt them."

He was out of the door, stumbling down the stairs, paying no mind to the glint of the river lights through the half-moon window, muttering, "Wouldn't want to hurt Lize and Darcy, see, can't go round hurting people. . . ."

Wait till he found out who he was, he thought, and could stand up to any situation. Iris would discover that he was indeed Somebody. A legal wizard, maybe, he thought wildly, if he was the child of George Terrence. A real writer, as big as Hugow in another way, if his father proved to be Alvine Harshawe. He thought of the pile of Harshawe published works in the drawer of his desk at the café, works he was reading carefully in the hope of finding some veiled allusion to his mother or a plausible connection with her life. He thought of the journal he had always kept, as people do who have no one they trust to understand them. Tonight he would write a sardonic bit about Iris and the folly of sudden love.

Jonathan walked hurriedly toward the shop, across Carmine Street, still smarting at being an unwanted third. He was being properly punished for losing sight of his true quest, that was it. Tomorrow he would confer with Earl Turner as to an interview with Harshawe. Miss Van Orphen was arranging a visit with the George Terrences for him too. Before he dared to fall in love he must find his guiding star.

6

AT FIRST Earl Turner showed only a pessimistic interest in Jonathan's attempts to get a response from Alvine Harshawe.

"That guy wouldn't give five minutes to his own mother if she wasn't photogenic," he said. "Maybe he's in Hollywood, or China. You wrote him at his agent's and at the Cape Cod address and at the town house. Nothing much you can do now."

"The *Times* said Zanuck was coming to New York expressly to see him about their picture," Jonathan said.

This was news to Earl, and apparently very interesting, for he meditated in silence for some time.

"You leave this to me," he said finally. "If Harshawe's in town I'll go see him personally and fix it up."

Jonathan was enormously grateful for this kind offer, having no idea that his good friend was going to "fix it up" for him by first putting the bite on Harshawe for himself. Earl had been beating his brains trying to figure out a way of asking Alvine for money again without having to crawl. It irked him that his recurrent need to beg emphasized the hopelessness of his own career and the triumphant infallibility of Alvine's. No chance of their positions' ever being reversed. Oh no. Fate, that cheap opportunist, never lets a winner down.

"There's a piece about him in *Esquire,*" Jonathan said. "It says he misses the old days in the Village when he was in dire straits."

"I miss those old dire straits too," said Earl. "Dire straits, my foot! Better than being broke, I can tell you."

It was a good thing to have Jonathan's interests as an opening wedge to call Alvine, Earl thought; anything to vary the monotony of his usual routine. Every time he made his touch he found himself making grandiose allusions to big deals in the offing and the loan being only for a fortnight. Old Alvine never failed to shrug ironically, foreseeing in his damnably rude way that Earl wouldn't have the nerve to show up again for years, then not to beg but to borrow again, past loans never mentioned as if time had worn away interest and principal.

Galling to admit that Alvine, as always, was his last resort. Earl's system of Paul-Peter financing had caught up with him, as it did periodically, and suddenly there were all Pauls and no Peters. Creditors seemed to be converging on him from all over the world. It must be Earl Turner Festival Year, he thought, and all of these pests were as menacing as if the debts were for hundreds instead of piddling little fives and tens. Whenever a stranger glanced twice at him on the street, he knew he must be a collector. When an old friend crossed a street toward him he knew there was some buck or two he had forgotten to repay. Even the sun coming out was just a promise of tomorrow's rain, a reminder that the very heavens had their own collector. His wretched hotel, the One Three (not to be called Thirteen) had been goading him with ultimatums. So, on our knees again to old Alvine, Earl had thought gloomily.

At least the case of Jonathan Jaimison was a change of

gambit, and there was a chance that Alvine would like the crazy angle.

If he could get through all the flunkies and chichi to Alvine, that is. The great man's stock must be slipping, however, for his agent's secretary readily admitted that he might be reached on the agent's cabin cruiser up at the City Island yacht basin, or else at his own town house. Earl tried the house number, and sure enough, Alvine himself got on the phone. How the hell did Earl know that he was here hiding out?

"Broke?" he asked. "What is it—bail, rent, blackmail?"

"All three, as usual," Earl said. "But that's only incidental. I can put it to you in about fifteen minutes when I see you. It's an episode from your past, fella, that might interest you if you've got the time. Nothing serious—maybe funny."

Alvine was in the mood to be curious. Earl should drop in around twelve and tell him his story. Earl could have been there in five minutes but he passed the time in Central Park feeding the ducks, then strolled slowly eastward, scattering peanut shells and thinking about old times.

His usual daydream was running through his head, the one about Alvine, with the background changed now to East Sixty-fourth Street. The picture was always the same. It was the one where Earl saw himself at the wheel of his Cadillac-Rolls-Jaguar-or-whatever, slowing up to notice workmen busily piling up furniture on the sidewalk. Some officials are standing about, and then Alvine himself comes out of the house, pleading with the officials. Earl sees at once what is up—Alvine is being dispossessed. Hastily he leaps out of the car and rushes up to the scene, bulging wallet in his hand.

"Why didn't you tell me things were bad?" he demands of Alvine kindly, thrusting bills into everyone's hands. "Didn't I tell you I would pay you back someday when you needed it? Now the tables are turned and I'm tickled to death to help you out of the jam, old pal. Come, come, Alvine, no blubbering—good heavens, man, what else would you expect from your oldest friends? Let's be systematic about this, now. Men, put that furniture back where you found it; I'm taking care of everything, spot cash. And you, Alvine, buck up, old chap, men don't cry! No, don't explain! The main thing is I've got everything under control, so let's forget it and go have a drink. Twenty-One okay with you? What do you mean your clothes are too seedy? Hell, man, they know me—a tie is all that's necessary. Okay, hop in, and we'll stop off at Bronzini's and buy a dozen."

Earl knew that the grade of his daydreams had not improved since his Peabody High School days, but he was hooked by them, no matter how cheap, the way he was still hooked by Almond Joy candy bars, sneaking into telephone booths to wolf them down. He absently fumbled in his pocket now to see if he might buy one, knowing that he should be careful of his change. This brought on another dream, the one about finding money in the street, and his eyes darted expertly along the gutter. He had stopped hoping to find bills of any larger denomination than a twenty, reasoning they would be too hard to explain and too hard to change in his circle. You could change an imaginary ten-dollar bill easy enough, but a dream fifty could get you in trouble. Actually he had found coins on several occasions and was always scrounging around in mud puddles and in the teeth of oncoming trucks to pick up dream quarters that turned out to be real bottle caps. Once, spotting a possible dime in a gutter, he had bent over so suddenly his bursitis nipped him in the back and he couldn't straighten up while a Fifth Avenue bus braked to a screeching halt at his very coattails. Since then he had made it a sporting rule not to bend over for anything less than a dream quarter.

The Harshawe house suddenly leaped out of the block at him, and there was no use denying that the imminence of seeing old Alvine again—in a matter of seconds—excited Earl, and he knew a silly grin was on his face as if he were right in the presence of Scott Fitzgerald. He forced himself to stand quietly a moment before the little brownstone house that flaunted its iron balconies and old-fashioned lamp-posts in the teeth of the surrounding modern apartment houses. He reminded himself of Alvine's childish weaknesses—his pose of hating New York for its social demands, his pretense of hating publicity. He wasn't seeing a soul this time, he had assured Earl on the phone, just wallowing in solitude and work, and was only pausing in his intense concentration long enough to see Earl.

Satisfied that his grin had changed from hero-worship to sardonic detachment, Earl was ready to proceed. Following Alvine's instructions, he rang the caretaker's basement apartment and was told to go on up to the third floor, where Mr. Harshawe was still in bed. The living rooms were done up for the summer, the furniture in shrouds, the smell of camphor all over, floors bare, shades all drawn.

"That you, Turner?" Harshawe's voice boomed from behind an open door, and there was Alvine lying in bed, unshaven, bags under his eyes, hair a little grayer than five years ago falling over the crooked black eyebrows, the brown eyes still keenly probing, calculating every flaw in your own appearance. He was a big hunk of man, Earl noted, and all those years of gracious living had left their mark. Earl patted his own flat belly with quiet ostentation, as if it were the result of rigid abstinence.

One thing that never changed about Alvine was the wild disorder of his bedrooms, no matter which wife was in charge. He always had great giant beds, for he wrote, ate, snoozed, read, entertained, did everything in bed. "Alvine's playpen," his present wife, Peggy, called it, and was constantly complaining about the difficulty of making Alvine get out of pajamas. There were stacks of newspapers, every edition, magazines, notebooks, manuscripts, proofsheets, a bathrobe, and a typewriter skidding over the counterpane. A tray with a box of potato chips and a highball glass was on a chair, and a half-opened suitcase on the floor spilled out a tangle of shirts, socks, and ties. No sign of any feminine life, Earl noted, but then in all of Alvine's ménages the female was boxed up out of sight whenever Earl made his calls.

"You old bastard," Alvine greeted him, propping pillows behind his head and sizing up his guest. "I made out a check over there under the ashtray, if that's what you're looking for."

Earl flinched. Same old Alvine. Kick 'em right in the teeth before they can put on their poor little show.

"I was merely looking for wife tracks," Earl said coolly. "Don't tell me you've booted Number Four."

"I left Peg up at Chatham with a houseful of crumbs and waiting for more," Alvine said. "Anything to keep a man from working. 'You're so dull when you work, honey.' " Alvine mimicked his wife's boarding-school accent. "Or 'Really, dear, you're not having brandy before breakfast?' "

"She'll be sore you left," Earl ventured.

"Peg? She'll act sore but she'll really be glad she can sound off about my opinions without me shutting her up," Alvine said sourly. "She won't have to apologize to her pals for my insulting them. Oh, she'll give me hell but she'll be having a ball. Have a drink, or is it too early for a dedicated littérateur like yourself?"

Earl poured himself a short one from the Jack Daniel's bottle on the dresser and noted the empty glasses and overflowing ashtrays on floor and chairs.

"Big night?"

Alvine gave an impatient snort.

"You're as bad as a wife, Turner," he said. "You find somebody in bed an hour or so after you've managed to drag your own can out, and right off you start pointing and yelling big night, big night, aren't you ashamed, it's after ten, Bergdorf's is open, Saks is open, Irving Trust is open, get up, get busy, do something, do your crossword puzzle, tear up your mail, get on all the phones, start apologizing for last night and tomorrow too, while you're at it, get on the ball, don't just lie there minding your own business."

"Well, now, Alvine, really—" Earl protested.

"I should have married you, Turner," Alvine said. "I could have had four wives' worth of nagging without changing mistresses."

"Sorry, old man. I forget I'm day people and you were always night people," Earl said.

"Who says we're people?" Alvine yawned. "There's the check, don't you want it?"

Earl picked up the check and put it in his pocket. The minute he had it there he didn't give a damn what Alvine said. Needle away, boy, he thought, nothing bothers me now. Maybe he'd get around to his Jonathan errand and maybe he wouldn't.

"What happened to that system you used to have of getting advances from publishers?" Alvine asked. "They used to be tickled to death to hand you out advances on a mere idea. They were so sure they wouldn't have to bother reading anything. What spoiled it? Did you turn in a manuscript?"

Earl laughed too, as if it were a great joke instead of being in a small way—two chapters—all too true.

"I haven't had an idea myself in ten years," Alvine admitted graciously. "Sit down and talk, man, fill me in."

You got mad at Alvine, insulted and humiliated by him, but you couldn't resist when he raised his little finger toward you. So Earl sat down on a chair full of *Esquires* and *Trues* and told him what the old ironworker had told him in a Myrtle Avenue bar about his son being a junkie and pinning the stuff on the old man. . . .

"This fellow tells you this for true?" Alvine yawned again, and when Earl nodded, Alvine snorted. "Earl, how many times do I have to tell you that what a simple workman tells you in a low bar in a Brooklyn accent isn't necessarily true? You're safer swiping straight from De Maupassant or O. Henry, somebody out there in good old public domain. These bar confessions are always straight out of *Reader's Digest* or the *Post,* magazines a literary type like yourself wouldn't be reading. No, my friend, I'd be afraid to use that little idyll. And nobody likes a worker hero any more, anyway."

That was good old Alvine for you, first encouraging you to talk, then knocking your wind out.

"Who said anything about that?" Earl said. "The junkie is your hero these days. Where have you been?"

He knew he shouldn't have flared up, trying to take Alvine down, but the damned check in his pocket made him feel like an equal. He was ashamed as soon as he saw Alvine's eyebrow shoot up in its old Clark Gable way. You shouldn't take advantage of your betters, Earl reminded himself savagely, especially a great genius who hasn't had an idea in ten years. The genius had poured himself another drink and Earl held out his glass to the spout, reflecting that the old boy was hitting the bottle but then, with the favorites, the bottle never hit back as it certainly would with himself.

"Otherwise, how's life?" Alvine asked amiably, pushing himself up with another pillow to watch his caller—to count his crow's feet, Earl thought, see the grease spots on his shirt.

"Nothing new. A review now and then—eight bucks for fifteen hundred words of new criticism in a little magazine, or forty for six hundred words of old criticism in the Sunday book sections. A pulp rewrite of a De Maupassant."

"I mean what kind of place do you live, what about dames?" Alvine interrupted.

Material, Earl thought. The sonofabitch was always scratching for material like a dog scratching for fleas.

"I'm in this Hotel One Three, men only," Earl said. "Way over east in what they call the New Village. A real fleabag. Signs in the lobby, NO LOITERING IN THE LOBBY, kind of funny considering that the lobby is only five feet square. Signs in your room, ONLY ONE PERSON AT A TIME IN THIS ROOM. FOOD IN ROOM FORBIDDEN, and all that. I have a little electric plate hidden."

Earl saw that Alvine was amused. Probably already figuring how he could use the stuff. Okay, let him have it.

"A fellow there wrote a song from the signs," he said

obligingly. " 'Won't you loiter in the lobby of my heart.' "

Good. The master was grinning.

"Dames?" Alvine persisted.

"A few favors from old friends, that's all," Earl said. "They throw me out regularly. Damn it, I'm a lonely man."

"Lonely!" shouted Alvine, suddenly coming to life. "What do you know about loneliness! Why, you're not even married!"

Earl had to laugh.

"Let alone four times like me. Oh, it's no laughing matter," Alvine went on bitterly. "You played it smart so you've still got your freedom. But me. There's nothing left of a man after he's parceled himself out to women four ways—five years lost here, five there, eight there, another six here . . . Believe me, that's loneliness! This door of your past to keep shut, that one mustn't touch, this one a booby trap—so what the hell have you got left of your own life? You can't even run around naked in your own mind!"

"You can think about all those front-page reviews of your books," Earl said with what he hoped was a good-natured chuckle. "Or having supper with the royal family after your play opens. Or editors wrastling on your doorstep. Don't get me crying over you, old man. It isn't that tough."

Alvine reached out for the highball glass on the floor and poured himself a drink.

"Write a story about a poor old writing stiff, a very complicated, well-educated, rich old author, perfectly adjusted to his lousy environment. Don't you see that great new Cinderella angle? The poor old slob, when he walks in a restaurant strangers flock to his table, put their drinks on his check; they visit his country home with their picnic hampers, they pick his roses, throw their banana peels around, urge their kids to swim in his pool, and when he shows up—it's his home, after all—they tell him they don't see what's so hot about his books or plays; in fact they don't even know them. They have no intention of leaving until they're chased off, so they can tell how mean he is. They ask if it's true he's 'interracial,' is it true that O'Hara writes all his stuff for him, that his present wife was a call girl in Las Vegas, that his mother spends most of her time in a straitjacket, that his kids are test-tube products, and that he's been living on dope ever since he left the breast—"

Earl had to shout to override Alvine's tirade.

"Stop breaking my heart!" he cried. "Who would read an old story like that? Talk about bar confessions! Where's your sympathetic character? Where's your struggle? Who cares about one man's most embarrassing moment?"

"Oh forget it!" Alvine said, lying back wearily. "Forget I said a word. It was just that I thought with your determination to write and my determination not to, between us we'd make one hell of an author."

Earl knew he shouldn't let Alvine get his goat but it always happened and he hated himself—and Alvine more—for it. He hated that wave of affection Alvine always felt for the person he had just kicked in the face. Good old Earl, he would say, how lovable of him to be a confirmed flop! He might be a nuisance but never a competitor. Other old pals might forge ahead and get stuffy—take old George Terrence, for example!—but you could count on old Earl to be down there at the bottom of the ladder, looking up at you like a dumb old mutt that can never learn the tricks.

What burned Earl was that Alvine no longer made any pretense of believing in his big projects, as if they were windy lies or so unfeasible that only poor gullible Earl would be taken in. He might have pulled off one of his deals, Earl thought, if he hadn't felt Alvine's skeptical eyes on him. Skeptical, hell—absolutely certain of Earl's failure. If others were always so damned sure you'd need the safety net, you usually ended up in it. You did what people expected of you. Look at Alvine. Everybody from high school on had always expected Alvine to make good, so he did. Everything worked out tick-tock. He turned out a play or novel, then sat back for years on his yacht or somebody else's and let the profits roll in—television, Hollywood, road companies, musical adaptations, foreign rights, revivals, with every gossip columnist beating the drum for him. Industrious, they called him, when every little word earned its own living again and again for years without Alvine's turning a hand. Yet people were always saying to Earl, "Why don't you get down to work, Turner, write something?" Sell something, was what they meant. He wished suddenly that Alvine would get sore at him, dignify him with a little decent jealousy, tell him to go to hell, get him off this hook somehow, let him fail in his own way without rubbing in how easy it was for others to succeed.

Well, they were each other's oldest friends. Not that it meant they liked each other. Some old friends went to their graves without learning to like each other, without even getting to know each other.

Earl and Alvine had become friends through geographical necessity at first—graduated from the same Schenectady high school, into the West Side Y, then Greenwich Village, always planning to write, talking endlessly about writing, getting down all those upstate characters and legends, yak-yak-yak. Earl realized he should have got the picture then and there, because while he rolled into bed at daylight, perfectly content with their discussions, Alvine went right to his damned typewriter to get it all down. Next time they'd meet, Alvine would have a fat manuscript to read to him instead of resuming their talk as Earl wanted to do. "Where's your story, Turner? The one you talked about all week?" Alvine would ask. Earl would explain that the material needed more time; he was too much the perfectionist to rush right in and mess up a great idea before he was ripe for it. He never could get over Alvine's reckless plunge from idea to typewriter. Cheating, he thought; not really playing the game. You could have a depth talk about murder, couldn't you, without tearing right out and killing somebody? Earl had a vague feeling of having been robbed, too, he wasn't sure of what. But what had he said that always set off Alvine without starting his own motor?

When Earl got the *Sphere* editorial job they shared an apartment with George Terrence, a rich young lawyer, on Irving Place. By that time Alvine had published some sketches about Schenectady boyhood, things about places and people Earl knew as well as Alvine did. Editing them for *The Sphere,* Earl felt robbed again. They were bits he intended to put in his novel when he got around to it, only now it was too late. They didn't see much of each other after Alvine married his literary agent, Roberta somebody, and don't think she wasn't a big pusher for his success, typing, selling, making him into a big enough shot for his next three wives. Not that Alvine ever gave any of them credit. He could use up their money, their life stories, their profitable connections and then complain they blocked his work.

"Do you mean to tell me you still hang around the Spur?" Alvine asked. "Next you'll be telling me that you still get grain alcohol from the mad druggist and make your own gin in the umbrella stand."

"At least the Spur is still alive," Earl said, remembering not to get sore. He wished he dared remind his chum of those old days when they were tickled to death to gouge the cash out of old George Terrence for a night at the Spur. "How about visiting it one of these nights?"

He was surprised that Alvine didn't laugh at the idea.

"Damned if I wouldn't like to, Turner," he said thoughtfully. "I need to freshen up on that background for the thing I'm working on, but how can I drop in a place like that and get the real picture?"

Conceited bastard.

"You mean you'd be recognized right away so your fans would tear your clothes off," Earl said, oh, very sympathetically.

Alvine nodded.

"Not that bad, but you know how it is. Old has-beens needling me for making it when they never could with their genius. Dames yakking about my mystique and their boyfriends sore and claiming I'm trying to rape them."

"I see your problem," Earl said. "Still, maybe I could handle the stampede. There's a young fellow around there now looking for you, and we could pick him up. He wants to know if you remember his mother. She had some pleasant memories of you."

"Pleasant memories," Alvine mused. "Sounds like a belated paternity suit."

You're not kidding, Earl thought. No reason for that big grin.

"Just the thing for writer's block," Alvine said. "A paternity suit ought to start you thinking. A real blockbuster."

So it was going to be a big joke.

"Her name was Connie Birch," Earl said. "She typed for you. Mean anything?"

"There was a Connie," Alvine recalled. "Sure. I promised to pay for the typing when I sold the piece. Lived way over on Horatio, Connie did. What became of her?"

"Died some twenty years ago. You can cross her off the bill."

"Dead or alive, Connie's got forty bucks coming to her," Alvine stated piously. "I'll settle with her heirs."

"You used to get 'em to type for free if you slept with them," Earl said. He could still get mad remembering how lucky Alvine used to be. "What was the deal with Connie?"

"Don't be a cad, Turner," mocked Alvine.

"You mean you don't remember," diagnosed Earl. "Anyway, this kid, Jonathan Jaimison, is crazy to see you and hear about his mother's New York past. Maybe he wants to write a book."

This was the wrong approach.

"Too many goddam writers already," Alvine said. "Why does anybody want to pick a lousy trade like that?"

"Look who's complaining," Earl said. "Nothing in it for Harshawe, of course. Just a million bucks and a passel of Pulitzers."

"I've never had a Pulitzer," Alvine corrected him with a rather brave, wistful smile. "A drama prize once, never any for my novels. Worst damn play I ever wrote, too."

So you did know that much, Earl thought.

"The picture deal was all loused up, you know."

Now wasn't that just too bad? Earl kept silent.

"Oh sure, I've had a couple of book-club breaks," Alvine granted, getting the message that he needn't expect sympathy. "But I've never gotten the critical reception for my novels that the plays get. That's why it's a challenge to me. I'm thinking of concentrating on novels, get out of this damn Broadway muck, give myself a chance to breathe. Keep to myself."

"Here?"

"Could be. Peg hates New York." He must have been mulling over what Earl had said earlier, for he said, "Say, what does this Jaimison kid you were telling me about, Connie's kid, look like?"

"You, come to think of it," Earl said. "By George, he does!"

Alvine sat up straight, both eyebrows up, incredulous but pleased.

"No kidding," Earl went on with delight. "I've been trying to think who he reminded me of all along. He's blond, and his eyes are different from yours—instead of his looking right through a person as you do, you can look right through him. But the build and profile are straight Harshawe, by George."

"Clean-cut American youth, standard model, that's all." Alvine shrugged, but he was amused. "Maybe I'll look him up at that. I ought to know more about that generation."

"For the new novel," guessed Earl, but Alvine only smiled enigmatically. Okay, make a big secret of it, Earl thought, but then Alvine always claimed it was no good talking about his writing, the way it was no good talking about cooking or dancing or singing—you just did it or you didn't, that was all there was to it. The born genius.

"What about you, Turner?" Alvine asked. "What do you want out of your writing, anyway? Dough? Kicks? Immortality?"

"I just want to be overestimated," Earl shouted, "like everybody else, goddammit."

Alvine burst out laughing. He liked that. He liked other people's hard-bought cynicism, but Earl was embarrassed at having betrayed himself. Now that he was standing up, ready to go, Alvine was suddenly crazy to have him stay. Have another drink—okay, one for the road then, and what have you read of the current trash? "You always read more than I do," Alvine said graciously. "When a book's bad I'm disgusted with the whole trade, and when it's good I wonder how such an oaf could turn out such good stuff. But you've got real critical sense." So Earl was beguiled again into trying to placate the master, telling him all the things wrong with Faulkner, Hemingway, Sartre, and the English crowd, till Alvine was crowing happily.

"We'll have a night going the rounds," he promised. "I'll have a look at this Jonathan kid."

Oh sure. Earl had sense enough to know that Alvine's geniality came over him only when the guest was headed for the door. Now was the time to leave.

He was able to congratulate himself, once outside, that this time he had not stayed too long. He had lived so long in cheap little hotel rooms that whenever he got into a regular home he couldn't bear to leave. He was as sensitive as the next one, but hints that hosts wanted to dine or sleep or go out bounced off Earl's consciousness once he was lost in home-hunger, standing in the door, half in, half out, not sitting down again, mind you, but not gone either. The few times before when he had succeeded in visiting the Harshawe ménage, he knew well enough he had overstayed, and it was funny too, because the minute he got in the door he kept watching Alvine anxiously to see if he looked bored or annoyed, which he did in a very short time. Then Earl got privately enraged and stayed on out of pure stubbornness. He could laugh at himself afterward.

"I know what old Alvine will have put on my gravestone when I go upstairs," he merrily told people. " 'We Thought He'd Never Go.' "

A good visit on the whole, Earl thought, walking down Lexington. Alvine had cheered him up in spite of everything. Suddenly he realized he had not even looked at the check. Maybe Alvine, who thought like a cagey rich man these days, was letting him have a measly fifty. Earl's lip curled. Already he regretted not having given a few straight criticisms of the last masterpiece, instead of buttering him up exactly like the disgusting toadies Alvine always managed to make of everybody around him. He regretted the faint twitch of affection he had felt when Alvine asked if he had time to wait for the restaurant next door to send up a bite of lunch. A real proof of Alvine's friendship, Earl had first thought, wanting to have an intimate little snack right there, just the two of them, instead of taking him out to phony chic spots like the Pavillon or Twenty-One, where his phony success friends would crowd around him. On second thoughts, the hell with this cozy little snack business, why didn't he invite him to those good places where he could meet those phony new pals? If phoniness was what he liked, his old pal Turner could be as phony as they come.

Earl reached in his vest pocket and took out the check. For two cents he'd tear it up and mail the pieces back to the old bastard. Then he peered at the figure written out. Three hundred dollars. Yes, three hundred dollars.

Three hundred cool dollars just like that. He stood still, breathing deep of the wonderful diamond-studded air, looking down beautiful Lexington Avenue, a street paved with gold, saw the little jewelry-store window right beside him and decided instantly he would go in and buy the silver wristwatch on the blue velvet.

It was true that Hotel One Three had promised to lock him out of his room if he did not pay today, but such catastrophes would not happen to a man armored with this beautiful check. A fine sense of accomplishment flooded his being, as if his own honest labor and not Alvine's generosity had brought about this reward.

Then a pang of irritation beset him, and he wondered how in heaven's name this piece of paper could be translated into cash. If he presented it to the hotel they would take out not only what he owed but a month in advance and probably raise the rate besides for such a rich guest. If he tried to get the bartender at The Golden Spur to okay it, then he would have to pay the old tabs he'd been hanging up at the Spur, and, besides paying all the customers from whom he'd borrowed a dollar or two over the years, he'd have to loan them money. He saw a branch of the bank on which Alvine's check had been written and thought of starting an account on the spot, but it would be days before he could draw on it. Passing a Riker's luncheonette, he saw that today there was steak-and-kidney pie, and it reminded him that he hadn't eaten today, and very little yesterday. Visions of great steaks of the past rose before his gaze; he thought of Cavanagh's, old Billy the Oysterman's, and the old Luchow's before it went Hollywood. He realized he was still walking and the great places he thought of were far, far away. Keene's Chop House then, he thought, and his mouth watered at the dream of those fat chops with Old Mustie Ale and a go at George Terrence's pipe always preserved there. But even Thirty-sixth Street was far away. And what good was a three-hundred-dollar check anywhere—no better than his cash treasure of a dollar and sixteen cents.

He was one of those doomed people who simply were not made to have money, he thought indignantly, child of eight generations of solid, substantial, bumbling Americans, born back in their rent—back eight generations with compound interest, the way old George Terrence, for instance, was born on top of eight generations of trust funds, so that he was honored as a success in his career before he'd made a dollar. He and Alvine used to sneer in the old times when their roommate, old George Terrence, would complain of being broke—less than fifty bucks in his wallet, maybe—might have to sell a bond, go into his savings, then after that go into one of his trust funds, and after that into his stocks, and then get an advance on the inheritance from his grandmother, then from his mother or uncle. Men like George honestly thought that to be broke meant just that. No, Earl conceded, George had never experienced the thrill of finding an extra one-dollar bill in his pocket after a week-end party—hell, George probably didn't even know they made one-dollar bills. George never had the exquisite ecstasy of spotting a dime in the gutter—dimes he knew, as any other born rich man does, merely as the coin used in tipping. Poor George had nothing but unlimited credit and could never be made to understand how a man with a big check in one pocket and a dollar sixteen in another could still be financially inconvenienced.

The gourmet lunch would have to be foregone, Earl saw. The sensible thing was to take the bus down, get some provender in that new supermarket near the Spur, stock up on coffee and eggs, and fix up a snack on his electric plate in his room. Once in the market he added a pint of milk and a bun to his eggs and coffee order, but when he offered his coins to the cashier she suddenly took a close squint at them—why hadn't she done this to the other people's money? he wondered—and cried out, "This quarter is no good!" The ladies behind him, who were battering at him with their pushcarts, stared indignantly at him. Crook. Pickpocket. Blackmailer. Forger. It seemed, the cashier stated with growing suspicion, that the coin was offensively Canadian and never mind about its being worth twenty-seven cents in United States money, it was worthless in the supermarket. Earl, goaded by the righteous, scornful eyes of the ladies wheeling about him menacingly, took the milk and bun off his order and skulked out.

He started on the walk back to the Hotel One Three, automatically ducking back and forth across streets, swerving around corners from Sixth to Broadway and east across Fourteenth to avoid passing a certain dry-cleaner's, a certain drugstore, Teddy's Barbershop, Smart Shirts, Inc., a dentist's office, and a few bars, in all of which he owed varying sums. It occurred to him that he had almost worn out his present neighborhood, but where was there left for him to move? He had lived up and down town, East Side, West Side, in furnished rooms and fleabags from Chinatown to Harlem, pushed by creditors from Avenue A to Chelsea and even across the river to Hoboken, where he had holed up in a six-dollar room on River Street, living on beer and free broth from the Clam Broth House, then swung back across and up to Yorkville, Spanish Harlem, down again to the dingier fringes of the East Thirties, then westward ho again, widening his orbit as obliged by his little debts. He needed a helicopter, he thought savagely, to skip his pursuers and land *bingo* right in his own bed. Only a day ago he had been speculating on how long before he maneuvered himself right out of the city into the Atlantic Ocean. Never mind, all this would be changed when he cashed his check, and he should be glad he didn't have to make this simple trip by way of Woodlawn Cemetery.

The walk cleared his mind and he began appreciating the wonder of Alvine's forking over three hundred bucks. He began to figure out little tranquillity pills to various creditors, and he visualized the new suit—almost new, in the window of the Third Avenue Pawn Shop near Twelfth Street. He had promised himself that he would buy it with the first eighteen dollars he laid his hands on. Already he was enjoying the anticipated cries of joy from all those creditors as he passed out tens, and twenties.

"What's all the excitement?" he heard himself saying. "Didn't I tell you I would pay it later?"

Figuring all he had to pay out left him with the sudden desolate realization that a fortune had passed through his hands and nothing was left for Baby. Supposing he did manage by some miracle to cash the damn check, by night he would be as broke and desperate as he had been yesterday. Yes, and hungry too.

Earl did not realize that his feet had frozen into the sidewalk, as if his mind had commanded *Whoa* and they waited like patient old cart horses for a new command. His hand absently groped in his vest pocket, where, surprisingly enough, the check still reposed. As long as it was there, uncashed, he was a rich man. As long as he didn't cash it there was a choice left open. He could, for instance, simply take off for Mexico on a cheap flight and live pleasantly for six months. Write a novel. Like *Under the Volcano,* maybe. Mexico would do it for him. The instant this grandiose idea occurred to him, he knew it had been garaged in the back of his brain all along. His feet seemed to recognize the change of plan, for they automatically turned around and started in the other direction. Earl was not sure where they were taking him, but the knowledge of the uncashed check in his pocket gave him a dizzy glow of unlimited power.

At the corner of Twelfth Street he caught sight of a couple coming toward him, the lady in paisley-trimmed horsehair picture hat, flowered taffeta suit, and purple gloves definitely Claire Van Orphen, the young man Jonathan. In a flash he knew what he would do.

"Friends!" He made a deep bow to her and another to Jonathan. "I was just about to call both of you to say good-by."

"Good-by, Mr. Turner!" Claire exclaimed in dismay. "Where are you going?"

"Acapulco," he said. "Later the interior. I can really write in Mexico."

He would have gone on babbling, for he did feel guilty at having done so well for himself on a mission that was supposed to benefit Jonathan, but while he was casting about for some definite word to give the boy, Claire placed a detaining hand on his arm.

"But you can't go, Mr. Turner," she cried. "I've just been telling Jonathan the good news. You remember your theory about updating my old stories? The switch, you called it. Making the heroine the villain and vice versa? You said they would sell in a minute that way."

"I couldn't have been that definite, come now," Earl said warily. "I only revised them as a little game."

"You said in the old days the career girl who supported the family was the heroine, and the idle wife was the baddie," Claire said gleefully. "And now it's the other way round. In the soap operas, the career girl is the baddie, the wife is the goodie because she's better for *business,* didn't he say that, Jonathan? Well, you were right. CBS has bought the two you fixed, and Hollywood is interested. Jonathan and I have been looking for you all over. Isn't it wonderful?"

Earl drew a pack of cigarettes from his pocket, negligently selected one, and offered the pack to Jonathan. He felt quite faint.

"Not surprising when you know the score as I do," he said. "One does learn a little in twenty-five, thirty years of professional writing."

"You see you can't go away now, with all my other manuscripts for you to revise," Claire said anxiously. "And I have your check right here in my purse, fifty-fifty, just as we said."

"Check?" Earl repeated vaguely.

Mexico vanished. Escape vanished. There was nothing but checks.

"Supposing we stop in here at Longchamps and talk about it over a brandy?" he said, exuberant confidence suddenly overwhelming him. "I've just left Alvine Harshawe and he is delighted at the idea of meeting Jonathan, here. We talked for hours about you, boy. Wants to see you. Any day now you'll be hearing from him."

"Maybe I should telephone him," Jonathan suggested radiantly.

"Wait a bit. I'll be in touch with him again," Earl counseled. "Never fear, I'll fix it up. Come on, now we celebrate."

Claire was already being seated at a sidewalk table.

"You must let me be the hostess, then," she said.

"If we must we must," Earl said with a gallant shrug.

7

The Then-and-Now Café did so little business that Jonathan worried over its survival. The real-estate man upstairs, who owned the building and half a block of houses beyond, was well pleased, however. A nice little capital loss, he gloated, rubbing his hands happily, just the break he needed. Moreover, he proposed to put more money into it for the same mysterious tax reasons, and since Dr. Kellsey's generous suggestions had not seduced trade so far, he was invited to submit more of his profit-proof ideas.

It was Dr. Kellsey's inspiration to have the walls covered with blown-up photographs of Pfaff's Beer Hall (of the 1850s), O. Henry's hotel on West Eighteenth Street, Henry James's early home on Mercer Street, Stephen Crane looking like a Bowery bum, John Masefield tending bar at Luke O'Connor's saloon, Richard Harding Davis dining on the Brevoort *terrasse,* and other nineteenth-century literary figures of the quarter. These reminders that other writers had been there before them merely annoyed the new crop of poets, subtly hinting that they themselves might end up tomorrow as blown-up "Thens" on these very walls. Dr. Kellsey himself realized this and thought all the better of the idea. Besides, he enjoyed his position as chief and sometimes only customer, with a big table to himself and no wide-eyed apprentice poets to watch him pour cognac into his espresso under the table, a routine that put him into a nostalgic mood for the old Prohibition days.

Jonathan was learning something new about the city every day, but there was no use trying to make today's lesson fit onto yesterday's. Each day the blackboard was erased and you began all over, yesterday's conclusions canceled by today's findings. Darcy, for instance, had confided often in Jonathan that there was something dangerously feeble-minded about a girl (Lize) who could hook up with a creep like Percy Wright. But now Darcy went the rounds at night with this very same creep, generously making him spend a couple of dollars at the Then-and-Now sometimes, admonishing Jonathan not to mention this to Lize.

"She'd really flip," Darcy prophesied. "It burns her up that so many men fall for me when she tries to hang on to them. God knows she's been doing her best to get Percy back but she hasn't figured out yet that I'm the reason he's holding out. He's just too nice a guy for Lize, that's all. He's kinda cute, too, the way he hangs onto his budget until you get him gassed enough to forget it. He says we aren't being fair to Lize, when she's so hot for him, but I say let's face it, Lize is just one of those women that can't hold a man, that's all, it's not his fault."

Jonathan obediently wiped Darcy's earlier statements about Percy from his memory and with the same open mind listened to Lize's stories of Percy pursuing her, begging her to come back. Sometimes Percy himself, deserted in some bar when both girls had found better fish to fry, attached himself to Jonathan and confided his own troubles, which were not frustrations in love but anguish that his idol, Hugow, was unmistakably shunning him. It was because Hugow's girls could not keep from falling for his unworthy self, Percy sighed. He told Jonathan it was not all roses having that terrible power over women, always breaking up homes, but what could a man do?

"If Hugow would only let me explain the situation," Percy said wistfully.

Jonathan told him he must not blame himself too much. It occurred to him that there was truth in every lie if you waited long enough, and you might as well believe everything while you waited.

Earl Turner said he was helping Claire Van Orphen "update" her fiction, and Miss Van Orphen's story was that she was helping Earl Turner get back on his feet professionally. Jonathan admired both of these people and felt fortunate in their friendship, just as he did about Dr. Kellsey's. The doctor brought his class papers to correct at a table in the Then-and-Now, enlivening this chore with helpful hints to Jonathan on his newssheet. He summoned his anecdotes of the past by running a beautifully manicured hand through his lordly gray mane, then pressing the hand to his closed eyes, a fascinating gesture that Jonathan could not resist imitating. Sometimes he caught himself performing in unison with the doctor and would peep out through the fingers over his eyes to see if his friend had noticed. Then the doctor would shake his mane (Jonathan would do the same), smile sadly (Jonathan would return the smile), and both would sigh, perhaps over the beauty of the past, perhaps over the folly of youth, perhaps over their shared sensitivity.

Jonathan took pride and comfort in the doctor's remark that he was the only young person who had the gift of curiosity. Students used to have it, oh yes indeed, the doctor said, but not any more. Everybody used that new word "empathy," said the doctor, but actually the word for the present age was "apathy." Apathy was what drove him to drink, said the doctor, apathy laced with either hostility or sheer ignorance in the young, apathy mixed with resentment and moral complacency in his wife, apathy with long-suffering and sulky envy in his lady-friend and departmental associate, Miss Anita Barlowe.

"But you, my dear Jonathan, you are eager to know things!" the doctor had said. "You want to know what I can tell you, what anybody can tell you, and you listen, too, by George. You make me feel alive."

So Jonathan was glad to have the doctor peer over his shoulder the night he was writing his historical items for the week.

"Have you mentioned that Poe wrote "The Raven" over here on Carmine Street?" asked the doctor.

"Last week I said he wrote it on Third Street above Bertolotti's," said Jonathan. "They gave us an ad."

"Ah yes, I keep forgetting that the function of history is to bring in advertising," Dr. Kellsey said. "How about noting that Stokes killed Jim Fisk over Josie Mansfield right in the Broadway Central Hotel just below Third Street? Mention that the hotel was redecorated with the tiles and fixings from the old Waldorf Peacock Alley. And say that poor old Hearstwood, in *Sister Carrie,* spent his last days there—committed suicide there, didn't he?"

"Will they think of that as a plug?" Jonathan debated.

Dr. Kellsey sipped his coffee judiciously.

"Very well, then take the Brevoort. Jenny Lind stayed there, and in Edward Sheldon's play *Romance*—played by Doris Keane, incidentally—her suitors unhitched the horses and drew her carriage right from the theater to the hotel. And it wasn't even air-conditioned then."

"That was the *old* Brevoort," demurred Jonathan.

"Try the Fifth Avenue Hotel, then, across the street from where Mabel Dodge had her peyote party forty years ago."

"No ad in that," Jonathan objected cautiously. "The Narcotics Squad might get after them."

The doctor chuckled.

"By George, you're getting to be a regular public-relations man. Must run in your family, that knack, or maybe it's plain Scotch caution."

Jonathan winced. Any reminder of the Jaimison family virtues sickened him, and it depressed him that his friend could find any trace of them in him. He made up his mind to tell the doctor the circumstances that made him definitely non-Jaimison, though Earl Turner had advised him against confiding in anyone else for fear it would block useful information. He opened his mouth to give a mere hint, but the doctor's delighted interest brought out everything Jonathan could remember from his mother's documents. When the doctor lifted a skeptical eyebrow over a point or two—"Are you sure she meant The Golden Spur and not The Gilded Lantern; that was a gypsy tearoom? And are you sure she took a poetry course at the night school, because I myself was teaching there then?"—Jonathan pounded the desk, ready to offer affidavits.

"Of course I'm sure. What surprises me is that you didn't know her yourself since you were teaching there. Look." Jonathan pulled the snapshot of his mother from his pocket and pressed it on the table before Kellsey. "Doesn't the name Connie Birch mean anything to you?"

The doctor obligingly took out two other pairs of glasses from his briefcase and studied the picture intently. Then he folded up both pairs of spectacles, readjusted his regular glasses, and handed back the picture to Jonathan. He stared at him in solemn silence for a moment.

"My boy," he said impressively, "we have here a most extraordinary coincidence. I did know your mother. She was in my poetry class. It was the braids that reminded me, and the unusual wide eyes. Connie. Yes sir, little Connie Birch. Amazing."

Jonathan felt faint and gripped the desk. Through a whirling mist he saw the doctor's fine hand rumpling through the handsome mane and heard his classroom Barrymore voice echo dimly in his ears.

"The very child who took me first to The Golden Spur, as a matter of fact," he was saying. "I forget names, but I was new here then, and this dear child with braids around her head had cried when I read Alan Seeger's poem, 'I have a rendezvous with death—' "

"Yes, yes," cried Jonathan. "She always cried over that."

"I invited her out after class for a beer and sandwich to comfort her," said the doctor, his rich voice choked with memories. "I found her naïveté refreshing, but it was she who suggested The Golden Spur. Usually I dropped in to Lee Chumley's, maybe the Brevoort or Jumble Shop. It surprised me that she should know such an out-of-bounds place as the Spur. Sporting types, jazz singers, writers looking for color, wandering trollops—yes, I was shocked to see that my naïve little student was devoted to this place."

"And after that—"

"After that I often took her there after class," recalled the doctor, stroking his head rhythmically as if this stimulated a special department of his memory. "She was always affected by love poems, and I'm afraid I got in the way of specializing in them—Sara Teasdale, Millay, Taggard—

just because of the charming way this little student reacted to them. Gave me an excuse to console her, you see."

"You saw her home, then," Jonathan said, beginning to wonder uneasily if he had pressed the wrong button. He admired and respected Dr. Kellsey but he was not sure he wanted a closer connection.

The doctor reflected on this question and then nodded. "I must have," he said. "It's true I was having some marriage problems at that time—in fact my wife was having me followed, as I recall, and my friend Miss Barlowe was having my wife followed—ha, ha—so little Connie Birch was my only refuge. Yes, she led me to the Spur. Curious, eh?"

"She wanted to meet someone there, perhaps," Jonathan suggested. "She knew Alvine Harshawe, don't forget, and he went there."

Dr. Kellsey shook his head fondly.

"Your mother was far too sensitive a girl for a big extrovert like Harshawe," he said. "Oh yes, she pointed him out to me—strange I remembered the incident without realizing it was Connie Birch—but a delicate child who cries over poetry would never be taken in by your Harshawes."

"But there was someone," Jonathan persisted. "She did meet some man at the Golden Spur—don't you remember any of her friends?"

The doctor twisted his mustache meditatively and stared into the dark street outside.

"I don't remember how I got the impression she was alone in New York and without friends," he mused. "I remember being surprised when Louis, the old waiter at the Brevoort Café, spoke to her by name when I took her there. And I was startled to run into her at a Pagan Ball at

Webster Hall—she'd come all alone, she said, imagine! Strange, come to think of it."

"She must have known someone would be there," Jonathan suggested.

The doctor frowned thoughtfully into space.

"I didn't recognize her because her braids were down, the hair flowing. I knew she didn't realize the type of party it would be. Later I looked around for her to take her home, but she'd disappeared. Frightened, I think, for it was a real brawl."

He stopped short. A sharp suspicion had crossed his mind that he had indeed found Connie that night, must have taken her home, for how else could he account for having been found by police next noon asleep in Abingdon Square in his tattered Hamlet costume? God knows his wife had flung it in his face often enough later so that he couldn't deny it.

Jonathan wondered if his mother had ever been frightened at the idea of anything, especially a wild party. Even in her weakest stage of invalidism she welcomed any excitement. He was sure she was like himself, always ready to accept whatever occurred as the normal.

"Don't you think she went alone to the party and to the Spur because she knew a certain man would be there?" he asked. "She said in her letter that this well-known man would always be there and would walk her home later."

The doctor's eyebrows lifted. He looked pleased.

"I did get some recognition for my reviews in the *New Republic* then," he admitted thoughtfully.

Jonathan choked back an impatient exclamation. He hadn't foreseen this angle and he wished he could keep the doctor from pursuing it.

"It was a long time ago, my boy," said the doctor with a

faintly mysterious smile. "And the whole episode had slipped my mind until now, but I assure you I would certainly have known if your mother was seriously interested in some other man."

Here was the closest he had come to an actual friend of his mother's, and it was leading nowhere, or if it was leading anywhere it was no place Jonathan wanted to look. He knew the doctor was studying him carefully and he became very busy at the typewriter, determined to drop the subject. But the doctor's speculative gaze made him uneasy, and he found himself tousling his hair in the doctor's familiar gesture. Presently the doctor rose and put his papers back in the briefcase.

"Remarkable," he murmured. "Incredible. I must put my mind to it and see what comes up. I'll do my best for you, my boy."

The tender way in which he said "my boy" made Jonathan berate himself for asking the doctor's aid. He rose politely to say good night, and the doctor stepped beside him.

"We seem to be almost exactly the same height," he said. "You have perhaps half an inch in your favor, due probably to all that spinach and orange juice of your generation. Well, good night."

"If she wasn't meeting Harshawe, what about George Terrence, the lawyer?" Jonathan cried after him. "Miss Van Orphen is sure Terrence went to the Spur in those days."

"Claire Van Orphen must be getting on in years now," said Dr. Kellsey. "I used to meet her at little affairs at the New School in the old days. She's probably a little confused about the past. It's hardly possible that a legal eagle of Terrence's standing would have haunted the Spur."

"But my mother knew him well," Jonathan insisted, unwilling to let the older man go without some leading answers.

The doctor raised skeptical shoulders.

"My little Connie? George Terrence? Possibly, possibly."

He gave Jonathan a soothing pat on the shoulder and tossed his hair back. Jonathan was annoyed to find himself tossing his own head again and meeting the doctor's quixotic smile.

"Amazing," murmured the doctor as he strode out.

He was humming, Jonathan noted with misgiving. Earl Turner had been right in advising him to confide in no one. Instead of getting helpful information he had let himself in for some unappealing doubts, for the doctor's suspicions had been quite obvious. Might as well be a Jaimison, Jonathan brooded, as to find his veins coursing with academic ink. He had a lightning vision of himself in future trudging over dreary campuses, briefcase bulging with student papers, growing a mustache like the doctor's, cultivating a rolling classroom voice, goading young Jonathans into becoming future Harshawes who would have all the fun and glory while he poured bourbon whisky over his poor frustrations.

"Can't you shut up the joint now?" a female voice urged, and there was Lize in the doorway. "Come on over to the Spur with me. This place is a morgue, how do you stand it?"

Lize didn't explain how she happened to be wandering in this dead end at one o'clock in the morning. She motioned Jonathan to a waiting cab when he locked the door, and he saw that the seat of the cab was taken up by the sleeping person of Percy Wright.

"Come on, we'll take the jump seats," Lize commanded. She cast a disapproving glance at the third passenger. "I asked him to meet me at Jack Delaney's after work for a talk—I wanted to borrow fifty bucks and I knew I'd have to get him stoned to get it—and the silly thing thought I wanted to come back to him and he got all emotional, blubbering away about not wanting to hurt me and all that, so I kept lining up double grasshoppers for him, and look at him! I had to tear out the lining of his coat to get the dough to pay the check. *I'm* perfectly sober. What's the matter with men?"

The sleeping figure mumbled.

"Don't try to wake up and be a nuisance now," Lize admonished him. "We'll drop off at the Spur and shoot him off to Brooklyn with the cabby."

She gave instructions to the driver and turned to give Jonathan a warm smile and a fond pat on the knee.

"I drove past half a dozen times to get you," Lize said, "but you always have that old goat from the college in there. What on earth do you pal around with him for? He's old enough to be your father."

"How could he be my father?" Jonathan exclaimed, stricken. "You have no right to say so—I mean, he's not as old as he looks."

"Okay, okay," Lize said, quite surprised by his fire. "You don't need to shout or we'll wake Junior here. I'm only asking what the old boy's got on you that you're so nice to him."

She patted him on the knee again.

"Dr. Kellsey hasn't got anything on me," Jonathan said tensely. "He's nothing to me—nothing at all."

Dr. Kellsey, after leaving Jonathan in the Then-and-Now, walked down the midnight streets in a kind of trance, crossing Seventh Avenue with speeding taxis shouting at him, finding an exotic charm in the smell of decaying bananas near a market, oblivious to the moist August heat. Bleecker Street along here had not changed much from the Bleecker Street he had known when he first came out of the West in the twenties. Granted that he had never been a man to observe his surroundings, his mind being taken up with a great file of indignant letters he had never gotten around to writing to deans, editors, women, creditors, anybody. In the early days he was always half-sprinting along Bleecker, he recalled, because he was due at class, or due to meet his wife for a showdown, and all along the way the little magic doors used to send out fragrant invitations to stop in the back room for a bracer.

Tonight, however, he was wafted along on a mysterious dream and he passed the strident bar cries of even the San Remo without turning his head. Jonathan's story, and the amazing discovery that he himself figured in it, had shaken his mind. The misty wraith of Connie Birch befogged everything. He was determined to fetch up a clearer picture and a proper sequence of memories, but so far he had experienced only the lightning flash of recognition at her photograph and name, a fleeting echo of a soft, apologetic twang, a hint of unexpectedly eager lips in a dark vestibule with sweet words lost in the roar of passing El trains. There was more, oh, there surely was more to it, but when he tried to force his memory through the door and up the stairs he lost the Connie image and the lips. He had been drunk at the time, that could always be guaranteed for episodes of this nature at that period, or else he had drowned guilt later in a healing binge. But this episode was special, Dr. Kellsey moaned, pleading with himself to produce clearer proof. The possibilities in Jonathan's story seemed to have transformed the world for him, and in his vague new rapture he walked across Washington Square and all the way up Broadway across Union Square and Gramercy Park to the Knowlton Arms.

There was an untapped quart of Old Taylor in his closet, and the idea had struck Kellsey that he might induce the proper memory chain by repeating the conditions of the original scene—plunge himself, say, into an alcoholic haze. He accepted the phone slips the desk clerk handed him, two calls from his wife and two, of course, from Anita, but he crumpled them into the wastebasket without noting the messages they'd left, only musing on how infallibly the two ladies kept neck and neck in their race to brand their ownership on him, almost as if—he did not know how right he was—they were partners against him instead of rivals *for*. Certainly their taunts at him were similar. "Too selfish to raise a family like any decent, normal man . . . too neurotic to live a proper married life. . . . No wonder he disliked children—probably couldn't have any himself." He grinned, thinking of their combined wrath when they found out about Connie Birch.

Tonight Dr. Kellsey entered his pleasant large bed-sitting-room with a purposeful air. Instead of getting into pajamas as he usually did, he pulled the serape over the open bed and rearranged the cushions. He turned on the pretty little lights over the unusable fireplace, hummed the march motif from *The Love for Three Oranges* (his favorite opera) as he tested the effect of the three-way floor-lamp—should all three speeds glare down on the rather shabby Chinese rug, or should just one muted bulb gently spotlight the big easy chair with the table of Vichy, cigarettes, and glasses hospitably beside it? He adjusted his prized *shogi* screen around the refrigerator with the electric plate and toaster on top, carefully closed the bathroom door, and then removed his tan cord coat, damp with perspiration from his brisk walk, hung it over the "gentleman," and put on his best black Chinese silk robe, quite as if he were expecting a lady of distinction.

Gratified that the ice was plentiful, he planted a bowl of it with his bottle and giant glass on the table, poured himself a generous sampling, and sank down into the chair, ready to entertain as many dreams of the past as Old Taylor could induce. Old Taylor would, sooner or later, get rid of his damnable monitor, the fear of losing his job, fear of scandal, fear of commitments, fear of failure, the composite bogey that had made his sober existence so disgustingly continent and had blacked out the bold Rabelaisian adventures that he would have liked to brighten his memories if they had not threatened his position. Yes, he had to admit that half the time the monitor, with its blessed anesthesia, had been an ally against his accusing wife and angry mistress, enabling him to shout, "How can I be blamed for something I did not know I was doing?" When he was braced alcoholically for his classes, there was never a passable female student that he had not considered hungrily and, properly loaded, approached. Even complaisant girls, however, either froze or fled at their professor's greedy but classical advances. An unexpected goose or pinch on the bottom as they were mounting the stairs ahead of him, a sudden nip at the earlobe as they bent over the book he offered, a wild clutch at thigh, or a Marxian (Harpo) dive at bosom, a trousered male leg thrust between theirs as they passed his seat to make them fall in his lap, where he tickled their ribs—all these abrupt overtures sent them flying in terror. Brought to his senses by their screams, Kellsey retreated hastily. Some of the more experienced girls, after adjusting their skirts, blouses, coiffures, and maidenly nerves, realized that this was only a hungry man's form of courtship. They reminded themselves that old, famous, and rich men played very funny games, and they prepared themselves for the next move. But Kellsey, repulsed, became at once the haughty, sardonic, woman-hating pedant, leaving the poor dears with a confused impression that they were the ones who had behaved badly, and sometimes, baffled by his subsequent hostility and bad grades, they even apologized.

Deborah was his wife, Anita was his mistress, but Amnesia had been his true friend, the doctor reflected candidly, permitting him to stare straight through some little sophomore trollop who thought she had something on him after his passes of the previous evening. Amnesia gave him back his arrogance and dignity, the proper contempt for students and fellow men that was necessary to a teacher. But alas, Amnesia had also taken away the love of his life—little Connie Birch. If, as he was determined to believe, a child had come of that dim encounter, then he was romantic enough to be convinced it was true love. He assured himself there was proof in the mere fact that he had been drawn toward young Jonathan from the moment of their first meeting, and he detected family resemblances now. He took a long drag of his drink and forced his mind into the period when he had taught Connie. He knew well enough he would have turned the case over to Amnesia if it were not that his true love was conveniently dead.

"The biggest thing in my whole life, and I can't remember it." He sighed, and he thought that poor forgotten little Connie was the only woman who had ever given him anything.

There was Deborah, still his legal wife, though long since living apart from him. She had been a blind date when he had been teaching out in UCLA in 1926. He had drowned his distaste for her in corn whisky, and next thing he knew she'd accused him of getting her in a family way and he must marry her. A plain, smug little party, morally convinced that "sex" itself, let alone her groom's idea of honeymoon pranks, was woman's cross, Deborah had later confessed that the pregnancy was a lie to win his hand in wedlock. Walter was so burned over this trick that it was all he could do to put up a polite husbandly front for his job's sake. Deborah was perfectly satisfied to be let alone, now that she was a missus, and they managed to work out a successful façade. Deborah did his secretarial work, as well as working for other faculty members, so she was on the inside track of academic promotions and finaglings. Presently she became secretary to a rich foundation whose board members were too busy to attend meetings, and powerful decisions were left to mousy little Mrs. Kellsey.

Deborah's *sub rosa* importance enraged Walter except in his periods of pious sobriety, when he was allowed to share it and flaunt it in the faces of his colleagues. Her grapevine information got him a fellowship at the right time, and got him the New York job when she was promoted to the foundation's New York office. Drunk and in his right mind he hated and feared her, but in his nightmares of remorse, financial catastrophes, or professional embarrassments, he turned to her. These were their happiest times, he wallowing in shame and she wallowing in virtue. If his reform lasted as long as his binge, then the doctor became fully as smug as Deborah. They dressed up to attend banquets and foundation affairs together, where

Deborah's undercover power was lost in her official insignificance. She was glad, then, of her extra status as faculty wife, and the doctor was equally glad of his temporary edge over her. Penance done and complacency soon exploded, he went back to his other doghouse, the one kept in constant readiness for him by Anita Barlowe, an assistant professor in his department with whom he had conducted an affair for several years.

This was a curiously spasmodic romance, grounded regularly whenever Anita insisted he divorce Deborah and marry her, and sparked again by their common jealousy of some associate's triumph. Anita took a spiteful comfort in keeping him away from his foundation-superior wife, and Kellsey took a manly satisfaction in having one woman clever enough to catch his subtle gibes at her. They usually went to bed together quite happily and got up infuriated, physically appeased but psychologically defeated.

The greatest thing they had together was a permanent fight subject (i.e., divorce), money in the bank, you might say, when they were bored and their love needed a neat whip. Of course he was bound to Deborah too by a perpetual fight subject, i.e., she had tricked him into marriage, yes. But hadn't he got along better career-wise through her wifely conniving? Yes. Hadn't she pulled the right wires many a time to save his ungrateful hide? Yes. What would he have done without her? Plenty, the doctor thought to himself, but he knew none of it would have been good, which was unforgivable of her.

What burned both women everlastingly was the memory of the time Anita had pounced on Deborah and demanded she give a divorce because Walter had never loved her anyway and why did she go on refusing him his freedom? Because he never asked for it, Deborah had replied with one of her smug smiles. Never even mentioned such a thing, she repeated, how very, very strange for Miss Barlowe to ask. Hysterical and humiliated, Anita had tried to pin down the doctor, who was properly enraged that she should have approached his wife. He had never loved Deborah, true. But did he want to marry Anita? No. After this climactic scene Deborah deliberately started calling herself Mrs. Walter Kellsey instead of plain Deborah Kellsey, Anita went into analysis with a Dr. Jasper who looked like a caricature of Kellsey (that helped a lot), and Kellsey resumed his secret binges and blackouts.

Trying to concentrate on his long-ago student romances, Dr. Kellsey was plagued by reminders of the two women who dogged his career. Everything he ever did seemed for the purpose of spiting or appeasing one or the other, and he wondered if there was anything left in him of untainted personal feeling. His surprising burst of joy at the mere hint he might be a father, for instance. Was this an example of a long-mocked philoprogenitive instinct, evidence that he had more of the simple average male in him than he'd ever suspected? Or was it malicious glee at turning the tables on Deborah for that unforgivable old lie about her pregnancy? Or was it a delicious slap at Anita for her bitchy taunts that he feared a "normal married relationship" with a "normal female" like herself because he knew he was sterile? Old Taylor blinked consolingly at him in the lamp glow, calling him back to that magic long ago when something or other had happened.

The Spur had been a speakeasy then, yes. He hadn't gotten mixed up with Anita yet—that didn't start till World War II—but he was still tangled with Deborah, yes. And he used the excuse of his weekly night class to make a night of it, yes. And he had split-second images of that pale sweet girl and himself in a booth, in a dark vestibule, in a kitchen making drinks (the doctor took another gulp of his kindly potion, for now he was on the right track), trying to dance to a squeaky record from *The Vagabond King,* and falling down in a laughing huddle, with the girl and the record whirring round and round and round, and the ruff getting in his way when he tried to kiss—yes, he was in the Hamlet costume still. . . .

Each time he got to the record part the curtain descended. Doggedly the doctor went back from the Spur to the classroom, to Alan Seeger, to blond braids, carried the story along faster, upstairs, kitchen, gramophone, *Vagabond King,* giggling, sprawl—but the blackout always stopped him there. Just once he got past it to a third shadowy image, another man, an objectionably sneering presence, and a wave of poignant indignation swept over Kellsey that there was always some last-minute intruder, the triumph was always being snatched from under his nose, he was always too late. . . .

The telephone rang. Only Anita would telephone him this late, and it meant she had been phoning around for him all evening. He must have forgotten a date with her. He listened to the ring, clutching his glass, blaming Anita for spoiling his dream continuity, finally snatched the receiver and heard her whimpering reproaches you-said-you-said, you-always-you-always-, you-never-you-never—

"Anita," he interrupted sternly, "you sound as if you'd been drinking."

He grinned with evil satisfaction at the outraged sputtering this accusation brought forth and when it died down he spoke with pious kindliness. "If you're in condition by

Friday, then, my dear, I'll meet you to talk over all these problems you find in our relationship. I have certain things to tell you."

There! If she will break in upon a man's private dream life, let her stew over the consequences.

8

JONATHAN'S NOTE to Mrs. George Terrence at Green Glades, Stamford, arrived in the same mail as a certain letter in green ink to Mr. Terrence. George recognized the ominous green ink, for it was the third such letter he had received, and he fervently hoped his wife and daughter would have mail of their own to distract their attention.

"Who in the world writes you in green ink, George?" his wife inquired, but he was glad she was preoccupied with her own letter.

"I'll read it later," he said, stuffing it into his pocket. "Nothing of any importance comes on Saturday, you know. Why are you scowling over your own letter, my dear?"

"Someone is bothering me again about an old roommate," Hazel said crossly. "I do think it's a nuisance to be expected to keep up with everyone you've ever known."

"That's not like you, dear," George remonstrated severely, glad to have the subject of green ink sidetracked. "As I recall your stories, you had some very happy times at college."

Both George and Hazel were excessively loyal, as a rule, to any demands from their alma maters, though George had been miserably lost at Yale and Hazel had barely finished one semester at Sweetbriar.

"This wasn't a college friend," Hazel said. "This is concerned with a girl I lived with when I was studying the theater. You wouldn't remember her."

Their daughter Amy, who had been patiently staring at the *Stamford Times* society page while her parents loitered over their coffee and mail, looked up.

"I never knew you were interested in the theater, Mother," she said. "I've never heard you mention it."

"I never mentioned it because I forgot all about it. I was young and foolish, like most girls," Hazel said impatiently. "There were all sorts of little drama groups starting up then. Naturally I would never have seriously considered going on the stage."

"I do recall your having a few lines in some little production on Cherry Lane," her husband said, knowing well enough the lasting wound a newspaper criticism of the performance had made on Hazel. "Some of my best clients make their fortune in the theater."

"I can't see why they should write you in green ink," Hazel said, goaded.

"I see no reason why they shouldn't," said George.

Daughter Amy observed the grimly set smiles on each parent's face and sighed, recognizing the signs. Father and Mother were about to engage in one of their obscure duels, flailing delicately at each other with lace-edged kerchiefs that concealed from the observer the weapon and the wound. She had never understood what hidden taunt started the hostilities, but she really couldn't care less. She wondered again how they had endured each other all these years, or did they have some normal human feelings invisible to outsiders? In the tense silence she applied herself dutifully to the newspaper items her mother had marked—MISS ALLIMAN'S PLANS, ETHEL FEIST A BRIDE, JO-

HANNA TRUE TO WED, and other careful hints that Daughter Amy was being left at the post.

"How nice about Ethel," Amy murmured sweetly.

"About this old friend you lived with, my dear," George said to his wife. "It wouldn't have been that nice child from the West, little Connie Whatsername?"

A petulant frown came to Hazel's fair brow.

"Now, why in the world did that come into your head?" she cried. "I thought it was strange that Claire Van Orphen should be writing me about her after all these years, but after all, Connie did do some work for Claire. Then this son writes me, as if I were a blood relation instead of a chance connection of his mother's. But you barely met her. I cannot understand how you should remember her at all."

His wife's irritation soothed George's own uneasiness, and he pushed his chair back from the table with an indulgent laugh.

"I see I need a lawyer for my answer to that," he said. His wife and daughter fetched a dutiful laugh. "What I need is a good lawyer" had been George's joke for years, but the laughers, aware only of George's highly successful legal career, never realized how true it was.

In his entire life George Terrence had never been able to present his own case in any matter, seeing the vulnerability of his own side more clearly than any other, his fine professional mind cruelly operating as prosecutor against G. Terrence, defendant. He took a dour, rueful satisfaction in arguing himself out of the good spots in any situation, sternly denying himself jubilation over triumphs, complacency over good fortune. Detaching himself from his person, he had watched people exploit his money, name, and abilities with ironical amusement. In time he acquired a monumental complacency over his brilliant victory over complacency, and his lengthy sardonic stories of defeats and minor mistakes were more boringly egotistical than other men's boasting.

As a precocious only child of a rich, cultured old family, he conceded (intellectually) that he had no more rights to the pet pony, the toy railroad, the privileges and spending money than the sturdy playmates who were constantly appropriating them. It seemed to him that the superior man degraded himself by fighting over material possessions and proved himself by gracefully conceding. He acquired a defensive ironic bluster and a haughty sulkiness that consoled his pride but did not protect him. At Yale other boys got girls and popularity using George's expensive clothes, cars, credit, and family contacts. They bragged of their rich society pal George Terrence, without letting George share the luster. He stood on street corners in New Haven, watching classmates he hardly knew race by in his Packard, wearing his sport jackets, their arms around lovely girls who would, he knew, rebuff him. (A rumor had gotten around that George Terrence kissed with his mouth closed!)

When he started his career in a distinguished firm on William Street in New York, he took a modest apartment on Irving Place and soon found that, through the pressuring of friends, he was sharing the place with two agreeable younger men interested in literature. At least he wouldn't be lonesome, George was told. It was true he did not suffer in that respect. The young men kept the apartment lively with their girlfriends and all-night gab-fests, and when one or the other was conducting a big love affair, George was likely to find himself locked out. They were as strange to New York City as he was, but they were not handicapped by conscience over privilege as was George. They crashed debutante parties, barged in on good people's dinners, borrowed money from him cheerfully, passed his bootleg gin around, and laughed heartily over his occasionally ironic outbursts.

It had comforted George to know, as he used to sit in his hall room preparing his brief while the living room rang with merry voices, that fun might be fun, but he was the one with the money, the background, and the industry to succeed. Harshawe, a tall, quiet, arrogant fellow, had had a novel accepted for publication, which gave him the edge over Turner, his friend. Harshawe was too tall to wear George's suits, but shirts, sporty vests, ties, socks, and jackets were acceptable. Turner confided in George rather bitterly that the reason Harshawe slaved so hard at his writing was his inferiority about not being a college man. Neither man could understand George's unwillingness to use his Yale Club privileges, where a man could have his liquor in the locker, swim, lounge about, and finally they bullied George into taking them there. It was embarrassing for George, since both interlopers knew all the routine of getting in better than he did, and nobody there knew him or, if anyone did, had a warm greeting that would set up his stock. He felt like an impostor and inwardly vowed never to put himself through such a miserable trial again.

Three months later, however, coming out of Grand Central Station on a Sunday and needing cash, he braved the club. He half expected to be refused entrance, actually. Once inside he saw a familiar pair of long legs stretched out in a big chair, showing Argyle socks made most positively by Mrs. Terrence, Sr., a newspaper obscuring the face, a highball glass nearby, with the arm reaching for it encased in a familiar Terrence tweed. It was Harshawe, who greeted him with lazy good humor.

"How did you manage to get in?" George asked, mystified.

Harshawe shrugged and nodded toward his glass.

"Sit down and have a drink, Terrence," he said hospitably. "Oh, I like the place. I drop in every day to read the papers and have a smoke or a drink."

George wouldn't have known how to manage this himself, so he said, "But how do they let you in?"

"I use your name," Harshawe said. And at that moment a boy came up to him and said, "Your call is ready, Mr. Terrence."

"Thanks, Joey," Harshawe said and rose to stroll over to the telephone, leaving George frozen with outrage, staring after him. In a burst of courage he snatched the *Wall Street Journal,* of all things, which Harshawe had been reading, and resolutely plumped himself down in Harshawe's chair. There was a touch on his arm.

"Pardon me, sir," the boy said firmly, "that's Mr. Terrence's chair, and I don't believe he's quite finished with his paper."

By this time George Terrence was madder than he'd ever been in his life, but, being unaccustomed to shabby shows of temper or pettishness, he could think of no way of handling the situation. All he could do was to gulp down Harshawe's drink and stalk out, forgetting to cash his check. He went straight to the apartment, packed up his things, and moved to the Hotel Lafayette. His anger appeased, his conscience bothered him about allowing a poor underprivileged, undereducated chap of inferior breeding to upset him. He sent a check for the quarter's rent on the apartment, said he had decided the Hotel Lafayette was more convenient for him, and graciously urged both Harshawe and Turner to be his guests at the Yale Club whenever they chose. The gesture restored George's *amour propre,* though it was periodically shaken whenever the three dined at the club and many members slapped Harshawe and Turner on the back, waiters beamed at them, but no one remembered George. The others did the ordering, made the suggestions, sent dishes back as they chose, and in all made George deeply relieved to get back to the Lafayette, where he could enjoy the pale eminence of being the youngest man in the café.

He was doing well in his profession, but when George did well nobody seemed to know it. Other, bolder members of the firm took entire credit in court for George's briefs. George tried to tell himself that the office and people who counted knew it was he who had done the real work, just as the important people at the Yale Club knew he was the real George Terrence, didn't they? But he ought to have learned that people believed whomever shouted the loudest and pushed the hardest. Crushed between his office pals and his old roommates, George appealed to psychoanalysis, a process that occupied two years and afforded that eager healer named Dr. Jasper a good living and some much-needed experience. In the nick of time Hazel Browne flung herself upon George and married him, remaining awed and grateful for this triumph, insisting on being bullied and masterminded, so that there was nothing for George to do but oblige her.

When people praised the powerful change in his character, George declared it was all due to his superb analysis. Hazel dutifully agreed, never realizing how colossal her own part had been in the transformation. She forgave George for his wild playboy youth, ruthless philandering, fascinating mistresses, and mythical past until George had the pleased conviction that he'd really had all that. Hazel must be right. It was the facts that erred. He allowed Hazel to worship him as a man of the world and dropped an occasional allusion that kept her ever fearful that she might lose him yet to the sexpots surely clamoring for him.

It was a good marriage for these twenty-odd years, with Hazel putting her whole soul into living up to the Terrence tradition of unimpeachable respectability and George always hoping to live it down. When their opposite views might have led to bickering they used their daughter as a buffer, and had grown so accustomed to speaking to each other through her that they hardly thought of her as a person but as an intercom.

"Your mother had a charming habit of being late for appointments when I was courting her." George now addressed his daughter. "While I waited in her living room her roommate very graciously entertained me. Naturally I remembered her kindness."

"I'm sure she was trying to get herself invited," Hazel said to her daughter. "Poor Connie didn't have many beaux as I recall her. At any rate I cannot understand why I should have to give out interviews to her relatives after all these years. Why should Claire Van Orphen suggest it? What could I possibly have to say about her?"

"What do you think Mother should do about it?" Amy obligingly passed the query to her father.

"If I were your mother I should write a nice little note inviting the party to come in for tea if he is in the neighborhood," George said judiciously, feeling for the offensive green-inked envelope in his pocket. "I gather that little Connie has passed on and they merely want to patch up some memories about her. No harm."

Hazel bit her lip.

"I still don't see why she should have mentioned me.

You can tell your father, Amy, that I did write a polite note saying that we didn't get into the city often and that I didn't see how I could tell him anything about his mother. But he wants to see your father too. I think it's very strange. And he suggested coming out today."

A stranger asking to take up his own valuable time was a different matter entirely, and George was on the verge of protesting that the intruder must certainly be put off, but Hazel took the words out of his mouth.

"It's all very well to say I should have him here, but when we only see our daughter once a month and when your father prizes his reading time at home above every other consideration—"

"Not above an old friendship," George said, perverse as usual. "If it's Connie's son, of course I will see him, whether your mother cares to or not, Amy, my dear. It's certainly too late to put him off now, anyway."

Both Hazel and George were getting red in the face, the only outward indication that they were having what would be in other families a knockdown fight. Amy looked from one to the other parent with languid curiosity. This was a game her parents had been playing as long as she could remember, a game which excluded her, but it afforded her privacy and freedom.

Many was the time they conducted a polite discussion through Amy regarding the suitability of a school, a dress, a companion for her, both their faces getting redder and redder but their voices never rising in their careful "your father"ing and "your mother"ing. Amy could have gone off to the wrong college with the wrong people in the wrong clothes without her absence's being noticed. She knew that her meticulously coiffured, massaged, and prim-mannered mother lived in awe of her trim, neatly turned-out father, quite as if his possible disapproval meant violence or excommunication instead of a delicately sardonic comment or a mere cough. Amy had given up puzzling over what their hold was on each other, devoting herself to the full-time job of concealing her life from them. If they were flaring up now, the cause was certainly more trivial than usual, a silly matter of receiving or not receiving somebody's son.

Mrs. Terrence, always the first to surrender, beckoned the Chinese houseman, Lee, who had been popping his head in the door every few minutes.

"Lee's in a hurry to clear up because he's going to the ballgame," she said. "Do you want to come with me to the Flower Show, Amy?"

"That sounds very nice, Mother," Amy said obediently.

"Mustn't let your mother tire you out," George Terrence admonished. "I'm sure you have lots of studying to do. Sometimes these special summer courses are tougher than the regular ones. Get back in time for a little rest before you leave, my child."

"Thank you, Father, I will," Amy said.

"She'll have all day Sunday," her mother said, "since she has to go back tonight."

George waited till the two ladies had left the table and Lee had started brushing up before he went into the library to his desk. He had to think, but he could never put his mind to anything properly if there was a chance that Hazel would interrupt. She had been remarkably suspicious today about his dreadful mail, he thought, and what with her twittering about little Connie Birch's son, she'd gone out of her way to be irritating. After a few moments he heard her calling, "George, we're off now. Tell your father we're leaving, Amy, dear." At the moment George felt like snarling, "So you're going, then for God's sake be off," but he controlled himself.

He wished fervently that something, anything, would keep his womenfolk away till he could collect his thoughts. He hoped he had remembered to ask where they were going, that was all, and if they were walking to be sure they wore the right shoes. He didn't care if they went barefooted, really, but he did care about showing interest. At any rate they were gone, and the next minute he heard Lee taking out the station-wagon, putting off toward the highway. Thank God.

George fumbled in his desk drawer for a minute before he remembered that he had destroyed the other two letters. He had kept them for a few weeks, intending to give them a completely detached legal study, but there had never come a moment when he could even think about them without panic. Their destruction had seemed to relieve his mind for a while, but the worry had only gone underground, and sprang up at sight of this last communication.

George spread the note on the desk before him, then covered his eyes with his hand. It was childish. He needed a brandy. Standing at the french windows, shot glass of brandy in hand, he looked out at the lush garden, the espaliered pear trees against the stone wall, the purple-blossomed Empress of China trees fringing the rock pool, the heliotrope-bordered paths, the twin fig trees by the gate. What would *you* do? he asked each one of them in turn and went back to his desk, forcing himself to read the letter.

"Dear Terrence: You know damn well I'll keep writing until I get some action or an answer. As a matter of fact, I like to write you. It gives me a chance to unload some old burns and a private laugh or two, like the laugh of you always calling yourself Roger Mills of Toronto. I knew who you were the first time you picked me up at the King Cole Bar but I went along with the Roger bit for laughs. I never could figure out why you picked me, when the other boys were so much prettier, but I suppose a closet queen has to pick the mutt type like yours truly to keep off suspicion.

"I wasn't planning to keep at the trade, really, not having your problem of being too afraid of dames to lay them. I could say you made me what I am today if I wanted to be real mean, doll, but you saved me financially that summer and I thank you. I know I saved you too, for you confessed you couldn't go for a dame that wanted you until you'd gotten excited over me. (I thought I'd mention that bit if I have to write to your wife, who, I guess, was the only one you ever made out with.) You taught me to like nice things, though, and Roger-George-baby I've got to have them now for an amusing little punk of my own that I've got on the hook just the way you got me.

"I'm a lousy actor, as any critic will tell you, so I can always get a job, but I can't make enough to keep this little punk in the luxuries I taught him to need. I'm laying it on the line, Rogie-Podgie, I'm nuts about this boy and it's driving me crazy when he has to screw some old woman for his bar tab. Love and honor are at stake when I repeat I've got to have $5000 to square things or I write Mrs. T. about that little summer's idyll. Daughter Amy—yes, I know you did make it once, anyway—will be grateful that she owes her existence to your great good friend and pupil.

"I'll be waiting, let's say till the first."

George looked at the writing again, commanding his

mind to detach itself from his panic and take charge as it would do for a frightened client. The green letters curled around one another like snakes, y's and g's and f's had corkscrew tails, capitals writhed through loops before identifying themselves, even the letter T managed to spiral on its cross. You didn't need any legal training to deduce that the writer was abnormal, even criminal. How simple it would be if this were a client's problem instead of his own!

"Send the chap to me," George could hear himself loftily advising the worried client. "I'll get him to show exactly what he has on you and in that way get a line on his own record. You'll find we can scare him off, lucky to get away without a prison sentence. Leave it to me."

Hah. Leave it to me. Not when he was his own client, George thought morosely.

If only he dared consult Doctor Jasper . . . But it had been Dr. Jasper, after all, who'd gotten him into this mess. He'd been an eager young psychiatrist in those days, all hopped up over the new science, and George was his first paying customer. He'd believed in the doctor implicitly, George thought with a sigh, probably because it was all new and exciting and he was as eager to be a guinea pig as Jasper was to have one. If you're so afraid to sleep with a girl, said the doctor, then try it out with your own sex, maybe that's the answer, let's have everything out in the open. Once you know, then we can handle the problem. Jasper never expected he would be taken seriously, then, by anybody. Lucky Hazel appeared on the scene about then and simplified everything; no further dealings with old Jasper.

George picked up the note and tore it up carefully, made a little snake nest in the ashtray of the pieces, and set a match to them. A slight sound outside made him look up from this operation. Someone was coming up the garden path, the pebbles crackling underfoot. George stayed motionless, smitten by the dread that the green-ink writer himself might have cornered him. He realized he could be seen from the garden and, from the sound of the footsteps pausing, knew the intruder must be directly outside the window, no doubt staring at him. George forced himself to walk toward the window. He saw with almost a sob of relief that the young man was a stranger with only warm friendliness on the fair, smiling face. He pushed open the french windows, half locked by rose vines.

"The bus driver told me this was the Terrence place," the stranger said.

"I am George Terrence," George said.

"I wrote Mrs. Terrence I would pay a call today. I'm Jonathan Jaimison. My mother—"

George felt a wave of deep affection for this young man, unexpected savior of his peace.

"Connie's boy!" he exclaimed, holding out both hands with an enthusaism that would have astounded his family. "What a splendid surprise. Do come in—no, no, right this way, never mind those tulips, just step over them."

As it had never occurred to Jonathan that he would not be welcome, he was pleased but not surprised at the warmth of his reception. He sat back in the elaborately comfortable red leather chair George had directed him to, accepted a cigarette and a stout highball, refused George's urgent offer of a sandwich, coffee, cake, icewater, protesting that he had breakfasted late. He would not stay long; all he wished was information about his mother's New York life from those who must have known her best. Miss Van Orphen had suggested—

"Splendid!" George Terrence exclaimed happily. "Yes,

a splendid idea of Claire's. I must get in touch with her one of these days, it's been so long. A pity Hazel, Mrs. Terrence, isn't here, since she was such a dear friend of your mother's."

"Perhaps I'd better come back some day when Mrs. Terrence is in," Jonathan suggested tentatively.

Indeed he must not think of leaving, George insisted. After all he too had known the young man's mother, perhaps in some ways even better than his wife had. There had been times Connie Birch had confided in him, for instance, while he waited for Hazel to dress or come home for an appointment.

"You mean she confided in you about her—love life, say?" Jonathan leaned forward eagerly. "About the men she knew?"

George realized that, in his anxiety to detain his caller, he had gone too far. He had only the vaguest memory of Connie; all he remembered was his disappointment when the door used to open on Hazel's roommate instead of Hazel herself.

"No, no, nothing like that," he said hastily. "Surely you never thought your mother was not circumspect in every way. No, we discussed her work with my firm's clients, the Misses Van Orphen, and music, books—"

"But she did know several men," Jonathan persisted, and then asked doubtfully, "You don't mean to say she was not—attractive to men?"

George saw he was on the wrong tack.

"My dear boy, she was charming! Utterly charming," he declared. "You must see that in her pictures." He wished the boy would produce a photograph to nudge his memory. "As a matter of fact, if my wife had been late a few more times I cannot guarantee what might have happened."

"She wrote my aunt that you—or the man her roommate was engaged to was tremendously clever," Jonathan told him. "She seemed to feel as you did, that if you had not been already committed—well, you know how those things are. You were a man of the world, she said, and had so much to teach a girl."

"She said that?" George was touched.

"You explained Marx to her," Jonathan said, "and Freud and that sort of thing."

Those had been courting subjects in that day, George recollected with some embarrassment. Now he did have a sudden picture of sitting on a sofa with the sweet girl, reading aloud from Freud while she consoled him with bootleg gin and orange juice till Hazel came home. He could almost swear there had been a slight hassle, a furtive embrace, a scurrying when Hazel's key sounded in the lock.

"I do want to find out the man in her life then," Jonathan said. "It wasn't you, sir, that winter of nineteen twenty-eight?"

"Nineteen twenty-eight," George repeated, and his eyes fell on the ashtray, where he fully expected to see green ashes. "Why do you ask?"

"I'm looking for my father," Jonathan confessed. "I was hoping it might be you, now that we've met."

The ashes were gray like any other ashes, George saw. A sweet sense of relief was surging through him, and an excitement was beginning in the back of his brain that meant a subtle, hidden point was about to be flushed out into service. He carried the ashtray to the window and poured the contents over the rosebush with great precision.

"Ashes are splendid for the soil, you know," George said.

Hazel Terrence would have been astonished at the behavior of her husband that Saturday afternoon. He had always professed a manly aversion to the details of the home, he disliked all social encounters that demanded small talk, and he particularly avoided contact with the younger generation.

Yet here he was showing Jonathan Jaimison over the grounds, pointing out the foundations of the old mill, leading him through the grape arbors and confessing his ambition to have a real vineyard (Hazel would have been surprised to hear this), explaining the herb garden with great pride: *this* was what you did with the *Waldmeister* in Maywine making, this was tarragon, this was rosemary, delicious with roast lamb, this was mint—by Jove, they'd have a julep!

"Next time you come up we must take you for a swim in the brook," George said, as if this was only the beginning of a deep intimacy. Hazel would never have dreamed he knew or cared so much about the flowers she and Lee nursed so tenderly. Her firm, dimpled jaw would have dropped to hear her husband's deferential interest in this young man's opinions on the state of the world and his benign advice on futures for talented lads. She would not have believed her ears had she heard the many times George exclaimed, "Splendid! How right you are!" to the stranger's shyly offered remarks.

Hazel had given up trying to break into her husband's moody silence at dinner with her harmless little anecdotes of town scandals, a tiff with the butcher, a pleasant encounter with an old neighbor, a report on a new supermarket's advantages. George had a way of smiling at her across the carefully chosen table flowers and shutting her up with "My dear, must we clutter up our minds with all this trivia? Isn't it hard enough to manage our own major patterns without dragging in the inconsequentials? We are not curious about others' private lives."

But here was her same George eagerly asking young Jaimison for more and more trivia, listening with deep absorption to a description of the Then-and-Now Café, nodding approvingly at Jonathan's praise of Claire Van Orphen.

"A splendid soul," said George. "I was fortunate enough to handle their father's estate and got to know the two sisters very well, particularly Claire, a most talented woman. And this writer friend you mention, Earl Turner, was an old friend of mine, too. We shared an apartment once with Harshawe, the now famous Harshawe, of course, and frankly I always felt Turner had the better brains. I've often thought of looking him up sometime, but since my semi-retirement we spend very little time in New York—my wife hates it."

Me hate New York! Hazel would have exclaimed, had she heard this statement—as if I had any choice about it! And "looking up" any old friend of his past was the last thing in the world George Terrence would ever want to do.

Whenever Jonathan suggested leaving, George Terrence thought of something else to detain him. So The Golden Spur was still going. Amazing. Jonathan must tell him more. Mrs. Terrence would be heartbroken to have missed him, and she should certainly be back before four. Living in the wilderness as he did, George warmly assured his guest, he found news of the great artistic world a godsend. It was seldom, moreover, that he found a young man who had so many of the same interests and reactions to life that he himself had had at that age. He was only surprised that Jonathan, with the acute perceptiveness he displayed on all subjects, had not taken up law.

"You really think so?" Jonathan asked, highly pleased. "As a matter of fact I did think of law at one time. My mother talked about it when I was still in primary school. Perhaps she was thinking of you."

Another wave of tenderness for his wife's long-lost roommate came over George. In the course of their talk a far clearer memory of Connie had emerged, and he had fleeting pictures of himself and Hazel, all dressed up for some fancy social affair (it was Hazel who had started him on accepting these invitations), while little Connie lonesomely bade them have fun. Connie had been shy, just as he was, and he should have noticed more things—her interest in him, for instance. But Hazel had rushed him through to the altar so fast he hadn't had time to be even polite. Connie had written him a little verse on his birthday, though, by Jove, he suddenly remembered.

"Your mother was a very fine person, very sensitive," George said broodingly. "Too bad you're not a lawyer. I could be of some use to you now in getting started in New York."

Jonathan had the impulse to declare that he would plunge at once into the study of law if it would please this kind gentleman. He stole furtive glances at him, telling himself that in spite of his being a good four inches taller than Mr. Terrence, and blonder and blue of eye, there was a suspicious resemblance in the set of the ears, the shape of the brow, even in the timbre of their voices, though this might have been because his host's academic style of delivery was contagious. Jonathan was always susceptible to other people's mannerisms and he was already handling his cigarette in the same way George did, waving it like a baton to illustrate some remark, then plunging it up to his lips as if to stop an emergency hole in the dike. George, suddenly glancing over, caught Jonathan in the very act of synchronizing the gesture with his, and smiled.

"A daughter is all very well," George went on confidentially, "but a man who has worked his way to the top in his profession, learned a lot along the way, has a lot to give, needs a son to carry on, don't you see? For instance, if you were my boy—"

But I am, I am, Jonathan wanted to cry out, quite carried away as George paused to light another cigarette, I could be! He did not speak, but he had a feeling that George Terrence had the same thought. Under the circumstances they could not come out openly with the idea. But they would know, and that was the main thing.

"I think I am only being realistic when I admit to you that my daughter is not a clever girl," George said suddenly. "Her mother and I have had to make all her decisions, and we are grateful that she is a good, obedient child. She has had the best upbringing and every opportunity, but she has no ambition such as I always had, very little interest in society even, clings to her home so much she did not want to go further off to college than New York. I dare say in our old age this sort of clinging will be a comfort. And yet . . ."

He sighed and stroked his chin. Jonathan stroked his own chin in sympathy.

Suddenly his host banged his fist down.

"By Jove, it's not too late even now!" he exclaimed. "I'll put you in our office as a starter, send you to school nights, no reason you shouldn't make the most of a good legal mind such as yours. Not necessarily in the courts of law precisely, but there are other angles. How about that?"

"That's too good of you, sir," was all Jonathan could say.

George Terrence wrote something on a card, which he handed to Jonathan.

"This may be a day you'll remember all your life," he said. "I'll be making arrangements for you, and you come to the office a week from Wednesday. I'll come in myself!"

Behind him on the mantelpiece a cuckoo flew out of a clock, and Jonathan jumped up at the stroke of four, remembering he should take the four-thirty train back to the city. Mr. Terrence leaped up at the same time as a pair of black cocker spaniels tumbled through the french windows.

"Good heavens, the girls must be back!" he said. "Wait while I tell them you're here."

Jonathan stared blissfully at the card in his hand as George left. Incredible that his future should be solved so simply and suddenly. He wandered around the library, studying the family portraits with new interest, measuring his resemblance to them. It occurred to him that if George Terrence was really his father, then it would be awkward meeting his wife. She might even see the resemblance and feel bitterly toward the old girl friend who had betrayed her. Perhaps she already knew. Jonathan found himself weighing all angles of the situation with the shrewd legal slant of which he felt suddenly possessed. Naturally she would be considering the danger of financial claims. Jonathan was smitten with embarrassment. That his desire to claim a parent might be construed as a raid on the family fortune had not occurred to him before, and he fixed his gaze broodingly on the garden, stroking his chin just as George Terrence did when pondering a problem.

He heard a feminine voice enunciate softly but firmly, "I'm sorry, my dear, but you'll simply have to explain that my head is killing me and I must lie down. I'm going straight up to bed. Amy can speak to him."

There was a patient sigh from George, a soothing murmur from another feminine voice, and then the library door opened again to admit George, smiling rather grimly, followed by a young woman.

"This is my daughter Amy, Jonathan," George said. "You must meet this young man, my dear, child of one of your mother's and my very old friends. Will you excuse me, Jonathan, while I go upstairs and see what I can do to relieve my wife?"

"I'm afraid I'll have to say good-by now, Mr. Terrence," Jonathan said nervously, stretching out his hand. "The station bus will be along any minute."

He stopped short. Mechanically he went on shaking the hand of the young lady, dropped it, and grasped George's outstretched hand.

"Amy can drive you to the station, can't you, my dear? Take the Volkswagen, and Lee can pick it up at the station later," George urged. "Amy has to take the same train back, don't you, my dear?"

"I'll be glad to look after Mr. Jaimison, Father," Amy said, and then their eyes met.

Jonathan stared at her incredulously. He barely noticed George Terrence clasping his hand again in farewell.

"We'll be seeing each other, of course, Jonathan," George Terrence called out from the door. "This has been most interesting. Sorry Mrs. Terrence is under the weather. Ah well, the ladies—you understand!"

Jonathan did not hear. Amy stared back at him defiantly.

"There—there must be some mistake," he stammered. "I had no idea you were—I mean—"

"Hush!" She seized his arm petulantly and pulled him toward the garden door. "Come along, they know we have to make that train. They'll be arguing for hours. Why did you have to come here? What have you told him about me?"

"But I came to see him about my own problems! I never even dreamed—"

"I knew it would happen sometime," Amy said, leading him across the terrace to the lower gate where the Volkswagen stood. He got in while she waited to wave dutifully toward the house. Jonathan took the cue and waved too.

"Oh, they can't see us," she said, taking the wheel. "I was just waving good-by to Amy Terrence like I always do."

"I'm confused," Jonathan said, once they were on the highway. "You are Iris Angel, aren't you?"

"Now I am. I thought you'd come out to tell Father, for a bad minute."

"But I didn't know—I still don't understand."

"Anyway, you didn't goof when you saw me, so I forgive you," she said. "I absolutely shook when I saw you there!"

"But which are you, Amy or Iris?" Jonathan asked, mystified. "Aren't they your real parents?"

"Of course they are, when I'm with them," Amy said with an obvious effort to be patient with childish questions. "I'm Amy Terrence for them. You don't think they'd ever let me be anything else, do you? But the minute I'm out of their sight I'm Iris Angel."

Jonathan thought it strange that to his own daughter a great lawyer like George Terrence should be as unsympathetic as a Jaimison.

"But he understands ambition so well," he said. "You could have explained to him."

"Explain!" Iris mocked him. "There's no explaining to your family. You can waste your whole life fighting them, if you're a fighter. But I'm no fighter, and how can you fight when they make you doubt yourself? I'm an actress and the only way I can survive is to play the part called for.

They want their Amy, so I play Amy Terrence for them, and everybody's happy with no argument. See?"

"We're in the same spot," he confessed. "I couldn't start being myself till I'd blanked out the Jaimisons."

He started to blurt out his own story but had the good sense to reserve the vital facts. Iris was fascinated with the hints he gave, and they agreed it was small wonder they had been drawn to each other at first meeting. They were still congratulating each other on the coincidence when they got off the train. At daybreak they were learning even more about each other, lying on Iris's floor on Waverly Place.

Amy Terrence had had secret names for herself all during her childhood, but "Iris Angel" was the one she stuck to after her fifteenth birthday. By that time she took for granted that the girl Amy was a dummy daughter invented by her parents, a proper doll wound up by them for family performances, while the real creature, Iris Angel, used the dummy as armor to hide her private self.

To all appearances Amy had been a quiet little girl, approved but scarcely noticed by teachers in the convent school, later practicing her piano, ballet, skating, and languages at home exactly as required, showing neither unseemly aptitude nor more apathy than was stylish. It had been a mighty feat of silent diplomacy for her to make her father feel it was his inspiration to allow her to live in New York for special courses instead of going to Vassar. A colleague in George Terrence's office had a daughter doing this very thing. The two men agreed that their daughters were too timid and overbred for modern times, and girls' schools would make them worse. The thing to do—if the girls were ever to hold their own in the race for husbands—

was to push them out of the nest, put them on their own (suitably protected, of course) to prepare them for the day when no more spoon-feeding was possible.

The colleague's nice little daughter was persuaded to take Amy into her nice little flat in a nice little made-over house in nice little Turtle Bay. All four parents congratulated themselves on their liberal point of view, and they chuckled at the paradox of their own modernity and their daughters' shy Victorianism. They reminded one another of what mature men and women they had been at that age and what irony to have hatched these tender doves.

Amy dutifully followed her parents' suggestions in registering for secretarial courses, art and cooking classes. She had membership cards at the Museum of Modern Art and the Metropolitan, season tickets for the Philharmonic, charge accounts at suitable stores. She then proceeded to ignore the whole plan and quietly set about getting into the theater, visiting producers and agents with a doggedness that would have amazed her parents. She got a part as a bawd in a *Merry Wives of Windsor* production that played only two weeks but established her, in her own mind at least. She took a basement apartment on Waverly Place as Iris Angel, but arranged with her roommate to keep the Amy Terrence name on the Turtle Bay apartment. For three years she had managed to conceal her true activities, rushing up to her proper apartment when her roommate alerted her that a parent was imminent, appearing at the Connecticut parental home on alternate week ends in the guise of docile student-daughter.

A number of things had happened to Amy during that time. She had taken her turn at falling in love with the painter Hugow, dogged his footsteps through Village bars, phoned him at least twice a day, managed to be seduced by him, had the usual agonies of an abortion, and then was rescued by a summer stock job in Canada. For her parents' information she was on a painting trip with an art class. She then followed him to Haiti and spent three blissful months with him while her roommate dispatched prefabricated notes from Europe, where she and Amy were supposed to be on a tour of the château country.

After her first few panics Amy had become so expert in conducting her two lives that she switched from Iris to Amy as easily as she played her other stage roles. She was helped in the masquerade by two factors. One was the fact that her shy girl friend was in an equally dangerous spot, having a serious affair with a married university teacher and needing reciprocal protection, and the second was the convenient blindness induced by the imperturbable complacency and complete self-absorption of George and Hazel Terrence. Devoted parents as they were, they had never taken their responsibilities easily but had worried and consulted and nagged over every tooth, every mouthful, every sneeze, every freckle of their little girl, smothering her with their anxieties till they lost sight of the girl herself. Secretly she was their weapon against each other. Such a good child, such an obedient daughter, such a treasure! But what heaven to have her being good and obedient some place else, leaving them to their mature, well-organized selfishness!

Amy must have sensed her position the day she was born and seen the advantage it gave her for her own selfish ends. She could have been plotting like a trusty in prison, building complete confidence in good little Amy all those years, while grooming Iris Angel for the escape. She had seldom uttered a thought in the company of her parents, always listening obsequiously, receiving their admonitions with a prim "Yes, Father," "I shall certainly think about that, Father." "Thank you very much, Mother, I am sure you are right."

Fortunately neither George nor Hazel liked the theater, certainly not in its new off-Broadway aspects, so Amy did not feel her Iris Angel identity was imperiled. At first she had feared not disapproval of her stage ambitions but interference in them. There would have been formal discussions, Mother would have escorted her to auditions arranged through suitable social channels, Father would insist on a program of plays to be studied, private tutors would be chosen from distinguished old stars of their own day who would teach her how to beat her breast and nibble the scenery. She knew they would explain to their circle that they had chosen theatrical training for her as invaluable for a future hostess, not really as a career.

If her parents had been able to forget themselves long enough to really observe their little girl, they would have noted that her manners became glibber every year, her Yes, Fathers, and Thank you, Mothers popped out mechanically, while Amy stared into space, increasingly bored by her daughterly role. Hugow and her stage and Village pals never once doubted her Iris Angel personality. Amy would have died of shame had they discovered her bourgeois background, but luckily they were too self-centered to be curious.

Now that Jonathan had found her out, she was surprised that it was a great relief to tell him everything. She had never thought of her double life as wrong; it was merely complicated at times, and inconvenient. Sometimes she was Amy, and sometimes she was Iris, she explained to Jonathan, never both at once, any more than a two-timing husband plays both his roles at once. Besides, it was absolutely necessary if she was to get what she wanted from life.

"I just do what other girls do, only they don't use two names," she said. "They just keep fighting it out with their families, but with parents like mine, I wouldn't have had a chance. I had to play it like a stage part."

Jonathan was such an admiring audience that she played up the part, describing narrow escapes from discovery both by her family and by her Iris Angel set. Now that she was Iris Angel again, her black hair fell loosely out of its prim arrangement, her arms and legs swung freely, she seemed bigger, as if even her flesh had been compressed in her Amy role. The voice changed from the colorless precision to the appealing huskiness that had first attracted him.

Funny, Jonathan kept remarking, that she should have to throw off her family mark to find her own identity, whereas his own problem was the opposite. It made the reasons for liking each other all the stronger, they told each other solemnly. Presently Iris bethought herself of danger and implored Jonathan not to betray her confidences. He was shocked at the idea.

"I am only wondering what would happen if your parents found out the extent of your Iris Angel life," he said. "As an actress, of course, you may have another name. But your union card, your contracts and lease here, and the false Iris Angel background you've given out . . . Can they stop you from appearing in a play, let's say?"

Iris had raised herself on one elbow on the rug where they lay and she was staring at him curiously.

"Or you find yourself unjustly accused in an accident," Jonathan went on, "and your double identity comes out. What is your legal position—"

He stopped when Iris put a hand over his mouth.

"You're just like Father!" she cried. "I can't stand it if you're turning out to get legal about everything. Jonathan, you scare me! Stop looking like Father."

"Do I really?"

"You do! You put your fingers together when you say the word 'legal' as if you were praying, just the way he does, and I can't stand it! It makes me afraid of you. You even say 'splendid' just the way he does."

Jonathan trembled.

"You know I wouldn't tell your father—" he started to assure her, but she interrupted him.

"What I don't understand is why you should have called on my parents," Iris said. "Mother never mentioned having lived in the Village or studying the theater. Until that note of yours came I never heard her mention your mother's name. And I simply can't believe she had all those beaux and dates as your mother said. Oh no. You've no idea how stuffy she is. Even worse than Father."

Curious that Iris had caught the resemblance in him to her father. If he couldn't make any headway with his wishful thinking about Alvine Harshawe, he would be content to be the byblow of a distinguished legal brain, Jonathan decided. Iris's long arms drew him closer, and joy filled him that he had found father and true love at the same time.

"Do you really want to go in Father's office as he said, and study law, Jonathan?" Iris said dreamily. "It will take years and years, darling, and there are so many other wonderful things we might be doing together. Why should he pick on you to be his successor?"

"Don't you see, it's because—" Jonathan started and then froze. Good God!

If he'd found a father in George Terrence, then he'd found not his true love but a sister!

"What is it, darling? If you're worrying about Hugow, you mustn't," Iris whispered. "The past is the past."

Jonathan forced himself to draw away from the warm golden cheek against his, and untangled his legs from the long brown ones. It was an effort to get to his feet.

The past was the past all right, and he should never have stirred it up.

"I've got to go," he said. "I mean we mustn't—I shouldn't—it's a mistake—oh, Iris, I do love you. Good-by."

He dashed out before she could speak, which was well, because any word from her would have brought him back. The faster he walked, the more frightened he was by the wheels he had set in motion which he must now brake as best he could.

Obviously he could not explain to Iris, and he dared not see her. His only hope was to get proof somehow that George Terrence was not his father. Until then he would hide.

For the first time he wished he had left an escape hole, even if it led back to Jaimison, Sr.

9

Ever since Jonathan Jaimison had brought magic into Claire Van Orphen's life she had been fervently longing for her twin sister, Bea. It was no use reminding herself that Bea felt no reciprocal yearning, and had never kept an engagement with her without postponing it at least twice. Bea was perfectly sweet about gossiping over the phone for an hour, but all Claire needed to do was say, "It's such fun talking, let's have lunch," and Bea was ready to hang up, almost as if she felt her good nature was being taken advantage of. Then Claire would pick up her poor pride and remember not to phone for weeks, because it was too obvious that Bea used the phone not to keep in touch with her but to keep her away.

Earl Turner doesn't find me such a bore, Claire told herself, and if I know Bea she would be mighty flattered to have an ex-*Sphere* editor like Earl call on her the way he does on me. And Jonathan is the sort of attractive young man she is always making a fool of herself over. And if she could just see me having my Manhattans at The Golden Spur with those two men, she would do her damnedest to make them like her best, the way she always used to do.

But Bea hardly listened to Claire's reports of her new life, or if she did hear she put her own interpretation on Claire's news. Maybe her little books on gardening, travel, careers, or kiddy life, and the occasional nice little love stories in nice women's magazines, weren't great literary triumphs, Claire conceded, but my word, it did mean something to do a job well enough to have it sold at a counter, and it wouldn't have hurt Bea to throw her a compliment. Oh, Bea tried to be kind, but her compliments were always laced with insults.

"I do think you're amazing to go on and on writing those little things you do, Claire," Bea would say. "I must send you that little avant-garde magazine my friend writes for. I'm sure you could catch on to the modern manner. It's such a shame to waste your talents on this other sort of thing. You really should catch up with the times, dear."

Well, what about those sales to TV of the old stories Earl had revamped? What about the old one he'd turned upside down and sold to the *Post*? Even Bea wouldn't dare call TV old hat. Claire didn't want to risk having the joy of her new triumphs crushed, and didn't confide them at first. Not over the phone, she said to herself. But how she ached for the old blind loyalty of their younger days! What good was happiness if you couldn't tell it to a loved one, share it and double the joy?

She herself, at least, tried to put on an act of being interested in Bea's obsession with the music world, all the greenroom tattle about the Met and Balanchine and Bing and Lenny Bernstein, all the inside chatter that the ladies around Carnegie Hall feasted on. She may have worked too hard at feigning interest, Claire reflected, for Bea usually shut up abruptly after some comment from her sister. Once she had been downright angry, Claire recalled, after telling stories about Bing all during lunch so that Claire innocently asked how long she'd known Mr. Bing. It turned out Bea had never even met him and was annoyed when Claire expressed surprise at such passionate interest in a man she did not even know.

As Earl says, I probably bug her more than she bugs me, Claire sorrowfully admitted.

In the night the new loneliness for someone to share her success, the ache for Bea, the sister of long ago was unbearably painful. Maybe they could take a cruise together, the way they did when they were girls. They could talk over the family history, go over memories of Father and that dreadful second wife of his (still alive in a nursing home in Baltimore, determined to hang on till every penny was gone). They could fill in the gaps of old stories they had forgotten. They might even live together again.

The idea of suggesting this to Bea was too bold for Claire to entertain at first, but it grew on her more and more. She had a vague suspicion that Bea's money must be running out. Bea had never mentioned what sort of financial conditions her husband had left, but there had been astonishingly little insurance, and once she had told Claire she was lucky not to have had a smart businessman husband like hers to lose half her capital by "shrewd" investments. Claire had confessed that her own ignorance of money matters was all that saved her from the poorhouse. She had stubbornly rejected all expert advice on reinvestments, and therefore still had her small income, which sufficed, with her intermittent royalties. But Bea had always lived on a much higher scale, joking about her creditors and about Claire's naïve terror of bills. It struck Claire that perhaps Bea had been avoiding her lately because she didn't want Claire to guess that the game was up and that the bills were closing in.

Bea had not seemed impressed or even curious when Claire hinted at her new fortune, probably thinking it was only a matter of a few hundred dollars instead of dizzy thousands, with more to come. If Bea would only meet her halfway, a quarter of the way—no, if she would only open the door and let Claire come all the way alone, Claire would offer her a choice of Paris or Rome for a year or two. Claire could hear her heart thumping in terror at the thought of leaving her dear little closet of a room and the new friendships Jonathan had brought to her. But if that was the only way to win back her twinship . . .

She began to speculate on how she could get around Bea without that proud beauty flaring up at any implication she wasn't on top of the world as always. Maybe she would have to make all the arrangements before she even put it up to Bea. Maybe she would have to buy a cooperative apartment in Bea's own neighborhood, the West Fifties or Central Park South, and simply announce to her that a home was waiting just a few doors away, with no troublesome change of habits involved.

But *what about me?* Claire shuddered. At the thought of giving up her breakfasts at the Planet Drugstore, her two-Manhattan binge at Mac's Bar and Grill, her little book gossip with Jo and Lois at the Washington Square Book Store, the Sunday twilight walk through Washington Square, with the young people clustered around the fountain, plunking their banjos and chanting their hillbilly songs, the Good-morning-Miss-Van-Orphen all down the street, in Henry's delicatessen, where she bought her staples, in Schwarz's stationery shop, where she bought her *Times,* Claire felt a childish panic. Childish, oh, definitely. If she was going to win her way back to twinship she would have to grow up as Bea had and face change fearlessly—yes, even enthusiastically. Bea would see that they were indeed sisters.

Claire's twin, Mrs. Kingston Ball, was having her hair done in her hotel room by Madame Orloff-Gaby. Madame Orloff was another hotel widow, picking up a living by tinting other tenants' hair, doing their nails, walking their dogs, feeding their birds, or reading to them in her Russian accent, all her services costing only half the standard charge. Bea was given to claiming that it was not the cheapness that made her loyal to Madame but the marvelous musical background gladly shared with her clientele. In her Odessa youth Madame had been a singer, a true mezzo, as she would tell you, but a great career was nipped in the bud by a stupid coach who tried to make her into a lyric soprano. It was a miracle, she said, that the creature had left her with even a speaking voice. It was indeed a lovely voice, Beatrice felt, chocolate-rich, rumbling around in dark baritone cellars and exuding confidence and consolation. You could tell Madame Orloff absolutely anything, for she'd been everywhere and seen everything. Nothing surprised her, yet she was always interested, always deeply sympathetic, supporting you in any folly, or even crime, if that was your mood. Today had been an unusually quiet session, Bea silent and brooding, and Madame gracefully taking the cue. Finally, however, as she took the pins out of her customer's hair, she ventured gently, "Mrs. Ball is troubled about something today."

"Do I seem cross?" Bea asked apologetically. "I'm sorry. Yes, I am bothered. It's about my sister, you know, the one who lives down in Greenwich Village."

"I've seen her with you in the hotel," Madame said. "She is in trouble and has come to you?"

"No, Claire's all right. It's just that she's suddenly gotten the idea we should live together," Bea said. "We did when we were young, and had to do everything together till I flipped and got out. But now here we are, getting on in years, both of us alone, and Claire's idea is that the time has come for us to close ranks, so to speak. Go to the grave together, I guess."

Madame Orloff's smooth plump hands deftly arranged the other's locks, then patted the top of the head as a kind of sign-off. She took a cigarette pack from her apron pocket, offered one to Bea, and lit them both before she leaned back in the low slipper chair behind Bea, who continued to sit frowning at the mirror. Although bright sunshine leaked through the window, the heavy rose-embroidered curtains were drawn and the electric lights were on. ("There is nothing the matter with my complexion," Bea always said ruefully, "except daylight.")

"We got a very nice tint today, dear," Madame said, eying the image in the mirror. "I added just a dash more of the silver to soften the gold. Very softening. Points up the eyes. So you may live with your sister, then. It would save expenses, eh?"

Bea gave a preoccupied nod.

"It makes perfectly good sense, of course," she said. "I don't know why I'm so bitchy about it. Poor Claire. I almost snapped her head off when she first suggested it. Now why should I blaze up and be so damn nasty when Claire is so patient and amiable?"

"Being twins, you are opposites, that's all."

Bea shook her new crop of silvery blond softly curled locks.

"I don't think so at all. I think we're just two lefts or two rights and we don't complement each other at all. I'm not sure I don't understand Claire because I don't understand myself or whether I understand both of us too damn well."

"It looks so gay, being twins," said Madame.

"I suppose we got a kick when we were little with Mama always showing us off and everybody taking second looks." Bea tried an Oriental effect with her gray eye pencil. "Then I took to having tantrums when Mama would say, 'The twins want this' or 'The twins say that,' as if I personally had no identity at all. Claire loved it because she was shyer and felt that being two was a protection. But I hated seeing my own weaknesses doubled. I was stubborn—you know how stubborn I can be, Madame! No matter what I liked, I was bound to do the exact opposite of what my twin did: Half the time I never knew what I wanted because this mean streak made me automatically take the track contrary to Claire."

"Perhaps you are more alike than you wish." Madame smiled understandingly.

"Sure we are." Bea sighed and rubbed out the experiment in gray shadows around the eyes. "We're probably just one fat case of schizophrenia between us."

"She wants you to leave the hotel?" Madame tried to keep the fear of losing a steady sixty dollars a month out of her voice.

"She sold some film rights and thought of investing in a cooperative apartment right near the Hotel des Artistes—yes, I grant you, it sounds good. She has it worked out even to having a Japanese couple keep house for us, but then I hit the ceiling. It's her money and she means it so well and goodness knows I need money these days, but I said I wouldn't dream of leaving this hotel; then I was ashamed and said I'd think it over, but she was so hurt. She just can't see—"

"You don't get on at all," Madame deduced.

Bea took a comb and began carefully to rearrange her hair in less formal style. Madame subdued the disapproval in her eyes.

"It would mean being clamped back into the grave," Bea went on intensely. "Breakfast and dinner and over our nightcaps remembering anecdotes about Grandpa Sterling's Panhard, and do I remember Father getting ossified at our coming-out dance at Sherry's, and can I still do my imitation of Laurette Taylor in *Peg o' My Heart,* and what fun those tango lessons were at the Castles'. My God, Sonia, I like to watch life while it's going on, be in it if I can, but Claire won't let you. She's got to drag you back fifty years to those good old days when I'm damned sure I didn't have any fun, watched and chaperoned and shadowed every minute. It's as if she has to have a transfusion from the past every day in order to get through the present, and it makes you feel so old and sunk and hopeless, as if everything's over, the game is up, good-by, world!"

Madame Orloff listened to Bea's outburst with a thoughtful smile.

"I live in the past too, Mrs. Ball," she admitted. "Perhaps I bore you too, talking about old days in Paris and Moscow."

"Never!" Bea assured her. "You see I don't know your past, so it seems alive, but my own past and Claire's is dead. I can't have her burying me in it—I really can't. You must see how interested I am in young ideas."

Madame chuckled.

"No one could say Mrs. Ball lives in the past, certainly," she said. "Indeed not. But you say she will pay all expenses?"

"She says she's making pots of money now," Bea said

moodily. "I can't believe it's by her writing, but on the other hand Claire is not one to lie. Neither of us ever cared anything about money"—she gave a dry laugh—"that is, so long as we always had it. But now, with everything hocked and all my bills piling up . . . It would be heaven not to have those worries. And when I have my frightful headaches or rheumatic spells, believe me, I whimper around for some of my own kin just as much as Claire does. The thought of being left alone to die . . ."

"Don't tell me you have such morbid thoughts." Madame laughed incredulously. "You who are always so gay and full of life."

"I don't give in to them, that's all," Bea said. "But if I took on Claire it would be giving in. Not only that, but I'd have to give up my private life."

Madame stumped out her cigarette and studied her hands. Bea, holding the hand mirror, examined a wrinkle in her neck and impatiently turned out the dresser lamps.

"Luis," Madame said quietly.

Bea flung her cigarette into the bowl already filled with barely touched cigarette stubs and lit another one.

"It would be good-by, Luis," Madame murmured. "Good-by, those charming Sunday lunches."

Bea blew a smoke ring jauntily. It was amusing the way she maintained those little flapper mannerisms, Madame thought, blowing bangs out of her eyes, pouting, tossing her head, shrugging her shoulders, ishkabibble. Was it Clara Bow?

"That can't go on forever, anyway," Bea said. "You don't need to tell me."

"What *can* go on forever?" Madame said. "I always say, So far, so good. A family motto. You have gotten some entertainment and some consolation from Luis, as you have from other young men in the past. And the sister would not understand."

"It would be utterly out of the question," Bea said. "Claire's no fool. She's read everything, even if she hasn't lived it. I wouldn't even dare sneak any *chéris* into the set-up, so I'd be furious with Claire for making me give up Luis, and I'll never forgive Luis if I give up Claire's money for him. Maybe if Luis wasn't such a rude little beast—"

"He resents having to have his love bought," Madame said.

"The way I feel about Claire buying me, I guess," Bea said.

"You could give him the money to go back to the island," Madame suggested. "You say he's homesick."

"He says they'd make fun of him if he went back," Bea said morosely. "All he ever wanted in his life was to get to Miami. When he was a kid diving for pennies when the ships docked he'd follow the women tourists and say, 'Take me to Miami, mama, take me to Miami!' He was still saying it when I found him in that inn back in the hills, and I promised I'd take him."

"And you did." Madame chuckled. "Only it turned out to be New York."

"Everybody on the island was mocking him by that time, calling him Mr. Miami," Bea went on, brooding. "I bought him clothes, and he was just too grateful, that was all, so I brought him here, afraid I'd lose him in Miami. Now he says if he ever goes back, they will follow him down the streets yelling, 'Mr. Miami, Mr. Miami.' I suppose I made him the little monster he's turned out to be."

"You were a very unhappy, lonely woman when you met

him," Madame reminded her. "Rushing off to Rome or Rio or London, packing and unpacking to keep from thinking."

"I missed my husband dreadfully," Bea said. "It got worse every year instead of better. Claire wanted me to live with her then, but how could a pious virgin comfort a haunted widow? Not that the trips did any good either. Wherever I'd go I'd say, 'How K. would have loved this,' and it didn't seem right to enjoy myself."

"K. loved travel?" encouraged Madame.

Bea laughed as a thought struck her.

"That was the funny part of it. If K. had been alive he wouldn't even have gone, because he hated going any place. If I'd bullied him into it he would only have loused it up for me. I'd have been in a rage all the time with him lying in bed in the hotel refusing to budge, or roaring around the ship's bar about women dragging their men away from home and making them change their bartenders. I don't know why on God's earth I missed him after he was dead, because I missed him more when he was alive."

Both ladies burst out laughing.

"We miss the man we wish he had been." Madame sighed pensively. "We never quite believe he is really what he is."

Bea, pleased at the way Madame articulated her thoughts with such understanding, reached for her purse, and Madame withheld a faint breath of relief. Instead of losing this steady income, perhaps she could double it, was the thought that hopped into her head.

"Perhaps your twin is not such a pious virgin after all," she said seductively. "Now that she is successful, as you say, perhaps she would like to be rejuvenated too—a nice rinse, the proper make-up, an introduction to an amusing man, eh?"

Bea considered this, then shook her head.

"I doubt it. The only man she went out with in the last twenty years, so far as I know, was our friend Major Wedburn, who lived in her hotel. That couldn't have been anything. No, I'm afraid it would be me joining Claire's life instead of her joining mine."

She leafed through her checkbook, frowning and clucking softly at the stubs. Then, with a deep sigh, she wrote out the check for Madame, fanning it idly for a moment while Madame's eyes followed its flutter. Bea was thinking that once she'd given Claire a definite no she could scarcely dare ask for the small loan she desperately needed. She gave her pretty reconstructed coiffure an impatient shake, as if she could shake off her utterly selfish, unfair attitude about poor Claire. She hadn't even asked for details of Claire's new success, she had been so stunned by the decision that was being forced upon her. Instead of being mad at Claire she should be mad at Luis for making her into such a silly old fool, really. But she didn't dare get mad at Luis. She was darned lucky to have him at any price, at his own good time, and they both knew it.

"Does Luis still live with that old actor?" Madame asked.

"Luis shares Gordon's apartment, yes," Bea said haughtily, knowing exactly what Madame was driving at.

"I was thinking your sister might like the old actor," said Madame soothingly. "Being on TV, you know."

"If you mean we could start double-dating again, no," said Bea. "Thank you, no."

Madame lifted her majestic figure out of the chair, collected the tools of her operations into a large green leather bag, folded her green working smock, and zipped it inside the bag. Bea was still fluttering the check with a vague feeling that while it was in motion it could not be substracted from her slender balance. Madame regarded her indulgently.

"Maybe it would be a good thing to get used to your sister again little by little," she suggested.

"I hate getting used to anything," Bea said. "I hate the very words. I don't think you're alive if you let yourself get used to things."

"Think of it as a test curl before the permanent," Madame said. "Start doing little things together again—going to movies, the theater. Go see her in this new life she says she is having. What would it be to you—only a few hours a week while you postpone the decision."

"I suppose it would help me stall for time." Bea reflected. "I could stay with her for a week or two."

"Twice I went back to my husband and got used to him all over again," Madame said. "I still did not like what I had to get used to, but it was a sensible thing to do. When he died, my conscience was clear and I could dislike him with justice. He left me his collection of military buttons of great sentimental value. I was able to trade it for passage to America."

Bea wasn't listening. There were tears in her eyes as she thought of how horrid Claire's importunings were obliging her to be, and how unfair it was of her dear twin to make her face her foolish weaknesses. Good people forced you to use them, betray them, hate yourself. . . . Bea dabbed at her eyes angrily and handed Madame her well-earned check.

10

EARL TURNER would have been mightily surprised to know the effect that his visit had upon Alvine Harshawe.

Alvine himself was surprised. At first there was his usual impatience at having his day shot full of holes by a morning caller. But then he was obliged to concede, in all fairness, that he couldn't hold this against old Earl. For the last five —no, ten—years he'd been holding out his day like a live target for anybody to shoot full of holes. He could not claim that his precious train of thought had been wrecked by that ghost from the past, for the simple reason that his thoughts didn't come in trains any more, or, if they did, they stood loaded on the siding, like a freightful of lumber waiting for a powerful engine to shove it to port. Mostly ideas came to him somewhat like office memos, stamped and questioned by the higher-ups before they reached him, the idea and its dismissal in the same message. "Why bother? Chekhov did this once and for all in *Three Sisters*." "You're sticking your neck out with this stale Steinbeck." "Why try to top Graham Greene?"

Why try? That was the hook to get each idea out of the way before he even tackled it. He was as bad as those conceited old stage stars rich enough to float through society for years, protesting that they just couldn't find a play that was good enough. In the same way he was always telling himself it was no use starting work before lunch or before Peg got out of the house, so then it was always too late. God knows it was no use trying to retrieve an inspiration after he'd mentioned it to Peg and she'd made her usual comment, "Do you really think people are interested in that sort of thing?" He didn't kid himself that anything or anybody was deliberately blocking his work; he didn't permit himself that alibi. On the other hand a man who'd worked as hard as he had at other times didn't just stop out of laziness. It wasn't all his own fault. What he really could say was his own fault was the easy way he deferred to Peg's plans, which never had anything to do with his work. That was why he'd been nursing the notion of skipping out, getting off Peg's social leash and holing up in the place where he'd done his best work.

That meant, of course, the New York house, which was closed most of the time and which Peg loathed. Maybe the old magic would start flowing again, he had figured, and even though he'd be lonesome and uncomfortable, used as he was to having Peg around, it was all the better for his work that she wouldn't be there.

One reason Peg wasn't keen on the place was that it was a holdover from Kay, his third wife, who had lived there with him for three tempestuous years. Kay he always regarded with a certain admiration as his emotional wife, always ready to throw a vase (cheap) or glass (empty), choking and panting in her rage, howling and abject in her penitence. The emotions all had to do with property, he had discovered. No bereft mother or betrayed virgin could storm as Kay did over his refusal to give her control of his finances. How childishly happy she was over the first book he dedicated to her, and what a tantrum when she discovered this did not entitle her to all the royalties! He'd managed to get out of that marriage with his shirt—in fact more shirts than she realized. He had been forced to give her this house as part of the divorce settlement—"My first real home since I left Sweden as a tiny little girl," she had pleaded sentimentally, then put it on sale that very same day. Alvine had foxed her by buying it back himself. The couple Kay had hired still lived in the basement, looking after things in return for their rent, and available for extra domestic service when he and Peg came to town.

Well, he supposed Peg couldn't be expected to like the house any more than she could be asked to like old Earl Turner, who wasn't in the *Social Register* or even in the telephone book. But Earl, like the house, belonged to the good old time when inspiration was flowing, and for that reason Alvine had rather welcomed his visit.

Looking back, he reflected that Earl was probably the closest friend that he'd ever had—that is, they'd been around the same places at the same time with the same ambition. Then Alvine had gotten married and later famous—two conditions that forbade a man to have a best friend. Best friends from that time on were his agent, his producer, his director, his leading man, his editor, his broker, plug them in and out of the switchboard as the deals changed. You lost one set of friends with each marriage, another when it dissolved, gaining smaller and smaller batches each time you traded in a wife. Mostly now his friends belonged to Peg, had to be okayed by Peg. Peg liked "amusing" people. By amusing she meant rich or titled or European social, certainly no literary clowns.

Alvine thought when it came right down to it he liked old Earl a damn sight better than he liked Peg. All day long he kept wishing he'd gone along with him, wherever the hell he was headed. Some crummy joint, probably the ideal setting for the new novel. Earl knew the spots all right. Lucky Earl! But let Alvine Harshawe try to get that kind of background! Let him try to pick up a conversation in a waterfront bar. Somebody was sure to spot him. Alvine Harshawe of all people! Was he there snooping for a story or was he really on the skids, as so many would love to hear?

He envied Earl, who could roam all over the city, from arty Park Avenue salon to Bowery mission, talk to strangers, do and go as he pleased, pack away enough juicy human material for a dozen Zolas. Not that he'd ever make use of it, bless his lazy old heart, except conversationally. The more he thought about Earl's opportunities and his own prison of fame, the more drab his present life with Peg seemed. (Wasn't this sterile period Peg's fault?) For years he'd been wanting to write about an ordinary young man involved in an ordinary situation with some ordinary everyday people. The Harshawe trademark, of course, was taut high drama in strange colorful backgrounds, and it was Alvine's plan to apply the same kind of swashbuckle to an everyday plot. But what did he know about everyday? Earl knew, because he wasn't hamstrung by a social dame like Peg.

The idea of envying poor old Earl set Alvine to sulking all day, and he was not cheered by his agent's good news of foreign royalties nor by viewing photographs of his agent's three sons, all great guys and a credit to the father. He began thinking of the son old Earl had found for him and by bedtime, after a few nightcaps, his head was bursting with the possibilities of the case. Could be, could be, he muttered dreamily over and over, and wished now he had gotten more particulars from Earl. He couldn't sleep as the situation began to branch out like a brand-new comedy plot.

What does a man do when he finds he has a ready-made son, twenty-six years old, mind you, by a female he scarcely remembers? Alvine found himself chortling out loud every few minutes. It was great, really great, he thought. In the first place he needed to find out for his comedy what a young man today was like, and here was one handed to him on a platter. By George, he'd announce him as his son, too. What would people say? he wondered.

It was characteristic of Alvine that he thought first of his public and only afterward of his wife. His earlier wives would have taken such news of a mystery son in their stride, he thought—Roberta would have been noble and modern, Ad would have cried a little, Kay would have seen it as a threat to her financial security—but what would Peg do? Alvine sat up and lit a cigarette, grinning. He had been with Peg longer than with the others, eight years—too goddam long, really—and the one thing he knew about her was that Peg didn't care what he did so long as he was in proper evening clothes. He could insult his host, rape the guest of honor, fall on his face with blind staggers, but by George, let him be dressed, black or white tie! All her complaints had to do with his being in a dirty old sweater or T shirt when he did whatever he did wrong—maybe was late or loud or lecherous. No matter how they'd quarreled over something, he could always win her over by dressing up for some fat nothing of a little party. She was prouder of him for having kept his waistline, he reflected, than for keeping his reputation.

What would really make her burn would be the embarrassment, Alvine realized. Peg embarrassed easy, God knew, and here was a real first-rate embarrasser in any family. She would think of all the little trivial social things before the big major thing hit her—like would this son move in with them and would they have to take him places with them and was he going to call her Mummy and all that. Or she might surprise him by throwing a real fit. Alvine figured, with an increasing glow of pleasure, that it might be the means of chickening out of this marriage. He hadn't written—or at least finished—any work since the wedding day. All his other women had kept at him in one way or other to get-to-work, write-write-write—you're-such-a-genius, or we-need-the-dough-for-that-cabin-cruiser or you-owe-it-to-your-public so get down on that typewriter and DO something. They stopped him in his tracks with their helpful yakking. He had thought, when he married Peg, it was going to be an inspiration just to be left alone. It had been amusing, at first, to see people's faces when Peg would say, "My goodness, how do I know what he's writing? I hope it's a space book because that's all I read." The other wives had always been ready to explain him and his work. It had amused him too that Peg, herself a much-admired beauty, was never jealous of the fuss women made over him. Indeed she never saw anything, wherever they went, but women's clothes, men's clothes, and interior decorations. She was always so absorbed in these subjects that when he described some brawl or contretemps that had occurred she would say, "Why, Ally Harshawe, you're making that up! I was right there."

It seemed to Alvine he could do nicely without ever having to hear "Why, Ally, you're making that up!" at the end of every one of his anecdotes. He could stand not hearing her brag of never reading her husband's works, too. His taunt of "illiteracy" only made her preen herself with a yawning, "Darling, you always said I was just a fine big animal." So he was stuck with a fine big animal who took all one winter to read just one of the space novels she often mentioned! He had gone back to separate bedrooms after being kept awake by paperback Ray Bradburys slithering off the bed all night.

He couldn't honestly say he'd lost anything by not writing these last few years. Peg often pointed out to him how much more famous he was now than when she'd married him. There hadn't been any new Harshawe, just revivals of the first two hit plays and all the usual anthologies and reprints of his stories. They'd traveled a lot, been interviewed all over the world, visited maharajahs and accepted decorations or honors. Damn it, you didn't have time to write if you wanted to keep your fame in good condition. Peg was disgustingly right in that, but that didn't stop him from wishing to God he could just sit down and knock something off like he used to. He could do it, too, if he could get Peg, that fine animal, off his neck. How these fine animals hung on, he marveled—he couldn't kid himself she loved him too much, but she loved the life he offered, and she wouldn't give that up.

Hell, he liked the life too, that was the trouble. He liked it best in those rare periods when he was left alone, though. He liked sleeping alone, and best of all staying awake alone, enjoying his insomnia, thinking his own crazy thoughts that Peg could never understand, listening to the all-night programs on the radio, reading a paragraph here and there about the secret of lobster gumbo or Gregory Peck's love life, figuring out what came next in his own life. The finding of a long-lost son would certainly shake things up.

"Peg, my dear, I'd like you to meet an old son of mine, Jonathan. . . ."

The thought tickled Alvine and he dozed off on it, the bedside radio gently clucking away, piping its program straight into his dream about Son Jonathan who was zooming around on a space-ship chased by his agent's three husky oafs in their space-helmets. This blurred into a Long John program about UFOs. The flying-saucer people, it said, particularly the Venusians (a pair of Venusian visitors having been interviewed by a reliable Hightstown, New Jersey, expert; absolutely a fact, affidavits right there in black and white) have a real brotherly interest in our civilization and will not do anything hostile to Earth until we're in a position to threaten them. A Mrs. Ethel Holm, ordinary housewife of Dingman's Ferry, Pennsylvania, also testified she found a very friendly attitude in the two Martians who landed their saucer in her back yard, and she testified in a signed statement right there in black and white so you knew it was God's truth that neither one had lifted a hand to her when she accepted their gentlemanly offer to take her for a ride around Clarion, a small sort of summer-resort planet behind the moon. Drowsily Alvine tried to fish the Jonathan image out of the planetarium ceiling.

Son Jonathan, a cross between a funny-paper space-man and a musical-comedy angel, materialized from a foam-rubber cloud, but just as he was changing into the Creature from the Black Lagoon Alvine woke himself up enough to reach out and switch the dial to Big Joe's all-night show, where more earthly experts discussed alcoholism. One man declared he was not alcoholic, just allergic to alcohol. A mere bite of rum-cake would set him off, stirring his allergy so hard he didn't show up for work for three weeks, you wouldn't believe what an allergy. Glad to have his new son driven out of outer space, Alvine sat up and poured himself a stout highball. He switched to a West

Virginia station where a gentleman farmer was describing how he bored holes in his prize beefsteak tomatoes, filled them with vodka, let them age in the icebox, then ate them for breakfast. The Built-in-Snapper. Delicious. Alvine was about to yell out to Peg to fetch him some beefsteak tomatoes, when he remembered she wasn't there, that he was alone with his darling insomnia.

If he did get rid of Peg, chasing her out with a secret son, he'd probably get somebody else, he reflected, sitting up wide awake now. He didn't want a helpmeet or inspiration or even a bed-broken round-the-clock lay, but he did like to yell out to somebody, say around four a.m., and get a response. If Peg were here and had stumbled, yawning, into the room at his cry, dragging her blanket behind her like Linus, the kid in the *Peanuts* strip, she would have slipped sleepily in the bed beside him, taking a sip of his nightcap, but then she would have complained, "I don't see why you kick about my space books when you listen to the stuff all night on the radio." And then they would have heckled each other back to separate beds again. So why pretend he was missing Peg? He switched back to Long John on WOR and poured himself some more allergy.

Now some very sincere fellows on the air were talking about the darrows, not outer-space people but the ones that live in the bowels of the earth. A scientific fact! It seems the way the experts discovered the existence of these darrows was that an ordinary everyday steel-worker took an elevator from the tower of an unfinished building—this was in Chicago a while back, affidavits in black and white on request—down to the basement. Down there the car slid sidewise—the fellow was sort of surprised—and started plunging down another shaft for almost two miles. Then the cage door opened and the darrows, these little fellows with big pointed heads, started talking to him, and they couldn't have been decenter if he'd worn his lodge pin. They had nothing against the Earth—naturally, they lived in it—and they intended no mischief; they were just out to get Chicago. Similar elevator adventures had occurred in Providence, Rhode Island, and in West Yonkers, all absolutely bona fide, sworn to in black and white by ordinary people. The darrows were, if anything, even friendlier than the Venusians, though of course not so personable. All they asked was to destroy Chicago, the wickedest city in the world. An Elizabeth, New Jersey, cop, a guest of Long John, added that these darrows often surfaced to take night jobs, naturally in work involving extreme heat. Many people reported seeing them working away after midnight in that little bakery near the station in Perth Amboy.

Now there was a tranquilizing thought, Alvine mused. When Peg asked him if they would have to take the new son around to parties, he would tell her to go ahead by herself, he and the boy were going to look up some darrows over in Perth Amboy. Or they might hunt for some of their own, up around the Con-Ed diggings in Columbus Circle, say. Take an elevator down to the basement of the St. Moritz after dinner . . .

"Be sure and dress, then," Peg would say.

Alvine, awake, leafed indolently through the magazine sprawling open on the bed. Dr. Norman Vincent Peale's face smiled benignantly out at him, advising a young man unhappily engaged to a selfish beauty to give up looking for beauty and get himself a girl who had something on the ball spiritually. That's the ticket, Alvine thought. He closed his eyes, wondering if his life would have been richer had he settled down with Jonathan's mother, dear long-ago Connie, instead of skittering around from wife to wife, Venusians to darrows, jumping from flying saucers in Massachusetts Bay to instant sons in Greenwich Village. The more he thought about it the more repugnant the thought of going back to the Cape became, and the more intrigued he was by the idea of the kid, Jonathan. He would stick around town for a while longer, he resolved. He would go downtown and hunt out the boy.

My son Jonathan. It couldn't be. And yet— One thing was sure, he wouldn't pass up the opportunity of announcing to Peg that the boy was his. If the idea of a long-ago love coming to light made her holler, then he would simply say it all happened when he was in his white tie and Meyer Davis's orchestra was playing.

"That makes it legitimate." Alvine chuckled.

The people were the same, the places were the same, but suddenly there was a difference. It seemed to Jonathan that the city had been coquetting with him, persuading him it belonged to him until he was confident, then mocking him for his complacency.

It took all his will-power to keep from calling Iris, and he spent hours trying to write an explanation of his flight the other night that would not reveal the true dilemma. He was so sure she was hurt and unhappy that the note from her was a grievous shock to his pride.

"Jonathan, dear, I know you've wondered why I haven't been in to see you at the Espresso after our heavenly night —I longed to see you—but a part has come up for me in the new Jeff Abbott play and I am studying every minute for the audition next week. I'm not daring to see a soul—not even Hugow—because this means so much to me. So here I am, shut up like a nun as we have to be when the big chance comes along. Please don't be hurt because you do understand your Iris is first of all an actress. Love, love, love."

There, Jonathan told himself, that makes it easier, but it was disconcerting to have his own role switched. In the same way he felt betrayed by Miss Van Orphen when he called up to apologize for not keeping in touch with her lately and had to listen to her own apologies.

"I've been meaning to invite you for cocktails soon to meet my sister Beatrice," Claire said. "I've told her about you, and she wants to meet you. But Earl Turner is working with me over my old stories for this wonderful TV producer, and I haven't had a minute. I owe it all to you, Jonathan, because you brought Earl into my life and it's been so lucky! Please don't think I'm ungrateful, you dear boy. We'll get in touch with you the first possible minute."

He went to The Golden Spur, hoping to chance on Earl there and find out if he had heard from Alvine Harshawe, but he was pounced on by Percy Wright instead, which meant that he was quarantined for the evening. Even Hugow failed him, but then, as the bartender and everybody else in the Spur realized, Hugow was deep in preparations for a great new show.

Dr. Kellsey alone was loyal, relaxing at the café table with his espresso and flask of brandy. But this was no longer any comfort to Jonathan. Instead he found the friendship increasingly oppressive. There seemed a new note of possessiveness in the doctor. His invitations to a midnight steak at Delaney's or a nightcap at Luchow's had a note of command. He spoke of having Jonathan dine with a lady friend of his, an assistant in the English department who worked with him occasionally.

"I'd just like to see her face when I introduce you," said the doctor, and when Jonathan looked perplexed he explained mysteriously, "You see she never knew me when I was your age."

The doctor spoke of moving to a larger apartment in his building, a place ideal for two bachelors. He wanted to know if Jonathan didn't think it was a capital idea. When Jonathan, taken off guard, agreed, the doctor nodded with satisfaction.

"I thought you'd get tired of shacking up with those two little harpies." He gave him a knowing wink. "I dare say you have to sleep with both of them."

The doctor gave a roar at Jonathan's embarrassment and patted him fondly on the back.

"Confidentially, I wouldn't mind it myself," he admitted, chuckling and wiping tears of laughter from his eyes. "I must say I can't see myself turning down a nice piece of cake like that, even though I was just as shy as you are, when I was your age."

"It's nothing like that," Jonathan protested, but the doctor brushed him aside.

"Nothing to be ashamed of, boy, we've got to have it. Only thing is the living with women! Always tidying up your papers so you can't work, or hiding the liquor, and their own junk all over the place. How can you write your novel there?"

"But I'm not writing a nov—"

"Nonsense, you don't have to keep it a secret from me. I know the signs. My guess has been right along that you're writing a novel about The Golden Spur, and I'm all for it, boy, because I always wanted to write it myself. So you've got to have privacy, not women. Women are forever washing either their hair or their stockings. No wonder you're looking worried lately."

There was no use trying to persuade the doctor that he was perfectly satisfied with his living arrangements, and since the doctor had not openly stated that he expected Jonathan to move in with him, Jonathan could not risk offending him by a premature refusal. He decided to simplify his position by finding a room of his own some place else, maybe in Earl Turner's old hotel.

But before he could make any move, trouble started in the Tenth Street studio. Lize, after a fight with Darcy, took off for a printers' convention in Atlantic City. Darcy was going to stay home from work, she said, because she had a "virus," and wasn't it lucky she had Jonathan to look after her? This meant that she had time to wash her hair and launder her stockings and lingerie constantly, draping them over his books and shelves, using his shirts as housegowns, his socks as house-slippers, his writing table as ironing board. She implored him to come home early, bringing a sandwich, and exclaimed what a relief it was to have Lize out of the way so they could really get acquainted. When Jonathan found his books dumped on the floor to make room for gallon jugs of wine, Darcy explained that it was because she had decided to go on the wagon and that always required a stock of wine on hand.

"Everybody else goes on the wagon, why shouldn't I, just for spite?" she said in answer to Jonathan's baffled query. "It always makes people so mad. They think you're on the wagon so you can put something over on them. Lize will be furious. It does give you an edge in a fight, you know." Later she added dreamily, "Anyway I like the way everything looks so crazy when you aren't drinking."

Too kindhearted to desert under these circumstances Jonathan found Darcy waiting up for him at night, and often sitting on a stool watching him like a cat while he pretended to sleep. Too ashamed to confess his fear of living alone with a female, he developed a prodigious snore to protect himself.

"You have the nicest snore of any man I know," Darcy told him. "I really mean that sincerely. It makes me want to cuddle right up."

He tried to spend as little time as possible at the café to avoid Dr. Kellsey. He would move out of his apartment that very night, he vowed, but when he got home there was Darcy, waiting to confide in him, over a chianti nightcap, the fruits of her serious meditations.

"A couple has the most fun," Darcy said. "A person by themselves has to keep thinking up things to do."

She held out her glass, and Jonathan obediently poured more wine into it. It struck him that Darcy drank more when she was "on the wagon" than she did when she was drinking.

"I think we shouldn't pour it out from the jug like this," she said, looking at the gallon jug of chianti on the table with sudden displeasure." I think we should pour some off into a vase or something. It looks nicer."

Jonathan found a milk bottle and carefully decanted a portion.

"Oh, fill it up," ordered Darcy.

Jonathan did. It left the jug almost empty.

"I mean when you're a couple you can do things together," she said and waved at the kitchen table where they sat. "Like this. When a girl gets home she wants somebody to have a nightcap with. And they can do other things together, like—oh, like going to auctions or double features and doing crossword puzzles, I don't know.

"One of the reasons I broke off with Hugow," Darcy went on, ignoring Jonathan's blink of surprise, "was that he never liked doing things together. Half the time he never even told me where the party was till it was all over. I guess I'm just an old-fashioned girl but I don't think it looks nice for a girl to go to a party alone, especially if she hasn't been asked."

"Don't you have to be asked?" Jonathan inquired.

Darcy gave him a pitying look and patiently explained that in New York City people didn't get invitations to parties, you just found out where they were. Oh some uptown women like Cassie Bender passed out invitations, but it wasn't to have people come, it was just a mean way of trying to keep people out. Hugow, for instance, never liked invitation parties or jigger measures or blue-white hair or avocados.

"Too mushy, he said," Darcy explained, holding out her glass. "You see what I mean about a couple having fun, don't you?"

"Like you and Percy," Jonathan said.

"Oh, Percy drags me," Darcy said impatiently. "I can't go a step without him tagging along. It's all right for an hour or two, we talk about Hugow and all that, but I guess I just don't like rich men. A person like Lize would think a girl was crazy to say that, but that's the way I am. Is that the end of the chianti?"

It was, Jonathan said hopefully, but Darcy recalled there was a spot of rum in the kitchen, and one real drink would not seriously affect her wagon, and it was such fun talking things over.

"You take a rich man and what have you got?" she said, holding out her hands and ticking off her points on her fingers. "You've got dinner in some dingy little Armenian dive or Chinatown where there's no bar to run up the tab, you've got a neighborhood movie rerun, you've got waiters hiding from you once the place knows the kind of tipper he is, you've got pink plastic pop beads instead of pearls and cologne instead of perfume for your birthday, and the only reason you get taxis instead of subways is that he gets that thing claustrophobia in subways. That's your rich man for you."

"Was he that bad with Lize?" Jonathan murmured.

"Of course not." Darcy blazed. "Lize is big enough to clobber him into expensive places like the Stork Club and she can get him blotto and carry him home, but I don't think that looks nice and besides I'm not big enough."

Her eye traveled from her empty glass to the empty milk bottle to the empty jug and to the alarm clock on the icebox. It was after two. Jonathan, reading her mind, said that the liquor store had closed hours ago.

"I don't have to drink," Darcy said. "A little wine, that's all, especially lately, now that I've been thinking over things. Living with a girl like Lize makes you see how you could waste your life with the wrong men. Hugow, for instance, was all wrong for me, that's why I walked out. Not so much his being an artist as his being so much older. Of course my folks always hoped I would marry a real-estate man or car dealer, somebody solid."

Jonathan took the glasses to the sink and washed them. Darcy stabbed a cigarette into her lips and waited for him to light it, nodding approvingly as he emptied the ashtray.

"That's what I mean, a younger man takes more interest in the home, washing dishes and straightening things up, not just chasing after women all the time. All the time Hugow lived here he never made the bed once, honestly it was embarrassing. I could always tell he'd had some new woman in when I'd come home and find the bed all made up. I knew he hadn't done it himself. Older men just don't care about nice things, they can't seem to take their mind off sex. That's why you and I get on, Jonathan, don't you think? Take Lize, she doesn't care if the place is a dump, but I mind terribly. Look at that lumpy old couch! Cracked old plaster walls, beat-up old chairs, dirty old curtains! It's all right for a girl like Lize, but for nice people like you and me, Jonathan, I mean, I could just cry."

If Darcy was going to cry, and she was, it meant another all-night session of confessions, and Jonathan had no consolations to offer, even to himself.

"I thought you liked the place when Hugow had it," he said.

"I wouldn't take Hugow back if he was the last man on earth." Darcy sniffled, dabbing at her eyes with a handy dishtowel. "I saw him in the Spur with that Angel girl the other night and I walked right past without speaking, that's the way I feel."

"With—" Jonathan came to attention suddenly.

"That dopey kid that's been following him around for years, says she's on the stage, but she's really just on the prowl for Hugow, that's all, following him around till he's too tired to go anywhere but bed."

Moral indignation was drying Darcy's tears. Jonathan wanted to ask questions but then he would have to listen to cruel answers. So Iris wasn't seeing Hugow any more, so she was absorbed in preparing for an audition next week and was simply so concentrated on this big chance that she forgot everything else. Dedicated! "Like a nun"!

Bad enough to have to renounce the girl you loved because she might be your sister. Bad enough to renounce a possible father because you'd rather make him a father-in-law. But to have your misery compounded by having the girl indifferent to your show of will-power, busy as she was claiming credit for her own, then lying to him!

Was the whole city out to betray his blind confidence?

"I can understand his going back to Cassie Bender"—Darcy was stroking her infinitely well-known wounds—"because she's just like a mother, that's why I was never, no never, the least bit jealous of her like Lize used to be, but what does he see in that big goony-eyed kid? Why we all used to laugh the way she'd come into the Spur and just sit and moon at him, never talking, just watching like she was hypnotized or something. That was three years ago, and now she's at it again, all goofy-eyed. Goodness knows you'd think she'd have learned she wasn't his type by this time."

Yes, you'd think so, Jonathan said to himself, but you couldn't learn when you didn't like the lesson. He ought to learn that Iris was carrying a torch for Hugow just like all the other girls, just as he had suspected at the very first. He ought to be angry now at hearing Darcy's news, but he wasn't mad at Iris, he was mad at Darcy for telling. It meant he had been foolishly trusting in Hugow too, so sure Hugow had no more interest in Iris and was a real friend, even though he no longer came to the espresso café to see him. Earl Turner too busy, Miss Van Orphen occupied, Iris gone, Dr. Kellsey a vague menace—there was no one left but Darcy, and Darcy without Lize to balance things was almost intolerable.

"Don't you think that's a good idea?" He heard Darcy's voice babbling urgently. She had found a miniature bottle of Southern Comfort and was sipping it. "After all, that awful little dive where you work can't make any money for you."

"It's not a dive," Jonathan said.

"Of course it's a dive, dopey," Darcy said. "Nobody goes there but your old goat professor and some funny-looking eggheads and social workers. It's a front for something, pushers or spies or bookies—just like the Metropolitan Museum and that Eighth Avenue subway station—and you ought to get out before you get caught. I mean you should get a job with the real-estate people right in their office, because you'd be wonderful in real estate, Jonathan."

She had her head cocked, with that pouting smile that meant she was feeling cuddly and would wiggle onto his lap in a minute if he didn't stand up, which he did, pretending to want a drink of water.

"You'd make a lot of money and wouldn't have to be spending your savings and you'd have first crack at some nice little apartment in the West Village, over on Horatio or Bank, maybe. We could live there. Let Lize keep this place, if she won't get out."

"We," Darcy had said.

"We could have a big housewarming and invite Hugow and the whole Spur crowd and everybody would bring a bottle," Darcy went on dreamily, still holding out her hand as if it encircled a wineglass, though this had fallen on the floor and was rolling about with a life of its own. "We'd make friends with the cop so we could make noise all night if we wanted, and we'd always have room for company to stay, that's the thing I like about being a couple, don't you? If we had to we could get married, too."

"Percy would want to live in Brooklyn, though," Jonathan said cautiously.

"Now Jonathan, you know perfectly well I'm not talking about Percy," Darcy said impatiently, then relented and flung her arms around his waist exuberantly. "You know I mean us. I'm surprised I didn't think of it before, but then Lize was all over the place."

Jonathan winced, marveling that such a tiny girl could have such a powerful hug.

"I don't think I'd be good at real estate," he quibbled, but this only brought more reassuring hugs from Darcy. Her curlered little head was strategically thrust against his breastbone and was butting him into retreat toward the living room. He remembered his magic words just in time.

"Scrambled eggs!" he cried, pushing her aside. "I'll make scrambled eggs, and maybe there's bacon left."

It worked, as it always did after his first error. Darcy was detoured by the flurry of cooking but not entirely appeased. She watched his operations pensively, ate her share, and handed him her plate to wash. He was able to get into bed and turn off the lights without further personal talk, and pretended to be fast asleep when he heard her call out plaintively from the bedroom, "All men ever think about is cooking."

There was no more time to be lost. As soon as the coast was clear, Jonathan escaped.

It should have but certainly would not have consoled Cassie Bender's shattered vanity to know that Hugow's flight from her magnificent summer party brought happiness to many vacationists now drifting back to the city. There were all the artists whose work she had rejected, all the ladies whose artist boy friends she had snatched, all the

Cape summer people who were not important enough to be invited to her Big Do, and then the anonymous strangers who loved any story about an honest, poor artist putting a rich, snobbish, overaged lady dealer on the spot.

"What I like best is the idea of old Bender being stranded on the Cape with no man of her own"—Cape oldtimers chuckled—"like everybody else."

For there is no place on earth a man is so rare and so prized as Cape Cod. A clever woman plotted for months ahead to round one up for summer, so that instead of being one of the ravening packs of Extra Women she could qualify socially as a "couple," a couple on the Cape meaning one man and at least four women—wife, mother, sister, girl friend, and possible house guest.

"I'll bet she's still burning," gloated Darcy Trent. "She stole him from me and thought she could show him off as her private property and she got what was coming to her. I *knew* he had something like that in his mind when he left me!"

"But what about the big show she's supposed to give him in the fall?" Lize said. "Maybe she'll get even with him by calling it off."

This was exactly the reprisal urged on Mrs. Bender by her faithful maid and confidante, Beulah.

"You done too much for that Hugow," Beulah said. "You gotta lay it on the line now, kick him right out of our gallery."

God, how she'd like to be able to do it, Cassie thought, but there was no point in telling Beulah why she couldn't.

"He's been kicking you around long enough," Beulah said. "It ain't gonna get any better, and what's more you ain't gonna get any younger. That's not saying you look your age."

Beulah was understanding, too damned understanding, Cassie often felt. She knew too much. She could never be fired, certainly.

"You don't act your age either, that's the trouble," said the sage, dusting the knickknacks on her mistress's dressing table as Cassie lay in bed. "Time you settled down. Have the same man to breakfast two days running, take your make-up off when you go to bed, and all like that."

"My own fault for letting friendship louse up a good sex deal." Cassie whimpered. "I get to liking a guy and trying to help him out of jams, and first thing I've lost myself a good lover. If you want to know something, Beulah, the older I get the more I love that stuff."

"What else you going to do with men?" Beulah said. "That's all they're good for, so you got to make the most of it. You ain't going to get anything else out of 'em."

"After all I've done for him he makes me the laughingstock of the whole Cape." Cassie's tears began to gush again as they had been doing for weeks. "Then all of New York hears about it and men wonder what I did to make him skip. I'll be lucky to find any more lovers. In another ten years—damn it, Beulah, all a hotblooded woman can get in her fifties is a choice of drunks. A drunk who snivels about the good old days, or one that breaks up the joint getting into the mood, or else one that falls asleep before he even begins."

Beulah gave her mistress a comforting smack on the bottom as she passed the bed where Cassie sprawled. Cassie was large, fair, and showy, handsomer in her forties than she had been in her eager, shrill, and scrawny youth, before her hair had turned to gold. Nobody knew what had happened to her husbands or where she had found the mysterious millionaire who had set her up in her own gallery. Beulah had heard that Mrs. Bender had gone into the art racket as an excuse to raid the art quarters of cities all over the world for lovers, but Beulah declared that was just the mother in her. She was the same way herself, just couldn't stand seeing a good man lonesome and starved for love when there was a good bed in her room going to waste.

Cassie was forty-three—well, all right, forty-eight, if you're going to count every lost week end—and Hugow's betrayal had happened at birthday time, when she was frightened enough by the half-century mark reaching out for her before she'd even begun to have her proper quota of love. She was making more and more passes at the wrong men, then trying to recoup with stately cultural pronouncements in her refined Carolina accent, which she kept polished up like her grandfather's shotgun, ready to bring recalcitrant suitors into line. In this crucial period she wavered between her passionate need to be thought of as a splendid roll in the hay and her other urge—a good retreat position really—to be recognized as a Lady.

One trouble, which Cassie refused to admit, was that she forgot to adjust her courting technique to her encroaching avoirdupois. It was one thing for an impulsive, jolly girl to jump on an attractive stranger's lap, crying out that she just loved that Down East accent, but a hundred and sixty pounds of solid female doing the same thing was likely to cause buckling in the property before it was even sold. Gay solo dances, skirts flung overhead to stereophonic cha-cha in bohemian cellar parties might have incited men to lust at one time but now only brought on the janitor complaining of loosened plaster, or an astonished exclamation from younger fry: "Good God, Cassie doesn't wear pants!"

I mustn't ever go to those artists' dives downtown again, Cassie reminded herself over and over. It's all right whooping around in the country places with the old ones, the ones that have it made, like Sandy Calder and that set —even Eleanor Roosevelt or Emily Post couldn't lose anything by that—but it's these young, jealous little bastards that can ruin you, blabbing and getting things in the papers. The trouble is when the party gets wild I forget I have my professional name and dignity. Instead of going home, I go wild too.

Loving men and love as she did, Cassie had a constant struggle to maintain a proper aloofness. Those handsome, fleshy arms were ever ready to be flung around the nearest animate object while she nuzzled its head in her banquet-style decolletage. It was no feather-bed embrace, however, but more a bruising hug from a statue, for Cassie's flesh had no nonsense about it, a nose could be broken on those marble breasts, and young men, touched by the demonstration of warmth, were surprised to find no cuddle comfort here, but more the implacable rejection of a good unyielding mattress. No soft little-boy cosseting, no waste of affection, there was work to be done. With their heads butting into inhospitable crannies and curves of Cassie's neck and torso, they would hear her voice, a Charleston-lady coo to the last, rising above them, as far off and seductive as a steamship whistle inviting them to tropic islands. "This darling man must see me home." Cassie would be third-personing him fondly, and sometimes, it was said, he was never seen again, and only Cassie could tell whether he had escaped or been broken on the wheel.

Beulah's set in Harlem knew much more about Cassie's prodigious appetite for love than Cassie's artist set did. They followed her affairs as they did TV's *Brighter Day,* pleased with her triumphs, shedding tears over her failures. Beulah declared herself as one who believed in minding her own business: she was not like some, noseying in and blabbing one madam's business to the other. This was the pious prologue to each installment of Cassie Bender's Loves, absolving the narrator of all guilt, enabling her to enjoy it the more comfortably, just as confession perfumes the sin. In Beulah's accounts she herself had the leading part, giving full details on all the advice and general theosophizing which guided a grateful Mrs. Bender to success in love and business.

"No sir," Beulah reported herself as saying to Mrs. Bender only a few days before, "you do plenty enough for those paint men without giving them the run of your bed. You do for them and do and do, like this Mr. Hugow, and they takes what they wants when they wants it and then walks out, leaving you bawling. Then you kick some fine rich customer out of your bed the minute Mr. Hugow feels like coming back, and that ain't right. 'I knows all that, Beulah,' she says (here Beulah imitated the whining ofay lady voice), 'but these rich buyers of mine is too old and anyway by the time I've poured enough scotch into us to close the deal I'm so punched up I want to get in the hay with a real man, somebody where I don't have to do all the work. When that damn Hugow shows up I forget I'm mad at him, and there goes the ballgame.' 'Don't you be a fool,' I tells her, 'you hang on to those old men or they'll take away your gallery and you won't have those painters to lay around with.' "

That turned out to be one of Beulah's soundest warnings, though it came much too late, even if Cassie had ever been in the mood to heed it. Right now Cassie had no intention of letting Beulah crow over her good guessing but allowed the girl to believe her weeping was caused by a mere broken heart. She was out of pocket plenty too, since her tender solicitude for Hugow's comfort, the redecorating and repairing of the cottage for his studio, and his own casual treatment of cash, had nicked her bank account. Her grandiose plans for his fall exhibition, too, went far beyond the expenses allowed for business, but she had been excited and, let's face it, hopeful that she and Hugow could make a permanent team. Broken heart, wasted generosity, wounded pride—all these Beulah understood, but if she had any inkling that the Bender business was in imminent danger of collapsing, the tenderhearted girl would have demanded her two weeks' pay, cash, and flown out the door, for, as she herself would say, a person's got theyself to think of.

So Cassie, after her first stormy declaration that she wanted no part of Hugow's work, now saw that she could not afford the luxury of pride or revenge. The boom had been lowered from another direction. She should have seen it coming and insured against it. After all, the once doting gentleman who had put her in business was well on in years and had been due to pass on any minute in the last decade. But he had no family to interfere with his private expenditures; he had kept his interest in Mrs. Bender and their financial arrangements a secret through all the years, spreading his beneficences through several banks. Asking no questions had been one of Cassie's virtues, but it was only because she thought she knew the answers. Of course he would pop off one day, but of course arrangements, in his discreet, thorough way, would have been made for the continuance of the Bender Gallery.

But the gentleman had absconded, just as Hugow had, and it was no excuse that his flight had been through the pearly gates. Cassie had waited, after the newspaper reports of his passing, to hear from the estate manager, his lawyer, or his bank, but weeks passed and nothing happened. In the hysteria of the Hugow business she had found time to ask her own bank to look into the gentleman's last papers to see how her inheritance was to be handled. The bank reported there was no provision made. The gentleman, cautious to the very end, had left nothing to indicate any connection with the Bender Gallery or with Mrs. Cassie Bender. His bequests in other directions had been infuriatingly generous, according to the report, the largest going to a completely unknown woman.

"Why, the old goat!" Cassie raged when she heard of this from her lawyer. All those years—her best years, at that—she had been the old man's darling, graciously accepting his largesse in return for assembling a masterly collection of horns for him, and the monster had been unfaithful to her! When he had taken her to the Lafayette for lunch—yes, it was that long ago—and told her he could not see her again as he was on the threshold of sixty and could not do her justice, he must have been already starting something new! It was a sentimental lunch, Cassie recalled savagely, accompanied by her tears and the final affectionate clasp of some nice bonds and his word that the gallery would be supported indefinitely.

Instead of throwing out Hugow, she would have to beg him to stay, Cassie saw. She would make money on him, for he was on the way up, but she had to make it a big plunge, double his prices, build up the show as if he were another Pollock, which God knows he was not likely to be. And then what? Why, he would drop her for a bigger dealer, naturally.

So Cassie wept and raged and cursed, partly at the dead

gentleman who had been no gentleman and at the lover who had decamped and now must be wheedled back and rewarded with the greatest show of his life. It was a gamble, but she had to do it, even if she had to close shop later on. So here she was, knocking herself out buttering up Texas tycoons and museum heads, hiring the most expensive public-relations firm, planning the most de luxe preview party, playing with her credit, and running after Hugow in all his wretched dives where she knew they jeered at her importunations.

If she hadn't been desperate, and if he hadn't become her most profitable talent, Cassie would have loved to play a vengeful game with him, letting him make all the moves, not committing herself to a show until she was good and ready, letting him realize how necessary she was. But she was in too precarious a spot.

Her lawyer was the one who gave her hope. "Perhaps the fortunate lady who got the quarter-million you expected to get is interested in art," he suggested. "It may be she knew the gentleman's taste and may even have discussed continuing with the investment on her own."

It was not much of a hope but it was worth a try, and after some preliminary investigation Cassie managed to write a discreet note to the heiress hinting that a partnership might be arranged that would be not only just but profitable. While she waited for this barely possible rescue she was obliged further to humble herself with pleasant, even merry, little notes to Hugow as if nothing in the world had happened between them but the exhibition plans.

"If this show is a sell-out," Cassie declared to Beulah, "I'm going to take my cut and buy myself the best-looking lover you ever saw."

"What if it's a flop?" Beulah chuckled.

If it's a flop, we're out of business, Cassie could have answered, but instead she said, "Then I'll start looking around for that first husband of mine, if I can remember his name."

Hugow was immensely relieved that Cassie showed no bitterness toward him. He was lazy about business and a coward about making enemies by switching dealers, framers, even waiters. Maybe he'd sneak out someday, the way he did with his women, but he was glad now that he didn't have to offend Cassie further.

Cassie plunged into preparations for the show and at the same time kept on the trail of her dead sponsor's heiress with propositions of partnership and appeals to sentiment. When her lawyer reported no reaction to her pleas, she meditated on the possibilities of polite blackmail. The late gentleman had been so experienced in clandestine affairs that he had left no trace of evidence of his past attentions, and her claim would have to be on a personal basis. The problems multiplied, Cassie made giddier and giddier plans, until both her gallery's future and Hugow's show were given hope by an unexpected visitor.

11

ALVINE HARSHAWE was in a foul mood the day he set out to find this Jonathan kid old Earl had told him about. For weeks he had been lingering around New York, enjoying himself in his own little sport of driving his agent and wife crazy. He quibbled and postponed closing the movie deal, allowed Peg to bombard him with telegrams and phone calls begging him to return to the Cape.

"My wife doesn't like the terms," he told his agent.

"My agent won't let me leave town till this is set," he told Peg.

Guests, important English directors, Italian film stars, "fun people," were due on Chipsie's yacht, Peg moaned, and he must realize his poor Peg couldn't entertain them alone. They didn't want to see her, they wanted their lion, as she knew perfectly well. Alvine knew it better than she did, and thought it did Peg good to be reminded of it once in a while. He'd pop up, he thought, just as they were all bored stiff and ready to go, then watch how they decided to stay, with the king back on the throne.

But suddenly Peg's telegrams stopped. After a few days came her cable triumphantly announcing that dear old Chipsie (Lord Eyvanchip, of course) had felt so sorry for her loneliness that he had simply kidnaped her to join the party sailing down to the Caribbean, dropping off at spots as whim suggested. She might leave the party in a month or even go on to the Mediterranean and then to Paris.

What am I supposed to do with four loose weeks on my hands? Alvine felt like bellowing indignantly across the ocean. He'd be damned if he'd fly over to join her in Paris, if that was what she was counting on. But she had not even suggested it, he thought with some surprise. What could be more baffling to a husband who yearns for his freedom than to have it handed to him gift-wrapped? Alvine pondered over Peg's unprecedented silence, studied her last cable for some clue, and became increasingly outraged.

And then the truth hit him.

It could not be—oh, *couldn't* it?—that for the first time a wife was shaking *him!* Alvine had never believed in fighting to get or hold any woman. Shake them loose little by little was his system, and let them drop off by themselves. Always the good people, the richest and most famous, stayed on his side through all of his divorces, dropped the old wife when he did, accepted whatever new wife he presented. Chipsie, being rich and titled, would never have stopped off had he known Alvine was not there. Chipsie couldn't stand boring wives, having just gotten rid of his own. Why, that made Chipsie a free man now, and this thought brought Alvine up short.

Peg wouldn't go in for any hanky-panky, he was sure of that, at least not for kicks or for spite and certainly not for mere love, but she was a snob. No use kidding himself that she wouldn't rather be Lady Chipsie than a mere author's wife if she had the chance, and the minute he had the thought Alvine knew what the game was. Peg was getting back at him with a ladyship. Alas! His agent had heard talk confirming the suspicion! What made Alvine burn was to think what a smug ass he'd been, so sure he was the one who pulled all the strings. He would never have dawdled around New York, half the time in his house and other times lounging around his agent's cabin cruiser up at City Island, drinking with a couple of actor guests at night, waking up at Port Jefferson or some Connecticut port, then starting all over next day—oh, never would he have enjoyed this except for the pleasure of infuriating old Peg.

But there was Peg hitting it off with old Chipsie and his world of envious enemies chuckling to think the arrogant Harshawe had been kicked out!

Raging about for some way of restoring his vanity, he remembered Earl Turner's talk of the kid who might be his son and he knew that was the answer. Let tricky old Peg have it right between the eyes. Winning a ladyship wouldn't be such a triumph if people knew it was a consolation prize after having her husband bring home a full-grown bastard son. Alvine set out at once to get Earl and find the boy Jonathan. He'd make the first move.

He took a cab from the City Island yacht basin, intending to stop off at the Sixty-fourth Street house and clean up, but it was a hot afternoon and he needed a drink after several days of salt air and bourbon. He dropped off at a dingy First Avenue bar where no necktie was demanded, then made another start downtown, with a few stopovers at some Third Avenue bars.

"Anybody ever tell you you're the spit and image of Alvine Harshawe?" the bartender in the first bar asked, after his second scotch.

"No," said Alvine.

"Of course he's a good bit taller and ten, twelve years younger, ha ha"—what was so funny about that? Alvine wondered testily—"but there's a resemblance, if you were dressed right. Many's the time I've fixed him up after a big night. The screwdriver's his drink."

"Must try it next time," Alvine said and paid his check.

At the next bar, where he ordered a screwdriver, a fish-faced blond man bared shark's teeth and extended a fin, saying, "You don't know me from Adam, but, by George, my mother's one of your greatest fans. I don't read Westerns myself, Mr. Steinbeck, but let me buy you a drink anyway."

"Buy your mother a drink," Alvine snarled and marched out.

He caught a glimpse in a shop-window mirror of an unshaven big bum in a stained white jacket and faded slacks. He smiled grimly, thinking of how Peg would carry on if she saw him going about New York like that. Never mind, he was a free man now, the hell with Peg. A wave of affection for his old pal Earl came over him, and he thought it would be only fair to appeal to Earl, show him that even foxy Harshawe could get in a jam. The trouble was he never took note of Earl's address, being sure he'd never want to look him up. He remembered something about the Hotel One Three and got a cab to cruise around the East Side looking for it, but it was no use. He and the cabby stopped off at Luchow's and had some drinks until a waiter came up with a necktie, suggesting that Alvine put it on. Alvine had a counter-suggestion and stalked out, too outraged to call the inside headwaiter, who knew him well.

Never mind, Earl was bound to be at one of the old haunts. Alvine had a dim recollection of a café Earl had mentioned on Bleecker Street, where the boy Jonathan worked, the place that used to be their favorite bakery lunch, but where was that? The poor good old days in the Village with a mailbox full of rejection slips were blessedly dim in Alvine's memory, and all that he remembered, as they passed the lane of lights on Fourteenth Street, was the feeling of excitement, promise, and youth, a wonderful feeling that he had never expected to recapture. He paid off the cabby, forgetting about Peg and revenge in the sudden joy of the moment.

"Sure you'll be okay, bud?" the cabby called after him for some reason, but Alvine waved him on, amused at the unnecessary concern.

The clock in the Con Edison building beamed down familiarly, and Alvine, surprised that night had come so swiftly, thought then of the old days in George Terrence's apartment on Irving Place when the same clock had beamed in their window and bonged them awake each morning. Old George had been top man then, with his money and family, decent in his way, and it was probably a shame the way they used to exploit him, use his charge accounts, sign his name at restaurants, use his clothes and liquor and girls. Once in a while Alvine had encountered him in later years, and it gave him an inner laugh to see how their positions had changed, George now eager to be host instead of sulking at being "used," as in the old days. Old Earl Turner had had the edge then, for a brief period, having a salaried editorial job instead of being a chancy freelance writer. Where was old Earl right now anyway?

Alvine wandered down toward the square, stopped in a corner bar for a double Johnny Walker to sustain the pleasant glow of memories. When he came out, the neighborhood seemed to him to have changed beyond recognition, old landmarks swallowed up by great new apartment houses and supermarkets. The Planet Drug Store was still there, where they used to drop in for contraceptives, leaving the girl standing, all innocence, on the corner. On such a night as this, mused Alvine, in such a place he had made his preparations for a pass at Connie Birch, while she waited outside, clutching his manuscript. The boy Earl talked of was surely his, Alvine thought, crossing a side street now, pleased to recognize the old auction gallery, with the hamburger stand next door now a pizzeria, and the old candy store now a bar. He looked in, half expecting Earl to be there with a welcome, but nobody spoke to him, the drink was terrible, and the seedy-looking customers scowled at the stranger.

Alvine found himself passing the Planet Drug Store again and realized that he had forgotten his way around this neighborhood. He began to be annoyed with Earl, and the good feeling blurred into a suspicion that Earl had ganged up with Peg, but that was fantastic, of course, for Peg was a snob. "Fantastic, fantastic," he muttered, going down the street. Coming upon his reflection in a window unexpectedly explained why women on the street gave him a wide berth. He laughed aloud, thinking again how embarrassed Peg would be if she could see him looking like a panhandler. It made him feel good to be a natural part of this neighborhood instead of visiting it as a well-dressed slummer. Earl would like to see him like this, that much was certain.

"Do you know Earl Turner?" he asked in the next bar, a dark place, clammy and stenchy with stale air-conditioning.

"He hasn't been in lately," the bartender said.

What was the boy's name?

"How about Jonathan?" Alvine asked.

"He'll be around later, maybe, after midnight," said the man.

Alvine stood at the end of the bar and ordered. He

laughed aloud again, thinking how fantastic it would seem to Earl to come in and find him there. Fantastic, he repeated, absolutely fantastic. There were several empty seats at the bar and at the tables but Alvine did not want to commit himself to such a permanent step, for the customers were not ordinary bar types or even bohemian types but seemed a collection of Rorschach blobs in the watery pink light. Another curious feature of this bar was that no one looked at Alvine or nudged someone to point at him. He was so accustomed to ignoring such attention, staring straight at his drink or at his *vis à vis,* that the absence of it made him look around more carefully, squinting at the blobs to make them form reasonable contours. Good God, I'm drunk, he suddenly decided as the blobs began twinning and tripling before his gaze. This particular kind of old-fashioned plain drunkenness had not happened to him since the old Village days, and now that he recognized it, he was amused and delighted with the game.

"It's the old rotgut," he reflected aloud.

With the fine labels to which he was accustomed at home, he could sip highballs for hours, knowing his Plimsoll line was reached when he retreated into icy silence, subtly insulting Peg's gayer guests by an occasional sardonic grunt that would make them turn anxiously, knowing the king was bored. He would saunter out of the room, bearing his glass, indicating that even drinking with such company was intolerable and that he preferred bed or a really intelligent talk with the cook or the dogs. No crazy, fascinating multiple visions such as his bar tour tonight was affording him. No three-headed long-eared blobs drinking triple drinks. Just boredom, blah blah boredom.

"Rotgut, yes," said the blob next to him. "But I find it has a tang to it that the good stuff doesn't have. They've got a brandy here that is terrific, sort of like sword-swallowing. We'll have some and you'll see what I mean."

The blob turned out to be absolutely right. The brandy was black and brackish, thick and smoky.

"The swords are rusty," said Alvine, gulping. "Instant tonsillectomy. Fantastic."

He found this curious sensation even more charming than the other effects. Instead of going down the little red lane, this raging drink shot up to the top of his head, where it separated the cerebrum from the cerebellum in one clean cut and then bubbled mischievously behind his eyeballs, so that the blobs all around changed their shapes with dizzying speed.

"Are you a darrow, by any chance?" he asked his friend, for the blob was now elongating into a pointed head which might conceivably have made him a Martian or Venusian except that he was too short.

"How did you know?" asked the sword-swallower. "My name is Wright, Percy Wright, but my grandmother was a darrow from Plainfield."

"Did she work nights in a bakery in Perth Amboy?" Alvine asked, intensely interested.

The fellow did not think she had, but he conceded that there were a lot of things about the darrows that he had never known. He did not know how often the darrows came up out of the earth, for instance, but he recalled an uncle who had to have a cement slab over his grave in Maryland because he kept floating out at high tide and indeed had once been waterborne in a tornado right into the village bar that had been his ruin. The wind had blown in the saloon door, and there was the uncle, perpendicular, pushed right up to the bar, ready for a nightcap.

"Fantastic, those darrows," said Alvine, delighted.

Out of the corner of his eye he could see the darrow's head lengthening and then squashing down like an accordion, an accordion with a tiny mustache. Under ordinary circumstances Alvine meticulously avoided that borderline in drinking when he was not master of the situation. He disliked slovenly drinking because he respected alcohol too much, he claimed, to see it degraded, used as a mask, weapon, or means to an end. Tonight was different.

He looked around to see if there were any other darrows present, but the bar was too dark to see well. His companion clung to him whenever Alvine started to leave, for he complained that nobody appreciated him in this bar, his girl friends were always insisting that he wait for them there and then they always came late and latched on to some other guy. It did strike Alvine that whenever his friend hailed a newcomer the person shied away to the farthest end of the bar or else left, probably afraid of darrows.

"Darcy, come have a drink with us!" the friend cried to a girl who walked by, a beautiful little blob of a girl with penetrating oyster eyes, or no, little clam eyes, tiny little Seine clam eyes that cut right through you.

"Not unless you get rid of that bum," said the girl. "You been down to the waterfront?"

"Now, wait a minute, Darcy. Now, Darcy."

The darrow began to cry, and the girl melted away into the Seine mud.

"Bitch," said Alvine, pulling up his friend, who kept sliding from his stool. "They're all bitches, popping off with the first title that comes along."

Rage at Peg came over him again but he couldn't remember what Peg looked like, except for the clam eyes. A fresh drink of the delicious house brandy made him happy again, and he thought of how Peg would screech if she saw him bring home all these blobs. His companion clutched his arm and maneuvered them to a vacant booth near the bar, where he laid his head down on the table and sobbed, little hiccupy sobs. Alvine watched his head stretch and contract like Silly Putty until the rhythm of it made him sleepy. He tried to keep his eyes open by staring at a menu card.

"Golden Spur." He made out the words finally. "I used to know the place once. Let's go there."

The darrow was sleeping now, snores punctuated with tiny hiccups. A disgusting lot, these darrows, Alvine thought. He tried to get up, but the other's legs sprawled out, locking him in.

"Okay," Alvine said, giving up and sliding back. "Might as well have another brandy."

"The boss says we can't serve you any more," said the waiter.

"Make it Johnny Walker, then," said Alvine agreeably, but the waiter had gone.

"Better get out of here before Percy comes to," far-off voices said, and then other far-off voices sounded familiar, addressing him by name.

"You get his other arm, Jonathan," the voice said. "Come on, Alvine, we'll get you to a cab. Here we go."

"Nasty lot, those darrows," Alvine said in the cab drowsily. "Where the hell were you, Earl, old boy? Looked for you all day. Let's go to Golden Spur. Old times' sake. Got to meet my son."

He was peacefully asleep.

"There's your end of the rainbow for you!" Earl exclaimed sarcastically. "You were so hot to find the guy, and see what you've got now. I don't know what on earth got into him, but here's your hero for the taking. This is the way it happens."

"He was looking for me!" Jonathan said unhappily. "Don't ever tell him we found him, Earl."

"You think it would bother him?" Earl laughed. "It's material, isn't it? Nothing bothers a genius but lack of material! Come on, we'll get him to bed."

"A good guy is always on the spot," Earl Turner said. "Everybody wants to take a crack at him. He doesn't have a chance. You've got to be a real bastard to get out of a jam, excuse the expression."

Jonathan looked at his notebooks stacked with his laundry package on the unpainted table of his room at the Hotel One Three.

"I should have left word where I was moving," he said.

Earl snorted.

"You can't tell a woman you're leaving until you're gone," he said. "Darcy wouldn't have let you get away, and Lize would have tied you up."

Jonathan knew it was true. What worried him was how he could resist capture once they started after him.

"I don't suppose I dare go in the Spur." He meditated. "All those messages on the bulletin board for me to get in touch. I can't go to the café on account of Dr. Kellsey. He's waiting for me to move into his apartment with him. He says he owes it to me."

There had been an unsigned note to "J.J." also, that would have been from Iris, saying, "The past is the past, but what about the future?" Earl had relayed other mysterious messages to him and had brought a letter from George Terrence.

"I can't tell you how disappointed I was when you did not appear for your appointment," it said. "Thinking it over, however, I could understand your hesitancy. We are both, I think, aware of our true relationship, though we have not discussed it candidly. I can see that the secrecy of the relationship would be a burden to you, since you want definite cause to cut yourself from the Jaimison name. I myself should like to sign papers admitting my paternity, which papers could be shown under special circumstances, but for appearances' sake I should like to "adopt" you. This would avoid unpleasant effects on my wife and family, for I would propose this step to Hazel as a sentimental gesture toward her old friend.

"I think this will put you in a much happier position. I shall proceed with these arrangements, confident that you will get in immediate touch with the office. I cannot tell you how much it will mean to me to be united with my unknown son."

Jonathan gloomily handed the letter to Earl. Weighed down with his own problems as he was, he was still able to note with surprise the new sporty jacket Earl was wearing, the natty shoes and pink shirt. Success had gone straight to his back, evidently.

"What about Alvine?" Earl asked, after scanning the note. "He'll be out in another couple of weeks. Every day he asks about you. It's damned awkward, after I laid it on for you."

"He doesn't know how we found him?" Jonathan asked.

"He doesn't remember what happened after he took the elevator in the Big Hat bar and landed in the bowels of the earth with a tribe of darrows," Earl said dryly. "They told him we were expected, so he waited for us. And that's the story he told that made his agent and the doctor hustle him off to the hospital. Oh, he's still mixed up, all right, but it's just shock."

"I haven't got over the shock myself," said Jonathan.

"With Alvine it's the shock of having something go wrong for once in his damn life," Earl said. "A wife leaves him instead of him leaving her. Shock number one. Then the shock of hunting for me instead of me hunting for him. A guy like Alvine can't adjust to upsets like that. He's either kingpin or crybaby."

Earl looked at his watch. Now that he had a wristwatch, Jonathan noticed that he was forever looking at it, as if important people were waiting for him elsewhere. Apparently it was gratifying to use this gesture instead of having it used against him.

"Well, do you want to come along and see him or not? I can see why you don't feel like claiming him right now as your rightful parent, but so far as I'm concerned I like him better as a drunken slob than I ever did as the king of cats." Earl frowned at Jonathan. "Okay, you were looking for a big hero daddy and you back away when you come on him getting thrown out of a bar."

It was the truth, and Jonathan couldn't understand himself.

"I guess I was disappointed on account of my mother," he said. "I couldn't picture her with him. I didn't want to."

"If he hadn't been flipping he wouldn't have even bothered to look for you, just think of that," Earl said. "You would still be hoping to find him, hoping he was your man."

"I know."

"So you've got your wish, and whenever that happens it's always too late and all crossed up. He's got it in his old bull head that a lost bastard turning up in his life will put him one up on his wife. He wants to throw you in her face. I guess that isn't the way you pictured it."

"No."

"I told him I'd bring you up if I found you," Earl said. "Can't say I blame you for chickening out, but I'd like to help Alvine right now. I used to get sore at Alvine always being on top of the world, everything working out for him, but damn it, I don't like a big man down. Funny, eh? I'm used to Alvine always running the show. I'm used to being jealous. That's my security. Alvine's my old North Star, I mean he's got to be up there in the sky."

That was how he felt too, Jonathan thought. He was ashamed to admit that his dream of a father was of a man infinitely superior to John Jaimison, a man it would be a victory to claim, not a responsibility. It was no triumph to be captured himself, to round out some frustrated man's picture of himself as a father. He hadn't asked Fate to send him a great man who appeared to have gone off his rocker and stood in need of a son's tender devotion. Damn it, he'd done his time as dutiful son, yessirring and nosirring. He didn't want to begin that all over with a new candidate. He wondered why it had never occurred to him that his father would expect him to make up to him for the lost years—as if he owed it to him.

"I hoped I'd never see this damn dump again!" Earl exclaimed in sudden petulance. He yanked down the mottled yellow shade on the narrow court window, and the fabric tore off the roll. He swore. "Same view of garbage cans, dead cats, and broken baby carriages. I'm through with all that. Why do I have to rub my nose in it again just for some kid that thought he wanted to find a father and then wants to hide out?"

Jonathan was embarrassed.

"It was getting too much for me," he said patiently." The girls and Mr. Terrence and Dr. Kellsey all expecting to take me over before I'd found out what I wanted. I was so sure Alvine Harshawe was the answer, then coming on him that night blubbering and wild, I couldn't believe it—"

"I couldn't believe it myself," Earl interrupted. "I couldn't believe I wasn't laughing, either, because he'd been so snotty about not wanting to go to the Spur for fear his public would mob him. I could have laughed, but the funny part was that I hated it. Hated seeing him stuck with a punk like Percy, a guy he'd never speak to in his right mind. I'd like to take you up to him, damn it. I'd like to see him get the edge on Peg the way he always had."

"I don't want it that way," Jonathan said.

Earl kicked the fallen shade angrily under the bed.

"If he really thought I was his own son he wouldn't use me to get even, that's all," Jonathan said. "Later on he'd probably admit it was all a joke on her, but the joke would be on me."

This made Earl meditate for a moment. Then he brought out more missives from his pocket and tossed them to Jonathan.

"Dan said these telegrams were forwarded around town to the Spur," he said. "You may have something there about Alvine. Maybe you'll think differently in a week or two when he comes around. Maybe he'll change his tune too. I'm staying at the De Long now if you need me. Don't expect me to come back to this fleabag again."

"It's only temporary," Jonathan said.

"I've stayed here temporarily all my life, boy," Earl said. "Don't get started."

"I hate the word 'permanent,' " said Jonathan. "I've got to pull out of the café job before it's too late. But what can I do? How will I get by?"

"You've got nothing to worry about," Earl said. "You're young, you've got looks, you've got a blue suit and a pair of black shoes, hell, the world is your oyster. All you need is a list of bar mitzvahs, walk right in, eat all you want, help yourself to a fat drink, shake hands, say Irving never looked better. You won't starve."

No use expecting sympathy from a battle-scarred trooper like Earl.

After the door closed, Jonathan looked at the telegrams. All were from John Jaimison, Senior, summoning Jonathan to visit him at the Hotel Sultana on Central Park West as soon as possible.

12

Four months ago Jonathan would have been outraged that his own special city should be defiled by the presence of a real Jaimison. He would have been indignant that the city had broken its promise of asylum and let in the enemy. He would have been shocked that his kind Aunt Tessie had given away his hiding place.

It surprised him that his chief feeling was mild astonishment that these people still existed when they had been erased from his own mind. The letter from Aunt Tessie explained a little.

"I wouldn't have given him the address but I got the idea it has something to do with money. I heard he was going to New York to see a specialist and it struck me he might be wanting to make up to you for everything before he dies. Now Jonny-boy, you take whatever you can get out of him, and don't open your mouth about his not being your own father. Goodness knows he gave you as bad a time as your own father could have, so let him pay for it. You go see him and be smart. Let's see if he'll let go a few dollars at last, ha ha."

Jonathan decided Aunt Tessie's theory must be right. He needn't worry that the old man would have made a trip to New York to retrieve a lost child, when he had not noticed his absence all this time. Nothing to be afraid of, really, in facing him again. If he wanted to atone, let him atone plenty.

Walking toward the park from the Seventy-second Street subway, however, Jonathan had time to worry about what kind of scene he would have to face, supposing the old man had reached a state of sniveling penitence. He might be propped up on his deathbed, surrounded by nurses and weeping Florence, and expecting Jonathan to join in tears of mutual forgiveness. But it was too late to back out now. In no time he heard himself being announced from the hotel desk, and there was his stepmother at the door of 9 B, one hand extended and the other at her lips.

"He's resting," she whispered. "He just got back from the specialist's examination."

At least she showed no signs of weeping.

"Pretty sick, eh?" Jonathan whispered back, tiptoeing into the vestibule.

Florence threw up her hands.

"You know your father," she said.

Jonathan looked startled.

"He will overdo," she said. "So when he had to make this trip I made him promise to see this expert. A hundred dollars a visit, so he must be good. And this hotel—twenty dollars a day, mind you, without counting the garage rent. Well, well, Jonathan!"

As she talked her little brown eyes shopped over his person busily, price-tagging his corduroy slacks and checked shirt, recognizing his old sport jacket and mentally throwing it out. Her frown centered on his hair as if the barbering bore Darcy's own signature. He followed her gingerly through the vestibule. Evidently there would be no deathbed scene, judging from her high spirits.

"My goodness, Jonathan, you certainly haven't got the

New York look yet!" she exclaimed. "I should have thought you'd have a whole new suit by this time. Those trousers—"

"Cost eighteen dollars," Jonathan said obligingly.

If Florence was reducing him to his net merchandise value, Jonathan was just as curious about the obvious rise in the fortunes of the Jaimisons. Packages with the Saks Fifth Avenue label were piled on the hall chair, a new fur stole hung over its back, and the living room revealed not only an expensive view of Central Park but a corner bar cabinet with a full bottle of scotch visible. A closer look at his stepmother showed that she had gotten herself up to hold her own in the great city. The effect was not a New York look but the small-town look multifold. The rouge was redder, the jaw firmer, the coiffure browner and kinkier, the bracelets bigger and noisier, the Alice-blue silk dress bluer and tighter, the patent-leather sandals higher-heeled.

The smell of prosperity was here, Jonathan thought, mystified. A familiar cough announced the emergence of Mr. Jaimison himself from the bedroom. He stood for a moment framed in the doorway, squinting his eyes, mustache and famous Jaimison nose quivering as if testing the psychic temperature of the room. Jonathan squinted back, surprised that his onetime father was shorter and stockier than he remembered, but then he had usually seen him in lordly command of a desk or steering wheel. Without his props of authority the old man seemed at a loss for a moment; then he squared his shoulders and plunged masterfully across the room, arms swinging as if ready to put up a stiff defense. He cleared his throat.

"Well, son," he said, giving Jonathan's hand a firm disciplinary squeeze.

Jonathan cleared his own throat.

"Well, sir," he said and returned the other's bleak smile.

"I guess you never expected to see me in New York City," said Mr. Jaimison, plumping himself down in the regal wing chair his wife pushed toward him. "Never expected to find you here either, for that matter, but that's life, eh? I had this business matter to attend to—we'll talk about that later—and I promised Florence that while we were here I'd let a specialist go over me just to satisfy her, but let me tell you, I'm not as close to the cemetery as you think."

"I didn't—" But there was really no use, as Jonathan knew, in trying to make conversation, for Jaimison, Senior, always pitched right into a strident monologue, which was a deaf man's privilege.

"Yes sir, do you know what this doctor told me? Said I had a little liveliness in the kidneys, perfectly natural in a man of sixty, they say, a touch of firming up in the arteries, usual too, and they tell me I've got the liver of a man of forty. Doctor couldn't believe it. 'You've got the liver of a man of forty—maybe thirty-five,' he says. How about that? Ha ha ha!"

"Ha ha ha!" said Florence, nodding toward Jonathan in an invitation to join the fun.

"Ha," ventured Jonathan, and wondered if he was expected to ask for a peek at this splendid organ.

"Tell Jonathan what he said about your heart," she urged and leaned toward Jonathan confidentially. "I thought it was a heart attack but it was only gas. Ha ha ha."

"Ha," agreed Jonathan and nodded politely while Mr. Jaimison delivered a full medical report, straight A's from sinuses to urine, minuses where it would have been promiscuous to be plus, prophecies of future gains and natural losses declaimed in the cheery manner of a smooth treasurer reassuring doubtful stockholders. When he paused to cough for emphasis, Jonathan coughed in sympathy; when he bared his dentures in a stiff smile, Jonathan arranged one on his own face. For there was no doubt about it, the old man was doing his best to be civil, flailing his olive branch around like a horsewhip, determined to bring up a bucket of bubbling geniality from the long-dry well. But why? Jonathan wondered.

Having finished off the medical report, Jaimison, Senior, launched into an equally gratifying and equally confidential description of his new Chevy, enumerating on his fingers (with Jonathan checking the tabulation involuntarily on his own fingers) the reasons he had chosen this car against other candidates, the real reason being that he never changed his mind about anything, so why would he change his car? During this talk Florence's eyes kept seeking out Jonathan's anxiously for approval, and if he smiled her hard enameled face cracked open wide enough to show a king's ransom in porcelain caps. When she saw his eyes straying in the direction of the bar, she whispered, "The lawyer sent the bottle to us as a gift. Would you like a highball? Okay?"

Extraordinary, Jonathan thought, nodding dumbly. The spectacle of a drink in Jonathan's hands stopped Mr. Jaimison's oration sharply. Forgetting his new warmth, he gave a disapproving snort. He himself never drank except for business, just as he never laughed except for business. It infuriated him that a man could drink half your bottle before your eyes and not even make a fool of himself. If he would only fall on his face, have a fit, or do something to give a non-drinker legitimate excuse to feel superior!

However, an admonitory glance from his wife made him content to mutter only, "More accidents from drunken driving."

"I've never had a car," Jonathan said.

"Throw away your money on taxis, eh." Mr. Jaimison grunted.

"Now, Father," chided Florence, evidently bent on maintaining a truce. She startled Jonathan by giving him a conspiratorial wink, saying, "You know how your father always travels by car, business or pleasure, ever since we bought the Chevy for our honeymoon. He isn't really himself till he's behind the wheel."

No need to remind him of that, Jonathan thought, remembering the blue Chevy tooling up Aunt Tessie's driveway in response to a dozen or more pleas from her for Jonathan's schooling, clothes, or even for simple advice. He recalled how determinedly the gentleman had shunted off appeals by launching into endless travelogues on trips he had just taken with his new wife through the Great Smokies, the New England lakes, the Berkshires, the Adirondacks, Route this and Thruway that, detour here and ferry there, just jump in the car and away, away through those great open spaces between Esso and Gulf. Dizzy from these vicarious tours, discouraged by the inability to interrupt, Jonathan would give up and dreamily observe the caller's evasion tactics. He had a vague image of Jaimison *père,* in the plaid cap and goggles of the early motorist, perpetually gypsying through cloverleafs and underpasses, skyways and byways, oblivious to everything but Stop and Go, knowing it was South by Dr. Pepper signs and Hot Shoppes, North by tonic ads and Howard Johnsons (allowing for the recent exchange of these clues), but happy in the one sure thing that he was safe at the wheel. What a fortress! Nobody and nothing could ever get at a man behind the wheel of his own God-given car. Nor was there any talent in the world as valuable as Mr. Jaimison's superior gift for parking.

"Your father thinks you should have a car," Florence said radiantly, just as Jonathan was musing that he hated the automobile.

"Every good citizen ought to have a car," stated Mr. Jaimison. "Something to show for himself, as I see it."

"Maybe Jonathan thinks owning his own home is most important for a young man." Florence again smiled at him with the coy wink. "Okay?"

Jonathan mumbled something about cars and houses being furthest from his mind, but Mr. Jaimison did not hear him, nor did he hear Florence's murmured explanation that Father should really get a hearing aid, and didn't Jonathan think the high cost would be justified? Jonathan wanted to reply that next to his gift for parking, Father enjoyed his deafness, for all he ever wanted to hear from anybody was "Yes, sir." He didn't want to hear persiflage, or requests for loans, or tales of woe, and the resulting lack of wear and tear on his emotions kept his brow unfurrowed, his eye clear, and his pockets full. What were the pair of them getting at, anyway, with their talk of cars and houses? There must be money in it somewhere, just as Aunt Tessie had prophesied, and Jonathan began dreaming of hundred-dollar bills, or why not five-hundred-dollar bills? Whose face was on a five-hundred-dollar bill? he wondered. For all he knew it might be that of Jaimison, Senior. He'd take whatever the old buzzard offered, he decided, and run.

But Mr. Jaimison had gotten on an even more curious subject as he twirled his cigar. He hoped, he said, that Jonathan had not been permanently discouraged by failing to make good in Silver City. He would admit frankly that Florence had blamed him for not taking a firm hand with him when Jonathan was falling down on his jobs, but the way things were turning out now he would guarantee that Jonathan could go right back home and open his own offices as big as you please and have the town behind him in no time.

"I don't say you could do it alone, mind you," said Mr. Jaimison, "but I've built up a solid business reputation back there, and with me behind you you've got nothing to worry about. I'd retire in another few years from the mills, anyway, and with our own business started I could step in full time. I looked at offices for you in the Gas Building—"

"Offices? For me?" Jonathan thought the drink must be affecting his own hearing, gu'ped it down hastily, and then decided another one would clear his head. He jumped up and poured it, not even seeing Mr. Jaimison's instinctive gesture of disapproval. Florence gave a little gasp and leaped up to snatch Jonathan's glass and plant a coaster firmly beneath it before restoring it to him. Mr. Jaimison watched this operation and Jonathan's greedy gulping of the second drink with tight lips.

"I did not realize that alcohol was so necessary to you, Jonathan," he said.

"Everybody has his own fuel," Jonathan said. "You have to have gas, and I have to have alcohol."

Mr. Jaimison saw no reason to reply to this flippancy. He drummed his fingers on the arm of his chair.

"Now about your office," he began firmly. "I can see that you can be set up by the first of the year. Give you time to straighten out here in New York and get back home and look over the situation. Being on the spot myself will save you a lot, of course, while the lawyers are speeding up the settlement—"

"What's he talking about?" Jonathan asked Florence.

"The inheritance," Florence said. "Your father had to handle the whole thing when nobody knew where you were, and then the chance to buy this real-estate business came along at the same time, so he thought he'd settle that too, advancing you the money himself. Too good a chance for you to invest in a permanent job, so to say."

Jonathan looked from one to the other glassily. Either he was dreaming or they were both crazy.

"I guess you'll be glad to get back home, eh, son," said Jaimison, Senior, with a benign chuckle. "We Jaimisons never like city life. I suppose I've traveled through every sizable city in the country and you can have them all—Detroit, Columbus, New York. Another thing. That money will be a nice little fortune back home, but it wouldn't last you five years in New York. I guess you realize that."

"What money?" Jonathan asked patiently.

"This money we're telling you about," said Mr. Jaimison with a hint of his old irascibility. "The money this party left your mother when he died. Naturally they had to come to me trying to locate her, and I handled it as far as I could till Tessie told us how to locate you, get your signature on things and all that. The way I see it, you'll be set up in a foolproof business for life and can hold your head up with the rest of them. The lawyer—he sent me that scotch you're drinking, by the way—says I've done everything his client would have asked by way of protecting your interests. You'll be seeing him."

Jonathan made an involuntary move toward the bottle, but Florence forestalled him, hastily pouring out a few drops into his glass.

"Jonathan's more surprised than we were." Florence giggled. "Wasn't it foxy of your mother never to mention any of those investments she was making in New York when she worked here?"

"Had me paying through the nose for years, mind you, and all the time this fortune tucked away in New York!" Mr. Jaimison interrupted. "By George, I was mad when I found out, but, come to think it over, it works out all the better all around. Seems her employer invested her money so well that it's mounted to real sizable proportions. A couple hundred thousand dollars is a neat little nest egg, Jonathan, even in these times."

"Whose nest egg? What employer?" Jonathan shouted.

Florence put a finger to her lips, smiling.

"I don't blame you for being excited. Your father didn't write because he didn't know where to find you at first and he kept holding off the lawyer while he sort of got things ready and straightened out the details. The Major, it seems, never knew of your mother's death, so that had to be straightened out."

"Major?"

"Her employer, Major Wedburn," Mr. Jaimison said. "I don't suppose you ever heard of him, either. I never listened to your mother gabbing away about New York, so I daresay it's my own fault for not knowing she was making a whacking lot of money, but—"

Major Wedburn. The man whose funeral was being mourned by the De Long that first day in New York. Claire Van Orphen had said Connie Birch had typed for him. So the Major had left her a fortune in the guise of "investments." Jonathan sat clutching the arms of his chair, trying to keep his thoughts from plunging toward the inevitable conclusion, while Jaimison, Senior, talked on and on, waving envelopes and papers at him, thrusting memos into his hand, and sugaring his voice resolutely.

"Why don't you want your offices to be in the Gas Building, my boy?"

"Because I don't like gas," Jonathan said feebly. "Anyway, I don't need any offices."

Mr. Jaimison was controlling his impatience admirably. "But I leased them for five years out of my own pocket!" he said. "Naturally I knew you'd settle with me later. There's your real-estate business all set up for you, son."

"Not real estate!" Jonathan cried, seeing Darcy's greedy little face.

"Okay, your father could get you into the bank," Florence said with a firm nod to her husband. "You've got to have everything safely settled. These people trying to get your mother to back them because they had claims on the Major are likely to come after you, and you'd have no protection."

"Once you're dug in they can't get at you," said Mr. Jaimison. "Let 'em sue. Claiming the Major wanted his money used to support a dirty little art gallery. Claiming there's some mistake somewhere."

"Show him the letters," Florence urged. "You'll see that your father was very clever, planning your protection from those sharks."

Jonathan read the letters Jaimison, Senior, thrust into his hand as a final argument. Cassie Bender wished Mrs. Jaimison to be her partner in the Bender Art Gallery, inasmuch as they seemed to have been partners in the late Major's affections. In a later letter Mrs. Bender reminded Mrs. Jaimison of how much they both owed him, and how beholden they both should be to his well-known tastes, creating a monument of sorts to his beloved memory, carrying on his torch, so to speak. A third letter begged the fortunate heiress to regard herself as heir to the Major's responsibilities as well as to his rewards, and Mrs. Bender was confident the Bender Art Gallery was the Major's prime concern before his untimely end.

"She doesn't know my mother died." Jonathan cut into the buzz of Jaimison's voice going on about stocks, percentages, taxes.

"We ignored her letters, of course," Mr. Jaimison said, a note of weariness creeping into his tone, for it was only his wife's admonitory glances and headshakes that kept his temper down. "As I say, we've saved you all we could."

"But she's right," Jonathan said. "I must talk this over with her."

"Jonathan!"

This time Mr. Jaimison's honest rage over his son's blind stupidity was too much for him and he shook his fists in the air.

"Twenty-five years old, and the boy still can't think straight! Twenty-five years old!" he exploded.

"Twenty-six," interrupted Jonathan, his courage restored by the exhibition of the old Jaimison temper. "Born November twenty-eighth, nineteen twenty-nine, just six months and a half after your wedding day."

There now, see what that brings up, old boy, he exulted.

"Premature, yes, yes," Mr. Jaimison snapped back savagely. "The only time in your whole career that you weren't backward!"

"Father, now Father!" pleaded Florence with an imploring glance at Jonathan. "All of us having such a nice reunion here, and the future so rosy, and here we are quarreling. It does seem, Jonathan, that you ought to be grateful to your father for protecting your interests after the way you ran away without so much as good-by, and the lawyer hunting for you too."

"I'll see him myself," Jonathan said, stuffing papers into his pocket.

"But what are your plans? You've got to plan your future, son, all that money going to waste instead of into a nice business," Mr. Jaimison wailed. "What will you do?"

"I'm going into the art business," Jonathan said. "Just like Mrs. Bender said. Sort of a monument to my—I mean to Major Wedburn. Good-by, sir, and look out for that liver."

In the hall he heard his name called and saw Jaimison, Senior, standing in the doorway, mopping his forehead helplessly. He mopped his own brow as the elevator went down, then put his handkerchief away.

"Maybe it was one of the Major's habits too," he reassured himself.

He came out into the early autumn twilight of the park and sat down on the first bench he saw. He felt giddy. He saw the Sultana lights go on and wondered if it was all a dream. But there were the papers in his pocket. He glanced at the address on Cassie Bender's letter. Her gallery was just across the park.

Jonathan headed eastward.

13

Claire Van Orphen looked smaller and older when Jonathan finally paid her a visit. Just a few months made a difference after sixty, he thought, or was it the trimly modern black wool suit, paler make-up, and tidier coiffure that her sister's influence had brought about? To tell the truth he could not conjure up a picture of her old self, blurred as it was by his intense concern with his own problems, and having seen only himself in her eyes.

"Don't you think it's too grand for me?" she asked, with an apologetic wave toward the McKinley plush decor of the De Long Presidential suite. "I've been budgeting and scrimping for so many years I can't enjoy splurging unless I balance it by doing without something else. My sister Beatrice is just the opposite. That's one reason our plan to live together didn't work out."

Jonathan looked admiringly at the sooty but imposing chandeliers, the huge marble fireplace with its electric logs, the balding bear rug sprawled over the faded rose carpet. Arched doors at either end of the room were closed on one side and open on the other to reveal bedroom walls gay with frolicking cupids, bluebirds, and butterflies from a giddier period. There was a combined air of Victorian closed parlors and musty potpourri that seemed deliciously romantic to Jonathan, more luxurious by far than Cassie Bender's bleak modernity.

"It's exactly the way my mother described it when she worked for you," he said. "So this was the place."

"Indeed no, my rooms were much simpler," Claire corrected him. "This was always Major Wedburn's suite, right up to the day he died. He kept it just this way no matter where he was traveling. I took over his lease, thinking of Beatrice, of course, but instead it turns out to be useful for Earl Turner, my collaborator. He has the Major's library there." She nodded toward the closed doors. "You know Earl Turner. Oh dear, I forget. You introduced us."

"I haven't seen him for some time," Jonathan said. "I'm afraid he went to some trouble to contact Alvine Harshawe for me and it—well, it didn't work out as he thought."

"We've been so busy on our scripts, as I told you," Claire said tactfully, remembering that Earl was annoyed with the young man. "He feels we must ride our luck while we've got it. Goodness knows how long we can last. Do you mind ready-made Manhattans?"

"I missed our little parties," Jonathan said, sinking into a titanic overstuffed chair beside her coffee table. "So many things have been happening."

He did look different, Claire thought. Was it the handsome vest or was it something about the eyes? She wished she had not been affected by Earl's and George Terrence's disappointment in him, but it had been naughty of him to get poor George Terrence in such a state, especially since she had been the one responsible for their meeting. And Hazel phoning around like a mad creature, saying George kept confessing to a mysterious past and getting himself analyzed and that she was coming into the city to help with her daughter's career, and why had Claire set him off with that sinister young man anyway? Hazel was a fool, true enough, but still—

"I hope everything is going well," she said, feeling guilty for the many times she had had to refuse his visits in the last few months because of her own new preoccupations. How selfish of her, no matter how mischievous he had been with others, when he had brought so much light and luck into her lonely old age! It was the old ones who were the heartless ones, drawing all the blood they could out of the young and then shrugging them off. Even as she was repenting she found herself peeping at her watch to see how much time she had before the conference with the CBS director.

Jonathan had been eager to share his news with his mother's old friend, but he saw now that her life was filled without him, and there seemed no way to begin again.

"I've had a little luck," he said, but it was no good wasting his dramatic confidence on the polite, strained atmosphere. Besides, people accustomed to advising and helping you were often ruffled when you became independent, as if they liked your need of them more than they liked you.

"I came to ask you about Major Wedburn," Jonathan said. "I should like to have known that man."

Claire could not keep back a laugh.

"You and the Major! I can't think of a funnier combination!"

"I'm sure we would have gotten on," Jonathan protested. "That's why I want to know more about him."

"I'm afraid you would have found him pompous, but he was a great gentleman for all his quirks," Claire said. "Our families were very close. I was touched when he left me the Cecilia Beaux portrait of his grandfather, which hangs in the bedroom."

"My mother spoke of a Cecilia Beaux picture," Jonathan said. "Funny she never mentioned the Major."

"Very strange," Claire said. She and Earl had come to the private conclusion that Jonathan's mother had been a very strange young woman in many ways. She was glad to be asked about the Major instead of Connie Birch, for she knew her disapproval would show.

"He must have been a gay old dog," said Jonathan.

"I don't think anyone could ever have called the Major a gay dog," Claire said. "A man of the world, I grant you, but a most discreet one. I daresay there were women in his life, but he took care that no one knew it."

"Then he could have had a secret affair," Jonathan persisted.

Now what made him pry into that?

"He was a secretive man, very fussy about hiding his lady friends from the world, and from each other," she said, controlling her impatience with the young man's curiosity. "At one time he was courting my sister Bea and myself at the very same time, and we didn't check till years later. He'd been playing us against each other. I suppose he fancied himself a strategist."

Jonathan smiled.

"Sometimes a man has to be," he said, thinking of Lize and Darcy.

"Bea was put out when she found he had left me the portrait," Claire said and sighed. "But then Bea has been very touchy these last few weeks. Quite by chance I bought a new suit at Bonwit's, and it turned out Bea had bought the identical suit that very morning at Bergdorf's. Our minds used to work like that in the old days. But Bea was so horrified at being a twin again that she raged at me. Sent her suit right back. Do you know that I cried myself to sleep for the first time in twenty years? No one can hurt you like your own twin!"

Tears came to her eyes again and she only nodded sadly when Jonathan asked permission to look at the picture.

In the bedroom Jonathan studied the portrait of the Major's grandfather seated at a great desk, quill pen in hand, open record book before him, a pair of black Dachshunds at his feet. He was a stout dark man, and though Jonathan could trace no resemblance to himself, in an odd way he looked familiar. The strong Roman nose, the beetling eyebrows, the bullish shoulders—why, he might have been Jaimison, Senior! He was grasping the pen as if it were a steering wheel, the notebook was a ledger in which he was adding up his toll fees, the keen gaze was searching beyond for the next Howard Johnson. Quite shaken, Jonathan came back to Miss Van Orphen's side.

"The Major looked just like him." Claire answered Jonathan's unspoken question.

"There must have been something else about him," Jonathan mused, "something my mother found and loved."

Good heavens, not the Major too!

"Oh, no!" Claire said, wincing. "You can't do this to my old friend, Jonathan! I don't care how dead your mother is, she ought to be ashamed of herself, stirring up the poor Major's ashes, a fine man she barely knew—no, no!"

"But you yourself told me he admired her so much!" Jonathan protested, confused by her genuine indignation. "You told me he advised her to go back home and marry and have children. You told me—"

"I was making it up!" Claire cried. "I couldn't remember

anything except that he had sent her to me for typing, but I didn't want to disappoint you, so I made up little lies!"

"They weren't lies," Jonathan said. "It was truer than you know. That's why he left his money to her, and now it's going to be mine. I tried to tell you before, but you were always busy on your work. Major Wedburn was my father."

Claire drew a long breath, poured another drink from her shaker, and filled Jonathan's glass as an afterthought. Everything was so upsetting—Bea's recent tantrums, the Terrences in her life again, and now the shock about the Major.

"Why do you young people have to stir up everything?" she burst out passionately and was immediately contrite. "Oh dear, it's not your fault. Forgive me. I should be thinking of how upsetting it must be for you, finding that your mother had so many lovers."

"But that explains so much to me," Jonathan said, surprised that she did not see this. "She wanted to be whatever anybody expected her to be, because she never knew what she was herself. That's the way I am, you see. And now that I know the Major had several different lives too, I understand myself better."

Claire was silent, trying to piece together these missing pieces from the Major's past. It was hard to work up sex jealousy thirty years later, but she could, at least, feel a sense of outraged decency that her first and only affair, a romantic secret between her and the Major, should have its memory fouled by that appalling young woman. How blind she had been not to see it all under her nose, but as usual she always missed the obvious, thinking of the little typist with her wide, eager eyes as charmingly naïve, and herself, ten years older, so worldly-wise! Thinking herself sophisticated with her one love affair in thirty-odd years, when the little country mouse, barely twenty, was having an affair with every man she met as if it were no more than a curtsy! And the Major leaving a fortune to the girl, tacitly admitting his paternity! But then old men always fancied themselves as dangerously fertile, and a girl could persuade the canniest Casanova that his merest handclasp had born fruit. George Terrence, of course—"of course" indeed, when she had never even guessed it at the time—was intent on producing living proof of a guilty past to cover up that brief experiment in homosexuality. Bea had told her about it. Bea always knew those things. Her little circle uptown doted on such tidbits about priggish old gentlemen like George.

"It did seem to me that Alvine Harshawe was the logical man in your mother's life," Claire said. "I understand he admitted it freely to his wife when her divorce suit claimed he was sterile. Of course he can't convince anyone he's sane when he insists on staying on in Harkness Pavilion, soaking up background for a psychiatric play, so Earl says. But what your mother wrote fitted him far more than it did George or the Major."

"I found that what she said fitted everyone," Jonathan explained. "She thought every man she met in New York was Prince Charming and whatever they asked must be the proper thing. She was afraid to seem ignorant or small-town. It's the way I am. That's why we were misfits in our small town. People there—especially the Jaimisons—are *proud* of their ignorance because it's been in the family such a long time."

Claire felt herself melting again under his radiant smile. He shouldn't be blamed for shaking up all these little tempests, and she would say as much to Earl. Considering their own change of luck, they had no right to mistrust the boy's windfall, no matter how preposterous the circumstances.

"I'm investing the Major's money in the way I believe he would approve," Jonathan confided. He handed one of his new cards to her.

"Jonathan Jaimison, Associate Director, Bender Gallery," she read aloud in bewilderment.

"Mrs. Bender thinks I have inherited the Major's natural flair," Jonathan said. "The lawyers consider it a good deal."

Now why should he have to apologize for coming up in the world? Jonathan asked himself.

"But what about your own talent?" Claire said.

"I never could find out what it was," he said. "All I know is that I do appreciate other men's talents, and this way I have a career of other people's talents. I hoped you'd understand."

Claire knew she was squinting suspiciously at the card, trying not to speak out her doubts and warnings, when she should be rejoicing at his news. But that Mrs. Bender! The Major would surely be shocked at such a collaboration. She read in the boy's face that she was failing him, not responding at all as he expected. But he was old enough to know she could not help being loyal to her own generation.

"I'm afraid the Major's tastes in art were totally opposed to the Bender Gallery's," she said bravely. "Winslow Homer was his idol, you know, and he loved Albert Ryder. When the gallery next door had a few Hugow paintings on show I remember the Major getting absolutely indignant."

Jonathan's face clouded.

"I thought of him as more cosmopolitan," he said. "I thought he was someone I'd want to be like."

"The Major was terribly proud of his family," Claire said. "He always tried to go to the family reunions at Christmas in Hartford. And he loved touring around the country in his Lincoln, until the last few years. He was a very conservative man."

Maybe family reunions were different in Hartford, Jonathan thought gloomily, and maybe touring the country in a Lincoln was not as dreary as in a Jaimison vehicle.

"You don't think we'd have gotten on, then," he said.

"I can't picture your having a thing in common," Claire said, shaking her head. "Indeed this all seems incredible, Jonathan."

She was relieved to see Earl Turner come in at that moment.

"Just left the Spur," he told Jonathan. "They tell me you don't come in any more since you made it uptown. Can't say I blame you now the West Coast bums have moved in. The old crowd seems drifting down to The Big Hat."

For a man who had come to success after decades of failure, Earl looked very morose, Jonathan thought. The frozen boyishness now seemed old and dried, petulant more than cynical. The familiar beret was gone, that was it, and the revealed bony bald head added years.

"So Cassie Bender's got you under her wing," he said, tossing back the card Claire passed to him. "It's part of the course. And the grapevine has it that your family came to the city and handed you a fat check."

"Something on that order," Jonathan said.

"Maybe you could advance me twenty until the first," Earl said.

Claire looked at him in amazement.

"Why, Earl, you just got a check for five thousand dollars!"

Earl threw up his hands.

"I can't help it!" he said. "You spend your life thinking in two-bit terms, and that's the only money that's real. Now, when I realize it's my own dough I'm spending it doesn't seem right. With nobody trailing me with duns, nobody hounding me to pay up, honest to God, I get withdrawal symptoms! My whole system is geared for the old way."

"Never mind," Claire comforted him. "It probably won't last."

"It's not just money," Earl said. "At the Spur I started to tell Dan about the new series we're doing for CBS and I saw he didn't believe me, but I didn't believe myself either. Damn it, it was true! I was bragging. It's all right to lie, but a man can't brag when it's true."

He rose impatiently and started toward the library doors.

"I'll straighten out that ending before our man gets here. We have twenty minutes," he said.

"Shall I reserve a table downstairs for dinner?" Claire asked him. "It's roast beef night."

"I can't eat the slops here," Earl said. "We can order tuna-fish sandwiches sent over from the Planet."

"I wish you'd visit the gallery sometime," Jonathan said, unwilling to accept their indifference.

"I can't see how that old warhorse Cassie Bender hooked a smart kid like you for a patsy," Earl observed. "It just doesn't figure."

"She hasn't hooked me. I think of it as the opportunity of a lifetime!" Jonathan exclaimed. "I'll be traveling all over, meeting wonderful people—look at my credit cards!

Cassie arranged everything for me. I know what people say—"

It was no use, he saw by their shocked faces. He picked up his own card and the credit cards he had childishly flaunted and stuck them back in his wallet. It was tiresome having to defend bighearted, overbearing Cassie wherever he went. It was no use expecting these old friends to receive him back into their arms, eager for his confidences. Old people thought only of themselves. Each one alone might be his champion, but together—and he had combined them himself!—they closed ranks, leaving the young intruder outside once again.

"I just wanted to say hello," he said. "I'll run along now."

The boy's feelings must have been hurt, Claire thought remorsefully, but after all one had one's own work and one's own life to live. The young never seemed to understand that. But you had so little time left, and it seemed as if you dared not stop running for a minute. You didn't run to win the prize as you did in youth. Indeed your dimming eyes could not tell if you'd passed the goal or not. You went on running because in the end that was the only prize there was—to be alive, to be in the race.

14

DR. KELLSEY was amazed to find himself installed in the larger apartment next to his old one within a month after he'd suggested it to the landlord of Knowlton Arms. He had been talking of this change for twenty years and it might have taken that long again to put his decision into effect. But here he was, books, screen, and pictures moved over in a trice, the studio couch for Jonathan in the living-room alcove, snug as you please, his own couch in the bedroom, empty closet and dressing room for Jonathan, separate door to bedroom so they could have their privacy. Everything settled but Jonathan, and he had left that to the last.

Now the die was cast, the professor reflected, a little frightened at the *definiteness* of things. Jonathan had been evasive when the hint to share his quarters had first been made, but he was a shy lad and would need to see that the place was all ready for him, no trouble was involved, and any responsibility was on the doctor's side. As they were both sensitive fellows they probably would be embarrassed to admit their secret relationship in so many words, but Jonathan must have recognized the facts just as the doctor had.

What worried the doctor was the problem of his lady friend, Anita. She had been urging this move on him for years, as part of her program for his divorcing Deborah and marrying her. A larger apartment would only mean to her that he had surrendered at last, and he would be in for a bad time explaining first the move and then Jonathan. The excuse of "private reasons" was a red flag to women anyway, sure to make them flip.

Pondering these matters sent Dr. Kellsey into a flip of his own for the period between the close of his summer term and the opening of the fall term. He spent this vacation, as he often had done in the past, in civilized drinking, a relaxation conducted in his two-and-a-half room apartment exactly as it had been in his one-and-a-half. It meant days on days unshaven, pajamaed, phone unhooked, incinerator clanking with empty bottles and broken glasses, a copper bowl of quarters by the hall door to hand out to liquor deliverers, delicatessen messengers, then a rehabilitation period presaged by a doctor's visit, drugstore deliveries, valet and laundrymen bringing and taking, a visiting barber, the public stenographer, newspapers, signs indicating reform was under way. Finally, the phone back on the hook, the hand and voice a little shaky but curable by the usual restoratives, the professor was ready to resume a gentleman's life, academic duties organized, the new autumn taken in stride.

He had not heard from his messages to Jonathan but was not concerned—young men were always dilatory—and it gave him time to butter up Anita meanwhile. He had agreed to meet her uptown at five and then escort her to Cassie Bender's preview party.

Pausing for a pair of quick ones at the club made him late at the start, and he had built up an even greater sense of guilt by the time he glimpsed Anita standing in the green glass shadows of the Lever Building. It struck him that she looked uncommonly calm for a girl who'd been kept waiting on a street corner for a good half hour. He had feared to find her pacing up and down, angry little eyes rolling from north to south to wristwatch, lighting a cigarette to place in holder, puff-puff and throw away, then lighting another in that fierce way she had, as if she was cooking his goose, but good, and snorting out smoke like Fafner himself.

"Hi!" she cried, waving her purse at him as merrily as any film star welcoming photographers. "Here I am."

No reproaches for breaking dates. No words about being late. Suspiciously Dr. Kellsey gave her his arm and they turned up Park.

"Good to see you," he said experimentally. Instead of saying, "Well, it's about time," Anita turned on him a radiant smile. Now that he was about to break up with her, he realized that years of familiarity had blinded him to Anita's good points. The sharp gypsy-dark face had good features, nostrils flaring a bit like a nervy racehorse's, upper lip too long and sulky, true, and the thin mouth shirred into a sort of bee-bite in the middle, fixed for a perpetual umlaut. Or an *œuf* or *œil.* More likely *eek,* he reflected. But good chin lines, he admitted generously, good planes, photogenically speaking, decent figure; she always boasted of walking right out of the store in standard size 12, triple-A shoe size 8, 32 bra—oh, there was nothing the matter with Anita's looks except that a mean fairy had taken them over at birth, squinching up everything somehow.

"I didn't mind waiting," she said. "I love watching the characters in this neighborhood. They fit the new architecture, all spare and bleak and hollow-looking. I'm sure their X-rays look like the blueprints for a modern sky-scraper."

"The women with all their organs out and the men with all their ulcers in," Walter retorted, feeling thrown off by her beamish mood, unable to utilize his prepared defense.

"No, really, there is a kind of stark purity—a sort of Mondrian quality that gets me," Anita said dreamily.

"What about a Hugow quality, since this is his day?" Walter said, falling at once into the clumsy-witted state that Anita's arch fantasy moods always threw him.

"Now, Walter, please!" Anita twittered. "Hugow has depth, mystery, all the things you lack, darling, so of course you wouldn't understand. Oh, poor Cassie Bender will make a fortune out of this show."

Walter glanced uneasily at the sunny uptilted countenance usually clouded with discontent, and sure to be when he got around to giving her his news. Yes, she had the smug well-fed look of someone who had just done in her best friend for his own good. And here she was with a good word for Hugow ("terribly overrated" was her usual opinion of him) and a tender word for Cassie Bender ("a vulgar nymphomaniac" was her habitual epithet). The simple exhibition of good humor alarmed Walter much more than her needling could. In fact Anita's caustic view of their acquaintances was a major charm for him, blotting out his own aching jealousy of all forms of success and permitting him the nice role of bighearted forgiver. ("Now, now, Anita, let's be fair. No one can be that bad, dear girl, they must have *something*.") And if she wasn't going to attack him for his neglect, he would have to make the first move himself.

"I'm sorry to have missed your calls and our usual Friday

dinners," he began, "but I was busy moving, you see—"

"So they told me at the club," Anita interrupted. "Don't give it a thought, Walter. I understood perfectly."

"But you see a strange thing happened," he went on doggedly. "It turns out there is a young chap in town who is the son of an old friend of mine, that is to say, she was a pupil of mine years ago."

"You do too much for your students, Walter," Anita said. "I've often told Dr. Jasper that that is our only trouble."

Suddenly the reason for her serenity dawned on the professor. Why, of course! She had just left her analyst's couch and had had her ego stroked for an hour by Dr. Jasper! He'd forgotten she had started that again. For a few hours after each consultation she enjoyed a state of glorious euphoria that merely having the money to buy analysis gives some people. Walter began steaming all over at the thought of the intimate revelations in Anita's folder on her "relationship" with himself. No use getting into that old psychoanalysis hassle, though, when there were bigger arguments ahead.

"He's given me so much help in adjusting to our relationship," Anita said somberly.

Help. Adjust. Relationship. How he hated the words, Walter thought irritably. Anita's problem was not a sense of inadequacy in herself but in her feeling overadequate to handle other people's inadequacies. She certainly didn't need a doctor to reassure her of her superiority. What she really wanted was for everybody else to be analyzed into admitting their wretched inferiority.

"He says the reason you don't have the normal philoprogenitive instincts is because you are compensated by being the father image to your students," Anita confided.

Father image!

"Does he think I was born a father image?" Dr. Kellsey exclaimed. "What about the students I had of my own age years ago? Doesn't this shrinker know there are a lot of other images in his old sample case? Doesn't he—"

He stopped, for Anita was giggling girlishly.

"I do think you're jealous of Dr. Jasper," she said. "That always happens and you're afraid I'm transferring."

Transfer! But he mustn't let her throw him. Instead he pointed toward the latest glass building under construction.

"Goldfish, that's what these damn architects would have us turn into!" he declaimed. "But the trouble is that some of us are toads and ought to be decently hidden."

Anita gave a silvery laugh.

"Oh, Walter, don't waste your marvelous epigrams on poor little me," she cried. "There'll be all sorts of clever people at Cassie's who can appreciate your wit properly."

"Look, we don't have to go to this show," Dr. Kellsey burst out. "I'm sick of this Hugow worship wherever I go. I can't stand that faded blond art madam, either. Let's skip it and have a quiet steak down at Costello's where we can talk."

Anita drew a white-gloved hand from his arm and batted her beadies at him reproachfully.

"I didn't realize you felt so hostile toward Cassie Bender," she said.

"Hostile!" echoed Dr. Kellsey savagely.

"And you can't downgrade Hugow's painting. Everyone says he's the best this year," she said.

Now the professor was really angry.

"I'm sick of this new cultural Gay Payoo," he shouted. "I can't stand Picasso or baseball or Louis Armstrong or boxers or folksongs or people's children or new faces, but if I open my mouth to say so a crowd closes in on me ready to get me deported. What about a little freedom of thought? You're as bad as the others, Anita, afraid to have an opinion of your own."

"Just because I don't agree with you, Wally, isn't that it?" Anita laughed, infuriatingly, above his heckling. "Come along, you silly boy, there'll be champagne and you'll love it. La la la."

She was humming "Three Coins in the Fountain" again and fondly resumed his arm. The shrinker had certainly filled her up with self-confidence this time, Walter thought, and he wondered how long before it would start chipping off like the lipstick and eyeshadow. Whatever was making her so satisfied made him jealous, but then he was jealous of everybody nowadays, jealous of the President of the United States for all that free rent and gravy, jealous of cops for their freedom to sock anybody who annoyed them, jealous of students who could skip his classes, jealous of Hugow or anybody stupid enough to believe in his own genius, jealous of happy believers and bold infidels, and jealous of young men with a whole lifetime ahead to louse themselves up as they wished. Ridiculous to be jealous of poor old Anita, especially when she had his bad news coming to her.

"All right, then, let's go," he snapped, taking long strides to throw off Anita's prim little high-heeled steps, her thighs never parting as if afraid of wandering rapists. "I haven't much time because I must see this young chap I mentioned, the son of my old student—"

"What's his name?" Anita asked. "Who was his mother?"

He had almost forgotten.

"He is Jonathan Jaimison," he said. "Mother was Connie Birch."

"I can't understand this sentimentality over an old student," Anita said. "You always claim your classes are just one big moronic sea, so what did this one do to stamp her?"

The familiar indications of a fight soothed and warmed Dr. Kellsey. There was chance of a little sport after all.

"It was long before your time, my dear," he said. "I had just come East and barely begun my classes. This girl had a slender talent—"

"You've always hated slender talents." Anita was now smoldering nicely. "Why do you have to waste time on her son?"

They had reached the entrance to the brownstone where Cassie Bender's modern window stood out, bravely anachronistic.

"For very special reasons that I can't go into right here," he said, amused to watch the chipping-off process begin in earnest as Anita, scowling thunderously, drew back and stoned him with a look. "The father image, as you call it, owes something to the father seeker, wouldn't your good Dr. Jasper say? Here is a too permissive young man with no sense of security in a sea of hostilities and unrewarding relationships. It is my plan to help him to adjust or project, rather, by taking him into my home as if he were, let us say, a son image."

"You wouldn't!" Anita choked. "You mean you took that apartment for him instead of for us! You really meant it to be good-by."

Now he did feel guilty and remorseful, for the poor girl looked white and wild under her careful make-up. As soon as she had put his plan into words he realized that he couldn't say good-by to Anita, any more than he could say good-by to his conscience or, for that matter, to his wife.

"It's to help the boy out till he can look out for himself," he said cautiously. "Think of him as a lost boy, Anita, without friends or money in this big city, no place to turn but to that father image you mention. You shouldn't criticize me, Anita, for feelings you used to scold me for lacking!"

Ha. He was turning the tables on her, and Anita was too smart not to know it. She was sniffling a little but softening. They went into the gallery, through the hall to the glass-roofed patio, where the party was assembling under a chandelier mobile.

"At least you can be decent to Cassie," Anita muttered in his ear as the gallery queen swooped toward them, white bosom bursting from purple velvet beamed toward them like truck headlights. "I'm so glad you came early," cried Cassie, clasping a hand of each guest. "The most marvelous news for you! I want you to meet my new partner, this heavenly, heavenly creature, Jonathan Jaimison. Darling, come meet Dr. Kellsey and Anita Barlowe, such distinguished scholars."

"Jonathan Jaimison?" Anita said, looking at Dr. Kellsey.

The young man was far too handsome, Anita thought, but then that sort of looks always went fast, thank God. Cassie was crowing over him in that revolting possessive hungry, sexy way she had, pawing him as she introduced him. But Dr. Kellsey's face was more interesting at the moment than Cassie's new partner, who was vigorously shaking the doctor's hand.

"I don't think I heard right," said Dr. Kellsey. "Did Mrs. Bender say she had a new partner? But that can't be you, Jonathan."

"Yes, it is a surprise, isn't it?" Jonathan said happily. "I couldn't think of a better use for my money than to buy into a business like this."

"I'm teaching him everything I know!" said Cassie with a splendid gesture.

"That's so generous of you," said Anita sweetly. "And so like you."

She could tell that her lover was thoroughly unprepared for this encounter, and, whatever the situation was, it comforted her to have him be the one to squirm for a change.

"So you've left the café," Dr. Kellsey said, "and the East Tenth Street apartment."

"I've caged him in the downstairs studio next door," Cassie said merrily. "Wasn't that clever of me?"

"It's best to be near Teacher, isn't it, Mr. Jaimison?" Anita asked Jonathan. "One never knows when one will need a lesson."

She was annoying Dr. Kellsey, she knew, but she felt she had the right. Poor lost boy with no money and no home indeed! A millionaire, from the way he was dressed, and the talk about buying the business!

"I knew his mother, you see," Dr. Kellsey mumbled, trying to collect his wits in the face of Anita's curled lip. "It was a long time ago. I found some old snapshots, Jonathan, that perhaps might help you in your research."

"Good," said Jonathan. "But I've dropped that research. I've been meaning to tell you."

"I see," said Dr. Kellsey, smiling but stricken. "That happens, of course, to all researchers, as Miss Barlowe here can tell you. The researcher comes upon findings that don't fit in with his preconception, so he loses interest in the game."

Anita was pleased and touched to be mentioned and moved closer. She could tell by the professor's trembling voice and nervous mustache twigging that he was immensely disturbed. Jonathan too was aware of a new sarcastic note in his old friend's voice.

"It was a game, as you say," he conceded warily. "As soon as I talked to Mrs. Bender I saw that here was my future."

"It's absolutely miraculous!" Cassie Bender linked arms with Jonathan, enveloping new visitors in her perfumed aura, clutching one, smiling at another, and speaking into a third one's ear. "You've no idea what a flair this boy has! Don't you agree, Dr. Kellsey, that *appreciation* is a talent in itself? Absolutely apart from criticism or promotion or diagnostic approach? Jonathan *appreciates*."

"It must be heaven," Anita murmured.

"Why, I'd never even heard of Percy Wright until Jonathan brought him to my attention. Wright has taken a good deal from Hugow, true, but Hugow's at his peak and Wright is new, one of the new romantics."

"Hard Edge," explained Jonathan.

"But Soft Middle," said Cassie.

"Ah," said the doctor.

"Champagne?" Jonathan motioned toward the bar. "There's scotch if you'd rather."

"I prefer Hugow," the doctor said absently. "Where is he?"

"He still stands up, doesn't he?" Cassie agreed. "But he makes me so mad when he won't come in! He says he can't stand openings and being talked about as if he was dead. He says the kind of people who like him make him want to give up art and drive a hack. Just between us, I'm glad to find a *gentleman* painter like Percy, after my struggles with Hugow."

"We've tripled his prices," Jonathan reminded her. "Sold out, too."

Cassie was loaded, he thought, and more Southern belle by the minute.

"Then you're no longer the little lost boy without friends

or home," Anita said to him with a charming smile, edging away from her escort's savage nudge. "You've found yourself."

"Of course Dr. Kellsey was a great help to me," Jonathan said, knowing he had failed the doctor miserably and wondering how he could atone for getting lucky. "You understood me, sir, and it meant a lot to me."

It meant too much for the professor.

"Ah, but I was mistaken all the while," he said. "It wasn't the father image you sought, after all, but the mother image. And now you've found your true mother."

Too bad Cassie missed that one, Anita thought. Men were so bitchy.

"How much he looks like Dr. Jasper!" she whispered to Walter. "It's amazing!"

"Really, Anita!" reproved the doctor. In his annoyance, the professor rejected the highball offered by Jonathan, suggesting pointedly to Anita that they must leave. It was Jonathan who was the offender now, greeting new visitors as Cassie drew him away.

"You were so right about Mother Cassie," Anita murmured, following Dr. Kellsey to the exit. "She's absolutely clucking today. I suppose she's sleeping with your little hero. Let's go before she makes us look at the pictures. I can't understand what anybody finds in Hugow."

There was his old Anita, the professor rejoiced, the shrinker's salve all worn away and the dear acidulous, embittered girl back again.

"Now, now," he rebuked her gently. "Cassie isn't all that bad, and you can't miss the basic strength in Hugow, crude though it is. Sure you don't want to stay for the crowd? It would be interesting to see how Jonathan handles them in his new role."

"I hate that Spur crowd and Cassie's rich oafs and the disgusting noises the critics make," Anita said. "Let's go to Costello's for a little honest air—unless, of course, you're afraid your wife will be there."

"Nonsense, Deborah would never be in a place like that," he said, which started Anita all over on a very old tack.

"Like that? Like what? You mean it's too good for me and not good enough for your wife? Or maybe she'll be at that new apartment of yours, meant for everybody but me."

It was like old times, before Jonathan had stirred up his life. The professor tucked Anita's hand under his arm when they got into the taxi and gently reminded her that a man's wife did have first rights to his apartment, new or old. By the time they got out at Costello's for steak and quiet talk they weren't speaking to each other.

It was good to be back in the ring.

The Hugow opening was a sensational success by Golden Spur standards. One minute before eight, the hour the party was slated to close, an entire new saloonful of art-lovers roared in from the Muse's farthest reaches. A sea of arms reached in the air for drinks as if for basketballs and passed them over heads of immobilized figures. Museum directors, critics, dilettantes were pushed into the paintings they admired; oldtimers accustomed to snubbing each other found themselves glued together, buttocks to buttocks, lipstick to hairy ear, beard to bra. The barstool artflies took over, and Jonathan's nightmare began.

"Jonathan, you stinker, get out the hooch, you know where the bitch keeps it! . . . Can you imagine that jerk locking up the bar when his old pals walk in? . . . Hugow would kill the guy if he knew they were holding out on his old friends. . . . Get it out, you dirty scab."

The more distinguished guests were being knocked down as they fought for their minks under the mountains of duffel coats, and leather jackets, and there were cries of "Thief! . . . Get the police. . . . Get Hugow! Get a doctor."

Jonathan's efforts to sneak more bottles into the party only reminded his old buddies that he was in a position now to do even more for them, and they despised him for it.

"I got to have forty-five bucks for my loft, Jonny-boy. If I get Hugow to put down a few lines on a card, how much will you pay for it?"

Whatever he said or did was wrong and brought forth jeers, none louder than when Cassie obliged him to announce the doors were being locked. He knew they regarded him as an informer now, but he hated himself too, wishing he could be put out with them instead of putting them out. He had looked forward to this great day as a kind of debut for himself, the more so because Cassie had kept postponing it for greater thunder. He would show his old friends that he was going to be a friend indeed. He had hoped to show Hugow too, but the artist had disappeared on some private binge, and Jonathan found himself agreeing with Cassie that an artist should be more *responsible,* more *mature,* more *considerate.*

"Is that what I'm going to be?" he asked himself, shocked. "Am I going to think Percy Wright is a finer painter because he takes off his hat in elevators?"

Long before the mob had poured in, Cassie, following her usual practice, had siphoned off the plummier guests to her own private quarters for caviar and champagne and inside chatter.

"Do get rid of everybody and come back here," she begged Jonathan. "Tell them I have a headache or passed out or anything."

"Jonny is Cassie Bender's bouncer!" jeered someone as Jonathan tried to guide a sneaker-footed stumbler to the door, and Jonathan was annoyed at Cassie for humiliating him, at the victim, at himself, and at the taunter for speaking the truth. His anger gave him strength to push the intruders outward, though they rushed out as suddenly as they had advanced when word spread that the Jackson Gallery party further down the avenue was still on. There was a hint that Hugow himself had gone to that party instead of his own, which made everyone gleeful.

In the gallery Jonathan stood panting from his exertions, brushing his sleeves, straightening his tie and hair; a regular bouncer, he thought, and his name in gold letters on a door meant just that. He picked his way over the floor littered with broken glasses, sandwiches, and forgotten rubbers to the patio which led to Cassie's exclusive quarters, where the cream of the party was assembled, the big shots he would now be able to swing behind deserving talent, providing the talent didn't double-cross him first. He wished he were going with the mob to the other party, cardless, thirsty, mannerless, tieless, absolutely free.

Immature, irresponsible, he told himself.

Cassie was arranged on her favorite sofa, one plump but shapely leg thrown across the other high enough to reveal chiffon ruffles and a charming suspicion—no, it couldn't be! —of pubic curls, coquettishly hidden as soon as the peek was offered. One gray millionaire sat at her feet for the view of lower joys, while another leaned over the back of the sofa, gazing down hungrily into the generous picnic of her decolletage. Cassie waved her cigarette holder around both admirers and spoke in her Lady Agatha accent of the mystique of art collecting. Jonathan pretended not to see her gracious gesture making room at her feet for him to crouch, look, listen, and learn. He sipped his whisky doggedly, feeling like a child left with the dreary grown-ups while the other boys were having fun in forbidden playgrounds. These important personages of the art world had no value in themselves, only when presented to men like Hugow for their needs. None of them would ever be friends or people in their own right, he thought. Just as he was speculating on how soon he could break loose from his new duties, he saw George Terrence coming toward him, smiling.

"My dear boy, you look as if you'd seen a ghost! Don't apologize, I understand now why you didn't answer my letters, and believe me, I think it's splendid. I've taken up painting for my nerves, on the advice of my doctor, and I will say that there's nothing like it. I don't blame you a bit for preferring it to the law. Even my wife is taking it up. In fact, she just purchased a Hugow from Mrs. Bender, that's why we came."

A lean, lantern-jawed, crew-cut man of distinction, barber-tanned and vested in lamé brocade suddenly detached himself from a manly cluster around the fireplace and reached a beautiful hand toward George.

"Roger Mills, as I live and breathe," he said. "How long has it been—let's see, ten, twenty—no, don't tell me—why, I believe it's nearly twenty-five years, isn't it?" He smiled brilliantly at Jonathan and favored him with the next handclasp. "So you're one of Roger's protégés, too. I've heard about you from Mrs. Kingston Ball, Miss Van Orphen's sister."

"I think you're mistaken about my name," George Terrence said, taking a firm grip on Jonathan's arm as Jonathan was trying to get away. "Terrence is the name. Would you like to meet Mrs. Terrence, Jonathan? She's been anxious to meet you, now that we're so interested in artists."

The trimly dieted little matron summoned from her corner was the same one who had avoided him as Connie Birch's son but was eager to make amends to the promising dealer and was equally pleased to meet the glitter-vested Mr. Gordon.

"Did I hear you mention Claire Van Orphen?" she asked him. "Claire and Beatrice used to call on us years ago. And Mr. Jaimison here is the son of a dear old friend as well as a friend of Claire's. What a lot we have to talk over!"

"Indeed, indeed," said the stranger. "I knew your husband before he was your husband, Mrs. Terrence, when he was quite the gay bachelor, in fact, eh, Roger?"

Mrs. Terrence burst into arch giggles.

"You don't need to remind me, sir," she cried. "George was a very naughty boy when I first knew him and I did my best to reform him. But do you know I do love hearing him tell about his escapades, because sex standards are so much freer now, don't you think, Mr. Gordon, and what shocked us then just seems amusing these days? I really blush at my own ignorance more than at George's naughty affairs. Imagine George using an alias, like royalty!"

Mr. Gordon toyed with the jeweled buttons of his vest and looked from Mrs. Terrence's bisque-matted façade to George Terrence's steely smile.

"Indeed," he said. "So you knew about Roger Mills."

Mrs. Terrence giggled again.

"That was so clever of George. His family owned the Roger Cotton Mills, so sometimes he called himself Roger Cotton and sometimes Roger Mather when he was out on a lark. I nearly died laughing, but it would have shocked me if I'd known it once."

"It still shocks me, Mrs. Terrence," said the stranger.

Jonathan wanted to leave the happily reunited old friends to their reminiscences, but this time it was Mrs. Terrence who detained him.

"My daughter has told me about you," she said. "Really my taking up art, modern art, that is, has made Amy and me much closer, just as it has made George and me understand each other. You must let us come and browse around the newer galleries, Jonathan, because you're the expert and we're amateurs."

"What made you take it up?" asked the stranger, brooding. "Nerves—like Roger's here?"

"Oh no," said the lady. "I knew it was all right because Mrs. Crysler was collecting modern art."

"Don't go, Jonathan," exclaimed George. "Please stay," cried Hazel and Mr. Gordon. "Come sit with me, Jonathan," commanded Cassie.

It was a trap, he thought gloomily. He thought wistfully of the pack of gallery-flies prowling through the night, battering on doors to be let in, brawling and bruising down to The Golden Spur, and he thought those were the real backers of art, those were the providers, the blood-donors, and Cassie's salon of critics, guides, and millionaires, were the free-loaders, free-loading on other people's genius, other people's broken hearts, and, when it came to that, other people's money.

Well, he'd learned something more about himself, and if

all he'd lost was some of Major Wedburn's money, that was okay. He didn't have to save his life by collaboration with the enemy, did he? He found Percy Wright trying to be sick in Cassie's bathroom.

"It's not the liquor, it's my awful problems!" Percy gasped. "I mean, naturally I'm terribly flattered that you and Cassie have taken me up and let me meet these great people, but I still admire Hugow—my master, really—and I want to tell him he mustn't blame me for my prices boosting and those reviewers saying he's through, because he isn't. Would I still be trying to paint like him if he was through, I mean? And if he gets through, where does that leave my work when it's like his?"

Yes, it was a problem, Jonathan agreed.

"I'll make a fortune when my show comes on," Percy said, "but nobody likes my money anyway. You'd think it was leprosy, the way Darcy nags me about it. But how can I stop my stuff from selling?"

"You can buy me out," said Jonathan, inspired. "Be a dealer. That's where you belong. Everybody you like will like you."

"You wouldn't sell," Percy said, cheered at once.

Jonathan handed him a towel filled with ice and a fresh glass of scotch, and the deal was started.

Jonathan hurried down Madison and looked for lights from the side-street galleries along the way where other opening parties had been held. By this time the old crowd must be heading toward The Golden Spur for post mortems and wakes, and he stood waving for a cab. A green taxi was parked in front of a Hamburger Heaven and as he waited the driver came out of the restaurant with a paper bag. He opened the cab door.

"Just the man we're hunting. Get in," he said. "How do you like this job? The best thing I ever painted."

Hugow took off his cap and grinned.

"I knew it," said Jonathan. "You're still in your green period."

"My fare's buying Pernod, a love potion rich debutantes give to taxi-drivers—green, of course."

Iris was hurrying out of the liquor store with her package.

"Darling, we've been looking all over for you," she cried, climbing in. "We've got everything ready for the trip."

"You never guessed I'd be at the gallery," Jonathan said.

"I figured you'd be too smart to stick that one out," Hugow said.

"I was only watching your doodlings pull in a fortune," Jonathan said. "It gets boring."

"Hugow's got it all spent already," Iris said.

It was lovely to be in each other's arms in the back seat of a taxi once again. It didn't matter that she'd been with Hugow, and the truth had no part in love anyway, except for the truth of finding each other at the right moment.

"Not spent, invested," said Hugow, heading the car north. "There won't be any money in art in the year two thousand, so I'm in a new business, the coming one."

Jonathan didn't care what business it was so long as they were all together once more.

"Demolition, that's my business now," said Hugow. "Cab for a hobby, demolition for real. My firm's hoping for this contract."

"The Metropolitan?"

They were passing the Museum, heading for the park entrance.

"We call that a ball job in my business," said Hugow. "The iron ball, that's our god. I'm picking up the lingo too. No art corn, just the simple, brutal words."

"Already it's arty," said Jonathan. " 'Demolition' for 'wrecking.' I've got some money to invest in it myself."

"I'll take it," Hugow said.

Jonathan wondered where Hugow was taking them, but if nobody else wanted The Golden Spur, he'd be the last to suggest it. He wanted to ask Iris where she had been all these weeks, but she was here now. Wasn't that all that mattered?

"Your parents were at the show," he told Iris.

"Parents are getting into everything now, spoiling all the fun," Iris complained. "Now mother wants to go back into the theater, she says, now that she knows about me. I told them all about me so I could leave for good, but instead they wanted to come too. Father painting, mind you! That's what that analyst Dr. Jasper did!"

They were tooling over to the West Side Highway. Maybe Hugow was taking them up to his shack up in Rockland County, where they would freeze to death. Maybe he'd turn around before they hit the bridge and go down to the Spur after all. Iris had her head cozily on his shoulder and was babbling away between sandwiches and drinks about the frightful hazards of getting on good terms with your family after all these years.

"That's why I love you so much," she said. "You simply have no family pride, Jonathan."

"On the contrary, I am very proud of my family," Jonathan said. "The Jaimisons happen to be one of the oldest families in Ohio."

He was very glad that Hugow had turned back downtown, perhaps to the Spur, where they could begin all over.

Dawn Powell was born on November 28, 1897, in Mount Gilead, Ohio. When she was six her mother died, and Powell later wrote that she was "dispatched from one relative to another, from a year of farm life with this or that aunt to rougher life in the middle of little factory towns." She made her way to New York in 1918, and over the next forty years she wrote more than fifteen novels, two dozen short stories, three plays, and articles for such magazines as *Life, Harper's Bazaar, Mademoiselle* (where she was a book critic for a year), and *The New Yorker*. She married in 1920 and lived in Greenwich Village in New York City, where her literary group included Malcolm Cowley, Edmund Wilson, and occasionally Ernest Hemingway. She was the toast of bohemia's smart set and continued writing until her death in 1965. "True wit," Powell once wrote, "should break a wise man's heart. It should strike at the exact point of weakness and it should scar. It should rest on a pillar of truth and not on a gelatine base, and the truth is not so shameful it cannot be recorded."